THE
OMEGA
PORTAL

A NEAR DEATH EXPERIENCE OPENS A COMMUNICATION BRIDGE WITH A MULTIDIMENSIONAL BEING

BY

ANONYMOUS

ISBN: 9798511154077

The Omega Portal:

A Near Death Experience Opens a Communication Bridge
with a Multidimensional Being

TheOmegaPortal.com

CONTENTS

PART ONE: THE OMEGA CONSCIOUSNESS (Saturday Afternoon) 1

SESSION 1

Introduction 2

Chapter 1 22

Chapter 2 28

Chapter 3 33

Chapter 4 39

Chapter 5 45

SESSION 2

Chapter 6 54

Chapter 7 59

Chapter 8 63

Chapter 9 67

Chapter 10 75

Chapter 11 81

Chapter 12 88

SESSION 3

Chapter 13 96

Chapter 14 102

Chapter 15 107

Chapter 16 115

Chapter 17 123

Chapter 18 130

PART TWO: THE OMEGA CONTINUUM (Saturday Evening) 137

SESSION 4

Chapter 19 138

Chapter 20 144

Chapter 21 151

Chapter 22 158

Chapter 23 162

Chapter 24 169

Chapter 25 176

Chapter 26 183

SESSION 5

Chapter 27 190

Chapter 28 198

Chapter 29 206

Chapter 30 214

SESSION 6

Chapter 31 223

Chapter 32 228

Chapter 33 236

Chapter 34 244

Chapter 35 249

Chapter 36 256

Chapter 37 261

Chapter 38 265

PART THREE: THE OMEGA ORACLE (Sunday Afternoon) 271

SESSION 7

Chapter 39 272

Chapter 40 280

Chapter 41 288

Chapter 42 295

Chapter 43 301

Chapter 44 306

Chapter 45 314

Chapter 46 322

Chapter 47 329

SESSION 8

Chapter 48 336

Chapter 49 344

Chapter 50 353

Chapter 51 361

SESSION 9

Chapter 52 369

Chapter 53 377

Chapter 54 384

PART FOUR: THE OMEGA PRACTICUM (Sunday Evening) 393

SESSION 10

Chapter 55 394

Chapter 56 402

Chapter 57 411

Chapter 58 416

Chapter 59 422

Chapter 60 430

Chapter 61 437

Chapter 62 444

Chapter 63 450

SESSION 11

Chapter 64 460
Chapter 65 467
Chapter 66 473
Chapter 67 480
Chapter 68 485
Chapter 69 492
Chapter 70 497
Chapter 71 502
Chapter 72 510
Chapter 73 516
Chapter 74 523

SESSION 12

Chapter 75 532
Chapter 76 540
Chapter 77 547
Chapter 78 554
Chapter 79 559
Chapter 80 567

PART ONE:
THE OMEGA CONSCIOUSNESS
(SATURDAY AFTERNOON)

SESSION 1
INTRODUCTION

Alright, they're both recording. Here we go. So like we've talked about, I'll start with setting the stage a bit and then give an overview of the layout and what we plan to talk about this weekend, and then we'll get started.

Sounds good.

So the short version is, you had a serious medical situation in the last year that led to your heart stopping, and then you were resuscitated a few minutes later. And during that time, you had a very impactful near death experience, to say the least, in which you found yourself in a Light-filled Space, deeply connecting with a Multidimensional Being, which you now call the Omega Being or the Omega Consciousness, or just Omega. And you not only had some amazing experiences and had a lot of really intriguing information come in, but through that a communication portal somehow opened, so that you now regularly have, not quite conversations, but communication sessions – you call them bridging sessions – with this Being, during which you receive what to me are also – the ones I've heard so far – really fascinating information downloads. Which you call inflashes or flash packets. So far so good?

Yeah, or sometimes I call them inwaves or data streams. Downloads works too.

So you've received some really interesting downloads of information about a variety of topics, including a map or model of how

Multidimensional Reality is basically set up, and you and I have been talking about a lot of this over coffee about once a week for the last six weeks or so. And today and tomorrow, we're having what we're calling a marathon weekend, where we're going to go into a lot of this in a lot more depth than you and I have so far, and then I'm planning to transcribe it and turn it into a book, if you end up feeling good about how it went and give me a final thumbs up. How's that for a quick intro to our intro?

Yeah, that's basically the lead. And like you said, the word *conversations* isn't really it, but we could say connecting and communicating, and receiving data streams of information and experiences and impressions and images and understandings. And during these bridging sessions, the way I experience it is, everything in a data stream flashes in all at once, or close to it, and then it can take a few minutes or sometimes longer for me to really open it all up and kind of read it or take it all in. Things I never knew anything about or thought about or had any interest in before, and that my mind just wouldn't have had any room for or openness towards, before the Big Event.

And by the Big Event you mean your near death experience.

Yeah, that made every other event that's ever happened in my life relatively small and uneventful.

And I'm still the only person you've talked to about any of this?

Yeah, maybe eventually I'll tell more people, but so far you're the lucky winner.

And can you say why?

Well one reason is, this whole thing's been a really personal, out of the usual range of experience kind of thing, and most people I know, the people in my life and the people more peripherally in my life, they just wouldn't really get it or feel that comfortable with it or know what to do with it. And that could add some tension and difficulty and kind of wonkiness in my connections with people, close and not as close, when I'm already still trying to process both the Big Event and the ongoing bridging sessions. And I can't untell someone once I've told them, so it's just felt like better taking care not to tell anyone.

And then a couple of months ago, you and I started having coffee, and by the second or third time, I found myself starting to open some of this up with you, which I've appreciated the chance to do, but that hasn't changed where I'm at with telling anyone else. And I realize that might sound a little strange or extreme or overprotective or closed off, not even telling the people I'm closest to, and maybe it is, but it's just what's felt like the best way to navigate something really important to me and really delicate, so far.

And also since the Big Event, I've been feeling more sensitive and raw, and more impactable by other people than I was before, kind of like my old comparatively tough skin suddenly shed and I don't yet have much new skin very fully formed yet at all. Not much of a buffer.

So my best sense has been to just lay low about it all, and to be really careful and deliberate about if and when I start to bring even a little of this up with anyone. I *have* communicated to a couple of people in my life that I'm still processing some things from that whole medical emergency situation and being clinically dead for a few, and that I'm not yet ready to talk about any of it, but you gotta be careful who you even say *that* much to, or they can really become like a zoomed in magnet about it, taking it personally that you won't share it with them or trying to figure out what the deal is, which is counterproductive. So mostly it just makes sense to me to not even bring up a hint of it at all. Maybe down the road I'll be less protective about it, not as sensitive and raw, I don't know, but for now this is what's feeling right.

But at the same time, it's been hard having this huge thing that happened and then also this whole other thing of ongoingly dipping back into that portal some through the bridging sessions, and not saying a word about either of those to anyone. That's not ideal either. So like I've told you a few times, it's been really nice for me to finally feel like I can talk with someone, who's genuinely interested and open and not judgmental, about what happened during the Big Event and about this whole ongoing aspect of my life that's still opening up with the bridging sessions. So yeah, something along those lines.

Ω

And to add a bit more background on how we got here today, you and I have known each other for some time, though we haven't known each other well or spent much time together, and when I heard about your medical situation, I started texting you here and there, wishing you well, letting you know I was thinking about you.

Yeah, you even sent me a book for while I was lying around recovering, which I really appreciated a lot. Both the book and also the thought.

I was happy to do it. And eventually that led to us meeting for coffee once, and then we started doing that weekly, and somewhere in there you started sharing bits and pieces of this with me, and then going into more detail about it all.

Yeah, it felt like you were really hearing me, really open to what I was saying instead of just placating me while thinking I had lost it. I could feel your energy was genuinely open and responding to what I was saying. Plus the book you gave me was indicative of you appreciating deeper currents. So added up, I felt like I could trust you pretty quickly, and that you would hold all this in confidence, which sounds funny considering you've now coaxed me into your lair with our phone recorders on.

And to expand and clarify what got me to coax you into my lair, I've been impacted by our conversations, first by just the story of what you experienced and your ongoing experiences with the bridging sessions, and second by the content that's come through, the downloads themselves, and then also sometimes I've felt a Deep Quiet Space showing up when you're talking about some of the more subtle levels of reality and what you've directly experienced.

So I'm clear you have a very interesting and unique story to share, with some fascinating and thought provoking downloads and experiences, that are also tapping into something more profound than most of us usually tap into, and I strongly felt that I shouldn't be the only one to hear it. So for a month or so I've been urging you to write a book or make some sharing videos or start a blog or anything that would get some of this out there, and you've been a hard no because you feel like – well actually do you want to say why you were a no on those ideas, and why you're giving this weekend a try?

Well, everything I just said about it being too soon to start really sharing about this yet, plus we both know I can be pretty introverted or just not that into attention or people seeking me out, and I just prefer to keep my life as simple and even keeled as I can, especially now. So bringing in this kind of attention into my life, about something that I think most people or a lot of people either wouldn't have much space for or would have a lot of quick judgments or strong opinions or reactions around, or maybe even assume I'm delusionalb – because what I share about my experiences and the flash packets might clash with their own beliefs and their familiar world view – opening all that up just doesn't sound appealing to me in the slightest.

Or the opposite, which I know isn't that likely but I'm still wary of it, where some people might think everything I report that Omega communicated must be The Truth about The Way Things Are, and/or they might think I'm somehow special or like oozing spiritual energy that they could get something from. So it just feels pretty unruly and messy and like I'm almost asking to have my work life, my private space – all of it – potentially disrupted or imposed on or damaged or weighed down, and maybe I'm completely wrong, but you can't put that genie back in the bottle, so yeah, I'm just a hard no on that for the foreseeable future.

Plus so far I haven't felt – and maybe this will open up later or maybe it won't – but I just haven't felt any authentic pull in myself at all to put any of this out there, and most definitely not to put *myself* out there around it. It just hasn't come up in me, and it pretty clearly won't anytime soon, if ever. So it's hard to get enthused and on board with any big project that might take a lot of my time and energy, and might lead to some backlash or personal costs that I'm not interested in dealing with, just in general, and especially while I'm still processing it all myself and still feel pretty tender and you know, raw and protective around the whole thing.

So all added up, I've been a hard no, but about a week ago – I guess I'll just go ahead and explain this part – last week you suggested, I think it was maybe your one last attempt, but you said how about if we just take a Saturday and Sunday afternoon and evening, and record a marathon conversation about the Big Event and also about what's been happening since then, what I've been experiencing and seeing in the bridging sessions. Then you would transcribe it and self publish it, completely anonymously, so that not even one person, not even the people closest to you – you would just tell them you were working on a confidential project, which you said would be workable – but not even *one* person would know who put the book out there, making it two steps removed from anyone finding out who I am.

And you incredibly enthusiastically jumped at the chance.

I think maybe you and I remember that conversation a little differently. But that did get us talking about it and coming up with some work arounds that helped me feel okay about showing up today and giving this a try. And even though I haven't felt a pull in me to do anything like this, I *did* feel a response of availability to the obviously strong pull in *you* to do it, if that makes sense. It's admittedly a little more muted now that I'm actually here and our phones are recording, and I've got the whole weekend in front of me, but it was there and got me in the door.

Ω Ω

And this might be a good place to mention, since it will be an anonymous book, just to have some bare minimal orientation of who's talking, we're both American or Canadian males, between the ages of 30 and 65. How's that for vague?

There goes our anonymity.

Sorry, how inconsiderate of me. And the next thing on my cheat sheet is to lay out what the basic structure of the weekend is. So to make sure things don't get out of hand and turn into something bigger than you signed up for, our agreement is we're limiting this to today and tomorrow, afternoon and evening, starting at one and going as late as ten, if needed. Minus about an hour or so total each day for a few short breaks and a 30-45 minute dinner break, and that should be up to around eight hours each day of talk time, if we end up needing that much.

Hence my quickly intensifying feeling of dread and my growing attraction to your front door.

Hence the padlocks. How about if we stick with it for an hour or so and then see where you're at?

Yeah, I'm not actually going to bolt, I'm just being transparent that I'm a little tentative and ambivalent, way out of my comfort zone here, and pretty daunted out by the task at hand. And I'm also pretty eager to get past the next 15 or 20 minutes, to hopefully start to loosen up and see how I do trying to express some of what we're here to talk about, in more detail than I've tried to so far. So let's just keep moving through your list and I'll probably start to relax into it.

Alright, then next up, we agreed on an outline of four main topics, which we may stray from a bit now and then, but our intention is to follow it to keep us basically on track for the four sessions. So the plan is, this afternoon we'll be talking about your near death experience, and this portal or bridge that opened for you during it, where you started being in connection with a Multidimensional Being, the Omega Consciousness.

And then by this evening, if not before, we'll move into the second main topic, which is your ongoing bridging sessions, where you relax in a chair and plug back in to that connection, and as you do, information comes in about more subtle levels of reality, about consciousness, and a variety of other topics, some of which you and I have talked about a bit during our coffee conversations. And I've found some of those really interesting and impactful, so I'm looking forward to drilling deeper into them.

And then we'll divide tomorrow between two other general topics that I felt were worth setting aside half a day for each, if we need that long. And the afternoon topic will focus on how during your near death experience one of the things that happened was you were flooded with scenes and information about a possible future. One potential way the future could look.

Or you could say I saw different possible future situations and circumstances and scenes and events, that might or might not come about. It didn't feel like all or nothing, like *one* future. Maybe some actually happen and some don't. Or maybe it was all just produced from my unconscious while my body was otherwise indisposed. But yeah, I saw some glimpses of what very convincingly appeared to be potential future events.

And some of the ones you've told me about were right in line with what I would've expected, and some I've never heard of or thought about before, and I found a couple of those to be particularly thought provoking. And I also want us to include in that discussion what we got into a bit a few weeks ago, around another download during your near death experience, where you saw some of the dynamics or influences that have led us to where things are, and how we might be able to shift them. And then tomorrow evening's topic – well first does all of that sound right so far?

Yeah, that was the second flash packet, and then there was also a third one too, and it had the really optimistic and encouraging future scenes that I've mentioned to you, but I probably didn't clarify they were a separate, third inflash. So yeah, that's basically what's on the docket for tomorrow afternoon, though it's hard to really convey a clear thumbnail of some of these topics and subtopics without getting into them, but that'll have to be good enough for now.

Alright, and then tomorrow evening's topic – I don't know that I can do it justice either, and I've only heard bits and pieces so far – but a few times you've talked about some practices and processes that the Omega Consciousness has given you during your bridging sessions, and – well first, some of the background you laid out for one of those in particular, the one you call Influencing Your Unfolding, was really interesting to me, and got into some territory we hadn't talked about before around the connection between consciousness and reality, and some other related things, so I wanted us to get into that.

And second, it seemed good to designate some time this weekend for you to go into some of those practices, or you said the word that came through was invitations, in case any readers find them helpful, and also just to bring some of these big concepts down to Earth a bit. So tomorrow evening will include looking at some ways to apply some of what we'll be talking about, that have come through during your sessions, along with some background I found really interesting. Is that a fair way to say it?

Yeah, and one of those invitations that I haven't talked about with you yet is a process that came in during a bridging session not that long ago, and lately it's been noticeably impacting my life in a good, supportive way. After the bridging sessions it's probably the most supportive thing in my life right now, in terms of really getting acclimated to my post Big Event life, and it's a big part of my gradual coming around to starting to appreciate a life that's so relatively cut off from the experience of being profoundly connected to Greater Reality.

And it's kind of a – well it's hopeless to try to give a quick snapshot of these – but it's a quick little process for when we're feeling dissatisfied with our lives or things are just difficult or hard or not going the direction we want them to go in, or there's something we really need or want in our lives that's frustrating or painful or contractive to be without. So this is a way to work with that kind of thing, and at least in my experience, it can really shift and enhance our internal experience pretty quickly, like in a few minutes, and also accumulatively, even if things just aren't yet lining up the way we want them to in our lives.

Sounds good. I'm looking forward to hearing that one. So I'm sure we'll stray into other territory at times, and I've got my list of questions at the ready, about things we've talked about that to me were especially intriguing or fascinating, and things I want to hear more about or make sure we cover, as well as some things I haven't asked you yet, but that's the basic layout I suggested for the weekend, and you said sure.

Yeah, it's your rodeo, I'm just the bull. And we'll see what actually happens – best laid plans – but that feels like a good basic outline.

Ω Ω Ω

And next up, I wanted to just spell out a few of the things, in addition to keeping things anonymous, that we agreed on to help you feel good about giving this weekend a try, and one was, you're free anytime in the next month to let me know you'd rather me not move forward.

Yeah, that puts this weekend into the giving it a try and testing the waters category, instead of a full on commitment that you can publish the transcript when I don't have any idea how I'll feel about it when we're done.

And if you know sooner, great, but I don't think I'll really have time to start pecking away at transcribing this for a couple of months or more. And another one was you asked me not to involve you in anything about the book after this weekend. It will just be my project to attend to, solo.

Yeah, I just feel like if you and I started sending the transcript back and forth for revisions and additions and other decisions, I might keep feeling like I need to clarify this and edit that and remove those sentences and replace them with another attempt, or maybe I wouldn't be satisfied with how I talked about a whole topic, or I might want to add a cool new inflash from a bridging session the week before, and before I know it I'm getting heavily involved in some endless project that I don't even actually have an authentic pull to keep getting involved with.

And maybe suddenly it's three years later and we're still fine tuning and adding to a project that's become some huge multi-volumed Frankensteinian hodgepodge time suck, that might end up have fewer readers than the months we spent on it.

So yeah, I just needed to enter into this with really firm boundaries so I know there isn't a risk of it sliding into some kind of entrenched mess I didn't even consciously choose to get all involved with. But I did mention, I think it was in a text, but the one exception being I do feel like I want to have a vote and veto rights with the title, just to make sure it resonates with me. It would feel off if it turned out we weren't on the same page, and you went with something like, you know, "My Stupid Friend's Ridiculous Story." Or something that you genuinely liked but that didn't vibe with me. So we had our attorneys add that to page 84 of the contract.

I can't believe I wasted twenty bucks on MyStupidFriendsRidiculousStory. com.

Live and learn. And I was thinking about it last night– I didn't sleep that well actually, a little nervous about trying to do this – but I was thinking about it and I do feel like if this does get to the book stage, it should have Omega in the title. Probably not "My Stupid Friend's Ridiculous Story About Omega," but something. But we can text or email or coffeetize about it to pin it down.

Sounds good, and another request was you've said you'd rather me not do much editing.

Yeah, that's what sits right in me. I mean minimal stuff makes sense, removing ums and uhs, and maybe stumbles or false starts or interrupting each other, smoothing those kinds of things out a little when they distract or interfere too much and it doesn't change anything being conveyed. Or of course if I obviously misspeak or leave out a word that leaves the opposite impression of what I was going for, things like that.

But overall, I like the feel of just keeping it more organic and not trying to perfectize it. And another reason is I don't plan to proof-read it, or read it at all, and I really wouldn't want the meaning of something I said to be inadvertently changed when you were just intending to clean it up a little, and us never even realize it. And like I said, I really don't want to get into us having a hundred rounds back and forth, so this was the only way I was going to resonate enough with giving it a try. We spend a couple of days, then go our separate ways. At least with this little project.

And the last request or condition, which wasn't my preference but you were clear about it, was that you wanted it to be published as fiction. Do you want to say why?

Yeah, so a few reasons. First, I know I'm probably more concerned about this than the situation really warrants, but it feels like that supports maintaining the anonymous piece. The fewer people that confidently believe I really exist, the lower the odds someone will get serious about trying to suss out my identity, which just feels better. Adding that to the mix brings in one more buffer or protective layer there.

And second, after staying anonymous, my biggest hesitation about doing this – also probably more than the situation warrants but it's just how I feel about it – is the concern that some people, not most, but some, might just really take in everything I'm reporting Omega to have communicated to me as The Way Things Are, without filtering it through their own tuning fork or compass. That they might unconsciously give more credence to what I'm saying because I'm reporting or claiming that it came from a Higher Multidimensional Being, and therefore it must be the capital T Truth, and I get *really* uncomfortable with that.

To me, what should matter when we're reading a book or taking in information about things more subtle than current science and evidence can yet sort out, is not so much how amazing the source is that it purportedly or even verifiably comes from, it's more how much the words – or ideas or the vibes interwoven with them – resonate in us, how much they vibrate our own tuning fork. Really noticing or discerning which things actually ring true within us and which things don't, and not just digesting the whole thing unquestioned. Like during the bridging sessions, most things so far have profoundly resonated, some things not so much, and a few I have filed under just doesn't fly for me, just doesn't resonate with my own compass.

Interesting. I want to make sure we talk about one or two of those at some point.

Yeah, we probably will anyway, but if not, feel free to ask. And I fully admit, a lot of my concern about that is actually self serving, because I really get skittish and avoidant about potentially feeling responsible for what someone else might do with anything I say this weekend. I mean, maybe they misunderstand something, or just give too much focus on one little piece I might not say so clearly or explain fully enough, so for me to feel okay about even attempting this, I wanted that added disclaimer or escape clause or reminder, of it being categorized as fiction, to reinforce that it's each reader's *own* responsibility to sift through it and run it through their own resonance system or sorter machine. It's innocent til proven guilty, but maybe with more out there things it's fiction, or at least questionable, til proven fact, or at least til you check it out for yourself and see if it resonates for you. So just another reminder of that.

And a third reason is just that because of the first two, it helps my shoulders relax about trying this, it just feels more spacious in me, less responsibility on me, less pressure, just feels better. So all added up, even if it doesn't really make sense to anyone else, it was one of the conditions I needed, to get to where I was up for giving this a go, and since it's a seller's market, you had little choice but to buckle to my extortionate demands.

Ω Ω Ω Ω

And I don't mean to suggest most people don't run things through their own tuning fork, but, you know, I've heard tell that some people have been known to at times believe things just because they read them on social media or hear them somewhere. And with this being put out there anonymously – if it gets to that stage – they won't have a lot to go on, which calls for even *more* cautious skepticism than usual. Though even if it's *not* anonymous I still feel like these kinds of topics, that are beyond the limits of current scientific understanding and evidence, really call for checking in with our own internal compass a lot.

So not assuming that what comes out of this weekend isn't miscalibrated here and there, or even theoretically the whole thing. Which is another reason I don't love categorizing this as nonfiction, because that can be interpreted to mean factually inerrant, and *that* could be interpreted to mean I'm representing that what I've understood Omega to communicate to me about Multidimensional

Reality and Greater Consciousness, was first of all correctly translated and secondly was perfectly accurate to begin with, and I can't possibly absolutely know either of those.

I mean, just looking at it skeptically for a minute, even if we accept this at face value, maybe some of the information that comes through is off to start with. We don't actually know how perfect Omega's perception is, right? Are we sure Multidimensional Beings are inerrant and can communicate distortionlessly? And also, maybe I misinterpret some of what comes in, or contaminate it with my own unconscious predispositions and filters and biases. That's probably almost a certainty with anyone who experiences receiving subtle information, at least some small percentage of the time, if not more. And even if everything I say is actually 99 percent accurate, then if we talk for even half of the time we've allotted, that means, just by the numbers, there's going to be some places I'm off, right?

And you know, it's also possible that something shifted in my brain during that whole event and I'm innocently imagining all of this. Could be. Maybe it's actually all coming from a newly reorganized part of my unconscious mind, and I'm not yet able to recognize it as the source of everything going on. I mean dying does funny things to a person, sometimes permanently. So it could theoretically be that's what's going on, we can't absolutely know that's not true. Though if it is, you know, kudos to my unconscious, I didn't know I had it in me.

And actually, in addition to those possibilities, you and any readers also have to consider – well I guess you don't *have* to, but my whole point here is to strongly *urge* you to consider – another possibility here is that maybe I'm deliberately making it all up, lying to your face. Well not the medical event part, but the near death experience part and/or the bridging part. Maybe I'm desperate for attention or I'm really insecure, which I pretty much am sometimes actually, and maybe I want you to think I'm special, which on some level I probably do at least a little. Or maybe I've decided that using my physical death and resuscitation to give more gravity to some ideas or gleanings I've secretly had percolating around for a while is the best available option and that the end justifies the means and I was testing them out on you, and then you suggested this book thing just as I was getting ready to put these ideas out there somehow anyway.

Or another level out, for anyone who reads the transcript, maybe everything I'm reporting is accurate as far as I can see, but I'm making you up as a kind of literary device to share all this. Maybe I'm even recording myself playing both me and you, hopping from couch to chair, but everything I'm reporting and talking about is my actual experience. Or another juicy option, maybe *you're* making *me* up, and either *you're* the one who had these experiences, or it's just a way for *you* to share things *you* wanted to share, right? Could be.

Or maybe – and I think this is the last level out – but since this is anonymous, readers can't really – they have even less to go on than usual, so they actually can't assume either of us exists at all. Maybe someone *else* created this whole thing as a way of communicating some ideas, maybe working off their own actual near death experience and/or bridging sessions, or other direct experiences, or maybe not even that, and they just feel like this is the best way to say what they have to say. Which on the bright side would mean I don't actually have to finish paying my not insubstantial medical bills, seeing as how I wouldn't actually exist and all. So any of those could be the real situation here, as far as anyone reading an anonymous book could know.

And of course, me naming these possibilities doesn't remove any of them from what I think is reasonable for any readers to keep in their awareness. I don't think – or put it this way – I think anyone who reads the transcript, or the *purported* transcript, of our weekend should really hold this whole, I guess presented scenario, lightly, and just tune in to what resonates and what doesn't in the words. That's the point more than the purported Great and Perfect

Multidimensional Wise Source from whence the information comes, you know?

So yeah, I knew I wanted to say something along those lines at some point today, didn't know I would do it right off the bat, but I just really think it would behoove any readers to look at it like, "I can't know the truth of this guy's story and experiences and inflashes, and I can't even know this alleged transcript really is what they're saying it is, so what it gets down to is, am I up for giving it a chance anyway, at least for a while, knowing I'm not sure about the context here, and just seeing which things resonate in me – if anything – and which things don't?"

And then just holding everything lightly, keeping what does resonate, and putting aside or throwing away what doesn't. Not sure what else you can really do in this case, and actually I feel like that's what we should *always* do with *any* unverifiable incoming information, even if it's from a source we really know and trust. I mean, all humans have distortions and filters and mind tangles, no matter how consciously connected to deeper levels they are, and *I'm* not at all, most of the time.

So we all need to be our own authority of what resonates with us, especially when there's not much else to go on. Not throwing out anything that really does speak to you just because the source might not turn out to be the pure and perfect translation of like an inerrant Higher Multidimensional Being, and conversely not keeping or accepting anything that *doesn't* speak to you, just because you think the information might be pretty cleanly coming from a Higher Multidimensional Being, or maybe a respected spiritual leader, or some other presumably clearer source. So, skeptical compass checking, being your own authority.

And it's not that our own compass is perfect, never miscalibrated when we're assessing this kind of thing, but at least it's *ours*, and it's what we've got when there isn't much else. Okay, I know I started soapboxing there a little, just wanted to make sure I said something about that at some point, and it turned out it was all just ready to sprint right out of the gate.

Ω Ω Ω Ω Ω

I think it's good you laid that out. And I just want to suggest we add the word openness in there too. Skeptical openness, or there's probably no point in someone reading the transcript.

Yeah, I guess that's fair. Skeptical, compass-checking openness. That's probably a good way to say it. Or maybe skeptical, compass-checking, self-authoritied openness. I would just rather someone not be open to a word of this weekend than blindly believe most or all of it without running any of it through their own compass and critical thought, which would then leave me feeling responsible for what they do with it in themselves, even though I know that's their responsibility. But I'm definitely biased in that direction of the spectrum. So yeah, skeptical openness. Okay, I got that all expressed, feels good to have just named it. I can feel my shoulder's dropping a little.

Good. Alright, so back to my check list, just a few more notes. First, you wanted to make sure we mentioned about skipping forward. Do you want to do that or want me to?

Yeah, I just wanted to make sure we say, since each of the weekend's four sessions have pretty distinct topics – at least in theory – if any of the four main topics or any subtopics aren't really vibing with someone, then instead of dutifully sludging through anyway, just feeling free to, you know, skim ahead or skip ahead some, until something else sparks a little more. Like maybe "The End."

Or ideally a bit before that. And second, we're going to try to cover a lot of ground and we aren't sure how long it will take. We might not need as much time as we've carved out, or we might end up using all 16 hours of talk time and still not get to as much as we wanted. And the more I talk the less time there is for you to share, which is why we're here, so instead of hitting the tennis ball back

*and forth like a typical conversation, I see me mostly in the inter-
viewer role, hopefully chiming in just enough to ask some questions and keep things moving when needed, but otherwise, sitting
back and not saying much.*

So you're saying this is basically a two day monologue. No pressure. We might be done in an hour. Which you could still turn into
a book, you'd just have to use pretty big print.

*Well anytime you're not sure where to go next, it's absolutely my
job to get us moving again with another question, so you don't
have to take on any of that pressure. And if we're done in an hour
then we're done in an hour, that's not yours to carry, you're just
answering some questions and sharing what comes to mind to
share. But based on how fast the time goes when we get into these
things over coffee, and based on all the basics I want to make sure
we lay out and all the questions I still have, and how genuinely
intrigued I am by all the different aspects of your story, I'm really
not concerned that will happen.*

*And the last note on the list is to set the scene a bit in case that's
helpful. So we're sitting in my living room, I'm in a typical recliner
type chair and you're sitting on the sofa, though we might switch
seats tonight or tomorrow if either of us needs to. And I'm not sure
how long it will take me to transcribe our marathon and put the
book out, but we're recording this in late August, 2020, the year of
Covid, so I wanted to at least acknowledge that, and also say that
we both have people in our lives who have lost people they loved.
And just to acknowledge it's been a stressful, difficult, painful several months for more people than not, all around the world.*

*And hopefully it gets under control and stopped in its tracks at the
early end of the wide range of projections out there, but we don't
know for sure at this point what the trajectory will be. So, I just
wanted to acknowledge that, and we talked about doing this on
Skype but we both have a fairly low risk of having been exposed
the last ten days, and we both felt it would be smoother and more*

in sync to do it in person. We're also opting to not wear masks for this, but I scooted the recliner back a bit to give us a little more distance, and opened the windows and the sliding door, and I have the central air fan on, and even brought in a fan that's on low in the doorway, so there's some good air circulation. Anything you want to add about any of that?

No, I think you said everything. I just wish everyone the best, and wish them some subtle sense of Connection to something Deeper inside, something Deeply Good inside, to maybe provide a little support and comfort and settledness during difficult times.

I'm with you on that. Alright, what else? I have my notebook here with some notes and questions, and I'll most likely jot down a few more now and then as we go, instead of interrupting you or trying to remember a question while listening to you, so don't let that distract you. And as you mentioned, we have both our phones recording, just for redundancy, and they're sitting on the coffee table between us, plugged in and on airplane mode.

Yeah, thanks for letting me borrow a charger. Hopefully that was our glitch for the day.

I'm glad we have two phones, just in case. And I think that catches things up to this moment. Anything else before we dive in?

No, let's do it. Like I said, it feels a little high pressure and daunting to have all this time lined up, empty in front of us, recorders on, and I'm supposed to lay all this out, so please feel free to jump in and save me more than you described a couple of minutes ago, especially at first as I'm kind of finding my sea legs here, which ideally happens sooner rather than never. But yeah, let's get to it, and like I said, hopefully pretty quickly I'll forget about the phones and start to relax into it more.

And I guess I'll just add one more time, if this does become a book, my hope is that anyone who reads it, you know, uses their head and their heart and, like you said, open skepticism, or skeptical openness, and as they read, just checking their own compass and their own self authority, to see what resonates and what doesn't. Otherwise I just wouldn't feel at all comfortable sharing what's in front of me to share here. So that's my, well not just my invitation, but my sincere request.

Well said. Alright, then let's go ahead and dive in. First up, your near death experience.

CHAPTER 1

So I know you don't want to go into potentially identifying details about exactly when it was or the medical situation that caused it, but aside from those things, can you talk about what happened and what you experienced?

Okay, so basically for a few minutes there, my body took the phrase "Be still my heart" a little too literally. And I didn't experience like lifting up out of my body or anything like that, it was more like I was just suddenly in a completely different environment or world or level of reality, and it was this vast, oceanic, warm, safe, embracing, Love-filled, Light-filled Space. All of those descriptors were like the substance of this Space, what it was made of and what it was radiating through me.

And somehow I didn't feel disoriented or confused or concerned or shocked, and I didn't feel any residue or baggage from my body or any of the intensity I had just been going through. I just knew – and I never had a spiritual or religious background at all or any interest in those things, and I always assumed death meant the end and it was wishful thinking for anyone to believe otherwise – but in that Space I just *knew*, as sure as I've ever known anything, it was absolutely crystal clear, that my body had stopped functioning and I was still alive, still conscious, still me, and somewhere else entirely.

And this Space was overflowing with Peace and Contentment and Well Being and Okayness and Acceptance and Goodness and Love, and like this very subtle, almost invisible, yet very feelable Pure Living Light. Like I was surrounded by and immersed in an Ocean of Shimmering Loving, Light-filled Pure Essence. And I just absolutely *knew* that I was safe, and that I always *had* been safe and always *would* be safe. No question. I felt incredibly held by the Loving Benevolence emanating through that Space. And I felt absolutely special, but not like more special than anyone else. This Specialness was equally disseminated, it's just our inherent, irrevocable True Substance, our True Essence, our True Beingness.

And I felt really met, deeply loved, completely whole. Unsplit, unbroken, unwounded. I felt absolutely unencumbered, unweighed down by the gradually increasing shoulder weights of life. For the first time in my life I felt really, through and through, complete. Through and through enough. And I felt far more fully alive than I had ever felt before. I just felt profoundly filled up and complete. Wanting and needing nothing and lacking nothing. Nothing unfinished, nothing unresolved, nothing to hold my breath for or to tighten for or to delay or reject really being here right now for. All contraction, all tension, all holding anything old and worn, it was all just gone.

That sounds like an amazing experience.

Yeah, it was completely off the charts. And you know what it kind of reminds me of as I hear myself talk about it, I read *Chronicles of Narnia* as a kid, and in the *Dawn Treader* one, Euclid, or I can't think of his name but the selfish spoiled cousin of Edmund and Lucy, he had turned into a dragon because of his greed, and Aslan came to him and used his sharp lion claws to cut into and really peel away his thick and kind of life-dampening dragon skin, and then he was free again. Fully alive again. So maybe kind of like that, where I just suddenly shed all my old, thick, dampening skin, that I hadn't even ever realized weighed me down so much.

Ω

And I absolutely *knew* that the loss of all those layers that had suddenly fallen away – both the loss of that space suit or wet suit, meaning that body that I had been wearing to live a life on Earth, and also the loss of the emotional and energetic layers of old stuck wounds and patterns and tight beliefs – losing all of that just wasn't a tragedy at all from this completely new and more vast perspective that was opening.

Being free of all the old energetic structures and patternings that had been holding on to me, or that I had been holding on to, that was a huge and hugely freeing gift. And the death of the body was simply a natural continuation of how life moves on Earth. The most natural progression, the most natural cycle, the most natural unfolding. *How* someone dies might not feel natural at all, but *that* we all die *is*. Exactly as natural as coming *into* a lifetime is sooner or later leaving it. As though at birth, sand gets put in our lifetime hourglass, and sooner or later it runs out, for every single living thing that has ever lived. And it's guaranteed to not be evenly, fairly distributed.

What do you mean by fairly distributed?

Not everyone gets the same amount of sand in their lifetime hourglass, or the same kind of sand. Not everyone even gets to live a few decades. Not everyone gets an equal start or has equal luck or gets the – let's say the emotional nutrients they need in childhood, as well as physical nutrients. Not everyone lives a long healthy life or has basically a healthy body or a healthy brain or a healthy living or working situation. Not everyone has basic financial security or a safety net or a support system. Not everyone lives somewhere basically safe. Not everyone has good friends or close relationships or a significant partner or love in their life, and so on.

Life is absolutely guaranteed not to be fair for everyone. Part of the fine print of taking a turn experiencing the amusement park ride that is Earth. Number one, you *will* die. Number two, no promises or guarantees that will only happen after 85ish easy and beautiful and blessed and happy and healthy and safe and love-filled years. It doesn't work that way here most of the time.

I mean there might be some kiddy rides near the amusement park entrance where that's the deal, but they're just those old mechanical horses that slowly and boringly go back and forth without ever going anywhere or doing much of anything, so they tend not to be that popular. But on this little planet, sometimes life's the best, sometimes it's a bust, but sooner or later we all turn to dust. That's just the deal. The terms of participation.

So in that Settled, Quenching Spaciousness, the inarguable unfairness of the amusement park ride of living on Earth, the unevenness of how things are distributed here – which sometimes includes, along with everything else on the list, dying years or decades earlier than you might have – that was completely understood and accepted as part of the deal. So then feeling short changed just wasn't possible, it just didn't compute. There just isn't guaranteed justice or a guaranteed fair shake for everyone, which isn't news, but I was seeing that fact as just the nature of life on Planet Earth.

Ω Ω

You're living a nice, safe, well fed life in the lovely, quiet little town of Pompei, sitting around the table with your family planning your week, and suddenly a volcano has other plans. Same with a tsunami or a wildfire, or a texting driver not watching the road or a thousand other examples. Sometimes one twin dies as a child and the other lives to be a hundred. Sometimes someone dies in a car wreck on the way to a funeral, or after their own wedding. Sometimes someone just happens to be at exactly the wrong place at the wrong time when there's a freak accident or a mass shooting or a bridge collapse or whatever else.

I had a friend whose husband died when a big truck took a corner too fast and tipped over on his car. I mean what are the odds? And actually, another friend got hit by a truck too, on a country road in the middle of the night at an intersection. He was just in his twenties, and he was doing good, meaningful work, and just like that it was over. So the point is, a lot of times there's no rhyme or reason, bad things happen to good people, good things happen to bad, no justice or fairness to be found, at least, not pre-baked into the cake of this planet.

But in that Spaciousness, there was a deep acceptance of that reality, that truth, that fine print of riding this Earth ride. There was a lightness that opened up around all that, where I had had a chip on my shoulder for a long time, that would come and go, and it was partly because of my two friends and some others I had known who had died way too young – a distant cousin, just 17 years old, from another car wreck, and a school friend from leukemia, and a few others – and also because I often felt like I didn't really get a fair shake in my own life in some ways, that I had it rougher than a lot of people. That some seemed to be born into life with gold leaf toilet paper, and some of us had to use – well I don't know whether to go with sandpaper or with a cold, dark spidery outhouse, which I've experienced a few times actually, and it's not particularly pleasant. And the spiders didn't seem that thrilled about it either.

But now, that heavy chip of injustice had just fallen away with the other extra layers I had hardly been aware of. Dying sooner than expected had not the slightest hint of *that's not fair*. It was so clearly just understood as within the range of the terms of participation on Earth. Life inevitably ends with death, and it could happen anywhere on the bell curve. That's exactly what bell curves are – reflective of more common and less common eventualities – but every dot on the curve is possible and happens to some, and this was my own end-of-life plot point. It wasn't personal. It was a natural part of a larger whole.

And somehow that opened into feeling completely free of any residue of hard feelings towards anything and anyone I've ever felt hurt by, which was a huge, huge weight off my shoulders and chest and heart, and my whole being. Even though I didn't experience myself to have a physical body, I still had the self concept of one, and felt that deep, dissolving relief flowing through the energetic after-resonance of it. I really had no idea how heavy a weight all of that had been. How much it had been weighing me down and burdening me.

Ω Ω Ω

But in this incomparable Loving Space I felt so completely free of all of that, and of any confinement and constrictions in general. Of any weight at all, any heaviness. I could see so clearly that anything bad that happens in a life is, from a Greater perspective, temporary. Fleeting. Not inconsequential to us when it's happening, for damn sure – I'm not minimizing it or saying it's no big deal, I'm not discounting real hurt and real pain and real woundings and stress and fear and suffering. But in that larger timeless Space I was experiencing – or if not timeless, definitely way looser time, way less strict time, way less beholden to the gravitational pull of Earth time, not limited by our little universe's time as we're used to experiencing it – but in that larger, Light-filled Space, I just absolutely knew – from a deeper, more all encompassing perspective – I just knew in my soul's bones, that all was well.

Deep, deep inside me, which on that level of reality didn't really seem different than outside of me, all always had been and always would be well. In spite of all appearances and experiences that absolutely didn't feel okay at various times, like "Don't you dare tell me all is well when I'm going through this hell, going through this injustice, this run of bad luck, this great difficulty." And there's truth in that perspective, no sugar coating it. Things *aren't* always okay for us on this planet. But from where I was now existing, from where I was now vibrating or reverberating with the amazingly soothing soul healing and heart healing energy of Pure Liquid

Light and Oceanic Love that was everywhere around me – and also more and more within me – I felt absolutely Content, absolutely Accepted, absolutely Loved.

And I felt absolutely Pressureless, meaning no pressure anywhere, nothing I had to get right. Absolutely unable to blow it. Absolutely unable to mess up. Absolutely allowed to just fully be exactly as I was. Absolutely free, absolutely off duty. Everything was instantly beautifully Resolved and Safe and Infilling, and Deeply Good.

And probably for the first time in my life I felt Absolute Enoughness. I *was* absolutely enough and I *had* absolutely enough. And I hadn't been cheated, dying when I died. Everyone having their own amount of sand in the hourglass, or sometimes even the hourglass getting a crack, or suddenly shattering unexpectedly, that was just all part of the fine print in the brochure. I was suddenly sandless. Case closed.

Except it wasn't.

Yeah, funny how that turned out. "Will he be okay, doctor? I don't know, he's lost a lot of sand." But they were able to do a tricky little sand transfusion and got some sand back in the top of the hourglass. Or maybe they just turned the damn thing over, probably would've been easier. But during the Big Event, while I was experiencing everything that was opening, I had no idea I would soon be returning to that physical body that was quickly fading from prominence in my awareness. Or really, it already had.

CHAPTER 2

And how much time would you say had passed in real time, at that point in your near death experience? Or how long was that happening, where there was just that Light-filled and Love-filled Space?

I know what you mean by real time, but since the Big Event, it makes more sense to me to refer to it as physical time or Earth time. Easier than our universe's time. But yeah, I really can't say. Was it just seconds? A minute? An eternity of Timelessness? Time wasn't working the same as it does in our little corner of the Omniverse, and also the part of us that tracks time, that part of me had taken off its smart watch and put down its phone and didn't have a care in the world, just absorbed in what was happening, so I really have no idea. Probably not even 30 seconds in physical Earth time, based on all that happened after it, but that's hard to even imagine, because it was so filled with so much. It felt like, bare minimum, an hour or two, maybe a lot more.

But how much time was passing wasn't exactly on my priority list. What *did* matter was that for the first time in my life, I was experiencing something that felt along the lines of Home. I had never even known that a Deeper Home could possibly exist. Or maybe deep, deep down I vaguely remembered it and longed for it, but if so, that had been completely obscured my whole life.

So my experience was, I had no idea, no idea at all, that this degree of Homeness was always here, always so close by, always waiting for me. That it would always be where I would get to be after my life ended. If I had known that, if I had realized that or somehow remembered that, it felt like my whole life would've been so different. So much less fear and anxiety and tension. So much less stress and worry. So much less tightening and bracing and closing and shielding, and being inauthentic and feeling hurt and feeling done wrong.

And so much less concern about not having enough. About not *being* enough, or not being *good* enough. Not having enough basic value, *exactly* as I was. Pre-existent value. Without having to earn it with fleeting and ultimately pretty damn meaningless accomplishments or accolades or affirmation or praise. And there would've been so much less worry about what difficult things might happen soon or down the road, and about what anyone else was thinking about me or feeling about me or judging about me. None of that mattered in the *slightest* compared to this indescribably quenching Light-filled Space of Soothing, Settling, Healing, Belonging-filled Homeness.

The whole experience of living a life would've been so much lighter and more easeful. And both, lower stakes and more able to – well take two, I would have been more able to more fully play the game, without getting totally limited by it, or being limited to it, because of having a rootedness in Safe, Loving, Contented Home. Always. Always knowing the truth that Profound Acceptance, Profound Belonging, Profound Home, was never truly far away at all. And that it was completely guaranteed.

What I was seeing so clearly was that sweet relief is guaranteed for every single one of us. Heart Quenching Homeness is guaranteed. That was just such an amazing thing to absolutely and directly *know*, through and through, in every atom, every cell, or whatever the subtle level energetic equivalent of those would be. In the marrow of my soul. It was just really impactful.

Even just hearing about it is having an impact on me, so I can imagine.

Ω

Were you starting to be aware of another being at that point, or was there just the Space itself?

At first it was just these qualities of capital L Love and capital A Acceptance and capital C Contentment. Overflowing Enoughness and Profound Homeness. All these words that are describing like an order of magnitude beyond what we usually experience, I see as starting with capital letters. So these higher level versions, original versions, of Love and Enoughness and Safeness and Homeness, they were completely surrounding me and encompassing me and permeating me and flowing through me. They were all just different expressions or qualities or experiences of the Light-filled, Effulgent, Shimmering Substance that this Space was made from, and also that was just really powerfully radiating through it, meaning that Substance was radiating through itself, into me and through me.

And it was just so completely natural on that level, like it was just the air that surrounded you and that you breathed in and out. It was just the particular rejuvenating, fresh and invigorating, kind of ocean air of that amazing Space, and it was quickly becoming more and more what was inside of me as well. It was flowing through me, circulating through me, and actually becoming more me, or I was becoming more it. Like raising the vibration of my cells or I guess my energetic patternings, to a whole nother vibratory rate or pattern or flow or frequency.

And if one year ago me had heard me talking like this, I would've smacked myself upside the head with a rolled up science magazine to try to snap myself out of it. Well, first I would've gone to a museum and taken a science magazine out of its protective glass case since they're now extinct in the wild, but yeah, that was my experience. So I was just taking it all in, this Oceanness of Supra-Loving Light, and letting it move completely through me and impact me, and wash through every vibrating energy wave of my being. And I just said *letting* it move through me, but I don't know that I had any say in the matter, not that I wanted to stop it.

Did you have any awareness of or connection with your physical body at all?

Not one iota. I assumed it was dead, more like I knew it was dead, which it was at the time, and I had no concern or thoughts about it at all. How often do you think about your wet suit when you come out of the ocean and take it off and then put it in the closet? It's just not relevant anymore. How often does an astronaut think of their space suit once they're back home?

I'm a little hesitant to be that blunt about it, and I'm wanting to add things like of course life is precious and our bodies are precious, and both of those things are definitely true, absolutely. And at the same time, honest reporting, immersed in that Space, I cared about as much about my sloughed off body as you would a wet suit once you were done swimming. Good job, wet suit. I'm on dry land now, so I'll be putting you in the closet til next time. Except I guess these are disposable wet suits. Once you take it off, you probably aren't putting that one on again.

But you did.

Yeah, go figure. But like I said, at the time it didn't cross my mind that this could turn out to be a false alarm or a temporary thing. I would've bet all the money you can't take with you that my human life was over, and I wasn't missing it even a modicum. Like if you go on a trail ride and during it you appreciate your horse and you bond with your horse and you enjoy your horse, or sometimes you struggle with your horse not cooperating so much, and then when it's over you pat it goodbye and give it a few baby carrots or a sugar cube, and you probably don't think about it again. A little like that, except when my trail ride was seemingly over I wasn't saddle sore, and slightly more importantly, I was suddenly in Perfect Quenching Living Enoughness, Absolute Unconditional Acceptance and Belonging, finally really feeling how it is to be Home. I was more alive dead than I had ever been when I was alive.

That's an interesting way to say it.

Yeah, who'da thunk?

CHAPTER 3

And did you hear any sounds? Any music?

Definitely not music music. There was a subtle background, soothing, so natural I might not have thought to mention it, multi-chord like harmonic droning. A steady, slowly shifting, continuous background wide-spectrum harmonic. A perfectly balanced range of slowly shifting multi-note and multi-octave chords, that was beautiful and settling and heart-melting and that just fit so naturally and perfectly. That just felt so perfectly right. But it also didn't seem like created music, or even like normal auditory sound as we're used to it. It felt more like just part of the whole package of this oceanic Flowingness of Supra-Enoughness and Light. Like if you're standing at the ocean, hearing the natural sounds that emanate from it, it's soothing to your soul but no one's deliberately creating it. It's just a natural expression of the deeper harmony that's just inherently, organically happening.

So my experience was, if you take in the Beautiful More that's surrounding you with something like your sight, you see what you see, and if you take it in through something like hearing, you hear what you hear, and if you take it in with your suddenly wide open Original Heart, you feel what you feel. But this Quenching Space of Living Oceanic Light, it wasn't separated into different things, it was more just how you were currently perceiving it, and safe bet everyone would perceive it a little differently.

Really interesting. Which I'll try not to say after every new thing you share. So you were experiencing this amazing capital S Space for a while, and then what happened?

Yeah, so after those first timeless flowing moments of just feeling that deep washingness in Profound Acceptance and Belonging and Expanded Vast Beingness, I was suddenly aware of a Light-filled, Presence-filled, Love-filled Being in front of me. I don't know if it approached me, or if I automatically zoomed to it, or if it just materialized, or if it was already there and then came into focus, but suddenly it was right there with me.

Could you see it visually? Similar to how you normally see?

It was more like I was getting impressions and energetic inputs and senses, and then my mind created corresponding visual phenomena, in an attempt to match what I was taking in. So to me it looked as though this Being's Heart Center was kind of like a hugely powerful, glowing, translucent, subtle level electromagnet, with gold and blue and other colored energy ribbons streaming and flowing and arcing around it and through it and into it and out of it. A shimmering electromagnetic field of colored light streams, glowing and scintillating and oscillating all around it. Like hundreds or thousands of interwoven multicolored light threads, and sometimes thicker ribbons, orbiting and radiating and pulsing around.

It was a little like those glass plasma lightning globes. Vibrating colors of light flowing in and out and around and through a heart-stunningly beautiful, mostly gold and blue heart center, with other colors moving through also.

And it quickly intensified – at least my experience of it did – until it was kind of like psychedelic, kaleidoscopic shimmerings, of a million vibrant living colors, more vibrant than our physical eyes can see, of like oscillating energetic expression. And those visuals – and not just visuals but that whole sensory experience – was accompanied by exquisitely beautiful, almost annihilating waves of Complete and Total and Unconditional Love and Acceptance and Belonging and Joy and Rightness and Peace. So, you know, it caught my attention.

I might have happened to notice it too in that situation.

Ω

And maybe what I saw was influenced by movies or TV shows or pictures I've seen here and there in my life, in terms of my brain creating visual impressions that matched the essence of it. Maybe someone who died before electricity and sci-fi movies would've seen it really differently, influenced by their own cultural imprints.

And, you know, did I see what I saw because of subtle unconscious influences from images and movies I've seen here and there over my lifetime, or are those kinds of visuals what's in some images and movies because they're a somewhat accurate portrayal of a commonly experienced phenomenon for those who've glimpsed it? Or a little of both? I don't know, but there was a real immediacy and legitimacy and intimacy to the experience, where it felt like I was actually seeing purely and clearly and undistortedly what I was seeing. Pristinely. Like my inner seeing was pure and accurate, even if my mind interpreted it with visuals that were influenced by images I've seen in my life, if that happened.

Can you say that last thought one more time?

Yeah, so my experience of it was that whether or not the exact way my mind was perceiving what I saw was perfectly accurate – I mean if there even *is* perfectly accurate nonsubjective visual experience on that level, which there really might not be – but whether or not what I saw visually was influenced by past images I had seen, I still *knew* what those visuals were pointing to. On a deeper level I was perceiving that original pristine emanation really clearly and accurately. And there was absolutely no mistaking those unparalleled, profoundly deep waves of Undistorted Light and Absolute Love, and Deeply Quenching Belongingness, which were all the same Singular Pristine Thing. They were unmissable, unconfusable, unmisinterpretable, even if the visuals themselves were influenced or distorted by images I had seen.

And how long did this go on?

Until something else started happening? I really don't know how to answer that kind of question. Time stopped or slowed to a crawl or just — it was a different current in the river of time, in the spectrum of time.

So you're floating there, or existing there, in that Space, and then—

—Yeah I guess floating there, but I'm not sure that adds any clarification to the experience, because it's not like I was floating in definable coordinates a mile above the Earth. This was another level of Reality, another frequency of the radio dial, and there just wasn't space as we think of it. But there was *something*, that I was effortlessly floating in, or just *being* in, and it was a Pure Living Ocean of Vibrant, Light-filled, Essential, Loving, Intimate Homeness.

So you were floating there, in that Light-filled Homeness, in front of this Being. And how big did you experience them to be compared to you? And how big did you experience yourself to be, or did you notice?

There really wasn't size there like there is here. And I really shouldn't be saying there and here, I should be saying something like on that more subtle level of here, but I'm probably not going to remember or bother to do that every time. But when you think about it, without my physical body and without physical atoms, what would dictate or lock in your size? Maybe something does, but not the physics we have here. But my self concept was still that I was my size, so that's what I was relating to anything else as.

Did you see other things? What else were you relating to besides this Being?

No, I just meant that's what I would've related to anything else in comparison to. Me as my size. And this Multidimensional Being was definitely bigger than me, in terms of my perception. Not huge, maybe twice my size, but I think I was seeing more my mind's representation of its size. If I had seen it as the size of a planet that might have been hard to relate to, and if it was the size of, you know, a golf ball, maybe it would've been harder for me to really have anything like the same experience of it, so it just kind of showed up perceptually in a perfect size range.

And it was ovallish, a little taller than wide, like if you imagine an electromagnetic or energetic field, or an aura I guess, a couple of feet out around a person standing in front of you, but without a clearly defined human shape. At least that's how I perceived it. Like an elongated, Light-emanating orb.

$$\Omega \, \Omega$$

How close to you was it?

Well I'm not even sure there's spatial size and distance at all there, so this is all my mind's perceptions, but maybe 20 feet at first, then it felt closer as the experience progressed til it seemed maybe four feet away.

And was your self image still as a person? As yourself? Arms and legs? Did you notice if you were wearing your usual daily clothes? Same hair, same age?

I'm not sure. I was looking outward and feeling outward, but I didn't really, there aren't that many mirrors up there, which again isn't actually up there, like in the sky, halfway to the moon or just past the farthest satellites. But in this more subtle level of reality or dimension of existence, I just didn't ever notice or think about any of that. My guess would be, which isn't worth much, that I was an energetic presence about the size and general shape of me, but maybe less precisely defined or in focus, more energetically oscillating and flowing. And also that as the time or non-time passed, my self concept was less and less unconsciously identified with a physical human body, so I might have been becoming less and less loosely shaped like a human and more and more amorphous and undefined, but I don't really know.

So, as I became aware of this magnificent Multidimensional Being, that I didn't have a name for yet, I felt a new influx of more personal, more connected, more in focus Deep Presence and Settledness and Acceptance and Enoughness and Love. And point of reference, I've never been someone who uses the word *love* in my daily life outside of my closest relationships, except for like I don't love cilantro, or I'd love to help you move but I'm busy whatever day you decide on. But this was Real Love in its Essence, like the foundational energetic substance of Love flowing through and around me. This was like the highest and purest thing the word *love* could possibly ever describe. Absolutely Undiluted, Uncompromised and Unconditional.

So I'm just floating there or just *being* there, with this Multidimensional Consciousness in front of me, and there's this new inflood of Pure Love, Pure Joy, Pure Contentment, Pure Acceptance, Pure Completeness – capital letters as usual for these things a level of magnitude beyond our usual range of experience. And just follow your own sense about that when you transcribe all this, it's not high stakes – but it was such a completely different degree than most of us have access to in our lives either ever or maybe aside from very rare experiences. Orders of magnitude greater than I had ever experienced.

So even though I had already been feeling most of that in that Space that I had suddenly found myself in and was surrounded by, it intensified even more when I became aware of this Being, and also there was a personalness that showed up. A soul relatingness and intimacy. Two heart centers, profoundly meeting, interconnecting, which hadn't been there before.

And I felt such a response of just completely opening to it, to this Multidimensional Being, and of knowing I could absolutely trust it, and of being completely in sync, like my resonance was effortlessly matching this Being's resonance, or like a tuning fork in me was really, really vibrating. And it was so strong it was almost overwhelming, almost too much to bear. Like a cosmic ultrasonic toothbrush, in a way, this high vibrational energy was kind of smoothly shaking the old, stale, stained, crusty plaque out of my consciousness and energy field, which was a little intense, a little uncomfortable, but at the same time it all felt absolutely and completely right and completely natural, and so Deeply Good.

So a growing sense of profound familiarity and recognition and personal connection. A quickly growing clarity in me that this Multidimensional Being wasn't a stranger, wasn't unknown to me, and I wasn't unknown to it. Like we were having a profound and Joy-filled Heart reunion. I had come Home.

CHAPTER 4

And when you call it a Multidimensional Being, what do you mean by that, and how did you know that was the case?

Yeah, I just absolutely *knew* I was in the presence of a Being, of a Greater Consciousness, that was operating at least one or two or three dimensions beyond our three dimensional experience of reality, but more likely, you know, eight or ten dimensions or so – not that I understood at all what that means, or really understand now – but just a vast and deep and timeless Consciousness, that clearly occupied more dimensions of existence than we do, or at least than we're usually aware of occupying.

And also, from kind of the opposite side, what I felt wake up in me – to be able to perceive the More that this Being was – that wouldn't have been elicited, wouldn't have been activated, unless this Being actually *was* More. Your depth perception doesn't come into play or get activated unless you're seeing depth. Multiple inner ear hairs don't vibrate simultaneously unless you're hearing more than one frequency. Something like that, just with more subtle perceiving and more subtle dimensions. And I don't feel like that answer really does it, but it's hard to describe, which is going to be par for the course for a lot of this weekend I think.

So, the connection between us was deepening and deepening, and it was feeling more and more familiar, a little like – and this isn't it but just to make an attempt – somewhere in that broad range or spectrum of like reuniting with a long lost family member or with a significant partner, or with your beloved childhood dog you loved with all your heart. That heart delight and recognition, except, at least in me, it was exponentially more than any of those.

And this Being so clearly remembered me, or more accurately had never once forgotten me, is what it felt like. I was so clearly so dear to it, so precious to it, so loved by it. And I don't know if there's anything that could ever be more humbling and heart piercing than to have this amazingly beautiful Multidimensional Being of Light come to you, the most beautiful Being you've ever experienced by a factor of a thousand, and for them to be filled with Heart Delight and Love and Happiness to see you again.

And I'm starting to feel it again, or at least a taste of it, as I talk about it. It was so exquisitely – a word I've probably never used in my life – but so exquisitely, perfectly quenching and touching and life changing. Who would've ever guessed I could be that loved, that loveable, and that a Being like that could be so joyful to see me again? And it felt like joy was just how this Being experienced existence anyway, but this was like a specific joy, related to us reuniting.

But that I could be received by such a Being with such Love and such total Wholehearted Reunioning was just almost unbelievable, except it was happening during the most real thing I had ever experienced. I was just floored and touched and humbled and filled up with Joy and Homecoming like I never knew I could be.

I never would've imagined this degree of Connection and Belonging was possible. A year ago I would've thought this was just – well probably just wishful thinking delusion, or delusional wishful thinking, by someone in serious denial of the reality that physical death is obviously the end, case closed. But this was the belief-shattering opening of a completely new and vastly Greater Reality. It was the Purest, Deepest, Most Real and Quenching Homeness I had ever experienced. Times a thousand.

Ω

And it wasn't just that I was in front of what felt like almost a holy Being, that was overflowing with Complete Acceptance and Enoughness and Belonging. I also was feeling myself starting to dissolve away or melt away more and more, *into* that Greater Being that I was having this indescribably profound soul re-uniting with.

So all of that was opening in me, resonating in me, first through my connection with the Light-filled Space around me and now even more so through this growing and deepening connection to this just stunning and mind droppingly – which I don't think is a phrase but it kind of fits actually – just mind droppingly Beautiful Conscious Presence. And I was just merging more and more into this Being, as though I was melting into my One True Home. A snowflake into a beautiful hot springs. It was so deeply satisfying and just so – well actually deeply satisfying doesn't even begin to touch it. It was so far beyond anything I had ever experienced in my life before, or ever had the slightest gleaning could be possible.

It was Contentment times a thousand. Relief from any tension or tightness or pressure or holding times a thousand. Quenchedness times a thousand. Needlessness times a thousand. Freedom from having to be a certain way and from having to get anything right and from not being enough or not having enough or not being valuable enough or lovable enough, times a thousand. And that's probably underselling it, actually. Maybe five thousand or ten thousand. Way off the charts.

I was loved without having to earn it, I was complete without having to be a certain way first, I was enough without having to get something or get rid of something or accomplish something or accrue more trophies first. I was in irrevocably good standing without having to lift a finger. Which was convenient because at the time mine happened to be dead tired.

But I was free of all burdens and all responsibilities and all pressures, with no way I could possibly blow it even if I tried. This was irrevocable, unblowable, unruinable, Joy-filled Completeness and Belonging. I was being seen all the way through, every energy strand of my being – no thought or feeling or any part of me left hidden – and there was nothing to feel shame about. Or lack about. Deficiency about. I was still loved and met with open arms and so deeply, fully, incomparably welcomed and accepted. Just fully, fully Loved, just as I was. No hiding, no faking, no presenting a facade, no strategizing my next move, no hyper-extending my radar to make sure I wasn't being harshly judged or negatively thought about. I was so unconditionally accepted, so absolutely enough, exactly as I was. Exactly *who* I was, exactly *how* I was, exactly *what* I was. Times ten thousand.

And I could feel how this Being recognized me as so, so dear to it. I had no details or memories or specific information, but I recognized our connection to be the closest of close, closer than close, not even two. And there was less two and more one all the time. Or at least my awareness of the Oneness and of the releasing of my no longer needed and no longer wanted individual identity structures were both increasing all the time. This was my very Home, and more and more, I was becoming less of me and more of it. And this dissolvingness into that Greater Consciousness, that Greater Being, it felt like the most natural and organic and right thing in the world. Absolute Rightness. Times ten thousand.

Like has happened sometimes over coffee, as you're sharing about this, I'm starting to feel a bit of a subtle peaceful, still quiet Space, what you've sometimes called Presence, arise in the room.

Yeah, I always appreciate when Deeper Presence shows up, which has been happening sometimes when we're meeting to talk about these things. It's always nice to feel the subtle Flow of Beingness when it visits.

Do you feel it often?

Not most of the time. To varying degrees during bridging sessions, and then like I said, sometimes when I'm talking about these things, which I've only done with you. A few hints now and then at other times, but not often.

Ω Ω

Alright, so next I'd like to ask a few questions about this Multidimensional Being, that you later came to know as the Omega Consciousness or the Omega Being, or just Omega.

Yeah, I think I've used those first two sometimes in introducing the whole idea to you, and you can use them if you want, but really I just think of this Being as Omega. Feels more casual and closer and more connected. Less formal and distant.

I don't feel like I'm quite on the same first name basis as you are, so I'll probably mostly stick with the Omega Consciousness or the Omega Being.

Sure, up to you.

Alright, so first question, I think so far today you've been talking about this Being as though it's a singular consciousness, but in our coffee conversations, sometimes you've described it as plural, as a unified group of beings.

Yeah, it's really hard to pin down a Consciousness that's multifaceted, multidimensional and multi-leveled. So I go back and forth between singular and plural, like *it* and *they*, and I can't quite even explain why sometimes I use one term and sometimes another. A

3D language trying to describe a 10D or whatever D Being just isn't going to be that smooth sometimes.

Most of the time I think of Omega as one Being. I don't yet really have a space in my brain for both simultaneously, so I've kind of settled on singular as a default more often than not in my own mind, but I do move around. It felt like and continues to feel like it's both at the same time, which isn't something the human brain can usually easily accommodate. And sometimes I perceive it as leaning more one way or the other.

During the Big Event I experienced it more as one unified coherent or I mean cohesive Being, and at the same time, there were sometimes subtle wisps of a hundred beings gathered as one. Or maybe a thousand beings or uncountable beings, a family or tribe or soul group of beings, and they were all one Consciousness, but also with individualness, uniqueness, singularness. Individual souls, individual consciousnesses, all deeply interconnected, interwoven, as one Greater Soul. One Oversoul.

It definitely felt like our usual way of delineating one being from many just didn't apply there at all. Both/and. Yes, one Being. And yes, a multitude of unique beings that were actually flowing and breathing and being as One Seamless Being, one Seamless Consciousness, one Seamless Energetic Organism at one focal point of Awareness. Maybe a little like a huge solar power array where there are, I don't know, tens of thousands of concave magnifying mirrors, all amplifying and aiming their light towards one single, unified Hyper-energized Center. The many and the one. Both/and. Not either/or. Kind of a Multitudinal Singularity. I like that way of saying it. A Multitudinal Singularity.

And could you tell if this Being, or this group of unified beings, felt more masculine or feminine?

Both/and, plus neither. Somehow both were embodied, if I can use that word, energetically embodied. But it was always oscillating, ever changing, so it couldn't possibly be limited to a definitive answer to that question. And the same thing back to your last question. Is the Omega Consciousness one single Multidimensional Being or a, well some people might say a heavenly choir of Beings, though that preconceived idea didn't fit my experience. But a group of beings in unison, a perfectly synchronized tribe of beings. A unified family of beings.

And maybe us trying to really grok this is a little like a two dimensional being looking at a sphere and saying, "Is that a circle?" No, a circle is way too limiting a concept to describe a sphere, but that's going to have to be good enough in a 2D world. Or maybe calling it a capital C Circle works a little better, considering the limitations of a two dimensional being's ability to perceive a three dimensional object. So Omega's a Singular Collective. And simultaneously, a Collective Singularity. A Multitudinal Singularity. Something a little like that.

CHAPTER 5

And I have one more question cued up, you used the word holy a few minutes ago. Did you have any moment of wondering if this Multidimensional Being before you, that was radiating all those amazing qualities, was God, or an angelic Being of some kind?

I definitely never had the slightest sense it was God, and also not like it was God's Assistant Director of New Arrival Processing. This was a dear, dear long lost connection, and it never felt like – well, take two, there wasn't ever any thought of like should I bow down and worship this On High Godlike Being, or anything along those lines. It was a magnificent – that's also a word I just wouldn't have ever used before all this – but it was a magnificent Being of Pure Love and Goodness, it just didn't evoke – well it evoked awe and a reverence at the Sacred Pristineness of this Being compared to myself and anyone on Earth I knew of, but not – I mean the way it greeted me wasn't as though I was beneath it, or that I should bow down and praise it, or that it had all the value and I had none. Nothing like that at all, and that really informed my experience of it.

Can you say more about that?

Well, there just wasn't anything at all like I'm not worthy or subjugation, if that's the right word. And nothing like this is *the* Creator and Sustainer of All of Existence. I didn't get that vibe at all. And it was way too intimate of an experience to feel separated by station, by level, by On-High-ness – by how expanded and Light-filled and Pristine and one with the Beautiful More each of our consciousnesses was or wasn't, compared to the other – if that wasn't too muddled to make sense. And also, there wasn't a sense that just because this Consciousness was more multidimensional and more evolved and more awake and aware and connected than me, it saw itself as more valuable or superior or above me in any way at all.

And you know, from a larger perspective – and this is something that came in later during a bridging session – it's kind of like a fruiting tree isn't more valuable than a sapling. A tantrumming snot nosed three year old isn't less valuable than a brain surgeon. I don't love either of those analogies, but what I'm going for here is we're all playing our part, being humans on the Earth. It's usually a pretty tough gig but apparently someone's gotta do it. That's no less admirable than being in the easy breezy tropical paradise of existing in Everpresent, Conscious, Living Connection to Pure Beingness, outside of the heavier, thicker and dimmer, amnesia-inducing gravity of our level of reality. We've got the tougher gig. By far the more painful one at times. That isn't lost on Higher level Beings.

$$\Omega$$

What do you mean that's not lost on them?

So in kind of a counterintuitive way, we aren't looked down on because we're less conscious, any more than an astronaut that's brave enough to walk around, far, far from home and from real safety, on a desolate, rough-weathered, high gravity planet, would be judged for not being able to jump as high or walk as far, or hear as well or feel textures as accurately through their space suit, or just in general be as clear and connected as they would be back on their home planet. *Of course* they can't. They're facing *way* more gravitational and dampening and experiential limitations.

But amazing they're living there, exploring that world and walking around out there, with just a little thin fabric protecting them from death. Exposed and vulnerable and cut off and weighed down in an unfamiliar and difficult and heavier and more dense and more unpredictable world, far from home.

That earns respect and honoring and warmhearted care, and so much spacious grace, for when they so understandably lose their bearings and their footing and misstep and clunk and crash into things in the dark and fall down, and lash out at shadow monsters that sometimes turn out to be nothing and sometimes turn out to be their fellow travelers doing their best. Spacious grace for when they sometimes have trouble standing back up again after stumbling or being knocked down by the harsh winds, weighed down by the massive gravity and dense atmosphere of this far from home planet.

So there's not condescending judgment from a higher, superior place, there's loving compassion and understanding and respect from a higher, much easier and expanded and more Connected place, of being in lighter, more fluid and flowing, and more Light-filled and Love-filled gravitylessness, surrounded by the everpresent Fragrance of warm, safe Remembering and Belongingness and Home.

It would be ridiculous to judge another being without taking into consideration the impact of the heavy density surrounding them. Like judging someone as slow and unathletic when their race track lane has two feet of wet cement all the way around. That has *nothing* to do with them at all. The limitations and difficulties of being on this planet have *nothing* to do with our deeper and truer and more fundamental heart or soul or spirit or consciousness.

And once that astronaut is off that distant planet, back at home, space suit in the closet, then they're fully back to their lighter, less weighed down self. It wasn't their *own* flaws or weaknesses that weighed them down and limited them, it was just the very nature of the heavy gravity environment they were exploring, and the clunky imperfections of their spacesuit and its antiquated and glitch-prone processing systems and navigational systems and threat assessment and response systems and home base communication systems.

So *of course* they were walking right into boulders and tripping and falling down and not hearing home base clearly and losing track of where they were and how to navigate. Damn near *anyone* would. Astronauting on a far away planet is just hard and way-losing for those who do it. Not the slightest iota of judgment towards those of us in that situation. Only warm, loving, compassionate, real understanding and genuine, genuine respect.

Ω Ω

So from the perspective of Higher level Beings, on the one hand, they always deeply and intimately *know* that actually, from a larger, much more zoomed out perspective, all is well, and all will always be well. And on the other hand, it's really recognized and understood that most of us living a life in denser levels of reality usually won't remember much or any of that truth at all.

Along with beautiful moments and meaningful connections, and all the other gifts here, there can also be real difficulty, real pain, real fear, real sadness and despair, real isolation and aloneness, real illness and loss and grief, real unfairness and injustice, real atrocities, and the whole list. Which would be hard enough of itself, but that coupled with the complete or very near complete forgetting of our True Nature and of our Irrevocable, Safe, Loving Complete Belonging, it can be a pretty damn rough toll road here at times.

What do you mean toll road?

It can really take its toll. So all of that isn't lost on Higher level Beings, and there's a genuine respect and reverence and compassion and kind Heartfulness and appreciation and natural honoring towards those of us currently on one of these sometimes rough rides, one of these often not at all amusing amusement park rides, like Planet Earth.

It naturally hurts consciousness to not be able to feel connected to – or fully or even partially remember – its True Nature. To not be able to connect with its Ever Present but not currently accessible, Love-filled, Joyous Homeness. Its natural state and its Greater Self. Conscious of it or not, it tends to weigh down the heart, and take its toll.

So bottom line, we aren't judged for our ineptitude. We live in a realm where ineptitude is part of what's unavoidably elicited. *Of course* it's not easy to be cut off from the Deepest Love of our Heart. You get the idea by now, but I see those as capital letters. But *of course* it hurts sometimes. *Of course* it's a tough planet. And *of course* we feel the inherent isolation of the loss of our Truest Self and our Greater Oneness and our Deepest Home and our Deepest Love, even if we aren't usually in touch with that consciously.

So they respect and hold us as precious, for being on this precarious ride, and certainly don't need us to hold them in the highest subjugated esteem, just because we're temporarily weighed down in our thick astronaut suits, on a dense, heavy, mostly cut off planet.

I really like that perspective. I haven't heard it put that way before.

Yeah, I mean no one would judge or look down on like a firefighter for getting smoke inhalation or getting burn wounds, or moving slower because of all the equipment on their back weighing them down. Just respect and appreciation and compassion and even a genuine honoring them.

And no analogy is perfect, and we aren't *actually* cut off or far away from Pure Homeness, it's always right here, and it's what our very Essence is truly made of. But experientially we damn sure *are* cut off from most or all of it, most or all of the time. And I also don't mean we don't have any responsibility – any response-ability – to do our part the best we can. But it's just recognized that things are a lot harder here, and that's not – We're not blamed for that just neutral, inherent fact, as we live with relatively very limited awareness, on this dense and challenging planet.

Ω Ω Ω

So, I didn't feel judged or looked down on or like I was being seen as lesser than this Being. I felt so, so met and so held and appreciated and valued and loved and something along the lines of respected and even honored. But pretty quickly, the distinction between this other Being before me and my own sense of self identity began to melt away. The thin sense of otherness was dissolving more and more.

What do you mean otherness? Separateness?

Yeah, separateness. Two-ness. Distinction between the two of us. And mostly, there was this constant yet ever increasing feeling that this was where I belonged. That this Being was much, much more my True Home than anything on Earth. Like I'm a finger in the ice water, and I got totally lost in just being a finger in an ice water world, splashing around, no longer consciously noticing how cold it is, forgetting my larger, warm and cozy self. Without any awareness at all of the greater body I was always connected to. But the rest of the body, that that finger is never not a part of, is of course still there, sitting by the warm, safe, relaxing fireplace, wanting for nothing.

So this Greater Consciousness has always been here and connected to me, and what I now know to be true – which of course doesn't guarantee it objectively *is* true – but what I know in my *bones* to be true now is that when I die, at some point I'll be merged back into that Higher Self, and that that's much more the real me than this limited extension of it, that's for now living this comparatively cut off and two dimensional and not infrequently dissatisfying and challenging life on Planet Earth.

And ever since the heavens basically opened up and I found unimagined Okayness and Acceptance and Contentment and Love and Belongingness, things have felt a little flat and grayscale down here by comparison. That has been starting to change, bit by bit, and more so lately – which I'll talk a little about tomorrow – but it was just always in my face those first several weeks, and I still find myself sometimes comparing my daily life now with the incomparableness of then, of the Big Event, and finding it so comparatively flat and coming up so massively short.

And, you know, maybe after more time has passed I won't even be comparing anymore, I'll just be more fully content right where I am, which I definitely feel I'm progressing at least somewhat towards, slowly and shakily. It still feels like quite a ways away for me to really solidly more fully get there, or to more fully get *here*, without dissatisfied resistance, but I've actually started to see it as a real possibility in recent weeks – having a good, content, satisfying, rich and deepening life – which I couldn't see at all at first.

Ω Ω Ω Ω

But there are still definitely times I just feel ready to fast forward to the good part, and then sometimes when I feel that way there's a sense of heaviness or a falling short, like I should be more grateful and stop comparing. And of course ideally that sounds good, and

I'm inching closer, but it's still just not yet where I am a fair bit of the time. And in one of the earlier bridging sessions, just as it was starting – and I'll just do the short version of this – but I was really giving myself a hard time about that, that I should just feel so grateful to be back alive, yet almost all I could think of was how soon am I going to be back with my True Home, that this world couldn't hold a candle to for me.

I knew I was falling short of a higher possibility of being more present and content here and now, and I was trying to kind of strong arm myself to get with the program, and make myself be more present and open and grateful and content during this bridging session that was just starting. But instead, I was getting tight and down on myself for not being more grateful to have more time to live this life, and for not really being fully present for the bridging session – that I should be feeling really grateful for but wasn't particularly that day – and I was just getting really tensed out.

And then suddenly this inflash or flash packet whomped in, and by whomped in I mean when a flash packet hits, I suddenly get these images and this felt sense, and this whole data stream of understanding – and sometimes there's some degree of a Deeper Presence along with it, that just hits me and impacts me as soon as it hits – and then I unpack it, or it unpacks itself, for maybe a few minutes or more, depending how dense or detailed or how deep the material is.

And sometimes a bridging session whomp is almost like a slow motion, gentle energetic punch or push to the stomach – that's where it usually lands. That's where the delivery is usually dropped off experientially, and then it opens up and kind of spreads around like evening out the icing on a cake.

So this inflash just suddenly whomped in, and I experienced it in a really visceral and also a really visual way, that solidly landed in me, that – well the short version is, it never works, it never actually serves, in spite of our best intentions, to push away what we're feeling or experiencing just because we feel like we shouldn't be feeling it. Or to try to make ourselves feel something we *aren't* feeling because we think we *should* be feeling *that*.

Doing either of those just adds to the tension layers, the pressure layers, the self disconnection layers, and doesn't really support the unraveling of the constrictive structures. It's moving in a way that doesn't match who we truly are at the Core, and interferes with us being more connected to that, even more than the original presenting feelings we're trying to change do. That's the Cliff Notes version anyway.

There's something about what you're saying that's leading me to want to hear the longer version. I'm tempted to ask you to go into it more now, but we don't yet know how our timing is going to go, so maybe we could revisit it this evening or tomorrow somewhere if we have time.

Yeah, I'll leave that up to you. But we don't have that much foundation laid yet, that much orientation, and that flash packet went pretty deep, so it might be a little easier to connect with it when we have more miles behind us anyway.

Alright, adding it to my list. So how about if we go ahead and take a short break here and then finish up talking about your near death experience. Then we'll get into your bridging sessions after that.

Yeah, sounds good. I'm ready for one.

SESSION 2
CHAPTER 6

Alright. I want to get back to your near death experience itself, and open that up a bit more. So first you were experiencing an amazing Light-filled Space, then you experienced the Omega Consciousness there in front of you, and then your experience of those amazing qualities you described deepened, and you were also feeling profound Belonging and Recognition and Reunion.

So – well let me start with, how did you know this Being recognized you and was reuniting with you? How did you feel that or register that?

It just felt so familiar, like coming Home. Like seeing someone you really care about after a long, long time, a long, long journey, but again, times a thousand or ten thousand. I could feel this Warm, Joyful Love radiating towards me. Recognition, Reuniting, Re-union, Re-membering. Re dash union. Re dash membering. I remember thinking, why would this magnificent High level Being be so touched and happy to see me? I didn't get it, but I absolutely felt it and loved it.

On that level, that larger me never really left, and yet paradoxically, simultaneously, there was still some fresh re-uniting and re-membering and re-merging and re-unioning, that was only as possible as it was once the me that had been amnesiacally living my life as a human on Earth had returned there again, free of the temporary, Connection-dampening wet suit I had been wearing.

Can you say that again?

Yeah, so we'll probably unpack this more as we go, and I've already touched on it, but the feeling of being with Omega during the Big Event – that feeling of Belonging and Homeness – was so complete and unmistakable, that it was clear on some level – or on every level in me really – that that was my True Home, my true Greater Consciousness. And the larger, more real me is always completely a part of that Greater Consciousness. And on that deeper level, from one perspective I never ever left, because you can't *actually* leave your True Self. It's closer to you than your amnesiac, temporary small self could *ever* be. Always. It's just usually hard to connect with the truth of that when you're in the density of our level of reality.

When you play a video game or board game, you don't actually leave yourself and fully become the Monopoly wheelbarrow or the video game character or avatar. From that larger perspective, that's a ridiculous thought. But of course, my awareness has been relatively bogged down in the thickness of the amusement park ride, Planet Earth, so this feeling of returning to my One True Home and being met with open arms and a happy Heart – or a unified Soul Group of happy Hearts – that was such an amazing, off the charts experience.

And somehow even though my Greater Consciousness had never left Omega for a moment, there was still, kind of paradoxically or mysteriously, a re-unioning that could happen when the me I'm familiar with returned to the proximity of the level of reality where Omega resides. And like I said earlier, I just never knew little ole me could elicit that kind of response from such a beautiful Being of Light. Really impactful to feel that loved by a Being that's on that level of Pristine Consciousness.

Like those coffee mugs that say "I'm kind of a big deal," except this wasn't at all in an ego building way, but a really humbling, grounded, heart melting way, and of course it applies to everyone. There wasn't the slightest hint or misunderstanding that there was anything special about me in relation to anybody else, it just felt really amazing to be so met and welcomed and loved and unconditionally accepted by such an amazing Being.

Ω

And did this Multidimensional Being say anything to you, or communicate anything to you?

So at first the only communication of any kind was along the lines of the joy of re-union and re-membering, just energetically showering my thirsty heart and my weary soul, filling me with that Loving Presence, that Flowing Beingness. And then while that was happening, just being bathed in this healing beautiful Love and Belonging, far beyond anything I had ever experienced, for a few minutes or a few eternities – which might have just been like 10 or 20 seconds of physical time, I don't know – but while that continued to happen, I had my first little inflash.

And I want to make sure it's crystal clear that when there are words, they're never exact quotes, it's not dictation, and I don't have a photographic memory to be able to repeat them verbatim even if they were. But my experience of it is they're like a translation or interpretation of a direct communication, and then my mind converts it the best it can. Which potentially leaves room for misunderstanding or misinterpretation or unconscious leanings shaping things a little, without my awareness.

But this Benevolent Consciousness conveyed a thought bundle that matched really closely with the words "Now the bridge is in place. Bridges are still rare but they're becoming easier. This one will strengthen with time and attention. We'll be bridging again soon."

I didn't fully understand – well I didn't understand at all – but I was just soaking in the most profound experience of Acceptance and Love and Belonging, and that was really quieting my mind. I didn't need to understand anything, just let me have this Space and I'm good. I was so saturated with, you know, everything that was inflowing, with all these gifts coming in so strongly, just orders of magnitude beyond anything I had ever known, and that was just so much more than enough. I wasn't really thinking about my decommissioned body, aside from just an early fleeting, "Oh I guess that body is done. I guess that life back there is finished. Strange, I'm still here. I'm not snuffed out. And this was always here waiting for me. Who'da guessed?" Something along those lines.

And whether I ever saw again the connections, the people, the places that in my usual life really mattered to me, just suddenly didn't. I couldn't be bothered to leave this Deep Showering of Healing Light and Love and Belonging. I couldn't be bothered to step even the tiniest step away from this complete immersion in Settled Melted Beingness to think about anything or try to figure anything out.

I didn't care about getting my bearings, I didn't care about understanding what bridge this Being was talking about or what's going on or how did I survive dying or what are the rules here. None of that mattered in the slightest. Maybe at some point it really would have, I don't know, but it just didn't. I was Deeply Quenched and I was Home, and that was all the bearings I needed. This was the end of the Great Quest that I had never even started to embark on. That I never even knew existed.

Ω Ω

And what happened next?

Well at some point, this whole other slide show opened up. I meant side show, but I guess either works, except it was more like a full on movie, or a trilogy actually. But this whole other side show started playing out simultaneously, like they were happening in two completely different currents of a river or an ocean, totally separate from each other. The main event, of Belonging and Home, was by far what I was most interested in and drawn towards, but this side event started playing out too.

And it consisted of three flash packets in a row, that we'll go into tomorrow, but in the first one I started seeing images and getting senses and seeing scenes of possible future global events and situations, and just getting different kinds of information about possible future unfoldings. And then that was followed by two other related flash packets, including that one that to me was really optimistic and promising.

So those were happening on the side, and I won't go into them more til we get there, but it was such a singularly wild experience to have these two completely simultaneous and dissimilar experiences or frequencies or currents happening, and for my awareness to be able to really fully be in both, and take in and track both, without being overwhelmed or just shutting down from too much input. I definitely would've had brain strain if my usual daily mind had been tasked with all that – at least I can't imagine being able to handle that much bandwidth at once. Like an old dial up modem, with that lovely sound coming through it, trying to stream two 4K movies at the same time. But this was happening just effortlessly.

So I was fully taking in both currents, but the main event, the big tent, was what I was the most interested in and attracted to and responding to. It felt like I was just dissolving and dissolving and dissolving into this Greater Consciousness of Loving Presence, just enveloped by it and one with it. And everything else was quickly in the rearview mirror, getting smaller.

What do you mean everything else?

I mean, not the side show but my whole life and everything it had been comprised of. It felt like that had all been just a warmup to this, the Real Deal, and I was just dropping more and more deeply into a space of Settled and Quenching and Content Love and Acceptance and Peace. And along with that was the resolution of everything still unresolved, the untangling of every remaining tangle, the wafting away of every remaining contracted story or structure. Fully feeling that I had returned Home.

And at that point, I had no sense of if just moments had passed, or hours or days, since I encountered this Being. If I had to guess, maybe I would've said several hours bare minimum, but the whole experience felt before time or beneath time or outside of time. Pre-temporal or nontemporal or supra-temporal. I have no idea how so much got so packed into so little actual physical time, but it did.

I remember the next day when they told me how long – or how briefly – my heart had been on strike, I just couldn't believe it at first. I even asked to see the write up. I just couldn't match up that brief physical timeline – a few minutes – with all that I had experienced, all that had been opened. It was just so clear they happened in different worlds. Different levels of reality. Different temporal currents.

CHAPTER 7

And can you share anything else about the main event, or describe it more?

So just – well if you think of when you've had a really good, soothing, quieting hug or holding – where you really melt into it and everything just slows down and drops inside, and you feel really safe and still and quiet and content – multiply that times ten thousand. I was just in this deeply settled Quenchedness and Enoughness and Peace. The term *Quiet Repose* comes to mind, though I'm not sure exactly what it means. But it was really Spacious and Settling and Resolving and Light-filled and Love-filled. There was Complete Acceptance. Irrevocable Safeness. Absolute Goodness.

And somewhere in there, I was also receiving something a little like full on rays of Pure Healing Sunlight, burning through me – or if that sounds too harsh, melting through my no longer needed, antiquated ice shell – in such a deeply purifying and cleansing and rejuvenating way. And I was just dissolving more and more, or my old outdated outer shell was. But that dissolvingness was perfect and not the slightest problem.

Why would I hold that old, limited clay brick and straw structure together at the cost of fully opening to this Healing Showering or Flowing or Inwaving of Pure Loving Beingness, just moving through me, wave after wave? Except there was no break between waves. One continuous Flow Wave. It wasn't even a little tempting or at all worth it, to try to hold my old, no longer relevant shell together to resist this Newness. It was so clear that this was where the Real Gold was. This was where the Prism Gems were found.

What do you mean Prism Gems?

Yeah, I knew when I said that I would have to fill it out some. I'm making up some of the languaging here as I go, with hits and misses along the way, but what I was going for was something about an invaluable gem or precious jewel, that when you turn all your attention to it, it takes you all the way through, connects you all the way to the other side of the First Prism. Before the One Pure Clear Light separates into different colors, different heavier frequencies. Before the Indivisible Oneness, that's before created reality, becomes the many, within created reality. Becomes everything that exists. Something with that kind of vibe. And if that didn't quite track, I'm sure we'll come back to it.

But yeah, I knew I had found the Greatest Treasure, which I didn't even know or suspect existed just a minute or two before, at least in physical time. But now that I had found it, I wasn't even slightly split about losing my entire life for it. To me, in the midst of that full on experience, it was just crystal clear to me it was the greatest bargain.

Maybe kind of like a sandcastle on the beach, or let's say an ice castle on the beach, knowing not only that it could never brace itself tightly enough or for long enough to stop itself from being absolutely dissolved back into the incoming ocean waves – that it could never stop itself from returning back home from whence it came –

returning to that pure flowing liquid essence it always truly was, but also knowing, why would it ever even *want* to resist that?

I mean what's the cost benefit analysis here, of trying to protect a separation that no longer serves anything but the instinctual drive and the self identification drive of self preservation at all costs, and prolongs a fundamental misunderstanding of what we really are? Why choose grasping onto that for dear life, no matter the trade off, over letting my old stubborn structures be completely and beautifully and nurturingly melted by Enoughness and Acceptingness and Belongingness and Pure Flowing Beingness – not to mention Pristine, Light-filled, Incomparable Love – if all of that's being offered so freely to me, with my physical shell or wet suit long gone?

Ω

So I'm losing you a bit. Do you mean it was easy to choose this treasure over your physical life, or to choose it over holding on to your identification as an individual, free floating consciousness, separate from this Being in front of you? Or something else?

Well no wonder you're confused, I'm kind of going back and forth with both of those. So when this was happening I was assuming my physical body was kaput, but I still had my self identity and a lot of that whole package of structures and me-fullness that I was identified with. And the apparent fact that I had lost my wet suit for this Treasure – I mean if it had to happen – this felt like nothing but the deal of the century.

And also as I felt my remaining energetic and mental structures of self identification begin to loosen and soften and waft away in the Oceanic Light Substance all around me, and really felt those outer layers of protective energetic and mentally sustained shell or skin beginning to release, as I felt the ice shell begin to melt and evaporate from the Pure Sunlight hitting it, that too just didn't feel like the slightest cost at all, to let all of that get washed away by the ocean waves of Deep Belonging and Love and Free Unhindered

Beingness. I'll take it. No contest, no conflict or ambivalence or angst of a heavy price, no forlornness. Sold.

There just wasn't a shred of grief to let that old, well worn ice castle, that I had lived in my whole life, just dissolve away, and/or to continue to allow whatever structures in me might still be a hindrance to just dissolve away. It all felt like a good trade, to be able to be Deeply and Intimately and Irrevocably Connected to my Source Substance. To fully return to the Profoundly Quenching Home of the Effervescent Flowing Liquid Nectar of Pure Conscious Beingness, that was so strongly emanating in the Space around me and through the conduit of this Multidimensional Being I was so profoundly re-merging with.

So I was just fully in all that, while also having that sideshow happening, high speed, high def streaming of images and information and understandings, mostly about possible future events. So both of those parallel currents were happening, with no conflict or difficulty or overwhelm that they were both 100 percent full on. And in the main event, I was letting go of more and more of my old identity structures, feeling more and more merged and connected with this Benevolent Light Being, and it was just Deeply, Deeply Good.

And then, like a million miles away, a million universes away, this faint but strangely familiar, from so long ago, distant sense came in. An energetic tug, a subtle pull, some sensation, some activity, from some distant physical body that wasn't – well that I didn't even at first recognize as mine. Just this annoying interruption from some far away, vaguely familiar wet suit, that I might have been connected to somehow once upon a time, two or three forevers ago. It was maybe a little like an exponential version of being in the middle of something you're really into, and then your phone rings and knocks you out of it.

And by the time that happened, I was so deep in what I was in that it took me a few seconds to put it together, to remember, to understand what was happening. Oh right, there's a place called Earth on a heavier level of reality, and it has physical bodies that hold a greatly reduced trickle of our Full Awareness and our Multidimensional Vastness and Aliveness. And one of them is tugging at me, which is disruptive and annoying, and rude, and just leave me alone, I'm in the middle of something here.

There was something way more important to me in that moment than some pesky mosquito buzzing around my ear, annoying me. Than some irrelevant, invasive spam call disrupting That Which Is Most Valuable.

CHAPTER 8

And then a little more memory clicked back in, oh yeah, that's *my* old body. That's right, I had a body. I had a life. Rings a bell. Oh right, that body stopped working and died, I remember now. Weird, I guess it didn't take. That's disappointing. I mean don't get me wrong, I don't mind if it lives, knock yourself out, you did your best and served me well for a long time, a trusted steed. You deserve it and all, more power to you, just don't get *me* involved. You're not my business anymore. Maybe I could just say nobody's home and get back to what matters. Just swipe the call to voicemail.

But what started as a prodding, an annoyance, an inkling of something pulling me back, it quickly became stronger and stronger, like you're trying to relax on your couch and your dog keeps jumping on you and barking because there's a ninja squirrel outside threatening your territory. You're gonna lose that battle sooner rather than later and won't get any dog gone sleep.

And then it suddenly all flooded back to me, the whole kit as well as the caboodle, and the current situation got crystal clear, and I knew that my body was being revived and was coming back to life.

And I also just knew that the laws of subtle level physics, or the fine print at the bottom of the amusement park entrance ticket, or whatever it was, meant there was an imperative or an ordinance – that I couldn't fight even if I tried – that my presence was kindly requested elsewhere. And if I refused, the matter would be quickly and involuntarily escalated, like a police officer kindly suggesting you get in the back of their car if you don't terribly mind, watch your head, to go with them down to the station if you have time and it isn't too much trouble.

And as I was realizing this – which this whole thing was maybe ten or 20 seconds physical time, but really I have no idea, time was so slow and zoomed in and so rich with so much – but I just started almost like falling backwards or being pulled backwards towards this quaint old wetsuit or space suit – let's call it an Earth suit – of a physical human body. And even though it was so far away and so insignificant, it clearly had *all* the power here and I had none, or I wouldn't have been so rudely interrupted.

Some bodies are so selfish.

Exactly, that's how it felt. Just me me me me me. "Pardon me, but if it's not too much trouble, I'd like to spend more time alive before my final death, seeing as how they've already brought me back to life and all." Talk about greedy and self absorbed and narcissistic. Dude, you're harshing my mellow here!

And as my awareness was quickly being pulled back towards it, it was like I was falling away, or being pulled away or yanked away, from this beautiful Multidimensional Light Being, and it was also like this Being was zooming away from me, and also like neither of us moved at all but like it just kind of all started fading – like changing the channel on the radio doesn't move the radio waves of your old channel or stop them from waving through at all, you just can't experience them anymore. Except this was so fast, and also like a slow motion fade out, all at the same time.

And then it felt almost exactly like there was suddenly a cable attached to a harness around my ribcage, and it must have been attached to one fast mother cranker, pulling that sucker in. And *I* was the sucker. Forced to leave my newly discovered One True Home to re-enter that weak and limited and diminished and probably for a while pain-filled physical shell again.

I felt hoodwinked. It felt really disrespectful, and even kind of violent, how abrupt and fast I got yanked back, involuntarily. No permission, no vote, no consultation, no mediation, no how would this be for you? No let me tell you what's about to happen so you aren't whiplashed. I didn't even have time to take a stand and protest, and proclaim, you know, "Over my dead body!"

Ω

And there was a, like a brief parting message from this Being, after I was already being pulled away, during the fade out, but it didn't help anything. It wasn't enough, it wasn't what I wanted. I wanted to *stay*. But I was just whipped back with this great force. Just Boom Zip Thud, and I was *whammed* back into that fragile, tired, barely re-ticking body. Just so harshly whomped back in. Not even an airbag or a slow down at the end for a more comfortable re-docking experience. Just *wham*.

You know how when they connect train cars, it's like this really loud echoing, jolting, ramming thud-bang. It was kind of like that. And for all I know it was actually a pretty gentle re-entry, but in comparison to what I was just experiencing and embodying and being filled with, and with so much of my comparatively thick skin energetically wafting away, leaving me way, *way* more sensitive than before – and I was already pretty sensitive – it *felt* like I was just violently slammed back into this long forgotten and still struggling physical body.

And the simultaneous awe of all I had just experienced – including the three side shows I haven't gone into yet – plus the sudden, abrupt shock of being torn away from my Deepest and Truest Home that I had only just discovered, it was all *way* bigger of a shock or a thing to deal with than that pesky little run of the mill thing called dying and being resuscitated back into a tired and struggling Earth suit.

It was just way rougher than all the huge physical discomfort of being back in a body that had just been a little on the dead side and still wasn't a very happy camper. It was the mother of all rude awakenings, and it hurt like a mother too. I was disoriented, and I was in physical shock from my body dying and being resuscitated, but at the core I was broken hearted. My heart was whiplashed and left for – well I almost said left for dead, which is actually really how it felt. In death I had found true life and in returning to life, my heart felt dead.

I had found a Joy and a Completeness and a Love and a Belongingness beyond anything I would've ever been foolish enough to dare believe could exist – I mean gullible dreamers and hopeless romantics just get hurt, it's safer to be a little cold and caustic and callus and cautious, especially since, let's get real, there's nothing out there, nothing beyond here, what you see is what you get – but then I found this Great Living, Healing, Unparalleled Jewel of Invaluable Preciousness, that was then unceremoniously just ripped away from me, with no warning or explanation or chance for closure. The run of the mill, salt in the wound physical difficulties completely paled in comparison.

What do you mean salt in the wound physical difficulties? They just made the situation worse but weren't the biggest thing?

Yeah, nice deciphering. And just in case I haven't quite made this clear, I did *not* want to be back in that subpar Earth shell, that ragged Earth suit. I did *not* want to return. I had some wisp of a thought of compassion and appreciation for that struggling body that was going through a hard time and that had served me so well my whole life, like when you trade in your trusted old car you're so fond of, that short lived little tug in your heart when you leave it behind for a newer model.

But being locked into it again? For probably *years*? Hell no. Why would I? Nothing could compare to where I just was, what I was just beholding and being with, what I was just immersed in, and what I was for the first time in my life actually *being*. Nothing in my old, outdated physical Earth life could even hold a candle to that Pure, Flowing, Healing, Love-filled Sunlight. The candle would just melt.

So to be ripped away from that without any warning was as big a jolt for me as dying and being resuscitated was a jolt for my body, or even bigger. The word that's coming – and again, I've never used this word in my life, unless maybe in high school English I read it out loud from a Shakespeare sonnet or something – but I was ripped away from my One True Beloved. The Source of the Deepest Love I've ever had access to, times ten thousand. My One True Home.

CHAPTER 9

And what was the message? What did the Being say as you were being yanked away towards your body?

Yeah, so the whole pull back or rip away or the cable being cranked in, I experienced on one level in slow motion, and while it was happening I could feel this Multidimensional Being kind of inwardly gently smiling, without the slightest concern about me being pulled back, because from that level, none was needed at all. And I don't mean coldness, I just–

–No concern was needed?

Yeah, no concern was needed. And it's not that the vibe felt cold or uncaringly indifferent, just unconcerned. And the words that came in – interpreted through my brain as always – were along the lines of, "All is well, Dear One. Yes, you have the privilege of going back to your Earth body for a time, which is really no time at all. And then you will return here, and for us, from where we reside, you never truly leave, and your return is more than certain. So enjoy the rest of your brief and precious Earth journey as you can. It's not so easy to get a ticket. And always, always know that from our vantage point, in truth, all is well. All is, and all shall be, deeply, deeply well."

I really felt the reverberations of that as you said it.

Well I don't mean to minimize it, but it just wasn't enough, it wasn't what I wanted. Easy to say all will be well and all already *is* well when you're on high, up in your castle, your every want and need met. Or beyond that even, just no longer really wanting or needing anything, in a continuous state of Quenchedness. Us common folk just don't have it so easy. It just didn't comfort me or help with the shock of being slammed back into my Earth suit.

And after that jolting crash landing, during those first few miserable weeks there were two very weak consolation prizes that I wasn't interested in at all, because I only wanted the Big Prize. They were almost like little mementos or worry stones or comfort stones, that I could keep in my pockets and wrap my fingers around if I wanted. But I was so jaded, they just felt like painful, bitter reminders of what I had lost, instead of tender pointers to what I had found.

And one was the amazing experience of the Big Event itself, and it was such a sore spot because I had lost all access to the Space and Connection and Belonging I had found during it. It was bittersweet, with the sweet being ripped away.

And the second was that parting message, a reminder that all was well and would be well, even though for now, on a more surface level, it was such a harsh, abrupt, hugely unpleasant and uncomfortable re-docking with my damaged Earth astronaut pod, and then having to inhabit it, empty gray day after empty gray day. Not just during the uncomfortable recovery, but projecting forward, being stuck in this miserable cut-offness until my body stopped working the final time. So that second uncomfort stone, it was salt in the wound too, just a reminder of how cut off I was from being free and truly alive and joyfully melting into a Space of Pure Acceptance and Love and Freedom and Beingness and Expandedness, without a care in the world.

So yes, I had those two little reminder stones in my pockets, the memory of the Profound Homeness of the Big Event, and that sense that for that Multidimensional Being I had connected so deeply with, there wasn't any problem with me returning to my Earth life-time for a while, and that in the Deeper Reality I wasn't actually cut off in the slightest, all was well and always would be. But I felt so hurt and disappointed and jaded and betrayed at being forced back that it felt like, "Easy for *you* to feel that way. *I'm* the one that was forced to leave the Oneness for cut-offness again, except now I know what I'm missing. What every moment isn't but could be."

Ω

So it wasn't comforting at all, and I was trying to process everything those first weeks in particular, and yeah, of course it was impactful to realize that we not only survive death, but also that That Which Is Waiting is so Infinitely More than that which is usually available here. And again, it's not really here and there. It's here, and then capital H Here. Full frequencied Here, instead of very dense and narrow frequencied here.

But the deep grief and shock of losing the off the charts Love and Belonging and Joy and Expansion I had found, that was much more negatively impactful to me those first weeks than the positive impact of what I had found or the parting words that all is well. Yeah, sure, all is well for *you*. *You* didn't fall down, comparatively, a mineshaft, to be stuck maybe for years in relatively isolated, sunless, cold and dusty darkness.

I guess it's a little like if the love of your life suddenly says, "I'm leaving you, but don't worry, it's all good, and I'll see you again in maybe a few decades, give or take a couple." "Oh, it's all good? Great, okay, in that case have fun and see you then." Not the most likely response.

And it's fair to say that I was basically tantrumming there for that first month or so, refusing to be comforted by the gifts of everything I had experienced. During the Big Event, all complaining or tantrumming at the unfairness of life instantly fell away in that Oceanic Light-filled Completeness and Love, and in my sudden deep understanding that the randomness of what happens here isn't personal. It's just the terms of participation. But now, any remaining subtle afterwaves of all that were overshadowed by the loss of it. Better to have never loved than loved and lost it all.

And I couldn't see that I was, you know, detrimentally tantrumming, getting more entrenched in the hole I was in, I just felt bitter devastation. I just – it took me a while to even begin to see I could at least climb the stairs out of the dungeonesque basement into a dark dusty living room, with at least a few window shades I could pull back, and maybe even open a few windows a little. Or, what a concept, maybe even actually step out onto the porch. I couldn't even see any of that at first.

And when you first realized you were back in your body, was there any sense at all of it being good to know you were alive again, even if it didn't feel good physically? Or was there just the despair of losing what you had found?

Yeah, not even slightly. I wasn't a happy camper, and I didn't feel like I had any viable options to get things back the way I wanted them. Somehow it was just understood in me, you don't cut short your life to get back to melting in Perfect Love and Contentment and Expansion and Belonging. You just don't. *Wanting* to return

ASAP, that's an understandable response when the heavens have opened, and then slammed shut. But to not take good care of this life, or to take action in order to hasten the conclusion of it, there was just like a gentle but stern, crystal clear *no* around that. Or maybe more accurately, a gentle but firm invitation or directive to accept that you're back in your physical life on Earth, and that's rightly where you are until the time arrives, unbidden by you, when you aren't.

There was just a clarity in me – and I can't say for sure it's objectively accurate – but there was a strong sense that doing anything to speed up the ending of your life to get to That Which Is Waiting, without any real, physically mitigating circumstances like terminal illness, it just might be that that adds a weighted cloud that would need to be somehow cleared first before the big payoff that I was so craving. Meaning I'm not even sure it would have worked, at least not right away or effortlessly. It might not turn out to actually be a shortcut at all.

So at least in me, it was just de facto clearo that deliberately speeding up my return to Home wasn't on the table. It's hard to explain, I just *knew* that, without any big deliberating. So I had no viable options to get what I wanted. I was stuck, and I wasn't happy about it. It all just felt like the greatest betrayal of the promise of finally being truly irrevocably Home, a hugely deflating and disheartening and unjust interruption of finally finding Perfect Love and Belonging. So yeah, finding then losing the Great Treasure I never knew was even worth searching for – that leaves a mark.

Ω Ω

And did you have any moments of really feeling those comfort stones? Feeling at least a bit connected to what had opened during you near death experience? Did it revisit some now and then?

Well, there were moments here and there, of like feeling a quieter current inside, that radiated a hint of a sense that everything actually *was* deeply okay, and that coming back into my body wasn't a – that it wasn't a betrayal or a personal jading towards me. It was just what was happening for now, temporarily, and I knew I couldn't fight it and didn't need to. Moments of knowing that actually, loathe as I was to admit it in my solo pity party, all was and would always be well.

But it was a pretty faint, occasional current, and one little drop of water here and there doesn't do much for you in the desert. Maybe if I had put all of my attention on focusing on it and following those little drops of water, they would have gradually led me to a watering hole or a stream or even an oasis, or maybe even led me completely out of the desert.

But at first I was too insistent in my hurt and jadedness and done-wrongness to really notice that current or give it any space or attention, and when I did here and there, at least a little, it just felt like so not enough, so I rejected it. Like a few bread crumbs now and then if you haven't eaten in days. I was too busy noticing it wasn't enough food to check out if those bread crumbs could gradually lead me to more food if I followed them. Kind of like if a hungry young robin after a rain sees the very tip of a worm tail sticking out of the soil and thinks "That little mini-worm is way too small to be worth flying over to it for a meal."

But bottom line, I just wasn't interested in a puny consolation prize, or a delay of however many years before I got to return again to really being with the incomparable Quenchedness of Pure Loving Beingness. So I was pretty God forsakenly miserable for most of that first month or so. And even when I did feel a hint of that Deeper Current, it didn't undo or counteract how intolerable the surface waves were. It just gave it – it just gave the surface a little more perspective for maybe a few hours.

If you're pushed into a mine shaft and now you're trapped, being told don't worry, sometime in the next few decades – give or take a few – you'll be free again, so just relax and try to enjoy yourself, and you're being told that by the one who pushed you in – which was how it felt – that's not gonna do a lot for you. A toddler with a lot of teething pain isn't that comforted by giving them their blankie and telling them they'll feel better in a month or two. Yeah thanks, but just give me the damn baby Tylenol and a double shot of milk on the rocks, pronto.

And for my own inner tantrumming toddler, a few decades, give or take, sounded excruciating. You meet the love of your life, times ten thousand, and then they abruptly and unexpectedly kick you out of theirs. Whether it's with or without the promise of eventually reuniting what could be decades down the road doesn't really make much difference. Your heart, and even your soul, still go through the ringer.

Ω Ω Ω

Was there – well I have a couple of questions cued up but let me ask first if there's anything else you want to say about the first minutes or hours or days after snapping back into your body, or those first weeks? Did it start to get easier?

Not really. Meaning I don't really have more in mind to say. Just that for those first weeks I was 98 percent devastated to be ripped away, wasn't happy about that at all, and two percent of a wavering hint of a lightness or a sparkle in my heart, because a door had been opened and now I knew something I had never known before, and I had been just completely bathed or immersed in something exquisitely Beautiful and Good that I didn't know could possibly exist.

And the promise of returning to that, and also that subtle sense that even though it was mostly lost to me, I wasn't lost to it – I could *never* be lost to that Light-filled Space, or to that Being of Love and Goodness and stunningly Beautiful Presence – the little hint of knowing the promise of that, I *did* know that was always holding me in the background, even if I mostly couldn't feel it and wasn't at all satisfied with the minusculity of it. No matter what my experience was, that *did* stay with me, at least to some degree.

Two percent.

Right. 2.27 but I rounded down. And in retrospect, I don't really doubt it would have been at least somewhat more if I had just been a little more willing to really receive the available reduced Goodness instead of rejecting it because of how short it fell. So two polar opposites that were born of the same – one very quiet and easy to miss, and one louder and stronger and more jaded and tantrummy and getting pretty much all of my focus. I was feeding the poor me one with all of my attention and emotion and belief, and starving the delicate, lovely, amazing new Greater Reality one. So things–

–Could you talk about – oh go ahead.

Yeah, just to finish this thought, so things felt bleak and gray, and being back alive but cut off just felt pointless. Valueless. Like why the hell would I want to stick it out here any longer if I had any real, viable choice in the matter, which I didn't feel I had. And as my life started to return to normal on the outside – recovering, working, living my daily life – I was still just hugely empty on the inside. In comparison to what had opened, I was just – well there was just clearly nothing here for me. Nothing.

Making a barren, bone-dry, lifeless desert your surrogate home until your body eventually dies so you can really live again – not a very joy inducing or thrilling prospect. What's that term? Life affirming. Not a very life affirming thing. Although I was wanting to affirm Deeper Life, which had so affirmed me, before abruptly jettisoning me out again. I just didn't have any access to it from the desert.

So it seemed obvious there was nothing to do in this empty but weighed down shell but to try to go through the motions of a normal life. To try to take care of my life and my responsibilities and my work and my relationships as well as I could. To ostensibly get back to living my life. But my heart wasn't in it. At all.

CHAPTER 10

And what were you going to ask?

Well there's two things I want to circle back to. One is your clarity that even though the life you had been pulled back into was profoundly empty to you, you didn't consider it an option to shorten it. Anything more to add about that? You never had a moment of despair where it crossed your mind?

Well, I mean longing to be back to what to me was an unmeasurably more Real World, that was with me all the time at first, and of course that constant aching to be somewhere else mostly kept me from noticing the little mini-gems of Goodness that *do* come and go, along with the thorns, which just further reinforced there was nothing here for me that would ever even *begin* to help compensate for the loss of That Which Was Waiting.

So there were definitely thoughts of, I wonder how soon I'll be done with this suffering and be back Home, and sometimes thoughts of, I can't wait til I'm the hell out of here, like a kid on the last day of school before summer vacation, staring at the clock.

And there *were* a few just pass through thoughts of calling it done, but I was never once close to actually taking any action around that. Would I have been sad if I suddenly woke up dead? Nope, not for a second. Or maybe for a second or a minute, but honestly maybe not, I mean I wasn't at all during the dress rehearsal. So I'd probably be 99 percent relieved the slog was over, cue the New Orleans brass band parade, my Real Life could finally begin. That was how I honestly saw it.

I remember once early on, I was eating something and started to choke for a few seconds, and while my body was doing its thing to try to clear my airway, I had the thought come up, I'm actually not so sure which way I want this one to go. All I *really* wanted was to be in that Love and Melted Oneness again. Nothing on Earth could compare, at least not in *my* life experience. But there wasn't any serious thought about speeding that up.

Somehow I just knew, or it was just so apparent that I didn't even *have* to know it, that that wasn't on the table. Like maybe if you have a teenager who's going through a phase of absolutely driving you crazy lately – just the last five years or so – and maybe you secretly just guiltily can't stand their personality at *all* these days, but you still know, so deeply you don't have to even realize you know it, that it's not an option to just send them away somewhere forever.

I mean maybe for summer camp, sure, the longest one you can find and hallelujah, but not permanently. You might google "List of colleges that accept ungrateful, entitled, self absorbed and just between you and me not that bright 15 year olds" but that's about as far as you'd go. You can't and you wouldn't and you won't actually sever your right relationship and responsibilities as their parent. Not even a starter discussion. So like that. Just obvious. I'm my body's steward, and it's my ward, til death do us part. Death unhastened by me trying to speed things along, like it or not.

In me it's just been clear, you don't trade your life on Earth before its time for the Deep Love and Contentment that's safely and assuredly waiting for you anyway. It just doesn't work that way. It was just so pre-known in me I didn't need to know it.

Ω

And also, like I said earlier, there was that sense that that kind of attempted shortcut just doesn't turn out to be one. Sometimes shortcuts are actually detours, that slow things down more than if you had just stayed the seemingly slower course, if you had just been patient in what's currently the excruciatingly slow lane.

And I just feel like I should add, because this is pretty tender territory, I'm not trying to say anything at all about anyone else's circumstances, I'm just saying in *my* case I wasn't struggling to stay afloat in storm sized waves of massively heavy darkness and full on despair, it was just – compared to the Big Event – my life was profoundly gray and barren and desolate and purposeless, and I wanted to be back in that Indescribable Quenched Homeness more than I wanted anything else, including wanting my empty gray life to continue. My pendulum had swung from being convinced all there is is our human life all the way to the Really Good Stuff only happens after my life is over, so my perspective was suddenly skewed in the other direction, but I was still just crystal clear that hastening things in that direction wasn't on the table for me.

But damn, maybe like slogging through your last year of med school when every fiber of your being wants to quit and go be with your long distance relationship, I was just mostly going through the motions. Sometimes I still am, and I'm still more pre-Christmas Scrooge than post, a poor excuse to pick a man's pocket every 25th of December, though like I've said, the needle's been moving in the right direction. But that was a cold, bleak, empty desert winter, those first weeks.

Reminds me of *Groundhog Day*, when Bill Murray's character is at the height of hopelessness, stuck in this endless bleak winter, and during a live, on location weather report he's asked what the prediction is for the next six weeks – spring or more winter – and he says, with all the weight and jadedness that disheartenment can bring, something like, "Prediction? I'll give you a prediction. It's going to be gray, and it's going to be cold, and it's going to last you the whole rest of your life." It felt like that.

And a little couplet came to me somewhere in there, that I would repeat sometimes in my softer, less bristled moments, like a heart prayer or a deep soul longing: Life's not enough, without your Love. The coldest winter. Please let me in, again, into your Endless Center.

Ω Ω

So at first I was just biding my time, waiting. Life's still largely flat and empty by comparison, but more and more I'm coming to terms with that, relaxing into that, accepting it. And as I've leaned into that more, there've been more good moments and even Deeply Good moments seeping in now and then, without me really even trying to hunt them down and haul them in. Of course a huge, huge part of that has been having the bridging sessions in my life, but that doesn't magically transform all the other mundane or empty or dissatisfying or challenging moments of daily life.

And another part of the shifting that's been happening is what I mentioned I want to share when we get into the final topic tomorrow. A little process that came through in an inflash, that I'm starting to find myself doing spontaneously – like it's doing me more than I'm doing it. And it's helping me be more content and open and less resistant in daily life, even when things don't feel the way I wish they did, or I don't have things the way I really want them, which is a fairly big chunk of the time.

And also I think just time passing helps us get at least a little more acclimated to a new, more difficult situation we find ourselves in. So all in all, I'm still not exactly thrilled, but I have less resistance and less myopic focus on what's wrong instead of what's not so bad and even what's sometimes good or really good. Yes, I would *prefer* Deep, Unwavering, Everpresent, Expanded, Presence-filled, Quenching, Connected, Light-filled Unconditional Love and Acceptance and Belonging, I'm funny that way. But gradually I'm – let's say my tantrumming is getting less frequent and less strong and doesn't kind of commandeer all of me as much. It's not taking over the steering wheel and taking control of the whole car.

And I do recognize that I'm really lucky in that there's this portal that keeps opening, so that I can have regular moments of bridging with Omega, sometimes pretty deeply, not to mention the value of the inflashes themselves. Having that regular connecting, even though it's usually a faint whisper of the original experience, it's still definitely *of* the same. It resonates with that same Presence, even though usually a few orders of magnitude less.

So bottom line, it's been getting easier and better, and when things were rougher, I intellectually knew that might start to happen over time, even though I couldn't feel that in the slightest, and I also just knew it wasn't an option for me to try to cheat the system, plus there was that innate sense that that kind of attempted shortcut just wouldn't actually pan out as a shortcut for me. And you had one more thing you wanted to circle back to.

Ω Ω Ω

I did, but let me ask a new one first, instead of writing it down for later.

Kay.

You said the bridging sessions are usually a few orders of magnitude less off the charts than what you experienced in the Big Event, and I was struck a bit ago, when you were talking about being pulled back into your body, that the Omega Being called you Dear One. That sounded so intimate and deeply caring, and I'm wondering if that happens during the bridging sessions too.

Yeah so, *Dear One* was the closest matching term for the sentiment being conveyed, but at the time there was too much happening, and I was too resistant about suddenly being whisked back into my body, to really let that sentiment land. And it partially landed here and there those first weeks when I occasionally connected to that goodbye – that comfort stone in my pocket that all was well – but I didn't have a lot of space or bandwidth to really feel it and fully let it in. But when I shared that story earlier, that was the first time I've ever said it out loud – and probably the first time I've really thought about it in months – and I *did* feel it this time some, in retrospect or retroactively. The real tenderness and love and dearness that was emanating my way in that moment. It was nice to tap into that a little, to feel it revisiting. It touched my heart some.

And I don't think Omega has conveyed anything since then that I've translated as calling me any name at all, including any terms of endearment like *Dear One*. But during the bridging sessions, I definitely *do* feel a toned down version of the Benevolent, Spacious, Warm, Connective, Supportive, Accepting, Expanded Presence of Omega. I feel it whomp in and hang out in the space with me, though nothing at all like the indescribable Oneness that was opening up during the Big Event.

But for Omega, for our Oversouls or Higher Selves or Greater Consciousnesses, we're never truly separate from them in the slightest, and we're always authentically and naturally and irrevocably so, so dear to them. We don't have to earn that through doing, it's inherent in our very *Being*. It's unbreakable and unconditional. Unearnable and unlosable. We're *all* Dear Ones. Always. No matter how lost we become here, no matter how badly we miss, and even though in the dampening density of this world, and in the stirred-upness and tightness of our own minds, we usually can't feel even a *hint* of it.

But feelability doesn't have to be a prerequisite for taking a little comfort in the possibility that what I'm saying might actually be so. We don't have to be able to *feel* it first to be impacted by the *possibility* of it. We just *are* cherished and loved and held and valued. The very Core of us is the very Core of *all*, so our Core is *always* in Resonance with Pure Essence. We don't have to get everything right first or earn it first or do something to deserve it first. We just *are* always and effortlessly cherished and loved and valued and held, even though while we're in our restrictive Earth suits on this dense level of reality, the direct experience of that is mostly or completely lost to us. And what was your second question?

CHAPTER 11

Alright, this is one I circled to come back to, and it's, is there anything more to say about why you didn't tell anyone about what you had experienced, especially at first, when you were so impacted by the finding and the losing of that larger world? It seems like it would have helped people in your life understand what you were going through, and might have helped you to talk about it. It must have been a lot to only hold within yourself for months.

I know I'm being annoyingly picky here, but it wasn't really a larger world that I was so drawn to, and so disheartened that I had lost, it was the Melted, Joyful, Loved, Connected, Free, so deeply Quenched Belongingness. Yes, I felt incredibly expanded, but for me it wasn't like excitement there's limitless worlds to explore, I just wanted to fully, completely *be*, in Simple, Complete, Free, Loved, Melted Enoughness and Absolute Okayness and Wellbeing. Maybe after a good long rest I'd be more interested in exploring the larger Omniversal world, like after two or three trillion years. Five tops, wouldn't want to get too lazy or complacent.

But to your question, I don't know if I can explain this to the satisfaction of anyone else, but I just couldn't find in me anything like urgency or need or desire to communicate it to anyone, and I *could* find a lot of protecting of it, taking good care of this vulnerable thing. It felt deeply personal, by far the most personal thing I could ever disclose, and I knew, or felt I knew, that no one in my life would really get it. Maybe condescending head nods like, "I believe *you* believe that happened." Along with unspoken thoughts of "That poor guy must have suffered oxygen loss to his brain." Or maybe a genuine care and wanting to understand, but just not really getting it, and not resonating with what I was sharing.

And it was way too intimate and raw and beautiful and tender to expose it to that kind of reaction or nonresonance. To put this rare, precious, not commonly understood thing in the hands of people who just innocently – just from a lack of understanding – might not hold it carefully. Like handing a kitten, fragile and delicate and precious, to someone in the middle of their busy workday, texting while walking across a busy intersection, and who had never held a kitten before and didn't quite know how to.

So it just wasn't – I mean even for people who really would want to be a support and would want to understand, they probably just wouldn't be able to really get something so far out of our usual framework. And I don't mean no one could possibly navigate it supportively, but the people in my life aren't really – this kind of thing probably isn't their cup of rational explanation tea. No blame, it wasn't mine either, for sure.

So it just felt like I would lose something, that something really important and pristine and delicate would be lost or de-pristined or sullied, if I shared it with someone who didn't already have at least *some* aptitude or established openness, some pre-connection to at least the basic idea, which I could tell you did. It's like you want your first piano recital or two to be only warmly and openly received, not people in there whose world doesn't really include music and they're just sitting there surfing their phones, wondering why you'd waste four years to get an expensive degree in this cute little pointless hobby.

But worse than that, because at least they would know pianos actually exist, music actually exists, you're not imagining it. And you're also not potentially majorly activating threats to their own maps of how reality is set up.

And the word *judgment* comes in again. I just *really* don't like being judged superiorially by people. It's not worth it to me to open myself up to that, it impacts me way too much. Always has to some degree, but I'm so much more sensitive now, and my best sense is it would actually be an unkindness to my nervous system – and to my body that's been through enough for a while – to stand in front of everyone and proclaim – well not proclaim, but speak my truth about what I experienced and what I'm now regularly experiencing, and then deal with some blowback.

Their judgments and placations would slice right through me now more than ever, and I know that's on me not them, that I would be so affected – not that I thought as a young kid, "Wouldn't it be fun if I was extra sensitive to other people's thoughts and judgments about me? Yeah, let's do that!" But it's just always been the reality more than average, and then now there's just even *less* protective skin than before, plus now there's this delicate, valuable thing to care for that I didn't have before, that really diverges from most people's spectrum of experience and understanding.

So all added up, nope, I'll pass. And the other side of that coin I mentioned earlier is the possibility of some people treating me differently, as though I have something special or I'm more Awake or have Magic Spiritual Energy or something like that. Hard pass there too. There can be a Flow of Presence when anyone is, for the moment, connecting a little more to Greater Reality, but that doesn't mean they have anything special, and if they *think* they do, watch out. It's the most natural thing in the world, just, in our neck of the cosmic woods, it gets covered over, like spring flowers buried in the snow, waiting for the thaw to let them breathe in the sunshine again.

So, like I said when we started, I've been a hard no towards spreading the word, but I thought why not give this a go since you've had what to me is clearly a genuine pull in you for us to do this, and we're addressing my biggest concerns – doing it anonymously, and also with me dropping reminders now and then for anyone who reads the transcript of this to be skeptical, openly skeptical, skeptically open. And then also putting it in the fiction category to support both of those.

Plus having a finite timeline – just this weekend and then aside from some title input I'm out, nice and neat. I don't want any – I can't remember if we specifically said this in our extensive contract negotiations – but I wouldn't want to get into like interview requests, or people asking you to ask me something, or asking you to share more about me or about yourself, or whatever else might come up beyond the scope of this project, that could jeopardize the whole anonymous thing or gradually get us into some bigger or ongoing project. Just a hard firewall around all that.

And eventually, I probably *will* share with at least a few more people, those closest to me, and maybe beyond that. Maybe I'll have a big exploding glitter reveal party. But me telling anyone else would only be on my terms, in my own way, in my own timing, and just to those I choose, as I get less raw and less blow-around-able by the winds of other people's thoughts and reactions and judgments. And also as I get more confident I can still take good care of what's opened up and what's still opening while sharing it more. But I'm just not there yet. No one else really has to fully get it for me to just maintain those care-taking boundaries, he said defensively.

And especially, *especially* those first days and weeks, I was just – it was all *way* too new to even *consider* sharing about it before it was clear to. I was still just getting started with trying to process and come to terms with it all, and how to live my life now, what place this would hold, where it would fit in, while also being heartbroken and empty from being abruptly cut off from That Which Had Opened. So I wasn't walking around with joy and love in my heart, bursting to share the Good News. As opposed to my unmissable, big hearted, bear huggy, jolly Friar Tuck vibe now.

So yeah, that first month or so, before a milder, more subdued version of the portal opened again through the bridging sessions and gave me some hope again, I felt like the moment I started spilling it all out something precious would become less pure, and this pristine thing would suddenly be mingling with the unpurified air – the judgments and concerns and understandable doubts of the uninitiated, plus my own inner reactions to that – and it might get diluted even more than it already had. So all together it just seemed best to hold the whole experience inside myself and not risk it getting trampled, and not risk it stressing relationships when there was already more than enough to deal with. So yeah, something along those lines.

Thanks for opening that up a little more. It sounds like keeping it to yourself has been you doing your best to take care of something really important to you and really delicate.

Yep. Exactly.

So I want to ask you a question from my Be Sure To Ask list, that you just alluded to, and then I want us to move on to when the portal opened again and how your bridging sessions started.

Kay.

So the question is, you said you're more sensitive since your near death experience. Could you talk about what changes you've noticed since it happened? Aside from the emotional impact of finding and losing what felt like your Truest Home.

Yeah, aside from that little inconsequential thing. Okay, well probably the one that's most kind of noteworthy is I'm not afraid of death anymore. Averse to pain and suffering, yes, and my body would still do its adrenaline thing if I was almost in a car wreck or was in sudden physical danger, but I'm just not afraid of death itself now. And another thing is I've been just effortlessly eating healthier. Not like scared straight or something, and I didn't eat all that horribly before, but I just find myself enjoying more fresh organic vegetables and having less processed foods and less sugar. I still like me a good dessert now and then – let's not go overboard – but definitely higher eating scores overall than before, and same with drinks. Less sugar and high fructose corn syrup, and less artificial sweeteners.

And I also enjoy being – well both – I enjoy being in nature more than before, though it was something I always enjoyed, and I also find myself doing it more often, making the time for it more. It's not like it gives me some big experience or I feel my connection to the heavens massively opening up or anything, I just find myself doing it more, and it feels grounding and connecting and refreshing in a really normal way, but more alive than before. More feelable than before. A little richer and maybe quieter than before.

And another one, I'm still introverted – maybe even a little more than before as I slowly process and kind of guard what happened and continues to happen – and my personality still doesn't love socializing, even on Zoom, so I'm not more social or more outgoing. But I *do* tend to feel more of a subtle, beneath the surface, let's call it a familial connection, with people I encounter throughout the day.

And I don't want to oversell that, I don't mean my heart always feels warm and open to everyone, and there are people I just flat out don't like the personalities of, believe me, I just mean there's like a subtle pre-existing camaraderie and a sense that everyone out there – it's like we're all in the same greater tribe or clan. In the same extended family. Like everyone's a cousin, or something along those lines. You might not really like all of your cousins, but there's still a connection there. A familial well-wishing.

Ω Ω Ω

But at the same time, another one would be that there have been a few people I'm just no longer feeling like being in connection with. They've just fallen away. Those connections were suddenly more discordant and disresonant, less of a fit than they were before. And I can't say if this is a trend yet, but I'm sitting here with you and I do resonate with connecting with you over coffee, so it may be, you know, in a year or two I'll have more newer connections that feel like a better fit for where I'm at now. So yeah, those are a few things.

And another one would be when I do sit down without any devices and just kind of stop moving – which I pretty much only do to be available for a bridging session that might or might not come about that day – I usually feel a baseline settledness and a little quieter mindedness pretty quickly, and I don't think that ever happened before. I don't mean I go into some profoundly deep meditative state or something, it's just easier for me to settle and get a little more still than it used to be, at least when I sit down to become available for a session.

And yeah, probably the biggest one, and the first one that was really in my face, was like you mentioned, being a lot more sensitive to everything and everyone. To light, to noise, to uncomfortable fabric, to smells, to sounds, to those quiet electronic humming and buzzing noises I never noticed much before. Sometimes it seems like my hearing is better now, but it would make more sense for it to be more of just a sensitivity thing. And I'm more sensitive to temperature, to discomforts, to violence or just harshness on TV shows and movies, that kind of thing. And probably–

–*What do you mean by harshness?*

Like crassness or meanness, or extreme darkness or bleakness or negativity, or the nonstop use of the F word. When it's just a constant barrage it can really start to feel harsh and draining and grating, which – it never bothered me before.

And the most obvious way I'm more sensitive now is to people's energy and their inadvertent emotional broadcasts, which I never thought was really even a thing. But even quick runs to the grocery store would leave me kind of buzzing and wired, which I hadn't ever experienced before. Walking by someone I would get like a – maybe kind of a fragrance in a way, of their inner emotional and energetic landscape. Tensions or fears or anger or anxiety or depression or happiness or eagerness or excitement or just whatever they were radiating, both front and center and more down a few layers, I was probably picking it up to some degree. And I started talking about this in past tense, I guess to convey the difference from before, but all of it still applies, except I've just learned to navigate it a little better, and to tone some of it down a touch.

CHAPTER 12

And do you have the experience of picking up other people's thoughts, or only their emotional states?

Not like reading someone's thoughts or content per se, though once in a while I get images or information, almost like an inflash, so I'll sometimes just have the experience of knowing something about someone, which I don't often try to verify, and when I have, it's mostly been right on, sometimes with a really specific, out of the blue thing, extremely unlikely it was just chance – which is pretty confirming – but a few times it's just been off, a complete miss, so I don't really know what to make of that.

But people's emotional vibe, or we might even say their emotional packets, usually comes my way to varying degrees, even when they're more layered and subtle and not so active in them in the moment. And that happens pretty much whether I want it to or not, and actually I'd be quite fine with not, but thanks everyone for oversharing anyway. But at least I've gotten more used to it and learned to turn it down a little. At first it was pretty overwhelming.

Can you give an example of a time that happened, that stands out to you?

Yeah, I mean there's been literally thousands of times by now, just when I'm in proximity to someone, in person or also on the phone or on a video call, which diminishes it a little, but not that much. But before I throw out a specific example, I want to just say that one thing this has done is it's normalized difficult states and difficult background or beneath the surface emotional threads for me.

Can you elaborate?

Yeah, so it turns out – and it's not shocking news but to directly see it, again and again, that has an impact – but just about everyone has some degree of tension and worry and anxiety, and sadness and unreleased grief and suppressed hate, and you know, frustration and impatience and jadedness and hurt. And insecurity and envy and jealousy. And just about everyone has some degree of feelings of scarcity and not enoughness and self-harshness, and tight judgments towards themselves and others. And shielding and inauthentic facades or shells, and tight defenses, and whatever I forgot to name. The usual top 20 or top 40.

And I'm not sure I really need to be adding the qualifier *just about* everyone. We all have our own unique combinations of most or all of those things churning around – largely unconsciously – with some being bigger areas for us and some being smaller, and some being more outwardly apparent and some being more under the surface or suppressed or currently dormant. But even suppressed or dormant emotional energies can still give off a faint wafting of kind of an energetic fragrance.

So that's actually kind of a – sounds strange to put it this way, but it's kind of a nice thing. Kind of a relief. It points to the universal truth that with trillions of neural connections in the human brain, there's just gonna be some tangles, some crossed wires – or less than ideally arranged wires – in every single one of us. So you could say we're all beautifully flawed together. We're all in the same boat, with similar kinds of leaks we're trying to plug, and different degrees of water building up in the hull at different times of our lives. Something about that is just kind of a relief.

And kind of like how all unique colors can be created through just red, yellow and blue, at the core there's a whole lot of overlap between people – a limited number of core emotional primary colors – even though the specific story might have unique shades and hues, and it's easy to feel like no one really understands your particular situation or difficulties. But we all have our own special unique recipe of what works pretty well or really well in our lives and what really doesn't. Our own not always so secret blend of 11 herbs and spices. Our own unique combination of riches and glitches.

Ω

So when you get right down to our inner emotional landscape, we're all still in, if not the exact same boat, pretty similar boats in some ways, even if sometimes we're in different seas. Everyone wants to be loved, and to be able to love. Everyone wants financial and physical wellbeing and safety and security, everyone wants to feel good about themselves and sometimes wants others to feel good about them too.

And also everyone wants to be left alone by the people they want to be left alone by when that's what they want, and to get their needs met by the people they want to meet their needs when they want *that*. Everyone wants to be enough, to be of value, to be affirmed and appreciated. We all really want to matter, whatever that specifically means for each of us.

And everyone wants to be happy, to feel fulfilled, to feel good about the world we're in. To have our basic needs met, plus some nice wants. And everyone has some real blocks that interfere with the full, unfettered expression of our life with empowerment and strength and kindness and care and happiness and connection, and love and aliveness and wholeness.

And we all have some at least small pockets of unexpressed and unassimilated frozen hurt and grief and fear and anxiety and anger. At least residual hints of icy hate and burning rage. We all have younger places in us that have intense inner reactions to feeling hurt by someone or to not getting what we need, which we often either act out reactively, which can be destructive, or we stuff down, where it can fester and build up and deplete and deaden us. And the list goes on. The usual universal human emotions.

And navigating all of these different things, or trying to avoid some of them, is a lot of work, and a few layers down, or all the way through, most people are a little or a lot tired of trying so hard to make this whole configuration work in their life, day after day. Or tired of not being able to muster the energy and care and motivation to get themselves to try much at all. So we really are in the same boat or similar boats, even when we feel really alone, which kind of ironically, is one of the most common things I feel from people.

Feeling alone is?

Yeah, it's one of the – well probably one of the top five most universal human emotional broadcasts. At least based on my involuntary field work.

Can you name the other four?

Well, this isn't an official list, and there could always be some expectation bias on my part, influencing my tally, but yeah, in terms of the most common struggles or difficulties or so called negative emotions, there's loneliness, not enoughness, deep buried hurt and done-wrongness, not feeling lovable or not feeling loved, not really feeling deeply safe or that you can trust yourself or others or the world, even feeling like you don't have basic, fundamental safety and security – which is of course up hugely these months, it's been a real worry fest out there, which isn't that fun to feel all the time from other people. Well, not all the time, but a lot. Just more practice I guess in learning to turn it down a little. And what else? Well, the need for deeper meaning and the need to matter, which both seem to be a little more subtle, but they still show up a lot.

So those seem to top the charts pretty universally, at least in my neck of the woods. And if you asked me again in an hour I'd probably omit a couple of those and add a couple of new ones. They're all a tale as old as time – it's not like we need my recently upgraded emotion sensing radar to name them – and of course I pick up positive emotions too, but it seems like those waves wave through faster and don't have as much longer term resonance in most people.

What do you mean?

They usually come and they go pretty fast in people, but the woundings tend to stick around longer and root in deeper, and for a lot of people they gradually harden and weigh things down more. The joys of the human brain and its negativity biases. It's the negative stuff that tends to be more Velcro-ish. Everyone's wired a little differently, but for most people, one negative experience can have more impact than five or six or ten or more positive ones, which was something I was already aware of, but now I experience the truth of it more directly, pretty much anytime I pick up someone else's broadcast, which is basically all the time. I slightly exaggerated that, but really not by much.

Ω Ω

But you asked about a specific example. So I remember once in a doctor's waiting room, it was almost empty, and I was just looking at my phone, and suddenly I just felt these tears wanting to come out. Strong waves of tears out of nowhere, a pain behind my eyes that wanted to be released. It was completely out of the blue, no context for it, I wasn't in a raw or sad or emotional mood or any-thing. I didn't really feel that was the time or the place to faucet out some tears, to cry me a river, so I took a few breaths and just a couple of gentle quiet tears showed up, and they were welcome to be there, even if I didn't know what their context was.

But then, a minute later or so, I felt a strong wave of sadness com-ing from the other side of the waiting room, and I looked over and saw a woman quietly crying. I guess I can't know for sure, first of all if the two things were connected – though I know in my bones they were – and second, if she caught my wave or I caught hers, but this kind of thing has happened a lot since the Big Event, with different emotions, and I've just learned, you know, situations like that, it's usually or maybe always not mine, it's theirs, and at the same time, it's fine for me to just let it pass through me if that's what seems to want to happen. I don't have to shield myself from those waves, they're welcome, though I don't have to let them take over my body or my experience either. I'm still the one driving the car.

So it's been a process, adapting to suddenly being hyper-sensitive to other people's unintentional emotional broadcasts. I've always been pretty emotionally sensitive, meaning my feelings would get hurt more easily than average, but I was never energetically sen-sitive before, like picking up someone else's emotional waves just because I'm in some kind of proximity.

And you feel like you're getting more used to it?

Yeah, I've learned how to manage it better, so it's not as overwhelm-ing or interfering. And I was going to name another change, if I can remember it. Yeah, the language part of my brain is definitely different than before. I probably use the wrong word a little more often, but the bigger thing is that in some ways it feels like there's more creative language expression than I had access to before. I used to be squarely in the science and rational analytics column, a little intellectual, a lot skeptical, sometimes hyper-mental, but never that creative with words, or really with anything else. But now it's maybe a little like I see more colors more crisply whereas I used to see more grayscale, except with words.

Can you say more?

Like I have a wider ranging verbal color palette available, and expressing myself while feeling connected to what I'm saying just comes easier now. I've noticed it the most when I'm talking about these deeper things, which has just been more recently, with you, but sometimes I've noticed it in other situations too over the months. It's just most obvious with these deeper topics.

$$\Omega \, \Omega \, \Omega$$

Can you give an example of that, too?

I don't know about one specific example, but one thing is that sometimes words just come out while I'm talking that aren't real words, at least not yet, though they're usually based on real words, but they make sense to me, and they help me feel more deeply what I'm saying, or help me say it from a more connected place sometimes, which I don't think ever used to happen.

And words are more multi-sensoral now, meaning I can feel or see what I'm saying more deeply than before, or maybe I couldn't at all before, didn't know it was an option. So now I can actually enjoy – well it's maybe a little like if you always ate food just to feed yourself, but now you suddenly find you can cook with spices and just kind of enjoy that process more of building a flavor profile. So I don't know how it lands in anyone else, but I find it richer than I used to. Words just feel more alive to me now.

So that's another change, and I don't know if, when the communication bridge was opened during the Big Event, that somehow stretched and changed that part of my brain – maybe to help me be able to take in and convert what comes in – or maybe it's the reverse, and somehow my body going on shore leave for a while changed my brain some, and that's what made it possible to bridge with Omega on that deeper level of reality.

So yeah, those are the main changes I think, but those first few weeks, the main thing was just being a lot more sensitive to everything and everyone. And there was also that clarity that after my body died, I would return to that Light-filled Oceanic Space, and to that Multidimensional Being. But like I've said, that wasn't doing much of anything for me in terms of lightening my mood in daily life. It definitely didn't feel like I was walking around on a higher level or anything, and I didn't feel like a totally new person now that I had seen the Light. Mostly I felt emptiness and desert, because I once was found but now was lost, could see but now was blind.

I had been rudely and abruptly thrown from the warmest, softest, most beautiful, bloom-filled springtime into what felt like in comparison the coldest, windiest, most barren and isolated winter. And my pretty impressively stubborn sourness about that, it pretty much vinegared away any subtle sweetness that might have stopped by for a visit now and then, which left me in a pickle. My life was mostly just stuck in that sour jadedness, that jaded sourness, and I was just half heartedly trying to adjust to going through the hollow motions of flat and empty daily life.

And yeah, those two reminder stones were in my pockets, the Big Event as a whole, and then specifically the promise that all is well and all *shall be* well, regardless of our current experience, but I didn't even really like to touch them, they hurt too much. Like looking at a picture of the love of your life, that you can't see again for maybe decades. It's bittersweet. Except like I said earlier, without much, you know, sweet. But then, one normal, par for the course, flat, unsatisfying, not nearly good enough no good day, that portal of connection opened again, and I had my first bridging session.

And before we switch to that, this might be a good time for another break, and that should get us through until we stop for dinner.

Yeah, sounds good.

SESSION 3
CHAPTER 13

Alright. You were about to talk about your first bridging session. How did it happen?

Yeah, so it was four or five weeks after the Big Event, it was morning, I wasn't all that awake, just the usual mind chatter, and I was walking by my couch, and I felt this urge to just sit down. Not turn on the TV or open my laptop or look at my phone, just sit. So I did. I just sat down, which was rare for me or maybe unheard of, to just sit there, without something happening to give my mind something to focus on.

And I started to feel a little mini-wave of becoming more relaxed and content, just sitting there not doing anything. And after maybe four or five minutes, I felt a whomp – a kind of slow motion gentle impact in my stomach – kind of like when you feel impacted by big news, like that kind of roller coaster dropping that can happen in your stomach. Not necessarily negative or unpleasant, but like you've been impacted in your psyche. And then a thought wave bubbled up, and the words were something along the lines of, "Good, just allow the bridging to happen."

And then I felt a wave of deeper settledness and relaxedness and dropping, and I felt quieter. I would've assumed I'd be really hyper-investigating what those words meant and where they came from, but I wasn't. I was just being. It was relaxing and enjoyable and refreshing and relieving. Not at all groggy, but not my usual busy mind either. Not the usual thought-pumping mind looking for a target. Quiet mental clarity. And somewhere in there I closed my eyes – and looking back I think I might have been directed or asked or instructed to close them, as well as to sit on the couch – but at the time it felt like it was all just happening.

So I was drifting and dropping more and more deeply into a really settled, quiet space. Definitely the nicest space I had been in since the Big Event, no doubt. Nothing like the original experience, but compared to the flat, barren, empty-hearted winter my life had been that last month or so, it was a really, really appreciated breath of fresh, pristine air.

And were you consciously connecting what was happening with your near death experience or with that Being you encountered during it, at that point?

Not at first. I was just enjoying it. The space I was in might be like what you think of when you think about someone going into a deeper state, maybe along the lines of what some long time meditators or yogis or people in deep prayer go into, I don't know. But my mind got a lot less busy than usual and my body felt quiet and settled and present, just sitting on the couch.

And then after maybe a few minutes of that, I felt this second whomp – an unmissable Presence whomping into the space. And I knew immediately it was of the same energy or feeling as that Multidimensional Being, which I didn't have a name for yet but I absolutely recognized. Even though it wasn't nearly to the same degree, it was clear to me it was the same energetic fragrance, the same Essence, the same frequency. It had extended itself to visit me, to come meet me. It was so crystal clearly and unmistakably that Light-filled Being.

So the experience wasn't anywhere near as intimate and powerful as the shimmering waves of Enoughness and Completeness and Acceptance and Belonging and Love and Light that were coursing through me during the Big Event, but it was definitely the deepest and quietest experience I had had since. And probably before.

You mean ever in your life?

Yeah, probably. Nothing like that had every really opened before the Big Event. And so much more important than feeling deeply good in the moment and getting to connect again to some degree with this Multidimensional Being – that I knew I was deeply and irrevocably connected with and that during the Big Event I recognized to be my True Home – I now suddenly realized there was a chance, a real chance, that I wasn't doomed to just live stuck in a barren, empty, relatively lifeless life until my body died. Maybe there really could be *more* moments like this. It was like if someone you were inexpressibly close to had moved far away, and then unexpectedly seeing them one day in your neighborhood, but so much more importantly, getting the news they've moved back into town, so they'll be able to really be in your life again.

Ω

But this was way, way more significant to me than something like that situation would be. This was, first I found Home, then I lost it, then I was limping through a listless, lifeless life, lost in the desert, bracing for that to be where I'm stuck for the rest of my life, but now, now my True Home came to *my* door and found *me*. It was potentially a total game changer. A total *life* changer. Not the same as being fully plugged in, but still such a deep reprieve from that relative mineshaft I had been stuck in, from that basement cell I had been feeling locked in, which was at least partly due to my own resistance and myopia.

And as I was feeling so grateful that the portal had opened again, even if it was muted, I heard myself kind of whisper out loud something like, "Oh my God, this is so nice. Such a relief. I'm so beyond glad to get to feel this again." And then I felt this response, that hard to describe light impact in the stomach, and then there were words unpacking and forming right after, and I knew it was this Multidimensional Energy Being.

And the sense of this inwave that came in was along the lines of, "We wanted to give you some time to recover and settle into living your life again, but now it's time to begin." Begin what, I didn't know yet, and I didn't much care, as long as I got to feel what I was feeling – the re-awakening of a Living Connection to Greater Reality and to this Light Being. Even if it wasn't nearly as full on as the Big Event, the portal had undeniably re-opened.

And a minute or two later, this Being conveyed that the bridge was holding nicely, almost like a surgeon looking at their work a few weeks later to see how it was healing. And then I heard or felt – once I translated another inwave – something along the lines of, "Now we can start to show you more of what you've always longed to know, and more of what you've always truly been."

And honestly, I don't remember always longing to know about any of this stuff, any of the things that they soon started telling me and showing me. For starters, because I never knew anything beyond our known space-time universe even existed. I like reading science headlines and skimming or reading articles and books, watching science documentaries and Ted Talks and YouTube videos, that kind of thing, I've always been interested in how things are set up, but it's not like I've lived my life always pining for the Deep Answers. I had never even believed there *were* any Deep Answers to uncover. Never believed in anything multidimensional or spiritual before the Big Event at all.

So I don't know where that came from, or if they were talking about a deeper part of me I wasn't aware of, or maybe they were just flat out wrong. Got the wrong address. Mixed up the case files. An embarrassing data entry error up in the cloud. Was I wanting to get back to the feeling of being immersed in that Oceanic Space of Love-emanating Living Light, and back to being Deeply Connected with Expanded Easeful Belonging with that beautiful, exquisite Multidimensional Consciousness? Absofrickinlutely. But was I aware of always – or even since the Big Event – having burning questions about Greater Reality that could finally be answered? Not so much.

Your near death experience didn't awaken in you a desire to understand Greater Reality more?

Well, when you're desperately thirsty in the desert, you're way less interested in the science of how water exists or how cups work than just having a nice long refreshing drink. I hadn't spent that last month aching for more information and understanding. I had been aching for a full on return to what had opened during the Big Event.

Ω Ω

So then for the next maybe 15 minutes or so, the portal was open. There was this bridging that was happening, this exchange, this interplay. This communication and connection, where they were showing me some things, inflowing information and understandings, through these little inflashes that would come in.

And sometimes I didn't quite get what they were showing me, or I had a follow up question about it and asked them, meaning in my mind I just had a wondering – that was the same as asking them a question. And sometimes they answered and sometimes they seemed to disregard it, but more than anything I was just glad to be with them. Even if it wasn't anywhere near as fully as during the Big Event or as much as I wanted it to be, I was still *with* them. They hadn't forgotten about me, and I wasn't completely relegated to a dim and dank pseudo-existence in a basement, completely cut off from them – from what mattered most to me – for the rest of my life.

And I realize that sounds like a pretty low opinion of daily human life, but that's what I was stuck in – comparing everything to *that*, and being chronically hugely disappointed. But now, now it felt like I wouldn't have to wait til I died to start living again. So I felt this *huge* relief. That I just might be able to have some degree of real aliveness again, real color again, in my flat, limited, grayscale life. It was just really, really impactful.

And I guess I couldn't absolutely know that was true that first visit – that they would show up again and show up regularly now – but it *felt* like I knew it, and it really changed everything. I don't mean my life was suddenly all butterflies and rainbows those next weeks, but I started to be able to touch in, which isn't the same thing as being fully there, but it was so, so much better than nothing.

On a scale of one to ten, me knowing this could be in my life was worth about a hundred and twelve, and my relative appreciation of the content or material in the inflashes they were giving me was comparatively more like a two or a three, or maybe a 3.5 on a good day. Maybe a couple of fives or sixes. Sometimes really pretty impactful – some really good stuff on that TV channel – that I sometimes really recognized as deeply good to be opening to. I'm not trying to minimize the content, but just saying, bottom line, I just wanted to *be* with them. *That* was what I was looking for. If them showing me some things was the context for that, the condition for that, I'll take it. And somewhere around there I thought about the bridge they mentioned during the Big Event, and started to understand *this* was the bridge they meant.

When was that? Somewhere around when?

In the middle of that first bridging session. Maybe halfway through or a little sooner it started to dawn on my that the bridge they meant was this portal, this communication bridge, that let me connect with them while I'm still alive in this life, instead of being totally cut off, til death do us start. I was so relieved and happy about that.

And I'm still not a carefree barrel of joy, or maybe a happy hearted Friar Tuck after *imbibing* in a barrel of joy – but my life started again that day – when I didn't think it ever would. I was *alive* again. To me, *that* was the day when I was resuscitated, after about a month of my heart not truly beating with life. And I was really, really immeasurably grateful.

I can imagine.

CHAPTER 14

And how soon was the next bridging session after that?

Three days later. And the third one was two days after that. I haven't tracked them, I just remember the spacing of the first few because I was really eager and antsy to make sure they kept happening.

And how about now? How often do they happen?

It varies, but it's been two or three times a week on average since they started. So far it's never been two days in a row or more than four days in between, except a couple of times when I was traveling. Usually it's every two or three days. Omega conveyed once that it was good to give me some integration time in between. I don't know if that will always be needed or if it's just an adjustment period and I'll get more acclimated to it.

Do you know in advance when the portal is going to be open for business? Are these sessions in your calendar?

No and yes, actually. I never know when they're really going to happen, but I did start putting in my calendar, "Bridging time" every couple of days, to just make sure I sit down, no devices, and just make myself available in case the portal wants to open and Omega wants to drop by and chat for a few. If I never slow down the whole day, always occupied – never just putting everything aside and sitting for a while – it's not going to happen, there's no opportunity. Maybe half the time I sit there with some anticipation and there's nothing. Then I'll usually try again the next day if I have time. After a while I learned if I didn't get anything after 15 or 20 minutes, it wasn't going to happen so move on.

Are you disappointed when it's a no show?

Well it's definitely not my first choice, I'd much rather have mutually agreed upon appointment times, but obviously getting uptight about it isn't going to help anything, and by now I really trust it's going to keep happening, at least for a while, and I think for a long time. My running theory is Omega wants me to sit there for 15 or 20 minutes without my phone or computer or anything, even when we're not having a bridging session, because that's good for me and good for, kind of bridge maintenance. So this is a way of getting me to sit there, where if I was like told I should do that as an assignment some nonbridging days, I probably wouldn't. But that little theory has yet to be confirmed or denied. Just crickets when I asked.

Ω

And this is one from my Be Sure To Ask list, what's your understanding of what's happening when the portal opens? Is the Omega Being descending down to you, or is it more as though you are lifted up to that level? Or is the tuner on your radio changing to pick up a station that's always broadcasting? Or something else?

Yes, yes, yes and yes. Next question?

The next question is could you elaborate on the <u>last</u> question a bit.

I had a feeling. Okay, so you could make pretty fair arguments for each of those options, from different perspectives. But more and more I'm seeing it as more like the third one. Opening up and tuning in to the Omega Channel on the universal cosmic satellite radio. That frequency is always there and when the portal opens I can tune in to it, and once I'm tuned in, the inflashes start. It's like my awareness shifts to include the level Omega's on.

I asked once how it was happening, and the answer was along the lines of – once it went through my own felt sense of it and my mind converting it into words – something along the lines of, "We're always with you the same degree. It could never be otherwise. We're never with you more or less. We could never be closer to you or farther away. You're always equally connected to your finger whether it's touching your nose or your arm is fully outstretched. Your connection to your finger has nothing to do with that perceived distance. The bridge helps you be aware of this truth, and helps you fall into a Deeper Awareness within your consciousness, that's more aware of our Everpresent Connection. And that opens the interflow that lets information and connection come through. The bridge opens your conscious awareness more to the level of reality where you're always with us, with no distance at all, and lets there be more conscious interflow between us." So yeah, something like that. And on the one hand—

—The word interflow, was that theirs or yours?

The words are me doing my best to match what I experienced to be conveyed. So something like interflow was the best match I could find, and can find right now, as I try to relay the felt sense of what came in. And of course, if I conveyed the same inflash another time, even if I repeated it right now, I wouldn't use the exact same words in the same order, and I might forget something or add something I forgot this time. Like I said earlier, it's not crystalized, it's just conveying my closest sense of what was expressed as it currently shows up in my imperfect and non-photographic memory. It's the felt sense that stays with me, but my languaging of it would change at least some every time.

And it's also just impossible for that kind of transcribing – or not transcribing but translating – to not be at least a little influenced by the receiver's filters and mental configurations and enculturations and biases.

By receiver you mean the person who's getting the download?

Yeah. With the human brain, at least small, occasional distortions and some unconscious filterings just go with the territory. That's a big part of why I'm so adamant that we check things out with our own tuning forks, and don't just take the words I attribute to Omega as The Inerrant Word of a Great Being. I'm just really uncomfortable with the thought of me being in any way involved with anything approaching that, as I might have happened to mention.

And again, as far as any readers know, well, it turned out the Great and Powerful Wizard of Oz was just a balloonist from Kansas, with a lot of hot air. He still had some wise things to say, and he did help our four heroes realize they already had within them the – I guess the power or the ability or the potential – to have what each of them was feeling was most deeply missing for themselves, which actually connects pretty closely to something we'll get into tomorrow, but those words were coming from a normal person with gifts and glitches, not from a Great Source of Knowledge Who Must Never Be Doubted.

Ω Ω

And are we assuming every Multidimensional Light Being, or for that matter every self help guru or spiritual leader or some other Great Seer of Truth, is infallible and always correct in all their perceptions and understanding of how the Omniverse is all set up? Even if you take all this at face value, and you also assume for a minute that I'm a pretty clear receiver of Omega's intended communications – pretty much free of translation errors and filters and biases – which is a big assumption, we still don't know for sure that the original intended communications are free of their own filters or assumptions or misperceptions, right? We just don't know.

I mean a fifth grade teacher or a respected professor both presumably have a whole lot more knowledge than their students, but they can still sometimes make a mistake, right? So, who knows, Omega could be the most Love-filled Being in all of Existence, and simultaneously, for all we know, could just be not that bright.

Innocently misunderstands a lot of things. Maybe compared to the average Multidimensional Oversoul Being, Omega's pretty much an Einstein, or maybe more the sharpness level of Einstein's basset hound. We don't actually know where the average run of the mill Multidimensional Light Being falls on the perceptual clarity IQ spectrum. We just can't say we know for sure.

Or maybe there's some prankster up there, or some matrix simulation program coder, making up this whole Omega character to have a little harmless fun with those cute but gullible humans. Or again, from the reader's perspective, maybe I'm confusing unconsciously generated experiences with real ones, or one of us made up the other, or someone else made us both up. And in any of those scenarios, the details of what I've been sharing could still be someone's honest report, or it could just be a way to share some things that resonate for the sharer, or it could be some kind of mix and match.

So for any readers of an anonymous book, those are all real possibilities that can't be dismissed, and even when it's a known, verified respected, obviously good hearted person presenting unverifiable information, how much does that mean you should bypass your own tuning fork? They later might turn out to have been wrong about some key things they confidently espoused, or they might turn out to not be as respect worthy and power worthy as generally believed.

So we're all self responsible for sifting through the mud to find the gems, and that can't be completely based on who purportedly said it. I mean Einstein was a patent clerk, Will Hunting was a work release janitor, Charlotte was a spider, and little known fact, Einstein's basset hound taught physics at Cambridge. Mostly focused on Schrödinger's cat. And it's safe to say that more than a few Great and Powerful wizards of Oz – more than a few esteemed way-showers of deeper levels of reality and of ourselves – have turned out to be either charlatans or to have shadow sides that could rival the dark side of the moon. Or at the least, have turned out to just be innocently really wrong about some things, which sometimes just comes with the very subtle territory.

So instead of making it unduly about any of that, instead of making it about something that isn't solid enough to base how we assess the material on, it's more letting it be about how the words and the energy they carry land in us. How much they do or don't resonate. So yeah, I guess I could've just said copy and paste my intro speech about being skeptical – being openly skeptical as you said – and using your own compass. Apparently it's one of the terms of my participation in our marathon, mentioning that a few times. So that mention should tie me over for another hour or two, no promises, and it looked like you started to ask a question a couple of minutes ago and I kept rolling.

CHAPTER 15

I was just going to ask, we've touched on this, but sometimes you refer to the Omega Consciousness as singular and sometimes plural, and I was wondering if there's something that shifts, that sometimes more implies one or the other, or is it more just on your end you happen to go back and forth, so don't read anything into it?

Yeah, more the second one. I don't think Omega has any self concept of singular or plural or anything like that. There's no need on that level to narrow that down. Omega is 100 percent one Being and simultaneously 100 percent a Multitude. A Multitudinal, what was it? I'm blanking. A Unilarity?

Singularity.

Yeah, a Multitudinal Singularity. Though I kind of like unilarity too. But Oversouls are always completely both, which is tricky for our brains, so mine tends to go back and forth. The only thing that shows is that neither *it* or *they* fully capture it, neither *I* or *we*, *me* or *us*. So I'm still, without consciously thinking about it, going back and forth between the two.

But to get back to what Omega was conveying, about what's happening when the portal opens, what came in was, it's not that they're lifting me to a higher level of reality where I wasn't before. It's more, from the perspective of a through line or a continuum – where there's a part of us on every level of reality all the way up, or all the way in, all the way to Pure Infinite Consciousness – that they're just kind of opening up the aperture of what I'm able to take in and perceive to a larger degree. Making it more open and more sensitively attuned. Like a radio telescope, which isn't actually picking up things far away – it's not actually reaching way up into the stars – it's picking up signals reaching it, touching it, hitting its receiver, that are just really, really faint, really subtle, really quiet.

Somehow the Big Event seems to have opened that possibility up, and I'm still not really clear about Omega's role in that part of it. Did Omega initialize it, make it happen? Or just keep a crack open that happened to get jostled open in all the commotion but would've otherwise closed? Or did they just take a good look at it and confirm it happened, that a bridge had been established? Not sure, but my feeling is they did more than just witnessing it and recognizing it, that they helped make it possible. So, I don't know—

—Have you asked?

Yeah, just one of those where there wasn't an answer, just kind of a warm non-answer, which happens sometimes. Where there's not a helpful answer, not any answer, but sometimes an increase in warm depth. The way I take it is, "We aren't going to respond to that question in a way you can recognize for now, and we won't be going into why not, but we're here."

Do you get a lot of non-answers?

A fair bit. When I ask Omega why, want to know what they say?

Not a damn thing?

Nailed it. Anyway I was going to say – what was I going to say? Yeah, so basically, I don't know for sure Omega's role in the bridging portal opening up during the Big Event. My strong sense is they helped it happen, but it's also possible that maybe something happened physically during that medical situation that opened it up. Whatever the case, whatever the cause, something shifted to make it possible for my aperture – let's call it my awareness aperture – to open more deeply and take in much more subtle level data streams than ever before.

$$\Omega$$

And my sense is that it's two things. I mean when I bridge with Omega, it's two things. First, my awareness aperture is just more open now in general – like it got jarred loose a little – and second, when Omega stops by for tea and scones, there's a way that something gets activated in me in that moment, to more finely hone my aperture tuning for a while. To help my radio telescope dish open even wider, and extend even more, and point in the right direction to pick up those faint signals so they aren't so faint for a while. That's my sense anyway.

But the upshot is, now I'm apparently somehow able to allow an externally assisted shift in my awareness, an opening of my awareness aperture, to tune into and receive data streams at the level of existence that Omega's on. Although I don't mean to imply that's the only level of reality Omega's on, like they're stationary or stagnant, like on one floor of a building. Things are way more fluid, or way less stagnant and regimented and delineated than that.

So when I use the word *portal* or *bridge*, that conveys a sense of it, and I've been using those words sometimes with you, but neither is exactly, exactly it, because the only thing that changes is that somehow my conscious awareness on this level, in this human body, expands its – I don't know what to call it – its receptivity or just its awareness, its radius of perception, to include more of the subtle levels of the seamless Continuum of Consciousness. It expands into the level of my Greater Consciousness that matches more closely with where Omega is. That's really all that changes.

My Consciousness isn't shuttled somewhere on a glittering rainbow tractor beam, and Omega doesn't descend from the heavens and grace me with their Presence, though it honestly feels that way and I've been saying it that way. But with a little help, my awareness aperture just opens. Its focus changes and expands, or you could even say that from a deeper perspective, it just relaxes and uncontracts.

When your eyes are the most relaxed in terms of their focus is when they can see the farthest. I actually have no idea if that's true, but the analogy works so let's go with it. The more you release any contractions, the deeper into Clear Subtlety or Subtle Clarity you can see. The more deeply into the Depths you can perceive. Exactly how clearly you're seeing should be kept a separate question, because we're all subject to our own interpretation glitches and beliefs and expectation biases and cultural conditionings and so on, but the more open your awareness aperture, the quieter the signal you can pick up.

And this relaxing your focus analogy reminds me of two things. One is how sometimes when I was sitting by the water as a kid – a stream or river or lake or the ocean – I would see if I could shift my focus from the surface ripples or waves, that are more attention-grabbing, to seeing the water underneath them. The surface of the water is just the thinnest layer of what's there, but mostly it's all we notice.

It's kind of like that, but in this case I'm not aware of *trying* to shift my focus or *trying* to open my awareness aperture, it just happens.

My experience is still really like Omega comes to me. I feel that sudden whomp, that sudden arrival of Deep Presence. I don't have to try to make it happen myself – which is convenient because I don't think I could – I just have to kind of move all the accumulated stuff off the guest chair, so Omega has a place to sit down. I close my laptop, silence my phone, and usually put them both in a whole nother room to really clear the space, and just show up to be available a little. It doesn't seem to take much, but you know, if you invite a friend over and there's no place for them to sit, they might not stay and visit, or even get the feeling you really want them there.

I like the way you put that.

$$\Omega\,\Omega$$

And was there a second thing you were going to say? That relaxing your focus reminded you of?

Yeah, it was – remember those Magic Eye 3D illusions where if you stare at them long enough, your eyes kind of relax their fixed focus and open up some, and then you start to see the hidden 3D image that had been there all the time? It reminds me of that too. That image doesn't suddenly swoop into the space the moment you've shifted your perception sufficiently, it's already there, waiting for you to relax your myopic focus, which naturally gravitates to the most obvious signals right in front of you over the more subtle ones, like only looking at the surface of the water.

And when you put on infrared goggles, the larger spectrum that you suddenly start seeing has actually been there the whole time. Same with turning the radio dial. So shifting your focus, opening your aperture, that just lets you tune into frequencies that are already there, waiting for your discovery.

I like that way of putting it too. I was seeing it more the first way.

Which first way?

The Omega Being suddenly swooping in, swooping down.

Yeah, that's still exactly how it feels, it's just not an accurate perception. We're never even one inch away from our Higher Self, the magnificent Multidimensional Being of Pure Consciousness that is more our True Self than the us we experience in this lifetime. Yes, experientially, most of us are cut off pretty much completely – or nearly completely – the vast majority of our lives. The avatar or game character isn't privy to the greater consciousness that has a small part of its awareness focused on being a player in that game world.

Basically, at the level of Pure Being, we're Absolute Consciousness, Infinite Presence, Undifferentiated Aware Oneness. And then from the level of Oversouls, we're absolutely connected with and one with our larger Consciousness, even while having this particular unique and myopic life experience. Our experiential separation from our Greater Beingness doesn't mean we're *actually* separate. Your Higher Self is eternally closer to you than your arms are, than your eyes are, than your brain is, than your own identity and sense of self is.

So in that sense, in spite of us not normally being able to directly experience this, your Higher Self is so much more the real you than your personality could ever be. Than your sense of identity, your sense of being a person on this planet, than your small self could ever be. It's much more you than *you* are. We're never *actually* only the game piece or the game character. It's a small appendage that we squeeze ourselves into and come to believe is the sum total of what we are, or at least the vast majority of what we are. But we have it absolutely bass ackwards. We so understandably, and maybe even at least at first unavoidably, perceive things exactly opposite of how they – from a larger perspective – actually are.

And when the portal opens and bridging happens in me, Omega isn't *actually* coming down to visit and I'm not *actually* ascending up into the heavens, a hundred miles straight above my couch, watch out for all those damn internet satellites. Just somehow something shifted in me a while back, either physically or on a subtle level or both, from my body having a temporary cease and desist order, or from the expanded experience that opened during that, and probably with some help from Omega.

And now, somehow, the aperture of the focal point of my consciousness shifts sometimes, and a part of my awareness resonates or vibrates or becomes attuned to the level of reality Omega's mostly on, without me trying to do it or having a clue how to do it consciously if I ever had to, aside from just sitting and making a little space and just *being* for a few.

Ω Ω Ω

And by the way, one inflash that came in included the little tidbit that a lot of times – probably almost every time – when people encounter their Higher Self after death or in a near death experience, or through other multidimensional experiences – not that that necessarily has to happen, but when it does – they often really understandably take that amazing Being of Love and Light and Beauty and Belonging and Acceptance and Home to be God or a High Angel or a great religious figure, because it's just too big a jump for us to go from such a limited human life to even daring to imagine – even it crossing our minds – that that exquisite Being before us could actually be our own Greater Self. Our own Unencumbered, Uncompressed Greater Beingness.

We can't really fathom that we could actually be *that* Beautiful and Light-filled and Love-filled, and amazingly magnificent. That we could actually be a Being that exudes an Oceanic Space of Homeness and Belonging and Wholeness and Peace and Contentment and Astounding Love and Acceptance and Healing and Joy and Oneness, all completely effortlessly and naturally and organically. It's just understandably too big a jump for us. Plus experientially, it just doesn't *feel* like us, it feels like an other.

And it's not for me to say people never actually *do* encounter what they know to be God or a High Angel or a religious figure – I couldn't speak to that, like you know, "Here's what *really* happened in your near death experience in case you were wondering, you're welcome, here's my invoice." – I can just say that per an inflash, most of the time when we encounter our Higher Self, we really understandably tend to interpret it as meeting a Great Other.

And in my case, during the Big Event, I wasn't saying, "Hey that Being right in front of me is actually me! Wow, I always suspected I secretly rock, but damn, I didn't know I'm *this* incredible! Can't wait to tell everyone in case they missed my greatness too!" I wasn't experiencing Omega as me or me as Omega, and I still don't. A finger wouldn't experience an entire body to actually be itself. But even in that short but timeless experience, the distinction between us was starting to melt away. I was starting to dissolve into that Being before me, with my tight identifications of my familiar self starting to loosen and dissolve, and the Oneness between us becoming more and more unmistakable. And that was all just in a few Earth minutes.

And the bridging sessions have continued to help me integrate and process this understanding – even though it's not nearly as directly and powerfully experienced – that in spite of how hard it is in me to fully grok it, we are all – every single one of us – so much unimaginably and vastly *more* than what we're currently aware of. And what we truly are is stunningly Beautiful, and is intimately and irrevocably Connected to Pure Infinite Loving Beingness, which is – well, which is one aspect of our Deepest Essence.

What do you mean one aspect of our Deepest Essence? You said that like there's more to the story.

Yeah, for a second I thought about opening that up, but my best sense is we table it for now and get back to it after dinner, after a little more foundation.

Sure.

But yeah, basically Omega doesn't come to the me I think of myself as, on this level, it's just that somehow my aperture opens, and a little like if a total eclipse comes in the middle of the afternoon and lets you suddenly see the stars that have always been there, I pick up the frequency or the energetic and Awareness Fragrance of my Higher Self, my Oversoul, my Greater Consciousness, which because I'm not fully experientially one with, I still relate to as an other, as a separate Greater Consciousness, this Higher Multidimensional Being, Omega.

CHAPTER 16

I'm feeling a bit of a Deep Quiet Space from what you're saying, some transmission from it. And at the same time, I'm not quite fully on board with this idea that the Omega Consciousness doesn't do anything at all to at least meet you halfway. Sometimes they show up for a bridging session, and you feel that whomp, and sometimes they don't, so it seems to me they sometimes have an intention to shift their awareness to you, which then intensifies your being able to feel their presence, instead of them just waiting for you to go to them.

Well, we're talking two different things here. Omega can lean into me, attune to me, in less than an instant, and I agree that does happen and is a part of what happens during bridging sessions. But what I'm trying to express is, as I understand it so far, that isn't what lets *me* be aware of Omega. That isn't what connects *my* side of the portal. A bridge has two points of connecting, and on my side it's the opening of my already loosened aperture – the tuning of my radio telescope – that lets me connect, that lets me catch the subtle signals.

I mean I could be standing in the middle of the subtle level 405 during Oversoul rush hour, and I wouldn't notice a thing without my awareness aperture opening up a lot more. To receive a radio signal, it has to be broadcasting *and* you have to be tuned to the right frequency. Takes both. And the frequency that Omega and I connect on, that's the frequency of the Higher level that Omega's on, it's not the more dense level of everyday Earth bound humans, the level we communicate with each other on.

And like I've said, I don't know how my aperture first got kind of loosened, and I don't know exactly how it attunes during a bridging session, it doesn't seem like I make it happen, but I do know I have to be available and make some space for it. I have to kind of get with the program, or there isn't one.

I think I see the distinction, that the Omega Consciousness can send you signals, but your radio telescope has to shift its focus or shift its tuning to receive them.

Yeah, exactly. Like for a sailboat to get cruising, the wind has to blow *and* the sail has to be up and correctly positioned. And somehow through mechanisms I don't understand, Omega *does* seem to support me in doing that, in lifting and positioning my sail, or in positioning and opening my radio telescope dish to change its focus. In opening my awareness aperture for a bridging session.

And fortunately, because of that first aperture shift during the Big Event, however it exactly happened, my part in it – just making space for it – doesn't require the slightest skill set or some higher level of like attained consciousness or anything. It just requires me clearing some space and settling a little and being patiently available for a few. Even a dog can do that when you've got a treat in your hand, so, you know, it's fairly doable for me. And believe me, I'm happy to take credit when it's deserved – I'm like number one at taking credit – just in this case, except for sitting down on my couch and mentally clearing my stuff off the visitor chair so Omega has some room to join me, I don't really get any.

That does make sense. Alright, let me – well speaking of treats, let me stop for a minute and check in about the dinner break.

Smooth segue.

Thanks, I try. So according to our schedule we've already gone almost 30 minutes over, but unlike tomorrow we're not switching to a completely different topic after dinner, so it doesn't really matter when we stop in terms of that. I'd like to get some more questions crossed off the list – a couple of which I probably should have already asked by now – so I'd like to keep going a bit more if you're up for it, and then after the break have a shorter evening session. But we can also stop here if you just feel ready.

Yeah, sounds good to keep going. Get a few more miles behind us.

Ω

Alright, so let's try some rapid fire Q and A.

Kay.

So first up, how long are your bridging sessions usually?

Usually 25 or 30 minutes or so, give or take.

And how quickly does a download come through once the bridge is open? Immediately or is there some quiet sitting or connecting for a bit first?

It depends. Maybe half the time there's just quiet settling with Omega first, being aware of the impact in me of that Presence whomping in. And those times maybe three or five minutes later, a flash packet comes in and starts unpacking. And other times it's like a tie and the inflash just shows up immediately. And now and then there isn't any inflash of material at all, just Silence and Stillness and Presence and Connection. No work to do, nothing to take in and process, just quietly sitting in a space of Beingness, in the subtle energetic fragrance of Home.

And how do sessions end? How do you know when they're over? Is there a goodbye of some sort?

Well there isn't anything like Sean Connery in *Highlander* saying, "This endeth the lesson." Or maybe that was when he was the beat cop in *The Untouchables*, not sure, but basically there's an ending to the unpacking of the inflash, so that just completes, and then there's also just a feeling of completion, and the intensity or obviousness of Omega's Presence dissipates. There's not a goodbye or see you later. Sometimes I throw out a "Thanks, I appreciate it, good to be with you," but I haven't ever felt like a "You're welcome" or "Our pleasure."

Do you think there's a time limit to how long the portal can be open that forces the end of a session? Is there some multidimensional mechanism, or your body or mind can't handle it longer? Or is it more that the bell rang and class is finished?

No idea, but it would be a little much for my brain to like unpack inflash after inflash for hours and hours. I don't think that would be good for my mind or body, or for really fully taking it all in. I don't have nearly the capacity I had during the Big Event, and after a few of the longer and more intense bridging session flash packets I definitely felt like I had a real mental work out.

Because they were emotionally intense?

No, I meant a lot of information waving through, and for longer than usual. That has its own intensity on the whole system. It's not just mental. It impacts. And a few of the really deep, deep Spaces that have opened up were intense too, not emotionally so much, just a really strong, deep whomp and after-whomp.

Did you ever – or let me ask it this way – have you ever had a session cut short or interrupted?

Yeah, twice I think.

What happened?

Well, once I was having a computer delivered and they knocked on the door so I had to attend to that. So I just said, sorry I gotta deal with this, and got up and did.

And then did the session continue?

No, I sat back down and kind of tightened and felt a little like a student that might be in trouble with the teacher, just because of my own stuff, and that started crowding up Omega's chair. And I tried to make myself relax and get back to being available, but I choked under the performance pressure I guess, or maybe Omega just left. And what hadn't unpacked yet, more of that unpacked, but it wasn't the same quality as when it's during a session where I'm really feeling Omega being present during both the inflash whomp and the unpacking of it.

$$\Omega \; \Omega$$

And the first takes just a minute or two and then the second takes – well let me ask you.

Yeah, depends how dense it is, meaning how much – how compressed with information the flash packet is, but maybe a minute for the inflashing, though some have gone on longer, and then the unpacking of it just depends, but could be the whole rest of the session, and sometimes little hits after a session.

But I'm not even sure those are real delineations, I mean I feel a whomp and then it immediately starts unpacking, and I'm not a hundred percent sure if, when it seems like the initial flash packet has been delivered, I'm actually catching the end of the whomping in of flash packet information or just the end of when that stops having such a strong initial impact.

Not sure that made sense, but I don't have anything solid to say there anyway. But there's a lot of feeling of space during sessions. Meaning it's not like, "We have a lot to get to so you better not let anything interfere." It's a pretty laid back feeling. Not lackadaisical or take it or leave it, but definitely not like I'm sternly rebuked or sent to the principal's office if I'm tardy or have to interrupt the session. It's not – I mean Omega's definitely not a Type A personality, but also not indifferent about the bridging sessions.

So in the next session after the computer delivery, did it pick up right where you left off or go to another topic?

I don't really remember, I just remember it was fine. No big deal. I said something like sorry about last time. I don't think I felt any response except just spacious warmth.

Did you say that out loud? Do you ever speak out loud?

Almost always just in my mind, but I've spoken out loud here and there too. But mostly my body is quiet and settled and still, and it feels better not to bother to speak out loud, and I definitely don't need to. It's not like Omega uses sound vibrations through the air that are vibrating nonexistent inner ear hairs to hear me.

Are your eyes usually open or closed during a session?

Usually closed. It's just a little easier to tune in that way, but I've opened them sometimes – heard a noise or something – and it hasn't thrown things off.

I assume you don't see any visual indication of Omega's presence in the space?

Nope. Would be cool if I did, but no visuals.

And what happened the other time a session got interrupted?

Yeah, the second time I just forgot to take off my smart watch and it vibrated with three or four new texts in a row, and then I wondered if it was urgent, since it's not often that happens, so without thinking I looked down and read the last one that was still displayed on my watch. And if it had been no big deal at all I would've just continued – well actually it *wasn't* a big deal, which is what became a big deal, meaning those three or four texts were activating and distracting and frustrating to me because they were about something I thought had already been all settled – well it *had* been all settled – so it felt like they shouldn't have needed to text at all, if they had bothered to read my last text, and definitely not three or four times in a row.

But they *did* text, right in the middle of a bridging session, of all times, and that shouldn't have been a big deal, but it really activated me, and then my mind was kind of off to the races. And I had been in a good settled space, but now I was tight and annoyed and couldn't get back into it. I had lost the connection. I had thrown a growing pile of stuff on the guest chair again. And you know, that's okay, I'm human, but I still was frustrated about getting frustrated. That I let it bother me so much. I tried awhile to get things back, but no luck, so then I just let it go for the day.

$$\Omega \, \Omega \, \Omega$$

Did that – were you in a worse mood for a while or for the rest of the day?

I was, actually. I don't know about the rest of the day so much, but for a while. One of those where I was also in a worse mood because I was letting myself be in a worse mood instead of just letting all of that have enough room so it could just dissipate on its own. And also mad at myself for forgetting to take off my watch and also for glancing at it, I just wanted to make sure there wasn't anything actually urgent, which was understandable. And I was trying to not be mad at myself, and trying to force away the tightness, which of course wasn't working. So yeah, I still get caught in that kind of thing, finding myself trying to boss my current experience around, which just adds more contraction to it. But I lived to bridge another day.

Did that come up the next session? That you checked your texts and then the session got cut off?

Well I mentally said I was sorry about the last session and that I've set up a reminder to take off my smart watch and leave it in the other room with my phone and laptop before I sit down to be available for a session in case it happens.

In case a session happens or a text?

I guess either, but I meant a session, since I never know if it will or not on any particular day.

Did Omega respond?

Yeah, there was a warm sense of acceptance and allowingness, and the words that connected were along the lines of, "That's such an understandable thing, it's really okay, and it sounds good you have a plan to try to help it not happen again. Because it's worth taking good care of these sessions. They're in service to you and beyond you."

In service to you and beyond you. That's noteworthy. Did you get any idea of how?

Well, I've said before, for me so far it's been more about the Space that opens up than the content of the data streams, though I appreciate them too for sure. And that process that came through – that's been happening spontaneously – that's been in service too, along with to a lesser degree some other inflashes. But there wasn't anything specific about the how of it. How they're in service. I feel like I already just get that they are. That they're good for me.

And do you have a sense of how they're in service to others?

I really don't know, probably too early to have any strong guesses. But what *is* clear to me is that the more open our awareness aperture is, in a grounded, healthy, real way – which doesn't describe me much yet – but the more that's happening in us, the better that is, in a small way, to everyone and everything on the planet. We become more and more of a touch point for Infinite Essence to have a little more room to breathe a little more fully and more freely in this world. Even if it's just a little, and just for a few moments, that still really counts.

So maybe the more I integrate from the bridging sessions, and the more any of us integrate a little more and get clearer and more open-apertured – in whatever ways each of us explores that and finds help with that – there's maybe just a little more space for Beingness to breathe in form a little more. Probably doesn't usually add up to that much with one person, but as we each attend to that as we can, in our own way, each of us doing our part, it could really add up. Which connects to something I saw during the third act of the Big Event side show, that I'll go into tomorrow.

Plus, you know, we've been having coffee, now we're having this weekend marathon you're intending to put out there as a book, so who knows, maybe there's other ways it trickles outward a little also. It's too early to really say.

CHAPTER 17

And you said a bit ago that sometimes there's nothing happening and you're just feeling the Presence that's in the space. You meant during those times you're just connecting with the Omega Consciousness and feeling that?

Yeah, sometimes there's not a big flash packet or several small ones or anything, it's just being in the space with Omega. Nothing to unpack, nothing to look at, just being settled and pretty quiet in a space of Connected Presence. Again, not comparable to that full on, unparalleled Homeness and Belonging during the Big Event, but still really, really nice to feel. It's settling and rejuvenating and nourishing. Some of my favorite bridging moments have been when there's nothing coming in, nothing to process. Just being settled in quiet content Beingness. Feeling connected to Omega and to the hints of Deeper Homeness that show up in the space.

Do you know if there's a specific purpose or something happening those times, or is it just a pause?

So a snippet I got once was that, at least in part, it's for strengthening the bridge and opening up my nervous system. That's all I got. I can't drill down on either of those but maybe it's like more precisely tuning the portal, and also like helping me have more space to be able to navigate all this, to be in it, and to take in and unpack the flash packets, that kind of thing. But I'm not sure every Omega move always has some deeper strategy or purpose. Might be wishful thinking, but sometimes it feels like we're both just enjoying the Rich Deep Quiet Beingness together, no agenda needed. I really like those moments.

And do you think Omega has a bigger desired outcome or master plan around the bridging sessions? You said there's not a type A, high pressure feeling, but is there any sense of some relative urgency or seriousness or heaviness to get you somewhere you aren't yet, to help you integrate and get clearer as you said a minute ago, or to get you to understand that day's material? And are you aware of a larger intention to help more people open more?

First answer is, during the bridging sessions there's an Everpresent Lightness of Being, that doesn't ever feel heavy or tightly urgent or deadly serious. But there clearly *is* an intention to be of service, to help my awareness aperture open more and more, and to help me integrate that and find balance in that. To help me be more aware of Greater Awareness and of my own undouseable connection to it, and to help me understand a map of Multidimensional Reality and of the Continuum of Consciousness.

And zooming out, it feels like – well first, definitely there's nothing special or specially chosen about me, just, the opportunity presented itself during my little health hiccup for my aperture door latch to be knocked a little looser than it used to be and looser than average. Maybe that happened with some help or maybe on its own, but either way, it made something rare possible with me, so they might have been like, "Welp, not exactly our dream candidate but we'll take what we can get."

And then zooming out, it's clear to me there's an intention to help this happen with more and more people. Well, not the clinically dying part, but helping the opening of our apertures more. And that touches again into something I'll get into tomorrow afternoon, that we've talked about a little over coffee, about things kind of, well, about a quickening happening, meaning more and more people waking up more and more.

Ω

I'm looking forward to us going into that more. Alright, next on my list, you said – probably a month ago or so – that you've had around 50 total bridging sessions so far, so would you guess around 60 by now?

Ballpark. I haven't been tracking the number but somewhere around there. Plus there's been a handful of times I've woken up in the middle of the night or in the morning, and had the strong sense the portal had just been wide open moments before, but no residual details.

No vague memories at all when that happens, like a fading dream?

Nope, not so far. I just feel good and refreshed and reset, like after a bridging session, and there's like the energetic fragrance that Omega had just been there. Which really just means that my awareness aperture had opened enough so that I could perceive the level along the Continuum of Consciousness where a greater aspect of my own consciousness always resides, the level where Omega is. Which like I said, gets a little hard to grok on this level, because really on that level, that's what we actually already and always are. That's where our Higher Self, our Greater Consciousness is, with no real distinction or separation between us and that.

But it's not quite that cut and dry, because it's more like my aware-ness aperture opens enough to relate to and communicate with and perceive Omega, but not enough to experience myself *to be* Omega. That would feel like a big, big jump, that I can't quite fathom so far, and probably won't really be fully able to while I'm living my human life in this Earth suit, though I guess I can't say for sure.

And also – and I started to go into this earlier but we had enough on our plate – this particular identified consciousness of the human me really *isn't* exactly the same thing as the Omega Consciousness. More just an extension of it, an arm of it, a finger of it. But when my awareness aperture is more open, I'm more consciously connected to my Greater Self, and then I'm able to perceive and resonate with and communicate with and feel intimately connected with this Greater Multidimensional Being, this Greater Consciousness.

But it's tricky because like I've said, for my usual awareness, the easiest way to interpret it is that Omega energetically or vibra-tionally descends and comes to visit me for a while. I would've sworn that's what was happening those first few bridging sessions. But I've gradually been getting more acclimated to the sense of me opening my radio dial, my space radio telescope dish, and kind of relaxing my gaze or my focus, to be able to tune into Omega. Not that I'm really *doing* it, but somehow that's happening.

Ω Ω

And has there been – over the 60 or so sessions – an organized, methodical progression of what comes in, building off earlier ones? Or does it seem more to be random, not particularly orga-nized topics that aren't part of a larger module or direction?

Yeah, the sessions are always building off of what's come before, except for when they introduce something completely new. And depending on how big the topic is, sometimes it's done start to finish in one session or less, but with a lot of topics it's more like slowly painting or filling in several different areas of a canvas over a few usually nonconsecutive sessions. Painting in one area some, then working on that area over there, then coming back around and filling in the first area more. The flash packets for bigger topics usually kind of spiral around and get more filled out maybe two or three sessions later, painting more and more of a picture.

But sometimes I get the feeling both the paint and the mural wall are basically infinite. Always more paint to add, and always more wall to paint. It just keeps on expanding with no sign of ever completing the process of filling it all out. And over time, seemingly unrelated parts of the mural meet in the middle and they create a bigger picture, a bigger sense of that topic. Or sometimes two not obviously closely related topics connect, so it gradually builds towards more and more understanding, even though it always feels like I'm just barely getting started in relation to all that's out there that could be known and understood.

And one thing that's interesting about these inflashes is after it's had time to fully unpack – maybe a few minutes, or sometimes it's still kind of percolating residually in the background even a few hours or more after I've moved on with my day – but a lot of times, my understanding of it feels like it's something I really *do* understand, like I really have the material down, without having to work at it. It's just there.

Of course communicating it to someone else is a different matter, as we're sometimes seeing today as we drill down more than we have over coffee. I'm not so clear how to go about talking about these things at times, but it does feel like I do have a basic understanding of a lot of what's come in. It's like once it's been unpacked I have access to it just as though I had put in the time to really understand it, even though I haven't. Like the roots of understanding grow as the inflash unpacks.

And I definitely don't mean I perfectly understand through and through all that's been received, not even close, and a lot of it really is mindboggling – which odds are we'll get into some of that after our dinner break and maybe some tomorrow – but I do seem to be able – like so far today – to talk about a lot of it from a place of some degree of understanding, even though that understanding was just something I opened to instead of something I sweated out, instead of getting it through hard work and time and study. My little hard drive connects to the Big Cloud and I have access to whatever the inflash du jour is, and pretty quickly it's almost as though I've always known it.

On some level maybe you always have.

Maybe. Maybe on a deeper level we all know massive amounts more than we're aware of, but I don't think my human brain and my regular human level of consciousness knows pretty much any of it til each flash packet gets whomped in. But it's still kind of a strange experience to – I mean a year ago I couldn't have talked for 30 seconds about all of this put together, and now, well let's just say so far today that's not seeming to show up as a problem.

$$\Omega \; \Omega \; \Omega$$

But back to your question, a lot of the time it's like spiraling deeper and deeper into these different threads and topics, dipping into one pool, then a different one, then deeper into the first one again, as though for some of these things it would just be too much to take one area and try to get me to grok the whole thing all in one sitting or even two or three in a row. Some of it gets pretty deep and mind stretching. Maybe a greater mind than mine could do it that way, but Omega's probably afraid of blowing a circuit in me. Just guessing, but that's definitely how the flash packets come in. All I've gotten from Omega about it is this is the flow that works best. They aren't very forthcoming sometimes if a question isn't related to what's already on the docket for the day. Or sometimes even if it is.

What was the first or one of the first major downloads that came through?

Well, we hit the ground running that first session with one of the major themes, and then it revisited some over the next few weeks, and it still comes around again here and there, because it's just – you know, *Introduction to Reality 101*. And that's that on a deeper level – and of course this would apply to all of us, but I was seeing it in terms of me – that on a deeper level, I'm not actually other than that Multidimensional Consciousness, that Oversoul or Higher Self or Group Soul. I'm never *truly* separate from Omega for one iota, and actually the Fuller Me, the Greater Consciousness that's the larger Essence of me, *that* me *always* exists at that level.

We all actually exist – our Core Consciousness exists – on every level between this level we experience ourselves to be on and the level of Oversouls, or Higher Selves – which is the level Omega's on – and also between that level and the non-level level, the pre-level level, of Pure Infinite Formless Beingness.

There's an unbroken, unbreakable, seamless Continuum of Consciousness, that goes all the way through. Our awareness of it on this level is usually mostly or completely broken, interrupted and obscured, that's a common condition on these heavier outer settlements of the Omniverse, like our cute little corner universe. But the actual Core of Consciousness itself never wavers or isolates – I meant oscillates, maybe both could fit – but never oscillates in and out of a seamless Wholeness of the Consciousness Continuum. So from that perspective, despite all indications, we're never *actually* cut off from our Greater Awareness, even when we aren't aware of it.

What we're cut off from is the *mechanism* of consciously being *aware* that we're always Deeply Connected to Greater Awareness. Or maybe more precisely, there's an extra mechanism that shuts that out, that limits our awareness of that which is so effortlessly available on less dense levels of reality.

On this level, our awareness aperture is almost completely and continuously contracted to or limited by or myopically focused on the identity of our small self and the smaller world around it. But we're not ever *actually* cut off from the Continuum of Consciousness itself. We couldn't be. Impossible.

And that same topic has spiraled back around from different angles I don't know how many times, like slowly filling out a jigsaw puzzle, but moving around in terms of which section you're working on. Slowly filling in the tapestry. Gradually painting more and more of the canvas. And what can sometimes seem like unrelated flash packets then become interwoven and click together, like Mr. Miyagi's paint the fence and wax the car turn out to seamlessly fit together into a larger picture of kicking some Cobra Kai ass. Sorry, Netflix last night, but you get the idea.

CHAPTER 18

You said earlier that the flash packets are a two or three out of ten in importance to you compared to just connecting with the Omega Consciousness, but it sounds like at least some of them are profound and impactful.

Yeah, a lot of them *are* incredibly profound, and some *do* have a strong impact, and I definitely *do* appreciate them, all of that's true. It's just that my deepest response is usually or pretty nearly always most drawn to and most grateful for and most appreciative of and most enamored by the connection with Omega and the accompanying Space of Flowing Presence. Just taking in that feeling of the portal being open, and by that I just mean feeling plugged in, feeling connected to that Larger Consciousness, feeling something shift like the energetic air pressure dropping, and then feeling this Deep, Strong, Quiet Presence whomp into the space. Which is just the experiential way to describe my own awareness aperture opening and tuning in to a higher, finer frequency that's already always here at a more subtle level.

And zooming out a little more, we could even say that all of *that* is actually just me ceasing the chronic continuous holding my awareness aperture closed – which then naturally opens my awareness to a different focal depth, a greater vantage point, where I naturally see through the surface of the water into more of the always present but easily missed Depths. Where it's more apparent to me, more transparent to me, that my Deep Interwovenness with my Greater Consciousness – and with Greater Consciousness in general – could never actually come and go, could never truly arise and dissipate, though my awareness of it does. But that Irrevocable Interwovenness is just always simply already so.

For me, that's the good stuff right there, whatever the content is that day. I don't always even remember everything that inflows, it's a lot for the brain to try to assimilate, though I think pretty nearly all of it still lands somewhere in there and then shows up later as something I know but I might not always remember exactly when I came to know it. But so far, none of that's really the first priority for me. It's mostly about, you know, I might not be the best student, but damn do I like class, and gee, the new teacher is just the best.

Have you ever put a nice shiny apple on the teacher's desk?

Yeah, regularly. Well, apple slices. Well, apple pie and ice cream – same basic nutritional profile – but since I'm one with Omega, and I'm the only one with physical taste buds, it just naturally seems best to just eat it myself. We do what we must to serve what is Greater.

You're a noble man.

I'm too humble to agree with you but I'm sure everyone else would. Probably not a great analogy, but if you're really in love with someone, and they're teaching you something on their laptop or tablet, the best part of that time isn't learning something new about how to use a new app or something, it's the eye contact and little touches between you that happen while they're teaching you. That's the good stuff right there, that you're really there for.

And again, it's not that I completely don't care about what Omega conveys, I don't mean to imply that at all. I've really appreciated a lot of it and some of it has really landed pretty deeply. And then there's a lot of it I'm still processing and trying to catch up with. And I'm also appreciating, zooming out a little, the overall slowly clarifying big picture as more pieces of the mural get filled in. It's cool and so completely unexpected for me to start to get a rudimentary picture or map of an Omniverse that I didn't even know existed not long ago at all. I can't swear to anyone else how accurate it is, and like I said earlier, now and then something comes through that doesn't really speak to me, doesn't resonate – which is on our list to talk about at some point if it doesn't come up naturally – but all in all it's really resonating with me, through and through.

I keep forgetting to ask, when you say the Omniverse, I'm taking that to mean absolutely everything, on every level.

Yeah, I don't know what the official definition of that word is, but to me that's what fits to express that. All that exists, on every level, and the levels themselves, and also that which is before created, formed reality. The Infinite Source Substrate in which all levels exist.

Ω

Another check in, we've already gone another half hour, so we're about an hour over, but I'd like to get to two last questions before we stop, if you're willing. Both I probably should've asked earlier so I'd like to cross them off the list.

Sure.

First, have you asked Omega about Covid? Has anything come through about it?

I did a couple of times. Once I just asked if there was a deeper reason it was happening. And what came in was, if you live on a planet where life evolves through random mutations, and the beneficial ones get favored and passed forward, there's just going to be mutating viruses and bacteria and other harmful microorganisms. DNA and RNA mutate through occasional random replication errors as they duplicate, that's just the way of things. You can't have one without the other.

Just making sure it's clear, you can't have what without the other?

You can't have evolving advanced species like humans without mutating, adaptive pathogens that threaten them. And with billions of people on the Earth – often in close quarters – and with hundreds of millions sometimes not taking reasonable precautions when called for, and with millions traveling around the globe, these things are going to happen, and spread and mutate. And some will be worse than others.

And also adversity often has within it deeper opportunity, intensified growth potential, but that doesn't mean there's always a deeper reason the adversity showed up in the first place. The human brain likes to have reasons for things, but sometimes things just happen – physics and chemistry and biology unfolding – no deeper reason. And that touches on some of that background we'll get into tomorrow. But yeah, those kinds of things are just part of the terms of participation of life on an evolving planet, and always have been, though now with more humans more densely packed and traveling more than ever before, they can be much faster spreading and faster mutating, and on a much more global scale.

And the second time you asked about it?

Yeah, this one's a different angle, but one day just before sitting down to be available for a bridging session, I had a lot of tension and anxiety about it come up, about Covid, which I had been feeling at times from the ethers out there – a lot of anxiety and heaviness floating around in the energetic space from other people – but this was my own, which hadn't been happening as much. That morning my front door happened to be unlocked, and someone just suddenly opened my door and stepped in, without a mask, confused about where he was.

And I could tell he didn't mean any harm, and he stepped out and closed the door, though not as fast as I would've preferred, and even though I knew the odds of actually getting Covid from that were really minute, it just kind of shook my sense of being in control of what I'm potentially exposed to. It popped my bubble of being really on top of all that and having the – well, the control.

So yeah, I got really activated, and felt like if I didn't think of that unlikely scenario happening, what else have I not thought about? I don't want to over perseverate on all the possibilities, but also I'd much prefer not to risk being hospitalized with a difficult illness given the choice, thank you very much. But I had my guard completely down in my own home, and then suddenly the lone stranger opens my front door and steps in – who *was* that unmasked man? – and then apologizes loudly for 10 or 20 seconds while standing there in my entry way, not far from where I was standing. It shook me or activated me more than I would've expected it to.

So all of that was going on in me when I was sitting there waiting to see if there would be a bridging session that day – which I doubted there could be, given my discombobulatedness – but it did happen, and as soon as I felt Omega in the space, I mentally said something like I'm really feeling activated and unsettled and anxious this morning about Covid. I mean, theoretically, I could be hospitalized for a month or more, with all that could entail, if I just overlook one little thing, like having my front door locked 100 percent of the time, lest a loud, maskless, talkative stranger just mistakenly step in, which had never occurred to me to include on the Covid watch list, silly me.

$$\Omega\ \Omega$$

And what did Omega say, or communicate?

At first there wasn't any translatable communication, just an inflow wave of deeply settling Peace and Quiet, which really soothed my frazzled nervous system and felt like such a relief. A warm bath or warm cozy fire after being in a sudden snowstorm. Warming and relaxing and relieving and softening and settling and soothing.

And then after a couple of minutes, the words that came in were along the lines of, "In your daily human life, you won't usually feel this Ocean of Warm Loving Okayness. But it *is* always here. Even when things feel very far from even a little okay. This Space is still here, and you can lean towards it in yourself even if you can't find evidence of it or feel it in the slightest. This Space is your Source, your Essence and your Destiny. It's *always* with you and within you, and closer to the real you than your thoughts or mental self images could ever be. It is *always* so softly yet so solidly holding you. Of *course* it's hard to connect with the truth of this in daily human life, but nonetheless, it *is* true, for every journeyer braving your planet. All shall truly be well." I can feel it seep in again a little as I say that. Feels nice.

Me too, a subtle, Still Presence in the room. It feels settling. Alright, last question, and the main one I probably should have gotten to a couple of hours ago, what's the story of the name Omega? When and how did that come into the picture?

Okay, so the second session I asked, or a question rose up in my mind – which like I've said, is the same thing as asking a question during bridging sessions – what should I call you? And the answer was along the lines of, "We don't have anything like a name, but that's a helpful construct for you, so you can call us Omega if you wish."

Do you know why Omega? Well first, was there any sense of this Being trying to think of a name, like "Hmmm, let me think of one. Okay, let's use this name." Or was it already at the ready?

It was instant. I don't remember a time where it seemed like Omega needed to stop and think. Which, again, if this is all my unconscious, it definitely got a hell of an upgrade during the Big Event. Nothing like a reboot to speed up the ole hard drive.

And do you know why Omega? It's the last letter of the Greek alphabet, "I am the Alpha and the Omega, the beginning and the end." I looked it up, and I had never realized it literally means Big O. Mega O. O-mega. There's also a small O in the Greek alphabet, Omicron, like O-micron. But why Omega? Do you have any sense?

I asked what the significance was and there wasn't an answer, which, like I've said, isn't unusual. So are there Deep Profound Hidden Meanings in the name Omega, that we should try to dig into and uncover? Maybe, or maybe this Multidimensional Being could just see that, deep in my own mind, that name was a good fit. Better than, you know, Bob or Myrtle. Or the Apple Dumpling Gang. Or maybe my own unconscious reached in there and dug up the name.

And intellectually, it could make sense that maybe Omega is the end of the journey of the me I'm used to, the me I'm identified with, even though also a new beginning at the same time. But that feels a little forced, and I don't need to generate some intricate explanation I don't know to be true and don't feel my tuning fork or compass resonating with, so I've just let it go. I'm not assuming it has any significance, and if it does, if something more ever clarifies around it, great. And if not, it's helpful to have a name to go with the Space, and for me that name just fits, which is probably why that's the name that came out. And I think that's about it for that one.

Alright. I'm glad to get those last two crossed off the list. So, time for our belated dinner. Let's call that a wrap for our Saturday afternoon session.

PART TWO:
THE OMEGA
CONTINUUM
(SATURDAY EVENING)

SESSION 4
CHAPTER 19

Alright. Let's get right back to it. I'd like to start with a question I was going to ask you before dinner but realized I needed to wait.

Kay.

You've said there are things that the Omega Being has conveyed that have impacted you and that you've really appreciated, even though you're more interested in the connection itself. And I'm wondering if one comes to mind that I wouldn't know to ask you to share, but that you appreciated, and also that maybe fills out the mural a little more.

Yeah, it's not like I just tolerate the data streams, I do appreciate them, I just usually appreciate the space of Connection itself the most because it – well you could say it scratches a deep soul itch and heart itch, that I didn't even know I had before the Big Event. But let me see if I can think of one that also moves us forward along the road we're on here. Well there's two or three coming to mind, but yeah, here's one that's probably already along the lines of the deeper waters that we're moving into anyway, and it shouldn't be too much of a mind stretcher. Not too high a diving board to start with, now that we've got some water in the pool.

Sounds good.

Okay, so basically, in one of the earlier bridging sessions I said to Omega – which just means I had the thought – now I know what happens after we die, meaning because of the Big Event. And there was an immediate inflash of like a gentle correction or expansion of my understanding that came in, that first of all, when someone has an experience of being conscious while their body has stopped functioning, that isn't necessarily a fully accurate representation of what really happens after permanent death, because they're still tethered to their body. You can't assume that experience is identical to untethered, final death. There's similarities and overlap, but we can't assume they're the same.

Weak analogy, but maybe a little like how those old scuba diving air hoses, that pumped air down from the boat's manual air pump, could impact how someone experienced trying to move around down in the depths. It does have an influence, it's not exactly the same as being completely free and untethered.

And second, our own filters and inner belief structures and cultural biases can influence how we perceive and experience the outer world, and that's much more true on more subtle levels, which are more easily and more quickly or even instantly impacted by our own mostly unconscious influences. And that makes us to varying degrees co-creators – conscious or not – of what we experience both during a near death experience, or other multidimensional experiences, and after death. Not the sole creators, but what humans experience after their body dies is in part influenced by what they bring to the table.

And third – I had a third one but I lost it. Oh yeah, the sheer scope of possible experiences after death. So created reality, with all of its levels, is a vast, complex tapestry of interwoven tendrils of Pure Consciousness, fractaling into near infinite form. So there are a *lot* of different experiences that could be experienced after death, not just one size fits all. And to try to squash all of that potentiality of what could happen, and how it might be perceived, into a really limited, narrow snapshot is just trading maybe some discomfort in directly facing the Vast Unknown for the unwarranted tight holding of a very limited and incomplete – and therefore incorrect – map.

Ω

So anyone who says they know exactly what happens after death – even if they've had a temporary tethered near death experience, or have heard about the experiences of others who have – that's extracting or extrapolating way too much from their own or someone else's experience or experiences. Which were not only one snapshot of the vast array of possible experiences, but were also unavoidably influenced to some degree by pre-existing internal influences.

Not sure I said that clearly, but it's extrapolating an overgeneralized assumptive picture of what happens to everyone, as though there isn't significant variation, and it's presuming a near death experience is a perfect preview of what will happen after final, untethered, no do overs, no refunds physical death. So saying, "Hey everyone, here's what I experienced during my near death experience," sure. But "Hey everyone, I now know exactly what happens to everyone including you after death because I had a near death experience or I heard about someone else's," that's an overreach.

But from what came in – which as always, we can't assume are the Infallible Words of the Great and Powerful Omega Being – one very common thing after death is that usually, regardless of the specific experience, there's much, much more of a connection with Presence and Re-membering and Pure Love and Pure Light and Homecoming. Because we've shed so much of the inherent limiting structures of experiencing a human life, which we naturally get so attached to and focused on and identified with, and the releasing of all of that makes us a lot more open-apertured.

Plus we're usually at a significantly less dense level of reality where Pure Beingness is less obscured – making that resonance easier to perceive and respond to – which helps our awareness aperture open even more, and helps us be more able to be much more aware of and connected to Infinite, Love-emanating, Light-emanating Pure Beingness.

Do you want to add anything to that word, usually? After death people are <u>usually</u> more connected and <u>usually</u> on a much less dense level?

Well, after death, after consciousness is freed of its wetsuit or Earth suit or planetary exploration astronaut pod, it does move to a less dense level than ours, but how much less dense can vary. Usually enough density has cleared away or been risen above, like an airplane rising above the storm clouds, that the Pure Loving Rays of the Infinite Sunshine are less obscured. There's usually more Clear Seeing, more Expanded Awareness, more Profound Connection and more conscious immersion in the Beautiful, Light-Filled More. But not always.

Just as someone can have brain fog – like when coming out of anesthesia, or when groggily partly waking up in the dark in the middle of the night, not sure where they are – they can also have Consciousness fog, or transition fog, where after the death of the wetsuit they've been inhabiting, they just aren't clear at first what's happening or where they are.

And if your attachment and tight gripping to your life is towards the end of the bell curve, could be for a noble reason or a less noble one, like a loved one having difficulty and you're concerned about them so you don't want to move on yet, or maybe someone deliberately caused your suffering or early death and you want justice. Or maybe the farmhouse you've lived in your whole life has been sold to a steampunk hipster couple that lives there ironically and converted the 200 year old icehouse into an espresso bar, and you just – who could blame you – you can't let it go. Or whatever it might be, those earthly attachments might keep your aperture narrowed and focused in on the life you were just in, at the exclusion of what's currently available to you and invited to you if you would just relax your contracted awareness aperture enough to notice.

If you're really tightly squeezing your aperture closed, which you're still able to do after death if you insist, since our consciousness has a lot more freedom and a lot less limitation than when we're alive – including the freedom to not be free – then things are probably going to be more dim and thick and obscured.

Ω Ω

And sometimes other circumstances can lead to that too, just the way you died or some other aspect of your situation. You might not even realize you're dead, depending on how smooth and gradual or unexpected and abrupt your dying process was and how strongly your drive is to resist the current situation, or I don't know what all can impact that.

So yeah, sometimes it's just a circumstantial obscuration or brain fog, maybe the way you died, and sometimes your energy can – well your consciousness can use its energy to propel it tightly to only being focused on the remaining attachments from the life that just ended. And that can create a kind of observational bias, meaning you don't even notice the larger context that you now actually inhabit, and you possibly aren't even aware your physical life is over.

I think I followed all of that except "to propel it." What was "it" referring to?

To propel your consciousness, which can direct your energy and power and capacity to keep your awareness aperture seeing very narrowly and obscuredly and unpristinely. And yes, people sometimes feel – or surviving loved ones sometimes feel – a genuine visitation, the unmistakable heartful presence of a loved one who's body has died, especially in the first hours and days and weeks after their death, and that can be a really healing, assuring thing. And some people after they die might stay pretty focused on what's happening with the people they love, sending them love and support and good vibes, that kind of thing.

And it doesn't have to be either/or – either moving on or staying focused on trying to help loved ones – because we're more of our larger awareness after we die, so it could be several things pretty much at once. Soaking in Deep Belonging, while also sending a loved one a sign or some love and soothingness and strength and all-is-well-ness, which they might or might not consciously notice, while also going off on some other adventure. Multitasking doesn't work so great here but it's a breeze there. Take that a little further – like by a factor of a billion or a trillion – and then in the Awareness Continuum, you're an Oversoul. A Higher Self, a Multidimensional Light Being, able to be effortlessly tuned in to almost endless things at once.

So sometimes people feel the good, healing, supportive, loving presence of a loved one who has died. But people can also feel, you know, semi-aware spirits or so called ghosts, or energy remnants, that are just lurking around, without them feeling very conscious or present or whole or clear or like a healing presence. And when that happens, those are the – well could be two things – but one is those are the obscured souls who are, just for a time – never forever but for a time – just stuck somewhere stagnant and gray and obscured for a while, confused and consciousness-fogged and cloudy in their awareness.

I think coming out of anesthesia is a pretty close way to say it, but it can take a while. Weeks or months or years, physical time. Kind of stuck in the gravity of Earth time and their Earth life, stuck in a stagnant habit loop or a confused default thought loop. Or a limited available perspective loop. Almost like a record player skipping and repeating without anything new happening. Or like in a stream or creek, a stick or a leaf that gets stuck in a whirling eddy and just can't get downstream for a while. But eventually, sooner or later, they always get unstuck and continue their journey onward.

And once in a bridging session, I saw that helpers of various kinds sometimes help those people or ex-people – which definitely doesn't sound quite right – but sometimes help those kind of post anesthesia consciousnesses, to slowly come out of their transition fogginess more fully, and help them understand they're no longer living that lifetime on Earth, that's now completed. And help them to reconnect with their actual current reality and connect more deeply to the Beautiful More, to Oceanic Light-filled, Love-filled Presence, and maybe to their own Larger Self, which doesn't necessarily happen for everyone every time they complete a physical life experience – a little like someone on a tour of duty might not come home as soon as one mission is finished. But helping them understand where they really are and what's really happening. Helping them snap out of their gray dream.

CHAPTER 20

So you said it could be two things, when people experience spirits, and I want to hear the second one, but first, what helpers? You can't just casually mention helpers and then move right on by.

Right, page 46 of our contract, sorry forgot. Okay, so you know how sometimes you sleep wrong and your arm's asleep and you kind of wake it up but it takes a while. So in a sense these are arm wakers, which isn't one of my stronger attempts, but basically sometimes other kind souls – literally kind souls – maybe a loved one who's already left their Earth suit, or maybe some benevolent guides or beings who are currently focusing on helping people with this big transition in their lives – or I mean after their lives – but maybe a kind soul helps point someone confused and disoriented and foggy in the right direction or walks with them or guides them to where they would naturally be drawn to go, or gives them what they need to shake off the fog and have more clarity. Gets them back on a path that will lead to Fresh New Connected Greater Aliveness.

And it could be someone who's been on the dead side of life for a while that helps a loved one out with their transition, or it could be a being that's never had a lifetime on Earth at all, but just has a response to be of service in this way, to be a Cosmic Walmart Greeter, or I don't know all the options.

Even still-living loved ones lighting candles and praying – or intending or sending heart love or warm thoughts or supportive energy – for someone who's died, to have a smooth transition or to relax into the invitation to a Deeper re-connecting, or to release any grasping or tight holding on to that which is now in the past, or to follow the subtle fragrance of Supportive, Loving, Expanded, Being-filled Healingness – or any warm intentional heart wishing – any of that can be a real, impactful support.

Just not trying to boss around the universe with exactly what should specifically happen, but sending warm-hearted well-wishing for Goodness and Connection and Healingness. It's not so difficult for our intentional thoughts to have some real impact on more subtle levels of reality, which we'll go into a little more tomorrow.

But yeah, sometimes people are a little foggy and confused for a while, or feeding off the fumes of their understandable strong attachment to being alive or to something else in this world that was really important to them. No one forces you to let go, no one can make you, it's just the natural response for most people instantly or fairly soon, because what's suddenly before them is so much more recognized as their Profoundly Good, Love-filled Home than what lies behind them. And it just does happen sooner or later for everyone. Kind of like eventually you get over even the roughest, most soul crushing break up and move on, hopefully while you're still alive, but sooner or later we all do let those things go. But this is the ultimate break up, with your whole life, every part of it, everyone and everything in it, sometimes all at once with no warning, instead of piecemeal or with some real notice to find closure as best we can.

So people naturally handle death in different ways, and also have just objectively an easier or harder situation to navigate. Sometimes there's immediately clear consciousness, and sometimes there's just a kind of post anesthesia fog and confusion, and that can be more likely if there was an unexpected abruptness, rather than real time to grieve and prepare and let go at least some while still alive. Beginning the completion process. With an abrupt death, there's more likely to be kind of a PTSD, Post Transition Stress Disorder. Not all that often as I've understood it, or at least it's not longer lasting that often, but sometimes.

Ω

So you talked about space-time being different during your near death experience and on more subtle levels of reality, and how you were free from time the way we're used to it on our level, but you also said after death some people can get stuck in the pull of time, and also that when someone dies, positive thoughts and heart wishes and prayers can all be a support to them. And just now you said again it takes some time sometimes to be clear after dying. So I'm not sure what my question is, really. Just, is there anything else you want to say about that contradiction, or apparent contradiction, around time still impacting more subtle levels?

Well it's just not binary, not all or nothing. It's not that either there's normal Earth time after death or there's no time at all. And there are a whole lot of levels between our more dense level and the highest levels of created reality, and then there's Eternal, Timeless, Infinite, Conscious Light-filled Beingness, the Central Hub and Pure Essence of All That Is.

So we're talking about *a lot* of different potential scenarios and experiences and levels that could be in the picture. And when someone dies and their consciousness is more obscured or limited or hindered or foggy – or more contractedly Earth life focused – it's like they're more caught in the orbit of our level of space-time reality, and so they're still under more influence of the gravity of time as it exists here. Not completely, but under the influence.

And even beyond space-time as we understand it, experiences can still happen – there can still be activity and progression – it's not that there's no movement or motion or experience, it just isn't constrained by the type of space-time that limits our level of reality.

And also, when love and warmth and support and care and kind heart energy are sent out to a being through the cosmic airwaves, nothing can stop that from reaching the intended recipient. That just happens, even if they're in a kind of gray, cloudy, foggy, stagnant, circling pool of looping nonmovement, or if they're in a pristine spaceless Space of Beautiful Timelessness. They may or may not be conscious of it, but it *does* reach them.

Let me – before we get too far away from it – let me circle back to that second possibility of when someone has the experience of sensing ghosts or spirits.

Oh yeah, good tracking. So sometimes that's actually just an energetic remnant, a small unconscious offshoot or tendril of the primary consciousness of that person. Sometimes if you look at a bright light you see after-images for a while. Or an echo might hang around a few rounds after an original sound has stopped. Or if you move to a new place you might unintentionally drive on autopilot to your old one now and then at first. And bathtub ripples keep going a while after you get out. So sometimes residual energy just kind of does its old thing, follows the old ruts, and it takes a while for it to get the memo or to get the latest software update, or just to lose more and more of its rippling or repetitive energy til it's spent.

Ω Ω

So all that was to say, sometimes what people perceive as chilling, off-feeling ghosts or energies or similar phenomena are just consciousless energetic remnants or remainders – energetic after-images – that will slowly dissipate, and aren't actually a confused, foggified post-physical person or soul that's stuck in their transition. So it's like an unconscious residual energetic after-image of a lifetime, that can kind of get stuck looping around, swirling in an old whirlpool, in a setting where that person spent much of their life or at what was a really important place. And that's most of what we might think of as ghosts.

So there can be lifeless energetic remnants or echoes, and there can also be getting stuck for a while, during the transition from being alive in a body to consciously being a Larger, Freer Awareness. Where you aren't yet aware of your Living Connection with your own Greater Consciousness and with Greater Reality itself, and for a while being in a kind of amnesiac fog of obscuration, maybe not even aware that the physical body has died.

And last thought, to me it feels likely that the traditional, centuries-old approaches for sending wayward spirits on their way to the Greater Goodness of the Beautiful More – things like prayer and candles and burning sage and performing ceremonies and so on – they all probably have some real energetic and consciousness technology that they tap into, that actually works.

Like I've said, conscious thought and intention can be a powerful influence on more subtle levels, which we'll get into a little tomorrow, but just because this whole area isn't understood by science yet, that doesn't mean it's not perfectly in line with the laws of multidimensional physics, whatever they might be.

Everything that exists follows some kind of template or laws, and the pursuit of understanding those is what science is, right? So all of this is in the purview of science, just not discovered by us yet. Eventually, as our understanding expands, all of this will be a lot more normalized, like we don't walk around amazed because we can surf the internet and watch videos on our phones, which would've seemed far beyond the realm of possibility a few – I was going to say a few centuries ago but even a few decades ago really. And now we not only take it for granted, we usually get really annoyed when we lose internet for 30 inexcusable and excruciating seconds.

This is all really interesting to me.

It is, and at the same time, it's safe to say there are people out there who've had a lot of deep, profound or interesting seeings about more subtle levels of reality, that have a different map for all this than the one that's been taking shape for me these months. Safe bet that Oversouls or Higher Selves don't come up at all in some maps, and that some have a different take around what I just said about temporarily lost spirits and residual energetic echoes, and maybe a different take on a lot of what I say this weekend.

Ω Ω Ω

And I haven't – well not only have I not been drawn since the Big Event to see what other people are saying out there or what other people have experienced or what they might be seeing or inflashing or their own version of that – however they come to see and understand things about Multidimensional Reality – I'm actually drawn to *not* check out other people's experiences or what other people are saying. I think I'm probably in the minority here, I haven't taken a poll, but I'm just wary of my own experiences and understandings getting diluted or influenced or tainted or mixed around by something I might read or hear or watch.

So *before* the Big Event I never had the slightest interest in checking any of this kind of thing out, it was obviously all nonsense by wishful thinkers, and then *since* the Big Event I've been wanting to not mix or water down my own experience by exposing myself to other people's experiences or teachings or maps. Maybe after more time has passed that will change, but so far, I'm just processing my own continually expanding experience and understanding of all this – and letting it continue to slowly grow and deepen and integrate – without getting into or checking out or comparing what else is out there. And also without making this map The One and Only Truth to defend and carry a flag into battle against other people's differing maps.

And you know, I think most of the time having a closed drawbridge around understandings and maps of reality isn't a great thing, but

I can't out reason my – I guess my felt sense or my – you could say my heart clarity – that for now it's good to just tread lightly and take extra care and keep giving myself some incubation space or integration space, and to just steer clear of comparing and contrasting with other people's experiences or understandings or maybe spiritual teachings, or anything else out there really. Because I feel a – at least for now – a response to keep this whole unfolding that's been happening as pristine and unblended with other influences as I can.

And just to tangent off my tangent here – I now this is self evident – but just because someone happens to read the transcript of our marathon instead of some other book with a different map – which probably Venn Diagrams with it, overlaps, but also has its differences – they can't assume the book they happened to start reading is the most accurate map out there, right? Same if they read another book first. Like assuming the religion you were born into is the closest one to The Real Deal, or even *is* the Real Deal, which is an understandable bias the human brain has, which we'll touch on tomorrow, but it isn't so ideal to unquestionably trust it.

So just because our weekend conversation is the book someone happens to be reading about Multidimensional Reality, etcetera, that doesn't automatically mean it's necessarily the closest map to the Real Deal. Same with some other book or video or workshop or whatever. So it always gets back to checking your own imperfect but faithful compass. Okay, I've lost the thread from two or three tangents ago. Do you know where we were or where to next?

CHAPTER 21

I'm not sure if you were finished with the original thread, about what opened during that bridging session around how we shouldn't assume a near death experience gives us a – we shouldn't assume it gives us the full picture of what happens after death.

Yeah, that's what we were talking about. We were so young back then. So to finish that thread up, basically, when we're living our lives as humans on this planet, and we get a glimpse of more subtle levels of reality from a near death experience or from some other expanded or multidimensional experience, then we usually can't help but interpret what we're taking in, and filter it through our preconceptions and beliefs and expectations, which already pre-impacted to some degree what we're experiencing in the first place.

Then to add all of that together and confidently call our description and interpretation of what we experienced an accurate description of what everyone will experience after death, and on top of that, calling it an accurate map of all of Multidimensional Reality, that's a little problematic.

Actually, Omega didn't convey a match for problematic, that was my own add on or commentary, which I'm trying to be really conscious of and either avoid or clearly label, but the sentiment was more like just be aware, just notice, that this kind of gap-filling really strays from the pure and clear and accurate understanding and sharing of your experience.

And it's really good to be aware of this, because humans tend to like things binary and tidy, with no gray area, which worked well for survival – like categorizing safe animals and unsafe animals, safe plants and unsafe plants, safe tribes and unsafe tribes – but reality is *way* more complex and vast and full of a huge variety of potentialities and seeming paradoxes than our brains might prefer. There are more things in heaven and Earth, Horatio, than are dreamt of in your philosophy. Times a trillion. Shakespeare spilled his coffee on those last three words so they were lost to history, but he originally wrote "times a trillion."

I'll make some calls and try to get that added back in.

Would be great, thanks. Also Romeo and Juliet were originally Fred and Ethel, but "Fred, Fred, wherefore art thou Fred?" didn't test well with focus groups at the time. But we're almost guaranteed – probably not almost – to interpret glimpses of Greater Reality from a limited perspective and in a limited way, and to lose a lot in the process, as well as to add some things in there too, through expectation bias. We can't help but overlay our own understandings and expectations and internal maps of this world on a completely new experience, and it's a very strong human tendency to innocently believe our resulting descriptions and understandings of it are filter free and accurate. We usually just take it for granted that our subjective experience is objectively tangle-free.

You know how sometimes when you're reading, you read the words you're expecting it to say next instead of what it actually says. Our brains pre-fill what we're taking in with what we're expecting to take in all the time, which colors our experience and how we describe it. That saves the brain a lot of processing time and energy, it's a great survival mechanism, but it does cost the immediacy of pure unfiltered, unaltered, direct seeing.

And our mind does that a hundred fold or more when it experiences more subtle levels of reality, because to our perceptions they're more ambiguous or ephemeral, and also they actually do tend to be more malleable, more subject to being influenced to some degree by the observer's thoughts and expectations and intentions. So all in all, our experiences of more subtle levels of reality are more subject to our own impressions and expectations and preconceptions and enculturations than our usual level is.

Ω

Reminds me of quantum physics. The observer influences what's observed.

Yeah I've never really understood that aspect of quantum mechanics that well – not that anyone fully does just yet – and there's still disagreement about what that's really indicating, but that sense of by observing something that's very subtle and malleable and moveable, we can inadvertently impact it or influence it, that does fit for subtle levels of reality, at least in terms of what's come in through the flash packets. But all added together, what I'm getting at is you can have confidence you experienced what you experienced, but not that your experience was unaltered by your own expectations – or by unconsciously overlaying your map of this level of reality onto other more subtle levels – and not that it was unaltered by other subtle unconscious influences.

And you also can't have confidence that it accurately describes the whole big map of everything. The whole shebang. Or even a sizable part of the shebang. I mean it's a pretty damn big shebang. There's so many different levels of reality and different worlds and sub-realities, sometimes with completely different laws of physics specific to that level or world, and so on. You can't describe Paris from a three hour layover at the airport. Much less all of France, or all of Europe, or our whole planet or solar system or galaxy or universe. That's not a problem unless we actually think we can, but there's a default human tendency to lean in that direction more than would be ideal.

You know a huge amusement park has room for a lot of different rides that have a lot of different themes and that do a lot of different things with gravity and centrifugal force, or have a lot of turning and twisting and spinning or entering a house of mirrors or riding a track car through a cave or through a haunted house, or up a steep incline then splashing down into the water, and so on. And these amusement park rides aren't really compatible with each other, there's not a lot of experiential overlap, each is their own unique setup, though some of the foundational basics are similar. So the way one ride works and what it does and how it looks might not have much in common with another one. Multidimensional created reality is a little like that on an unfathomably bigger, near infinite scale. And again, there are different fundamental rules and laws, to different degrees, on different levels and also in different areas of different levels.

So things just aren't as cut and dry and delineated as our brains like things to be. There's just a million ways – well you know the Cat Stevens song, "There's a million ways to be, you know that there are." It's like if we all lived in the center of the Earth, and different people found or built tunnels to the surface, and if someone asked what it's like, the answer would be so hugely different if they surfaced on a tropical island or in Antarctica, or in a summer forest or in that same forest during a winter blizzard, or in a desert, or in a busy downtown of a major city.

So there would be a lot of different possible experiences, and there would be a tendency, at least til there was more understanding, to say, "I've experienced the Great Surface everyone, here's what it's like! Here's what awaits all of us when we reach the Great Beyond!" When in reality, that was just one particular possibility out of many, and even the surface level isn't the end of things. There's sky above that, and stars and planets beyond that, and other galaxies and other universes, other levels of reality. Heavens beyond heavens beyond heavens. And someone who tunnels out to the middle of the Sahara Desert might understandably think now they finally know exactly What Lies Beyond.

I had a near surface experience, let me tell you what it's like up there.

Yeah, exactly, and to take this one step further, some worlds or levels of reality are very much in flux, and some are instantly hugely influenced by the experiencer of them, so that even if you're in the same neighborhood, standing at the same street corner, your description of the reality you're perceiving could be completely different than the person next to you. Or from you five minutes from now. And add to that your own preexisting conditioning and biases coloring and filtering your conscious experience of it, and this whole business about reality being a steady, reliable, unchanging thing held by the same knowable and consistent laws all the way through, on every level, and consistently perceivable as objectively the same by each perceiver each time, that just doesn't hold water.

And this idea that we can understand other levels of reality by applying the same understandings we've always used to navigate our own – well not only do we all have plenty of obscurative filters in our perceptions here, but also the consistency of physical laws might be a foundational aspect of our physical universe as far as we currently understand it, but we can't superimpose that on more subtle levels and other worlds and presume they're the same. Well, we can, and we do, but we shouldn't if we have any interest at all in more unfiltered, uncompromised and undistorted perceptions and interpretations and understandings and reporting.

And there are countless worlds so even if you get a glimpse – or a hundred glimpses – of something beyond, that might be basically the equivalent of wiping away a few layers of dirt from the ground with your hand and saying now you understand what the inside of the Earth is like.

So, that whole inflash or inwave, that whomped in as an immediate response to me declaring I know what happens to us after death, it really had an impact in me. I really got how easy it is to assume we know so much more than we do, and now that my eyes have been opened that there's way more out there than I ever imagined,

I'm more aware of how I tend to automatically apply the rules and regulations of this little neighborhood universe on the rest of the Omniverse. That's just what the brain tends to do.

And, last thought, it also left me really seeing how miniscule in some ways our own neck of the woods really is, when it's as though, relatively, this entire massive universe – which might be even exponentially more massive than science is currently aware of – is like just one cute little suburb of one little city on one little planet in one little galaxy out of billions. It was also a sobering reminder that no matter how sure I am of what awaits me after death, I can't really be positive exactly what I'll experience til I'm tether free, and my body doesn't pull another last minute Lazarus, bless its heart.

But I will say that even if I remind myself I can't know exactly what I'll experience after death, I do just know in my bones the feeling, the vibe, the Profound Goodness and Complete Belonging that awaits me. Theoretically I could turn out to be wrong, but it would be out of my integrity to not really trust what I know so deeply about that in what feels like the very marrow of my Being.

Ω Ω Ω

So bottom line, I was seeing just how vastly unfathomably huge all of Reality is – and that's a massive understatement – so to presume we pretty much have it all mapped out is to be a little more innocently arrogant and a little less authentically humbled by the unfathomably infinite scope of it all than the actual situation warrants.

Like imagine if our entire universe, with trillions and trillions of stars and planets, billions of galaxies – with more stars in the universe than grains of sand on the Earth – imagine if all of our entire universe was inside an inconceivably huge glass snow globe. And then imagine as many different and unique entire universes existing – unique snow globes existing – as there are stars in our universe. As there are grains of sand on the Earth.

And then imagine that whole thing, that whole collection, all those trillions upon trillions of snow globe universes, are each just one little snowflake in one big mega snow globe. And then, for the grand finale, imagine that there are as many of those big mega snow globes as there are stars in our universe. As grains of sand on the Earth. And then, for the grand grand finale, keep doing that again and again and again, as many times as there are stars in our universe. As many times as there are grains of sand on the Earth. Til your mind is thoroughly boggled. Then we're off to a good start and we've almost definitely scratched the surface of the vastness of the Omniverse.

My mind is considerably boggled right now.

Happy to help. So one of the things all this means is that even as I'm taking on talking about what I've experienced during the Big Event and my bridging sessions, and what data streams or inflashes I've taken in so far, all of that still has to be seen as a very limited take on it all. It's all just *way* too vast for any one person's one take or even a hundred takes to do it anywhere near justice.

And you know, like I said, someone else who has a mind blowing near death experience or similar opening might not experience a Multidimensional Being at all. Or even if they do, it might not be understood to be their Oversoul, like I understand Omega to be. The same mountain peak can look completely different from two different sides, or four or five different sides, or from above it or below it, or inside it.

So this is a fraught challenge, to try to share my sense of these things based on what's been opening in me. I mean what's opened so far has to be seen as an infinitesimally small snapshot compared to what all there is to potentially open. But as long as you – along with anyone who might read the transcript – keep in mind it's one limited perspective, one take on Greater Reality and some specific aspects within it, and take what resonates and leave the rest, why not come along for the ride? So yeah, I think that finishes up that whole piece.

CHAPTER 22

My mind is still trying to stretch enough to take in all those snow globes. But next question. I wanted to ask about, when you were talking about tunneling up from the center of the Earth, and how vast the sky is, you said something about how our physical universe might be exponentially more massive than science is currently aware of. And the way you said it, I wondered if there was something more to say about that.

Yeah, that's the second time you've caught something like that. For a microsecond I thought about trying to squeeze something more in there, but it was too many words to really stick with my main point at that moment, and you know what a stickler I am about not going on a tangent or using a lot of words. But yeah, we could go into it now.

So – well first, just an interesting tidbit that didn't come from a bridging session, all of the normal matter in the universe – planets and stars and nebulas and galaxies, everything we think of as what the universe consists of – all together it only makes up about five percent of the entire mass of the universe, and astronomers aren't sure where the rest is hiding. It's bad enough to lose your car keys, but they've misplaced 95 percent of the mass of our entire universe, which is pretty embarrassing. They theorize the rest is made of an invisible substance they call dark matter and a force they call dark energy, but bottom line, right off the bat there's 95 percent more mass in our universe than the matter we normally think of our universe as. But that little update could just be small potatoes compared to what else might be going on.

And I guess I'll just cut to the punch line and then fill it in, so basically, once in a bridging session, a flash packet came in about how our physical universe is just one of many, in an extradimensional physical structure on our level of reality that includes a myriad of them. So like if you picture – well let me start by asking, do you know what a tesseract is?

Do you mean that includes a myriad of universes?

Yeah, per the flash packet, this extradimensional physical structure on our level of reality contains huge numbers of physical universes similar to ours. And do you know what a tesseract is?

I take it you don't mean the glowing green cube from the Avenger movies.

That would be correct, I do not. So there's a concept that – I must have learned it in a math class – but there's a thought experiment about a four dimensional cube. So you start with a two dimensional square, and then if you add a third dimension you have a normal cube with six squares for the sides, like dice, six faces. So far, nothing strange. And we can't really imagine what it would be like, but just like we added a third dimension to a two dimensional square, you could theoretically add a fourth dimension to a three dimensional cube. And in math that's called a tesseract. So a tesseract is to a cube what a cube is to a square.

Ω

But from our three dimensional world, we can't really get a sense of what a four dimensional object, much less a four dimensional whole world or even multiverse, would be like. You can't really get a sense of 3D from 2D, if you're a 2D being, and you can't get a sense of 4D as a 3D being. Like 2D has north, south, east, west, or it has top, bottom, left, right and diagonal, and then 3D adds to that up and down, it adds depth. So then what does 4D add? We can't really get a sense of it from our 3D world.

But just because a 2D being, if there was one, couldn't really conceive of what a 3D square would be – this theoretical "cube" 2D scientists speculate might exist at least mathematically – that doesn't mean it *doesn't* exist. We're living proof it does. And yet we don't really – I mean it's hard for us to really be open that just maybe there's also a 4D world all around us, that there's maybe even 4D structures all around us, and we just don't happen to be able to perceive any of that from our limited 3D world, just like 2D beings couldn't perceive that their square is actually part of a greater theoretical and unproven cube.

So that's all a pre-ramble to saying that one image that came in during a bridging session – and it could've just been a mind stretching exercise or an analogy of how vast the Omniverse is, or it could've been literal – and even if it was literal, it could've been incorrect or misperceived, or it could've just been my unconscious, you know the drill by now.

But the inflash was that, just like a square can be one part of a cube – meaning like one 2D side or face of a larger 3D structure – our entire, unfathomably huge 3D universe is part of a greater four dimensional tesseract universe – let's call it a tesseverse – that has a whole extra dimension. So our entire three dimensional universe is like just one of its sides, in a sense. One of its many three dimensional faces or facets, or whatever the word would be for a 3D side in a 4D multiverse.

And you know how – well let's say you have a hundred of those flat square cardboard restaurant coasters. You could use six of them to make a cube, but then you could fill that cube with all the rest of them. A hundred – well I guess 94 – flat 2D sides or faces, stacked tightly inside a 3D cube. Like a package of sliced cheese, or maybe the most obvious example is a deck of cards.

So kind of along those lines, a four dimensional tesseverse could have thousands or millions – or I don't know the upper limit – of 3D universes like ours, kind of stacked right next to each other, on top of each other, or maybe with a little space in between, but all the way across the tesseract, the tesseverse.

$$\Omega\,\Omega$$

And for what it's worth, and I'm not assuming it's worth much of anything, but there was also in this flash packet an image of some distant civilizations being able to go card hopping, universe hopping, from one to another, within the tesseverse. That there's nothing in physics that prevents that, we're just a few hundred or a few thousand years or whatever from having the technology, if we ever develop it at all. And then that whole thing, that whole flash packet, ended with an image of a spaceship that just kind of flickered in and then flickered out of the sky. Appeared and disappeared. And I asked Omega to fill that whole thing out some more and explain what that was about, but just silence again.

So, I don't know what to make of all of that, and as to whether there are physical beings just a couple of frequencies over on the radio dial, that know how to, you know, push a button in their Wonkavator, and suddenly pop in for a visit, or if advanced civilizations in our own universe kind of dimension hop or transdimensionalize in order to travel faster than the speed of light – like hop over to another universe in the tesseverse, and then nearly instantly hop back here a billion light years away from where they started – I have absolutely no idea. But definitely more mind stretching stuff to even begin to think about.

Plus, you know, if there can be a third dimension added to a second, and a fourth added to a third, why would we presume it stops there? Or even why would we presume it stops at *three* dimensions? By definition, hypothetical two dimensional beings couldn't really bump into or meet or greet or interact with the three dimensional world in a way they could recognize, and that would be true for each additional dimension with the next one, right?

So I have no idea how many dimensions there really are in this little realm or level of reality that our universe and purportedly the greater tesseverse exist on, but the inflash was that this kind of multidimensionalism, it's all on *this* physical realm, it's all part of *this* level of reality – meaning these are physical, physics-based dimensions in our level of reality – and not the same thing as more subtle levels of reality that open for us after death or during other expanded experiences. So yeah, I don't know what to do with all that, I can't notarize it as Certified Accurate Information, but that's what came in.

That's all really intriguing. It would be interesting to explore it a bit more in depth sometime. Some of the implications of if it were true, and how to even begin to picture it, which may be a fool's errand.

Yeah, I really don't think us 3D-ers have much of a chance of grokking it. It's a 4D world out there, and we're just living in it. Or living in one relatively thin little 3D slice of it. Or I'm totally wrong. But at the least it's interesting to think about.

It is. Alright, on to another question.

Kay.

CHAPTER 23

Can you talk a bit more about what the Omega Consciousness is as you understand it, and how you're connected to it? How it's connected to you?

Okay, so first question first, Omega is an Oversoul or Higher Self or Multidimensional Being. A Conscious Spark of Pure Consciousness. A Conscious Expression of Pure Beingness.

And did Omega give you the term Oversoul?

Well, again, Omega radiates a transmission of waves and senses and images and concept seeds, and then when they land in me, some of it never needs to be converted into words – my mind already gets it fully without that – but sometimes words are involved in the unpacking and translating, and of course the expressing of it, and all of the unpacking happens a little like plant seeds sprouting and growing all in seconds or minutes, or sometimes more slowly for bigger flash packets.

And like I've said, there's room in that process for my misinterpretations or mistranslations or filterings. Anything that goes through the inner interpretation of the human brain is subject to filters and flaws and translation errors and expectation biases and cultural indoctrinations, it just is. Like that Mars space probe around 20 years ago, where the European side used centimeters and the U.S. side used inches, causing a big translation error, and then the whole project – probably hundreds of millions of dollars – just crashed and burned. Literally.

And for me, usually I find words that match up really well, a direct hit, you sank my babble ship, but sometimes I have trouble translating it, trouble finding just the right aligned wording that captures it. Or sometimes it's so unfamiliar that it's challenging to find a way to convert it to words and thoughts and feelings and senses and understandings my brain can really grok and store.

And like in Jurassic Park, when they mostly used dinosaur DNA but filled in the missing pieces with frogs, sometimes maybe the unconscious does its best to get the full translation, but it could theoretically fill in some missing pieces – pieces that are just too unfamiliar to really grok – with something more familiar, and that could potentially change the DNA of the information, if that makes sense.

So I just don't think anyone should be considered a completely reliable narrator about more subtle, less scientifically verifiable experiences and understandings. Most of the time my experience is that I've got a clear signal coming in and I'm able to understand what it's conveying, but I don't think that should carry a lot of weight for anyone else, and rumor has it being confident you're right – and/or projecting confidence to others – doesn't always strongly correlate with actually *being* right.

So, with the word *Oversoul*, I don't really remember how it rose up. Maybe I had heard it somewhere before and it came to mind as a good match, or maybe it just felt like it fit linguistically for what inflashed. I also use the term *Higher Self* sometimes, and I don't really have a word or phrase yet that really captures the sense of Omega being both many and one. Soul Group or Group Soul or Soul Tribe or Soul Family, but none of those are exactly it for me. We don't really have a way, our brains aren't really set up to contain both simultaneously. Multitudinal Singularity or maybe Multitudinal – what was the other one? Multitudinal Unilarity – they're about as close as I've gotten. A Multitudinal Singularity of Consciousness.

Ω

You know how some trees, like aspen, can spread through their root system, so on the surface they seem to be individual trees, unique organisms, separate life forms, but just under the surface, it's clear they're simultaneously one living breathing singular organism. Separate fingers of the same hand, of the same arm, of the same greater body.

Individual aspen trees can share water and nutrients and I think they can even send some communicative biochemical signals to each other, so if one tree is in a really dry, hot place, another healthier tree with deeper roots or wetter soil not far away can send it water through their interconnected root system. Or if one aspen is under attack by a pathogen, its roots can signal other connected trees and they can begin to redistribute their resources to build a defense in time to make it more likely they'll be able to resist the insect or fungus or whatever it is.

Not so different from setting mountain top beacon fires, one after another in a long chain, to warn of an approaching army. These aspen groves are actually one living organism, while also being a collective or a group of unique, individual living trees. So Oversouls, you could think of as something kind of like that, times a million. So we could add the term *Soul Grove* to the list of good try but not quite it ways to express the Multitudinal Singularitiness of it.

That sounds a bit like ant colonies. Individuals moving as a group mind.

Times a million. Or maybe a billion. I'm noticing in my mind the tree grove feels more evolved and closer to what I'm talking about, but maybe I just like aspen trees more than ants. They ruin fewer picnics and make better walking sticks.

And zooming in some, of course even our physical bodies are made of individual living cells that work together as one larger collective. But it's just hard for us on this level to really get a handle on a Multidimensional Being that's both – on the one hand a unique individual Being, one Multidimensional Consciousness – and also simultaneously, a single United Tribe or Family or Group or Collective, consisting of a great many unique soul sparks within the one Larger Spark. A Community of souls on one level or from one perspective, but from another simultaneous perspective, all one seamless Being or Greater Consciousness. One Oversoul, or one Soul Grove, that all of those individual sparks are intimately and inextrably, or inextricably and inexorably and irrevocably a part of and one with. A multitudinal singularity.

And trying to get our head around it is like trying to grok – speaking of quantum physics being over my head – how in some experiments light can be both an energy wave and a particle at the exact same time, without the slightest conflict or contradiction. Paradoxes are only paradoxes from perspectives or levels of reality that don't have enough dimensions to have the space to hold both apparent contradictions simultaneously. So with Omega–

–Could you say that again? Paradoxes are only paradoxes...

From levels and perspectives that don't have enough dimensions, or frequency bandwidth, to have room to hold both aspects at the same time. So with Oversouls, there's no contradiction or paradox on that level, it's just business as usual. So is Omega one Being? Yes. Are they a Multitude of Beings existing as One? Yes. Is it both of those, continuously, exactly simultaneously, without the slightest contradiction or conflict or paradox at that higher level? Yep. Can we really fully get that or grok that on this level? Nope.

So Omega is the name that lit up in my brain – however that exactly happened – to refer to this Being that is my Higher Self or Oversoul, and there are a lot more individual consciousnesses than just me that are all actually, on a higher level of reality, always one with this particular Multidimensional Light Being, that at the Core is never truly other than Pure Consciousness.

Ω Ω

Does the term Light Being have a specific meaning we haven't talked about, or is it just another way to express a Being whose Core is Pure Consciousness?

Well, *every* being's Core is Pure Consciousness, but yeah, I just throw that in there now and then. These aren't exactly everyday concepts I'm putting out, so I'm trying to say them, well sometimes the same way again, in case more passes help, and sometimes deliberately in different ways, in case a new one happens to click more. Just trying to shoot slightly different arrows and see which ones stick in the tree. Not an aspen tree from that grove I just mentioned, I wouldn't do that to them. But I'm basically building a lot of my lexicon, my language color palette, in real time as we go, for better and for worse.

So a few times I've used the term *Multidimensional Light Beings* – or MLBs for those of us in the biz – but just as a way to suggest a Being that's very, very connected to Fundamental, Pristine, Pure, Shimmering, Scintillating, Light-filled Essence. Pure Beingness, Pure Consciousness. Pure Infinite Living Light, before it's gone through that prism into the multicolored light, the multi-wavelength light of created reality. But as we go, I'm basically just throwing a lot of different spaghetti at the wall to see what sticks, so if you don't like how a piece lands, feel free to toss it in the trash. Or toss it with some olive oil and parmesan, your choice.

A light meal. So these other individual beings that are part of Omega – I'm not sure what I want to ask – but during your near death experience, and during your bridging sessions for that matter, did you hear or feel different personalities chiming in, like different members of a great council?

No, it's not like that, that I've experienced. You could also say there's only one Being, one Consciousness, no division or delineation at all, but that One Consciousness is simultaneously having a lot of different experiences. Has a lot of fingers in a lot of different stream currents.

Do you have any sense of how many souls there might be in an oversoul? And how many Oversouls there are?

So it's not like there's a thousand meters in a kilometer and a thousand souls in an Oversoul. Or like each Mothership has a precise capacity of ten thousand individual explorer pods that fly down to a planet or maybe several planets, like "Next stop, Andromeda 78, watch your step." There are so many different potentialities and possible alignments with all this.

An Oversoul might have a lot of different experiences and explorations and creative expressions happening on subtle levels but only a handful of extended fingers of the Greater Body living out a physical lifetime on one or more planets. Or maybe – I don't know the upper end – maybe trillions of extended fingers in billions of snow globe worlds throughout every level of the Omniverse. So at the risk of going out on a limb, an Oversoul has somewhere between just one and around a hundred trillion individually sentient consciousnesses, give or take.

Thanks for narrowing that down.

Anytime. And in case your mind wasn't stretched enough earlier, you could also say that with each Oversoul there's actually only one Soul, one Being – not subdivided at all or multitudinal at all – only one exploration pod per spaceship, and it flies its pod down to a planet or other amusement park ride, and experiences that, then goes and experiences a different one, and so on, totaling a million different planets or a million different video games, and playing between maybe one and a thousand different characters in each game, and all of that is happening all at once, because time doesn't exist the same way at the Mothership level.

Like you could theoretically be playing a video game where instead of just being one avatar or game character, you have a thousand, all playing at once, as thousands of years pass in the world of the game, but for you it's an hour. Or you could even change the settings and make all those centuries play out in five minutes. Or five seconds. Our physical brains wouldn't have the capacity to track all of that, but that doesn't mean a Multidimensional Light Being doesn't have that effortless and near limitless capacity.

CHAPTER 24

And you could also say there isn't actually a delineation at all between souls and Oversouls, and it's just the Oversoul, the Higher Self, this multitudinal singularity, dipping its hand in the water for a while. But with a hundred thousand arms it can dip a lot of hands in a lot of different water all at the same time. It's just the water's cold so the fingers don't have as much full flowing, warm and open consciousness circulation as the core of the body does. But we could say that's all that's happening.

If you're in a canoe and put a hand in the water on each side of the canoe, are there three or are there two or is there just one that's experiencing the water? Or if you focus on your fingers, the numbers go up. And fingers and hands just don't have nearly the same neural connections, they don't have the same awareness of the larger mind as the larger mind does of the fingers. So the larger mind can be more aware of ten fingers, or why not ten million fingers, than those fingers are aware of the larger mind.

So lots of ways to look at it, and if each of an Oversoul's million arms or hands or fingers is in a different world and is sentient and conscious and autonomous, experiencing its life, how do you add up the numbers? Is it one Being with a hundred thousand arms, or is it a hundred thousand sentient souls, all connected to the same Mothership, to the same central nervous system of their Higher Self or Oversoul?

And time passes for those individual extension fingers currently living a physical lifetime, but for the Mothership, those millions of experiences are happening at the same time, like when you're in a canoe there's nothing challenging about having your hands in the water and all your fingers experiencing the water slightly differently, with different little currents and eddies and leaves floating by, and one getting scraped by a rock a little, and one brushing against a tree branch. And all your fingers are having those different experiences at the same time, it's not like we have to reincarnate one at a time into each finger, right? One finger doesn't say to another finger, which finger were you your last life? It's just all one smooth flowing experience, in this ever living now.

So on that higher level, there's not space-time as we think of it, it just all is existing in the Eternal Nowness, without the straight narrow arrow of time we're used to. That doesn't mean there's no experience or movement, like I said earlier. But it's more easy, unrushed, non-instant, Eternal Spacious Nowness. Without the slightest contradiction.

So, there's a Consciousness Continuum or through line from Pure Infinite Undifferentiated Beingness down though the different levels of created reality. And you could say that while Omega is my Oversoul, there could be, up a few levels, a more centralized Being that in a sense is Omega's Oversoul and the Oversoul of a lot of Oversouls. It's just that to capture that kind of image you have to freeze frame the ever-flowing energetic fractaling of Pure Consciousness into subtle levels of form and beyond, and that's a false image, because it never stops swirling and flowing and swooshing and inhaling and exhaling in and out and through and into and out of. In and out of time. In and out of both higher and denser levels. In and out of Singular Merged Undifferentiated Oneness. And in and out of autonomous, unique, segmented individual Beings. In and out of the many and the One.

$$\Omega$$

I know that was all English, I recognized most of the words. Mindboggling again.

What would *really* be mindboggling is if your mind *wasn't* boggled right now. So Oversouls or Multidimensional Consciousnesses are like – what is it – E Pluribus Unum, out of many, one. To coin a phrase. They're simultaneously, one single Multidimensional Being or Consciousness, and you could also see them as a Being Group or a Being Tribe or a Being Family or a Soul Grove of many different individual autonomous consciousnesses. On one level or from one perspective, they're distinct and unique consciousnesses, maybe like highly conscious bees that leave and return to their collective nest, and on another level or from another perspective, they're all one Consciousness. Five fingers, one hand. Two hands, one body.

And there's no paradox in this simultaneous many and One. Nothing even slightly contradictory about it on more subtle levels of reality. It really smoothly flows so naturally and obviously. Try telling an aspen grove that it's impossible, that it can't exist the way it's existing, that it has to pick a number, is it one living thing or a seamless group of individual living things? It will just laugh in delight at your limited seeing, but you'll assume it's just the wind quaking its leaves. Little known fact about aspen, they have a highly evolved sense of humor, and most of the time quaking aspen leaves are just due to good jokes going viral through the grove.

I did not know that. Have an example at the ready?

Well, one good old aspen classic is, knock knock.

Who's there?

A woodpecker.

A woodpecker who?

No, that's the whole joke. Knock knock, who's there, a woodpecker. Our sense of humor isn't evolved enough to really get it, but trust, me, it's profoundly, chef's kiss hilarious to aspen trees. Sure, most woodpeckers don't appreciate it much, but we all know how self serious *they* can be. I mean, have you ever *once* heard a wood-pecker laugh?

I don't believe I have.

I rest my case. But yeah, Oversouls are simultaneously many and one, and at the same time, most fundamentally, each Oversoul or Soul Group is inextricably connected to, and one with, the One Seamless Conscious Infinite Universality and Essentiality of All that Is. Pure Infinite Beingness, Pure Essence, Pure Consciousness. The Eternal, Benevolent, Love-emanating Source Substance, from which all beings and all form on all levels of Reality arise.

So that brings up a quick little simple question. How do all beings and all form on every level of Reality arise from this Eternal Benevolent Source?

Here's a quick little simple answer. Two words. Ready?

Ready.

You're sure you're ready? It's gonna rock your world.

Let it rip.

Okay. Here it is. Drum roll. Ice bubbles.

Ice bubbles?

Yep. Next question.

My world doesn't appear to be noticeably rocked.

Crushed. Okay, so we'll add in a little more background and see if that helps. So, there's one undifferentiated Infinite Consciousness, one All Encompassing Everpresent Beingness, and then that kind of spiders out or tendrils out into created levels of reality. Structured, formed levels of reality. And I'm counting all levels of created reality as formed. Maybe some are really, really subtle and just wisps of minimally structured energetic patternings, but they're still part of created, formed, differentiated reality. Post-prism reality.

Remind me about the prism?

Just throwing more spaghetti at the wall. Pre-prism is the Clear, Undifferentiated Light of Pure Beingness, and post-prism is the multi-colored, wide spectrum, multi-wavelength light of formed multi-leveled reality. So this Pure Infinite Consciousness – which is also Pure Living Infinite Flowing Love, but not because it intends to be, it just by its very nature *is* Pure Infinite Flowing Love – so this Infinite Ocean of Pristine Essence is endlessly Flowing and Merging, and let's say *Yessing*, into all that exists on every level.

Ω Ω

And regardless of all appearances, this Pure, Omni-temporal Infinite Isness doesn't ever actually leave itself or stop fully being itself to enter formed reality. It couldn't. Preposterous. Not even slightly. Not for a nanosecond. And it's never one nanometer away from itself. Not possible. Its very Essence is infinitely intimate with all that is, which at the Core of all that is, is only this Essence. There isn't truly anything beyond this Infinite Essence or outside of this Infinite Essence.

So, if Essence is only Essence, if Pure Consciousness is only itself – with no differentiation or separation or segmentation or otherness or two-ness or form – if it's only seamless uniformity of Infinite Conscious Nectarous Isness, then how does the multidimensional sausage of formed created reality get made?

The multidimensional sausage?

You win some you lose some, just add it to your plate of wall-fallen spaghetti. But so then how do all the levels of formed reality and every thing and every being in it come to exist? How does the Essential Absolute Oneness of Pure Undifferentiated Omnipresent and Omni-temporal Infinite Love-emanating Consciousness generate and enter into temporary multitudinal reality?

Could you say that last sentence again?

Not in a million years. But how does the One become many? How does the singular, non-two Pure Isness become duality? How does Pure Seamless Oneness extend and express in multi-leveled reality? And one way to analogize it is, how could a drop of water in the ocean remain in the ocean, and keep its pure oceanness, but at the same time be able to have some uniqueness and individualness in form and shape and experience? Without ever leaving the ocean for a second.

And one answer to that question is to picture a liquid-centered ice- shelled sphere, but that's more of a mouthful than just calling it an ice bubble. A thin spherical layer of ice forming around a liquid drop of pure ocean water, to give it separateness, individuality, uniqueness and the ability to experience itself and other. Two ice bubbles could interact with each other, and they could also still flow with the one ocean, though maybe not quite as freely or amorphously or completely or mergedly. And then eventually, that thin outer individuality-enabling ice shell membrane – which is still only pure ocean water, just in a solidified form – eventually melts back into the oceanness it actually always was, and then that unique, individual drop of ocean is once more completely one with Pure Infinite Undifferentiated Conscious Oceanness.

I think I actually more or less followed most of that.

Me too. But let me take another pass to smooth it out a little. You know, I have a little photo printer and each pass it takes over the same photo paper makes the image a little clearer. So hopefully these different passes and angles and arrows and spaghetti strands on the wall help bring into focus at least a little more some of these things – and non-things – that are really difficult to talk about and convey and get a sense of.

So, pass number 17, there's Pure Infinite Awareness, Undifferentiated Isness. It doesn't have form or delineation or border or boundary or two-ness or creative – well, not sure what to follow that word with, but it doesn't have creator and created within it in its pristine undifferentiated homogenous, seamless non-two form. It's just Pure Infinite Seamless Singular Beingness. Vibrant Scintillating Living Essence, effusively overflowing with itself.

And then, like those thin-membraned ice bubbles within the vast liquid ocean, this Pure Overflowing Infinite Light-filled Beingness created – not out of need but out of superabundant and overflowing, let's say Joyful Expression and Uncontainable Creative Superpotentiality – it created individual membraned Sparks of itself, which could then have self awareness and individuality and autonomy and unique experience, and they could also relate to and interact with and respond to other Sparks of Consciousness, and to Pure Consciousness itself.

These newly individual Conscious Sparks of Beingness could connect and interrelate and experience and create. They could mingle with other Individual Sparks of Pure Beingness, over at the charcuterie board. But these unique conscious bubbles of differentiated Beingness are never for an instant *really* other than Pure Awareness. They're never for an instant *actually* anything other than Pure Radiant Flowing Essence. A Spark of Pure Source Substance, temporarily existing and experiencing and interacting and creating as an individual, unique, aware ice bubble. A light wave that temporarily solidifies into a particle, til it eventually waves back into the one Infinite Conscious Light, that it was never for a moment actually even slightly other than.

CHAPTER 25

To say it another way, pass 18, there's the Infinite Brilliant Shining Sun, and then there's individual Sparks of it, that can now have their own experiences and make their own decisions and even create with the painting canvas of subtle energetic realities and sometimes denser, more solid realities as they choose. And what separates them from Pure Consciousness, from Pure undifferentiated Essence, doesn't really separate them at all, but does create the mechanism for individual unique identity and experience and agency and expression.

And it isn't like a literal membrane or skin, that actually has solid separative properties, but more a kind of minimal light containment field of individuality, so that they can have unique experience and a unique identity in form, while also always being completely aware of and one with Pure Infinite Awareness. With Endless undifferentiated Beingness, their True Nature and Core Essence.

When you said a minimal light containment field, did you mean lightweight or like it was made of pure light?

I have no idea, that was almost 30 seconds ago. I don't even recognize that old me anymore. But I think both could work so let's leave it unspecified. But the bottom line is, Multidimensional Higher Beings like Omega, they're always individual Sparks of Pure Consciousness, with the thinnest of membranes that give them their own unique consciousness and experience and expression and autonomy and agency, and the ability to interrelate and interweave and interconnect and self navigate and create, and co-create with others.

And they can also extend individualized extensions of themselves – individual souls, conscious autonomous arms or fingers or tendrils or soul sparks – that can experience living a smaller, contained, boundaried, experientially separate, unique, temporary life in various levels of reality and in various snow globes or worlds within those levels.

And these individual souls or individual beings or individual consciousnesses, these individual Spark extensions, they can experience aloneness and all Oneness. They can leave and then return. They can forget and then re-member. They can experience the loss of Oneness and the re-uniting of it, like with me, to some degree, to some extent in the Big Event. And they can experience a completely unique and perceptually separated lifetime, with all its highs and lows and rewards and challenges, and then merge back Home, truly none the worse for wear.

They can experience existence as an individual autonomous being that's living a life on a planet – or in some other snow globe world very different from our universe of planets and stars – while simultaneously actually always being safe at Home, whether they're completely or mostly or slightly aware of that or not at all.

A Spark of the One Sun puts on a wet suit and goes for a swim, forgetting most or all of what came before and what waits patiently for after, and what still exists right now, beyond the oh so convincing holographic veil. While simultaneously and without contradiction never for a moment *actually* leaving the cozy hearth of Home, enjoying the warm safe relaxing fire, profoundly Safe, profoundly Content, profoundly Loved and profoundly at Peace. A gamer becomes immersed in an intense game world, becomes identified as their game character, while at the same time chilling on their favorite chair, safe at home.

There's a bit more of a Deep Presence coming in again. I was about to jot down a follow up question but let me just go ahead and ask it.

How did multi-leveled reality itself come into form? If the ice bubble analogy gives a picture of how individual beings came to exist, how did the levels themselves of what you're calling created reality arise?

Good question. It'll be interesting to hear how I answer it. Okay, so everything of every world is made of a Conscious Energetic Substrate, that at its most distilled is Pure Consciousness. I'm not saying a rock has the ability to do math, and definitely not calculus, but the substrate of that rock itself – the energetic building blocks of all energy and matter – that's of Pristine Fundamental Consciousness. And because All That Is is made of Infinite, Conscious, Living Light-filled Oceanic Isness, then all that is, all that exists, is a part of Infinite Conscious Oneness. Everything is, at its most fundamental Core or Substrate, one with Pure Flowing Infinite Living Light.

So in our Deepest Roots, we're already always one with everything, without exception. We just aren't experientially aware of it. And like a two way mirror presents to one side of it as a mirror blocking what's on the other side of it, and presents to the other side of it as a clear glass window where everything on the other side of it can be clearly seen, these thin membranes of differentiation and individuation, they're just the experience on one side of the glass.

And from that post prism perspective, or from the mirrored side of the glass – from the perspective of form and levels and created reality – which includes the most subtle levels of created reality, there really is the experience of separation and partition and boundary and self and other and me and you and this and that, and sometimes a little space-time thrown in to thrill up the ride a little. That's accurate on this side of the two way mirror.

But without the slightest contradiction, on the *other* side of the glass, the First Side – capital letters – on that Pre-prism side, from the perspective of Pure Seamless Infinite Isness, those partitions are merely insubstantial shimmering holograms, with no actual existence or real border or boundary or partition or delineation, or separation or inside and outside or here and there. From that First Side of the glass, all is one, all always *has* been one and all always *will* be one, and there's actually no glass at all. There aren't two sides.

But from the created reality side of the mirror, those wisps of holographic boundaries create the whole experience of formed reality, with all its levels and separations and unique individual objects and energies and fields and everything else in form. They make it possible. And on the most subtle levels of created reality – still this side of the mirror – those holographic membranes of individuality and duality and multi-ality, they're more see through, more translucent, more recognized for what they are. More permeable and more obviously hologrammatic. Less convincing and less limiting and less partitioning.

As though Higher level Beings on the most subtle levels of formed reality are standing exactly at the side or edge of the two way mirror, one eye seeing from the Undifferentiated, Non-two, Pure Awareness side of the glass, and the other seeing from the created reality mirrored side of the glass. One foot firmly planted on each side of the center glass line. One eye on each side, like a perfectly positioned tennis center line judge, if the net were the two way mirror. They're just always effortlessly aware of both.

So, with this separative membrane – or let's call it a holographic containment field – of delineation and boundary and energetic skin and individuality and uniqueness and self identity, individual beings can traverse and experience and explore and creatively express in the near infinite worlds and realities that are in subtle levels of reality and also in the more dense levels like our physical reality. You get on an amusement park ride, that might be thrilling or scary, and your greater life recedes in your conscious awareness for a while. But when it's over, you'll be back to your larger sense of experience and greater awareness. Less myopically limited in your awareness aperture. You're back to your more full and more complete life.

And maybe it changes and more bridging happens here soon, and gets easier, like Omega's conveyed, and like I'll talk about a little more tomorrow, but for now, living here means mostly or completely forgetting there, the Oversoul level, which again isn't really over there or up there somewhere, way up in the heavens, straight above the particular continent you're on at the moment. That over there, or that up there, is actually much more here than the here we usually experience as here. The here that's here usually isn't as here as the here that's there.

I didn't quite follow that.

That's okay, I didn't either. Let me take another photo printer pass, and maybe we'll both get it this time.

Ω Ω

So imagine levels of Multidimensional Reality spiraling around downward into denser and denser form, like a vertical Slinky slowly winding around, or like a screw thread or auger, or like those old barbershop spiraling signs. Actually I don't like any of those, but how about a really tall circular parking garage where you just wind around and around, slowly going up towards the top level or down to the bottom. As opposed to an elevator with precise and delineated segmented floor stops. And the car that's four levels above you is a minute or two away from you, but at the same time, it's just 50 feet directly above you. So the levels are spiralingly stacked on top of each other with some space in between, making things closer than you might think.

Or picture a bunch of circling airplanes slowly descending to land one by one when a runway is back open after an ice storm. If all the planes are slowly circling lower and lower, just following the wide, slowly descending spiral they're all taking, following the plane in front of them, the planes aren't that close together. They're like two minutes behind the one in front and ten minutes from the one that's five planes ahead, that's already a few spiral levels lower down. I don't know anything about how that really works, but just as an analogy.

And because they're stacked on top of each other, the actual distance to that fifth plane is, vertically, a lot closer. Maybe it's just a thousand feet below you and a little behind, because it's one or two big full circles ahead of you in the spiral. So it's true that it's ten minutes ahead of you in the spiral path, and it's also true it's just a thousand feet below, it's just one quick ten or fifteen second carefully timed jump to land right on the nose, just in front of the windshield, which would, you know, take a lot of guts. But it's a lot closer than you might be thinking it is if your thinking is limited to just following the linear, slowly spiraling path.

Or think of a wicker chair, where there's those long strands of thin bendable wood or soft bark strips, that wrap around the chair. And imagine one strand wraps around all the way from the bottom of a chair leg up to the top of the chair back, then it winds all the way back down to the bottom of the same chair leg where it started. So it would be a really long journey for like an ant to crawl that whole way following that one long strand. But since the starting point and the end point are actually touching, that little ant could also just be touching the beginning and the end at the exact same time, without going anywhere at all.

Time and space and distance as we think of them just don't apply to subtler levels. A film reel holds every point in the movie, start to finish, simultaneously. Your car radio doesn't have to do anything for 50 different transmission frequencies to be right here and right now, you just have to tune its receiver to the frequency you're interested in. They're already all right here. Radio signals are transmitted everywhere within range, not just selectively to your car radio or mobile phone when you're tuned to that frequency. It's raining radio signals and satellite signals and mobile phone signals and a lot of other radio wave frequencies all the time.

And just like the bigger the radio telescope the more faint the transmissions it can receive, the more open our own inner awareness aperture is, the more subtle signals it can tune into. Of course not having a lot of busy interference bouncing around helps too, but the more open the receiver, the more can be received.

Ω Ω Ω

So I think I lost the thread of what those analogies are pointing to. One thing you're saying is that the Omega Consciousness and other Oversouls aren't up in the sky looking down on us, other levels of reality aren't way up there, they're much closer than that. They're right here, overlapping, in the same space, just a different frequency. We just aren't attuned to them or our radio telescope isn't – it's not open enough I guess.

Yeah, I kind of moved around there, but the spiral analogy was trying to allude to how, first, levels of reality are more fluid and flowing than like elevator stops. Like rising in elevation in the mountains gradually changes the flora and fauna, but it's not a precise line or border. And second, while a more subtle level can seem far away, there's like a shortcut, a shift in perception, like the gutsy airplane jump or like the parking garage, or the wicker chair ant, where they're actually a lot closer than we might have been assuming.

And then the radio wave thing was just – yeah, where do we think those other levels are? Like we tend to think they must be up in the heavens, up in the sky above our particular location on this round planet. Every radio wave within range is literally passing through our bodies right now, but we tend to think higher frequency levels of reality, way more subtle than radio signals, have to be far away, in some physically far away distant dimension. Or we've been culturally ingrained to think of the heavenly realms as, you know, up in the sky, maybe 50 miles straight above our current

GPS coordinates, but definitely *not* in the sky on the *other* side of the world, straight below where we are.

But realms beyond our realm of time and space, why do they need to have spatial distance from us, as we think of it in our level of reality? Where else could they be but overlayed right here? Or from a zoomed out perspective, "right here" is more a holographically created set of coordinates that doesn't hold up as its own individual spatial location, once seen from the vantage of non-spatial or pre-spatial reality.

CHAPTER 26

This is all really hard to conceptualize.

Yep. It's almost a lost cause for our minds to try to really get the vibe of it. But it's not that more subtle levels of reality are farther out, farther away, they're closer in, they're just a subtler frequency. It's not like the higher the radio wave frequency the farther away its source has to be from us, right? Distance has zero to do with frequency level. Absolutely zero. Does a higher pitched noise have to originate from farther away? Does the higher end of the radio dial have to have transmitters farther away? So why do higher dimensions, higher levels of reality, have to be far away from us? Omega doesn't descend down and grant me a visit from on high, but is always right here, just a turn of the dial.

Like the 5,000 mobile and Wi-Fi and satellite and the whole spectrum of radio waves passing through us right now. And then there's that First Waveless Wave, that's before *every* frequency. Infinite Flowing Beingness, the Ultimate Everpresent Unperturbable Continuous Wave, that nothing could ever bump into or clash with. So we're used to the idea of radio waves overlapping the space that we inhabit and take up, without any noticeable contact or conflict or bumping, but Higher frequency levels of reality can't? Higher frequency Beings can't? Pure Infinite Beingness can't?

Those more subtle levels, those higher frequency levels of the Omniverse, they're always right here. I don't rise up to Omega and Omega doesn't descend down to me. But that's harder for us to conceptualize so I've been saying it like a Multidimensional Oversoul Being extends a tendril down into a world. An astronaut exploration pod comes down from a Mothership. It's a little easier to get some sense of it that way, at least for me. Something's always lost when you try to compress five or six or ten dimensional – well I can't think of a word – but ten dimensional perspectives or viewpoints or maps, or just 10D reality, into a 3D conceptualization. Just like trying to represent something that's 3D in two dimensions, or even one.

But however we talk about it and conceptualize it, an Oversoul can extend into different worlds, simultaneously, with I don't know how many tendrils at once. There's no logical limit. They aren't limited by a measly hundred billion physical neurons in a human brain. Their Consciousness has no pre-set limits at all. So they can experience many, many different lifetimes simultaneously, maybe even on the same planet in the same time period, so that you could potentially meet someone and they could be – you could both be tendrils of the same Multidimensional Oversoul. You could both be tendril extensions of the same Higher Spark of Pure Consciousness.

And you know, the idea of reincarnation as I've heard it is really linear and time limited. You live, you die, you rinse, repeat. But from the perspective I'm describing, that which you really are – this Oversoul, this Higher Consciousness Spark of the One Infinite Clear Light – it could have many, many different lives, on this planet and others. And not just lives as we think of them, but other kinds of experiences in other worlds, that are set up completely differently from the way we think of individual life forms living a lifetime and then dying. And since that Oversoul mostly resides on a level or frequency of Existence that's beyond space-time as we know it, it can have all of this happening at the same time. All in the same nontemporal unfoldingness of Eternal Nowness.

Ω

And again, zooming out a little more, every conscious being, every soul, is at their Core, always of One Pure Consciousness. Within the Continuum of Consciousness, we are literally One Consciousness, flowing into form, experiencing form, creating in form, creating with form, while on the Clear Glass side of the two way mirror, never actually leaving the Infinite Pristine Oneness – the Pre-prism, Undifferentiated, Love-emanating, Eternal Essence or Source Substance – that everything always actually is made of and is existing within and is substrated from and is never actually divided from or separated from in the slightest. Those holographic – what did I call them? Not holographic membranes, but holographic holding fields, or–

–Containment fields.

Yeah, those holographic containment fields, they aren't real from the vantage of that First Side of the two way mirror. They hold no real power or weight or influence at all. They do on *our* side, like autonomous actions towards others can cause real joy or real pain, real impact, to ourselves and others. But from the First Side, all is always only That. All is always seamlessly One.

So, we're having our experience of our life, and at the same time it's possible that other conscious tendrils of that same Oversoul are off in other experiences, maybe on this planet, or maybe they're on some other completely different amusement park ride or in some other snow globe or video game world.

And since time and space are deeply entrenched constructs of denser reality, it's hard for us not to apply them to more subtle levels and hard to really grasp how timelessness and spacelessness could possibly work, but time and space aren't inherent just because existence is happening, they're extras. They're bonus features found in some denser trim levels. Found in some snow globe worlds. They're not requirements for a snow globe to exist or for some levels of reality to exist or for conscious existence to happen or for beings to exist. They're optional. And they're malleable and spectrummable, not binary. Time and space can exist in a lot of different ways.

And an Oversoul Consciousness is aware of all those autonomous conscious tendrils having individual experiences, tracking it all, experiencing it all, intimately inside of it all, like how your consciousness knows when your finger is in cold water or hot water, but your finger doesn't have much awareness of the greater consciousness it's always connected to. And like I said earlier, that's equally true if your finger is touching your face or your arm is completely outstretched as far as it will reach. What we perceive as distance has zero impact on how connected we are to our fingers, or how connected our Higher Self is to us.

So this whole dance of an Oversoul extending through a conscious tendril into a world and then that individual tendril or spark of consciousness returning to the larger Spark that it never really left, that dance could happen with an Oversoul a few times to a few hundred times to maybe billions or trillions of times. And at some point, that whole Being Tribe or Group Soul or Soul Grove or Higher Self – that Overspark of Pure Consciousness – it eventually fully merges back and returns to Pure Consciousness Itself, which it never left from the perspective of the Pre-prism side, the First Side, the Clear Glass side of the two way mirror.

And by eventually I mean, and again I don't know exactly, but like over trillions of years if it's looked at from our space-time infused level. And also instantly, like it was never gone. And simultaneously, it *isn't* ever gone, like a gamer never disappears from their chair when they're identifying with a game character in a game world. There's just some holographic containment field shenanigans playing out that create that – not exactly illusion – but create that real but limited experience.

An Oversoul's Core Awareness, its True Essence, is absolutely *always* completely connected to and one with Pure Essence. Which is true with us as well, it's what we, in our Purest Core, at our most fundamental, indivisible Essence, actually always are.

So just as we – an individual spark of Conscious Beingness, that's also a tendril extension of our Oversoul – just as we return to our Overspark or Higher Self or Soul Group or Mothership, this Multidimensional Being – that's much more consciously connected to Pure Beingness, and which our conscious autonomous spark has never been even slightly separated from – this Oversoul eventually returns to Original Pure Infinite Beingness, and so we do as well, along with it.

Ω Ω

And neither the spark or the Overspark – neither the individual consciousness or the Oversoul – was ever, throughout this whole multidimensional journey, even *slightly* actually separated from the Infinite Pre-created, Pre-prismed Ocean of Everpresent Benevolent Conscious Essence. It's all one seamless through line. A seamless Continuum. From the Pure Undifferentiated Oceanic Infinite Love-emanating Source to our Higher Self to us, and from us to our Higher Self to the Pure Undifferentiated Oceanic Infinite Love-emanating Source. A complete circuit. The Exhale and Inhale of Pure Beingness. The Breath of Being. Okay, I think I got that whole big piece expressed. How are you doing?

Well, my mind is still getting stretched by all this of course. As I've said, it's hard to conceptualize. One thing that keeps striking me is sometimes people talk about the other side as though it's almost a 50/50 split, but that would be like – well you said it when you talked about wiping off one layer of dirt and thinking you know what the inside of the Earth is like – but I was going to say it would be like peeling one outer layer of an onion, if every layer was different than the next, and thinking now we're at the center, this is how things are beyond the veil. When actually it's just the next densest layer with a lot of unique layers to go until the Center.

Yeah, I like that analogy better, and just imagine that that onion layer is as thin as a regular onion layer, but the onion of reality is the size of say Jupiter, with each layer to varying degrees different from the next. That's a whole hell of a lot of layers. So the veil opening to the next few levels is just barely scratching the onion surface.

And it's not that this is the only level that feels solid and everything beyond our veil is wispy and floaty and ephemeral and translucent. It might seem that way to us because it's a higher frequency, a higher vibration compared to our usual orientation and our – let's say the calibration of our perceptual instrumentation. To an elephant, a mouse squeak might not even be hearable, but to other mice it's just a normal vocal expression, not experienced as a high pitched or fast sound. And of course, we can't hear elephants' lower frequency vocalizations, they're below our range, but they can travel a few miles or more. What's out of range from one part of a frequency spectrum is normal and solid and usual in another. So each level has in its own way some degree of substantialness, as perceived from that level.

And of course, even on our level there are vastly different densities, from solid rock – or let's say from solid ice to snow to water to clouds to invisible humidity, and then there's the whole electromagnetic spectrum, and quantum fields, and there's also thought processes and feelings and imaginations and dreams. So we can't take one snapshot or one experience and call it an accurate picture of any particular level, much less of the whole so called other side, as though it's only binary – here and there, this side of the veil and that side – instead of a near infinite number of sublevels and snow globe worlds in created reality. And that's not even bringing in Pure Infinite Light-emanating Oceanic Isness. And even what I've said about *that* so far isn't the whole picture, but it's good enough for now. Can't bring in everything all at once or we'd just be stuck in a traffic jam instead of actually moving forward.

And speaking of that not being the whole picture, which sounds intriguing, I want to jump to another quick little simple question I have down to ask you at some point, that's related to what we've been talking about but we haven't quite addressed it yet.

Why do I get the feeling it might not be particularly quick or little or simple? Okay, but since we're changing topics anyway, I'd like to go ahead and grab a quick break first.

Sure, sounds good.

SESSION 5
CHAPTER 27

Alright, so first a quick update since it's different than what I said this afternoon. I checked in with you during the break, and since we're changing topics tomorrow, and we got started a little late, and we spent longer on our introduction than we had thought, and also I stopped us for dinner about an hour late so this evening is flying by, you said you were good with going an extra hour or so, stopping around 11 instead of 10, which means we now have about two more hours. So, let's get back to it.

So it's time for your simple little quick question.

Alright, it's what has the Omega Being said about the why of it all? Why did Pure Consciousness start to have individual Conscious Sparks that can then create and experience existence on different levels of formed reality? And why would individual sparks of an Oversoul go experience what you're sometimes calling an amusement park ride, and then come back? Why would souls go live a life and then return? Why leave Home to go have experiences, some of which – as you've said – aren't very pleasant or easy? And at least in your experience, being in deep connection with your Oversoul was all you could ever want. So why leave?

That little question. I asked Omega once in a bridging session, what's it all for? This wasn't so much one sizable flash packet as an exchange of sorts, so that there were a few small inflashes, closer to a normal give and take conversation than usual, just with senses and impressions that I would unpack, instead of starting as words.

It was pretty early in the bridging sessions, but the honeymoon was kind of waning, where it was normalizing, and I still wasn't so thrilled about things. I mean I was glad the portal was opening again even if it paled in comparison to that first incredible experience when my body was closed for repairs, but pretty much every other moment of my life still felt relatively empty and barren and lifeless and gray in the shadow of the Big Event, except for waiting for and looking forward to the next bridging session, but that was really about it.

And I was feeling more down than average that day, as reality was setting in that the bridging sessions weren't like a cure all or permanent lift to a happier place. They helped, definitely, but I still had to live the other 23 and a half hours a day, plus the four or five days a week without any bridging at all. So I was sitting on my couch feeling all this, and once the portal opened up, even though I could feel the Presence of Omega and the usual Deeper Response in me to it, those feelings didn't suddenly disappear or get erased or get covered over. So both tracks were there.

Ω

And I asked, with kind of an edge of frustration and jadedness and disheartenedness, what's the point of this whole miserable setup? It had been such a slog for me, post Big Event. Just such a gray — I can't think of another word but slog. And why would any being want to be separated from off the charts Pure Loving Belonging and Beingness?

I mean a Higher Self residing in a Joy-filled, Love-filled, Contenting Space might not be exactly the same as the Pre-created Eternal, Infinite Ocean of Pure Loving Consciousness, but it's a hell of a lot closer than here, and most definitely a conduit, a bridge, a mediator between Pre-prism Perfect Beingness and our identified small self. And being in that Space with Omega was just exponentially more Quenching than anything I had ever experienced. So you know, not a bad consolation prize at all, to be in an Oceanic Love-filled,

Light-filled Space, in continuous Deep Living Connection with a Greater Multidimensional Light Being that's always co-infused with Infinite Loving Essence.

And that thinnest membrane of separation from Pure Being, that Higher level Multidimensional Beings have – that holographic containment field – it isn't the slightest problem for them because there's such a continuous Living Connection with Pure Infinite Essence. They always have one foot in the pre-multitudinal side of the two way mirror. The Pre-prismed, Unseparated, Infinite, Love-emanating, Conscious Oneness side. It's a pretty good gig if you can get it. Playing in form without getting lost in it. Very low attrition rates.

But for us planet-bound, mostly closed-apertured, Greater-Reality-impoverished lowlanders, most of us most of the time don't have even a modicum of that access. It can be a rough road, and even when it's not, even when life's pretty good or better, we're still mostly really cut off from Greater Reality, from our Greater Consciousness.

It's like having a pretty good life in a cave and not ever really know-ing there's a whole world out there. Brilliant sunshine, beautiful lakes and forests, mountain streams, waterfalls, wide open bloom-ing fields of wildflowers, peaceful high deserts, vast oceans, beau-tiful beaches and so on. So why the hell would they want to will-ingly tendril down to go live in a cave, or worse, make a sub-Spark of themselves go live in a cave and report back? You want to go experience life in a cave, *you* go yourself, and I'll stay home, nice and cozy, instead of being cut off from the Infinite Stream of Pure Living Essence. Hard nope on that.

I just lost you a bit. You're saying why would an Oversoul send down a conscious tendril to live a relatively cut off life on a planet, and if they want to do that so badly, they should just go down there themselves and let you stay relaxed at Home instead of the reverse, is that right?

Yeah, I was feeling like there's obviously a programming glitch somewhere for things to be set up this way. I don't mean to be negative about life on Earth – it's a full spectrum ride, not evenly distributed, and that can include experiences that are really beautiful and lifting and so deeply good, as well as the opposite – but during that bridging session, what was coming out was, now that my eyes had been opened during the Big Event, now that the Heart within my heart had been opened, it wasn't just that sometimes life hurts or is hard or scary or stressful or unfair or unjust, it was also that it's usually just so cut off from the Beautiful More, and from Deeper Connection with what we truly are. Normal, relatively closed off, pretty good daily life is pretty much a grayscale shadow world once you know how the Infinite Sunshine feels. At least that's how it's felt for me, and *especially* those first weeks.

Ω Ω

And over the centuries, and even right now, there have probably been a lot of people who have been able to have much more of the Beautiful More while living their daily lives than I have, but so far that's been the exception. So why go from maybe 98 or 99 percent plugged in to Perfect Home to just sometimes having pretty good or great – but still not very Deeply Connected – months or weeks or days or hours here and there, and the rest of the time it's fairly bland at best, and that's if you're lucky? And for billions of people alive or who have already come and gone, their lives are or were much, much harder and more difficult and with significantly more pain and suffering than that.

And when I asked Omega that, with an attitude of like, I demand to talk to the hotel manager, who made this ridiculous policy, what the hell were you thinking when you probably coerced this me-spark to leave the We-Spark to go live with the – I don't know – the greed sharks. I overshot the landing there, but why did I have to leave Home to be in this comparatively – now that I know what I'm missing – subpar, cut off and separated, hugely diminished life experience?

Sure, life on Earth can be beautiful and amazing, but mine hasn't been that way very often, mostly fair to partly cloudy, a bed of thorns at least a little more often than a bed of roses, and most of the time just kind of flat and neutral and not very full of life, with of course some upwaves and downwaves here and there. And I'm pretty sure I'm not the only one. And then, fresh from the heavens opening, my life down here in the lowlands became exponentially way more subpar, way less satisfying. So I was just laying it all out there, like what the hell's the deal here?

And what was the answer?

Well, you might not be very satisfied with it, because it was one of those non-answer answers, no mental information, but right after I asked, I felt maybe the strongest wave of capital L Love I've felt since the Big Event. It was so deeply good to feel that again, that strongly. Still not at the same level, but it was way closer to that than anything I had felt since and probably before the Big Event. Not off the charts but way up them.

And my mind got quieter, really quiet actually, and my body got really settled and content and relaxed and soft. You know when you close your computer and the whirring fan you weren't even noticing stops, or the fridge or the A/C or the heat turns off, and then suddenly it's really quiet in comparison. My mind just stopped whirring and things just got really quiet.

You said whirring, not worrying?

That's what I meant to say, but either one. So it was a really notable contrast. I felt deeply at rest, with no argument or frustration or discouragement or jadedness. No disheartedness. No background problem solving or discontentment or the subtle tightness or pressure to get somewhere or to get something done or to get rid of something or to try to catch and reel in something I don't yet have. All of that just rested.

Or like the motor shut off but my boat kept quietly gliding through the water a little longer, and then even the gliding forward stopped, and everything was way more still than usual. The residual momentum slowed to a stop, and there was just peace and contentment and settledness, and the gentle rocking of the lake waves of Deep Presence flowing through. So it was a really soothing deep relief. Really settling and quenching and quieting.

Sounds like the ultimate lullaby.

Yeah, the lullaby of Poignant Settled Quietness. But no mental answer came through at all. No answer to what the hell's the deal here? And even though now there wasn't a burning dissatisfaction leading the way, and there was a lot of quiet and contentment, the thought still bubbled up that maybe I should ask again, in case there was just a portal glitch, like a dropped call or a bad connection or something.

Ω Ω Ω

So I asked again, with a lot less charge than the first time, more open and spacious, but as I asked I did feel a little of the original charge re-show itself, reactivate some, just way less. What's the point of it all? Why does created separate form even exist, and why would any being trade the direct and continuous intimacy with Pure. Conscious. Loving. Home-filled Oneness – that Higher level Multidimensional Beings have – for the pain of forgetting, the pain of separation, the pain of a – in comparison – an isolated, cut off, tightly identified small self, that's locked in a tangle-prone mind? Locked in a really dense, heavy world, that hopefully has some beautiful moments and really good experiences, and close relationships and deep meaning in their life, but also almost definitely goes through times of real difficulty and pain, plus the mostly beneath the surface chronic pain of being mostly cut off from True Home.

And some lifetimes really skew towards the great difficulty and suffering end of the spectrum, while others have more that gold leaf toilet paper experience. And that whole injustice piece, that didn't bother me during the Profound Quenchedness of the Big Event, it was bothering me again as part of this whole formal complaint to the VP of customer satisfaction, like what the hell's the point of it all? Why the hell would it be set up this way? Where some have it way more easy and breezy, and some have it way more pain and hurricane. Some suffer way more, or die way earlier, or both.

And of course it's not lost on me that the dramatic difference, that was so in my face, of suddenly having it all during the Big Event and then immediately losing it all, has colored my perception of life on Earth, and especially at first. It wasn't a dream life for me before, it was kind of average I'd say, but definitely its approval ratings went way down once I knew what I was missing, what I had been shut out from. You're kind of basically okay with your salary until you find out how much more your annoying and incompetent coworker has been making all this time. Then suddenly, not so much.

So yeah, I put all that out there again, and this time there were words – or what my mind could translate into words – and the answer or the response was something along the lines of, "The First Reason can never be understood with thought. Any answer to that question that you can think with words is leading you down the wrong road. The answer is before explanation. The answer is on a different current than the current of mental understanding. The real answer is much, much closer to what you've been feeling the last few minutes, not in what you've been thinking. Those are two very different currents, and for this question, they can't meet."

Ω Ω Ω Ω

And even though I was still receiving this wave of Deep Love and Stillness, wanting for nothing, and even though my mind was really quiet – probably one of the two quietest moments I've ever had – I still felt this little wave of annoyance bubble up at the same time. Something like, that's pretty convenient, or that's a handy cop out, or that's bull, that this Multidimensional Being – that's so much more connected to Pure Loving Consciousness than I am, and has so much more understanding of all this – keeps taking a pass and refusing to give me a real damn answer that my mind can understand.

In my very first bridging session Omega had even said that now they could answer what I longed to know, and I didn't really long to know much of anything. That didn't stop them from deluging me with inflashes, which was fine, sometimes really good, but now I *finally* had like a legit burning question, *the* burning question, I finally *really* wanted to know one of the Great Questions of Existence, and I got back nada. Not a damn thing.

And I wasn't intentionally saying or asking Omega anything at that point, that was just what I was feeling, along with that Deep Quiet Fulfilled Stillness. Like sitting in a beautiful, peaceful forest and hearing one little tree squirrel that won't stop yapping at you to get off their damn lawn. And sometimes you just can't seem to help but give it most of your attention.

And the reply that came in was – and this might have been my projection, I don't know for sure – but like a little bit of annoyance or impatience or tough love or straight talk, around my ungratefulness or dissatisfaction that this wave of Deep Settling Love wasn't enough for me. That this beautiful gift had just now been given to me, and in response I was complaining. It was just a quick little pass through while there was still so much Flow of Loving Stillness coming through, but I felt like it was there.

And the words came in – once they went through my translator – along the lines of, "Didn't you feel our answer? Aren't you feeling Love and Stillness now? We *didn't* take a pass. We fully answered you. We *fully* answered you. Much more fully than words ever could. We just didn't answer at the frequency your mind was wanting us to. At a frequency your brain could pick up.

"Just because an answer is in a less familiar frequency to your mind does *not* mean it's not an answer. Just because it's not addressed to your mind does *not* mean the Heart within your heart didn't get the memo. That's a more limited perspective than serves you now, and not one worth grasping." Which to me felt like, "Come on, dude, stop your whining and complaining. You know better than that, you can do better than that, so step it up here a little, would ya? Meet us halfway here." So, yeah, that's what happened and that's the best I can offer you for an answer.

CHAPTER 28

Have you felt that apparent sternness or tough love from the Omega Consciousness other times?

Nope, not so far. Wasn't my favorite, actually. But I should add that the Deeper Space didn't go away during that. It wasn't revoked as punishment or anything, if that would even be possible. It felt more like a strong invitation to step up than anything else. Putting a little responsibility back on *me*. And the last couple of minutes, as I've been answering your question, tapping into Omega's nonmental answer, I've been feeling a pretty strong inflow of some of that Settled, Content Love and Silence that whomped in the first time I asked. I feel it revisiting. A weaker echo but still – well actually more than an echo, more alive than an echo. A weaker but definitely perceivable vibratory resonance of it, a more diminished wave, but still reverberating in me.

I felt it getting stronger too as you shared that. I've been really appreciating the subtle Presence that keeps getting activated in you when you talk about some of these things, and then it radiates outward towards me. And to me, the fact that we've both been aware of it showing up sometimes today is a validation that we're on the right track by doing this. And I don't know if any of these

Presence Waves will end up reaching anyone who reads the transcript, but if it they aren't limited by space-time, maybe it could happen a bit. Alright, let's move on to one or two unrelated questions I want to make sure I fit in somewhere, in case you've gotten any mentally communicatable answers for them.

Kay, but a couple of quick things first. One is that I feel like what you just said is one valid way of seeing it, about how because of the Big Event, sometimes something opens in me when I'm talking about these things, my aperture spontaneously opens more some, and then there's sometimes a little flow of Essential Presence that you can pick up. Like if you stand close to a boulder that happens to be in the sun, you might feel the warmth radiating from it.

But another way of seeing it, for what it's worth – and this wasn't so much a direct, head-on data stream from Omega as something that I just kind of absorbed indirectly from the bridging sessions, and I'm still not clear how much that distinction really matters – but another perspective is, you know that aspen grove, where any two trees seem to be individual separate trees but their roots are really connected. So it sounds like you're picturing it like one aspen tree radiating some Essential Presence that it's currently connecting with to a nearby aspen tree, through the air, through the space between them. Maybe. But what if it's different than that? What if it's more that those two aspens are connected through their roots, and from a zoomed out perspective, they're even part of the same greater organism, like they're both from the same deepest root? They're both of the same singular organism of the one unified grove.

So what if it's more like if one aspen could use a little water, and another one ten feet away is closer to a stream, then that quenched one just naturally shares that water with the parched one, but that isn't transmitted between the two trees through the air above the surface, it moves through the roots, up the thirsty roots of the drier one. And the same thing could happen in reverse. You could be particularly plugged in and I could feel that radiating up from your

Deeper Roots to me, impacting me, giving me some Essential nutrients of Presence and Stillness and Beingness.

Ω

So I don't have anything special here, for me to happen to be by a nice stream and have a little more access to water sometimes. If that was muddled, I just mean that doesn't make me special at all or more of a spiritual – like a spiritual somebody – in the slightest. Just through that little medical journey – or through the Big Event I experienced during it – my rusty and atrophied awareness aperture got knocked loose a little bit, the bolts loosened a little, so that now it opens easier than average. Maybe for the rest of my life, or maybe at some point it kind of reverts back and doesn't anymore. I didn't do anything to earn that, it just somehow happened.

And if our Deeper Roots aren't at all confined by or limited by space-time – aren't pinned to one point in the grid of time and space – then what if Essential Presence could flow not only if we're in person, but also if we're on a video call, or on the phone, or what if it could even happen – like you said – when someone reads our transcribed words from the parts of our conversation when this is happening more? Because if it's moving through the Deepest Roots then it can't be limited to only when we're a few feet away from each other. And it can't be limited to only when we're matching up temporally.

Ever been in a centuries-old place of worship, where you just feel a Peaceful Presence in the space? That Presence is radiating from centuries of people intentionally Connecting to the Deeper there. So this isn't limited to syncing up in time or linking up in physical proximity. And if you, sitting there, are really being impacted and staying in connection with the Presence you're feeling, that can radiate through *my* roots and help *me* drop a little deeper or be a little more consciously connected, which then can impact *you* again and maybe help *you* drop a little deeper.

So you can transmit or emanate – or let's say trans-root – Deeper Presence also, I don't have a corner on the market. There's already been a couple of times today when I felt you more deeply responding, and naturally and effortlessly radiating that response – or trans-rooting it – and that in turn dropped me a little deeper in that Presence that trans-rooted from you to me, and emanated up or waved up through my roots.

So just an interesting reframe to maybe be open to or play around with, that what if it's happening not so much through the air or the space between us, but through the Deeper Roots we have in common, that are nonlocal and nontemporal, and if you go deep down enough, that are completely connected to the Core Original First Root that all beings have in common. So just a different way to think about it that I wanted to bring into the mix.

That does add a more expanded perspective to it. I hadn't thought about how I could radiate or trans-root it back to you in a way that could impact you. I had assumed it was just one way, because of this portal you have access to, or because of your more open radio telescope dish or awareness aperture. I like the feel of that, that it can happen both ways.

Yeah, we're all just naturally radiating what's moving in us – and what's stuck in us, to some degree – whether we want to or not, and whether other people are consciously picking it up or not. So no one has a patent on radiating Deeper Presence when that's what they're connected to in the moment. It just happens effortlessly.

Ω Ω

I really like that perspective. Alright, I lost track, was that – did you have something else you were going to say or was that it?

Yeah but I lost it. You were talking about feeling a transmission, and I talked about that. What was the other thing you said?

I don't remember. Oh, that I see it as a sign we're on the right track, the fact that we're both feeling Presence in the space sometimes.

Yeah that was it. I just wanted to throw in a thought about that too, you know, to get over my shyness about expressing my opinion. So I'm with you that if we both perceive Essential Presence coming into the space, or up through our roots, while we're here doing this together, that can be seen as pretty solid evidence that we're connecting with something Good and Real and Deep and beyond our usual range of experience and our usual more confined consciousness. It shows we're bridging with some aspects of Greater Reality to some degree, connecting with the Beautiful More at least a little, and also connecting to a Deeper part of ourselves, because that's the part that can perceive and receive those frequencies.

But what I wanted to say is – and I'm not saying you don't already know this, but just so it's said – feeling Presence, feeling the Flow of Beingness, feeling trans-rooting happen, that doesn't by itself imbue what I'm saying – if imbue is the right word here – with the stamp of Accurately Described, Verified and Guaranteed, Correct and Inerrant Truth.

Feeling the Presence of a Deeper Flow doesn't automatically mean the details that are riding along with that wave are necessarily anywhere near flawless or perfectly true or accurate. The degree of Presence we're feeling isn't necessarily correlative with the level of accuracy of the information accompanying it.

I mean you could have a massive misunderstanding and still feel the Presence of Greater Consciousness filling you with Stillness or Joy or Presence or Love or Contentment or Peace. So something feeling right isn't the final evidence that the understanding piggy backing off that wave of Essential Presence is correctly perceived and instantly trustworthy. It's not indicative of how deeply accurate the maps shared by someone who's seeing more of what else exists and who feels more Presence are or aren't.

Kind of awkward phrasing there, but Deep Resonance isn't automatically evidence of Deep Accuracy. Think of all the millions of people over the centuries who have had profound spiritual or religious experiences, but they've understood or interpreted them within the confines of the particular cultural or religious belief structures they were indoctrinated into or enculturated into, that they naturally sponged up when growing up.

We can't help but sponge up the family and cultural norms that surround us, when we're young and sometimes even as adults, at least to some extent. Or sometimes people just currently, freshly misunderstand or misinterpret, while also clearly feeling a profound Wave of Beingness moving through.

So the arising of Subtle Presence, that's good and worth noticing and worth appreciating and enjoying, that's worth letting our heart have its response to and worth calibrating our compass to, to the best of our human ability. But there isn't necessarily – I mean we can't assume it's indicative that there's a correlation between, if a nice Presence is showing up then that therefore means what I'm saying or what you're saying – or for readers, what that part of the book they're reading is saying – must ergo be true and accurate. We just can't assume that.

Even a very flawed diamond can still stunningly sparkle. At least I assume, I only use flawless ones for all my phone bedazzling needs. But the legitimacy of Deeper Connective Experiences doesn't of itself automatically validate or legitimize one word that's being said along with them, or one aspect of the map of Reality that's being described or understood during those experiences.

So basically I'm just saying, not confusing the presence of a Flow of Being with a stamp of Higher Approval of the accuracy of what's being shared. Feeling waves of Deeper Presence doesn't mean the information waving through with it warrants pass-through status, like the pre-approved fast lane at airport security.

And it's easy – when we're feeling a response of yessing and open-ing to the Presence that's flowing through – it's easy to then have the gate wide open for all the information that's along for the ride, and to put it all in the "feels right" pile, because of course the Deeper Presence feels right, without really checking out how our tuning fork is resonating with the information itself – independent from how it's resonating with the Presence – which can be tricky, but it's still important to have in our awareness and to try to discern that.

Ω Ω Ω

So bottom line, still checking things out with our own compass even though we can't assume it's flawlessly calibrated to True North, or that we can always tell where our compass is pointing. But like I've said a couple dozen times, so only 76 more to go, what else can we go on when, at least for now, we're beyond the realm of scientific evidentiary validation? Much better to innocently be led astray by our *own* miscalibrated compass at times than to almost lazily and subserviently be led astray by someone else's, or even by their deliberate or unconsciously self serving or misguided agendas or false calibrations. So yeah, I just wanted to put both of those thoughts out there.

That's an important point too. Not conflating a trusting response to a wave of Presence with the trustworthiness of the information that's showing up with it. I'm not sure I've thought about there being a distinction between the two.

Yeah, it's easy to not really step up our discernment when we're feel-ing good vibes. There's a natural, inherent or instinctual response to open to waves of Essential Presence when we sense them, the vibrations and resonance of our First Home. But it's always our job to be conscious and careful and discerning about that.

The most beautiful slowly and gently approaching ocean wave in the world, stunningly heading your way as you stand on the beach, can still have a huge stinging jelly fish riding on it. So modulating what your open arms are being open to, so you don't get stung. A castle draw bridge is either open or closed, but a discerning immune system, or a security check point, is more selective about what really gets invited in and assimilated. Okay, got all that said. So what was your question or couple of questions from a few minutes ago?

I'm still taking all of that in, but, alright, so one question was, you've talked about how what we experience after death depends on different things, and there's a wide variety of possibilities, and you named some, but you said most of the time we're less – I don't remember how you put it – but less cut off or disconnected after death than we usually are in our physical lives. And I'm wondering if there's anything more you can say about what the Omega Consciousness has conveyed about that, and what tends to happen after death after the initial experience. Just filling it in a bit more.

So one thing I keep checking in with myself about all day is, am I getting ahead of my skis here? There's so much more I don't know or understand about these things and how it all works than I do, and I don't want to cross the point of saying something that's no longer reporting only what understandings have come in to me via Omega, either directly or through kind of a delayed unnoticed absorption which sometimes happens, like what I said about Presence spreading through trans-rooting more than radiating through the space between two people. That's an example, where I don't remember that inflashing, but as the zip files uncompress in me, sometimes there are more connections made than I consciously notice during that bridging session, and then later if that topic comes up in my thoughts or in our conversation, it's just there ready.

So delayed absorption is when you find yourself knowing something you weren't aware you had learned?

Yeah, but it still has kind of the fragrance of the bridging sessions, still has the vibe or resonance of Omega. So, in terms of trying to go into much more detail about the range of specific possibilities after death and where they each fall in the frequency bell curve, I think that would probably be getting ahead of my skis. But I can probably say a *little* more about that, and also, I've had a couple of data streams that were a little more generally about Oversouls tendrilling into living different lives in different amusement park rides or snow globes – different worlds – which is related and helps fill out more of the overall map that Omega's been slowly unveiling with me, so how about if I get into those some and we see what comes out?

Sure, sounds good.

CHAPTER 29

Okay, so if we leave aside the variations in individual specifics, two things usually happen after the conclusion of a lifetime. First, there's usually an effortless connection to all those qualities I experienced during the Big Event, like Peace, Connection, Completion, Expansion, Safeness, Joy, Acceptance, Belongingness, and Love – meaning both, feeling so deeply, deeply loved, and also feeling your own opened-up heart capacity to fully and effortlessly love as just a natural, no longer comparatively covered over, state of Being.

A fish doesn't have to learn to be in a state of water, but it's happy and free when the constricting ice finally melts around it. So those kinds of deeply quenching experiences of suddenly being more connected to more of both, our own Greater Consciousness, and to Pure Infinite Conscious Beingness itself, the Eternal Source of all that is.

And then second, simultaneously, as that larger perspective opens up with this influx of profoundly satisfying realigning and returning, your strong attachment to and identification with the lifetime that just ended – which when you were in it seemed to be completely or nearly completely the totality of who you are – that strong attachment quickly begins to loosen, lighten, and fade away in the rearview mirror.

A little like if you've been playing a board game or video game for hours or days, really completely into it, at first it can be hard to let that go and get back to your fuller life. But soon, as you're out of that room and attending to your larger world again, it just naturally begins to fade away, til sooner than you would've thought possible when you were in the thick of it, you've mostly or completely broken free, and maybe you even wonder how it had ever grabbed your attention and investment and attachment so stickily and convincingly in the first place. You might wonder how you had zoomed in so much, narrowed your awareness aperture so much, that you lost sight of your greater life.

And as time passes, if you think about it, you might be able to remember other board games or video games that you've disappeared into over the months or years, if that has happened. And obviously, not one of the roles you played in any of those games was more the real you than any of the others and none of them were the full larger you.

And til you have more distance from your most recent game, it's the one that's most likely to be more the one that isn't – Well take two, your most recent game is the one you're most likely to have the most attachment to because it's the freshest in your mind. But after some distance, they all start to blend together more, get lumped more together, become of equal, more distant importance.

Just objectively, the last game you played, say it was over a year ago, isn't actually any more important now than all the other games you played over the years. The question of which one was the most real or which one was the most you, they just don't make any sense. They all mattered at the time to the degree they mattered, but none of them were the full you and they've all lost their highest priority status with some distance in the rearview mirror. The identification and intensity and attachments of your most recent game, that maybe when you were in it felt like everything, like all or nearly all of who you are, it just so naturally fades away, and soon takes a more equal place with earlier games you played.

Ω

Or you could say the same thing about a long-past serious relationship, and how it was everything, and all you went through when it ended, but now – after so much road between then and now – it probably doesn't have a hundredth of the grip it had when you were full on in the thick of it. Or even a thousandth or ten thousandth. Maybe it helped shape who you are to some degree, consciously or not, but other than that it's probably just not really in the equation of your current awareness or of who you currently identify yourself to be and what's currently important in your life.

And another pass, if a sports team or maybe a solo athlete barely loses the championship, that bad taste can linger a long time, and they might get really focused on making things right next year, instead of feeling that freedom of, it's over, sweet resolution and completion. Or maybe someone's gambling in a casino and they just get hooked, they lost all that money and by God now they're gonna win it back, and they just can't walk away. That nagging unfinished gravitational pull might lead them to play another round, maybe in the same casino or another one.

Or back to a video game that a gamer is hooked on, maybe after finishing some gaming sessions, they feel really complete and resolved and it's easier to just move on and let it all go, but after other games, things feel unfinished, things are left unresolved, and it's harder to let it go. Harder to leave the headspace of that experience they were so invested in and that just now ended but doesn't really feel complete.

And maybe they're compulsively or almost compulsively pulled to play again, and the next game they might play as a different avatar or game character or game piece, maybe at the same game level or in the same game setting, or maybe they switch things up, and it's a different game level or different setting, but it's still the same basic game that they just can't quite let go of yet.

Or, last pass, imagine a kid spending a month at a summer camp, and it becomes their whole world, and when it's time to say good-bye to all their new friends that they bonded with so closely, then after their tearful goodbyes, as they're being driven away, the camp gets smaller and smaller behind them, and soon it's completely out of sight. There's a transition period and maybe they keep their connections with some of those relationships, but soon their current, bigger life is front and center, and that camp experience fades from their present awareness faster than they would've ever guessed when they were fully immersed in it. Especially during that emotional last night, tearfully singing songs around the campfire with a mouth full of s'mores.

And during that whole camp, they probably never even thought about the other summer camps they had gone to during previous summers, that felt so much less important, but maybe half a year later, that most recent camp has mostly faded back into the same mental folder as all the others, quickly becoming of about the same lesser importance – compared to their new current experience – as the ones before.

As we've all experienced countless times, the closer you are to an intense experience, the stronger the gravity. The farther away, the less the pull. Once there's some miles behind you, it was what it was but it's now what it is, and what it is isn't anything like what it was. It's faded in the rearview mirror, still present in your heart to some degree, but now it's just one fiber in the whole tapestry of the sum total of your accumulative past experiences.

Ω Ω

So all of that is loosely pointing to how the life you just completed recedes in importance, and any experiences your consciousness or soul might have had before your last life might or might not at some point open back up into your awareness to some degree, as your separate exploration pod returns back to the Mothership – your Oversoul – and reconnects with that larger perspective – the larger reality of your larger existence – which consists of far more than your most recent life experience.

But the whole way – well two things. First let me just clarify, I'm not trying to say everyone after death experiences reconnecting with their Higher Self. They might continue to have more experiences as an individual tendril or finger of the larger body they're always one with, without a complete re-membering and re-uniting with their Greater Consciousness, their Oversoul. Like I've said, there's a lot of permutations – if that's the right word – around what could be experienced, and that whole flow chart of possible experiences and what all leads to them is way beyond my pay grade.

And then the second thing is, the whole sequential way I've been talking about this, it makes sense from our temporal-centric level of reality, but as our proximity to the gravitational pull of this dense physical level lessens, so does the influence of space-time reality. So this idea of finishing a life, and then – after stopping at the water fountain for a minute or sitting on the bench for a few or stepping outside for some air – then getting back on the court for another game or going back in for another round, or maybe going off and playing some other game on some different court or field or course – or doing something else entirely – that linear-ness is pretty oversimplified from a fuller perspective.

After death, we might, after some R and R, go into some other experience that isn't being a life form on a planet or anything like that. Or we might just melt into our Higher Self for a while, or from then on. Or we might even melt back into the Pure Original Infinite Everpresent Eternal Essence of what we most truly are, which – well there's more to say about that but I'll wait – But from levels beyond space-time as we know it, all of that can be seen to be happening simultaneously, in the spacious, flowing, nontemporal or pretemporal Nowness, which our brains really can't grok from within space-time.

And like I said, I'm not nearly up to speed on the whole flow chart of what all determines where we go and what we experience, except to say sometimes one of the influences could be that you might naturally have more attraction and attachment to returning to the same summer camp or playing another round of blackjack at the same casino to try to beat the damn house this time for once. Or maybe you want to go be around a place with a lot of significance, like where you spent most of your last life experience, or maybe something you recently experienced pulls you towards something similar or adjacent or opposite of that. But really, there are a lot of other influences and there's endless options, it's a damn big amusement park, or a trillion damn big amusement parks, and some of those experiences might not even include forgetting your Larger Self at all.

Say more about that?

Well, some amusement park rides, some worlds, could include the full remembering of all of it, full access to full connection to your Greater Self and to Greater Reality, as you're living an individual lifetime on another planet in our universe or in some other snow globe or some other level. Or there could be living a life as a collective consciousness of several connected life forms that are also one. A collective grove, or a multitudinal singularity or unilarity. There's a lot of ways for all this to play out. A lot of ways to experience conscious existence, on a whole lot of different levels of reality.

And like we've coffeetized about a couple of times, it's very possible that even Earth will gradually become more and more a place where we're consciously and open-aperturedly connected to the Beautiful More and to our own Greater Consciousness, and maybe even at a faster timeline than we might think, which is – yeah, something that we'll come back to tomorrow afternoon.

Ω Ω Ω

And again, we think of all this as happening sequentially, but in the nontemporal levels where our Higher Selves experience Multidimensional Reality, there just isn't sequential time in the same way at all. I liked that analogy of if you have all your fingers in the water on both sides of your canoe, you can experience all of them at the same time, simultaneously, and it wouldn't even make sense to think it has to be sequential. Why could there only be one finger experiencing the water currents at a time? But none of those fingers has the neuronal bandwidth to really be aware of their connection to the other fingers or to the greater body they're actually always one with. You can be aware of all of them, but they aren't so likely to be even a little aware of you.

And when we really look at it, does a soul or individual autonomous sentient tendril extension of an Oversoul go have a life, then come home for the holidays and hang out with their Oversoul for a while, enjoying puzzles and hot chocolate by the fire, all the while keeping all their autonomousness and individuality and holographic containment fieldness and memories of their last individual lifetime experience intact – or maybe remembering all of them if they've had several – and then they pop a temporary amnesia pill and go out for another round? While other separate soul tendrils of the same Higher Self are doing the same? Maybe.

Or, upon its return after the end of a life, does it completely and totally dissolve into that Oversoul, fully returning into that Greater Consciousness, plugged into the mainframe, connected to the cloud? Fully becoming integrated into that Oversoul, along with a thousand or a billion other separate tendrils that do the same thing, all unifiedly being One Seamless Greater Awareness?

And in that case, each soul tendril would have one life experience and then melt back into the Greater Multitudinal Singularity of their Higher Self. Not annihilated but massively expanded, seamlessly integrated, being privy to the whole hard drive, to the whole cloud server, to the full and complete memories and experiences and hard earned wisdom of all the thousands or billions of individual tendrils of that Oversoul, that have lived a lifetime and then returned. And are those other lifetime tendrils absolutely you, just you having different lifetimes and experiences, but there's actually only always you? Or are they unique individual soul sparks of your Greater Self? Is each aspen grove tree uniquely individually alive, or is each one like a finger, an extension expression, of the One Seamless Grove?

Or is it mix and match, like maybe an individual soul has several rounds of lifetime experiences or other experiences, before really fully re-docking with their Mothership Oversoul, like a military scout that – like I mentioned earlier – might have several missions in a row before heading back home. Or could an individual spark of an Oversoul, after the end of an individual life – say as a person living on Earth – is it against the rules somewhere for them to just bypass the intermediary of their Higher Self altogether and just make a bee line and return to Pure Infinite Beingness, and just fully dissolve all the way back into the Eternal Home of the Infinite Undifferentiated Ocean of Pure Essence?

Or maybe, like it's hard to pin down if a particular unit of light is a wave or a particle, maybe the Continuum of Consciousness just isn't so either/or, isn't so regimented and delineated as I'm describing it, and all of these attempts I just made are basically trying to cram like ten dimensional existence into a nice, neat, steady, ironed out map, that might make some degree of sense in this small and limited three dimensional space-time based world, but the more nailed down a map is, the more it'll rust. And the less pristinely it reflects the truth.

CHAPTER 30

The more nailed down a map is the more it rusts. I've never heard that.

Me either.

That nontemporal, beyond space-time aspect is especially hard to get a feel for, not that the rest is easy.

Yeah, it's a brain boggler for our linear sense of time, but multiple lives, when they happen, aren't necessarily lived in sequential, chronological order from the level of Oversouls. Both perspectives are true, without contradiction. From higher levels beyond the gravitational pull of our space-time physics, multiple experiences of an individual autonomous soul spark can be simultaneously existent like fingers in the water. Not only all at once, but in a single, nontemporal Isness Space, of an unrushed, uncompressed, timeless non-moment. Or we could also call it an Ultra Wide Still Moment, in which all moments exist in the supra-temporal Now.

Like holding ten film reels in your hands, ten movies, and let's say they're all with the same main actor. Every frame of each whole film is simultaneously right there in your present. You've got the whole world in your hands. Actually ten worlds, that all exist independently, but they're also all right there in front of you, without colliding with each other, and without contradiction.

And some of these movies were in what would be our past, some in our future, some on another planet, but all the same actor. The same player playing a role that is smaller than their greater self. A subset of it. And yet, within the gravitational pull of space-time in our level, there really *is* a forward arrowness of time. There really *is* past, present, future. Progression. Time passing. The arrow flying forward. So temporal movement exists and doesn't exist at the same time, without contradiction.

Next you're going to say there is and isn't contradiction, without contraction.

If I had thought of it I would've. So, can we say that your individual soul spark consciousness might have experienced other lifetimes on Earth and just doesn't remember them while in another lifetime? Yes. And maybe on or within other worlds as well? Could be. I haven't inflashed yet the actuarial tables of the chances of each possibility, but why not? But can we also say that you're exactly simultaneously living all at once all the conscious tendril experiences – AKA lifetimes – on this and maybe other planets or snow globe worlds, that you have ever lived and will ever live? Sure.

Your Higher Consciousness, your Greater Self, is holding every film reel in its hands, and can simultaneously and timelessly experience each whole film, every frame. A hundred film reels, or a thousand, or a hundred thousand or more. Multidimensional Oversoul Beings can see through the clear, transparent film reel canisters, and take in and absorb every frame in all those different films at once. Each moment in each film reel.

And that's not really quite it either, because it's not like they're in a hurry so they just glance for an instant. Time as we think of it just isn't even operating, not quick as a snap or slow as the life of a universe. It's just outside of that whole pesky time spectrum that we have so much trouble imagining existence outside of, no matter how much time we spend trying.

Ω

And then imagine using scissors and cutting each individual frame of the film of a whole lifetime, and laying those frames out in order on a huge backlit table in front of you, so you can see each micro-moment at once. You can move your eyes forward, move your eyes backwards, however you want to take it all in. There's no rush at all. They're just frozen there, each individual frame, except each frame is fully alive and multi-sensoral. And then imagine the same thing, slightly bigger table, for a hundred or a thousand lifetime film reels. And each one has sound, and also feeling, and all the five senses and even more than our limited five senses, and you can effortlessly take all that in at once. You can effortlessly omnifocus. Multidimensional Light Beings aren't limited by physio-electrochemical brain processing, so they can literally take it all in.

And we could also imagine stacking all those millions or billions or more of those cut individual frames, those multi-sensoral moment snapshots, one on top of the other, however high they would go. A mile straight up or something, and this might be just more spaghetti on the floor, but a higher consciousness can look through every one of those stacked frames and simultaneously take it all in, all at once, in all its multisensoralness. Not as a chaotic sensoral overload cacophony, but as a flowing harmonic symphony.

We might think you have to kind of – or that that Being would have to kind of choose where they wanted to focus, along that tall, tall stack, but for Arch-Souls – for Multidimensional Oversoul Light Beings, for our Higher Selves – they can effortlessly focus on every single frame at once. Each frame can be the center of attention and fully taken in, *simultaneously*, without contradiction. The softer their focus, the more they can fully and completely take it all in without narrowing their focus on any one thing in particular. So we can—

–Could you just say that last thing again?

Yeah, so our eyes have to choose where they're focused, and our brain has to decide what sounds or conversations we focus in on, but for the soft focus, relaxed focus, of a completely open awareness aperture with limitless or near limitless processing capacity, everything observed is in perfect focus and everything within the field of awareness can be observed simultaneously. Even snakes can perceive in our visual range of light wavelengths plus infra-red too, at the same time, no moving back and forth or choosing between the two. And waterfowl like geese have monocular vision, which doesn't mean they wear a monocle like the Monopoly top hat guy or Mr. Peanut – not really the fashion anymore in most goose cultures – but it means each eye is taking in a completely differ-ent scene, which added up gives them a 360 degree view. We can't even imagine what that would really look like, or how our brains would process all that, but for them, it's the most natural thing in the world.

Ω Ω

So even though it's a stretch for us to imagine it, for Oversouls, omnifocus is just the natural way of open-apertured perceiving. It's only amazing or impressive or magical or mystical from our slow, heavy, clunky, dense level of reality, and from the perspective of our physiological brains – which can only really focus our eyes and ears clearly on one thing at a time, maybe occasionally two if we want to really fully take in that sensory information. Which reminds me of a little practice that came through in a bridging session, but I think I'll save that for tomorrow. But for Oversouls, multi-sensoral omnifocus is just business as usual.

So, can we say that from a deeper, pre-temporal level, it's not just that each life is unfolding simultaneously, it's that all of those lives together and every moment of each life – past, present and future – exist in one Unmoving Eternal Nowness of non-time – outside of incremental, measurable time – an endless, wide open moment, in a nontemporal unrushed Space of Eternal Isness, on a timeless level of reality? Yes, we can say that. Gonna get some strange looks, but we can say that.

And again, is it you that lives a thousand lives, or is it your Oversoul that does, through a thousand different tendrils, or a million, and you're just one of them? Is it a single exploronaut, exploring one lifetime at a time, on this and maybe other planets or other kinds of worlds, and forgetting all the previous ones during your current exploronaut mission? And is there a nice home visit between each one, or is it usually a long string of explorations without ever really coming up for some real Home air until you're all done?

Or what if these distinctions just don't make any sense on a higher level, and there isn't really even the *slightest* delineation between you and your overarching Greater Consciousness, and I've just been talking about it like there is to try to communicate about ten dimensional reality with 3D languaging? Because both distinction and nondistinction can coexist effortlessly in subtler levels of reality, even though they can't here in a world based on distinction.

So yeah, I realize most of what I just said sounds more like a Zen koan than really explaining anything. It's just not very grokkable and I don't fully get it either. And rather than kind of scrunching up our brow and giving ourselves a headache trying to get all this mentally, maybe letting these poor attempts at explaining of mine, letting them just kind of wash through and just see how they land, how they resonate or don't, how your tuning fork reacts. Holding all this gently, lest migraines ensue.

Our fish out of water minds trying to get all this is like a conscious 2D flat pencil line on a piece of paper trying to understand the physics of a balloon rising through the air into space. Good luck with that. But just softly relaxing the furrowed brow of trying to understand it all, and enjoying lightly trying different jigsaw puzzle pieces to see if any fit, while also checking in with your compass, while also appreciating the natural and obvious impossibility of the human brain very deeply getting much of this at all.

Ω Ω Ω

I understand the wisdom of that sentiment, but it's easier said than done, to take a step back and drop trying to mentally understand and organize all this. Especially this weekend, when I'm the interviewer and host and time keeper and the stand in for the readers.

Yeah, I really get that, and I'm not suggesting going from a nine out of ten to a one out of ten of trying to put together a mental framework. Especially, like you said, when we're in the middle of a book-bound marathon. But I'm just putting it out there that it could be an interesting experiment to dial it down a little from a nine to a four or five or six, and see how things go. And this is the ultimate setup, talking about things the brain just can't get. *Of course* it can't really capture all of this. *Of course* a pencil line being can't understand 3D geometry. *Of course* we can't really visualize a tesseract or a tesseractal universe. *Of course* we can't *really* grasp existence in motion – beings in movement and having experiences – beyond space-time. It doesn't compute.

But can we just enjoy the impact of lightly playing around with what's basically an impossible jigsaw puzzle for the brain? Not to complete it and glue it in place and hang it on the wall so it's stuck and stagnant in a position that was our best seeing at the time, but just because there's something in that unfurrowed exploration itself that somehow helps us be more in Living Connection with more of the exact same Greater Reality that our minds can't fully grok. Which is actually of more value than some elusive perfect, pinned down mental understanding or map. The more you pin down a map, the more holes there are in it.

So something in what you just said does ring true for me. It's natural for the mind to want to understand, but can we accept that it's really not going to get all this very fully, and let that just be alright, and enjoy playing with the puzzle? Still easier said than done, but I do feel like I can connect with that perspective. And that brings up another question – well first I should say I'm keeping an eye out for a good place to take one last break this evening, so if this opens something that will take a while, maybe we can go ahead and do that before we get too far into it. But the question is, is Pure Consciousness aware of all these lives and experiences and levels? Can Ultimate Reality experience and be aware of what's happening in created reality, if I can put it that way? Is it along for the ride?

Ω Ω Ω Ω

Yeah so, I've been watching for when it makes sense to bring this other big piece in, and there's not that much more time tonight, so since you used the term *Ultimate Reality*, I think this is probably it. So let me think how I want to at least crack the door open a little, then maybe we take the break and then dig into it.

Sounds good.

Okay, so I'll just start by saying that so far I've been talking about all this like there's two things. First there's Pure Beingness. Eternal, Uncreated, Undifferentiated Oceanic Essence. Pre-prism Reality. The Infinite Source Substance and Core Substrate of all that exists.

And then second, on the other side of the two way mirror, there's differentiated reality, created reality, formed reality, post prism reality. Or maybe we could say membraned reality or holographic containment field reality, meaning every level of created reality, no matter how subtle, that at the Core is still only Pure Essential Beingness. Like structured ice compared to water, so that it's differentiated from the Pre-level or Pre-prism or First Side of the two way mirror, that's only Pure Oceanic Boundaryless Isness itself. I think that's pretty much how I've presented it so far, or at least intended to.

And like I said earlier, since we can't really drill down on everything all at once without a traffic jam slowing things to a crawl, sometimes I'm spiraling back around today, going a little deeper on a topic we already touched on, which also happens to be how the flash packets often come in during the bridging sessions.

And this is one of those situations, where there's actually more to that story than those two things and I just haven't opened that folder yet. But if we zoom in on Pre-created Reality, there have been a few flash packets – plus some little touch ins in other sessions – that have included more depth about it, and how it can be seen as actually two things – or maybe one thing and one non-thing – but Infinite Pre-created Reality has two aspects or two faces or two facets to it. A yin and a yang, kind of. The one I've mentioned a lot so far today is Pure Beingness. Infinite Undifferentiated Pure Consciousness. Eternal, Scintillating, Light-filled Benevolent Isness. And this Pristine, Overflowing, Love-emanating Essence can and does always Flow anywhere and everywhere, which is a preposterous statement because it always already *is* absolutely everywhere. Everywhere is within it. There is no outside of it.

And yet, without the faintest hint of a real contradiction, both are true, it *is* always fully absolutely everywhere and there could never be more of it or less of it anywhere, there isn't actually a where that's outside of it at all, and at the exact same time, it *can* and *does* Flow everywhere in a ceaseless Sacred Dance of Endless Flowingness.

It's the Medium and the Substrate and the Essence of the subquantum field of everything and every energy and every wave and every particle, and every energetic form and physical form of every type on every level of created reality. Everything that exists is always *of* that and *in* that and *from* that and destined to return to that, while simultaneously never being truly *other* than that for even an instant. It's the Source Substance that creates and permeates and infills and exists as all of created reality. And everything and every being is, at the Core, that Pure Living Flowing Beingness, and never truly separated from it in the slightest.

But that Pre-prism Essence isn't actually the Most Fundamental Ground of all that is. It isn't the Most Ultimate Reality, the Absolute First Foundation, that holds all, including that. And that other thing or other non-thing – which is the most Absolute or Ultimate Base or Ground of all reality – that's what I haven't opened up yet and what I wanted to make sure we get to before we stop tonight.

So yeah, that's what's next on the docket, but odds are it will get a little on the dense side, to try to conceptually convey it, which is ironic because from one perspective it's Absolute Density-lessness, while also being Absolute Solidity from another perspective. But yeah, we should probably go ahead and get the last break in so it's not hanging there, and then get into it.

Sounds good. You've set up a nice little teaser there. Alright, let's take five or so.

SESSION 6
CHAPTER 31

Alright. You were about to start talking about something more fundamental than Pure Beingness.

Yeah or about some non-thing. It's kind of hard to find a way in to talk about this First Ground, this absolutely indivisible Foundation of all that exists, so probably a good time to practice unfurrowed, light hearted seeing how the words land, rather than trying to mentally solidify a map of it in real time. And anything I could say to kind of point to it is already too much, not Empty enough, to be it. Because it's not – it's not any thing, it's before any thing. It's non-existence in a sense, and yet it's the Deepest, Most Fundamental, First Foundation, the Ground of All Existence. It's the most Solid Eternal Non-Thingness. The profoundly Peaceful Pre-dawn, Still Silent Darkness, that gives birth to the Pure Infinite First Light.

And from one perspective, the higher into Multidimensional Reality you go, the more dimensions there are, deeper and vaster. But from another, you could say this Absolute, Ultimate, First Reality is one Single Point, one Infinite Still Point. No time, no space, no size, not small, not big, undefined. In a sense, it's Pre-dimensional. It's Dimensionlessness. And Pure Infinite Beingness and all of formed, created reality – every dimension of reality, every layer of the Cosmic Onion – are originally born of That.

So Multidimensional Reality is incredibly complex, and Pure Infinite Loving Beingness is Simple, Infinite Clear Living Light, overflowing with Infinite Potentiality. And then this Richly Empty,

Pre-dimensional, Still Absolute Ground, on which all else rests, it's Absolute Simplicity. Absolute Non-thingness.

And it's nothing like cold or barren or lacking or harsh or lonely. This Absolute Emptiness is profoundly Rich and Benevolent. Its Empty Nothingness is actually Superabundant with unmoving Love. Love before motion. Love before Flow. Love and Light and Joy before expression or movement. This Pre-Dawn, Benevolent, Peace-filled Night is the medium, the clay, the substrate, the substance – or maybe the Absolute Nonsubstance – that precedes even Pure Beingness, Pure Undifferentiated Infinite Flowing Living Essence.

And pretty much every word I could use to describe it, every concept we could use to talk about it, it's all way too much, too dense, has too much weight or mass, it's too busy. So yeah, like I said, it's hard to talk about, hard for the brain to tune into. Well, I don't think the brain really *can* tune into it, but it's hard for us to catch enough of a whiff of it to follow the bread crumbs, and also just hard for the brain to even begin to grok the basic concept of it, when there really isn't any thing there to grok.

So that's a first swing, a first attempt at introducing this Absolute Fundamental Stillness. This Infinite Unmoving Silence. And let me just kind of take a step back and swing my bat a few times and spit in the dirt, and then step back up to the plate and try a different route here, that might not pay off, but we'll see if it can add to the conceptual or experiential tapestry a little more, of this pretty much impossible to talk about Absolute Foundation of all of existence.

And as I start attempt number two here, just another reminder to maybe just relax your brain and brow and your efforting a little, and just see if you can catch even the faintest breeze of the Essential Presence of Absolute Silence, subtly trans-rooting up into your experience, as I give it another swing here.

Swing away.

Okay, so, in the beginning, was the Pure Infinite Unmoving Silence. Absolute Stillness. Infinite, Eternal and unchanging. Only Itself. No motion, no flowing Light or Love, no differentiation, no variety, no thought, no creative expression. And no experience, no experiences, no delineated, unique, individual, self contained consciousnesses that could be experienced and perceived or that could experience and perceive.

No ice bubbles.

No ice bubbles. Just Deep, Silent, Ceasing, Infinite Pre-Light Stillness. The Deep, Silent, Peaceful, Infinite Night. The Source and Final Home of everything in reality. That which always underlies all.

So, in the beginning was Absolute Reality, and it still is, just as it was. Eternal, Infinite, and Unwaveringly Still. So thick with Emptiness, so unshakable in its Still Silence, that it has its own fundamental, absolutely undamageable and indestructible Solidity.

And then, at some point, the Unmoving, Presence-filled Nonbeingness of this Ultimate Pre-Dawn Stillness somehow bubbled upward and outward, through itself, and expressed its Overflowing Emptiness as the Infinite Living Light of Pure Scintillating Consciousness. As the Eternal Flow of Pure Infinite Oceanic Beingness. Pure Essence.

And I'm not really saying it wasn't Pure Consciousness before, there was just nothing at all to bounce off of, nothing to be conscious of. No other. No thought. No movement. No Flow. No moving Waves of Love and Light. No expression, no creating, no active consciousization. Just Consciousness in the Most Still and Unmoving Repose, thick with Endless Silence.

So, from this Undifferentiated, Undivided, Silent Stillness came the First Dawn, the Pure Love-emanating Clear Light. From Unmoving

Nonbeingness came Pure Beingness. From the Nonflowing Stillness of the Deep Sacred Night came the Pure, Love-emanating Living Sunrise. Even though they're two sides of the same non-coin. Maybe E Unum Pluribus. Out of one, many.

And this might not quite work but another little swing, we've talked about the two way mirror, and on one side is Pure Infinite Beingness and on the other is every level of created reality. So we also could say that on the Pure Beingness side of that two way mirror, farther back or farther in, there's another two way mirror, and on one side is Absolute Reality, upon which and within which All That Is rests. And on the other side is Pure Living Essence, that's overflowing with All Encompassing, Ultra-Vibrant Love and Light, and Endless Joyful Creative Potential. The Source Substance of all that exists in created reality.

So, there's the Unmoving, Silent Absolute Ground of all that exists, and from that, Pure Infinite Ultra-potentialled Isness bubbled up and bubbled out. Pure Overflowing Potentiality. And this Infinite Overflowing Isness is still an aspect of Pre-created Reality, it's still pre-formed, pre-differentiated, pre-segmented and pre-delineated. It's still pre-multitudinal. Non-two, Nonsplit, Nondual.

But this Light filled Infinite Beingness is able to move, able to flow, able to geyser up and out. And that's the aspect of Infinite Beingness through which the thinnest membranes of individual boundary arose and arise. Ice bubbles of experiential separation that allowed, for the first time, individual autonomous consciousness. Experientially separate Beings. Holographic containment fields allowing unique, conscious, individual experiencing and creating and contacting and connecting and communing and co-creating. Not trying to score an alliteration bonus, those are just the words that actually fit.

Ω Ω

And one of the images that flashed in was a huge endless ocean of pure golden honey, pouring into a vast empty honeycomb, with the honeycomb walls made of hardened, crystalized honey. Some of that Infinite undifferentiated Pure Golden Honey just naturally and effortlessly pouring into all of those empty – what are they called? The individual hexagons of honeycomb?

Cells, I think.

Yeah, it was pouring into all of those empty honeycomb cells. So now there were individual droplets of Shimmering Golden Consciousness, that could experience and create and interrelate as separate autonomous consciousnesses, with individual form and shape. Individual borders or boundaries or membrane or skin, made of crystalized Pure Essential Honey, or temporarily hardened Pure Essential Honey. And that allowed uniqueness and individuality and autonomy and agency of action, and creative and co-creative expression. An individual, differentiated cell of Pure Undifferentiated Golden Honeyness.

And this happened both trillions of years ago, or trillions of universes ago, and it's also happening every nano-moment. Like we inhale and exhale air, Pure Infinite Joyful Loving Oceanic Essential Beingness inhales and exhales entire universes, entire snow globe worlds, every breath. Ad infinitum. The Inflow and the Outflow of the Tides of Existence, the steady rhythm of the Infinite and Eternal Breath of Being.

Like water from the still, silent great ocean depths gradually rising up, churning up towards the surface, and then becoming waves and mist and splash droplets, filled with life and vibrant energetic flow, and then getting submerged again into the deep quiet still depths of the dark silent undifferentiated ocean. Pure Consciousness is always churning back down into Absolute Emptiness, and that is always churning back up and out into Pure Overflowing Beingness. So everything is always fractaling outward from Pure Stillness into Pure Beingness into formed levels of reality, and back again.

Outfractaling and infractaling. The outbreath and the inbreath. The exhale and the inhale. The Great Circle of Formlessness and form.

And the time does come when the very Core of every Oversoul, of every Multidimensional Being, and also every soul, every spark, every sentient consciousness that is a part of that Oversoul – every finger or tendril of that, including our own consciousness – does completely merge back into that Infinite, Purest, All Encompassing Still and Silent First Home, which it never actually left. Because all that is, everything that is, is always of, and always within, the Absolute Ground and Most Fundamental Source and Most Indivisible Substrate of everything in Existence. Which isn't way up there somewhere, at the top floor of the skyscraper of spiritual levels or Multidimensional Reality, it's right *here*. We're absolutely immersed in it always. It could never be otherwise.

CHAPTER 32

So, this whole schema is, there's the Pure, Unmoving, Richly Empty Absolute Ground, incomprehensibly dense in its Emptiness. The Solidity of unmoving Absolute Love in Absolutely Still Wavelessness. In a sense, it's a little like the solidity of solid ice, that as it melts, releases the Living Effervescent Golden Honey of Pure Essential Beingness. Releases Pristine Benevolent Light-filled Isness in motion. And that First Foundation is the Infinite Still Point Center of our very Being. The Ground of All Existence. Ultimate Reality.

And during one of the bridging sessions, when this was opening up and filling out, an inflash included that inevitable truth that the return to the Absolute Peace and Home of the First Ground will happen to all Consciousness eventually. That's just the way of things. It might be after trillions and trillions of years as we think of time, it's not exactly right around the corner, but it will happen.

And dissolving into the Love-filled, Joy-filled, Quenchedness of Pure Flowing Beingness, that's losing your sense of individual consciousness – losing your holographic containment membrane – to melt into the Great Fulfilling More, which can still feel scary to the identified small self, but there's so much Vibrant, Infilling, Quenching Beauty there to help counter that. Dissolving into Pure Belonging and Pure Love and Pure Flowing Isness, not so bad, as dissolving goes.

But this, this is losing yourself into the Great Unmoving Silence. There's not the Full Rich Muchness to entice you. So the first few dozen or few hundred or few million close passes by the event horizon of falling into what can feel like the Great Abyss – falling into the gravitational pull of that Absolute Source – the individual self is less likely to think of it as a particularly good trade and just go right on by, whistling overly casually to try not to attract attention.

And when I first felt that – the eventual inevitable dissolution of all individuality and unique selfness, the dissolving of the crystalized honey individual cell walls, the dissipating of the holographic containment field, all the way back into the Silent Unmoving Ultimate Ground of All That Is – it felt like the total, irreversible annihilation and extinguishment of all I identify myself as, without getting all the profoundly fulfilling and delicious riches of Pure Quenching Light-filled Beingness as a reward.

And my heart kind of – well my stomach kind of sank – like looking over a huge cliff from the top of a mountain or the top of a sky scraper or the top of a roller coaster about to go down. It didn't feel comfortable, I didn't like it. I felt a contracted *hell no* in me, like yeah, no thanks, I'll pass. I mean, letting a few layers of my individuality shell dissolve away as I merge with completely quenching Pure Loving Beingness, I can live with that, that's to die for. But dissolving every shred of my me-ness into the Absolute Silent Ground of all Existence, facing the Great Void, the Final Annihilation of my individual consciousness, no thanks, I think I'm good.

And as if in answer to my reaction, well, it *was* in answer to my reaction, I felt this sudden and powerful *whomp*, and felt a deep, deep wave of Absolute Stillness. Of the Eternal and Peaceful and Sacred Unmoving Night, from which the Living Light is endlessly born.

Not only sensing it in front of me, and in the space all around me, but suddenly I was *in* it. And it was in me. This Ultimate – this Ultimate Cessation, that I was just a moment before feeling woozy and resistant and rejecting about the idea of, was suddenly happening in me directly and intimately. Not hypothetical, not theoretical, not imagined. My consciousness was dissolving into that Absolute Silence, and I didn't have access to a certainty, or like a confidence, that it was just a temporary, reversible experience. It felt like the Real Deal. It was completely indistinguishable from the absolute end of the road of all traces of me-ness.

$$\Omega$$

And my mind slowed to a stop for a few timeless moments, and my awareness became Deeply, Deeply Quiet. My small self began to kind of waft outward, decompress, becoming less dense and less defined and less localized. And it felt like Omega also joined in the party, and fully stopped also, and dissolved into this Sacred Solidity of Absolute Stillness and Unmoving Love with me.

Both of us, just ceasing the continuous identification with our own respective versions of the autonomous individual conscious self. Ceasing the generation of the individualized holographic membrane. Experiencing the dissolution of the honeycomb cell walls into the Pure Golden Honey of Essential Beingness, and then immediately dissolving into the Absolute Empty Stillness of the Pristine, Unmoving, Pre-dawn Ultimate Silence.

And to my surprise, once I got over my initial hell no, it was actually – well it actually wasn't scary, it wasn't terrifying. It wasn't Oh my God I'm gonna die. Which when we're talking about my Earth suit, I'm pretty at peace with, but the instinctual individual self – the body and the brain – doesn't take too kindly to being suddenly extinguished, so it's going to try to have a say in the matter when it feels that encroaching on any level.

And beyond the body and brain, it's one thing for my temporary wet suit to cease functioning, it's completely another for my very consciousness, my most fundamental self identity, my very awareness, the most fundamental unique and individual and differentiated me, to simply cease as an individual autonomous unique being. That's upping the ante a little. I've been talking about being good with death when it naturally comes because of what the surviving individual me gets to have from that, gets to experience. Beautiful Loving Joyful Belongingness. But Ceasing into the Absolute Unmoving Ground of Reality, that's the Big Death, of all individuality. That's some real death right there. Not for the faint of heart.

And yet, as I had this substantial taste of it deepening within me – after the initial involuntary bracing against the sheer gravitational pull of Absolute Emptiness once I was in its event horizon – that initial hell no I won't go, it just softened, and there was just an effortless, profoundly deep relaxing into the experience. Falling into it. Yessing into it. Softening and melting and dissolving into it.

And you might think, "Yeah, but you knew you were safe, you knew it wasn't real. You were just sitting on your couch." But in the fullness of the experience, there wasn't anything like that. When a lion's mouth is around your head, being told, "Don't worry, Fluffles just ate a few hours ago," that doesn't exactly assuage your fears. This felt like the real deal. Nothing about it didn't. My mind really didn't know if I would come out the other side. Not of the lion but of the experience I was having, just to avoid any confusion.

I actually wasn't confused, but you can't be too careful, usually.

And yet, after the first nope, there was just a Yessing in me, a response of acquiescing, of letting go. Not fighting that unresistible strongest of currents, sweeping me choicelessly through the event horizon of this Solid Sacred Stillness. And what remained was simply the most comforting and contenting and relieving Silence and Stillness and Peace. Complete Resolution.

It was the Peace that passes all understanding. The Peace of Infinitely Resting in my Most Fundamental Home. My most – or actually let's say my least *something* home. Well let's not, that didn't work, but I'm trying to convey there's just nothing there. This Home has nothing at all. No structure, no flow, no differentiation, no moving consciousness, no creating, no Beingness in motion or Love in motion or Light in motion. Not anything at all that could be recognized and related to.

$$\Omega \, \Omega$$

But at the same time, it also has no sense of lack. No sense of missing anything. And there's no feeling at all of being terrifyingly trapped or lost in non-thingness. It's a completely Full and Rich and Content and Peace-filled Emptiness.

If you take a walk in nature at three in the morning, the air thick with living stillness, you probably aren't thinking this would be nicer if only the sun was up and sunlight was shining on your face. Both day and night have their beautiful place. And this Still Empty Night is perfectly Full of the Richness of its Solid, Complete, non-Flowing self.

And is this Absolute Ground infinite, or is it a Pre-dimensional Compact Stillpoint, that's completely outside of every rendition of space and any and all dimensions and levels? As though All of Existence is holographically projected out from it, yet still within it. Or is it somehow both? The only guarantee is however we're conceptualizing it falls significantly short.

But that very real and substantial direct taste of dissolving into the First Ground, with the cessation of all effort and all movement and all need and concern – and somehow all thought, while I also was still tracking it all – it just felt like the Deepest Peace and most Settling Stillness and most profound and complete First Home. It wasn't cold or desolate or barren or lacking. It had no deficiency or deficit in its so Full and Solid Emptiness. It was thick with Absolute Silence. Dense with Nothingness. Full with blanketing Stillness.

I couldn't feel Love or Light from it, because its Love and Light were motionless. But that still informed the experience, it must have, because I had never felt so deeply at Absolute Peace in my life, not even during the off the charts quenching and Love-filled and Belonging-filled Big Event. Not saying this Peace was as infilling and satisfying to my self as that was, but it was more Still. More Quiet. More the Peace that passes all understanding. The Peace before all movement.

And it was somehow so deeply familiar, even though all experiencing ceased as I fell into it. Not like scarily falling into a black hole all alone in the cold vastness of space, even though it had that kind of dense, dense gravitational pull, but it was Peaceful and Quiet and Complete. Maybe a little like a diver or an exploration submarine sinking slowly downward into the darkening peaceful depths.

And it was softly pulling me into dissolution, dissolving, disappearing. The Absolute Cessation of self into the most Restful and Complete Holdingness. And it wasn't that I was being snuffed out, a candle flame into pitch black coldness, it was that I was disappearing as an individual me and simply fully returning to and being one with that Singular Absolute Holding Ground, that was simultaneously my own Absolute First Essence.

And for probably in real time two or three minutes, my mind just completely quieted and rested. Maybe an EEG would've still showed some thoughts here and there bubbling up, neurons firing, and somehow I was tracking the experience, but any occasional thoughts weren't reaching me, weren't disturbing the Peace-filled Pre-dawn Stillness. I was dissolving into Ceasingness til all ceased. And yet all was fine. Such Deeply, Deeply Good All-is-Well-fullness.

So it was the Simplest, most Peaceful, most Complete Stillness, while being One with Absolute Nonexistence. It was Supreme Soul Contentment, Absolute Homeness. And I absolutely *knew* how profoundly Benevolent and Trustworthy and Safe and Solid and Core Home it was. Exponentially more so than – than I don't know what – but than I could ever describe. So yeah, that's about the best I can do I think, to try to convey it.

Ω Ω Ω

I've been really aware of a strong Presence in the space as you've been opening all this up. This time it's deeper and quieter and more sparse, but also more of a deeper Stillness and Peace, than the other times I've felt it today. It's like a slow motion wave of Profound Stillness that's been coming in. Or that's been trans-rooting. My mind is moving a little slower, and there's almost a thickness of Peace and a Sacred Silence in the space. I don't think I've ever felt this before, and definitely not to this degree. It's a bit humbling and also a bit disorienting, and also very poignant and deep. Deeply Quiet Stillness. And you've said nothing has compared to your near death experience, but from what you just described, it sounds like this was right up there with it.

Well, it wasn't as big and bold and beautiful and bright, it wasn't as infilling and let's say scrumptious and heart enlivening for my individual self, because the self receded into nonmovement. So it was Deep and impactful, but not as – not as much happening for the mind or heart or body or energetic nervous system. They all got a lot more juice during the Big Event, from the Loving Joyful Belonging, that felt so amazingly good, with so much Overflowing and Joyful and Loving Deliciousness, or I think the technical term is Yumminess.

Whereas this experience, it was also totally quenching, but in a different way. It wasn't as big or emotionally fulfilling because emotions quieted. It wasn't as Joyful and Love-filled because the heart quieted. It wasn't as self reflectively wish fulfilling because the mind quieted. And it wasn't as sensually kaleidoscopic because the body quieted. But it was Pure Perfect Quieting Restful Silence. It was so, so fully the Peace that passes all understanding, that passes all thought, that passes all relating to it. The Pure Peaceful Stillness of the Absolute First Ground.

What do you mean that passes all relating to it?

Well it's two things, both sides of the – of the bridge. The Peace that's so Still and Unmoving, there's not relating happening. There's not a you that's relating to the Peace. There's only Peace. And also, the Absolute First Ground can never be fully experienced as an other that you're relating to, only as a nondual direct immediacy of existing as That, where two-ness completely dissolves.

And it wasn't Love-filled, but it was Love Stilled. Love in Stillness instead of Love in motion. Love Solidified instead of Love in Flow. So way less experiential. And it was the Completeness of nothing wanted instead of the Completeness of having what you most deeply want. It was the Fullness of all lack simply *ceasing*, all wanting completely stopping in Perfect Content Peace, instead of the Fullness of being filled with the fulfillment of your most latent soul desires.

So I was just disappearing into this incredibly Quiet Non-Space, or more than that, I was undifferentiated from this Still Sacred Night. And then one lone thought bubbled up, like an air bubble slowly floating up from the bottom of the ocean to the surface, or I finally noticed a thought. Then another one. And soon I was back to thinking thoughts again, but like you said, more sparsely and clearly. My mind was just gently canoeing down a slow, smooth, easeful, unagitated river current, instead of the rapids. Not the usual incessant chatter the brain pumps out like the heart pumps blood, it was really a spacious and contenting and impactful respite, as I was slowly coming back online, to have been in such a Profound, incomparable, Ultimate Home-filled Silence.

CHAPTER 33

Do you remember what those first thought bubbles were?

No, probably like, this is so cool, or oh my God this is Absolute Cessation and it's amazing, or something along those lines. And it felt like Omega falling into reverent Cessation along with me is probably what made it so easy for me to follow close behind without thrashing around in the water. The unknown usually isn't so scary for a kid when they're holding a safe adult's hand, something akin to that, maybe.

But yeah, it was Absolute Peace, just dissolving into this Sheer, Empty, unfamiliar and yet so familiar and so right First and Final Home of Ultimate Completeness. I like that term, Ultimate Completeness. It was the Absolute Cessation of Being, even of Pure Infinite Flowing Consciousness. All stopped. All ceased. And it was only Good. Only Deeply, Deeply Good. And it was recognized as my First and Last Home. My Most Fundamental Essence. And as I – you started to ask a question?

Well I was about to, I thought you were done, but I'd rather you keep going.

Well, just a couple of last thoughts to express out. One is that in that Deep Completeness within Absolute Stillness, I didn't *not* exist, but I didn't exist as an individual anymore, or even as Consciousness in motion anymore, as hard as that is for our minds to fathom. We could say I existed simply as Stilled Consciousness, as Stilled

Peace, as Stilled Love. As Stilled Flow. Not stuck or stagnant, not deadened, just Richly Silent. The total Cessation of all movement within, even though my heart was pumping blood and my brain was functioning, which must have included neurons sparking with each other. I mean, my physical cells didn't all suddenly freeze. But at first no thoughts at all, or none I noticed, and no one to notice them.

Maybe they just weren't bubbling all the way up to my conscious awareness to reach me, or maybe they were but my conscious awareness was just absolutely absorbed in the Silent Absolute Ground. Just Absolutely Stopped and Stilled. Like a bee – or let's say like a hummingbird that's been in the air way too long, maybe it's migrating south to stay ahead of the deadly cold of winter, and after flying over one of the seemingly endless Great Lakes, it's finally able to just land on a sturdy, perfectly sized branch, and cease all movement and effort, and just really fully rest in still content silence.

And yeah, I just really saw that there's actually nothing ultimately or fundamentally costly about losing the self's individual identity for True Home. Losing attachment to it, but also losing the whole perception of experiencing existence through the filter of the individual identified self, through the holographic membrane of an individual separate consciousness. There's nothing actually highly costly about releasing that, in order to return to Ultimate Homeness. Nothing ultimately costly about allowing the dissolving of all barriers that interfere with merging with Safe, Perfect, Absolute Rest and Peace.

$$\Omega$$

So right now, in this moment, I'm kind of both, remembering the bridging session when this happened full on, and also experiencing a lighter version of it now, and those two are kind of intermingling and together helping me reconnect with what I'm talking about pretty directly. And just as if I were suddenly almost hit by a car my body would release some adrenaline and fear, my identified self can also knee jerk about its end, its final resting, as I experience a hint of approaching the event horizon of this Benevolent Original Eternal Silence that ceases individual experiencing. And yet stronger than that resistance to the extinguishment of the individual self is the resonance of how Profoundly and Ultimately Home this Absolute Stillness is. How Complete it is. Ultimate Completeness. Ultimate Landing on the Most Solid and Unshakable and Permanently Safe and Peaceful Ground.

It's before Joy in motion or Love in motion. Before Experience or Creativity or Flowingness. It's that which exhales into existence the Infinite Potentiality of Pure Beingness, which in turn breathes out the rest of reality into life. It's the Complete Contentment and Peace of Pre-Dawn Emptiness. Not desolate or barren or lacking, but Absolutely Rich. Absolutely Complete. And not just *at* peace, but actually *being* this Perfect Eternal Peace. Being Absolute Nonexistence. Pre-existence. The Absolute First Ground of all Existence.

More mind stretching.

Along with some mind quieting, as a subtle hint of this Deepest Stillness radiates through. And we have it so backwards if we think it's threatening in any way – the annihilation of the thinnest membrane – and also of all the stories we've attached to it and gotten attached to, and then the dissolving beyond even Pure Undifferentiated Infinite Loving Beingness, so that all that remains is Pristine Benevolent Unflowing Nonbeingness. Such Deep Relief and Such Deep Rest, to be One with that First and Final Home. It wasn't like an exultant experience, it was just Absolutely Still and Sacred and Clear and Complete and Quiet and Contenting, to be dissolved into this Ultimate Absolute Home of All That Is.

So wrapping this up, are there parts of me that prefer me-ness, and especially that perfect mix of me-ness getting to melt into Complete, Safe, Profound Love and Belonging, like during the Big Event? Are there parts of me that prefer Door Number One?

Abso-fricking-lutely. A lot of me really *doesn't* prefer the idea of losing everything that isn't that Pure Perfect Unmoving Complete Peace of Absolute Stillness. No thanks, I'll walk.

And yet, wow, it was really – I mean the Absolute Cessation of every shred of our self identity and of the holographic containment field of individuality, and of even the Joyful Dance of Pure Loving Infinite Flowing Essential Beingness – it was really – it really left an impression, and was the most at Peace and the most contentedly Still and Rest-filled and Resolved and Complete I had ever been. Dissolving into the Silent Reverence of the Deep indivisible Peace that passes all understanding.

And in this moment, as I feel the resonance of it flowing in, flowing through, and as I really remember those momentless moments, yeah, it's just only, only Good. But like I said, it's also not – I mean the Final Restingness in That – is also not something irreversibly coming to us, or us going to it, any time soon. We're never pushed there or forced, we never have final dissolution in That before we're completely 100 percent choosing it and yessing into it. It doesn't chase us, we just eventually Yes into it, in our own so natural and right time, which could be another few trillion Earth years down the road.

And as our awareness aperture opens more and more along the Continuum of Consciousness, this Ultimate Stillness can be related to – well not related to exactly – but can be dissolved into, anytime we wish, like Omega did, and like Omega helped me do in that bridging session. It's always right here, much more solidly and steadily and unwaveringly than any thing that's here or anywhere else. Every level of the Continuum of Consciousness is always right here, including that Spaceless Space where Consciousness can dissolve and cease into the Still Sacred Pre-dawn Night, from which comes the Brilliant, Eternal, Love-filled, Joy-Flowing Dawn.

Ω Ω

I'm still feeling the reverberations of what you're speaking of, emanating more as you've gone deeper into it. And it is quieting and peaceful, and it does open a feeling of a lot of Space. Almost a disconcerting amount of inner space in me the last few minutes, actually. A lot more than I'm used to so it's a bit uncomfortable. I do recognize there's something Deeply Good in it, but I think I would fight the annihilation of the individual me tooth and nail. So I'm glad to hear the perspective that we're never forced into it before we're truly ready, and that might be a few trillion years down the line.

But there is a Pure, Poignant Reverence to this particular Space of Stillness that I haven't felt before. And something that struck me as you were sharing is that it sounds like Oversouls can just instantly stop and not only return to being one with Pure Beingness, but can also just cease their own individuality altogether and return to being absorbed back into Absolute Stillness at will. And then return.

Yep. Higher level Multidimensional Beings like Oversouls can just open their aperture completely, and just stop continuously creating or maintaining their holographic membrane – the crystalized structure-holding walls of their honeycomb cell – and in no time, literally, they're just one with Pure Conscious Beingness. Or if they choose, even letting go of that last remaining membrane-ness that lets them experience that, and then they can just gently fall into the Incomparable Rest of Absolute Cessation within the Infinite Center of Perfect Absolute Home. So they always have instant access, with their All Access Pass. They're really living the high life. It's us tendril lowlanders who have it pretty rough sometimes.

But during that bridging session, that Deep, Deep immersion into Absolute Completeness was like that scuba diver or exploration sub, slowly floating deeper down into the Still Quiet Depths, safe and relaxed and in awe of the peace-filled beauty they can feel but not see. This was Eventlessness. Just Absolute Stillness and Emptiness and Completeness. But not cold, not isolated, not lonely, not yearning for anything at all. Absolute Quenchedness, not because you have everything you ever wanted, but because in that Silent Complete Peacefulness that passes all understanding, any wanting melts away into Stillness before it can even arise.

Say that again? I think I got it, but I'd like to hear it again.

How about if you give it a try yourself, and I'll be the bowling ball gutter bumpers if needed.

Now suddenly I'm feeling the hot seat. Alright, in that state of being, or maybe of Nonbeing, you're quenched not because all of your wishes suddenly are granted, or every state you could desire shows up, you're quenched because all wanting and needing just dissipates before it ever arises.

Nailed it. And you mentioned feeling an aversion to being annihilated, and I used that word a couple of times too, but it's such a strong, almost violent word for melting back into Ultimate Home. And yeah, there was that place in me for a few moments at first, that was a little scared or slightly freaked out looking over the ledge, that felt like I *was* about to be annihilated forever, the Final Death – not of my Core Existence, but of my individual experience and self identity. But somehow, probably at least partly because of Omega leading the way, it just didn't shake things up in me. Just a passing wave that didn't muddy the Clear Still Waters. And I absolutely knew in the bones of my soul, this was Absolute Safeness and Absolute Completeness and Absolute Contentment. Our Deepest and Purest First and Continuous Home. And even though it–

–What do you mean Continuous Home?

So like Infinite Living Beingness, Absolute Stillness isn't just the preface and epilogue of our existence, it's continuously here, and its gifts are ever-available, to the degree our awareness aperture and willingness are open and aligned enough to receive them. For Omega, that's an ever-available instant and effortless option. For me, and I assume for everyone or pretty nearly everyone else on

Earth, not so much, at least for now. But it's always right *here,* and it's always what we most fundamentally are, regardless of how aware we are of it.

Ω Ω Ω

But I was just going to say – last thought about all this – even though that experience, or that ceasing of experience, was the total cessation of my identified self, it was so right, so Home, it was like how could there be any problem losing any sweet and lovely extras to be in Absolute Completeness? Even merging in Profound Love, like during the Big Event, wasn't as full of Stillness and Peace and Absolute Return. Complete Contentment and Rest.

And our minds might kind of try to imagine this and assess the cost benefit analysis, but what the mind misses, what the mind can't really factor in, is this is our Core Core Essence. This is the most Home Home there could ever be. So what's kind of indescribable about it is, there's just *no* scenario where when you're really in that Absolute Stillness, one with it, it feels off. It feels like not enough. Because it's your innate Original Existence. It is your First and Final, most Profoundly Contenting and Peaceful Soul Home.

But still, like I said, given the choice I'd probably choose that yummified, joyful, heart-filling melting into Flowing Love and Belonging, that Delicious Quenchedness, well probably at least 90 percent of the time. Maybe 98 or 99. Just for a little while – like I said this afternoon, maybe just like the next two or three trillion years or so – til I've finally really had enough of feeling beautifully, saturatedly quenched in Superabundant Belonging and Love and Light and Unconditional Absolute Acceptance, and Profound Merged Fulfilledness. Because my self is still very much here and it wants what it wants, you know? And experiencing that is one of the most beautiful gifts – if not *the* most beautiful gift – available within the Continuum of Consciousness.

Say that last part again or differently?

We didn't come into individualized experiential consciousness to dissolve back into Ultimate Silence as fast as possible. Not a perfect analogy, but a butterfly doesn't finally break free of its cocoon just so it can immediately start to spin another one around itself and dissolve back into its most fundamental existence again. There's no hurry, there's no pressure, there's no prime directive around this, there's no instruction from above we're ignoring at our peril, if we simply aren't ready yet. *Of course* we aren't. Butterflies are meant to fly and drink nectar for a while. No rush, no pressure. We're invited to *enjoy* experiencing the journey, as we can, and at our own pace. So yeah, I'm with you, I'm not ready either, and no need to be. But at the same time, nothing else is as Profoundly Still and Complete and Resolved and Fundamentally Home as the Perfect Incomparable Peace of the Unshakable Absolute Ground that sources all of Existence.

And all these words are just shooting a quiver of arrows, hoping some of them stick in the tree. And we're both feeling the Silent Presence of the Absolute Ground, subtly seeping up into the space as we're here opening it up. Rising up from our Deepest Roots. From the very Deepest First Root. And there's such undeniable real Goodness in it. Such Solid, Strong, Steady, Absolute, Pre-Dawn, Silent and Still Goodness. So yeah, I think that's all I got about that.

It does feel like a rare privilege, to be in the Presence of this Deep Quiet Space arising into our field. And as I said, it does have a different quality, a quality of being almost sacred. That quiet reverence, that I haven't felt the other times a subtle Presence has come through, today or during our coffee conversations. There's a palpable Deep Stillness here right now. I almost feel like I should be whispering out of reverence. It occurs to me that the other moments of feeling Subtle Presence today have felt a bit like being in a nourishing, rejuvenating steam room, and this is more like being in a cleansing, purifying, still and quieting empty sauna. I don't know if people reading the transcript will feel any subtle arising of this Deep Silence, but in this moment it does somehow seem truly possible.

Yeah, like we talked about earlier, it's not such a tall order, that the timeless and spaceless resonance of Presence and Essence and Stillness and Silence could trans-root through our words and between our words, and the subtle fragrance of it could arise in the awareness of someone reading the transcript months or years later, Earth time. Not a stretch at all, really.

CHAPTER 34

Well, a part of me would rather just be off duty in this slower moving, quieter space a while, and relax in the sauna, but we're running out of time tonight and I want to keep us moving.

It could be interesting to just lightly explore if it has to be binary, one or the other. Just playing around with trying 20/80 as we move on to the next thing. 20 percent of your awareness on this rare Space you're noticing, while it's here, and on how you're feeling it in your body or in your experience, how you know you're aware of it, how you're perceiving it. Without chasing it or trying to keep it from leaving when it does, just letting it ebb and flow or fade away, while keeping most of your attention on the task at hand, and seeing how that goes.

This came in once when I was waiting to see if Omega would show up, and then it had a follow up a few weeks later, but with this one, I was about to give up and call it a no show, and before I felt the usual whomp of arrival, there was this little instruction flash packet that came in, and it was basically, while you're waiting to see if there's going to be a bridging session, and also while you're living your daily life, when you remember to and are willing to – especially if you're not feeling very present or you're getting contracted or reactive or more pulled into something than you would like – let a part of your attention land on different places in or on your body, different contact points, like your feet or toes, your hands or fingers, your arms or legs, your stomach or chest, your shoulders or neck, or your jaw or forehead, it really doesn't matter.

So landing on one or two, feeling whatever's there to be noticed, and when your mind wants to move on in a few seconds because it's getting bored, nothing new to see here, letting it move on to another contact point. And there was also something about how this is a deceptively simple awareness practice, because it can help anchor you, help ground you, and can help start to relax and open and uncontract your awareness. And with a little time and practice, it can actually support your awareness in being *more* capable and present and available in the moment, not less. And when you forget, which is inevitable, just gently bringing it back if you feel up for it. So that was the basic invitation, and–

–*By bringing it back do you mean starting to do it again? Or bringing your awareness back to a contact point? Well I guess those are the same thing.*

Right, just starting fresh. Just letting your awareness land on or tune into your body, doesn't matter where, and when it gets bored let it move on to another contact point. So that was the basic instruction or invitation.

Ω

Then there was another level of it in another bridging session, where again I was waiting to see if Omega was going to show up, and again this little inflash showed up before I really felt Omega's arrival. And it was like, while you're waiting, this could be a good time to try that practice. And then there was another round of briefly guiding me through it. So yeah, basically it's just let your attention gently land in different places in your body, and then moving on to a new place in a few seconds or whenever your mind wants a little activity. And when your mind wanders, which it will, kindly and gently bring it back to a new contact point or the same one a little longer. The wandering mind is baked into the cake, not the slightest failing or problem. It's expected and factored in.

So that second time was a quick like review of that practice, but then it added to it just the little twist of – and I almost talked about this earlier but was going to save it for tomorrow – but it's just a minute or two, and it added the little twist of, you can also explore, once you get the basic hang of it, adding in very gently, softly, not forcing it, noticing if you can be aware of two different contact points at the same time, while also letting most of your awareness focus on what's in front of you to focus on. Not being concerned if you're able to or not, it's more about the zoomed out soft focus required to even lean towards that invitation.

And you can also do it as a centering practice along the lines of meditation, where you're just sitting for a few and connecting with different contact points in your body – the list I named or you can add your own in there if you like – and then after you've done that a minute or two, gently see if you can be aware of two or even three of those contact points simultaneously, without really working your mental focus hard to make it happen. Soft focus. Zoomed out gentle focus. Not really being able to do it and the mind wandering are both baked into the cake, part of the deal, not the slightest problem. It's the practicing of it, not the so called succeeding. The practicing *is* the succeeding.

And it's not like – Or take two, you don't have to have any awareness of Presence at all to do that, that's not usually something we experience and that isn't the point. The point is just lightly exploring simultaneous awareness. Letting part of your awareness rest on these various contact points on or in your body, regardless of what you're feeling, which can help you be more grounded and centered and connected, and help your awareness open a little more. And you can also include sensory intake like sounds and visuals. If a loud motorcycle roars by like a minute ago, *including* that, instead of fighting with it as an intrusion and trying to partition it out of the experience.

So it might be something worth exploring as we go, or like you said earlier, if you understandably feel like you have more than enough on your plate this weekend – being the interviewer and host and emcee and time keeper and itinerary manager and question tracker and audience stand in and recording engineer and snack provider for our little marathon weekend – if you feel like this isn't exactly the most ideal time to add in starting to play around with this, then maybe some other time. Anyway, as with most things Omega, I felt a resonance with it when I saw it.

Ω Ω

Do you practice that sometimes? And do you have a name for it?

Simultaneous Awareness Practice is the kind of obvious name that came up. And I don't do it much at all, but sometimes it does me. I mean, I'm not the best student, I'm more like, just give me the Good Stuff and don't make me trudge through the dissatisfying tedium of working for it. I've gotten several of these suggestions or invitations or little practices or processes during bridging sessions, and I haven't been able to try all of them – or haven't been all that up for trying all of them – but it would be a lot to try to implement or incorporate even half of them really firmly in my daily life, and I've never felt that's expected. And also I've never been someone who's able to really rouse up a lot of discipline to consistently stick with things that might be worth doing.

So all of that was my slightly defensive excuse to say I haven't deliberately and disciplinedly tried to do this particular suggestion or invitation, or really any of them, except for sitting on the couch to see if Omega shows up, but that one's pretty self serving and I'm always up for doing it.

But with this particular one and a couple of others, sometimes I do just find it happening, I do just find myself doing it some, kind of from the inside out instead of starting with a conscious intention to do it and trying to dredge up some discipline. Usually this one kind of just happens when I'm sitting and waiting to see if Omega's going to show. I just kind of settle in and start naturally and effort-lessly find myself being aware of different sensations in my body, different parts of my body even if I'm not aware of any particular sensations there, like my feet or hands or forehead. And I do find it settling and clearing.

It sometimes happens at other times too, especially when there's a Greater Field of Presence in the space, which for me mostly hap-pens when I'm in a bridging session with Omega, and also some-times when I've talked about these things, which means with you when we've met for coffee or today. Part of my awareness just kind of sits in that Field or stays centered in it, while most of my aware-ness is focusing on, you know, our conversation and expressing the topics and so on. And maybe it roves from ten percent to 30 per-cent of my awareness, sometimes a little more, and sometimes it ebbs completely away for a while.

But I think the way Omega's flash packets come in, they impact me more deeply than just information, and I also had that aperture alteration from the Big Event, so when it's something like a prac-tice or process we can do, with a few of them I sometimes find that I'm just doing it here and there in spite of myself, without really mustering up anything. And the one I want to talk about during our last topic tomorrow is one of those, where I just find it happening sometimes, and more often lately, and it's starting to become a real support.

So I'm not quite sure where we are or what to ask next, and my mind is still moving a little slower – I think from the gravity of the Pure Stillness and Silence that's still lingering in the space a bit. Let's try some more rapid fire questions I still have in my note-book. A few are half crossed off because you've addressed them some, but I want to briefly revisit those, as well as a couple of others I've jotted down.

Kay.

CHAPTER 35

So I'll start with, earlier I asked you a two part question and I don't think we got to the second part. How many Oversouls do you think there are?

Absolutely no idea. Somewhere between a hundred million and 27.5 quadzillion. And it also depends on how you're counting. How many living tree organisms are in an aspen grove? One. And also, you know, a thousand. But if you dig in the soil a little, some of the younger ones are clearly just subsurface offshoots or root branches of older ones, which themselves are sometimes the same for even older ones. So then it's maybe also three hundred living tree organisms. Kind of like that.

Alright, next up, anything else to say about the whole layout between Oversouls and souls? What that connection is like between individual conscious beings, like people, and their Higher Selves? That whole layout is hard for me to grasp.

Yeah, better not to grasp, better to let all this wave in, and just allow what resonates to land, and what doesn't to wave on out. Critical thinking can be part of that, but it's not as helpful to have tight, contracted thinking trying to force understanding it all. And my mind tries to grasp all this too, of course. That's just what the human brain tends to do. But especially when we're exploring Multidimensional Reality and the Beautiful More, there's an opportunity, that's worth not unawaringly steamrolling, to just let all of this kind of whomp us, to whatever degree it does, if it does at all. And to just let the questions, and that subtle sense of Infinite Vastness, if or when it shows up, impact us, stretch us, make space in us. Open us.

And letting ourselves really not know, really not have it all figured out. Letting the floor fall out from under us – like one of those spinning, round room, centrifugal force amusement park rides – and letting that all be really okay, without trying to put it all back together in a nice neat tidy controllable way.

But to your question, so, like the aspen grove, the boundary isn't that clear cut between an Oversoul and the individual souls that are within it or connected to it or extensions of it. That delineation isn't fundamentally a solid, unwavering one, and a lot of it depends on the perspective and level you're coming from. But it's a little like, think of all the different avatars or game characters or Monopoly game pieces or Dungeons and Dragons wizards you've been over the course of all the years you've played various games. If someone asks how many game characters are in you, how many Monopoly wheelbarrows are in you, the question doesn't even make sense, unless maybe you inadvertently swallowed one. There's just you.

Zoom out, and the you that you usually think of as you, it has always been a game piece or avatar or game character – probably one of many – by a Higher Consciousness gamer, your Oversoul, your Higher Self, your Greater Consciousness. And that Being is absolutely you, but a you that's way more you than your current limited game character in your current game could ever approach.

Zoom out some more, and it's Pure Infinite Consciousness, the First Gamer, with maybe near infinite numbers of Oversoul avatars who each have their many avatars in various games or amusement park rides or snow globe experiences. Maybe some have millions or more tendril souls extending into different experiences, and maybe some have just a few, or just one. And some Higher level Light Beings have none, that's not what they're about. But maybe some Oversouls are just starting to try their hand at extending down some exploratory tendrils, with just one or two, just starting to put their hand in the water and let their fingers do the walking.

Ω

And we'll see how this attempt goes, but sometimes cartoons have an octopus doing eight different things at once because it can. So instead of eight tentacles, a Multidimensional Octo-Being has – I don't remember my guess earlier – but maybe somewhere between one tentacle and eight trillion, in somewhere between one and one trillion snow globe worlds, more or less.

And actually that's a good metaphor in another way, because octopuses have neural networks in each tentacle. Largely autonomous mini-brains in each arm, that can experience and sense and make their own decisions without having to check with the Mothership central command brain in the head. Their arms are like free thinking autonomous conscious tendrils, attached to a larger organism and larger consciousness that they're always a part of. Like a conscious version of individual aspen trees in a grove.

So an Oversoul is like an Octo-Being or Octo-Soul, with all those autonomous tentacle extensions off living their own individual lives. But the central nervous system of the main brain, the head of the Octo-Soul, is always instantly and continuously plugged right in to what the tentacles are experiencing. Those tentacles aren't usually as aware of the central brain, but it can be aware of them. They're all always one with that main Being even though they might not have much or any conscious awareness of it.

I think out of all the ways I've tried to express this, I like this analogy the best, at least for the moment. Not picturing literal octopuses, literal sucker tentacles, but whatever way works to get a sense of this. But I really like this octopus analogy, sans visuals, because it captures that individual souls or individual selves are like conscious, autonomous arms with neuronal networks and autonomous thought processing, yet they're always connected to the Greater Central Nervous System, and not truly ever even remotely separate from it.

And an octopus might reach one tentacle into a jar of sardines that someone left in the sand during low tide, to get the snack out of it, or maybe sometimes that tentacle reaches in with its own autonomy, while another tentacle is reaching into a different jar – turned out to be pickles, not really their thing, thanks for the thought though – and at the same time, not sequentially, another is checking out a shell next to the two jars, almost like a parent with eight identical octuplets – or whatever that word is – and all these tentacle arms are doing their own thing with their own separate neural brains, but they're also always, mostly without their awareness, plugged into and networking with the primary Mothership brain.

So for Multidimensional Light Beings with tentacles in various snow globe worlds, all this is happening both within and beyond time. It's temporal and also pre-temporal and post-temporal and nontemporal. So yeah, something like that.

I think from here on I'll just tell you when something isn't mind stretching. It's more efficient that way. So here's another question. You said earlier that it's possible for more than one person on Earth to be from the same Oversoul at the same time, and they could even meet. Would there be a recognition if that happened?

Ω Ω

So yes – at least per the bridging sessions, which should just be understood with everything I'm saying – but yes, an Oversoul could have more than one tendril or tentacle in a world at the same time, like a gamer having two game characters in a game world at the same time. Two avatars. And sometimes an actor plays two different parts in the same movie, sometimes even shown on screen at the same time, like Kirk Douglass in *The Man from Snowy River*, but we always understand, zoomed out from the story, there's always only one actor playing both roles.

And is it possible if you met another tendril or extension of your Oversoul, you would feel a particularly familiar and strong connection to that other person because of that? Yes. And is it also true that if you zoom out a few more levels, every person you've ever met shares the same First Oversoul, the same Ultimate Self, Pure Consciousness itself? Yes. The Infinite Source Point of the Continuum of Consciousness interconnects every being with every other being, along with Pure Beingness itself.

We're all conscious autonomous tentacles of Oversouls, which in turn are conscious autonomous tentacles of the One Infinite Mothership of Pure Conscious Beingness. Maybe, depending on how you look at it, with one or two or three Over-Oversouls in between, though I still feel like the way I'm talking about it has a little too much demarcation and hierarchy to really capture it.

But a strong recognition and closeness with someone you just met could be either of those – the recognition of having the same Higher Self, or something opening that allows a greater recognition of both of you coming from and being of the One Pure Eternal Consciousness. Every being is of and from Pure Living Conscious Beingness, so you truly are of the same Universal Tribe. We truly are all One in the Spirit.

Or there could be some other dynamic involved, like maybe your consciousnesses or souls or beings have been or are in connection with each other beyond this current life experience. Maybe you've—

—*Just making sure, you're using the terms your consciousness, your soul and your being to mean the same thing, not three different things, correct? We haven't really talked about or defined a soul.*

Yeah, there's no subtle differentiation, I'm using those words interchangeably to mean one tendril, one tentacle, one sub-Spark of an Oversoul or Higher Self. And I'm also using the terms Higher Self, Oversoul and Greater Consciousness, and let's throw Greater Self in there too, interchangeably. And all Oversouls are Multidimensional Light Beings, but not every MLB has tendrils or tentacles or astronaut exploration pods, they don't all have individual consciousnesses having individual autonomous experiences, so not all MLBs are Oversouls or Higher Selves to individual autonomous consciousnesses.

So, that deep, usually instant sense of unshakable familiarity and connection, it could be recognizing and re-membering the Essential Oneness we're all intimately and inextricably connected to. Our Deepest Root is the same First Root. Different branches are still one with the same tree trunk. And sometimes that moves from the default setting of mostly or completely hidden to us, to energetically obvious in a way that's really impactful.

Or maybe you've had other journeys together, already have a Profound Deeper Connection from before and beyond this life experience. Or maybe it's just a psycho-physiological thing, where you just really hit it off with someone, and feel a rare connection, because there's a lot of compatibility, in terms of what your mental and/or emotional and/or physical patternings offer and receive from each other. Or there could be some other explanation.

Ω Ω Ω

Those kinds of special connections don't have to mean you're of the same Being Tribe or Soul Group or Soul Grove or Oversoul. The more your awareness aperture opens, the more the doors open to more recognition of the familialness of everyone, of every being, who lives now and who has ever lived, and ever will. The commonality, the shared oneness, the shared – well not sure what to add – but the Common Ground we all share, capital C and G, the Common Ground of Being. The Deepest Root that we all are one with, which interweaves us with each other. All things of all levels were created from and through and by and of and with and within that First Common Ground, that Deepest Root, and that Essence is always *our* Deepest Essence.

And like I said this afternoon, that's a shift I often palpably feel in myself since the Big Event. A subtle and underlying default warm familial connection with everyone, in spite of having a pretty introverted and sometimes a little aloof or not that socially open of a personality that doesn't tend to love other people's personalities that much. As though everyone's a cousin or second cousin, even if not my favorite relative.

So from a larger perspective, it doesn't even really matter if someone is a conscious autonomous tendril or soul tentacle of the same Higher Self. Fundamentally, just one or two or three steps removed, yet not truly removed at all, we're all already and always one with each other through being one with the One, Love-emanating, Benevolent, Everpresent Essential Source. The Infinite Unilarity, to which we all belong and are, at the Core, completely comprised of.

I sometimes feel like my brain short circuits as you talk about these things, and sometimes that correlates with subtle waves of Presence coming in and getting stronger. Right now, it still feels a bit Silent and Quiet and Deep from a few minutes ago, like a slow motion water fall of Flowing Presence is still slowly pouring down on us. And then what you just said generates its own quality of Presence also.

Yeah, it's been nice to open all this up, and feel the impact of the arising of Essential Presence as we do. The arising of it from the Deepest Root, even though it usually feels like I can't convey these things well at all with the clunkiness of language and with my own linguistic clunkiness. A lot of times it doesn't come out as smooth as I would've liked, or just doesn't really capture what I'm trying to communicate, but you know, a book with blank pages might be a tougher sell. Or maybe a tie, depending on how this turns out.

Thanks for your vote of confidence in the project.

I'm confident in the goodness of us following your pull for us to try doing this marathon, but I really have no idea how many people will ever know that the transcript exists or will start reading it, or how much of it they'll read or how much they'll resonate with different parts of it, and in a real sense that's not our business, not our heavy concern. And I do feel confident the Presence we've been feeling throughout the day is somehow, through the mystery of natural multidimensional Consciousness physics – that for now is beyond current scientific understanding – is somehow encoded in the words and, like I said earlier, in the space between the words. So some people might be positively impacted by that on a subtle level as they read, whether they're conscious of it or not. Anyway, what's next?

CHAPTER 36

Let's do a few more rapid fire questions.

Kay, bring on the next RFQ. Even though the odds are I'll reply with another FLA.

So this is another half crossed off one – I think I just got that. But you've said you're not afraid of death since the Big Event. Could you say a bit more about that? You said your body still has fear sometimes, like if you were to almost have a wreck.

Yeah, if my life was suddenly in immediate danger, like a car heading straight towards me or something, my heart rate would of course increase and adrenaline would surge, and I would feel waves of fear like anyone else. Of course the body wants its safety and is deeply programmed to have a strong aversive and mobilizing reaction to imminent danger. Not so much slowly encroaching danger, but we'll touch on that tomorrow. But on that level, definitely, I can still have fear.

And like I said earlier, I still don't at all like the thought of suffering when I'm dying if it comes to that, or suffering like in a hospital with serious, difficult health issues, whether I'm dying or not. I still have a huge preference not to suffer, like everyone else. I've been through the physical ringer once and it ain't fun. So I'll probably always have some degree of a hell no thanks though to physical suffering.

But when I think of death itself, skipping past any unpleasantries, just the end of this individual person on Earth, the end of this lifetime, then even if I somehow absolutely knew there was nothing after death at all, if I could skip the pesky little dying part then I don't feel scared of death at all.

If we assume for a minute there's no experience, no nothing after death, then in me there's nothing to be afraid of. Maybe there's some sadness to lose the whole package of me, lost forever – I mean I'm one of my favorite people – but not scared. And when you think about it, if there's nothing after death, that means there can never be a moment we see that verified, like "Oh damn, there's nothing." We can't have that moment because we'll lose awareness before we have enough evidence to conclude that's the case.

But of course, my experience during the Big Event was very different than this possibility of nothing surviving death. You told me a few weeks ago that some people say near death experiences might just be a big release of some neurochemicals flooding the brain that create that experience, and you know, it doesn't ring true in the slightest for me – it's hard to imagine that accounting for and explaining everything that I've experienced, and I imagine a lot of other people that have had profound near death experiences feel the same way – but just objectively, it could theoretically be true I guess.

But in myself, I just know, I mean I *know*, that I absolutely will survive bodily death, that we all will. Not because I desperately need to believe that – if anything I just almost desperately need to believe I won't ever experience a lot of suffering, which is a little bit of an exaggeration but not by that much. But I just know it in my soul's bones, the Most Real me will survive death, beautifully. So when I check in about where I'm at around when this body actually dies, all nice and legal like, no take backs, what I feel – at least right now imagining it, which granted is definitely not the same thing – but what I feel is something not too far from peace and joy.

Because I completely trust and know and expect, even though I acknowledge that this could somehow turn out not to be the case at all, but I absolutely *know* that I will get to be back in that profound, deep, unparalleled, not found anywhere else – at least in my life – Space of Absolute Love and Acceptance and Settledness and Safeness and Contentment. Pure Relief. Pure Joyful irrevocable Intra-connection. Complete and Total Belonging.

$$\Omega$$

And that word *Belonging* is really landing in me today. Absolute Belonging. Complete and Effortless Belonging. Like finding your long lost family or tribe, and finding your truest self – your most authentic, centered, relaxed, complete, congruent self, your happiest, most empowered, most playfully mature and arrived self – and also finding your – let's say your soulmate or life partner, and earlier I mentioned even like reuniting with your beloved dog from childhood, so something of the feeling of all of those things together, plus returning to your truest, truest Home, and feeling absolutely safe and *at* Home, all rolled into one, times ten thousand. Plus a little merging with Infinite Light-filled Love and Essential Oneness thrown in for good measure. Something along those lines.

So it's a little late for a short rapid fire answer to that question, as I remarkably predicted, but mine would be nope. Not afraid at all of my own death. But if my life is suddenly in danger I'll still feel that. The body doesn't go, "Hey look, there's a hungry tiger running towards me, but before I react with fear, let me check with that conscious mind upstairs first, and see if it currently believes its consciousness will survive bodily death. And if it *does* believe that, I won't squeeze out any reaction time enhancing and strength and speed enhancing adrenaline to help me respond to this tiger that's now three feet away. But if my mind *doesn't* believe there's life after death, then it would perhaps behoove me to begin evasive or self defense maneuvers so that – Damn tigers have bad breath. And fairly sharp teeth." The body just does its thing, just does its automatic job, no consultation huddle with the conscious mind first.

But I definitely am at peace with the fact that this body will die at some point. It will be a relief in ways, and it will also be tender and sad and poignant to completely leave behind this unique life and all it entails. I mean, I'm the only me there will ever be. That's not an insignificant, no big deal thing. But from the perspective of the Continuum of Consciousness, what I just said still applies, and also, simultaneously, the ending of this personal self, unhastened by me, the shuffling off of this mortal coil – whatever that phrase exactly means – is such a relatively small thing to lose compared with expanding into becoming so much more of what we always – a few layers beneath the surface – truly are.

This is the great non-secret Secret, that's patiently waiting for all of us, but is truly in no hurry. Not quite it, but maybe a little like a parent that will be so happy to see their college kid, but wouldn't at all want them to drop out of college just to come home early.

$$\Omega\,\Omega$$

And you know, that whole, deep, through and through quenchingness that happened during the Big Event is still pretty recent in my life, so I don't know where I'll be in a year or two with it all. But for now, I still find myself now and then looking at this life as something like an inconvenient annoyance I need to tolerate and make peace with, make friends with, do the best I can with, til I can finally once again be back with my Fuller Self, my Oversoul, where I Deeply Belong, and where I'll be so much more connected to Infinite Beingness and Absolute Stillness, which are even more fundamentally my Home.

So even though it's been slowly shifting, my heart is still longing to be back in that amazing space of Love and Acceptance and Peace and Contentment and Settledness and Pressurelessness, with no to do list, no worries, no having to get it right, no way to blow it if you tried. Irrevocable Quenching Belongingness. Being unconditionally Held in Light-filled Love. Once you've had the best, it's hard to be content with the rest. Once you've merged into the Beautiful More, daily life is kind of a bore. Once you've, – well, I'll stop while I'm behind, but in my defense, we're pushing midnight. Been a long day.

It has, and I realize we blew way past our 11 o'clock extension, and I know we need to wrap up. How about if we stick with it about 20 more minutes, with a hard stop at midnight?

Sounds good. So, just to finish that thought first, like I've said, I do feel like I'm gradually getting more acclimated and more in alignment with more fully being here. That's obviously the higher invitation, right? Not spending years or decades of your life wishing you were somewhere else. But I can't speed that process along faster than it's happening just because I think I should, which would just add more knots to the already existing ones.

So more and more, I'm just appreciating what I can authentically appreciate about having longer in this life, when I genuinely can, to the degree I genuinely can, and not trying to bulldoze that on top of where I genuinely am in any given moment, which only tightens the knots, and helps nothing. Like trying to pry open flower petals because they aren't blooming as fast as your idea of how fast they should. Doesn't tend to work out so well. So yeah, that's my honest current report.

It sounds understandable to me. During that greatly impactful experience you found your heart's Home, that Space where you felt melted into the Deep Love and Belonging of being plugged in to Greater Reality through the Omega Consciousness. That's where your compass is pointing, and you don't think you'll feel fully complete until you fully have that again.

Yeah, like that. Exactly like that, I would say.

CHAPTER 37

And by the way, I almost said this a few minutes ago, but for now it's true that being plugged into the Field of Omega is what I have the most feelable pull towards, but once I die die, for realsies, no escape clause or return ticket, and once I'm merging with my Higher Self – which I still think of as that separate Multidimensional Being of Love and Light and Belonging I call Omega – it seems completely plausible that I'll realize that that which I responded so profoundly to and feel like I so completely found Belonging in isn't *actually* that individual unique Being, that thinly membraned individual Multidimensional Consciousness of Omega. But instead, it's the very *Core* of Omega, the Infinite *Center* of Omega, the very *Essence* of Omega, which is the exact same thing as the very Core of me, and which is *actually* Pure Eternal Consciousness, the Infinite Loving Beingness at the Center of all, that's so much more experienceable through the intermediary of a Multidimensional Oversoul Light Being than it is through all the thick walls and mostly closed apertures that most of us have in this world.

For now, Omega is a hugely appreciated go between, a conduit, a personification of the Purest Undifferentiated Isness and all the gifts that offers a thirsty soul, as well as a greatly appreciated source of support and wisdom and Connection, not to mention, you know, being my own Higher Self, so there's that. But I can't say for sure how things might progress once my post-life existence has time to actually get past the, you know, five minute mark. Maybe I discover my Deepest Response isn't towards Omega at all.

I mean it could be like – well I'm getting an image of an astronaut exploring a desolate strange world, getting back into their pod after decades and returning to their Mothership. So nice to be back. And then that spaceship flies back to their home planet, back to their true original home. Nothing compares to that. The Mothership was an intermediary, a necessary go between, that it was so, so nice to be back to after wearing an astronaut suit on a mostly disconnected planet for years or decades, and you're so grateful to be back on it. But when that Mothership lands back on your home planet, and the spaceship stairs open, and you see your real home and hear the sounds and smell the smells of it, and feel the heart resonance you have with it, no doubt, *that's* what it's *really* all about. That's your *real* home right there.

That analogy fails though, in that Omega doesn't have to travel back to the home planet of Pure Beingness, Oversouls are *already* continuously consciously connected to Infinite Flowing Benevolent Living Essence. *Always* simultaneously aware of every point along the Continuum of Consciousness, including their Infinite Core, the Source Substance itself, which makes them pretty damn good emissaries of it or emanators of it. Surrogates of it. But actually more than any of those, because they truly *are* that, in a way that's much, much more immediate and affecting and within their continuous awareness than the degree we usually experientially are, even in our most connected moments.

For our Higher Selves, there's no losing awareness of that. It's never something Higher Beings lose and then try to re-find. That's us lowlanders' situation, but never theirs. Joy and Delight and Connection is just par for the course up in Blissville, pretty continuously. It doesn't register for them as some rare, amazing thing, this Everpresent Living Flowing Connection with Pure Beingness. Living Homeness and Absolute Belongingness is their natural state. They are, at their very Core, in their very Essence, One with and the same as and undifferentiated from Pure Infinite Flowing Love-emanating Consciousness.

And of course, so are we, always. It's completely irrelevant if we can feel the truth that that's what we truly are, or if we believe it or not. We don't have to experience it for it to be true. There's nothing we can do to make it more true, and there's nothing we can do to actually cost us that irrevocable connection within the Continuum of Consciousness. Yes, our awareness aperture can be more closed or more open. But the degree of trueness that we actually are – in our own Infinite Core – the same as Pure Infinite Beingness, which is always one with all that is, *that* never ebbs and flows. How could it?

$$\Omega$$

And in case I didn't quite hit my daily quota when I said it a few minutes ago, to me Omega still *feels* like an other, a separate Multidimensional Being, that I will get to be with after this Earth suit stops functioning. But I do *know* that this Greater Being, this Higher Self, actually *is* the Fuller Me, my Greater Consciousness, the gamer playing the Earth lifetime game with a human character. That's the More Fully Conscious me, without the training wheels, without the blinders, without the limited aperture and without this heavy and dense level of reality clogging up most of the Flow.

And also, this idea of like four points on a graph, with a line connecting them along the Consciousness Continuum – first us, then our Oversouls, then on the other side of the prism, which converts Pure Clear Light into wide-spectrummed created reality, there's Pure Beingness, and then the Absolute Ground of Existence – those four graph points don't actually exist the way I'm talking about it and the obvious ways that work for us to think about it in our comparatively limited, three dimensional world based brains. It's just not that delineated and segmented and plottable.

Omega isn't *really* at one fixed knot in the middle of the long rope of the Continuum of Consciousness, with our small human selves at one end and Pure Beingness and Fundamental Ultimate Reality on the other. All of those points are overlapping, on top of each other, inside of each other, wafting through each other. They're different depth points in river currents that are always dynamically alive and changing and rising and falling. So I don't mean to convey a sense of inflexibility and rigidity and entrenchedness about all this. It's mostly our own awareness aperture that's understandably stuck in inflexibility, not the rest of it as much.

And ultimately, we could say, from one perspective, there's most fundamentally only One Universal Silent Still Point – the Infinite, Everpresent, Absolute, Non-spatial Ultimate Unilarity – and the rest is very impressive holographic illusion. Which doesn't make everything in created reality not real or not worthy of our care. You see a kitten crouched down against a street curb one morning, anxiously meowing all alone, you don't ignore it and say, "All well, that's just part of the hologrammatic illusion." *How* our reality comes into existence every micro-moment has nothing to do with the truth that, within this reality, we inherently *know* it's good and right and resonant to care for ourselves and each other and the Greater Earth Community – all of life and all ecological systems on this delicately balanced planet – and we hopefully, way more often than not, live as though these things are good to care for and really do matter, because we deeply know that they are and that they do.

And we'll open up this up tomorrow some, but just maybe, bit by bit, more and more, we grow in deeper capacity. We open our awareness aperture a little more, so that while we're caring for ourselves and each other and the Earth, we also begin to have one foot dipped a little more in the Living Waters of Greater Awareness. Or maybe just one toe at first, and then slowly more of a foothold, where we can directly know that from a larger perspective, even when things are difficult here, what we *truly* are is *always* fully safe, *always* fully held, *always* fully accepted, *always* fully loved, and *always* fully in Profound Connection to Pure Infinite Joyful Loving Beingness. Like Omega said, through my inner translating, that's our Source, our Essence and our Destiny. And it's always closer to the Core of ourselves than our identified small self could ever hope to be.

CHAPTER 38

My mind is swimming some again, in the wave that just opened as you were talking. But let me try to get in a few last questions for the night in our last ten minutes or so. The first is do you have any sense of how old the Omega Being is?

So that's one of those questions that just doesn't compute. Like if you're holding a film reel in your hand, how much time has gone by in the movie since you came into existence? It just doesn't make sense. But the words *ancient beyond ancient* resonate.

And another half crossed off question. Would you care to take another stab at why Oversouls or their soul tentacles, or tendrils, decide to leave their Higher Selves for—

—Tentadrils.

Tentadrils? Alright, why soul tentadrils decide to leave, and go experience a less connected and more challenging human lifetime?

Do you mean why they would leave for a lifetime that's especially less connected and more challenging, or why they would come here to this comparatively challenging and less connected place at all?

The second one.

Yeah, so this isn't really The Big Answer or The Big Reason, and it isn't really saying anything new, but a different angle maybe, Pure Infinite Consciousness naturally gravitates towards the Infinite Fractaling of creation and expression and experience. I don't know if we can say water enjoys flowing downward, that's just what it does, how could it not? That's its nature. I can't say for sure Pure Consciousness, bursting with Infinite Creative Potentiality, *enjoys* fountaining ever expanding fractals of creating and expressing and experiencing into form, that's just what it does. So that's at least in the mix.

Did Omega tell you that fractal thing?

Yeah, the image arose during a bridging session and that word matched. You know those fractal images and fractal videos, kind of like a full color ever expanding kaleidoscope, or like a multicolored, ever growing snowflake crystal under a microscope, where you just keep zooming in and zooming in, more and more, and these fractals grow or offshoot into more fractals, which grow or offshoot into more fractals as you keep zooming in. Ever increasing zooming in, ever more fractals, never stopping. They're based on some simple mathematical formula I don't remember, or maybe a few formulas, but they kind of tendril out in every direction, with beautiful, self reproducing patterns. They look really cool. There's a lot of videos of them, and you can also find some where they go in reverse so they're endlessly outzooming instead of inzooming.

So Infinite Superabundant Potentiality is endlessly fractaling outward, in all directions, not just 2D, and not just 3D, but in all directions and all dimensions, just Wonkavatoring everywhere. And all of those awareness fractals somehow *also* fractal back inward, and I don't know that you can say to report back, like a scout ship reporting back to the Mothership, but there's like an effortless thread of connection between Oversouls and their tendrils or tentadrils, their individual soul sparks, as well as a natural returning, of every soul spark, and of every energetic ribbon of created reality, sooner or later, back to Pure Infinite Beingness. Like droplets of water evaporating from the ocean, and then eventually, surely, even if it takes eons, finding their way back home. That happens with every Spark of Consciousness, and with all form, sooner or later.

Ω

And like everything your fingers experience is communicated fully to your brain, everything a sentient tentadril experiences, the Central Consciousness System of the Oversoul is connected to. Everything an autonomous octopus tentacle experiences, so does the central brain. Everything your game character is experiencing in the game, you're aware of. The Cosmic Through line or Continuum is always open, both directions, we just mostly lose the ability to tune into it when we drop our dime in the turnstile and hop on the Earth bound train.

But it's like the heart pumps blood out and also pumps it back in. Same with the lungs and oxygen. The Cosmic Circulation System. And while on our level, in these human forms, we don't usually get to be privy to the inbreath and outbreath of Infinite Beingness – we don't usually get to be consciously plugged into this natural expressive pull to fractal ever outward, and also ever inward – still that process is just a natural part of the inherent Joyful Expressive Isness of Infinite Consciousness, that's ever outfractaling and infractaling, ever exhaling and inhaling, ever creating and experiencing, expressing and exploring, connecting, and communing, living and loving, forgetting and remembering, and then inevitably returning to the Heart of All That Is, for another outbreath. Another Cosmic Circulation Cycle.

And cue another round of some subtle Presence. Sometimes I'm not sure how much I'm fully following what you're saying about some of these things, but that doesn't seem to stop me from catching the waves of that subtle field of Presence coming in. The trans-rooting of it, which, I'm still getting used to that phrase and getting reoriented to what it's pointing to, but I like the reframe of it.

And we need to stop, so just one last question, I asked this earlier, and that opened up a different thread you wanted to make sure you talked about, and I don't think we ever came back around to it. Is Pure Awareness aware of everything going on in formed reality the way you've described an Oversoul can be aware of what's happening with its – with its tentadrils? Is it along for the ride and experiencing it all?

Yeah, when you asked that before, I zeroed in on you bringing up Ultimate Reality and ran with it as an opening to talk about Absolute Stillness, and completely spaced your question. Maybe the shortest way to say it is, it's not really like a Mothership way up above, closely monitoring the goings on down on the planet. It's more like, well it's not more like, it actually *is* – at least based on the flash packets – that Pure Flowing Beingness, Pure Infinite Essence, is absolutely intimate with, and closer than close to, everything in all of existence. It's inside of everything. It's One with everything. It's what everything actually is made of and what everything actually fully is. It's closer to us than we are to ourselves. Far too close for us to find it by looking for it. We always overlook it, because it's *before* looking. And it's *within* longing.

I lost you.

Longing for it is *before* looking for it. And it's the longing that can create moments of finding. All looking for Pure Beingness is *over* looking, because it's closer than our eyes, closer than our ears, closer than our thoughts and concepts and maps and understandings. It's closer to us than our own self identity is. But our *longing* for it, when we let that breathe, when we give that some space, that's a ringing tuning fork, attuned to any faint relevant resonant vibration. It's a heartful solo wolf howl in the night, that's fully present and available for the faintest resonant response.

Ω Ω

And Pure Beingness is *always* along for the ride, because every ride is *within* Pure Beingness. Every aspect of every ride and of every being and of every thing and of every level is, at the Core, Pure Beingness playing dress up. Wearing a disguise. Out trick-or-treating in a convincing costume.

But is Pure Beingness, that's so Omnipresently Intimate with everything, also consciously tracking and observing and logging all that's going on, almost mentally or intellectually? It doesn't need mental thought or mental tracking or mental memory in order to intimately exist as all that is. Thought isn't the avenue through which its Aliveness and Intimacy breathes. Its intimacy is before thought. Before processing. Before information. Before agenda or reason.

On the Pre-prism, nonlevel level where it exists, on the First Side – the Clear Glass side of the two way mirror – there's *only* Oneness, and every apparent part and particle and wave and energy field of post-prism twoness is *actually* only comprised of that Pure Essential Oneness. For there to be one aware of another, that's what the ice bubbles are for. That's what post-prism holographic containment fields and individuation membranes are for.

Pure Beingness has no *other* to be aware of. It is Pure Singular Awareness itself. It's Pure Unilarity, before and beyond and within duality. It's Pure Undifferentiated Golden Essential Honey, before any crystalized, individualizing honeycomb walls or cells. It's the Great Oneness that holds within it all of created reality. So yeah, something along those lines.

Alright. Well it's only fitting we stop the evening session with another mind boggler and another Presence wave, both hitting at the same time. I have no doubt we could keep talking about all this another day or two easily, probably more, but it's definitely time to stop. I really–

–It's hard to believe I started the day, forever ago, worried about filling an hour or two. Didn't turn out to be too much of a concern after all. I could be way off about tomorrow too, but I really don't think there's as much ground to cover, and they should be less mindboggling and less unruly topics. A little more contained and orderly, at least in theory. But sorry, what were you going to say?

I was just going to add, I really appreciate you staying with it an extra couple of hours. As well as just showing up today, and giving this a go when you weren't convinced about it. It's been really good. Really rich. And actually my over-stretched mind is glad to hear tomorrow's topics should be a bit easier to talk about.

Well, right after I said that I had the thought, famous last words. Like we saw today, you never know exactly where we're going to go, what aspects of the main topic and what side tangents we might get into, and it's probably a safe guess that here and there we'll touch back in on one or two bogglers from today and fill those out a little more. Plus I'm remembering one or two things on the docket for tomorrow that are probably fairly mindboggling in their own way, so I guess we'll see how it all goes. But anyway, yeah, I've enjoyed today more than I thought I would, nice to try to open a lot of this for the first time, at least in that much detail, and also nice to feel Essential Presence in the space so often, which I wasn't expecting, at least to that degree. So yeah, I'm glad we're doing this.

Glad to hear it. Me too. Alright, then that's a wrap for the Saturday session.

PART THREE:
THE OMEGA ORACLE
(SUNDAY AFTERNOON)

SESSION 7
CHAPTER 39

Alright. So to set the stage for a minute, you got here about seven or eight minutes ago, a little before one, and we had a few minutes of small talk while getting our drinks and getting situated. And we both said we were a little tired but we're up for today. I mentioned I had trouble falling asleep last night, I was buzzing with energy as though I had had too much caffeine, and then you said something that didn't come up yesterday, that when the bridging sessions started, you usually had trouble falling asleep the night of each session – you felt wired – and you asked the Omega Consciousness about it, and they said it was due to the higher Energy or Presence coming in during a bridging session. The body isn't used to it at first, but it gets acclimated over time, which has happened with you. Is that right, and anything to add?

Yep and nope. I think I'm just going to give one word answers today so we can cover more ground.

Solid plan.

Yep.

And then a couple of minutes ago as we were sitting down, I named the two main topics for today to make sure we were on the same page, and then we talked about how we plan to keep today a bit tighter and on the original schedule in terms of the dinner break by 5:15 and then the 10 o'clock stop time. Then we both hit record and sat our phones on the table and here we are. I'm not sure if any of that was report worthy, but I thought I would orient readers to where we're starting this moment from. I didn't do that yesterday, but it was basically the same. Small talk, getting our drinks, making sure we were on the same basic page around our general topic outline for the weekend, and then jumping right in. So, that out of the way, before we get into this afternoon's main topic, it occurred to me to ask if you had a bridging session this morning or yesterday morning?

No, but I did Friday.

Could you give a quick summary or snapshot of it?

So it was one of those where there weren't any inflashes. Just being in Rich, Flowing, Alive, Settled Presence. And you can copy and paste the part about not being the same as the Big Event, but it was still really nice to experience. I got the sense afterwards – no idea if it's accurate – but I had the sense it was about deepening the connection, opening the aperture a little more for this weekend. Opening up a stronger field of Essential Presence for our marathon.

Well based on yesterday, it seems to have worked. Then it sounds like the Omega Consciousness knew we were doing this?

Not positive, but during a session it feels like my mind is pretty much an open book for Omega. I didn't try to consciously communicate anything about our weekend marathon, I just – there hadn't been a completely silent soaking session in a while, and I could be wrong, but it just resonated in me after it ended, it kind of bubbled up as I was about to get up from the couch and go on about my day – that it was for deepening my connection to the Deeper Roots, specifically for this weekend.

And you're calling it a soaking session because you're just soaking in the Presence?

Yeah. Both relaxing in it and absorbing it, kind of like a subtle energy Epsom salt bath.

Ω

So you didn't ever ask Omega about doing this weekend? It never came up?

You mean like asking if I should trust my resonating with your enthusiasm about this project? Didn't even cross my mind. I had a sense in myself, a yes in myself, a response to your response to your project idea, meaning I trusted where it was coming from in you enough to give it a try, while giving myself an out if it didn't end up resonating after all. But so far it has, and I expect it will continue to. But Omega isn't – well take two, Omega's role isn't being like an authority over my life and my decisions, that I defer to when I have a choice to make. There are no strings on me.

Is that – is that Pinocchio?

Yeah, I mean we're not living this life to be an out of control id that just does anything we want, like a kid alone in a candy store, but at the other end of the spectrum, if we find ourselves in communication or connection with what we perceive to be a wiser being or a wiser person, that doesn't mean we just cede all authority to them and become a puppet or a sheep or a, I don't know, a mindless, powerless, deferring zombie. I felt a yes in me, in my tuning fork, to give your yes the benefit of the doubt, with exit rights just in case, and that was that.

I'm with you about not ceding authority, and especially when that opposes your own tuning fork, but in this case, we're extending what Omega has been communicating to you to however many people–

–Once it's gone through my imperfect filters.

Once it's gone through your imperfect filters, to however many people end up reading the transcript. So I could imagine during a session, just seeing if there was any feedback or opinion or response from the Omega Consciousness about this.

But it's not like a – well there's like five different replies coming up at once, so let me try to just zip through them. So first of all, when you and I were having coffee and I started talking about Omega, would you feel like in retrospect maybe I should've run it past Omega first to make sure it was okay before I started telling you about it? And then what about if I decided to go into more detail with you? Like check in each new level of divulging? And what if there had been three or four of us having coffee? Would that change your answer?

And then imagine you had me over for dinner along with six or seven other friends, and the topic came up and I was ready to talk about it, like should I excuse myself and go sit in another room and see if an impromptu bridging session starts, so I could say, "Hey Omega, sorry to cold call you during dinner – no, I'm not a telemarketer selling anything, just a quick survey – I just wanted to ask, even though this is feeling right in my own tuning fork, I just wanted to check and make sure you were cool with me telling people about my near death experience and our bridging sessions."

And then what if we decide to have dinner again the next week and talk about it more, and there's more people? Then a few more and it keeps growing. 20 people, 30, 40. At what number does it suddenly become a situation where I need to check in with headquarters? A hundred? A thousand?

$$\Omega\,\Omega$$

And then second, it's not like Omega only tracks or hears what I internally intend to say, and the rest stays hidden. Like I said, it's like I'm an open book, maybe 24/7 but I'm more aware of it during bridging sessions. So it's not like there's a firewall and everything behind it is private, but once I inwardly intentionally communicate something, then that gets past the firewall and Omega can pick it up. It's not like that for me either when I'm around people, it's just more limited with me to feelings and energies, not much specific mental content, and not as refined and precise perceiving of the energetic and emotional landscape.

But fundamentally, like I said yesterday, whether your finger is touching your forehead or your arm is as outstretched as it can be, your finger is always equally connected to your central processing system. There's not actually any real distance or separation between an extension of an Oversoul and the Oversoul.

So it's just not – I mean it's understandable to see it more like the way things work here, where you have to deliberately communicate with someone to make sure they're up to speed, but that just doesn't translate to this situation, it's not like that. Your hand doesn't have to use sign language to communicate to your brain that the stove is burning it. The brain gets that communication quite clearly and naturally and directly already.

And then third, Omega just isn't possessive about all this, like "You're doing *what* with *my* material?! But I was going to trademark it and sell it as an online program, that's half off for the next five people who sign up in the next five minutes, before it's sold out forever." What's being offered through the bridging sessions is offered with Grace, capital G, not with any expectation from me or limitation on me. There's no quid pro quo or conditions. And – not sure if this is still number three or on to number four – but I'm in my own integrity or my own resonance here, as clearly as I can see, and that's – I mean that's enough. My tuning fork says I'm cleared for landing. That's about the best we can do as humans.

And if you feel like a little – well, take two, if you live near the ocean and you feel like going to the beach, and it resonates and there's not a superseding responsibility or consideration you're pretty clear to attend to instead – like going to work or taking care of the kids or financial repercussions – then you just go, because it's your delight, it's your response. And I was wooed by your enthusiasm, it was my – well *delight* feels a little strong here, but it was my genuine response to lean towards your enthusiasm to try this. It's not heavier than going to the ocean. Things just aren't heavy with Omega. A Light Being.

Ω Ω Ω

And then fourth or fifth, of course if Omega whomps in, in the next couple of weeks with a different perspective that I haven't seen, and if once I see it then I resonate with it authentically in myself – not just because of where I perceived it to come from, but it genuinely resonates – then I would take that under consideration, just like if – well it could be through what a friend says or it could be alone, but if you suddenly see things in a different way than you had, and it changes your take on a situation, you might change course.

So I guess that could still happen, I would just need to really recognize the resonance directly in myself, otherwise, my decisions aren't connected to my own roots, which would just make me a rootless tumbleweed, at the mercy of someone else's hot air. So that could still theoretically happen I guess, getting a different sense during a bridging session in the next week or two, I just don't see it happening. Omega's just not going to say, "Let's just keep all this between me and you, cool?"

And I guess last thing, I just want to add that I'm still getting my head around all this – around the original Big Event of course – but specifically the bridging sessions and the inflashes during them. It's kind of a lot that's happening, and remember, to one year ago me, you die, you decompose, and with some luck you become a rose. End of story. So this has all been a lot, and one thing I'm really watching out for in myself is not giving up my own autonomy or authority or my aligned congruence, to whatever degree I have some at any particular moment. I don't mean being arrogant or obstinate, or a cup too full to take in anything new, I just mean congruently rooted.

And I've never once felt Omega's trying to take my authority – there's just not that kind of energy of imposing on my life, or of dismantling my own sense of capacity to navigate – but it's, you know, kind of a trip to be experiencing all this, and one way I just check in on myself and do kind of a congruence check or an empowerment check is just making sure I'm keeping my autonomy. Especially since, like I said yesterday, I'm kind of sweet on the teacher, so I feel like it's particularly important for me to be kind of vigilant about not ceding my own rootedness just because I like the feel of the waves that pass through me.

Ω Ω Ω Ω

So that's why you probably felt me bristle a couple of minutes ago. I'm happy to sit for the bridging sessions, and really drink in what's offered, as long as I keep an eye on myself to make sure I'm not becoming like a codependent reverse zombie. And because I don't have 100% confidence in myself around that, I can get a little tight about it.

That really makes sense. What's a reverse zombie?

Not sure, but I meant like letting someone *else* chip away at or slowly eat away at your *own* brains, your own empowered agency and your own sense of resonance, your own compass, your own tuning fork. Becoming codependent and rootless. Leaning too far forward and glomming on to the trunk of another tree, to try to maple tap through its bark and only feed off of *it*, instead of a balanced diet where you're also taking in nutrients and nourishment from your *own* roots. Doing that just makes your own roots atrophy and shrivel up more and more out of disuse. Leaning forward can give you a taste, and awaken your longing, but it can also throw you off balance. And while others can help, only your *own* roots can in the end lead you back to the Pristine Homeness of your Original Root.

That's why I really like the sense of when you feel a field of Presence impacting you from someone who happens to be a little more plugged in to Deeper Rootedness at that particular moment, thinking of that more as being transmitted through trans-rootingness, impacting you by coming up through your own roots – that are being nicely watered at the moment – rather than that sense that it's emanating through the physical space between you and someone else, which can lead you to energetically kind of lean towards the perceived source of that Presence in a way that can knock you off balance and cut you off from your own inherent empowerment and congruence and groundedness and Deeper Rootedness, and cause your own roots to start to shrivel.

And, last thought, it's not that I'm concerned about Omega actively encouraging me to trade my own autonomous tuning fork for being mindlessly directed, I've never felt a hint of that. My concern is about me unilaterally doing it. Disregarding my own tuning fork because I'm leaning forward only listening to someone else, or staring at someone else's compass instead of my own. Becoming kind of a lazy sheep, mindlessly following the path plodded in front of me, without paying any real, mindful attention myself, to watch out for fallen logs on the trail that could cause a stumble, or to watch out for an unexpected cliff just ahead. So yeah, I think that's everything I wanted to say. Unless you have something else, let's call that steak well done.

Sounds good, and I'm glad you expressed all that. The last few minutes some arrows landed, or some spaghetti stuck. Something poignant showed up in the space. And I can imagine it would be a tricky balance, to be open to the Omega Consciousness and the bridging sessions, and the Resonance of Home that opens, while also trying to stay balanced in your own roots.

Yeah, well said. It's probably along the lines of trying to find that balance with an amazing new relationship that you just want to completely dive into, but you also know the goodness of not completely giving up your own autonomous rootedness as well. Most of us have been there once or twice in the past. When you lean too far forward you might hit the ground fast. So, I'm navigating balancing all of that the best I can.

Makes sense.

CHAPTER 40

Alright, so let's go ahead and switch gears to this afternoon's main topic, which is talking about what you saw during your near death experience, related to several possible futures or possible future events, and some related topics. So let's start with how that opened up and then get into what you saw.

Okay, but I wanted to start that off with taking a minute to talk about a related, kind of peripheral possible data stream, that I've sometimes glimpsed out of the corner of my eye during some bridging sessions, but when I've tried to look at it directly, I haven't found anything. It's not something Omega has directly shown me, and when I've asked, it's just crickets, so it might not – there really might not be anything there at all. But it's still kind of fun and interesting to think about just lightly, even as kind of a mental stretching exercise.

Since we didn't do enough of that yesterday.

Exactly, finally a chance to do a little mind stretching this weekend. So there's been a sense sometimes when I'm bridging with Omega of like peripherally glimpsing a packet or folder about this, but it hasn't ever gotten any clearer than that. So I'm not really solid in what to think about this possibility, and I haven't yet received any confirmation or denial from corporate, and I really could be flat out wrong.

Everyone who makes some educated guesses or has an intuitive sense of some things is right sometimes and wrong sometimes, and just objectively, probably a bigger chance I've got this one closer to wrong than right. But I just have this nagging, I don't know, a nagging wondering or resonance that it might be true, and I suspect sooner or later Omega will either confirm that it is, or help clarify for me what it is that I'm picking up that kind of seems to point in that general direction the way I'm interpreting it.

You've got me curious.

Well I can feel I'm a little hesitant, because this is – this seriously could just all be my own fabrication and I'm making more of it than I need to, I mean sometimes our brain puts thing together in a way that's a really nice intuitive leap that's right on the money, and sometimes it points us in a direction that turns out to be way off base.

But I'm bringing it up because it's – well first, I do have inklings there might be something to it, and if so it could be related to how the future scenes we're about to get into came in, but also because regardless of if it pans out in the slightest, it's still an interesting thought experiment, and I'm most comfortable if we just look at it that way. Just something to lightly play with. So, pre-ramble finished, here's the interesting little thought experiment.

Alright.

Ω

So in a minute, we'll be talking about a big info-packet or data stream of images and scenes and senses of possible future events, that came in during the Big Event. And if we take them at face value for just a minute, then how does Omega know about them? Omega isn't hobbled by pesky things like the space-time continuum, and one possibility is that they came from tendrils or tentacles, or conscious spark extensions, of Omega that are–

–Tentadrils.

Oh yeah, tentadrils. So one possibility is they came from tentadrils, or conscious spark extensions of Omega, that are living a life in our relative future, and are experiencing or will experience the events I saw. Maybe even future me will see some of this if I live long enough, and Omega will know some of it that way, I don't know, but Omega could be seeing all this – our past, present and future – from beyond time, like we talked about yesterday. A spacious, unrushed temporal array, without the steady forward arrow of time as we experience it.

Time is more that movie reel in a canister for Omega, so any frame can be seen or the whole movie can be observed instantaneously. To us it sounds impossible or magical or maybe deitical – meaning like a deity – to be able to be beyond time and to see the future, but that's no more amazing than that idea of a Multidimensional Being having the ability to hold a transparent film reel canister and focus in on any multi-sensoral frame they wish – beginning, middle or end – or even seeing and taking in the whole movie, every frame, all at once.

But here's where that explanation, of where these future scenes came from, just doesn't completely fit for me if we just leave it there. My really strong sense and understanding during that flash packet was, this wasn't just hey look what's going to happen, good luck with all that, you'll need it. My strong sense was these are *possible* future scenes, with some being much more likely – like it's too late to completely steer clear, or with some maybe it's too late to even steer clear at all – but some are really *not* too late – or I mean it's really *not* too late for some – if we get our act together.

So how can both of those things be true, if they are, that Omega saw it from the future but it might not happen? And one answer is, and it might be the simplest answer, and you know, Occam's razor, right? All else being equal the simplest answer is usually right – and I don't mean to suggest I've accurately narrowed it all down to only two options – but one option is just that maybe Omega sees a thousand or ten thousand possible unfoldings, potential future forks – none of them definitely happening, just varying degrees of potentiality that they will happen – and really that might be the answer, nothing too shocking there.

But there's another option, to add another dose of supra-boggled-ocity to this weekend's proceedings, even just as a thought experiment, and this is the core of what's been just barely too off to the side for me to really glimpse fully head on, but I just feel like it might be lurking. If nothing else, it's still interesting and mind stretching and paradigm stretching to just entertain the possibility of it.

And that is, just to lightly try on for size for a few, what if these future events that I saw actually came from a real future, but not necessarily *our* future? What if it's not just that Oversouls have tentadrils in up to a zillion different snow globe worlds, with sometimes simultaneous ones in one world – like several souls or people on Earth potentially having the same Oversoul – but what if also there are, drum roll, zillions of *alternate* universes or parallel realities or parallel timelines, where a whole lot of other potentialities are manifested?

What if the images and senses I was shown of potential future events wasn't our definite unchangeable future, which I feel sure it wasn't, and also wasn't just projected probabilities based on current trajectory plot points? What if the future scenes I saw are actually showing real existing futures – that from Omega's supra-temporal perspective have already happened and are happening and will happen – but they're from one or more of a myriad of parallel timelines, and we absolutely have the ability to impact to varying degrees how our *own* timeline unfolds, with there being a lot of different potential trajectories?

If we imagine Omega holding a transparent movie reel canister and being able to emanate enough light and perceptual focus and awareness to be able to see each frame simultaneously, then if that's possible, why not ten thousand film reels? Ten thousand different parallel unfolding futures? Or a million? Why assume Oversouls have an upper limit to what they can take in and perceive and process in their simultaneous Now? They can track a million individual consciousnesses that are tentadrils of themselves but can't track a million alternate realities? Or a trillion? All forking in front of us but appearing as one tapestry for them. What if in spite of all our mindbogglingness yesterday, it's all still exponentially more complicated than we've gleaned so far, with thousands or millions or trillions – or dare I say gazillions – of different unfoldings all happening in different parallel realities or versions of the same snow globe? And more specifically, of our little universe and our little planet?

And if that happens to be the case, if my peripheral inklings are correct, and Omega is just not ready to open that folder with me – maybe just because, you know, one step at a time, fractions come before trigonometry, or who knows – but if that *is* the case, then the hard news is that at least one version of the future that does or will exist has the various not so great events that I saw, and maybe more parallel futures than we could count do. But that would also mean the good news – I guess selfishly for us – would be that if all the events I saw do happen in one or more futures, then it's not set in stone that they all have to happen in *our* future. Meaning we could potentially change our trajectory some, steer away from some of what I saw, or reduce the impact somewhat.

Some of it is probably pretty unavoidable at this point, too late to steer the barge fast enough, and also not everything was bad news, and that one thing I mentioned yesterday – that I'll go into a little later – was particularly encouraging news, if it comes about, but maybe for a lot of the bigger icebergs potentially ahead, maybe the impact could be, to varying degrees, minimized or in some cases maybe even altogether evaded.

Don't ask me if I think it's very likely we actually *will* be able to hugely change course with some of the icebergs I saw, but we potentially *could* alter some of them. Maybe we don't steer clear soon enough to avoid *some* icebergs but we manage to miss others, or just nick some we were headed for head on.

But yeah, I just wanted to bring that little possibility in before we get into everything, as kind of a light thought experiment. Sometimes inklings are right on target and sometimes way off, and sometimes kind of in the middle, but regardless, it makes a nice little brain stretcher, that just maybe it's all exponentially more complicated or intricate, as well as way, way more vast, than we've been imagining so far.

And maybe right now there's millions or more parallel versions of every single person living a lifetime on Earth, and every being on every planet in this universe – and in the whole four dimensional tesseverse too if it exists, and maybe there are more dimensions in it than that just a measly four. So a myriad of parallel universes and tesseverses, with alternate unfoldings for individual people and for this planet as a whole, and beyond.

And it gets pretty unruly and untrackable pretty damn quick, to try to imagine all that. Like does every single choice point or some other split point cause a fork? And there are just unfathomable numbers of parallel Earths all playing out slightly differently, or sometimes greatly differently? I have no idea, I'm just spreading unsubstantiated rumors since word on the street is I'm an incorrigible gossip. But something in me, my spidey senses, have been tingling here and there around this whole thing for a while, and Omega's been rudely completely unforthcoming. "We'll tell you anything you want to know." Fine print: "Except for most of the things you're really genuinely curious about." Yeah, great, thanks Big O. You're the best.

And last thought, sometimes when I've started to think I've got a pretty good grasp of the whole zoomed out bullet point Big Map of Reality – including the Continuum of Consciousness stuff we laid out a lot of yesterday, and Pure Beingness and the Absolute Ground and all that – I've felt like kind of a patient smile from Omega, as though in spite of all my mental stretching these months, it's *still* so much bigger than I have yet to even begin to fathom. It's not conde-scending or patronizing, but it's like an ant starting to realize there's more to the universe than its underground ant colony where it's so far spent its life. "You mean there's grass out there? You mean there's a tree? A lot of trees? No way! A mountain? Impossible! An Ocean? Blasphemy! And by the way, what's a tree and a mountain and an ocean?"

Relatively, that underground ant colony might be about how much of Multidimensional Reality I've glimpsed so far. So maybe I'm onto something with this whole parallel universes thing, maybe I'm catching a scent, hot on a trail, or it's also a distinct possibility that I'm partly or completely misperceiving those glimpses – maybe I'm picking up the fourth dimension in the tesseverse or something – and my little multiple alternate realities theory is a red herring and not it at all. Who knows? I'm assuming Omega does, but a lot of good that's done so far. Anyway, interesting to chew on.

Ω Ω Ω Ω

Definitely intriguing, even just to mull over. We've already entered mindboggling territory again today.

Yeah, sorry to rebogglify your brain after you probably spent the whole night debogglifying it. But I just want to bold the point again, that I definitely do get the strong vibe that the words *big* or *huge* or massive don't even begin to touch how inconceivably and incom-prehensibly vast the whole Omniverse really is. That so far this weekend, in spite of my best and most loquacious efforts, we really haven't – well maybe we've scratched the surface, but we haven't done much more than that, in comparison to the actual vastness and ever expanding fractaling complexity of Multidimensional Reality, not to mention the Infinite Everpresent Benevolent Isness and the Benevolent Pre-Light Ultimate Ground of All Existence, that precedes and holds All That Is.

So we've potentially got the tesseverse, and maybe even extra dimensions of it beyond adding the fourth dimension – you know, maybe one tesseverse is just one face or side of a geometrical object that's a whole dimension beyond that, and then another one beyond that – and then we've got the snow globes within snow globes within snow globes of multiverses, more snow globes of entire tesseverses than there are stars in our universe.

And then either adding in our little thought experiment – of the possibility of two or three gazillion different parallel worlds or alternate realities for each of those – or if that's off base, maybe adding in a placeholder for something almost equally vast and complex and incomprehensible that might exist and that I've been misperceiving as parallel worlds.

And then bringing in a great many levels of greater Multidimensional Reality – each near infinite in scope, and with its own physics and range of potential expression and creative outfractaling and its own almost infinite number of unique snow globe worlds. So all of that added together, that's some high octane primo imboggliciousness right there. That's a fairly good sized Omniverse, as Omniverses go. So yeah, it's interesting to try to even begin to start to think about, but I just wanted to throw it into the mix before we got into the specifics of the future scenes.

Just in case I was starting to think I had a bit of a handle on any of this.

Yeah, just in case. And what sounds good to me, now that I've named that inkling of parallel worlds or diverging timelines or multiple realities, is to just close that folder again and take it off the table, and put it in a drawer, to keep things more simple and manageable as I get into the specific scenes that I saw. Just putting this idea away for now, and we can go with the working theory that Omega saw, you know, a thousand or ten thousand possible unfoldings, and saw which ones were more likely and which ones less, and that these are the events that are more likely on our current track.

Or I guess we don't really need to have any theory of where they came from at all, but we'll assume these scenarios haven't already happened in any future – they aren't already set in stone anywhere – and that they *are* impactable, influenceable, changeable to varying degrees, depending on how we navigate and how tall an order it is to steer clear of specific icebergs. That's how I'm most comfortable sharing some of these not so ideal possible future scenarios, and that was also my genuine sense as I was watching these scenes pass by. That there's time to change course on some of them, to varying degrees. Okay, I think I got all that said. So now let's get back to our regularly scheduled program. What I saw on my near death vacation.

CHAPTER 41

Alright, so could you set the stage a bit? You were connecting with the Omega Being, feeling really quenched in that connection, and then something else opened.

Yeah, so at some point there was this whole other current that started happening, maybe about a third of the way into the whole experience. But it's fuzzy, because it was all outside of time as we're used to it, and all that I experienced could never be crammed into the brief amount of Earth time that my body was legally deadish, and yet somehow my brain or my consciousness absorbed enough of it that I remember it.

So while I was immersed in feeling this Deep Belonging with this not yet named Multidimensional Being, just soaking in Peace and Goodness and Love and Presence and Homeness, while that was happening, this side current also started happening, where I was being shown a lot of different scenes and kind of info-packets, of potential future events and situations.

And just in case I haven't really driven this home, even if I had really felt like I was shown *The* Future, that of course still wouldn't necessarily mean it would turn out to be validated. Like I said yesterday, for all we know, maybe my brain was in hyper overdrive as my body was checking out of Hotel Earth, and I went into a dreamlike hyper creative warp speed state and created all of this out of my unconscious. We have to keep that as a possibility.

And then maybe my bridging sessions are merely residual brain wave re-synchronizations with that original trauma-induced, dissociative, internally generated illusional patterning. I'm not sure what I just said, but it sounded kind of impressive, and that's what matters. But really, that kind of thing is something I think we have to hold as a possibility, to keep our conclusion-leaning minds a little looser. But that whole side show started up, and part of my awareness was taking that in, while the rest of me was taking in this Light Being in front of me.

And actually instead of *in front of me* I prefer the term *before me*, because, you know, I didn't have physical eyes, or a literal physical body, even though I still had a mental concept of having one. So it was like I was taking in 360 degrees all at once, maybe you could call it omnocular vision, where *every* direction was right in front of me, there wasn't a behind me or beside me. And there wasn't even – like outer space – there wasn't even a default orientation of right side up or upside down, an above me or below me. But yeah, I was mostly focused on this Being before me, and then these images and scenes and info-packets started coming in at the same time.

What do you mean info-packets?

Like in addition to images and scenes, there were details or impressions of the larger picture behind and beyond what I was seeing. An infilling of more details sometimes, to help me understand what I was seeing.

Were there sounds or smells? Did you touch anything or feel a breeze or feel anything?

There were visuals and sounds and information. No smells or physically feeling anything. It wasn't like I was placed in the scenes, more like watching them from a distance – or not always from a distance but as a non-participatory observer.

Was it intense for you to see all these images come in? Was it emotionally charged for you?

Mostly no. Most of my emotional awareness was on what was happening with this Being, the Deep Quenching and Acceptance and Lovedness and Belonging. Some of it did have some real impact, and we'll get to that, but not like devastating or a big stomach punch, I was mostly pretty removed from it. Also I had never taken in so much information so quickly before, so it didn't really – there wasn't really time for it all to land as fully as some of its gravity would suggest maybe it should've.

Ω

And how long did it go on? Did it get interrupted when you got pulled away to return to your body or was it already finished?

Well, I'll go into this more as we go, but like I said yesterday during our intro, there were actually three different inflashes, separated by two little breaks or intermissions. And after the third one finished, that whole side stream felt done, just leaving me with the one main current of being with this Multidimensional Being. And then pretty quickly after that I got the Vaudeville hook and was yanked back into my body.

And was it clear to you that that Multidimensional Being was showing you these images? Did the two seem connected?

Nothing was conveyed about it, just the images and related information started streaming in, but to me it was just obvious this

Being was orchestrating it, fully or partly, rather than it just being coincidental.

Anything else before we get into what you saw?

I don't think so.

Alright. So you've talked about some of this in our coffee conversations, and a lot of what you've shared has been what I would've expected – like the impact of global warming – but some I had never heard of or thought about, and one of those that never would've occurred to me was around voluntary life completion. Could we start with that one?

Damn, you're going for the squirmy, cringy, controversial one right out of the gate? That's really courageous of you, to be willing to risk people being irate with me like that.

It's a risk I'm willing to take. But remember you'll be anonymous.

Yeah, til I'm not. I don't have any qualms about talking about the more obvious ones or the less controversial ones, but this one – it's like which of these things is not like the others, it was really its own out of the blue, stand alone thing – and I just don't love the idea of being maybe the first one to say this is possibly something that starts to happen, at least in one possible future unfolding.

And I know it's probably that inflated sense of potential influence rearing its persistent head again, but the last thing I want is for my sharing about this to somehow contribute in some way to it coming about. So yeah, I'm not overflowing with eagerness at the moment, I wasn't expecting us to jump right into this one, but really, we're going to get to it anyway – within the next hour probably – so I guess why not go ahead and get it out of the way right out of the shoot.

And also, just to reiterate, it felt like I was given a glimpse of these possible future events exactly because they *weren't* all set in stone for us, not because they were already chiseled into the marble of destiny. And since I haven't mentioned this in the last five minutes, the unconscious is amazing at synthesizing different pieces of hardly noticed information and turning it into something new, so this all might have just come from there. And as always, naming that as a possibility doesn't make it less of one. And how else can I delay here? Yeah, the requisite disclaimer, the views expressed in this inflash do not necessarily represent those of the messenger and should not be construed as such. Okay, that's probably about all the soft padding I can pre-gather as I brace for potential impact.

Ω Ω

So now that you're well padded, how about if we start with you giving some background about what led up to it becoming widespread? Voluntary life completion. Filling in a bit of the back story.

Okay, so one of the good things I saw was, as you'd expect, there was some real health and medical care progress, like cancer was mostly wiped out if not caught too late, mostly very treatable, and Alzheimer's, dementia and mental decline were greatly reduced. Some medications really reduced the whole – I don't remember what those brain proteins and toxins are called that cause a lot of the problem, but those were now able to be mostly nipped in the bud.

Also there were some real age extenders, youth extenders, that prolonged healthy years some in different ways. Like some medications or supplements that reduced appetite without any side effects and others that converted white fat to brown fat so that obesity was way down, and some other treatments to lengthen telomeres – those ends of chromosomes that contribute to aging as they shorten – and big breakthroughs connected to gene editing, which enabled taking care of a whole lot of diseases and issues. So all this together – all these different advances all together – added maybe ten or so healthier years on average. But of course, bodies still age and decline, and at some point give out, just the good to fair years got extended some, on average, before the inevitable declining years. So you know, 90 was the new 80, which was the new 70. And even though—

—I just realized we haven't said yet how far in the future these scenes were taking place in.

Oh right, good point. I would say just about everything I saw in the whole experience was mid to late century. Say from 2050 to 2090 or so, but don't quote me on that, you know, in a book. And actually the third flash packet extended beyond that some, but I'll name it when we get there. So anyway, this added up to a *lot* of seniors, and a lot more elderly than ever before, and the vast majority still stopped working in their 60s, but now they were living longer than ever. Many weren't that far past halfway through their adult lives when they quit working. You know, about 45 adult years behind them, and maybe 30 or so to go.

And even though some health issues were more under control, so more people lived healthier longer, aging seniors still had significantly more health care needs than middle aged or younger people, especially as they entered their 80s and 90s and beyond. And most needed more financial support than they had through their pensions and social security and IRAs and savings. Thirty plus years is a long time to live after retirement, and that was becoming the norm. And you mix that in with a lower and lower birthrate – with it becoming fairly rare to have more than one child, very rare to have more than two, and really common to have none – and things were getting really skewed in most countries, with way, way more elderly than younger, and the labor and economic numbers just didn't add up.

Ω Ω Ω

So in terms of working adults for all the different positions in a society, compared to all the seniors who weren't in the labor pool and who needed varying degrees of extra care and medical resources – as well as needing a lot of supplemental financial support, plus just usual needs like consumer goods and services – all of this added up to there being an increasingly dire imbalance to a degree that had never existed before. Fewer and fewer working adults had to be responsible for everything that needed to be done, including more people directly or indirectly working in the health care and support fields for the needs of people of advanced age than ever before.

And then on top of that, it was just no longer possible to ignore the massive effects of climate change as well as environmental toxification through human-made chemicals, and other human-caused environmental imbalances. And as we'll get to soon here, there were huge and growing environmental and therefore economic challenges – like shortages of food and water, natural disasters, dustbowls and wildfires and droughts and floods, rising sea levels, a whole list – plus a lot of accumulatively toxic particles pretty much literally everywhere, in soil and water and even floating around in the air.

So there were really huge global and regional challenges, and massive efforts were underway around climate rebalancing, like carbon capture and tree planting and hundreds of other things, and all of that was requiring a massive economic investment and resources, and a huge number of workers. Some things could be automatized and robotized, but people were still needed to manage and oversee that, and there were still plenty of things only humans could do.

So add it all up and we've got a situation here. Economically, countries didn't have the resources to have – on top of the usual percentage of working age people out of the work force – additionally almost half of all adults were retired from working, while still needing resources and financial support and medical and support care, and there also weren't the resources to take on these huge environmental rebalancing initiatives, but they couldn't afford not to take them on either.

And with more and more natural disasters, rising sea level, relocation, huge economic pressures, all kinds of environmental fallout for past actions, just a huge list of things added to the mix, it just wasn't sustainable. It wasn't tenable. It wasn't survivable as basically functional countries and societies. Something really drastic had to be done, or all might be lost. Governments and societies were incredibly strained and things were getting beyond desperate.

So that's the setup, and as I'm about to do the big reveal here, it's kind of interesting or telling that I'm not much afraid of death, but saying something controversial with two phone recorders staring at me, taunting me, *that's* pretty flusterizing. But it's just a slippery slope, what I saw happen, and it gets steeper as you go down it, and it's not pleasant to really look straight at this and to really – well I'll skip the pre-commentary and just say it. And for the tenth time, it's not a forgone conclusion that it will happen it all.

Understood.

CHAPTER 42

So basically what I saw was that one of the things that became really widespread in an attempt to try to deal with this untenable situation was voluntary life completion, an option for seniors a certain age or older. And the exact age was different in different countries, and changed and got earlier as time passed, but it wasn't allowed earlier than that legally mandated earliest age unless there were significant detrimental health issues.

And this was almost worldwide – not all countries did it but more and more – and some countries had more skewed demographics than others, had a lower birth rate than the already lower and lower average, and couldn't bring in enough workers through immigration anymore, and also there was a huge backlash in some counties, around so many non-native workers from different cultural backgrounds coming in.

Plus there was insurmountable government debt, there was civil unrest from shortages of essential products and services – due to the lack of available workers and climate and environmental changes and degradation – there was the huge increase in spending on environmental rebalancing initiatives, and whatever else the various influences were.

So all added up, the whole situation was just a huge, unsustainable economic and infrastructure and resource and labor burden on countries, that none of the technological advances were enough to sufficiently counteract and mitigate. Things were really strained and the whole fabric of society, of functional national and local governments – of functional cities and states and countries – was really at risk.

And it was beyond obvious at this point that carbon capture and Earth rebalancing initiatives weren't optional. They had to be the highest priority to at least *try* to bring the Earth back from the brink to avoid even further environmental and societal and governmental degradation and collapse. And that significantly added to the number of work positions that needed filled, along with health care and senior care related positions taking a really costly percentage of the already shrinking and limited labor force, that fewer and fewer young adults were entering because there were fewer and fewer people having children that could enter the labor market 20 years later. And all of that added together had huge economic and societal costs.

And with all the stressors making the fabric of governmental order really shaky, some countries or regions were teetering towards total disarray. There were militias and uprisings and skirmishes and violent, out of control protests – which, you know, doesn't take a crystal ball – and there were strengthening rebellionesque factions in a lot of countries, which had already been happening but it was getting worse and worse, which led to more authoritarian governmental responses, which led to more rebellion, so it was getting really dicey. Not a dystopian wasteland of full on anarchy in most places, but things were at best on edge.

I saw an image of – well, because of drones and common place jetpacks, and personal commuter drones, fences just didn't do the trick anymore, so I saw an image of the White House with a complete wire mesh chain link fence type dome, all the way around it and over it, starting at the perimeter, to stop people and drones from swooping in – from flying in alone, or even more dangerously, in organized flash droves – and overwhelming White House security, even though it was way more advanced that what it is now.

Ω

That's really interesting. A wire mesh dome over and around the White House.

Yeah, as well as around other federal and state buildings and other buildings and facilities that needed extra protection, in the U.S. and around the world. Perimeter dome fencing was getting more and more necessary and commonplace, as ground and road fencing and gates and barricades didn't do the trick anymore. So these were also getting more common around factories and plants and warehouses and some homes, and some were even retractable. Old fashioned ten foot fences just didn't stop people, solo or in organized infiltrations, and even advanced automatic defense systems at the White House and elsewhere couldn't stop every single drone in mass attacks, with fireworks level explosives or stronger, or sometimes they had like automatic guns, or different kinds of gas canisters, or other kinds of weapons, and they could break windows and so on.

The drones had those?

Yeah, so they could do some real damage and sometimes take lives, which gave rise to dome fencing. So all in all things were really getting shaky, but this population imbalance was one of the biggest pressure points. Bottom line is the ratio between working age people and retired, relatively higher needs seniors was just completely unsustainable, and even more so with all the environmental rebalancing initiatives.

So what I saw was, a couple of countries in the most dire situations adapted the earliest versions of it first – of voluntary life completion – at about the same time, and then a third country joined in soon after. Then the dominoes fell after that.

Do you know which countries?

Well I don't *know* that any of this is going to happen, and also I already really feel on thin ice here, and according to what I saw, pretty much every country and their dog got on board really soon after, so every country holds, you know, responsibility for their choice – whether it was a brilliant last ditch solution or an immoral one or some of both – regardless of who went first. And like I said earlier, I just want to be careful about what I say actually somehow having some negative impact on how things play out, or even towards how someone might feel about how they might play out. So I'll just say the first three were in some of the most dire situations a little earlier than most countries, in terms of age demographics.

And then once a few countries started kind of testing the waters, it quickly spread from there, like if *they're* doing it, it must not be that bad. So it got quickly adopted around the world, with maybe 75 percent or more of countries doing it in some form, and in terms of population like 80 or 90 percent were in countries doing this.

I lost you.

The total populations of the countries that got on board over say a 15 or 20 year period added up to around 80 to 90 percent of the Earth's population. And different countries had different fine print about how this worked and had varying minimal ages to qualify – which became earlier and earlier over some time – but this was seen as the least worst option to try to really start to balance out the numbers a little more, and to have a chance to be able to stabilize things and sustain things for all of society in a workable way. As opposed to the alternative of not surviving as a country, and maybe pretty much global societal collapse, along with people dying from lack of food and medical care, and from violence and so forth.

There was just so much pressure from so many angles, something radical had to be done. So this was like a desperate extreme austerity measure. And there's strength in numbers, and younger to middle aged adults largely supported it as a necessary evil or necessary best available option to help improve the chances that society didn't completely fall apart or leave tens of millions of people – or more in some countries – without their basic needs taken care of and with a very low quality of life, with things quickly worsening.

Ω Ω

So, without further ado, drum roll, the deal was, or actually I can repeat all that background again if you didn't quite get it.

No, I'm good.

You sure? I could probably cover it more succinctly the second time through, which would save us some time.

I'm very sure.

Your loss. Okay, so the deal was – literally the deal was – governments started offering a financial incentive to the family if a senior agreed to voluntarily end their life. And different countries had different ages like I said, but it started with around 90 years old as the youngest qualifying age to do this, partly to just kind of test it out and get people acclimated, and that got things started but it wasn't nearly enough to have anywhere near as big an impact as was needed given the circumstances. And then it pretty quickly started working its way down, to mid-eighties, and low eighties, and even upper seventies, and some countries even went to 76, which was the lowest I saw, except people younger than that – in their 60s or early 70s and later even younger – if they had significant resource-heavy health issues then they could qualify too.

So if a senior at the currently minimally allowed age or older decided to voluntarily end their life, voluntary life completion – and as always, I don't know exactly what these things are called and it would've varied, but that's what came to me – then their family got not just potentially more unused inheritance than they would've gotten five or ten or fifteen years later, if there was any – though most seniors needed most or all of what they had – but they also got a nice life completion volunteer survivors' payout.

And it was based on the actuarial tables of estimated likely savings in total medical and support related costs, and also estimated savings in federal and state senior support programs, plus social security savings and sometimes pension funds – maybe life insurance settlements were thrown in here and there – and similar. So a mix of federal and more local governmental agencies, and also private companies, that would all contribute if it meant most likely saving them a chunk of money in the mid and long run, especially when averaged out over a lot of people.

And you saw it being offered to people as young as 76? How long did it take to get down that low?

Yeah, I'm fuzzy on how many countries went that low and how long it took, but maybe over say a 15 or 20 year span it worked its way down, pretty commonly to 80 or younger, depending on the country and time point. It was pretty quickly adopted because of the dire situation. And there was also a gradual loosening of the requirements for younger than that as long as they had resource-intensive health issues, resource-heavy circumstances.

And remember, on average people tended to be healthier like ten years longer, so a lot of these volunteers still had some real healthy and enjoyable years left, but the more seniors that participated, the less resources would be used, and the more money would be saved – in general, and then specifically on extensive and expensive medical care that a fair chunk of seniors would eventually need in the last months or years of their lives.

So it was a numbers game, the law of averages. The more people that took part, the more money would be saved, the less resources used, and the more workers would be freed up to work in other fields – which with more than half of all adults out of the labor force in total, it was desperately needed, especially with the all the climate and environmental rebalancing initiatives adding even more to the already huge labor pressure.

CHAPTER 43

And it was about, do the right thing for your country and your family and future generations and younger current ones. Be selfless, be a hero, to help society make it through this unprecedented difficult time. You've had your turn, you've had a good run, and things are looking a lot rougher for those that follow you than you had it coming through, partly because of your generation's and earlier generations' selfishness and greed and using fossil fuels and toxic chemicals and over-logging and over-fishing and the whole list. Now don't suck up all the very limited resources that should be used to help rebalance the climate and the environment, and to help the next generations thrive, or at least to help them hopefully ward off or postpone the complete and total collapsing or meltdown of our society and our country, and of organized and fairly functional human civilization.

Do it for the children, who deserve a fair shake. Do it to so there are fewer people with health care needs over the next years, to help the system not be overwhelmed and to free up workers. Do it to help ease the tax burden and financial stress facing the next generation and beyond, and the huge debt and lack of resources facing governments and greater society.

Don't hog up all the resources that society needs in order to function. You've already had a good 80 plus years on the planet, mostly pretty damn easy compared to now. So now it's time to do the right thing to help younger people have a little more of a chance at some degree of quality of life, not to mention basic necessities and a basically working economy and a more balanced planet.

So that's how it was presented, and there was a huge media and social media push to get this normalized. A patriotic, selfless, generous, brave, heroic gift to society and to others and to the next generations. It's not too late to be remembered a hero. The ultimate gift. Your name added to a memorial wall, most towns or cities or states or provinces had a memorial wall for the heroes who gave their remaining sunset years to help there be more sunrises. Lots of memorial benches. A metal of courage and sacrifice going to the family, their name read on Volunteers' Day, the works. A fitting slogan would be something like, "Give the Greatest Gift. Be Remembered a Hero." So it was like, contribute to the best available solution for these dire times, and be honored for your brave and beautiful and selfless sacrifice.

And a little side thing that came in was that some adult kids would pressure their parents, couching it in more of this generous selfless offering for the future, but they actually wanted to cash in. It wasn't a massive sum, it was – I don't know, and it varied by country and specific situation like age and health assessment and genetic health profile – but maybe survivors of volunteers got a third or half of what was predicted would likely have been spent on that person if they lived another 10 or 15 years or whatever the averages were, based on their details and the actuarial tables.

And somewhere in there it's also catching the 20 or 30 percent or so who sooner or later would have hugely costly medical procedures and recovery and intensive care and around the clock nursing and support staff and expensive testing and so on. Plus it's easing up the sum total of things like social security and government senior medical care and other programs, and food and housing and other basic resources. So it adds up to a lot of money saved and a lot of workers freed up from home visits, hospitals, senior care facilities, and all those direct and indirect support positions, so they could fill other much needed positions like the usual range plus the huge global warming reversal and environmental cleanup initiatives. So along with economics, this was about freeing up resources, and having more workers available to do all that needed to be done to try to put a dent in things.

$$\Omega$$

So basically, once you were approaching more advanced years, and no longer contributing by being in the labor force, regardless of your wisdom or whatever else you had to offer, just absolutely coldly, the earlier your life completed, the more the different stakeholders would save, and the more resources would be freed up that were sorely needed elsewhere to help try to reverse course from where things were quickly headed.

So the more of a contribution that decision made, or was estimated to make over the next years, the more your family would get. Or you could give it to a charity, or government programs or to government debt, which probably got you a special memorial or something, just guessing there, but it could go wherever you designated it to. So yeah, that was voluntary life completion.

Could you describe that beach scene you told me about? That image really stuck with me.

Yeah, so this scene flashed in of an older couple at an end of life celebration. Instead of funerals after the fact, they had end of life celebrations, with the person getting to be there and take part in it and hear all the kind words while they still had ears to hear. And I don't mean one size fits all for all the different countries and cultures and individuals doing this, but that's what I saw. And this couple didn't look really old and limited and didn't feel old and limited.

So they seemed healthy? How old would you say they were?

Yeah, they didn't look like they had anything limiting their enjoyment of life and ability to really live it. Maybe they were 80 or 82 or so. And maybe there were 40 or 50 people there, plus more on live video all around the walls. The walls of this big hall or sanctuary or whatever it was, were seamless video panels, the whole wall was just all seamless video panels, all the way around.

Same with the center aisle floor. It was a really high def realistic creek running forward along that path, with sounds exactly like if it was real, and a little mist, and the walls were showing like beautiful forests. And then interspersed along the walls were people participating virtually. I remember wondering if the creek turns off when someone's walking down the aisle, seems like they'd get dizzy. But anyway, this couple of honor, they were sitting on the stage or in the front, facing all their friends and family so they could see each other, and someone was emceeing or facilitating. Different people sharing and speaking, honoring their lives, and there were videos of their lives, what you would expect from a memorial, except, they were there to witness it.

And actually, I think that makes a lot of sense, you know? Why wait and celebrate someone's life when they aren't around to hear it? Not sure how that would work when we don't know when someone will die in most cases, but maybe they could just hold them at like 75 or 78 to increase the chances you didn't wait too long. But anyway, with voluntary life completion it was just – the sense that came in was it became the norm to do it this way for volunteers.

$$\Omega\,\Omega$$

And then the scene changed and I saw them at the ocean, and in their case the life celebration service I had just seen was maybe a week before. It might be a little much to try to enjoy "This Was

Your Life" when you only had minutes left to breathe the air of Earth. So they were at the ocean on a beach, some days later, just out of reach of the waves, and family and maybe a few friends were gathered around, saying goodbye.

And they were sitting or lying next to each other in two reclining beach lounger chairs. They were facing the ocean, and there were maybe 10 or 12 loved ones around them and two – let's say life completion specialists, these two professionals who administer the injection or give the pills or hold the pillow over their face or whatever it is. Let's assume not that last one. And their family was taking turns holding their hands and embracing them, tears all around, and their dog was there too, on one of their laps, a big hug goodbye to the dog, and then the other one called the dog and it hopped on their lap and they hugged it goodbye too.

And then some of the family and friends left with the dog, including two kids – I assumed grandkids – so maybe the family members who would rather their last memory be of them still alive, who didn't want to watch them die, they went a few hundred feet away along the beach and waited there. And then, lying there side by side, with the ocean in front of them and some loved ones still with them, they faced each other, looked at each other, held hands with each other, closed their eyes, and that was that. Their bodies breathed their last breath.

It was somber, there was grief, tears, family hugging each other, consoling each other, but it was all by choice, all voluntary. They were healthy. They were fine. And they might have had five or ten really good years left, and maybe more not too bad ones after that. It was really poignant to watch.

And this is just occurring to me now, it wasn't part of what I saw, but I could imagine in the intensity of that final goodbye, some adult children might understandably change their minds, literally at the last minute, and you know, crumble into tears, begging their parent or parents not to go through with it.

Or even some of these life completion volunteers might be there about to take their end of life pill or whatever, and suddenly say "Screw this, shit's getting a little too real for me, I'm outta here. I just wanted to be there for the nice life celebration last week and hear everyone lie about how amazing I am, but now I'm going to the Bahamas with my savings, and good riddance to my selfish, greedy kids." You would think those two things would happen sometimes. It's a little easier to be brave before the dragon is actually walking towards you, staring you down, taking in a big, hot breath.

CHAPTER 44

But one of the main senses of this whole thing was how much and how quickly it became a social norm and a widespread social pressure, maybe as much of a social norm and pressure as back when divorce just wasn't often done by decent, moral, respectable, God fearing people, some of whom used the tried and true arsenic method of relationship completion instead.

But it became selfish to not do the right thing for your country and for the Earth and for your children and grandchildren or nieces and nephews or just for the next generations. Selfish not to free up health care workers and other support workers for other needed positions by ensuring you didn't live long enough to become a resource-intensive burden. Selfish not to call your already long life done, for a larger purpose greater than yourself.

So it was be remembered a hero, or else feel the silent or not so silent shame when you walk down the street, that you're putting your sunset years ahead of younger people just trying to have a present and a future anywhere close to as long as you've already had, while they also have to deal with the repercussions of climate change and environmental degradation and desecration and the resulting economic and social strain and fracturing, that your generation greatly contributed to.

So, that was the deal. And I really don't know what to make of it. I mean I do get the perspective that in this possible future, things were much more strained than ever before in modern times, and it just wasn't possible to plug all the leaks that needed plugging. They needed to reduce the weight of the boat or the whole thing would sink, and you know, desperate times call for desperate measures, the needs of the many outweigh the needs of the few, they already lived long and prospered, that kind of perspective.

And also I think we can safely say that for the bulk of human existence, for tribes and clans and villages and close knit larger family groups, the goal wasn't to live as long as biologically possible at any expense to the tribe, which would have to use scarce and precious resources to take care of you. And that also just isn't tenable in a larger society of tens or hundreds of millions, where more than half of all adults weren't working due to retirement or other reasons, and maybe roughly one or two out of five working adults were needed to help in some way in the care of nonworking adults, while new environmental rebalancing initiatives were desperately needing so many labor resources as well. Just clearly not viable.

But it also absolutely doesn't feel right to end the life of someone perfectly healthy, even if they volunteered – which from what I saw was sometimes through strong arming – when they might have had some real life left to live, several high quality years. It just doesn't sit well at all, removing the potential stragglers before they start straggling, to make sure they don't straggle down the already struggling pack.

Ω

And in terms of it being allowed for people below 78 or 76 – whatever the bottom age was of a particular country in a particular year – if there was a resource draining diagnosis, then where does it stop? What about a 40 year old who could live three or four more decades with a huge amount of medical costs and human support? Do they have that offer? Should they? Should they be under pressure to do the right thing for the greater good and not be a mean selfish resource drainer? What about a 30 year old? A 20 year old? As soon as you turn 18?

And once you open this whole road, the younger it is, the more money and resources are saved, so there's a lot of societal incentive there to keep the pressure on, but then where does it stop? 85 isn't wrong when things are this dire, but obviously 84 is? Well 84 is a nice solid even number but 83, that's clearly too young, and therefore that's a travesty and just plain wrong. Do I hear 82? 80? 78? Sold at 76 to the happy and healthy seniors with the selfish ungrateful kids eager for cash.

So I can get it from one perspective, to a degree, in a dire situation, more people needing supported in various ways than there are workers to help, plus other jobs need done to try to right the ship that past generations didn't take good care steering, including that senior generation. But it's a slippery slope, and in me there's this nagging sense that no, even *starting* to do that really loses something, puts a price on a healthy human life, and it just isn't okay, though what if the alternative is unavoidably way more dire for older and younger adults, and also children. For people who haven't lived much of a life at all yet?

If someone *has to* run into a burning building and save a child at the cost of their own life, makes sense for it to be someone who's already in or near their sunset years, rather than someone younger with more life left to live. But in this situation it's just not such immediate or zoomed in cause and effect – this child dies unless this senior does. But zoomed out, it still kind of adds up to something that's along the same lines, in that more younger people would die, over the next years, if some older people who had already had a long life didn't volunteer to lighten society's load.

And really, this kind of thing is already a reality in a way, like if someone was dying of cancer and they could be saved for five million dollars, does that happen and who pays for it? And if there are half a million people with that same cancer, that gets substantial real quick. And does their age impact that? If someone is 95, it just *does* feels more natural to me to let them die of cancer than an eight year old, which feels very, very different. And I assume for organ transplants, if they have to choose, they save the 20 year old and let the 85 year old's life come to an end. We intuitively get that.

And safe to say, close to a hundred percent of grandparents, if there wasn't enough food for the winter and there were no other options, they would probably choose to go out in the snow one night or something, and let their life end, so they didn't take any more food or resources, to help their grandchildren survive the winter. Even if they likely had 20 or more good years left in their life.

$$\Omega \, \Omega$$

So there's different perspectives, and like I said, I don't really know what to make of it, but it definitely created – and as I talk about it, creates – an uncomfortable, squirmy, something's not right here feeling. And again, at what age does it suddenly switch from an acceptable desperate solution into inhuman and inhumane? Kicking in the offer for people who are 85 is a sad necessity, but 84, now that's a moral abomination and we wouldn't do that, we aren't monsters. Or paying a healthy happy 78 year old to end their life, that's okay, extraordinary times and measures, but 77, that's obviously too young and morally reprehensible. And by the way, if this were to really happen, and in the time range I saw, then hundreds of millions of younger people, already alive now, will in their later years be faced with that choice.

Do you have any sense of the percentage of people in the qualifying age group who went that route?

I should clarify if I didn't already, you could do it later than when first eligible, but you got less payout, your kids or a charity or whatever got less payout the longer you waited. A hundred year old's sum total expected future health care costs and resource requirements and economic toll are on average going to be a lot lower than an 80 year old's.

You also got very little if you had a diagnosis that meant imminent death with low medical expenses. Little money and resources saved, little money offered. And moderate for moderate. "The bad news is, you've got six months left to live, some of that in the ICU. The good news is, we could just go ahead and take care of all this for you next week if you prefer, and give your kids a nice payout check. How's does 8am Monday work for you?" And by the way, if it's done by giving them a shot, I wonder if they rub alcohol on the arm first. Wouldn't want them to get an infection now would we?

But to answer your question, not sure exactly, and it increased as social adaptation or adoption shifted towards it, but maybe 15% were doing it pretty quickly after they were eligible, within say six months, and another 40% to 50% were doing it later, two or three or five or eight years later, once they were more limited and heading towards more real difficulty. Even though waiting meant less payout, it also meant more pretty good years, which feels better to me. Doing it once their quality of life was starting to significantly go down, that's easier for me to get my head around. My heart around.

And then even for those who declined the early and mid opportunities, once death was really on its way, some at that point chose to speed the process up, which didn't provide much money for the kids or whoever, but a little, and it saved some suffering. So this whole concept of checking out of Hotel Earth a little early was just much more in the zeitgeist than it is now.

Ω Ω Ω

And actually, calling it checking out of Hotel Earth feels too cavalier, not taken to heart. Of course it's a hugely significant, poignant thing, the end of someone's life. And I can say that kind of thing about the end of my *own* life – partly as a way to convey that huge shift of orientation that happened during the Big Event – but it didn't resonate to hear myself say that so casually about anyone else's. So let's try a take two, this whole concept of – let's call it preemptive conscious life completion – was a lot more in the cultural zeitgeist than it currently is. And that *does* resonate with me, no squirm factor there. And I like the way that came out, preemptive conscious life completion. Or maybe conscious preemptive life completion, but basically, when death is approaching, often along with some real suffering, having the freedom and the agency and the empowerment and the dignity and the self compassion – and also maybe the compassion for your loved ones as well – to make that decision if it resonates as best, once the end is really in sight.

And back to voluntary life completion, maybe I kind of said this, but there was a real feeling of the tide really turning in terms of social pressure to do it and some judgment and disapproval, even scorn, about seniors much past 80 who hadn't done it yet. Look who's selfish by not terminating their existence! And also I could imagine that some unscrupulous religious or spiritual leaders might urge their congregation or followers to do the right thing, and to go ahead and call it done, and have the money donated to them or their organization. Seems like a lot of potential for bad actors with their own agendas.

And one last side thought about it and we'll move on, there *is* something that catches my attention about – leaving aside the pesky little ethical aspects of all this for a second, who needs 'em, and good riddance – but like, just imagining a scenario where you just knew your whole life that if you lived to reach say 82, you would have one last year for a goodbye tour, or start earlier and have two or three years if you like, but the day you turned 83, that would be it. That would be the absolute top end of the length of your life.

Like if globally societies just happened to evolve where that was the understanding, the accepted norm – you do the selfless elder thing and not weigh down your tribe, village or country. You have a beautiful life celebration, and you hand the reins and keys over to the younger generations. If that had just been how it always was, for millennia. It wouldn't have taken too many tweaks in societal development for that to have become an ingrained enculturated norm that everyone adheres to and expects and understands. That human life just has a hard stop on the day of your 83rd birthday, if you're lucky enough to live that long.

Ω Ω Ω Ω

Or maybe imagine like if somehow our species just naturally had a hard biological expiration date, exactly 83 years after opening, and that was just the way things were biologically, so everyone knew that was just the deal. That's probably better for this little thought experiment, not as loaded – so strike the first one from the record – and just imagine for a minute it's just a biological fact of life, you hit 83 and your spirit's free. Or 85 or 80 or whatever you like for this little thought experiment, but just trying on that basic concept.

There's just something in that that kind of – that kind of gets my attention. Knowing there's a definite endpoint in your life, a finite number of grains of sand in the lifetime hourglass, if the glass doesn't break before that. I wonder if it would inform and impact and influence how people live, and make life a little more precious. When you hit 63, okay I have at *most* 20 years left, the sand is falling fast, and I've just been sitting here streaming TV shows and movies most of the month. Better get busy living while I can. Maybe help others or the Earth more. Or at 53, 30 years left at most, what else do I want to do with the remaining sand in my lifetime hourglass?

I'm just acknowledging there's something that sparks my – well interest is a little too casual, but there's something poignantly intriguing about what it might be like, how it might impact your life, to know your whole life that that's absolutely the last train stop if you haven't disembarked by then. There's something poignant about that, that I could imagine might potentially add some degree of richness and depth and non-taking-for-grantedness to the years passing. So just a wondering of what impact that might have. But yeah, all in all it's mind stretching in a different kind of way, to open all this up, but also for me it does feel pretty uncomfortable and – to use that technical term again – a little squirmy to talk about it.

I've been resisting the temptation to weigh in and get into another dialogue about it – which is my necessary modus operandi this weekend – but as I said over coffee when we talked a bit about this, I agree it's uncomfortable and brings up a lot, and I don't know exactly where the line is either, or how the cost benefit analysis comes out if things really were so dire that there would be more deaths and younger deaths without implementing something like this.

Yeah, I can really see why under dire circumstances that whole thing might be explored to some degree, but it's still quite a thing, and then it got all peer pressury and manipulated, with some non-transparent, self serving agendas getting in there, mucking it all up. Rather than that ancient offering of a selfless elder, freely choosing to generously serve their tribe in a way they intuit is what's most in service for the greater good. And third or fourth time to say it, but once you open that whole thing up, where do you draw the line?

Anyway, okay, now that I've just sprawled that lovely possible future onto the table, I guess we'll just leave it there conspicuously and move on to the next thing.

CHAPTER 45

Alright, so moving on, the next thing is, what else did you see during these future scenes?

A lot. The other things in that first flash packet weren't in as much depth and detail, but they also weren't as out of the blue or as completely outside my preexisting framework. But yeah, not sure where to start or the best way to get to all the main things, so how about if I just popcorn out a bunch of them to get things moving and get them out there?

Sure, sounds good.

So buckle up.

I'm buckled.

And lucky for you it turns out you're not far from an air bag. Okay, so, yes, global warming happened, or continued to happen, faster and hotter than predicted, yes, ice caps and glaciers and ice sheets melted, faster than earlier models predicted, yes, sea levels are of course also rising, more and faster than expected, and yes, ocean acidification through absorbed carbon dioxide is way off balance, and that's killing off a lot of species that have shells or calcium based structures, and hotter oceans are wreaking havoc too.

And everything's interconnected in terms of life thriving or dying so that works its way up the food chain to larger species. So the oceans are just really out of whack in a lot of ways. Coral reefs, as we've already been hearing, mostly die off, though a few that are better adapted to both warmer water and higher acidity are hanging on, and the jury's still out with them. Kind of hard to survive when your perfectly temperatured, perfectly pH balanced home is more and more being replaced by what's basically warm Diet Coke.

And what else? Ocean currents are really messed up. The major ones have mostly slowed or stalled, some have moved and/or sped up, and some new ones have formed. That's really impacted by – and then in turn impacting – salinity levels, with all the fresh water that's just pouring in, and it effects ocean temperatures, and all of that affects everything from plankton to migration patterns to species survival or extinction, to air currents and weather patterns – like temperatures and rainfall and hurricanes – and then there's all the fallout and chain reactions from all those first round of effects, both in the ocean and on land masses. I said all that a little awkwardly but we'll let it ride.

And there's just a huge amount of anger building up, that past generations and even older current ones did this, which also showed up in that social push to get those late septies and octies and older out the damn door instead of hogging so many of the resources of every kind. "You've done enough damage to the Earth and to our future, just call it done and exit the stage gracefully, as your penance and as your rightful selfless final act, to try to salvage to some degree a life that has participated in a world that has done this to the Earth and to our present and our future. Something's gotta give here, and it's just karmically fair for it to be you, in the sunset of your life, rather than many or most of those in the sunrise or morning or afternoon of theirs."

Ω

A *lot* of anger, and not much empathy, and of course not everyone was equally complicit, but in general, people *could have* – and from the perspective of growing numbers of younger adults facing the fallout, *should have* – taken more action in their personal lives, which has an accumulative impact, and they also should have risen up and demanded change, and they didn't. Not enough anyway.

So even if they didn't directly participate that much, not huge direct culpability – though a billion people driving gas cars and using disposable plastics day after day, and having better living through toxic chemistry, etcetera, that really *is* contributing to the situation – but for those who weren't obviously really directly culpable, they *still*, from the perspective of angry hindsight, didn't lift a finger enough times to really change the trajectory. So they're retroactively found guilty by association and by silent complicitness, by a trial of their younger peers, as what humans have done – over the last century or two in particular – has started to become more and more in your face obvious.

And what else? Oh, here's a fun one. Microplastics and nanoplastics are just everywhere. Hard to believe, and maybe I got it wrong or the flash packet got it wrong, but I even saw it in the air, like breathing in nanoplastics and other human-made – let's say nanofibers, nano-strands. So along with the obvious plastic bags and other larger plastics all throughout the ocean – and we've all heard of microbeads – but this is also the microscopic and submicroscopic micro and nanoparticles that are just everywhere, literally. I saw them like raining down absolutely everywhere, remotest places on Earth, didn't matter. Carried by the wind currents and inside raindrops, as well as all in the water pretty much everywhere.

And I have no idea if there's a technical distinction between nano and micro with these things, but I'm just trying to emphasize some were really, really microscopic, and just absolutely everywhere. Micro-strands of them swirling around in the air like dust or fuzz or hairs, and hard to imagine but every liter of water and every square inch of land had literally hundreds or thousands of them, and spoiler alert, that's less than ideal.

So plastic was not only a significant contributor to global warming through manufacturing it, but it was also just more and more understood to be really toxic to life on Earth. Both plastic itself and all the chemical additives in a lot of it for different specific purposes really mess with the biochemistry of mammals and other animals. More than we as yet really understand. So small, small amounts can really disrupt the body over time, really mess with a lot of different biological systems, and now it's everywhere and just leaching into everything. So that's become a huge, huge issue, one of several that are just, you know, forcing people to lift their heads out of the plastic-contaminated sand like, what have we done?

Ω Ω

And you said there were environmental efforts to reverse some of these things. They were pulling carbon dioxide out of the atmosphere? Did you see how that worked? And as for plastic, it doesn't seem possible to make much headway, if it's basically every square inch.

Not basically. Literally. Physically. Actually. At least based on what I saw. So some of these projects were akin to trying to empty the Great Lakes with a bunch of thimbles, pretty hopeless, but there were great global efforts to work on it all, all kinds of projects and initiatives. You know those old Westerns where the meek townspeople finally band together and take a stand and chase the Sarsaparilla Gang out of Tumbleweed Gulch? Like that except about three billion townspeople, standing together saying, "This. Stops. Now. The Earth and our future are more important than your wealth, and even than some of our own convenience and comfort and prosperity."

So a real shift, necessitated out of self preservation and societal preservation and next generation and future generations preservation. Out of real necessity, and to some degree out of an awakening of conscientiousness and ethical responsibility to the greater good, as well as the start of a deeper awakening of consciousness, that I'll get to before long here.

So to your question, one thing humans have done in the future – which is a phrase I never thought I'd say – is manufacturing massive systems, not exactly machines, no moving parts, but contraptions or arrays to absorb or capture carbon dioxide from the atmosphere. And also some kind of sludge that they spread out in the desert or open land, and it absorbs carbon dioxide and converts it into some kind of carbonate rock, locks it in for thousands of years.

And I don't know how many other projects and approaches, but it's just David versus a David-created Goliath, or David facing a Goliath created by David's parents and grandparents and that crazy coal baron uncle that always drank too much on Thanksgiving. But I did see gradual steady progress just starting to get into first gear. Literally moving mountains.

What do you mean?

Well, might sound like robbing Peter to pay Paul, but bulldozing some hills and mountains that had the right – I can't think of the word but the material or dirt or soil or gravel – with the right chemical composition, and then spreading it out in open field or desert areas, treating it with something quick and easy, and then it absorbed a lot of carbon dioxide.

That was just one of several things they were doing, coming at it from a lot of angles, some experimental and some full on. And the carbon capture contraptions, some of them were also catching some nanoplastics, they had some like added filtering, but that's just such a miniscule amount compared to what's out there and was more maybe a proof of concept or a prototype or a token attempt. Like putting your air purifier in your backyard to clear up the pollution in your city. Gonna need a bigger filter.

But it was *something,* and thanks to alternative energy and some kind of basic and cheap and nontoxic battery technology, maybe salt water or something simple like that, creating these things and doing what little automated maintenance work was needed – I guess refreshing or resetting or emptying the filters type work that was needed – that was all getting really cheap and easy to scale up. Mostly automated robotic factories creating all of this with fewer and fewer people needed, though you still need humans involved with getting the raw materials for the manufacturing and for the distribution, and also in the factories, overseeing and handling the unexpected and the less automatable tasks, and making sure the robots don't take too many oil breaks.

Ω Ω Ω

So some small but real progress, it just takes decades to even *begin* to put a solid dent in it, and they were throwing everything but the kitchen sink at it and hoping it all adds up. They tried kitchen sinks too but that was a wash. One bigger project I saw was massive iron powder or filings being dumped into the ocean around Antarctica, and that was to feed the – feed the plankton but specifically what are those small shrimp called? Starts with a K.

Krill.

Yeah, they were creating algae blooms to grow krill populations, which helped tie up calcium for centuries at the bottom of the ocean. And this is one that I think I had read something about – pouring iron in the oceans as a kind of fertilizer or jump start – so you know, did that show up because I had read it and it just came from my own mind and there's nothing else to it, or are some of the things that have been in the headlines over the last 10 or 15 years actually viable so they turn out to be used in the future?

And they were exploring dumping other – like truckloads of other minerals or sludge into the ocean for carbon capture too. I can't even fathom the scale those kinds of efforts would have to be to have a real impact, plus making sure the efforts themselves had a minimal carbon footprint or other negative repercussions, but it seemed like they were approaching it from every angle they could. They probably would've made exhaling illegal if that would've been viable.

And the sense was it would be another hundred years or more before all these projects would have any real discernable impact, depending on the exponential automation and implementation, how much resources they put into it, but it was – well I said it, but it was crystal clear, unavoidably obvious, that if that's what it took it was still worth doing. They had to try to put things back in balance where possible, or things would keep getting worse and reach a tipping point that would just really put things in an irreversible feedback loop of huge falling dominoes, which the Earth was teetering on the edge of.

The planet really was slow motion dying, and not that slow. At least dying in terms of its systems functioning in a way that would still be workable for all the complex life that had been adapting to for the last hundreds of thousands and millions of years.

But trying to right the wayward ship was a huge drain on resources and economies and human workers, even though it looked like a lot of it was automated, but not all of it. And there were thousands of factories creating these carbon capturing contraptions and other solutions, plus the mountain dirt or gravel moving and iron dumping and hundreds of other types of approaches being explored around the world, along with other initiatives to rebalance things, like drone tree planting, chemical and plastic cleaning to stop groundwater seepage, and so on.

So all added together, environmental rebalancing was another reason things were dire with resources, both economically and with human workers. Not enough plugs for all the leaks in the boat, but if they ignore the leaks, everything's underwater. In a lot of cases, literally.

$$\Omega \, \Omega \, \Omega \, \Omega$$

And also, in the too little too late but at least it's progress category, there were pretty much no more petroleum based plastics being made any more. There were global accords, everyone signed on, so it was all plant-based, and fully biodegradable plastics, and they were good substitutes – cheap and easy and strong – and depending on the kind and where they would end up, they would easily biodegrade under the right circumstances, but not easily before. And they were nontoxic, which is a nice bonus feature for ubiquitous substances that everyone, including children, are continuously exposed to.

And here's one I almost threw in with the plastics being everywhere but I bookmarked it to go into next and then got sidetracked, but it's a huge one and it wasn't on my radar that it was anything like this scale. Doesn't seem possible, if it turns out to be true. But I also saw, not just nanoplastics, but other toxic chemicals that just don't break down, or if they do its centuries or more, and they were also just everywhere – everywhere on Earth, every square inch literally of surface and every gallon of sea water or lake water or stream water. They were physically – or let's say biologically disruptive nanoparticles like plastics turned out to be, but even worse, even more harmful.

And they were literally in every animal in minute quantities, lower than plastics, but they're more toxic, so still enough to sometimes have subtle to not so subtle effects. I don't know the names of those, but along the lines of nonstick coating type stuff and waterproofing chemicals, and dozens or hundreds of industrial compounds with complex molecular chains that just don't break down, but do interfere with basic biology.

And I was already aware a couple of these things weren't good for you, like nonstick coatings, but that there was so much of them, and that they were absolutely everywhere, and really having an accumulative negative biological impact on animals of every species, to one degree or another, that was news to me, if it bears out.

So yeah, dozens, maybe hundreds, of these different long lasting human-made chemicals – along with other kinds of chemicals too – but just made in massive amounts over the decades – sometimes ending up in the ocean, including through illegal dumping or piping, or ending up in dumps that leach into ground water, and that are going to be around for maybe a few thousand years or more, and that are messing with everything more than we used to realize – meaning they're accumulative, so they become gradually more harmful and disruptive, and they can mess with bodily systems a whole lot more than we currently realize.

And one little snapshot I saw was the older chemical companies were facing, you know, pitchfork mobs almost, and being sued out of business, because they deliberately didn't ever really thoroughly check these things out and their lobbyists and donations made sure most politicians and governmental agencies didn't have much interest in checking out their safety profiles either. Gotta keep the stockholders happy to get those big bonuses, which is of course the highest value, worth bulldozing all other values for. Literally poisoning the Earth for at least centuries, for a nicer house and a feeling of having more financial security, future generations be damned. Along with those currently adversely impacted. And per your request, we'll go into that mentality soon here, what I saw around how we got the hell into this mess – which was the second flash packet of the three – but for now let me keep popcorning out things from the first flash packet a little more.

Sure.

CHAPTER 46

So, where to next? Yeah, connected to those chemicals and plastics disrupting physiological systems, amphibians are largely extinct in the wild, and not as easily kept alive in captivity, especially outside, and that's partly due to some new fungus infections and other new or very old and recently resurfacing microorganisms really decimating them, and also in part due to the precipitous drop in insect populations – if I used that word right – but also due to these nanoplastics and chemical compounds impacting their reproductivity, which also weaken their immune system, and make them even more susceptible to funguses and bacteria and viruses and parasites.

And the plastics and chemicals everywhere aren't just impacting amphibian reproductive development but other animals too. Not sure about reptiles, but fish and birds and mammals, including humans. They caused reduced sperm count, reduced fertility. And also sexuality and gender develop less binary more often, and one aspect of that – not the only one but one aspect that science came to clearly see and understand – as the biological impact of these human-created chemicals being so prevalent everywhere, and that impacting the physiology of reproduction and gender development in primates and all mammal species, and pretty much all animals. There's some universal signaling as the body develops, that can be impacted by these toxins to varying degrees.

And those chemicals impact the brain too, way more than we currently recognize. They can subtly impact a lot of different brain functions, and can cause this kind of – well what I saw as a representational image was like dark mini-dust clouds darkening and weighing down and foggifying the brain, and impacting functioning in different areas. And the meta-info around it was that these chemicals – that were just everywhere and especially in homes and offices and schools where a lot of products that have them were used, and they were even deliberate and incidental additives in foods from food packaging and preservatives and similar – they were causing an increase in things like behavioral issues, hyperactivity, autism, emotional reactivity, depression and anxiety, and other physio-psychological delays and deficiencies and imbalances, plus sometimes heightened fight or flight response, and just a host of other things.

The brain is a really delicate and easily impacted thing and these nano-chains or nano-molecules, even in really small quantities, can get in there and into other organs and systems and wreak some subtle but accumulative havoc. Really throw things off balance. Same with heavy metals by the way, which keep increasing in concentrations in the environment and particularly in water sources, so all of these things working their way into hundreds of millions of people or more, including children, and including pregnant women, which then can negatively impact health and brain chemistry starting in utero.

So yeah, at least in the future scenes and images and info-packets that waved through, these manufactured plastics and industrial chemicals are just effing with damn near everything, followed not quite as ubiquitously by heavy metals. And it's just such arrogance, you know? Such greedy arrogance and willful ignorance or disinterest in learning about the real impact before producing these things en masse and having them spread all over the planet, resulting in marine life, birds, amphibians, and I think reptiles and amphibians were kind of shown to me in the same class but not sure, but all animals, including mammals and humans, being sometimes subtly and sometimes like hit over the head with a brick level impacted by the chemicals we've been producing and not containing.

Just such unbelievable arrogance, and greed really, in not bothering to really check out the consequences of them first, not bothering to take possible toxic effects under serious consideration. And also not bothering to do much about it as we *did* find out a lot of these industrial chemicals are very, very bad news. What are the consequences of unleashing all these chemicals and plastics into the environment, land, air and water, and into homes and schools and office buildings? *Profit*. Next question.

Ω

And like I said, there will be a massive societal shift, from keeping our collective heads in the toxic sand way more often than not to the wide awake outrage of billions of people standing together, saying how the hell could those with power in the last few generations have been so unbelievably arrogant, and how could most everyone else have been so complacent? Maybe two or three billion people, standing strong, saying This. Stops. Now. Which will finally be enough to hugely reduce complacency, and also herd impunity.

And this whole human caused toxic contamination thing is like one massive, slow motion, harder to see, more subtle – but still hugely, hugely impactful – global wide oil spill, on the entire planet. Just one huge flustercluck. It's all just everywhere. That was one of the reasons ocean-caught seafood was hardly eaten anymore – along with there being such decimated fish populations – but also because of all the contaminants in fish. Plastics, other chemicals, garbage waste, human released mercury and other heavy metals, even pharmaceuticals, which is hard to imagine having the slightest impact in the vast ocean, right? But that's what I saw.

So a veritable smorgasbord of fun extras making seafood unsafe to eat. There were probably caution signs posted for the dolphins and seals and sea lions and see otters, but they foolishly ignored them and kept eating the contaminated fish anyway, which was one reason for their declining numbers, along with greatly reduced fish populations, and more pathogens floating around. So instead of eating ocean-caught seafood, there was a lot of fish farming or ranching – well probably not fish ranching, get along little doggies – but there were huge on-land facilities where that's happening and where most grocery stores and restaurants got their seafood.

Let me think what else. Well, of course, lots of extinctions. Whales were almost all extinct, which, I'm rattling these off and not really deeply connecting with the impact of what I'm saying, but I do feel that one hitting. Whales are almost all extinct. Not so easy to build a natural living habitat that's cut off from the ocean toxins and micro and macro plastics and other chemicals and contaminants, plus everything else in the mix, including declining food supply, more pathogens, less hospitable ocean environments, and yeah, I said it but way less plankton and fish. And a thousand pound bag of Purina Whale Chow isn't as cheap as it used to be, even with a coupon code.

And some whales were more sensitive to – I think it was PCBs, which I've heard of but don't know where they fall in the family tree of fun human made chemicals – but they were particularly harmful to some smaller whale species, which really hurt their populations. Not to mention being harmful to people who eat a lot of fish.

You wouldn't think, like pharmaceuticals, in the vast ocean a few human-made chemical chains, could impact whale species, but turns out to be hugely impactful to some, per what I saw, which is just mindboggling and infuriating and just staggering all at once. Seems like you'd have to be almost *trying* in order to get enough toxins in the ocean to effect whales. As well as to impact humans through eating fish. And like we've all heard, plastic bag strands and similar in the stomachs or digestive tracks of some whale species was a leading cause of death and decline too.

Ω Ω

What else with oceans, as I just casually move on as though what I just said isn't a massive, jaw dropping tragedy? Okay, so I already popcorned out this one, but also a massive increase in fresh water flowing in, which reduces salinity, which throws off and slows and stops some major ocean currents, messing with the whole circulatory system and the weather patterns that come from it.

And I saw Europe being a lot colder, because the Atlantic currents weren't flowing in the same way, warmer waters weren't moving as far north. I mean, Rome and Madrid, with their Mediterranean climates – Rome is actually farther north than New York, and Madrid is tied with it, which blew my mind. And Paris is more north than Maine, there's just these warm ocean currents that keep things milder, but it grinds to a near halt. And when you add in warming water temperatures and growing acidity, it just really knocks oceans all out of whack, mostly in just a few decades. And that has way wider ripples, or way wider shock waves, really. Far reaching ramifications.

And there were thousands and thousands of maybe solar or wave powered robot trash trawlers in the ocean, picking up trash and sifting out larger floating plastics and other trash, and some had filters to try to clean things up in terms of smaller contaminants, but again, so much of the plastic was micro and nano and bead sized and most of it was well below the surface, so those trawlers would basically be the equivalent of using a broom to try to sweep up the Sahara Desert. Gonna need a bigger dustpan. So it's really slow going.

Same with land. Can't exactly vacuum all the nanoplastics and microplastics and chemicals up from literally everywhere, or use a leaf blower to get those pesky things all tidied up. Turns out an ounce of prevention would've been worth about a billion tons of extinct animals, and a whole hell of a lot of suffering.

And as you can tell, as I've been talking about this I've been starting to feel some, I guess snarky anger coming up. Again, just the arrogance, you know? It's so obvious it's easier not to pollute things up in the first place than to try to take it out of there after the fact. Which still wouldn't get temperatures and acidification under control from carbon dioxide.

And of course, it's not just the oceans. As we've already seen early versions of, it becomes, just broadly, a whole lot wetter in wetter regions and a whole lot dryer and hotter in dryer ones, causing frequent disaster level, never before seen levels of flooding in some regions, and just massive monster megafires nearly every year in others, including in regions that had never been wildfire literal hotspots before, like the completely de-balanced Amazon, which was just mostly gone. Past the point of sustainable returnability without a massive, massive amount of help.

$$\Omega \, \Omega \, \Omega$$

And like the whales, it's almost unconscionable for me to just casually throw that into the mix and move on to the next thing like a shopping list. "Milk, bread, and oh, don't forget whales and the Amazon are basically gone." But all of these individual things – and none of them are actually individual, it's all interconnected – but each thing I'm naming, if you slow down and really take it in, is just profoundly heart boggling. Incredibly disheartening. And some of it was left – some of the Amazon – but so, so much less, and shrinking fast.

Thousands of extinct species of plants and fungus and insects and animals and birds, and those are just the ones that were known. Still a lot not yet discovered even 50 years from now. Not to mention, you know, fully understanding the medicinal properties of so many of those plant and fungus compounds, gone before they could even be discovered.

And efforts were still underway to try to salvage what was left and grow it back where possible, it's just tough going, post tipping point. An uphill battle. Yet another rebalancing project that just takes huge amounts of resources, funds and workers and drones and forest ceiling canopies and whatever else. A massive megaproject.

What do you mean forest ceiling canopies?

I saw like artificial shading canopies in places, to provide the shade needed for the under-canopy trees and flora and fauna to come back in areas that used to have that type of ecosystem but had been de-canopied. They also collected water from the air to help bring back the humidity and precipitation levels needed to bring back some rainforest ecosystems.

But yeah, it's just really infuriating, the self absorbed, selfish, me first arrogance that's a through line tendency in our species, including a lot of people with more power. Which I'm trying to hold off getting into til we get there in a few, but it just hurts the heart. The beautiful, perfectly balanced Amazon and all the living things in it, chipped away, burned away, cut away, in a matter of decades. Just squeezed and squeezed into too small a space, no longer self protected enough to have some chance to withstand the worsening outer climate forces, even as ever encroaching non-indigenous humans finally started to back off and try to reverse course.

So they're trying to bring it back, just, like I said, an ounce of prevention is worth 500 years of considerable difficulty or whatever it turns out to be. And Madagascar's rain forests are mostly gone too, along with Central America and others to a lesser degree. Along with mangrove forests, mostly from rising sea levels and destruction of habitat, and also mountain forests and boreal forests from heat and wildfires and droughts and insects and pathogens taking advantage of their weakened state. And let me think what else. Yeah, I'm kind of blanking. Anything coming to mind that I mentioned over coffee but haven't said yet today?

CHAPTER 47

How about natural disasters?

Yeah, if you can still call them natural, right? So changing weather patterns bring more extreme flooding and drought, another one we already know. Hundred year and five hundred year floods are just commonplace – I guess I said that. But weather systems moving slower and dumping more water in smaller areas. Also more frequent and more monster sized hurricanes from so much heat and moisture and slower currents. Plus bigger tornadoes, and in more places that never used to get them, and also more tornado-like wind events. And bigger and more frequent hail, harder deluges of rain and flash flooding, it's almost like, you name it they got it. The greatest hits.

The Earth just isn't doing well, and who would've ever guessed that all our greed and selfishness and arrogance as a species – or as the modern, more powerful, technically advanced, new and improved version of our species – could possibly ever come back and bite us? And bite everything else too. Who could've seen it coming that the Earth's ecosystems couldn't just keep taking more and more of our misuse and abuse? That they might actually crumble under the weight of all the extreme pressure we've been putting on them? Quite rude of the Earth not to just keep taking it without buckling.

And I know it's not everyone, not everyone's equally culpable, but they weren't going – I mean the hundreds of millions, standing strong saying enough is enough – they weren't going, "Oh it wasn't most people's fault, you get a pass if you were just living your best life fifty or a hundred or a hundred and fifty years ago." They were at least as angry and in as much disbelief about our complacency – the complacency of the masses, as we are about past societal wrongs, past societies ignoring or actively participating in obvious injustices and wrong actions.

They were outraged and heartbroken about the very real, very long term, and in some cases completely irreversible global wide harm, that will impact the next hundreds and even thousands of years and beyond, and cause some permanent changes to this planet, permanent extinctions and permanent imbalances in some places and some ecosystems. Plus a great deal more difficulty and significantly increased suffering for hundreds of millions of people. Even billions. We didn't join together to stop it, that makes us tacitly complicit, no excuses.

History won't look kindly on the 20th and early 21st centuries. Just in a matter of decades, it will all be seen so differently. The karmic chickens are coming home to roost, like for a hundred plus years we've been shortsightedly lighting really long and slow burning dynamite fuses, and now we're entering the phase where they all start blasting, to where it can't be ignored as "possibly problematic sometime in the future" anymore. Shit's getting real, and real fast.

Ω

And you said in spite of seeing all this devastation, it wasn't hitting you very impactfully at the time?

Well, remember, most of my awareness was still in the most Contentment and Quenchedness I had ever experienced, no contest. Being enveloped and infilled by Absolute Belongingness and Profound Love, and feeling profoundly connected to this Multidimensional Being before me, while in this exquisite Space of Pure Quenching Living Light. So I was seeing all this and taking it in more dispassionately, more distantly, not like I was in the middle of it. And like I said earlier, it all zoomed by so fast, there just wasn't – it didn't really have time to fully sink in on a deeper level. Which I'm grateful for, because yeah, most of these just by themselves would've hit pretty damn hard without some shielding or distance. And what else?

Well, here's more from the not exactly shocking news category, but huge areas that had more rain or snow not long ago are now bone dry, almost always in deep drought. And of course, coastal areas are flooding way more, from ocean levels but also from more intense weather events. And all that's leading to massive relocation, between droughts causing three or four or more months a year of intense wildfires in vast swaths of a lot of regions every year, and coastal and flood-prone areas getting worse and more frequent floods. And also ground water is mostly gone most places that were pumping it out way faster than it could ever replentify, and that shriveled up a lot of farms.

And there are huge air dehumidification systems, not sure what they're called, but to generate water for irrigation and homes, pulling water out of the air, with cheaply stored renewable energy, wind, solar, wave, geothermal, even some fusion, which is cracked but not all it was cracked up to be, not a panacea. Fossil fuels are done, everything's renewable energy. So it's fairly low cost to pull water out of the air, but it's just not able to generate water nearly at the levels ground water provided. Ocean water desalination is a lot more prevalent too, more affordable, but it's still quite the project to not only desalinate hundreds of millions of gallons per day – which with renewable energy works for coastal and near coastal cities – but it's a lot more energy intensive to send it hundreds of miles inland, and up elevation, where it's even more needed.

Also there are a lot more desert and semi-desert areas than there were. The next big dust bowl comes roaring in, looked like either two or three of them in a row or one long one with a couple of breathers. The Grapes of Wrath Part Two, with extra sour grapes, caused by hotter and dryer years and decades than ever on record, as well as decades of mostly corporate unsustainable farming practices that haven't taken good care of the topsoil, and with more frequent intense wind events thrown in – or blown in – for good measure. So add all that up, plus a lot of advances in indoor farming, and that's become the new norm.

Indoor farming has?

Yeah, it's climate controlled, uses minimal water, less fertilizer and no weed killer, no insecticides. A lot of old unused farmlands are being reclaimed by nature, though not back to how they were before. Invasive species, way fewer insects, different climate, all interfere with them returning to their original grasslands or forests or whatever they originally were. But still, a lot more reclaimed wildlands from farmland and ranchland getting freed up than we have now, so that's at least some kind of progress over miles and miles of homogenous crops. And a lot of the land that was burned down in the Amazon and other rainforests – for cattle and whatever else, and then from wildfires – they're trying to re-forest, like I mentioned, as animal meat has been largely replaced by plant based substitutes and indoor farming gets more standard.

$$\Omega \; \Omega$$

And bees are mostly extinct in the wild, but I saw some species starting to make some degree of a comeback somewhere in there, as chemical based insecticides and herbicides stopped being used, or were used way, way less, and more land had a natural variety of flowering plants. So some degree of more monarchs and other butterfly and bee species, and some other insects, and more renaturalized land, so some things seemed to be coming back from the brink of collapse a little bit, but still things were extremely precarious or post-precarious. Insect collapse had really wide ripple effects from pollination to all the species that depend on them and then up the food chain. Oh, and bee drones are big. I mean they're small but they're big. Bee drone pollination.

How does that work?

Well, they don't look like bees, at least in my mind's eye. More like kind of big toenail clippers with little drone propellers. And there are also small, autonomous ATVs that are kind of like their mothership, that they go back to frequently to recharge. They can't fly far or long at all, and I don't know how drone pollination would work but they re-dock to handle all of that and then go off for another round. Which sounds a little like Oversoul autonomous exploronauts, going out and coming back, actually.

And there are trucks that are home base for the mothership ATVs. So like a truck is slowly crawling along a road – or stops awhile then moves forward some – and maybe it has 30 robotic ATVs spread around the area, and each of those has say a thousand bee drones maybe. Those ATVs can also fly like a drone if they need to hop over a fence or something. Seemed like a pretty cool system.

So some crops are still grown on farms?

Yeah whatever isn't workable inside or makes more sense to. Maybe 15 or 20 percent of what it used to be, depending on when the snapshot was taken, but gradually declining. With 3D printing and robotic automation, building these giant multileveled indoor farming buildings wasn't prohibitively expensive at all, so that became the default for most. But things like fruit trees and some berries and melons and root vegetables, and also some grain crops and other vegetables when conditions made it feasible, were still grown on farms or orchards.

And outdoor farms used – instead of soil, a lot of them used some kind of a nutrient-rich, gel-like compound that needed a lot less water, and retained the water and nutrients for the roots without it dissipating into the larger soil, the surrounding soil, or mostly evaporating. So outdoor farms needed like ten percent of the water they used to need, and indoor farms even less than that.

I saw one image of like really densely stacked grain rows, which I wouldn't think would be as viable as vegetables indoors, but it looked really compact and efficient, with the bottom of one long platform or giant tray or level having lighting for the tray or level beneath it. These indoor farming setups were in every major city, meaning more foods were really fresh and organic and healthy. So it's not quite *all* doom and gloom, just mostly.

Ω Ω Ω

And I feel like I was about to say another one a second ago. Indoor farming, bee drones – oh yeah, I mentioned insect populations have mostly collapsed. Maybe five or at most ten percent of what used to be normal. There was an image of them being suffocated by the dark dusty clouds of human impact. Choked out. Weed killers, insecticides, chemicals and nanoplastics, disruption of habitat, drought, floods, higher temperatures, viruses, funguses, parasites, the usual suspects. The natural balance was just gone.

And let me think if there's any other big ones. Well, air circulation patterns are way off. For however many hundreds of thousands of years or more, the Earth moved everything around really nicely in a way that ecosystems evolved around, with ocean and air currents circulating and impacting each other in a balanced way, and now it's all shifted and moved and slowed down in places and sped up in places like the ocean currents. And yeah, there are exceptions but mostly the wet gets wetter and the dry gets dryer.

And I don't mean terrible weather events are happening every moment, people running in the streets in a panic with a monster firenado chasing them, but it's all just – climate patterns are no longer stable, not recognizable anymore, and it's a lot rougher a lot more of the time. More natural disasters of every kind.

How about earthquakes and volcanoes?

Well when I said every kind, I didn't think of those two. I think just about everything I'm rattling off wasn't just here's some possible big events in the future, but here's how humans have impacted the Earth. It's probably a safe bet that in the next say hundred years there will be some sizable earthquakes and volcanos, I just didn't, it's like the natural earthquake and volcano folder wasn't opened up for me to peruse.

But bottom line, in case I haven't adequately conveyed this, all in all things are pretty damn flusterclucked. Shouldn't be surprising, we razed paradise and put up a parking lot. We just have some hopefully not completely fatal flaws working against us, that weigh us down in terms of taking responsible care of hugely important things rightly and in a reasonable order of priority and in right timing. Not exactly our strong suit, at least so far.

Would this be a good time to – well we should probably take a break first, but then to go ahead and open that up more, by moving into that second flash packet of how we got into this situation?

Yeah, both sound good. I'm definitely ready for a break, this has been a long stretch. But let me just add, it's not like what came in from that second inflash was a lot of huge breaking news, it was just laid out in a way that woke me up more to a few primary causes of what's going on, in a way I hadn't ever thought about before. But yeah, I'll leave it there for the moment.

Alright, we'll pick it back up here after the break.

SESSION 8
CHAPTER 48

Alright. Can you set the stage for a minute? This was right on the tail of your future vision download?

Yeah, with a short little intermission in between. As that first data stream finished – of scenes and info-packets around possible future events – even though most of my enhanced attention was just soaking in that profound experience of being with this Multidimensional Being of Light and Acceptance and Love and Belonging, which was happening in that surrounding Space of Presence and Love-filled, Light-Filled Well-Beingness – that by itself was already amazingly quenching and Deeply Good and off the charts, even before Omega even showed up – But after that data stream ended and I was just being with this Light Being, I was also still in part just processing what I had just seen, and the massive flustercluck we had created.

And then this heart thought came up, how could we have done this? How could we, or how *can* we as a species, just be so diametrically off kilter and out of step with the Greater Balance? The Greater Good? And then this whole second data stream came in, and I guess I can't know for sure – maybe it was going to come in anyway, maybe the syllabus was already locked in – but it seemed to obviously be a response, like since your heart asked, here ya go. And like I said, it wasn't revolutionary news, though some of it was new to me, but I hadn't ever heard it all broken down like that, explained so obviously, and it just came through in a way that really struck me. So we'll see how I'm able to express it today and if it adds anything to the mix.

Alright, so I'll let you take it away unless you need a question to get started.

Well, I guess I'll just start by saying the biggest, or one of the biggest Achilles' heels that we as a species have is that there's a tendency to not objectively and balancedly consider the full impact of our actions and decisions. Especially if doing that might cost us or our family in some way, and to a lesser degree, if it might cost our tribe or clan or village, the people we think of as one of us. If it would risk costing us or those in our circle money or station or comfort or security, or even slow the continued accumulation of those things. There's a tendency to not consider the impact of our choices beyond our own circle, or even within our own circle much into the future.

Ω

And one image that came in was like an energetic shape or structure or programming in the human brain that just instinctually puts self and tribe first, and secondary ethics and values are much more malleable than we might like to think. Where we have much more of like a gravitational pull to take care of ourselves and our family and our immediate tribe than to make sure all of humanity, and the greater ecological community of the Earth itself, are getting a fairly fair shake. It's an influence or predisposition or strong, strong tendency, that's just in the genetic makeup of primates, including us. And it's in a lot of other mammals and birds and other animals too, but specifically we're zeroing in on primates in general and our own species in particular. Self and family first, then troop, tribe or clan second, though how we internally and unconsciously define the current version of something along the lines of our tribe is vastly different than it used to be.

But those kinds of decisions, that feel right – that successfully pass our internal senses of right and wrong – even though they could cause harm to others or to the Earth or to ecological communities or to future generations or current groups, they feel right because

our evolutionary predispositions and learned social maps emphasize taking care of yourself and your family, and maybe your tribe,
way before even considering anything else.

That probably worked pretty well for quite a while, from a survival
of the species perspective, and works well for other primates who
don't have the power to hugely damage the Earth or hurt hundreds
or thousands or millions – or even hundreds of millions of others
or more – not to mention the power to hurt other species and the
Earth's balance itself, by prioritizing themselves, their family and
their troop.

Some monkeys have skirmishes for territory, just like some human
tribes have since the dawn of our species. But when monkey troops
fight each other, it's with a statistically significant lower number of,
you know, spears and arrows and swords and guns and fighter jets
and nuclear submarines. That escalated quickly. And for tens of
thousands of years, there were a lot of more peaceful leaning tribes
and clans and ethnocultural groups, and a lot of more aggressive
ones, and there was suffering and hurt and death – and it's possible that human hunters contributed to the extinction of large land
mammals like the woolly mammoth and giant sloth, and definitely
caused some deforestation – but with evolving technology came
expanded reach and increased power, which as we know tends to
be used once it exists.

And for better and for worse, primate groups have a deeply rooted
instinctual sense of us and them, being cautious and suspicious
and distrustful and animositous towards those from another group
or from a different territory. Inherently not trusting that strange
group that lives over the mountains or up the river. We protect
what's ours, we defend our kind. We generally aren't so open armed
or trusting or generous or kind towards outsiders, towards those
others. Towards *them*.

Wouldn't surprise me if the word *kind* from kindness comes from
the word our *kind*, our *kin*. We're kind to our kind, and we're very

suspicious of those *others* over there. That served the survival of human groups pretty well for tens of thousands of years. Or really a few hundred thousand.

Ω Ω

But now, what's the current version of that tribe over there across the mountains that we don't trust? Some of it's the same, some different. It varies, but it's people with different religious beliefs or political views, people that look different and sound different, different ethnicities, different languages, different accents. People who have a different financial level or social status, people from big cities or from more rural areas, people with more academic education or less, different music preferences, style preferences, age group. Different world views, different values, which are of course wrong because ours are obviously right. How do we know? We check inside and our answer key tells us so. Case closed. Those suckers over there obviously have error-prone answer keys. Sure glad *we* don't, over *here*.

And as for everyone and everything that's not us or our family or our tribe, the default programming is for them to just not receive nearly as much concern or care or consideration or compassion, to a detrimental degree. This default setting of me and mine first, damn the rest, is a huge influence, wherever we are on the spectrum of it in various situations and scenarios. And if we don't wake up to it, what will continue to feel right to a great many people will be to, at least unconsciously, minimize our awareness and recognition of the damage or harm or difficulties we might be causing other people, other species, and the Earth itself, now, and even in just a generation or two, as long as me and mine are taken care of for now and for the pretty near future.

It's a scarcity based, zero sum based perspective, where one person's gain is another's loss. That fig tree only has so much fruit, and either our monkey troop is getting it or that enemy troop over there will, so let's make sure it's us.

And this perspective doesn't consider the more zoomed out perspective of Greater Consciousness, how we're all interconnected and of the same Oneness. Or even the planetary interconnectedness of all living things and ecosystems. What if the entire Earth is one tribe? But that's not our wiring and as a species we tend to let our wiring run the show. Not everyone all the time but most of us do a hell of a lot of the time, without even really being aware of the influences at play.

We think we're obviously clear about what's right and not right, good and not good, and we trust our value system, without really looking freshly and honestly, how much of this is primate instinct and human instinct that then also gets converted into social and cultural and family norms and values, that naturally feel right because they're both instinctual and what we absorbed growing up?

We usually don't think to ever question our sense of what feels right, but it *is* based on something, and that something has some really shaky ground in places. So if billions of people are making decisions based in part on presuming – without ever really stopping to check – that there's a really solid foundation where there's actually some partially shaky ground, and they're accumulatively building more and more on top of it, at some point things are likely to get awfully wobbly and maybe even collapse.

Ω Ω Ω

Like – and I know I'm just rolling through this, but I kind of feel it all lined up and ready to come out, everything I want to remember to name, so if you don't mind, I think I'll just keep steaming full speed ahead and then we can see where we are – So like–

–Sure, keep rolling.

So like the one percent, or the point one percent, those who are the most affluent, from one perspective they could be seen as a tribe that looks out for itself to keep away invaders who would scale the city walls for food and shelter and to take their gold and take more of their money in higher taxes.

What if, from the perspective of someone not in that tribe, who looks at them suspiciously, what if we give them the benefit of the doubt for a minute that the vast majority of them are good decent people following their best sense, that it feels right in them to protect their money and their family and if other people want more money they can work hard and get it themselves? And if the government wants more of their money, the very affluent sometimes use some of their money to help bring in lobbyists and fund election campaigns of lawmakers who will support their interests in keeping more of what's theirs.

Just to overgeneralize, from their perspective, it's not fair to punish them just because they worked hard or their parents did, or they had some good luck. And they naturally want to protect their territory, like a squirrel protecting their winter stash of walnuts. Sorry you other squirrels are running short this winter, but these are *mine,* they're *ours,* go find your own. Like monkey troops protecting their fig trees.

That perspective feels valid to them, not incongruous with maybe having a sense of strong ethical or religious beliefs or donating to some charities and generally feeling like they are a good moral person, a good global citizen. That it's actually irresponsible *not* to fight to keep as much of their money, their winter stash of nuts, as possible for them and their children and grandchildren. Or for their company or corporation or stockholders.

Meanwhile of course, fewer and fewer people own more and more of the pie, and they're likely – the point one percent are likely to feel animositous about the less financially secure tribes trying to take away what's theirs, unfairly, while on the other hand, a greater and greater percentage of people are struggling more and more, and becoming more and more animositous towards the point one percent tribe for taking more and more – and hurting more and more of the Earth and its inhabitants – and leaving less and less. Scorched Earth corporate profits and personal prosperity at one end of the spectrum and storming the castles with pitchforks at the other, with a lot of perspectives in between.

But there's a lot of us and them, with both sides damn sure they're right and the other side's wrong. Regardless of what might be objectively true, like if you could gather a thousand of the wisest and most objective judges on the planet and take a vote, even if it's a landslide, that doesn't change these deeply entrenched, feeling based, survival based, tribal based, us and them based instinctual mechanisms and their influence, as well as the deep influence of being enculturated into family and social group belief systems.

$$\Omega \, \Omega \, \Omega \, \Omega$$

So I was seeing all of this, and it was almost like a presentation of like dissecting an insect in science class, just objectively, look at what's going on here, breaking it down, deconstructing it a little. Just laying out the basics in a really obvious, easy to see way. We think our value system is this pristine unquestionable rock solid structure that has no room to be questioned, and watch out those who try to push us to. Obviously, *those* people over there – those strange tribes with funny ideas or funny names or different languages or customs, or different political or religious or cultural beliefs – they should clearly seriously question and update their ridiculous views and value systems, nothing could be more obvious. But *ours*, ours are rock solid. I mean, come on, why would you shake it down and start over when it's actually so clearly and so solidly the *right* one?

We don't even – it doesn't even occur to us to question if there's the slightest possibility that our right feeling answer key could possibly be off in places. When I check in and compare my values with the answer key that was drilled into me as a child, also influenced by instinctual primate and human prime directives, it matches perfectly, it checks out. So yeah, thanks but I'm all set in that area.

Those people over there, though, *they* need to take a good hard look at their, no offense, ridiculously off values ASAP, because they don't match up with *my* answer key, which is irrefutable evidence their values are wrong, bless their inferior little lost loser hearts.

So taking a step back, where did our answer key come from in the first place? Is it deserving of being presumed to be inerrant and infallible? Not much in the human brain can be seen that way, but our value system answer key legitimately can? So zooming out a little and looking at, where did some of our dearly held values come from originally?

Most primates just coincidentally *happen* to have territorial wars between troops – something that's been happening for millions of years – and we think that has nothing to do with political or religious or economic tribalism, us and them, or when tribes or clans or gangs or countries go to war with each other? There just *happens* to be a pecking order in primates as well as most human societies and work cultures and schools and social groups, with the physically or socially stronger sometimes bullying or mistreating or taking advantage of the physically or socially weaker, but there's no connection between the two? Really?

And we just both *happen* to have a tendency, since the dawn of all other primate species and our own, sometimes latent and sometimes active, to invade a different troop's or tribe's or country's territory – at any cost to them – to make sure our family and tribe has food and security and is prospering and is safe and has more and more so we can grow and grow, regardless of the cost to *that* obviously less worthy tribe over there?

And we just *happen* to try to grow our country's territories and land mass and power and resources for us, who cares if it leaves *them* with less? They're a different, and clearly inferior tribe or clan, they're from a different country or territory, they're a non-us group, and if they could they'd probably do it to us first, so survival of the fittest, right? It's just pre-punishing *them* for what *they* would do if *they* were stronger than us. Serves them right, for us to do it to *them* first.

They don't even behave as fully civilized humans anyway! Like the way they attend to their dead is completely bass ackwards! They don't even bury their dead in sacred soil to please the gods, they just burn them like common firewood! Such disrespect! Or, they don't even purify their dead with fire to please the gods, they just bury them in the dirt where worms eat them! Such disrespect! They only believe in one imaginary god and ignore and anger all the real ones! They believe in many false gods and ignore and anger the one true God! Their religion and their customs and their beliefs are different from ours and obviously completely inferior. And most importantly, they keep their toilet paper roll facing the wrong way, what more evidence do you need?

So it's this default, widespread, mostly unconscious sense that the entire planet is our tribe's dominion to conquer. Manifest destiny for our special, divinely blessed tribe or clan or family – or dynasty or empire, or ethnic or cultural group or country or civilization or corporation – to have more and more, and *they,* those inferior *others,* will just have to figure out how to divvy up our scraps on their own. Not our problem or concern.

CHAPTER 49

So it was just made really clear to me in this kind of startlingly in my face kind of way, that there are really powerful, beneath the surface influences on our values and the ways we make choices, and we personalize it and make it a sacred thing that can't be questioned and doesn't deserve to be questioned because, we don't mean to brag but unlike *them,* we nailed it the first time.

And you know, evidence and facts and reason, those things sometimes just generate a fear based reactive response in our answer key, in our inherited and injected and sponged up value systems. Those things often can't crack our defenses, especially if it's outsiders, other tribes, you know, *them*, probably with their own ulterior agendas, trying to cram their inferior beliefs down our necks. That's red alert stranger danger right there. Full on persuasion invasion. We can't let the outer hull be breached.

And of course that kind of "Ring the village bell, to arms, to arms" reaction doesn't have the space or field of safeness for honest self reflection, like "Wait, maybe that value I hold so dearly, that I've always been so sure is beyond question, maybe it was just indoctrinated or injected into me by my parents, and into them by theirs, and maybe 50,000 or 100,000 generations ago by monkey troops fighting to have more fig trees in their territory. So maybe it actually *isn't* inherently reflective of the highest possibility here. Maybe it actually *isn't* deserving of being categorized as obviously beyond question in me. Gee I'm glad I realized that, I'll just drop that whole antiquated belief system right now. Done. What's next on my to do list?"

That kind of value inquiry doesn't happen very often, which is fine because obviously *they're* the ones that need to investigate their values, not us. Not me. Not *my* family or *my* political tribe or religious tribe or economic or education level tribe or generational tribe or corporation tribe. We're good.

But at what point were these fundamental, instinctual and learned values of me and mine first thoroughly run through a rigorous test to make sure they really objectively hold up? That as long as you and yours are safe and secure and comfortable and in the money – or at least foresee a roof over your head and basic needs met, plus hopefully a few wants – nothing else outside of that needs to be given much of your heart's concern? Especially anything outside your territory, your property's borders or your family's or your tribe's. Beyond your clan's village. Too much concern for others, too much including them in your tribe, that would threaten the heart of the prime directive. First me and mine, for all time, and them over there, not my damn job to care.

But when have our basic fundamental belief structures been really fairly, openly questioned? Let's dare to assume most monkeys have never done a lot of deep and honest self reflection and soul searching about all this, and honestly how often have we?

Ω

Like religious or political beliefs, if say 70 percent of people have the same or similar ones as their parents, a lot of those people feel like they obviously have *the* correct one true religion or obviously have *the* correct political views, no question. Literally *no question.*

But what are the odds that out of all the different religions and belief systems on the planet, you just happened to have been born into a family that has it all exactly right? And that person over there – with a different religion or with different views of what's absolutely true – that person also is quite sure they're right, that they were born into the One True Religion, and everyone else is wrong to varying degrees, but of course that person is laughably wrong about that and you're right. You're positive. Sure, they are too, but you really *are* right, so you've got *that* going for you.

What good fortune, what luck, you're a proud member of the One True Club – maybe just like your parents and their parents before – and the rarified air is kind of nice up there, on the tall mountain of being right and knowing the High Truth. None of that fog and pollution of all those wrong beliefs flying around, like those poor lost souls down below.

Or maybe as an adult you left the belief system you sponged up as a child, and fortunately found the One True Religion, or the One True Perspective. You found *The Truth,* unlike most people. And someone else, born into the religion or political views or some other perspective you just joined, they just left *it,* to join the one you were born into, because they've realized *that's* the Right One. And maybe you both are absolutely *sure* you were wrong before, but now you've found *The One True Way*. Of course I'm exaggerating some, but there's something in this that's true to some degree with most of us, with a lot of different things.

Liberal or conservative, iPhone or Android, stove or microwave, reality TV or scripted shows, jogging outside or using a treadmill. What else? Mountains or ocean, piercings or no piercings, music or podcasts, butter or vegetable oil, and on and on. Or like which healthy diet you're into this year. A lot of people used to be vegetarians but now are paleo or keto, or they used to be low fat and now they're low carb or gluten free, or whatever their current but obviously right way is.

All these differences can trigger that automatic reaction of superior us, inferior them, to some degree. I can recognize that in myself here and there, smugly feeling my way is better than theirs, and then maybe five years later I've switched to their way, and again smugly seeing how my way is better than those other poor out of date saps still doing it my *old* way. And when someone from the 99 percent suddenly joins the one percent, their views might move from wealth redistribution and Robinhooding to keep your grubby little hands off my money and keep my taxes low. And vice versa.

Ω Ω

So all of this is really worth objectively questioning. But doing that – questioning the injected and sponged up value system that you were largely shaped by as a child, and/or that is strongly preloaded software from hundreds of thousands of years of evolutionary tendencies – that's just not – I mean that kind of earnest inquiry just isn't part of most value systems' programming. It's antithetical to most of them because by nature they're self defending, self protecting, self surviving, and self perpetuating.

I assume when cancer cells start spreading out of control, they aren't programmed to take a good hard look at themselves and self-extinguish if they're harmful to the greater good. Maintain and multiply is their mission, not "Let's really stop and reflect regularly on if our own growth and expansion is supporting or harming the larger body, of which we're a part and on a deeper level one with."

Questioning our value structures can shake them to the core and might lead to them being left out in the cold and replaced by a newer, better model, so value systems don't usually include self inspection that could potentially lead to self ejection. The immune system of value systems doesn't include a self check and self culling or self pruning or self termination mechanism. It doesn't usually have room for a really honest, piercing, skeptical and unbiased bird's eye look.

These are our most basic mental operating systems. Best not to look under the hood and start tinkering. Changing a few lines of code could destabilize the whole OS, the whole prime directive. It's much safer and way more comfortable to look at those other tribes with a good hard pre-judged look, from the vantage of being up in the castle of obviously the right and righteous and superior value systems and belief system and cultural views.

That tribe over there – those members of that religion or political party or social class or culture or educational level or age bracket or whatever it might be – *they* really need to take a good hard look at themselves. Sure glad I'm one of *us*. Best tribe *ever*. High five everybody, we rock, and they're a crock. *We're* the ones with the cool stars upon thars.

I didn't get that.

That old Dr. Suess story, *The Sleeches*. No, *The Sneetches* I think. Yeah, *The Sneetches*. Basically it's we're better than them, and you can identify us because we're wearing a cool elite star on our chest. So then the inferior, non-elite *others* over there, they start wearing them too, to try to be as good as us – probably a cheap counterfeit knock off knowing *them* – so then we change it to the superior elites *don't* wear those ridiculous out of style stars anymore. That's *so* last year, just for those *wannabees* over there.

And you know, we actually play that kind of thing out, where whatever the clothing style or hairstyle or facial hair style is this year, it's *so* superior to that laughable style from a few years ago, that some out of style, uncool, inferior people are ridiculously still wearing, the fools. When you take a step back, it's really just jaw droppingly unbelievable that we accept the enculturalization that someone wearing clothes that were perfectly in style ten years ago should be literally ashamed of themselves, and we should feel embarrassed to be seen with them. Especially if they're wearing socks with their sandals, the horror. Until it's cool again.

What a strange thing, if you really zoom out, like if there was a planetary social archeologist – or I guess anthropologist – from another planet that's here observing us, to try to comprehend that this intelligent species actually buys into clothing styles as something substantive, that actually impacts social status. That having a $3000 Gucci handbag or Armani sports jacket increases someone's value as a person, and zooms them towards the front of the pecking order. Which basically amounts to using money to cut in line.

Ω Ω Ω

And the roots of it are understandable, we're instinctually wired to try to keep our social status higher rather than lower, so we're influenced by the current snapshot of social norms, keeping up with the Joneses. We hitch some of our value and worth and instinctual comparative rank assessment to how well we're matching up with the top rankers, who are by default influencers. And if we're keeping up pretty well, with them and the latest must have styles or phones or earbuds or cars, we can feel some mostly unconscious superiority to those *lessers* over there, who don't have this year's stars upon thars.

All of that becomes mixed in with the whole value assessment program we sponged up long ago. We just can't help but absorb as children the world according to our parents or primary caretakers, watching and learning the ropes around how the world works, absorbing their answer keys as our own. Taking on our parent's conscious and unconscious beliefs and value systems, at least in our formative years.

But imagine if parents had the perspective to say, or even to just embody a stance of, "Listen, here's how I see things, here's my belief system, and deep in my heart I believe this is the best perspective, my internal answer key says it's right. And at the same time, the best I know to do to support you becoming an independent thinking, strong, solid, self-navigating adult in this world is to expose you to how I see things, while always holding a spacious place in me that has room for if you decide you don't agree with what I've laid out to you as what I currently see the truth to be.

"And I acknowledge I could be wrong, or my take on things just might not resonate with you as your own, or it might not even resonate with *me* in five or ten years, I can't know for sure. And as you grow up you get to explore and try on for size and see for yourself what your *own* sense of these things is, and I'll love you and accept you regardless. You don't have to fall in line with my beliefs, a lot of which I have because of the beliefs my parents happened to have when *I* was a kid.

"And it would be good sooner or later to really seriously question and investigate whatever beliefs and values and operating systems you feel you've sponged up from me, because the human brain *does* sponge up and take on what is witnessed and heard, from family and tribe and village – and now from virtual village – but that doesn't mean it's infallible and unquestionable.

"And there are kids all over the world that are sponging up very different belief systems and value structures than you are, so you know, it's good to add a question mark to all of this, to hold it lightly, and over time you can see for yourself what resonates for you, and reevaluate things as the years pass. And whether where you end up is really similar to my value system and beliefs or really different – or if it changes over time – whatever your journey, I will love you and respect your right to travel your own path."

And that whole speech would just be to get things started. During labor. Or maybe even during conception. You might get some strange looks, but a small price to pay, you just can't start too early with kids these days. But learning how the world works from adult caretakers is part of the deal for us primates, and I assume most other mammals. A baby monkey watching what their mother eats, watching how she breaks open hard nutshells with a stone.

Ω Ω Ω Ω

And as this whole inflash unfolded, I was literally seeing the tight inflexibility of human brain belief structures, position structures, not that they can't stretch and loosen and change, but there's a *lot* of resistance to ever seriously questioning them and we have strong defense systems to prevent our basic foundational beliefs from being shaken once they're in place. You just aren't supposed to question the root operating system. How do you know? Because the root operating system says it, so it must be true. Kind of a closed loop there. My answer key is right, because it says it right here in my answer key. That's a closed circulatory system that never gets any fresh air.

And again, that evolutionary development has worked great for young primates learning the rules. Watch, learn, imitate, integrate, habitualize, use that rock to open that nutshell, raid that other troop's territory to get some fruit, treat troop members that are higher on the pecking order with deference but bully those that are lower. Or is that middle school? Same innate rules.

For most primates, there was no need to question what's taught, it's tried and true and works within the confines of a very specific environment where they spend their whole life. But human life, and especially modern human life, is a tad more complex than that.

So you know, maybe it's worth getting more conscious of all of these innate, ingrained tendencies. Adding some conscious investigation, some real vigilant inquiry into it all, or else we're largely controlled by deep seated automatic belief structures that are a mix of genetic predispositions and learned patterns that were injected into us as children, plus a few tablespoons of social influence as children and even as adults, and we mostly don't even have the distance or perspective to realize how much we're under the influence.

They just – those belief structures and value systems and prime directives just feel like internal us. They just feel so right and natural and obvious. When we check in, what feels right to us feels right to us. Our answer key is unquestionably beyond question, end of story. Our belief system and value system castle guards only know how to look *outward* for threats and problems. They just don't know how to turn around and look within the castle walls.

Works pretty well for the survival of other primate species, though there are injuries and fatalities in raids and alpha male fights, and it's not so fun for those at the bottom of the pecking order. But with humans, that tendency of me and mine first, even if it scorches others and the Earth, that's been happening on a gradually increasing scale, and the last couple of centuries or so, it's been getting more and more precarious and problematic, and growing exponentially. It's pretty daunting, when you take a step back and look at it, the power we as a species now have, to impact other groups of people and other species and entire planetary ecological systems. A power that we as a species so far haven't demonstrated ourselves to be good and worthy stewards of in the slightest.

CHAPTER 50

So to bring the two main things I've talked about so far together, there's that injection of preset value packets learned from parents and tribe and culture – and now internet tribe – and then there's also the genetic predisposition to put ourselves, our family and our tribe way ahead of everyone else, to a degree that's out of balance and detrimental for the greater whole.

And since that matches our unquestioned answer key, which was itself formed largely by those influences, it's a feedback loop without checks and balances, so it doesn't usually feel off or out of balance that a lot of the time we aren't caring much for people and species beyond our own tribe – aren't caring for the larger human family or the larger Earth family – and aren't caring much for even a couple of decades down the road, aside from maybe trying to have some retirement funds, and if we have kids, wanting them to have a good start, a good education, maybe wanting to be able to help them financially.

And nothing wrong with working to have enough resources to meet your and your family's needs and to have some nice wants met too, but I'm talking about a skewed, outsized form of that, that's really prevalent, even though at the Core it's all – we're all deeply and profoundly interconnected. We're all part of the one Earth tribe and the One Universal Tribe, even if there's not conscious awareness of the Deep Interwovenness of every being and everything – that has existed and does exist and will exist – through the Universal Deepest Root of the One Pure Infinite Essence.

And our belief structures run so deep, they come with their own pre-loaded, in our bones, pre-rationalization coding, meaning we usually don't have to consciously rationalize making decisions that, zooming out, are out of balance and to some degree are adding harm rather than harmony. So even if we do self investigate or inquire about it, it can evade detection, kind of like asking a company to audit their own taxes. "Nope, nothing to see over here in our unsuspicious accounting department, everything looks good to us – all those deductions were legit – thanks for asking though, and feel free to ask us to self check if we're clean and green anytime, happy to do it."

But with this, the evolutionary origins are completely innocent, there's not usually strong deliberate malice going on, but they're just woefully outdated for our current planetary situation, with the power humans now wield. Which is mostly used for self, family and tribe, including the company or corporation and its stockholders, because when that's all doing well, which fair wages and pesky environmental and humanitarian considerations tend to hinder at least in the short term – which is what matters – then me and my family get more acorns for winter, a nicer house, higher social ranking, more trips to tropical islands, the latest espresso machine, and more of a feeling of solid personal and family security.

And there's a third main influence in what's gotten us into this mess that I'll touch on in a minute, but it's just – when I saw it all laid out it was so unmissably apparent, if we don't wake up some and snap out of our automatic assessment systems and default trajectories, things will only keep getting exponentially worse all around.

So the challenge and the invitation is, for us to just really recognize this, to hold it more in our awareness, to really be conscious of the everpresent, almost completely beneath the surface influence of our evolutionary and cultural prime directives, in our perceptions of us and them and right and wrong and how far our circle of good taking care extends or doesn't extend beyond us. Looking at how we weight everything, the cost benefit analysis of like our chemical company making some good money with this new untested class of chemicals, that *they* are going to make anyway, whether we do or not, so might as well, and how we weight the amount of fossil fuels we're nonchalantly releasing into the atmosphere, or overfishing or deforestation or insecticides or herbicides or habitat destruction, or the release of heavy metals. Or more individually, going through way more plastic waste than we have to, or not yet getting a hybrid or electric car because, you know, good reasons, and so on.

To see how easily and instantly and automatically and pre-judgingly – and actually we could even use the word *naturally,* because it largely originated in evolutionary predispositions – but to see how automatically and easefully we tend to make choices that are at a real cost to the greater good.

Ω

And of course this is a spectrum, not binary, and I don't mean everyone should be lumped into exactly the same group, but I'm talking about overall tendencies in the human species of primate. Yes, we've gotten pretty fancy as a species, with our soup spoons and fitness trackers and Mars probes and that phone controlled espresso machine. Tap the app from your bed and start the day ahead. But we *are* still primates, and on some level we still play out the prime primate troop directive, that those strangers over there are at best irrelevantly neutral and at worst they're life and death competition.

And these days for a lot of people, *my* tribe might largely or mostly be people on the internet who think like me. And those *other* people *not* in my tribe, they don't deserve much kindness or concern or consideration or care or compassion or camaraderie, or carrot cake or coconut cookies. And we also still tend to be disinclined to sacrifice having all that we can possibly have, in order to help make sure now and in the future things are more in balance all around, from a larger, more zoomed out, more all encompassing perspective.

A strong predisposition towards not even *considering* the Greater Earth Tribe, or the future of the human tribe, or the present or future of those outsiders, those *others*, those non-tribemembers down the road or in that strange distant country with the inferior cultural norms. My concern largely ends at my and my family's front door, or front and back yard, or maybe at the gate of my gated neighborhood. Or the virtual gated community of my social media groups.

And of course, a lot of times people *do* consider a larger perspective, and *do* extend beyond themselves, their family and their tribe, with conscientiousness of the larger local or even global community, and with generosity and kindness of heart, absolutely. But this was like a bird's eye view of the general situation, and how these circle the wagons tendencies are so embedded and pre-conscious and have so much influence, they're worth really pulling back the curtains of and magnifying and shining the light on.

If I approve that new chemical, if we build that new fossil fuel plant, if we sweep those studies under the rug and say our herbicide is safe, then our company will make a nice profit, we'll get a nice bonus, and I'll be able to pay the hundred thousand for that college admissions consulting service to get my kid into a prestigious university, so yeah, it works for me and mine for a decade or two, end of consideration. Or, I'll get re-elected if I deny human-caused climate change, because corporations in my state make money by releasing tons of greenhouse gasses, and they give to my campaign. That's good for me and mine, for a decade or two, end of story.

Or we'll bulldoze more rainforest to bring in more cattle because there's money to be made there, and I need to provide well for myself and my family, end of thought process. Or airlines and other industries with a huge carbon footprint completely ignoring the future costs they are causing, not factoring that in at all now, making future generations pay those hidden costs because, hey, we can get away with it. Or tens of millions of people buying new cars that burn more fossil fuels instead of increasingly affordable ones that burn less or none, for convenience or style or short term financial benefit. And even plastics in fast food and grocery packaging, etcetera, just massively add up over the lifetime of billions of people. So those big and small decisions, made again and again and again, on bigger and smaller and seemingly miniscule scales, are accumulatively devastating the planet.

$$\Omega\,\Omega$$

And also, the us and them threats of tribalism still trigger all the neurochemicals in our brains they always did, but instead of once in a while encountering a band of strangers while foraging or hunting, or seeing them approach your village on rare occasions, it can be a hundred times a day or more on social media and news feeds, getting that neurochemical hit, that shot of reactivity, just by lifting up our phones, which gives the brain something like a quick shot of a sugar high, addicting even if it's not of goodness. It gives us *something*. Not real nutrition, it's empty, but it's still perceived as an empty *something*. The brain really likes an empty, stress-inducing *something* so much more than a quiet nothing. A quick little drug injection. And we can really get hooked on the false nutrition of those repetitive, ever-more available micro-jolts, positive or negative.

So the upshot is, we can't only go by what feels right, because what we grew up with as familiar, that by default is likely to feel right. And amassing all the figs and acorns we can, all the territory we can, even if it leaves others without enough – which is on them, sorry, not our problem – that's likely to at least to some degree feel right to a lot of us. And doing everything we can, regardless of consequences, to boost our company's success – even if it potentially causes real harm out there – that's more often than we'd like to admit what's likely to feel right to a whole lot of people, and likely, at least to some degree, somewhere inside us, to feel right to ourselves. Increasing the difficulty of others or of the Earth, if that increases our own holdings – because it's my job to only take care of me and mine, and good luck everyone else except that one strange tribe over there with the threatening beliefs – that's all likely to feel right. And ignoring long term negative impact for short term gain, that's really incredibly likely to feel right.

Hunting beasts to extinction for the food and warm clothing they provide, or destroying habitat for farming or ranching, even though at some point that causes the permanent extinction of plants and insects and animals, that's likely to feel right. Not with deliberate malice, but it just passes through our integrity and ethics filters, usually without the slightest bump.

Letting future us or future generations pay for our own acorn hoarding for this winter, or even uprooting and dragging the whole acorn tree – or why not the whole grove – to our fortified territory to better protect our ownership of the acorns, not leaving any trees for other, less important tribes or species – or for less important future generations – and minimizing and ignoring the fact that we're hurting others now and hurting them later, as well as hurting the ecological balance, all of that's actually likely to feel completely fine, and not trigger any inner alerts or alarms, to huge numbers of people following their internal answer key, including a great many who are in positions of power and decision making.

Ruthless profiteering is greatly rewarded, and the costs often don't show up in your own gated neighborhood, and are often delayed, so you don't have to see them anytime soon and maybe not much within your lifetime. And trading a healthy ecosystem for a few more acorns, a few more figs, a little more honey, some more security in our cave, all of that's likely to feel right and pass our answer key core ethics checkpoints.

$$\Omega \, \Omega \, \Omega$$

One pretty extreme and just really infuriating example, I almost mentioned this earlier when I brought up ocean dumping, but just unfathomable amounts of DDT, the banned *Silent Spring* pesticide from 50 or 60 or 70 years ago, were not only piped into the ocean off the California coast for decades by a chemical company that made it, but also – and this was a year or two ago when I saw this so I don't know the latest – but also there's tens of thousands of barrels, and possibly even *hundreds of thousands* of barrels, as hard as that is to imagine, just dumped into the ocean, now just sitting on the ocean floor, that are filled with left over sludge from the manufacturing process of it – of DDT – so they had substantial amounts of it, and who could've guessed, more than half a century later, they're slowly leaking.

So things are still really contaminated in that area, and the concentrations in the fish and other sea life are still hurting animals that eat them, like seals and walruses and dolphins and sea otters, and it's also hurting the animals that eat those animals, like scavenger birds. It's even really impacting the recovery of California condors, making it a lot shakier. And it's just really incomprehensible to me that people would do that, that they *could* do that. And think of all the people that had to be complicit, over *decades*, in dumping vast amounts of toxic poison into the ocean, both through just unfiltered piping, plus tens of thousands or even hundreds of thousands of drums of toxic sludge. Just infuriating and incomprehensible.

And when I think about it, I just want to track everyone involved down and bang on their door and have them hauled away to prison. Which gets a little complicated when most of them are no longer alive, but I just have this visceral reaction of wanting them punished, wanting justice, wanting them to realize the egregious errors of their ways and to just crumble in a puddle of genuine tears and heartfelt contrition. And I want anyone who ever tries to do anything like that again to have immediate and harsh consequences, and for that to stop anyone else from doing it.

And that's actually another thing hardwired into primates, punishing troop members who put themselves ahead of the troop. Sometimes they'll even bite off a finger or toe as punishment, which, you know, does tend to make a point. You give us the finger, and we'll take one of yours. I'm not saying it's not appropriate to have justice and consequences, I'm just saying even *that*, the deep, passionate response in us for punishment and justice, is even more ancient than our species.

Ω Ω Ω Ω

And you know, that kind of F U to the environment and to the health of other species and our own has been so rampant – I don't know how many movies and books are out there that are based on true stories of things like chemical companies continuing to sell what they secretly learn are highly toxic chemicals, or corporations knowing they've put heavy metals or other contaminants in drinking water and just keeping it quiet, or radiation leaks or toxins in the air, dumping toxic waste into rivers, and so on – it's just been so prevalent, at the extreme end of the spectrum and less extreme, that just explaining it away by saying most of those chemical execs and politicians and CEOs and super rich are bad people, that doesn't really get to the core of it at all, it just provides a shot of neurochemicals and reinforces how 100 percent bad they and theirs are. We need more refined and discerning seeing than that to really snap out of all this and really move the needle.

And like I've said, this mentality of first me and mine, if we're good all's fine, it's a completely understandable, completely trackable back to its source, innate human and primate and mammalian and animal tendency, and it worked pretty well overall for a good million years of humanoid primating, but things are so much more skewed now, so out of balance in terms of the outsized power humans have, where we can really impact things incredibly negatively, faster and vaster than ever before.

And even when we know that the things we're doing are part of something that accumulatively will hugely negatively affect the future – even the very near future – or know that it will negatively impact tens of millions or more of other people's present and future – or even just a few people, why skip over that – we mostly can't be bothered. Good luck grandkids, good luck next gens. It doesn't look too good for you, but the stock market had a good day with those tax cuts for the wealthy while the national debt grows and industrial restrictions on oil drilling and fracking and toxic compound accountability are even more loosened, so I'm good. Reducing carbon emissions and tighten environmental restrictions? Nope, that might cost some jobs for a while, so obviously we can't do that. Nonstarter.

We don't even question that our tribe having our current jobs is more important than taking good care of the planet and the life on it, or than other people being displaced or detrimentally impacted in other ways, like their health. That's third rail stuff right there. It would sound crazy to us to say, you know, "If federal law makes it illegal to dump tons of toxic poison in big cities, people would lose jobs so that can't happen." But somehow when it's removed just a couple of notches, not in our backyard, not in our drinking water or air, that we know of anyway, with the polluting and toxifying not quite that blatant or immediate but no less harmful in the long run, it's mostly given a pass.

CHAPTER 51

And that brings in the third main glitch that's Titanicking us straight towards a thousand icebergs, and then I'll be done rolling out this whole big piece, but first maybe I should – well I just want to acknowledge here that I've definitely been mixing neutral reporting with some personal soapboxing, it just activates a lot of dormant mild to moderate infuriation as I open this whole folder up again, what our species has done and continues to do to each other and to the Greater Earth Community. And the incredibly high stakes, that I don't keep in my awareness all the time, really come back into focus.

But the third glitch is that we're evolutionarily biased to recognize and prioritize and mobilize against sudden or fast approaching smaller dangers much, much more than slowly approaching, slowly encroaching bigger ones. We see a bear or a flash flood raging straight towards us, we react. But we hear about global warming and everything else I've named, and how it's impacting the Earth and almost every species on it, and how we're creating changes that could cause great suffering and hardship and increased death rates for centuries – including for our own tribe members and our friendly neighboring ones, and for our whole species, as well as for other species and for our planet as a whole – and for the most part we read the headlines or watch the two minute news story, or even the occasional eye opening but inconvenient documentary, and then we usually move on. Most of us usually just can't be bothered to lift a finger. Except maybe sometimes the middle one.

Boiled frog syndrome.

Rings a bell but I don't remember what that is.

It's a myth, but the idea is if you put a frog in hot water, it will immediately hop out, but if you put it in cold water and slowly increase the temperature, it doesn't notice the slow incremental changes and just sits there. Which doesn't turn out well for the frog.

Or the spaghetti. Yeah that captures it. We're less evolutionarily inclined to notice slowly encroaching dangers, even huge ones, than sudden or imminent ones, even if they're relatively far less significant. So we mis-assess and mis-prioritize and misallocate energy and resources and time and attention, and basically ignore the huge and fast growing list of approaching icebergs, since they're out of eyesight up ahead.

It's like how much do you react if you're told the train you're on lost power and the breaks are out, and it's going to fly off a cliff in five minutes? There would be panic and pandemonium and screams and fervent praying on that train, and that's just from the internet going down. But what if – well I guess it would have to be a really long train ride, but just to make a point, what if you're told it's going to fall off a cliff in five days? Five weeks? Or how about if we discover a huge asteroid will definitely hit us in 30 years if we don't start working on a solution now? How quickly would people and governments mobilize and get in gear? When it's fast approaching, that's a five alarm fire. Defcon Five. Or Defcon One, not sure which is which. But the more in the future it is, the less we're motivated, even if the consequences are exponentially more dire.

Ω

If a doctor says I'm really sorry, but your results came back and you're definitely going to die in 20 years if you don't immediately change your ways starting today, what do you do with that? How much motivation and mobilizing energy does that really generate slogging through day after day, and can you find a shred of that motivation a month or two later, once the initial action-mobilizing jolt normalizes?

Reminds me of a joke, a doctor calls a patient and says, "I have good news and bad news." The patient says, "Okay, what's the good news?" The doctor says, "The good news is you only have 24 hours left to live." The patient says, "That's the good news? Then what the hell's the bad news?" And the doctor says, "Well, the bad news is, I kind of forgot to call you yesterday."

I've never heard that one. Pretty good.

One more since you're begging. A doctor tells a patient, "I got your test results, and it's not good news. I'm afraid you don't have much longer left to live." And the patient says, "How long do I have?" And the doctor says, "Ten." And the patient says, "Ten? Ten what? Ten years? Ten months? Ten weeks?" And the doctor looks at the clock on the wall and says, "Nine. Eight. Seven."

But the point is, we just really need to be more aware of all these evolutionary, and indoctrinated – or sponged in from childhood and beyond – tendencies, and we need to not trust our automatic danger level assessment system so much, which prioritizes immediacy over severity. Proximity over potential impact. Our mobilization systems are programmed to respond to the closer threat over the bigger one, and again, that just feels right to us because it's so deeply ingrained in the brain. It worked well when there were killer sloths and saber tooth chipmunks menacingly hiding around every other tree, and not quite as many fossil fuel power plants and unscrupulous corporations and gas fueled cars and forest-razing bulldozers and nuclear power plants and nuclear warheads.

And I've said this, but future generations will just be aghast that we so selfishly, head in the quickly sinking sand, let all this happen. The sheer audacity of the arrogance and self righteousness and self centeredness and self prioritizing and short sightedness and shirking rightful responsibility will be seen as just unfathomable. We're so influenced by cultural norms and the rest, it's hard to see outside of our programming enough to get to where people will be in a hundred years – or even 20 or 30 – about our choices, mostly over the last century. How harshly we'll be judged, as we judge those in the past for doing things our current cultural norms and understandings see so clearly as absolutely and unquestionably wrong. It's so obvious they must have known it was wrong back then. There's no way they didn't. And yet, here we are, and very soon the same will be said of us.

And that me first and my clan or tribe first perspective, it's always going to be a loud, convincing voice in the human brain. It's been a sound evolutionary survival perspective for hundreds of thousands of years, it's just so obviously *not* sound now, if we don't want to continue to barely notice repeatedly making choices that destroy more and more of tomorrow, in order to have it a little easier or more comfortable or more financially secure or well off today, or for the rest of our relatively short lifetimes, which we've already gone a long way towards doing.

I just lost you.

Our current trajectory is so obviously not a sound one, if we don't want to continue borrowing from our future with no viable way to repay, which is basically the same as pillaging and plundering and looting from tomorrow to give us more things we need or want today. And actually, I said it's always going to be a loud, commanding or convincing voice in us, but this outdated perspective doesn't even really need a loud voice, it's just so ingrained it doesn't need any volume at all to be convincing, to be followed, like staying in deep ruts on an old jeep road, it's just largely the autopilot default. The path of least resistance.

Ω Ω

Ask anyone, do you care about the oceans? About the ecosystem? About the Earth? Yes, of course I do. We just don't connect the big choices and our daily little choices with the accumulative big impact of billions of people and tens of thousands of corporate and government decision makers prioritizing me and mine first. What did we *think* was going to happen?

The level this operates at in the brain is basically the same level as monkey troops invading another troop's territory because they have more fruit trees, killing them if they have to. Cruel but effective in small doses from an evolutionary and troop survival perspective, but inconceivably disastrous on the larger scale it's playing out now.

And we think we're so enlightened and intelligent and superior, but which species has hurt the planet the most? Maybe other primates just had the greater wisdom not to take a bite of the snake's tempting apple. "Yeah that's okay, we monkeys and apes will happily stay at our current ceiling of intelligence and manual dexterity, because we don't want to get too big for our britches and mess with things with greater ramifications than our little territorial troop skirmishes. We can't even *imagine* what we would unleash if we had a trillion times more power than we currently do. Thanks, but too rich for our blood. We might have a little more suffering in our individual lives by passing up the magic apple – and even *that's* debatable – but this way we'll cause others in the Great Community of Earth way, way less suffering, soon and farther down the line. What kind of foolish species would take a bite, and possibly bring down the whole planet with them? Homo Idiotus, that's who."

So yeah, I'll stop soapboxing and we can move on, but bottom line, it was just so beyond obvious, almost like a mathematical formula certainty, that with our evolutionary imprints and our familial and cultural influences, *of course* this is our situation. Now what are we going to do about it?

Because just letting future us deal with the mess that past us and present us have made and keep making, and every year it gets worse and worse, really? That's the big plan here? Come on. We *do* know better somewhere inside us. In spite of all our influences that give us a feeling of permission – conscious or not – to turn the other way, to turn a blind eye, to keep doing what hasn't been working and has been so devasting and has already set in motion what will be exponentially more devastating in the coming decades. Doing the same thing, and half-heartedly barely even mustering a little non-action-taking, passive hope for different results.

So asking ourselves, ideally after we've gotten a little freer from those influences as we get more conscious around it all, okay now are we *really* going to, as societies, as governments, as corporations, as neighborhoods, as families, as individuals – because united and unified really can have so much more power than occasional smatterings of isolated action and dissent – are we *really* going to keep doing this, and allow it to keep happening, without making our unified voices heard?

Ω Ω Ω

So yeah, time to move on, and I feel like I haven't quite tied it all up with a nice neat inspirational bow, even though, you know, we need to be repeatedly inspired or we usually can't be bothered. So the too long didn't read version is, if we actually *do* want to change our iceberg-field-approaching-trajectory, we gotta wake up, get honest, be aware of our strong evolutionary tendency to ignore slowly encroaching dangers, be aware of our equally strong evolutionarily and also culturally shaped predispositions to automatically and unquestioningly and uncritically believe the value systems we were born into – or took on later – and this incredibly strong, blind tendency to put me, mine and my family and tribe way ahead of anything else and everything else, with the way we unconsciously define our tribe – and dangers to it – being woefully outdated for modern society and the current global situation. And then we gotta just roll down our sleeves and get to work.

Roll down our sleeves?

Yeah, all the damn mosquito pathogens spreading everywhere due to climate change, if I didn't mention those earlier. And by the way, full disclosure, I haven't made drastic changes these months to practice what I'm preaching right now. I'm not above all this or trying to represent I'm living the high life now and everyone else should follow my inspiring example. I actually haven't thought about all this that much since it opened up during the Big Event. I'm sure just one outraged tweet would change the world and make me a hero, but I have yet to take that bold and impactful step. But as I've been tapping into this whole stream today, this whole thing, it's really woken all this up in me again, and got me feeling the incensedness of it all. For, you know, maybe 30 minutes, after which odds are it's back to business as usual.

And that's a huge part of what makes it all so incredibly serious and precarious, or past precarious. Post precarious. Because even when we know the mechanisms at play, it's hard to muster enough rocket force to escape their gravitational pull, even briefly, not to mention in a sustained, impactful, transformative way. So it's quite the challenge ahead. Quite the long list of challenges.

But being more aware of these subtle dynamics and influences at play is a key starting place, to hopefully help us start to snap out of the deep rutted trance, at least to some degree, and start to really change course. Start to steer clear of all the icebergs we can, and start preparing for impact with the ones it's too late to avoid. Okay, I get the feeling I could keep soapboxing about all this for another hour, but let's call a hard stop here. So, I still want to bring in that third and more hopeful flash packet, but anything else to finish this up first?

No, but I'm glad we included talking about it. It does spell things out in an obvious, matter of fact way. And like when we moved on from voluntary life completion, it feels a little jarring to just hop right on to the next thing, but that's why we're here, and ending the afternoon session on a more optimistic note sounds good. We've talked about it some over coffee, but I'm looking forward to hearing it in a bit more detail, and I'm really glad we're including it in our marathon. So let's go ahead and open that up.

Actually, I could use like a two minute stretch break just to kind of refresh a little.

Sure, that sounds good to me too.

SESSION 9
CHAPTER 52

Alright. Take it away.

Okay, so let me just lead into it by saying that after that second whole data stream finished, about how we got into this mess, there was again just being with this Light-filled, Love-filled Multidimensional Being before me, while being surrounded by and immersed in that amazing, unparalleled, Oceanic Liquid Living Light that was just permeating me. So I was feeling all of that, being in all of that, without any side show or slide show happening for a few nontemporal moments, another brief yet timeless intermission like after the first data stream, and I was mostly just taking all that in, responding to it, soaking it in.

But there was a lingeringness in me, of like, ouch, looks like a rough road on that delicate little planet, that I used to live a life on, forever ago. A lingering of, based on what I had just seen in the last two flash packets – the possible future events and then all the factors stacked against really getting things back in balance and living in balance – there really didn't seem to be a whole lot of hope for the human species or for the Greater Earth Community. Considering how fragile things were, and with all those icebergs ahead, and with so much stacked against them – with all the internal structures that interfere with right, balanced, full-perspective based action – there wasn't any optimism in me that they could actually make much of a comeback, or right the ship to a significant degree.

It felt pretty hopeless and dark and disheartening. Nice to be shown the dynamics and understand them better, but as far as I knew, my time was already done on that planet, and even if everyone on Earth suddenly understood these hugely detrimental predispositions and influences and dynamics better, that's still a long, long way from things actually getting anywhere near back on track.

So part of my awareness was processing that, feeling some impact about that – that it really felt like it was probably too late for a real turnaround on that planet I used to have a life on – while most of me was still just completely enjoying being so quenched by this Ocean of Benevolent Living Light and by the Profoundly Quenching Connection with this Multidimensional Being, soon to be known as Omega. And then suddenly, again as a response or answer to what I was thinking and feeling about the first two data streams, this third and final one started up, that actually *did* have real, authentic hope in it.

And when you think about it, first showing where all the messes we've made – and keep making – might have us heading, and then showing what some of the main root causes of that are, and then showing that there's still some real hope, that would've made sense regardless of any reaction I did or didn't have, but it also perfectly matched up with how after the first round, the future scenes, I just naturally had that arising of, how did it come to this, and then after seeing how strongly programmed and predispositioned we are, there just naturally rose up a resigned sense of, this just looks pretty damn bleak and hopeless – for them to actually course correct in a significant enough way – which I wanted for them, even though that was no longer my own future. It wasn't my home.

And what started playing in this third round, and it was the shortest, but it was some images of the future that were roughly around the same timeframe of what I was reporting earlier – which was maybe 30 to 70 or 80 years from now, and then this new one including up to maybe a few decades beyond that, so up to a hundred years plus in the future – and I also saw that it's already starting to happen a little, slowly starting to ramp up, or maybe it's in the pre ramp up stage, but it will keep building and increasing momentum.

And basically, it was that people were starting to popcorn open everywhere.

Popcorn open?

Yeah, seems to be my word of the day. But their awareness apertures were loosening up and becoming more open like mine has been, but a lot more than that. I mean just an aperture opening doesn't mean much in terms of the kind of person you are or your – let's say your spiritual maturity or consciousness evolution or how much you've really integrated living a Larger Perspective and Deeper Connection – which includes Greater Reality and Greater Consciousness and your own Greater Self – into your daily life.

Ω

At its most basic, and this is overly simplistic, but just having a more open aperture is basically just a relaxing or loosening of the contracted focus of your deeper awareness on your small self – your daily life, your biological/physical/mental/emotional human experience – so more of your Larger Self and more of Greater Reality can be seen and connected with more deeply and more often, without disassociating or walling off your small self in any way.

And that's good, don't get me wrong, to have more moments of that, I mean that's great, but I didn't *do* anything to earn or deserve that, and haven't earned anything since. There's absolutely *nothing* particularly special or impressive about me in this whole area except I happened to take the fast train to Deadville Station and some doctors and nurses arranged a ticket back. And that little journey somehow left me with a more open awareness aperture, which has enabled this portal with Omega to be open, at least during bridging sessions, and sometimes I feel like it's still partly open to lesser degrees at other times, like when I talk about these things with you.

But I just honestly don't get much credit , well I don't get the *slightest* credit. It doesn't mean I'm really walking the walk, just because I'm talking the talk, and I'm only even doing *that* with you. And sometimes I *get* walked, like when the whomp comes in of Omega showing up for a bridging session, where I get some nice guided tours, or like when I just find myself effortlessly doing an invitation, like that one process that recently opened, that I'll go into after dinner, but that's not at all the same thing as really integrating your own awakened capacity around all this, which I haven't integrated at all yet, and don't actually know how much I ever will.

But what I saw in this third flash packet was, a whole lot of people were starting to – like their hearts and their, maybe you could say their beings or their souls – were starting to open, as well as their awareness apertures. And believe me, I don't mean Shangri La bliss, petting rainbow butterflies that poop golden glitter, but like a mature, powerful, empowered, grounded, compassionate, open hearted, open minded, full spectrummed, fully human, open energied, authentic, congruent, centered, solid, embodied waking up. With more awareness and more of a larger perspective, and less self centeredness or me-firstness or narrow, evolutionarily based perceptions and conclusions, less contracted preoccupations and obscured myopia. Less believing every thought and feeling the brain pumps out, less ignoring the larger ripples of the choices we make every day, and the sometimes hugely impactful decisions that decision makers in organizations and corporations and governments make. More authenticity and integrity. Less my tribe over yours, less us good them bad.

And definitely not martyrish self deprivation, and definitely not walking around with faux spiritualness, discongruently pretending to be flowing with peace and love while you're stuffing down everything else and barely holding down the lid. But less of that *us first no matter what* mentality. Because when you zoom out, there's only One Tribe. And when you *fully* zoom out, there's only One. Infinite, Interwoven, Benevolent, Light-filled Conscious Oneness.

And like I said earlier, of course, nothing wrong with, you know, taking care of yourself and your family and your finances and your retirement – taking care of what's particularly yours to take care of – and having and doing some things that bring you some enjoyment and enrich your life, just not in an out of balance way that would steamroll over others and the Greater Earth Community and even the future of your own tribe to do it. And also being aware that even the most well meaning among us are usually contributing not so insignificantly to the problem, so at least being conscious of the ways that could be happening, including that and meeting that in your awareness, being self honest about it, rather than in denial or defensively minimizing it.

Ω Ω

So, specifically, visually I was seeing – and let's just assume this was influenced by, you know, artwork and images I've seen here and there over the years, like I was saying yesterday – but I saw multicolored rays of light waving out, rippling out, ribboning out, radiating outward, from people's hearts. Not as dramatic as what I was seeing with this Multidimensional Being before me, which was all energy, no physical form, but what I was seeing in this third flash packet scene was in the same vein. And then the scene zoomed in to one particular shimmering scintillating Light-filled heart, and then zoomed out to one person sitting in a park or a field, and then slowly zooming out more to show there were dozens, then hundreds of people gathered with similarly awakening and awakened hearts, all with their own unique ribboning but similarly open.

And the scene kept zooming out and zooming out so that it was like I was seeing it from space, and then I started to see the curvature of the Earth, and then the continents, and I saw these rays of radiating energy and light coming out really brightly from tens of thousands and then hundreds of thousands of people, then millions and millions, all over the world, as the Earth was spinning around in front of me, or maybe my view was rotating around the Earth. Not every single person, but a big chunk of people, and quickly growing, and it would soon become hundreds of millions, maybe within just a few more decades after when I was seeing it. Maybe a little faster, maybe slower, but it was happening.

And there were also like almost meteor shower streaks, or more like northern lights, shimmering down onto the Earth and into the Earth from all around it. Healing, cleansing, awakening, aperture-opening Higher Level Light raining down onto the Earth everywhere, and that Pristine Healing Light Energy was helping with this awareness aperture and heart and mind and soul awakening.

And you know, that degree of worldwide seismic shifting, those waves coming through, it's just going to cause some real growing pains along with it, so I saw the friction increasing, between those whose eyes and hearts and minds and awareness apertures had been opened more and more, and those understandably clinging to older, smaller perspectives. It wasn't binary, there were gradations on both sides of the spectrum, but that was the basic idea.

And I think we're already seeing some of that friction, of less contractedness and less closed apertureness and less self-survival focus, that then bumps against more rigidity, more old status quo, more of a scarcity-based or a me and mine based mentality. More "I need to hoard walnuts or protect and fortify the fort for me and mine and everyone else can fend for themselves." From that perspective – an understandable perspective really ingrained and imprinted and injected and insponged from the first years of life as well as from our very DNA – these profound shifts can understandably be really threatening.

And it wasn't that everyone this was happening to was integrating it equally smoothly, there was some contraction in some of them at first or even some evangelical or zealoty, "I have found the One Truth," because, you know, humans do that. But there was some fracturing from the stress of these two fundamentally diametric views, between circle the wagons and open the wagons. Between our family and tribe first, no matter the cost, and we're all one tribe so let's take care to move as harmoniously as we can, really considering the greater impact of our individual and collective actions. That *does* still include working to help ourselves and our family and our tribe be in a good place and in good care, it just also includes others and the Greater Earth Community as well, the Greater Earth Tribe.

Ω Ω Ω

And unless these shifts that were quickly spreading around the globe genuinely really opened in someone, from the inside out, it would be really hard for them to relate to – much less to really embrace – that kind of One Tribe view, that's deeply Rooted in Infinite Loving Benevolent Conscious Oneness. Like I said yesterday, kind of like everyone on Earth is your cousin, that you spent Christmases with as a kid and have just a kind, fond, warm-hearted response to and inner connection with, even if these days you can't stand their personality and don't particularly want to hang out with them anymore. Not loving their personality or some of their views doesn't mean you kick them out of your greater family. If they are in your city and need help, you help, within reason and self-caring boundaries. Once a cousin, always a cousin.

And just trying to be crystal clear here, you're welcome to have success, you're welcome for you and your family's security and finances to be solid, you're welcome to have empowered personal boundaries and to say no when that's what's clearest. You aren't suddenly a wimpy doormat just because your heart is more open, you just aren't kicking everyone and the Greater Community of Earth to the curb along the way because your personal thriving – and your family's or tribe's – supersedes all other considerations by a mile.

But all in all it was definitely hopeful and good, and yeah, some growing pains as collective societies and countries, as well as individually, as more and more people were kind of waking up – well, not kind of, but were waking up to various degrees, and in various ways, opening their eyes to the Beautiful More. Opening their awareness apertures and hearts to Greater Reality and to their own Greater Selves.

There was no doubt this whole transition was Deeply Good. Capital letters as usual, Deeply Good. And I wasn't shown like fast forward a century or two and it's some utopian society with the Earth back in perfect pre-industrial balance and everyone teaching the world to sing in perfect harmony. The inflash just didn't go that far forward, and I didn't get the impression things will ever be some smooth, painless, perfect utopia on Planet Earth. That's just not the terms of participation here. But it *did* feel like a lot of things were going to get ironed out and more in balance, and things were going to get better and better after a rough, let's say a rough century ahead in different ways, mostly brought on or at least greatly, greatly exacerbated by our own shortsightedness and me-firstness.

Not that it will all suddenly be easy at the hundred year mark, but I saw a clear realigning and a heading more towards rebalancing, which will take real, real time, and yeah, some things from the list earlier just won't be able to be fully recovered, but still, millions, then tens of millions, then hundreds of millions of people living life on Earth while being much more consciously connected to the Continuum of Consciousness, to Greater Reality and to their own Greater Awareness, that's a really significant sea change.

And then future generations and the Greater Earth Community itself can receive the benefit of everything that this global consciousness shift opens and enables. All the healing from that. All the rebalancing and re-harmonizing from that. As Greater Connected Perspective and Awakened Balance begin to really integrate in the human species.

CHAPTER 53

And of course all of that awakening and awareness aperture opening and heart opening that I saw happening, with eventually hundreds of millions of people, it doesn't automatically take away all of their patterns and their identifications and their reactivity and their misperceptions and their mis-navigating and their baser conscious and unconscious motivations. I mean they're all still fully, fully human, with the full spectrum of what that means, the riches and the glitches.

But the high end of the consciousness spectrum is suddenly getting a lot more extended, and awareness of the influence of the low end is more, well more aware. More conscious. So the long tail of the higher end of the bell curve really opens up, and the average level moves in that higher direction, meaning the average level of consciousness on the planet really starts to rise.

And all of that definitely helps decisions be at a higher level, and helps more things be taken into consideration before daily decisions are made – that accumulatively add up – and also on a larger scale, before hugely impactful decisions or potentially harmful ones are made. And it also helps there be more cooperation and larger tribeness, and less win/lose and us/them cutthroat competitiveness and less scarcity mentality at the cost of real balance.

So people's radars start going way beyond the comfort and prosperity of themselves, their family and their tribe or company or retirement plan or financial investments. Basically I saw a quickly spreading maturity where way more people than ever were way more mature than I feel like I'll probably ever be.

No harsh judgment about a lower maturity level. A tree can't bear fruit til it's had however many less mature years with good soil and water and sun, which is normal and necessary, and can vary greatly from tree to tree and grove to grove. How soon and how much fruit and how nutritious the fruit a tree can bear depends a lot on how much water and sun and rich soil they have now, and also how much they had as a sapling, and through the years in between.

And regardless of where each of us is along that spectrum, we all have gifts and challenges, we all have ways we can serve, things we can offer, and also ways we get tangled, things that can knot us up.

But in this new phase, the healing and flourishing and thriving, and then the growing of fruit, was really happening more and more. Which was then a Real Gift, capital letters, or maybe we could even call it a blessing, for others. And this was happening on really deep levels in people, in their roots, as well as in their minds and bodies. It was happening in their very Being, in the Heart within their heart. And then it was rising up, rising through, trans-rooting upward and outward and spreading to others, and in the best way, catching fire.

And, you know, more mature tree still grows and develops and also has its imperfections and weaknesses, but it's now actually able to give back some serious fruit along the way, in spite of those. It's able to spread some sweet nectar and offer some nourishing sustenance. Real, impactful nutrients. For others and for the Earth and for future generations. That's the kind of thing I was seeing.

Ω

We all can have moments of offering real value, for sure, we all have ways to contribute and to support others, but I'm talking about a huge shift in the degree of millions of people's conscious awareness *of* and conscious connection *to* and conscious rootedness *in* the Beautiful Depths, the Beautiful More, their Greater Awareness along the Continuum of Consciousness. And that *does* have a whole nother level of real impact, it *does* bring a lot more nurtrients to the tired and weary and closed down and cut off and parched and wilted and depleted and walled off and hyper-protected places in others, and helps other people's tuning forks catch the resonance of what a more open awareness aperture and more awakened inner Heart really feel like.

And I assume over the centuries, over the millennia, there have been quite a few pretty mature, awake, Consciously Connected people to various degrees, but all and all, probably safe to say it's been fairly rare. Never a huge wave of awakening and maturing and of awareness apertures and hearts and minds opening more and more, by the millions, each in their own unique but integrated and solid and sturdy and flexible and healing way.

Kind of like a great, thick-trunked apple tree, that's not weak, not wimpy, not a pushover. Real maturity, real awakening, that includes love as well as the power to stand tall and strong and to solidly say *no* when that's what's needed, which can also be a clean expression of love. The love of true seeing and right action, the love of personal integrity, the love of empowered boundary. There's no world where saying *no* is less consciously or spiritually evolved, and being a falsely peaceful pushover is more evolved.

But yeah, I saw just this massive Springtiming of Empowered, powerful, awakened hearts and minds and awareness apertures. Millions then hundreds of millions of people. A benevolent force to be reckoned with. This was the spreading of a great Fire of Re-membering. A Great Wave of Awakening. And then that whole data stream ended and there was just the single current again, of just basking in this Content Belongingness, in that Profound and Luminously Alive Space, connecting so deeply with this off the charts, exquisitely Beautiful Multidimensional Being again.

That is hopeful and encouraging.

Yeah, especially after everything else that had been coming in, it was really good to kind of have some counter programming on the

Omega Channel with that. And there's one last piece to this, that we haven't gotten to yet during our coffee conversations, but I asked Omega about some of this during a bridging session pretty early on, about how during the Big Event they communicated that bridging would start to get more common and easier to have happen, and there was also this third data stream, the whole Great Wave of Awakening thing, and I asked how does that start happening? What causes the shift?

And the response was kind of cool – well it was actually really cool – and it filled this jaded Scrooged up heart with a little optimism and hope. And insert here the usual obligatory disclaimer, that maybe it was just something my own unconscious created by itself – a reasonable explanation – or, just maybe, Omega and all the resources of my hundred billion neurons worked together synergistically to create everything that flashed in as soon as I mentally asked that question.

$$\Omega\,\Omega$$

But this image came in of like trapped miners after a cave in, and they're digging furiously up, trying to get to the fresh air and daylight, and on the surface people are digging furiously down, trying to help free them. And then I saw that big breakthrough moment, where two hands, one reaching down from above and one reaching up from below, finally clasp each other through a little hole in the dirt and rubble. Literally a break through.

And then the digging gets easier and faster and the hole or tunnel gets wider and wider, and they lift the first few people out of there, and then more and more. And it was just really a beautiful scene. And along with it were the words, or pre-words that my brain converted, "There are many here digging down. There are many where you are, digging up. And more and more, we are meeting in the middle."

That's really, that's really cool. I just felt a little shiver.

Yeah, it was definitely impactful when it came through, and I've never shared it before so I'm feeling it as I say it. And there was an image of like a time lapse, with fresh sunlight and fresh air and food and water coming down into the mine, and people being lifted out, and the tunnel getting wider and wider til – fast forward – it was just this big, easy, safe open area, and there were like earthen stairs coming up and then a gentle spiral winding ramp or trail, and then it was widened out even more to just a big gentle grassy bowl or indention or dip down, so at that point it was just easy and natural to gently go up the gentle easy slopes.

So during that time lapse, things were just getting much easier, much more open circulation between above and below, with more and more people coming up above ground all the time, and plenty of hands from above to help get that really going, along with plenty of diggers from down below as well – who once they made it into the sunshine and were rested up on the surface – would help with the digging down and opening and smoothing and ease-ifying.

Who are the helpers? Who's lending a hand?

Yeah, I asked Omega that, and asked what does that really mean, the image of these helpers reaching down and helping to dig us out, meeting us in the middle. And what waved in was, the helpers are a variety of benevolent beings from a lot of different levels, and in some cases from different worlds within those levels, wanting to help us rise to the occasion – rise up out of our relatively dark enclosedness in terms of our consciousness level and awareness apertures, compared to the rest of the Consciousness Continuum – and help us enter a new time, a new phase, a new era, a new epoch, a new level of more open apertured consciousness.

And I got a little inwave where I saw a multitude of different kinds of benevolent beings gathered around, surrounding the Earth. Maybe twenty or a hundred miles above it, though that's more likely to be more my own limited 3D thinking, but a great Multi-Dimensional gathering of Benevolent Beings. A coalition of all kinds of subtle level Beings, from all kinds of levels and backgrounds and snow globes.

And they were all gathered to both, help birth a new phase on Earth – to help birth a new level of consciousness in humans – and also to witness it. To witness the rare uplevelling of a fairly evolved, but largely cut off and self serving species to a more connected and conscious level, with more awareness of the Beautiful More and of the Irrevocable Interconnectedness of all. To witness this transition, from almost everyone having a relatively mostly closed aperture to more and more people having a much more open one. A transition from almost exclusively smaller, more myopic consciousness to the inclusion and integration of more and more Greater Consciousness. From being almost universally not consciously connected to the Beautiful More and to our Higher Self and to Deeper Flowing Beingness, to becoming more and more connected to all of that, while fully living a more and more mature and fruit bearing life as humans on Earth, in much more harmony with the Greater Earth Tribe than most of us currently live in.

$$\Omega \, \Omega \, \Omega$$

And I mentally asked for more information about all these benevolent beings, but nothing else came in, just that poignant image of a Great Gathering of like ten thousand or a hundred thousand or, I don't know, millions – It partly depends on how you're counting along the Continuum of Consciousness, right? Whether you're focusing on five fingers or one hand, etcetera – but thousands or millions of – not sure what else to call them – but a Consortium of Benevolent Beings, all supporting us and our fledgling Great Wave of Awakening. Helping us reach critical mass, helping us finally break through to solid, sunlit ground. The arrival of a new Spring.

They can't do it for us, they can't dig us out unilaterally, but they can, almost literally, meet us halfway, as long as a lot of us are also digging up towards the sunlight from the – at least relatively – from the collapsed and cut off mineshaft we're stuck in.

And what was your sense, if there was one, of how we help dig up?

Yeah, well there's a thousand ways. And first just to be clear, we absolutely don't *ever* have to feel Essential Presence at all, which is fortunate since most people pretty much never do, or hardly ever do. I never once did in my life before the Big Event, that I'm aware of. So it doesn't need to be about that at all.

But I think we all have a sense, on some level, of what serves the digging up, in our own way, with our own specific resonances. Somewhere inside us, we already know – at least to some degree – what clears more dirt out of the way above us, and what adds even more dirt that we'll just have to dig out of later. But just in general, whenever we're letting ourselves really feel what's here to feel, instead of stuffing it down or pushing it away or instead of trying to get ourselves to feel something different because the current feeling is uncomfortable, we're being more real with ourselves, and that's a little bit of digging up.

And whenever we're letting ourselves get really honest and become aware of some things or feel some things that might be painful, or that really feel uncomfortable, to see and acknowledge and feel, but they're already lurking inside us and we've just been mostly unconsciously holding them back to try to be more comfortable and feel less pain, we're digging up. We're digging out. And whenever we're trying out just getting quiet and still – while our mind is still doing its job of pumping endless thoughts – and just seeing if we can be aware of our internal compass a little more, our internal tuning fork, and if not, just doing some type of awareness or mindfulness or meditation practice – could be Simultaneous Awareness Practice or whatever one you resonate with, or exploring several until you find one you like – that's digging up. That's digging out.

And also, when we get together with someone else, or with a small or large group of like-intentioned people – in person or in an online group, or a phone or video call – in support of getting more clear and being more connected to ourselves and others and to Greater

Reality, intending to be available for ourselves and each other in the opening of our apertures and our hearts and our minds, that's digging up. That's digging out. And whenever we're sincerely working on ourselves or connecting with ourselves, in the ten thousand ways we can do that, alone or with one or more others, that's digging up. That's digging out.

CHAPTER 54

And on the other end of the spectrum of inner motivation and mood and what feels possible for us, whenever we're just honestly not wanting to deal with any of that, and we just want to be off duty – to just mindlessly watch some TV or play games or read a novel or just check out for a while – and we just want to avoid feeling anything uncomfortable or challenging, and just need to avoid getting real or getting vulnerable about anything for a while, or maybe we just feel completely stuck and we just can't apply any of these stupid, over-simplified, pointless suggestions that never do any good anyway and nothing ever does, and we're feeling all that frustration and stuckness and hopelessness – or trying to *avoid* feeling any of that, which can be exhausting in itself – then even during *those* times, *exactly* those times, when we can just give ourselves a little kind compassionate warm understanding, give ourselves a break, *that's* digging up. *That's* digging out.

When we can just kindly say to our tired, deflated, discouraged, disheartened self, "Yeah, it's been one of those days, or weeks or months or decades, or even one of those lives so far, and I really understand you just want to be done trying for a while, and it's really okay. I'll just give myself full, guilt free permission to be off duty for now. Watch a movie, binge a series, play a video game, read a light novel, full permission to just take a kind break from trying. And maybe I can try again freshly tomorrow, or next week, or next month. But right now, *of course* this is how I feel. It's so understandable, and it's so okay. And for a while I'm just not going to battle with myself to be somewhere I'm not." Even *that* is digging up. That authentic and self compassionate meeting yourself *right* where you are, without shoulding on yourself, or adding even more pressure or weight.

And maybe sometimes, after some kind, authentic self compassion and giving yourself some R and R – or at least cutting yourself some slack – you *do* kindly and also strongly encourage yourself to take a few steps in the heavy wet cement that seems to be in front of you, and then maybe a few more, and then maybe sometimes you just give yourself full warm permission to take another break from trudging for a while. That's all digging up. That's all digging out.

And even when it just seems hopeless for us, when we still offer our kindness to someone else, maybe a helping hand from above, or a lift from below, or a kind, encouraging pat on the back from next to them – which is the same as making a foothold with your hands to help them reach the cavern ceiling and use their own pickaxe to chip away at the dirt – that's digging up. That's digging out.

And I could go on, but like I said, I think on some level each of us has a sense, to some degree, of what might bring us a little closer to the fresh air and fresh water and sunlight of the surface, closer to breaking through the dirt, and a sense of what's likely to make us more buried. And if we're completely stuck, with YouTube and local meet up groups and online groups and video gatherings and mindfulness apps and instant ebooks and audiobooks and talks and podcasts, there's a lot of places to explore to try to find something to infresh things, to maybe put a little fresh ocean breeze in our torn and weary sails.

Ω

And after dinner, I'll be talking about – well probably a few things that could potentially be helpful tools for the Big Dig – but I want to share that one in particular that's been helpful to me, in case it resonates to explore it some and give it a try, and see if it seems to be a good fit. But we all tend to presume that whatever we're currently finding most helpful for us should really speak to everyone else, and of course it often doesn't work that way – everyone responds to different things and at different times – but I do want to at least put it out there, along with the one you asked me to talk about, Influencing Your Unfolding, and there's one or two others I'd like to include along the way as well.

And, last thought, I think it's important that we keep in mind how we can, each of us, help others dig out as well, even while we're still digging ourselves out or even if we're in a phase for a while where we feel like we just can't really dig out at all. Even with all our flaws and imperfections and all the pre-programmed disastrous tendencies of our species – literally disastrous, for the Earth and its creatures and for future generations and even for current ones – we can still help others dig out.

Even with everything that isn't yet completely ironed out and healed and made right in each of us, even with the more general human glitches and our own personal top 10 ways we're uniquely glitched out, even with all the tangles we haven't yet untangled and might never untangle during this life – because the human brain, it just has tangles, it just has knots, it just has glitches, it just – with a hundred billion neurons and maybe a quadrillion connections, some of them are just going to be a little haywire for every single one of us – but even with all our inner messes and flaws and shortcomings and unresolved traumas and woundings and outdated and unhelpful patterns, each and every one of us can still be a sometimes intentional and sometimes synergistically accidental conduit for something Deeply Good to come through – in bigger or smaller ways – that supports someone else, or supports *something* else in the larger Earth tribe.

So we shouldn't underestimate, along with the power of humans to knock things *out* of balance – among ourselves and with the Greater Earth Community – we shouldn't underestimate the power or capacity or potentiality of every single one of us, just as we currently are, to play some part in helping to bring things *back in* balance, in big and small and tiny, tiny ways that can gradually add up. We shouldn't underestimate our capacity to truly contribute to someone else's more surface healing or their deeper healing, both intentionally, and by just being available for synergy, for synchronicity, for happy accidents to happen through us, sometimes in spite of ourselves.

Ω Ω

And also, what lands in me as really good news is, we aren't alone in this. If we either decide this sense of a great gathering of a Consortium of Benevolent Beings, coming to support us, if we either decide that rings true, or we decide the feeling of even the *possibility* of it being true is a warm support in and of itself – regardless of whether we believe it's already starting to happen and will continue to build – then we can let ourselves really feel the resonance of not being alone in this.

And even if not, even if that whole consortium piece just doesn't land for us, still, as dark and dusty and cut off and suffocating and endless and hopeless as it might feel in the most difficult times – which some of us might have a lot of and some of us hardly any – it's still true that as we try to dig out, there are, I don't know, hundreds of thousands or more likely *millions* of people, or even more than that, who are already hard at work digging themselves and others out, right alongside us, as best as they currently humanly can. And awareness of that can be a real support. Either by finding some of them locally or online, and having a real sense of being a part of a community of up diggers, of Big Dig workers, or by just taking comfort knowing they are most definitely out there. Our own benevolent consortium of human, slightly rusty and amnesiac pre-Light Beings, that at our Core already always *are* Benevolent

Beings of Pure Light, working to help a Great Wave of Awakening spread across the Earth, which sometimes looks like putting the oxygen mask on ourselves first, before getting too focused on helping the person next to us put theirs on.

But you know, we don't know for sure, so just *maybe*, just *maybe* in addition to that, we can also resonate with this sense of it just being *possible* that we actually *are* being met halfway, from the bright, fresh-aired, sun-cleansed surface. Just maybe there *are* a lot of helpers in the sunlight, and more all the time, who are digging down, ready to take our hand.

And it just *might* be that now, more and more, having that support helps a lot more progress happen, and helps it happen a lot more easily than used to be the case. Just maybe, the momentum is starting to exponentially build, and a new, Light-filled Dawn is approaching. We don't have to know for certain it's true, to let the sense of its possibility impact us and warm us and encourage us and enhearten us. We can still feel towards, if that were true, how would that feel in us? If that were true, what would that really be like? Which touches on part of where we're headed this evening. And just maybe we can be lightened some, around the heavy shoulder load we've been carrying to varying degrees, usually more beneath our awareness than fully consciously.

And even if that just doesn't resonate at all – this sense of making a little space for even just the *possibility* of being more and more supported by a Consortium of Light Beings, gathering around the Earth, contributing to and delighting in our awakening – even if that just doesn't resonate, it's not much of a stretch to feel into the sense of in the near future, and already beginning, growing and growing numbers of people – to varying degrees and in different ways – still being flawed, imperfect humans, and at the same time, stretching into and opening into being connected more and more deeply to the Greater Earth Tribe, to the Continuum of Consciousness and to Greater Reality. To their Greater Selves and to the Beautiful More.

Perfection not required. Every mind tangle being untangled first, not required. Every glitch being de-bugged first, not required. Never messing up royally, not required. No longer getting angry or reactive or triggered or depressed or jealous or hurt or petty or spiteful or jaded, or addicted or negative or hopeless or going full on unconscious, absolutely not required. And cutting off from ourselves what we see as the messy, ugly, unspiritual, unevolved parts of ourselves, because they don't fit the image of a movement towards open apertured maturation, most definitely not, I repeat, *not* required.

Ω Ω Ω

So, to bring this whole afternoon full circle, if what came in bears out, it very well might be that eventually, and maybe sooner than we might think, the Earth isn't – put it this way, that people aren't as cut off from our Higher Selves and Pure Beingness as most of us experience now. And if that happens, that would support societal change that brings things more into balance, not only in ourselves and in our species, but on every level of life on Earth, and for the Earth itself.

Some things it would probably be too late to salvage, but a lot could be saved or reversed or the damage could be mitigated or minimized. And even if some things we've done to the Earth just aren't repairable for centuries or ever – which is more than likely with some things, including irreversible extinctions, and some ecological imbalances, some toxic chemicals spread all around the globe and so forth – it would still be comforting to know, even if it was just too late to stop some things from the doom and gloom list earlier, it would still be comforting just to know that millions and millions of people are starting to wake up and become more responsible global community members, more responsible members of the delicate and beautiful tribe of the Living Planetary Being, Earth. Which *will* help course correct and rebalance a great many things, even if it's too late for some.

And, according to what I saw, there's more and more help coming our way, both from above and from all those around us joining in on the Big Dig. And more and more apertures are getting ready to recalibrate with much more Conscious Connecting to Greater Reality, to the Beautiful More. And more and more heart kernels are getting ready to pop open. We're gonna need a bigger popcorn bowl. So yeah, I guess time will tell, and that's all I got, but I just wanted to end this whole big topic on an encouraging, more optimistic, higher note here.

I really liked hearing all that. It does sound hopeful. I think that might have impacted me more than anything else we've talked about so far this weekend. Meeting in the middle. Makes it sound like it's possible we aren't completely on our own.

Yeah it really does. A Consortium of Benevolent Beings, gathering, digging, dropping us shovels and pickaxes and lanterns and water and apples and jerky, through the slowly widening vent holes that connect our comparatively underground collapsed mine with the sun soaked fresh Spring-infused world of open-apertured Greater Re-Membering. That free and open world isn't very far above us at all, and closer all the time.

And again, whether this turns out to be literally, factually true and accurate or not, there's something there that felt supportive to me when the inflash came in, just in letting that image and sense wash through me. And also that more and more people around us are also doing their part to support the digging out, in their own ways. I like the image of that. Okay, let's call this whole topic done and have some dinner. I definitely need a real break and some food. And maybe a throat drop and some caffeine for Round 4. They should make a caffeine throat drop if they don't already. Feed two birds with one seed. How did we do with time?

We went about 20 minutes over, but I'm really glad we didn't cut that last part short.

Well we should still have enough time for what's on the docket tonight. But then again, I keep thinking that, and it seems like there's always more than I would've predicted once we get into it. Kind of like those circus clown cars. Doesn't seem that big from the outside, but once you open the doors, more and more keep streaming out. So we'll see how it goes.

PART FOUR:
THE OMEGA PRACTICUM
(SUNDAY EVENING)

SESSION 10
CHAPTER 55

Alright. Back to it. So our fourth and final main topic is opening up some of the practices and processes that have come through during your bridging sessions – you said the word that matched for them was invitations. And our intention has been not to talk shop during our breaks, to keep things fresh when recording, but a few minutes ago I brought up that bridging session that you briefly talked about yesterday afternoon, where you were judging yourself for not being more grateful to be alive and then a download came through about it. It piqued my interest and I wanted to hear more, but I didn't want us to go down a side road so early in the weekend, and you also thought it was jumping ahead a bit. So I brought that up, and asked about returning to it this evening, and you said we've laid more foundation since it first came up, and it connects with some of what we'll be going into anyway, and it also goes deeper into an area we probably wouldn't otherwise really touch into this weekend, and there was one more I can't think of. What else did you say?

Yeah, that it had a simple practice or invitation, which would be apropos for tonight.

Right, so we both thought it sounded good to circle back to it, and you said you were up for starting things off with it.

Yeah, so, let me kind of find my way back into it. I gave the *Cliff Notes* version yesterday, but just to recap, so this was pretty early in the bridging sessions, and at that point a lot of the time I was still a lot more pulled to returning to that amazing space that had opened in me during the Big Event, and especially being with Omega, and

I wasn't particularly interested in or appreciating how fortunate I was to have a second chance at life again.

And that morning in particular, I was really fighting with myself, wrestling with myself, like come on, what's wrong with me? I should be more grateful to be back in the land of the living. And sure, that sounds reasonable, but that morning – and a lot of the rest of the time – that wasn't currently at all where I genuinely was.

So I was just getting more tense, fighting with myself, trying to force the space I was in to get with the program and change to where I felt I should be, which was just making things tighter. And this was all happening before the bridging session started but it was still going on when I felt Omega arrive. And for those first three or four minutes nothing had flashed in yet, and I was afraid my tightness and tension and agitatedness was going to blow the session, keep it from happening, so I was fighting with that too. And then out of the blue I just felt this whomp suddenly come in, and this flash packet showed up, and one thing that opened was that I could suddenly really feel – and also really see in my mind's eye – the tightness of my musculature and a tight energetic band wrapping around mostly my abdomen and chest and shoulders, but also even my neck and jaw and temples and forehead.

Ω

And I just so crystal clearly saw how every time we try to push ourselves to feel something we aren't genuinely feeling, or try to stop feeling something we are, that always causes more tightness, and a tighter mental tangling instead of a loosening. Like – well, let's say a loved one dies and you're at the memorial service and you just aren't feeling sadness. So then you judge yourself for that, and you maybe start trying to squeeze yourself into feeling some, and you're questioning maybe you didn't even care about them that much because everyone knows you're supposed to feel sad at a funeral and you just aren't feeling much of anything.

And then to add to it, maybe they're an older relative, and their death means you'll probably be getting a little inheritance, and you're sitting there kind of flat and numb at the funeral and your mind goes to wondering how much it will be. You've been wondering that at times, and feeling guilty for it, and now especially at the memorial service of all places, can't you just be a decent enough person to not be so greedily thinking of *yourself* when you're supposed to be tearfully honoring *them*? What kind of person *are* you? You don't even *deserve* to be in their will. And great, now you aren't even paying attention at all, which is really self absorbed and selfish of you, as usual. Can't you just for a few minutes think of anyone but yourself and just actually really *be* there for an hour? When this is their final goodbye in this world? What the hell is *wrong* with you?

So maybe all of that is running through you, trying to feel what you aren't feeling and trying to stop feeling what you are, plus now a big added serving of self judgment and guilt weighing it all down even more. And all that inner busyness is squeezing tighter these contracted energetic and also musculature bands around you, which makes it even harder to feel whatever else your genuine authentic experience actually includes right now. It tightens everything inside you and makes it harder to be in even a little authentic connection with yourself in the moment. It doesn't actually serve anything at all, it just lets you feel like at least you're trying. But it doesn't actually help anything any more than squeezing your fists tightly closed helps you tread water. A for effort. D for drowning.

So I was seeing how all that tightness and inner self forcing just begets more tightness and doesn't really serve, and then I also saw an image of kind of an energetic boa constrictor wrapped around me, circling around and spiraling up, and constricting all those same areas in me, all the way up my body. And every time I tried to force myself to feel what I'm not, or to *not* feel what I am, in this little high speed vision or imagery that I was experiencing, every time I resisted and rejected what I was experiencing, that gave the boa constrictor more of a foothold – well I guess a squeeze hold, and it tightened even more.

This constrictor squeezes some of the vibrant life out of us, and just doesn't let up as long as we're tightly fighting and resisting our genuine current experience. It just wasn't modeled in most of us to value that, if it's not, quote, *positive*. We tend to mostly unconsciously assess it and if it doesn't feel good, or if it doesn't match up with what we think we should be feeling, we usually try to use brute force to whip it into shape, or we wrestle it into the basement and lock the door. And the constrictor just does its only job, which is to tighten even more every time it's given a little more inroad. It has no choice. It's just reflex. We tighten, it tightens. We relax our grip, it relaxes its grip. That's just its energetic physiology, in a sense.

Ω Ω

So as this inflash was unpacking and kind of doing its work in me, I was really seeing and feeling all this constrictedness from trying not to feel something I was feeling – which was my readiness and even eagerness for my life to finish up already so I could go back to my newly discovered Profoundly Beautiful and Quenching Home again – and also constrictedness from trying to make myself feel something I *wasn't* feeling – which was a gratefulness and openness and nonresistance to being back in this world and having probably several years ahead of me in it.

And I was seeing all this, feeling it all, and then something kind of discouraged and a little hopeless, or at least a little disheartened, came up in me, like "Yeah, I get it, I see it, but I don't really know that I can do anything different." And right then there was this second whomp, and I felt this amazing inflow of Deep Settled Spaciousness, that was so opposite of all of that contracted tightening and self squeezing I had just been doing. In comparison to this new space that opened, the bulldozing myself around felt so unkind and self-aggressive, and almost even – from a more subtle perspective – like a subtle form of a kind of muted, unintentional inner self violence.

But this new energy, it was this Deep, Soothing Spaciousness, that reminded me – in a more subdued, dialed down way – of the Space I felt during the Big Event before Omega showed up. And the quality that it kind of – well put it this way, the Space that waved in during this inflash was one specific quality more than anything else, and that quality – the words that came in to describe it were Absolute Allowingness.

And the flash packet of it was that this was one particular aspect or quality of Pure Beingness, Pure Consciousness, Pure Essence, the Source Substance. The First Source and Pure Essence and Clear Infinite Center of everything that exists. And like we talked about yesterday, this Infinite Loving Ocean of Pure Beingness is always everywhere, fully and completely. There's nowhere that it isn't.

It's the First Substrate and the Infinite Core of everything that exists. And you could also call it Pure Undifferentiated Essence or Pure Undifferentiated Beingness or Pure Undifferentiated Consciousness, or a hundred other names, but this particular aspect, the words that matched were Absolute Allowingness. Same Infinite Pre-created Essentiality, different angle, different perspective, slight shift in focus.

And Absolute Allowingness has the qualities of Infinite Softness, Endless Openness, Absolute Acceptance, Unending Presence, Ceaseless Flowingness. Uninterruptible Love and Everflowing Oceanness. And nothing could ever be too dense or too hard for it to flow right through without the slightest bumping or blocking or resistance or obstacle.

It just moves through molecules and atoms and subatomic particles with ease. At their core they're actually energetic potentialities, not fixed structures in space with actual dense mass or solidity. If you zoom in even more, every atom in existence is made of subatomic particles that are made of quantum fields that are made of pre-quantum energetic potentialities, that are made of a Pure Flowing Energetic Substrate that is made of only Pure Essence, Pure Beingness, Pure Consciousness, Absolute Allowingness.

If you imagine a huge dense solid rock at the bottom of the ocean, the ocean water can't flow through it, but this Infinitely Open, Boundaryless, Flowing, Omnipresent Isness is maybe a little like a more subtle form of a living flowing ocean, and everything created is in it, and it actually *can* flow through hard solid rock, because when you magnify in enough, there's relatively more empty, available space between each nonsolid subparticle in every atom in that rock than there is in our solar system.

Kind of like a chain link fence is more space than structure. Then magnified even more, even those fence wire structures are themselves more space than structure, and do that a few more times, until it's just swirling – not just subatomic – but subquantum and sub-energetic potentialities. So this Open, Spacious, Endless, Accepting, Loving Oceanness, it can just flow through subatomic particles effortlessly.

And the energetic precursors to these subatomic particles are made of this Infinite Flowing Presence Itself. I think I said this yesterday, but it doesn't *try* to be any of its qualities, it doesn't *try* to radiate inextinguishable Love and Presence and Acceptance and Spaciousness. It's just naturally continuously *being* the Way of Love and Presence and Acceptance and Spaciousness. Effortlessly. That's simply it's unreducible or irreducible very nature.

Ω Ω Ω

So Absolute Allowingness can flow through anything and everything effortlessly. It could never bump into anything or be stopped by anything. It's impervious to the tightest, thickest, strongest, most dense object, and to the most tangled and reinforced and tight resistance.

And it never pushes back or becomes a hard resistant boundary. It never contracts or tightens or insists. It never rams into or through a hard structure, or demands anything to change or to be different than it is. It flows but it doesn't push. It Tai Chis but it doesn't tango. It doesn't engage at the level of otherness than itself. It simply can't, any more than water can hold itself up to be a hard steady wall without changing its organizational structure into compact snow or solid ice.

And like I've said, of course, in our world we *do* need to push back or resist or say hell no sometimes, it's part of the deal here, and what I'm talking about shouldn't be misconstrued as advocating for becoming powerless against disresonant power, or being meek when what's called for is standing up for ourselves or what really matters to us. A clear firm no can be as deeply good and true and aligned as a soft open yes. Depends on the situation, right?

And by the way, if somehow this flash packet had had a different message, that it's never okay to push back, that's it's never okay to stand firm under pressure or to rise up against adversity or oppression of any kind, I'd push back against that pretty damn hard, and keep on pushing back in life when that's appropriate, because that doesn't resonate with my own compass. What comes in during the bridging sessions isn't the final word for me. Each of us are.

Each of us are the final word for each of us?

Yeah, for our own lives. Though hopefully we don't turn a blind eye to science and evidence and wisdom and feedback. I don't mean we just get to decide the Earth is flat because we saw it on social media, I don't mean a closed loop. But the buck stops with us, so I don't just automatically accept everything in these inflashes just because they come in, I check and see how much I resonate with them, which we each need to do for ourselves. But this particular one was really landing, really resonating.

And I kind of said this, but not only does Absolute Allowingness *not* push back or bump into or clash or crash or brace against, it just doesn't even have the structural formations or the formedness to do that. To contract and harden and resist and push. It's not that it *chooses* not to, or gives its tacit approval of everything it isn't pushing back against, it's that it simply doesn't have the structures or the mechanism, or the dualness, to close down and tighten up and push against or bump into anything. That's just not in its nature. It's at the Pre-level, or Nonlevel of Absolute Oneness.

And nothing could ever disturb it or perturb it or push it or block it. That isn't even *possible* on its Pre-prism First Side of the cosmic two way mirror, which is beyond and before all formed levels of created reality, though it holds *all* levels and is in Oneness with all of them. It's one aspect of the Eternal and Infinite and Omnipresent Essence and Substrate and Source Substance of all that is.

So just like it can simply flow through the hardest rock as though that dense structure was just a hologram – which from its perspective or nonlevel level it basically is – similarly, someone's heart could be as tightly closed and hard and dense and shut down – and as just impenetrability walled off – as that deep ocean rock, and Absolute Allowingness can still just completely effortlessly, without agenda, without even trying – it wouldn't even know *how* to try – it can still just flow right into and through that closed heart, and fully reside in that heart, like it resides everywhere else, always. It passes through absolutely everything because it's at the Pre-level level of reality, where there's nothing solid to run into. It could never encounter a boundary or border or a barrier for it to hit. It could never meet any real resistance, no matter how tightly closed someone is.

CHAPTER 56

And like I said yesterday about finding a stray kitten, when I talk about created reality being like a hologram – that from the perspective of Pre-created Reality, everything in created reality, both in more dense and less dense levels, is in a way hologrammatic and has no real solid substance – I don't mean it's not real, I mean its realness doesn't come from the foundational solidity of dense matter. Because the foundational pre-energetic substance and substrate of formed reality isn't fundamentally solid at all, it's not as it appears. But a lost kitten still really feels lost and scared, and a person suffering still really feels pain. And a delicately balanced planet being treated like our species has overall been treating Earth, especially in the last couple of centuries as our power to impact has exponentially increased, that's still a terrible tragedy. There's no skipping over that, no bypassing that, and we should be highly skeptical of any perspective that tries to do that.

But in terms of Absolute Allowingness being both omnipresent and omniflowing, both are true, that first, it can effortlessly flow through and reside in the hardest heart, the most contracted personality patternings, the hottest anger or coldest hate or tightest closed down self protection, or the most painful, solidified, hardened hurt, or the most reactive fear, and second, at the same time, even the hardest heart, the most cut off consciousness, *always* resides, *already* resides, *only* resides, in Infinite Oceanic Absolute Allowingness. Pure Undifferentiated Light-Filled Essential Beingness. Nothing could *ever* be beyond it or outside it or other than it, not truly. So it always resides in everything, and everything always resides in it.

That hard ocean rock always resides in this Ocean of Infinite Allowingness, even if it isn't aware of it. So from the vantage of that Flowing, Accepting, Everpresent, Evertemporal Essentiality, it could never meet resistance wherever it flows, which is always everywhere simultaneously. It is absolutely Omnipresent and Omniflowing, and nothing could ever hold it back, or block it, or push against it or put up any real resistance to it at all. Not even slightly. And so, at the very Core of absolutely all tightness, wherever it might exist, is *always* Infinite Loving Flowingness. Absolute Allowingness. It's already so, before we even lift a finger. A fait accompli.

And that Core Essentiality is actually our True Nature. Our very Essence. Our very Source and our very Substrate. Our most inward inner Beingness, Pure Undifferentiated Consciousness, the Core within our core. It's that which we really are, most deeply. And it doesn't *ever* try to force or push or pressure anything to be different than it currently is. It literally doesn't have that within it. Either the agenda or the capacity.

So when I was beating myself up and trying to have different feelings than I was having during that bridging session, what opened up was this direct and immediate and impactful Space of our Essential Beingness. A Space of Absolute Allowingness, of Infinite Loving Flowingness.

And it just so gently wafted through me, and really softened me and melted me and contented me, not as much as the Big Event, but a striking difference from just a couple of minutes before, when I was mad at myself for not being more grateful and content with my life, and was just tying myself up in more knots, more tangles, by trying to force myself to be in a different place than I genuinely was in. Like "Relax and be grateful right now, damn it!" This was a pretty profound shift from that. A complete re-set.

Ω

So I was just sitting there, getting really settled and centered, feeling soft and open and soothed and flowing and spacious, with any remaining residual tightness and tension from arguing with where I genuinely was, all just wafting away. And then this kind of invitation came in, which was along the lines of:

When you can, as you can, without forcing it, inside yourself be this way with yourself. Be softly and tenderly and warmly allowing and accepting of exactly what you're feeling and thinking right now. Meet it with friendliness and kindness, to the degree you authentically can, and not with the slightest harsh judgment or self imposed pressure for it to change. Be with yourself as Absolute Allowingness *always* is so naturally and effortlessly with you, whether you're aware of it or not. Be with yourself as Infinite Spacious Flowingness always is with everything that is. That helps heal and soften and open the constricted places. That helps even the boa constrictor get so relaxed it releases its contracting and gently unravels to the ground, and then slithers off to sleep in some soft grass under the warm sun.

And there was an understanding that came in and really landed, that to whatever little degree we're able to be in contact with that sense, or that intention, we're being a way of being that's in harmony with and closer to our True Nature, closer to our Purest Essence, closer to our Higher Consciousness, and so it naturally brings us a little closer to – let's say a Deeper Congruence. A little closer to our True Self. To the Infinite Core within our core. The Eternal Heart within our heart.

And it just might be that that *does* end up changing our space, relaxing our contractions, or maybe relaxing our contractions about our contractions, helping us be in a place that we like better. It just might loosen the knots we were holding tightly in our very trying to get rid of them. But it doesn't–

–Say that again?

So being a little more that way, the way of Absolute Allowingness, just might loosen the knots and tangles that we were making even tighter by trying to get rid of them. In ourselves, the only way our tightness can try to untie a knot is by tightly pulling on the strings, and that just makes it worse. But taking our hands off the strings completely, that can give them the space to start to loosen on their own. They can start to breathe and have some room. The warm sun can shine on them and thaw the ice that was holding the knot closed. The fresh flowing breeze can create some space between and within the tangles, and loosen their self grip.

So life's just naturally easier when we allow that boa constrictor to just uncontract and go to sleep peacefully in the grass. But the more we try to use force to try to *make* it unconstrict, *that's* what it responds to, and the tighter it holds on. Imagine instead of a boa constrictor it's an energetic electric eel, and it feeds off of the electricity we generate through the friction of our struggling against it, which just makes its contracted grip stronger. Or the more you try to force a scared baby armadillo, that's rolled up in a tight, self protecting ball, to open up and relax, the tighter it holds itself closed for dear life. And side note, something along the lines of mostly harmless, subtle level energetic electric eels might actually exist, which I'll come back to shortly.

Ω Ω

And of course, not only is this *not* about not taking appropriate action, or not setting solid boundaries or speaking a hard loud no when we truly need to, it *also* isn't about giving ourselves permission to act out or indulge or shoot energetic arrows at others if we're angry or reactive. It's about, when we find ourselves arguing with the way things are inside ourselves right now, could we connect with – to whatever degree is available to us, even just a little hint, and even if it's just using our imagination – could we connect with our intention, which can be a powerful thing, to match that Deeper Flow of Essence, that is always being absolutely Soft, Accepting, Unagendad Allowingness? And could we invite ourselves to simply cease pushing against and wrestling with and trying to steamroll what's showing up in us in this moment right now, and stop trying to force the arrival of what actually isn't?

That availability and willingness and allowingness can bring us closer to and more congruent with ourselves on this level, and also helps us be closer to and more congruent with the Deepest of what we are. Because then we're being in a way that matches the natural and easeful and nonresistant Way of Being that's of Absolute Allowingness. Then we're being just a little more of the Way of Being of our Truest Essence, even if what we're allowing to genuinely be here within us right now doesn't feel so great or expanded or beautiful or ideal. Even if what's here is a huge contracted *no*.

It's not about judging and rating the feelings we're having and then wrestling them around or performing surgery on them to get them the way we'd prefer. It's about actually *being* with them. *That's* the value. *That's* what can bring a little hint of that fresh Spring breeze of nourishing, vibrant, flowing, alive Openness into our lives, even when we're feeling something uncomfortable or unpreferable in ourselves. Not carte blanche permission to act out in the world, but gentle, kind permission and self compassion, for what is circulating inside you to be circulating, because, spoiler alert, it already *is*. And trying to use a tourniquet on our feelings just temporarily freezes them, while cutting off more of our vibrancy and life force. So yeah, that was what came in that day.

Well I really appreciate you sharing all of that, and as you've been talking about it I've been feeling a bit of a subtle Presence that has some of the qualities you were describing Absolute Allowingness to have. Open and spacious and flowing and deep. It feels settling and soothing. Reminding me I don't have to get everything perfect to feel like things are okay and going to be okay. Some tension I was holding without being aware of it has softened some.

Ω Ω Ω

That was quite a response that showed up for you, to what you were feeling stuck in. The perfect balm for it. And a couple of others you shared yesterday were too. Has that happened often, where the content of a flash packet in a bridging session was a perfect response to what's happening in you in that moment?

Yeah, sometimes. Another one that was along the same lines was, and I'll keep this really short, but once I was saying – and I mentioned this yesterday – but I don't really fear death anymore after the Big Event, but damn do I dread the pain and suffering I might have to deal with just before it. The process of dying, whether minutes or hours or days or weeks.

And immediately there was a whole inflash about it. Similar vibe, but it didn't specifically invoke Absolute Allowingness, at least not by name, and it had a different angle. It was about our universal and so understandable tendency to brace against, to resist experiencing what's in front of us to experience, and how that cuts off our life force – our life flow, our vibrancy, our intimacy with ourselves and with this Living Moment – in an attempt to not feel something emotionally or physically uncomfortable or painful.

The more we deaden ourselves from feeling those things because we naturally want to avoid them, the more we deaden ourselves from our Original Vibrancy, our Pure Aliveness, our very Essence, which is already usually pretty limited in the human experience anyway.

And the more we just allow ourselves to stop bracing and resisting and tightening against the discomfort – of worry or stress or sadness or loneliness, or hurt or fear or anger or hate, or physical or emotional pain, or whatever it might be – then the more potential there is for the discomfort or pain or difficulty or great difficulty to cease to be experienced as having the same degree of suffering, and the more there can start to be hints of – and then more than hints of – some space and softness and breathing room and relief and solid trustworthy ground, all showing up as an innate support underneath and around and within the discomfort or pain or difficulty.

And then the more capacity there is to feel what's there waiting to be felt, even more, without it being too much or causing more suffering. The capacity to navigate difficulty can increase, because the inherent support and strength of our life force has more space to move and breathe and cleanse and integrate, and to be more fully alive.

Could you say that again or a bit differently?

Yeah, so basically, it's usually not the original painful or the original difficult or uncomfortable feeling or sensation that creates the most intense internal suffering, even if it does create real physical or emotional pain, real difficulty. It's usually our contractedness and resistance to the first issue – it's usually our bracing and tightening and pushing it away – that creates the most suffering, that doubles down or triples down on the original suffering, or at the least *adds* to the original suffering, without us usually really being consciously aware of it.

That's a universal mammalian response, completely automatic and understandable, to brace against discomfort. It just doesn't work very well, and it costs us humans, or it causes in us humans, a deadening of our intimacy and congruence and connection with ourselves and with our very life force, and it reduces our capacity to show up in the moment with presence and clarity and competence and groundedness, and with empoweredness and solidity and availability and balance and vibrancy, when the moment isn't a dream come true.

We tend to see pain and difficulty as synonymous with suffering, but what came through was, first, absolutely acknowledging the great difficulty of real pain of every kind, and everyone's unique journey with it, not minimizing anyone's experience in the slightest, and second, this invitation or possibility that if we allow ourselves to relax the tight, tight bracing against that pain or discomfort, to whatever little degree might be available to us, we just might discover more space and flow and even – blasphemy alert – more okayness, while we're right in the midst of that intense and difficult full on original pain.

Suffering equals pain plus resistance. Without the resistance, there's still the pain – a beast to be reckoned with, worthy of respect, absolutely – but not the same quality of suffering. It has more room to breathe as itself, and that can help to dissipate the tight contracted intensity.

Ω Ω Ω Ω

So yes, it's awful having a terribly uncomfortable or painful feeling, physical or mental, and at the same time, the invitation in that inflash was, could I just check out what it would be like to stop unconsciously minimizing my breath or tightening my stomach or gritting my teeth, or deadening my emotional or energetic vibrancy, or whatever it might be, in an outdated and usually mostly unconscious attempt to minimize my own suffering at the cost of my vibrant aliveness? Could I just try for a minute or two or three to cease suppressing my very life force in an attempt to avoid feeling that lurking or full on discomfort or pain? Because that's selling my aliveness to avoid uncomfortable sensations, and that's a Faustian bargain. Not a truly worthy trade.

So could I let a little light shine in through the contraction cracks, by letting the spaces get a touch bigger? Allowing a touch more daylight? Could I cease bracing against discomfort or pain in the moment, just a touch or two, even for a minute or two? Just seeing what happens if I stop automatically or unconsciously bracing against it so reflexively and strongly and steadily.

It's the difference between self deadening and self enlivening. Being comfortably numb and uncomfortably but vibrantly connected. Between distancing ourselves from this living moment and showing up within all its discomfort when that's what's here. Which gives us more access to our capacity to engagingly and centeredly and empoweredly and vibrantly navigate through difficulty, via the inherent support of our life force and of more open connection.

So just exploring allowing ourselves to cease our bracing against discomfort and pain, even for 30 seconds. Or 10. And this isn't about trying to unpry our tight bracing, or trying to force open the closed, curled up baby armadillo. Not trying to force the tourniquetting of our inherent energetic vibrancy and capacity in an attempt to stop contracting right now, damn it. It's just seeing if we could gently lessen it some, reduce it some, cease it some, relax the bracing and tightening and resisting and numbing, even briefly, and even just a little. Small steps add up to more than a leap, and you're less likely to twist an ankle.

It reminds me of, there's nothing you can do inside yourself to warm up cold fingers, to dilate contracted blood vessels. Nothing. But what you *can* do is so subtly and gently simply *cease* contracting them. It's a Releasingness, a permission, a cessation of an unconscious action. A gentle acquiescing, a loosening of a habitual grip. An allowingness of letting go.

So that was another one that showed up as an immediate response to what was happening in me. And yeah, that's happened probably at least seven or eight other times too. I don't know how it all works, how those packets or data streams are formed, but it's pretty cool that there can sometimes be this instant, full on, fully formed flash packet, that applies to exactly what's up in me in that exact moment.

That is cool. Amazing actually.

CHAPTER 57

Alright, so next up, I'd like us to go into that series of downloads you talked about a bit over coffee, that set the stage, and then opened up this process or invitation that you called Influencing Your Unfolding. From what you've shared so far about it and the background leading up to it, I thought it was worth including this weekend. So let's start with, could you talk about when and how this topic came up, and what Influencing Your Unfolding is?

Yeah, so that phrase was just what translated as the best match for the overall theme of a lot of that material, that came in over three or four bridging sessions. And of course there are a lot of different things that influence how things move in our lives, what happens to us, what happens around us, how our future unfolds. And some are obvious and some are more subtle, and some, according to these inflashes, are more a walk on the wild side and I'm not sure what to think about them. So we'll unpack some of those, and then get into looking at how we can try to tilt the scale a little more in our favor sometimes, in terms of how things go in our lives.

And even if it doesn't seem to work, if it doesn't seem to change what we wanted to change, attending to that can still help our brain create new neuropathways and new senses of what could fit in our lives that maybe we haven't had before, and infill us some with some essential nutrients and support, in a few different ways, so it can still be a really good thing for our lives, and also it just might help tilt the scale a little more around what could unfold later on down the road.

And I guess I'll just go ahead and throw in that the other main process I wanted to make sure we get to – the one I've mentioned that you haven't heard yet – it's related but different, and like I've said, lately it seems to be supporting me in settling more into my life as it is – helping me appreciate it more and show up a little more – instead of inwardly rejecting it til it's shaped more the way I want it to be, which for me would mostly mean returning to that completely quenching feeling of Total and Absolute Belonging and Love-filled Enoughness and Contentment and Connection. And when we talk about that one, it will bring in another quick, simple invitation or process that I liked. So those are the main things on the docket, probably with a few little hopefully scenic detours or points of interest along the way as usual. So how about if we start with me just laying some foundation.

Sounds good.

Ω

So, there are a lot of different categories of things that can influence how our lives are going and will go, what happens to us, what our experiences are, whether we seem to have more good luck or bad luck, more smooth sailing or rough seas, more success or failure, more happiness or heaviness, more money or financial stress, more health or illness, more relationships and above average relationships or more difficulties in that area, and so on. And some of these influences are obvious to us, like sometimes we're just in the wrong place at the wrong time. I mean, if you were excited to book a ticket on the biggest ocean liner ever, and you got on the Titanic, bad luck, bad timing. Your heart probably sank. Or let's go check out that swell new Hindenburg airship. Hottest ticket in town. Bad luck. Bad timing.

And just like a gorilla can be just living their life and happen to catch Ebola, humans in the region, even if they're taking careful care, can happen to catch it too, if they're at the wrong place at the wrong time. Same with Covid, or the whole list of other viruses – or bacteria or parasites or fungal infections – the whole list of pathogens. Sometimes preventable with more care, but sometimes just bad luck, bad timing. One little tick bite can rob you of a decade or more. One little mosquito bite, one little undercooked egg, one piece of listeria-contaminated cantaloupe, one little cough from someone near you, etcetera, can nosedive your health for a while, or for the rest of your life, or even greatly shorten it. Wrong place, wrong time, bad luck.

We touched on this yesterday afternoon, sometimes things just happen, and it isn't fairly distributed. On a wild, unpredictable planet, with billions of people and a whole lot of microorganisms and weather events and moving cars and unpredictable investment risks and lotteries and a million other potential influences – or maybe more like trillions depending how much you drill down – really fortunate and really unfortunate things are going to happen to people.

So, pretty self evident, one big influence on what happens in our lives is random events, random timing. Stuff happens on Planet Earth, it's just the way the dice land. We want to know why things happen, but a big part of it is it's a random, wild, unruly planet with trillions of moving parts, trillions of pinballs bouncing around. Sometimes they're going to bump into each other. Things happen.

A drop of ocean spray lands on the hot sand and evaporates, and its last wispy dying thought is why me? But it's a statistical certainty a whole lot of spray droplets will be landing on the sand all day every day all over the world. No particular deeper reason for what water splashes up and what stays in the ocean, just the random churn.

Or one snowflake lands in some shade and gets to have the whole winter, and another lands on a dark log under the sun that just came out, and burns away in moments. "Why me? It's not fair! Help me I'm melting!" I remember a *Far Side* cartoon of a butterfly that had just left its cocoon only to be caught in a spiderweb right next to it. It happens. Sometimes it's just how the numbers crunch, how the pinballs roll, how the wind blows, how the dice land. Just the luck of the draw.

So not much news so far, and of course also not news, genetics impact health, some jobs and activities are riskier than others, and some food is healthier and some more risky, which is one reason the McBlowfish burger hasn't really caught on yet. So a lot of things have possibilities or propensities or potentialities that can impact our lives, and a lot of it is random. Pretty self apparent so far.

So then we go one notch deeper, also probably not a surprise or a controversial perspective, our mental and emotional programming has a real impact on things. Like obviously, some people are bigger risk takers than others, some find it easier to take better care of their bodies than others, some are more defeatist while some are more anything is possible. More confident job candidates get hired more and gain more confidence, and less confident ones might not come across as well during interviews and might not get hired as easily, which reinforces their lack of confidence. Pretty self evident.

Or if two people are diagnosed with diabetes, maybe the first person has always found it natural and easy to really take the bull by the horns with challenges, they've just always had the inner resources to do that, and they completely create a new, healthier life for themselves, which increases the chances of it not becoming as big of an issue, staying at a very manageable trajectory, and maybe the second person has always found it very difficult to rise to challenges, hard to find enough available inner resources, and just kind of collapses into, "Why did this have to happen to me? It's not fair." And maybe they just can't find what it would take to really change their life, and they end up having a worse trajectory, reinforcing their understandable belief that life isn't fair to them.

Both people to some degree create their own self fulfilling prophecies, and both are very possibly doing the very best they can with their particular combination of strengths and inner tangles, most of which were most likely fairly established when they were children. There's *some* choice there, but a lot of it is a mix of genetic predisposition and early childhood experiences and learnings and woundings. They didn't start on equal footing, but they tend to be compared and judged as though they did, like that race track I mentioned yesterday, where one person just has wet cement in their lane, but is often judged in comparison to everyone in the normal lanes. We all understand that our genes and our past experiences can have a huge impact on our health and on our psyche, which can have a huge influence on our life now and in the future. But that doesn't mean we can't do our damnedest to heal and/or overcome some of those physical and mental predispositions and imprinting and residue, but that's usually easier said than completely done.

Ω Ω Ω

And then there's a whole host of less obvious things that can impact how our life unfolds. Like one thing most of us aren't very aware of, even gut bacteria can really affect our brain. If it's out of balance, it can create depression and anxiety and other brain chemistry imbalances, which isn't that conducive to healthy eating habits, which can exacerbate things and make them even more out of balance. It can also create a near irresistible craving to eat more sugar and carbs, to help multiply that particular out of balance bacteria. Almost like parasitic entities controlling our brains, putting us under their spell.

So if our biomicrome is a little – if our microbiome is a little off, that can really control or hugely put the thumb on the scale of some of our behavior, and then it can take so much energy to fight those battles that sometimes we just give in. Which over time can lead to worsening health issues and a worsening microbiome, which can perpetuate and worsen the cycle.

So some of our impulses and urges and actions are sometimes actually being controlled by microscopic nonhuman cells that live inside us and send chemical signals to our brain, and we think *we're* the ones making those choices. Kind of humbling. More than half of the cells we walk around carrying are not our own, not human cells – we're in the cellular minority of our own bodies – which understandably doesn't really make it into our self concept much.

And of course most of us can sometimes also be really influenced by what others say or do and how that impacts our patterning. Maybe you read a negative comment on social media when multitasking and you're not even aware of it really landing in you and getting in there and stewing and bothering you, and then later that day you tear into someone who didn't deserve it, and then they tear into their kid for knocking over a lamp, and then that evening that kid leaves a bullying comment on social media, which starts a whole wave of ripples in that kid's life and beyond.

So there are all kinds of things flying around, obvious and less obvious. Including more subtle things that we don't even consciously register that can be pretty significant influences in the short term or over time, on the unfolding of our life. But now let's take it another step deeper, into less conventional and probably more controversial territory, and this also gets into what you asked yesterday if I was going to get to this weekend, where there's a couple of these I'm just not personally sold on, I don't really buy it.

Good, I've been curious to hear one or two of those.

CHAPTER 58

Yeah, so on top of all of the influences from this level of reality that impact the unfolding of our life, what also streamed in was there's also various multidimensional subtle influences. And I don't know them all and don't understand them – if they even exist – but what came in was, there are things beyond our known physical world that can have an impact on what unfolds here.

So it might be a little like how the complex pattern of the Earth's magnetic field can direct a magnetized needle to turn a certain way in water, which at one time seemed like magic, but now we understand the mechanisms. So something like that, where there are forces and influences and energies that aren't against the laws of multidimensional physics, they're just beyond our current limited understanding.

So one of these potential more subtle influences that came in is one I'm not that excited to mention on the record, because it's in an arena that I've just flat out never believed in at all, and I've admittedly had some superioritis towards those who do. So maybe Omega was having an off day, maybe my signals got crossed and I got this one wrong, or maybe my own unconscious was having some fun. Or, just maybe there's some solid scientific explanations behind it that we're just not quite there yet around, and my arrogant judgmentalism isn't on quite as sure footing as I presumed.

But this one is that there actually are like subtle, something kind of similar to but different from electromagnetic and gravitational waves – some other waves or influential fields that our science doesn't know about yet – that can create an influence, a pull, an impact on how things unfold on the planet and in our lives, that are generated by the subtle gravitational impact of the positioning of the planets and the sun and maybe even objects farther out than that.

You're talking about astrology?

I don't know if I'm talking about astrology, that word conjures up daily horoscopes in the comic section of what used to be known as newspapers. Astrology could potentially be a very imprecise and hit and miss field of study that's actually based on some subtle intuition some people have had over the centuries that something like this exists, but basically what I saw – accurate or not –was that there's a scientific explanation to there being some degree of real influence there, we just don't understand it yet. Try telling someone a few hundred years ago about radio waves and see how that goes.

But just like you can physically turn a magnetized compass needle a different direction, it's not a big battle, those influences – if they exist – don't have to be the final word. So I don't know that it's true, and it doesn't personally ring true for me so I'm not holding it as true for now. It's off to the side in a folder with a big question mark on it. Preceded by an S and a B, not necessarily in that order.

And even farther out than that is another one I don't at all know is true, and it's one where I'm really skeptical but I also just don't really want to even engage in thinking about it. I'd much prefer it to not be true, and I have it categorized in a different folder, this time the cover has a question mark preceded by a W and a T and I forgot the third letter but I think it might have been an E or an F.

I have a feeling it was an F.

You could be right. If that's your gut feeling, I'd trust it. And who knows, maybe my sense of both of these things will change, I mean my sense of what's possible and what isn't has already been massively stretched since the Big Event, and it turns out the Omniverse is apparently a tad bigger than I used to think, so this might well be true also, but I'm just not there yet.

And just because there seems to be a lot more out there than I used to think, that doesn't suddenly mean everything that I'm exposed to or anyone is exposed to as a possibility is actually true. Just because I experience what I interpret as getting an info-packet from Omega doesn't mean I have to always accept it in myself as what I personally believe. Like I said this afternoon, that would be ceding *way* too much of my own autonomy and power and tuning fork assessment responsibility.

Ω

So, take this next one with, you know, more salt grains, and this is what I was referring to about there possibly existing like subtle level electric eels that feed off of the friction of our resistance to them, but basically it's that on a relatively nearby dimension on the radio dial, on a subtle level of reality not too far from our own – maybe a couple dozen notches over or deeper or farther up than where we are and any universe in our tesseverse is – there are these, well actually, let me try a take two here.

So kind of like, at least in some movies, there are or were some pedicure places that offered a thing where you soak your feet in a container of water that had little nibbling fish in it and they would nibble away your dead skin – and it sounds unsanitary and ridiculous to me, and probably not a dream come true for the fish, and I don't know if it's still a thing or if it ever really was – but something loosely kind of like that. There are lots of parasites and symbiotic – I think symbiotes is the word, according to every third sci fi movie ever made – but there are lots of organisms on Earth that mooch off of other organisms. Sometimes it's harmful, sometimes neutral, sometimes helpful. Like those birds that help hippos by eating flies from their backs.

So I saw subtle level, energetic – I'm still not sure what to call them, the word *entities* wasn't quite it, because these were closer to fish or leeches than sentient beings. Small and not powerful, no evil intent, barely conscious energy creatures, if even that. And they were on relatively nearby subtle levels of our reality, meaning not up on Omega's level or the level of the Big Event, which I don't know if I said yesterday, to me felt like it was maybe halfway between our level and Omega's usual level.

But they were like subtle level suckerfish, or energy nibblers – maybe energy suckers – that feed off of the energetic discharge we create when we're feeling strong emotions, or even when we're creating a closed circuit of tension and emotional suppression in order to *not* feel them. That's the energy range they feed off of, like algae living off of sunlight or real suckerfish living off algae. They live off of the natural energetic emissions of our emoting, and also the emissions of our resistance and tightness and frozenness. Like subtle level electric eels that feed of off the electricity we generate in our resistance.

And they kind of – well like I said, they aren't complex, conniving beings, not evil or hair stand up sinister, but they just know how to get a little more food than what was happening before. Like some gut bacteria, or like, there are some parasitic wasps that temporarily paralyze a spider with their sting, and then they inject their eggs into it, and then the larvae slowly feed off the spider for a while, nothing like fresh, locally sourced food, and then they somehow take over the spider's web building code, they inject a little malware, or maybe even literally a virus, the mechanism isn't understood yet, but they somehow force the spider to make a web it wouldn't normally ever make, that's ideal to support the larvae's cocoons.

So it becomes like a zombie spider that has no choice but to follow its rewired operating system, and it doesn't even realize it's been highjacked. Somehow the larvae release just the right chemicals to reprogram and steer the spider's brain in just the right way, and the spider is just perfectly following its unfortunately co-opted and rewritten and rerouted operating code, not recognizing anything is amiss. Pretty astounding.

That is.

But this isn't quite that extreme, it's just kind of, it's just little pokes, little nudges, little steerings. These energy nibbler fish just learn where the pressure points are, where to press down on a bar to get a food pellet, like a trained rat. If you tap just under someone's kneecap, their leg kicks out. So they just automatically know, like a hamster pushing up the water bottle ball bearing so it can get water, they just know how to nudge us to create a stronger reflexive emotional reaction sometimes. They aren't angry or mean and they don't care about us either way, if they even have enough understanding to really understand we exist as beings, and I don't think they do. They're just trying to eat, just trying to earn a living, like leeches or like the hippo birds.

Ω Ω

And actually, if I remember right, they aren't actually – hippo birds aren't actually just completely symbiotic. I think they actually sometimes poke the hippo's back with their beak, causing little wounds that attract more flies. So it's like, "Hey we've got a deal for you, let us stand on your back and we'll take care of those annoying flies for you." But then once they have their ID badges and are waved past the guard desk, they sometimes deliberately exacerbate things, generating more food for themselves at the cost of their not incredibly bright host. Like if those salon nibbler fish deliberately irritated the skin to generate more food for themselves. So what came in was, they're not just passively feeding off the emotional energy we offgas, but they're also instinctively pushing a few levers to generate more intense emotions from us, so they get more food.

And you know, mosquitoes seem to favor some people over others, and depending on your makeup, or the phase of your life, or the kind of day or week or lifetime you're having, some people are better candidates than others for these energy suckerfish too. So like the out of balance gut bacteria that send signals that direct our brain to go into the kitchen and eat sugary or carby food – which feeds them and makes them and their reflex hammer more powerful – it's similar with these little suckers, but they feed off of our energy releases. And they can nudge us, pull a lever, push in a ball bearing, tap a knee to make it reflex, they can do little pressure point pushes to get us riled up or get us emoting, get us juicing.

It's not that big of a stretch that, for instance, when we sweat, our skin bacteria flourish more, so they might eventually evolve in a way that increases our stress to induce more sweating, which as far as I know doesn't exist, but that wouldn't be out of the norm in natural evolution. And we don't really think about it, but it's not a crazy idea that more subtle levels of reality – that are kind of like nearby tesseverse adjacent energetic overlays to this level, just a few notches out of current scientifically perceivable frequencies – might have some energy life forms that have evolved or have found just the perfect energy food match to sustain themselves in the energy we release – let's call it the offgassing of energetic evaporation – from both emotional energetic discharge and from the considerable energy we use when we try to unconsciously suppress or hold in or shut down unprocessed emotions. It's not that wild of an idea when you take a couple of steps back. Imagine a simple solar powered robot that learns to tilt the solar panel in a direction that gets it more sun juice. Something like that.

This is really interesting.

CHAPTER 59

Did you get anything about if there are different species or subtypes of them, with some feeding more off anger, some fear, and whatever else?

If they exist. I would prefer a world a little tidier and simpler than one where this is true, and also I don't want – not only do I not want mindless colonies of gut bacteria forcefully lobbying me to have some cookies before bed, which might not hold up in court if I'm caught chocolate handed, but I *really* don't want some potentially real parasitic suckerfish manipulating me so they can get some energy food. Just no.

But I didn't get any like subspecies information or anything. One image was like those little skin nibblers, mostly harmless, except maybe as they grow bigger they need more and more energy sparking or radiating off us, so they help things along more. Maybe they start as nibblers, but as they grow they learn what prompts more payoff, more offgassing from us, more energetic evaporation. They aren't any more malevolent than a caged rat pushing on a food release lever. Just trying to survive.

So yeah, those are another example, potentially, of an influence that can affect what unfolds in our lives, what we experience. And it again could be self fulfilling or a catch 22, where some energy suckerfish attach themselves to you – to a more subtle imprint or blueprint or subtler level of you – and they squeeze out a little more reactivity, and then that causes more difficulties in your life, so then you have more negative emotions running, which feeds them more – the energy nibblers – and maybe they grow and get stronger, and then maybe some other ones that were just getting a few crumbs from that enlightened monk over there come join the picnic. And maybe with some more power, either through growing strength or growing numbers or both, they start to steer you more towards that negativity of emotional feelings and the expression or suppression that they feed on.

And someone without them, or with fewer of them than someone else, or smaller ones than someone else – I really have no idea what I'm talking about in terms of numbers or size – but someone with less of them maybe could go through life without those influences and so they could be on a higher road than if they did have more of them nibbling and tugging and pushing reaction levers all the time. Like the difference between walking down a road alone or with 30 leashed chihuahuas pulling on you every which way. So with enough pull from these energy nibblers, life could be harder, which might create more negative emotion – and a withered emotional immune system – which maybe lets those energy leeches grow stronger, making things even harder. A vicious nibblistic circle.

Ω

And like I touched on yesterday, maybe exorcisms and sage smudging and other clearing ceremonies and traditions developed as a way to call on an energetic technology of sorts, that activates more

subtle levels of reality to kind of electroshock away unwanted energies or mini-entities, or maybe to create a vibration they can't tolerate, fingers on the chalkboard, so they move on.

Reminds me, once I bought a little mosquito-repelling high frequency sound emitting device that you turn on when you're around
a lot of mosquitoes, and the point of this gadget, as you probably
guessed, is to trick gullible people like me into wasting 20 bucks
on a scam that doesn't do a damn thing. But maybe something like
that *does* work to get rid of these energy suckers, and maybe some
of those traditional clearing approaches were – or are – effective
ways of mitigating them and other unwanted visitors or energies.
That definitely isn't something I was shown in an inflash, just to be
clear, but interesting thought.

I mean, I would expect a lot of old spiritual traditions and ceremonies and beliefs to have had one foot in genuinely effective meth-
ods, based on accurate perceptions of some aspects of subtle levels of reality – or just based on trial and error – and one foot in
misperceptions and misunderstandings and inaccurate and enculturated beliefs. And actually, newer spiritual traditions could be
included in that too. So maybe there are ways to clear them, and
maybe some extra drama or extra steps get added to that process –
to that technology or methodology – that maybe aren't strictly necessary, but it's probably hard to isolate just the distilled effective
part from the ceremonial or belief system extras, like separating
the aspirin from the willow bark. And also if believing in efficacy is
an important ingredient, ceremonies and traditions help generate
that belief and confidence, which might strengthen the effective-
ness of the method or technology, if that made sense.

*It did, but backing up a second, just making sure, you're not say-
ing that anytime someone is feeling reactive or feeling negative
emotions, that's always the energy nibblers.*

No, definitely not. We don't need to bring energy nibblers into the
equation at all to explain strong emotions and emotional reactivity,

lots of causes we're all familiar with, sometimes a bad mood is just a bad mood, a tantrum is just a tantrum, fear is fear, anger's anger. And again, these are all just potential influences and I can't speak to how strongly various real and allegedly real influences *can* influence or *do* influence. I'm just laying out the tapestry here, as I saw it in the inflashes.

Does it work with positive emotions too?

Does what work?

Do these energy nibblers feed off of positive emotions too?

I don't really know. My impression is it's more the negative energy they feed off of, both expressed and suppressed, and when you think about it, fear and anger and arguments and disagreements and heated political divides and old feuds when they get reactivated, and social media comment fights, that us and them we've talked about, that defensive jaded clenchedness or attacking or reactivity, things like that tend to create the strongest charge in us. But did I get that sense from the flash packets or could that be an example of my own assumptive biases influencing the pristineness of what I was shown as I try to process it and share it? Not sure. But mostly negative is what resonates.

And about not needing to bring subphysical suckerfish into the mix at all to explain everything, I just want to add that just the way the brain is, stress can beget stress, hopelessness can lead to more hopelessness, reactivity can lead to more reactivity, anger can feed more anger, negativity can feed more negativity, and heaviness can feed more heaviness. And any of those, or jadedness or disheartenedness or closed drawbridgedness, whatever it might be, can filter what you see in a way that seems to give you more reason to feel that way.

Brain wiring and neural clusters tend to get stronger through repetition, regardless of if they're helpful or harmful. Like how driving to work becomes automatic after enough times, or like how muscles get bigger the more they're worked. So it's Occam's razor again, right? Why bring in this wild, currently unprovable idea when you could keep it more simple and say it's just the brain, doing all its brainful braining again?

$$\Omega\,\Omega$$

But for what it's worth, that was what I saw, that there exist subtle level energy suckerfish, or energy leeches, that feed off your energetic evaporation. Subtle level electric eels that shock you and then feed off your reactivity. They feed off two different energy sources: emotion expressed and emotion suppressed. And that they exist as actual, living, uncomplex, subphysical energetic creatures, that can be one influence in our lives, to greater or lesser degrees. And no I don't have any real idea of their size or if size even applies, or what percentage of people have them, and are they like a school of fish nibbling away around the energy cloud of one person, and then someone else walks by who's really triggered because of that damn comment someone made – verbally or on a social media post – and then they all jump ship and swim over to that hot new free buffet overflowing with food? I doubt those birds choose one hippo and stay with it through feast and famine, it's probably more advantageous to be opportunistic than host-loyal, but that's just unsubstantiated conjecture.

And I don't know like how many nibblers per person, anything like that. The image was like a handful, but I'm not positive that wasn't assumptive. And even if now that we've heard about this possibility, we started feeling like maybe we're becoming aware of them, that could easily just be us inaccurately interpreting chemical processes in the brain, mis-attributing it. So I don't think we get to definitively resolve this anytime soon, but it's interesting food for thought. That our thoughts are interesting food.

It is. More to mull over.

Yeah, and like I said, for me, for now it's just sitting in a question mark folder, to be determined, or maybe it never is. I'm definitely not interested in premature determination. If it's undetermined it's undetermined.

So, zooming out again, we've got the influences I've named, and there are probably a lot more subtler ones I haven't, like Oversouls or guides or beings on subtler levels influencing things here on Earth in subtle ways at times, if/when they can, or offering subtle support if/when they can. Like maybe that growing Consortium of Benevolent Beings helping us dig out and reaching down to us, and maybe loved ones who have died sending good vibes, and whatever else.

And sometimes maybe there are different forces or influences that are in competition or pulling things in opposite ways, a little like two wizards, ten feet apart, in an epic wizard battle, each trying to use their wands and sheer will power to pull a crystal ball to them that's sitting on the ground in the middle between them. Probably easier just to walk over and pick it up, but you know, wizards are gonna wiz.

And just to reiterate, back to where we started, sometimes things just happen in a complex world. Sometimes a broken ankle is just a broken ankle, a bad mood is just a bad mood, unexpected income or unexpected bills are just that, and facing a fairly serious health situation sooner or later is just part of the deal for a lot of people over the course of several decades of being in physical bodies. But according to what came in during these bridging sessions, there are also these other more subtle influences. Okay, so, let's leave all that aside and lay a little more foundation in one or two other areas.

Ω Ω Ω

A question before you do. I'm wondering what was your actual image or sense of these energy nibblers? Were they like amorphous energy balls, or multi-colored spheres, or more solid than that with internal organs just on a more subtle level? Did they have eyes and ears and a mouth? And can we get rid of them? Is there Deep Woods Off for these energy suckerfish?

Yeah, so my sense of them was that they don't have organs or differentiated body parts like on this level of reality, that on their level energy organizes itself as needed without specific more defined organs with specific functions. So closer to amorphous nebulous energy blobs, or amoeba like energy globules, maybe the size of a baseball or volleyball, but size might not even apply. So these are just individual subphysical mini-entities or energy creatures – maybe subtle level energy creatures isn't too far off – with a very limited perspective or a limited consciousness, just a barely conscious id if even that, just feed feed feed feed feed, that's all they live for, all they know.

And I don't think they can evolve or become more conscious, I don't think they can be reasoned with any more than mosquitoes or leeches or electric eels can, and I was going to try to go into this a little later anyway, because it connects with some of what we'll get into here soon and it also connects back to Absolute Allowingness and to a repeating theme that's come in a lot from different angles during the bridging sessions, so I wanted to give it its due, but we're running out of later so I think I'll just go ahead and bring it in now. So in terms of energy nibbler repellent, what I saw was a lot of it is no longer feeding them.

You lost me with that last sentence.

So the main way we can reduce their strength or their numbers or their power or influence, to the degree they have some – which by the way happens to be the same way we help ourselves not feed into negative mental cycles and ruts even if these shadow suckers don't exist – is just to no longer feed them. Not being a – well, not providing an easy and ample source of food for them anymore. If a mosquito never gets any blood from you, it's gonna buzz off. A leech can't leech if there's nothing to leech onto. So not offgassing as much strong or persistent negative energy, not being as reactive, outwardly or inwardly.

We might not feel like we have a choice a lot of the time, but that doesn't mean we're actually powerless about it, even if it's not easy and takes some time to uplevel around. We can practice and build the skillset and build our flexible solidity to stop reacting so much to our reactions, to stop feeding strong and not so strong negative emotions. What came in was, you just stop reacting, stop giving them your contracted attention, meaning stop fanning the flames of your negative reactions and emotions with more of them. Stop priming the pump.

Not stuffing down feelings at all, *not* building a strong vent cover or battening down the hatches to keep them locked up below deck – which still off gasses energetic evaporation – but just not feeding an endless feedback loop of reacting to your reactions about your reactions. Not continuing to feed and energize the toy top, which just energizes it and keeps it spinning around. Tops need energy to keep spinning, so if you just leave it alone it eventually falls over and becomes still. If you aren't feeding your spinning reactive thoughts, you aren't replenishing the energy that makes them spin. You aren't contributing to the offgassing they feed on.

That the energy suckers feed on?

Yeah. but really it's true for both, for reactive thoughts and feelings and also for these subphysical energy nibblers. If you stop feeding the seagulls at the beach, then after divebombing you awhile, they're going to finally move on to those kids over there that are about to be no longer enjoying their ice cream cones. But if you try to catch them and cage them in a lockless cage, where you have to keep holding the cage door closed yourself, that's not really going to settle them down or free you of them or create a genuinely freeing and calm environment all around, even if there's less divebombing going on for now.

CHAPTER 60

Can you say a bit more about no longer feeding them? The energy suckerfish, not the seagulls.

Yeah, but same answer for all three. The ceasing of habitually reinforcing and rewarding actions that create agitation. Maybe a better way to say that is just stop damn feeding them or fighting them or trying to freeze them or hold them down. So with shadow suckers, what it might look like in daily life, when we can't even see them or feel them and they might not even exist at all, is just really intending to not be as moved by the winds of emotional reactivity.

And when I say "just," I don't mean it's the easiest thing in the world, and again, I'm not talking about getting all tight or stuffing anything down or going unconscious. Not Pink Floyding your way through life, comfortably numb. So it's not shutting down or stuffing down, it's just over time growing the muscles of having a larger perspective and a more grounded center and stronger trunk and roots, and learning to not be so blown around by all the different winds that blow around in your life.

And this applies exactly the same if there are shadow suckers pulling on your reactivity reflex levers, or if it's people doing that – which in just about every social environment there's at least some of that now and then – or if it's all just brain reactivity, self tizzifying ourselves into more tizzification and reactivity. It might even be a little of all of the above, but whatever the composition of what's activating us – of what's getting our negative emotional electrical currents really firing – still a really practical response is just not feeding it with more reactivity. So growing our capacity to be more like a solid Sequoia tree trunk and roots. Practicing our stance.

What do you mean practicing our stance?

Well first, while I'm thinking about it, let me just throw in that there's probably a better word than *negative* emotion. No emotion is inherently negative when it's allowed to have its safe space to wave through and then dissipate, without you believing it sums up who you are – that you're a terrible person because some of your 30,000 thoughts and feelings a day, or whatever it is, won't win any saintliness competitions, which actually, the definition of a saint isn't someone with only pure holy thoughts, it's someone who doesn't let the rest of their absolutely normal and natural human thoughts and feelings drive their chariot, control their life – so not believing our thoughts and feelings define us, and also not needing to act them out in a way that's out of harmony.

It's just part of the terms of participation as humans on Earth to sometimes have waves of less socially acceptable feelings, like hate or rage or anger, self pity, envy, greed, jealousy, reactive hurt, evolutionarily crucial coarse sexual desire, the whole list. The waves that arise in us don't define us. But how we *navigate* those waves partially does.

When we're upset, hitting our bed with a pillow, or just hitting a pillow, or getting really into a video game, or moving some energy through pushups or jogging or dancing to a song with a driving beat, or some other physical activity – like maybe cleaning and organizing for an hour – or alternatively just sitting and breathing and letting all those feelings have space, while also doing an awareness practice like Simultaneous Awareness, so that you're touching in with an anchor of a more grounded perspective, all of those can help us navigate the wave, giving it permission to exist and to pass through and dissipate harmlessly. Whatever isn't self harmful now or later, and also isn't sending that energy wave uninvited into someone else's field for them to deal with, just so you can unload and depressurize the discomfort of having it in your own field of experience.

And really our whole concept of, some emotions good, some emotions bad, just contributes to our tendency to harshly self judge and judge others, and also to suppress and sometimes maybe explode, rather than just intelligently allowing those energetic waves to pass through spaciously and then dissipate. So one image that came in was having an open emotional aperture while you're still in the driver's seat. Not giving your power to the waves, but also not locking them in the dungeon. Which brings us back to having a solid but flexible stance, which we can grow through practicing it.

Ω

So, let's say you're on a fishing boat for a week and the waves are coming on pretty strong most of the time. The first few days you'll be knocked all over the place and generously make a lot of offerings to Poseidon over the side of the boat. But as you learn balance and a solid, flexible stance – as you get your sea legs – you're more and more able to move and groove with the boat, or dance with the way the waves are rolling, so it doesn't bother you as much.

You're in flow with it and not fighting it every step. You're more solid by being looser, more sturdy by being more flexible, more in control because you're allowing the waves to be as they are without fighting against them and trying to control them. You have a steady stance by rolling with the swaying of the forces encroaching on you.

And I'm not saying I've got my sea legs in the slightest, just saying I saw and felt this sense of patient nonreactivity, a solidity of grounded rootedness. Not skipping inner leg day. Just learning to either go with the flow a little more, or standing in balance and allowing that flow to flow past you, but not resisting it and fighting it, even if it's flowing in a way you don't love at the moment. So not habitually resisting and fighting against what's happening as much. And like I've said, I definitely don't mean not taking a stand when that's your truth, I don't mean not having the loudest strongest *hell no* in the world when that's truly called for, but most of the time in our daily lives, that's not the situation.

So it's getting a different – well getting some perspective, stopping and taking a breath, just realizing that in the scheme of things it might be healthier to not get so indignant and so worked up and so kind of tightly zeroed in on the justification of whatever the feeling is over those particular things that you tend to react to. Not sure I said that clearly, but maybe it's a little like a lioness whose cubs are crawling all over her, and she's just not adding more agitation to it, meaning she's just lying down, relaxing into it even though it isn't so ideal, and not reacting to it. Not counter-acting, not adding her own aggravated energy into the mix.

Her trying to pick up each cub by the scruff of the neck and move them all one by one to where she wants them to be still and take a nap, that's just going to activate them more. As soon as she sets one down it's going to be crawling around again. Any attempt to stop the romping around would just re-rompify things and make it worse for a while, as opposed to just leaving a little romper room. They would feel her agitation and just get more agitated them- selves. But if she just lets them crawl on her and around her for a while without reacting, then instead of the situation escalating into a full on feline hootenanny, eventually they'll get all tuckered out and cuddle up and go to sleep.

Ω Ω

I'm not so sure I want to cuddle up with an energy suckerfish, or with lion cubs with their momma nearby for that matter, but I get your point.

Well, when we ignore the pokes and reflex hammers of the sub- physical energy nibblers, they don't cuddle up with us, they just lose interest and go somewhere else. They go find someone else to play with. The only way they can sense the presence of a buffet is from the steam that rises off of it when the unwitting chef stirs the food pans. When we stop stirring things up, nothing signals them and they go on their way to another buffet.

So, what would it be like to stop stirring the buffet dishes, and just be uninteresting to an energy nibbler? And to be uninterested in, and unreactive to, their little nibbles? To not take the bait? Not playing dead, not tightly freezing all movement, not being hyper-intellectual and cut off, not being fake or shut down, not trying to tightly force yourself to stand perfectly still so the mosquitoes don't see you. And I'm not talking about some exalted enlightened state of perfect, saintly, equanimous – if that's the word – unmovingness in your thoughts and feelings. It's just relaxedly not getting all charged up and taking it personally when a lion cub tugs and bites your finger. When a mosquito bites you. Or when someone's having a high stress day and shoots a harsh energy arrow in your general direction.

So with these daily or weekly annoying, activating, aggravating, infuriating things, seeing what it's like – when it's not clear to take more assertive action – to just let what's here fully be here, since it already is, without engaging in fighting with it or giving more charged focus to it. Not engaging, not initiating conflict, not getting hooked. Resisting the temptation to take the bait. Not further exacerbating the existing charge with your own counter-charge.

No matter how right we're sure we are, and they're wrong as usual, or whatever the situation is, if we take the bait every damn time it's in front of us, we're just being Pavlovianally at the mercy of maybe a few thousand neural connections that take up less space than a pinhead. We're being completely controlled in that moment by an outdated neural cluster that's bossing us around, and we're just automatically obeying.

Are we really cool with maybe a few thousand neurons controlling our entire behavior every damn time that particular trigger shows up in our lives? Are we honestly good with just calling that a lost cause? So just, over time, growing the muscle of just not going there. You know, stoking a wasp nest to try get a handful of them to stop swarming outside their nest isn't going to pan out too well.

And there's just a huge difference between *suppressing* your life force and supporting it being relaxed, open, even, vibrant and flowing. A huge difference between a *flatline*, which I know a little something about in more ways than one, and a more steady but very much alive and dynamic and vibrant *flow line*. So it's just, not continuing to contribute to a self perpetuating cycle of offgassing reactivity, while also not squeezing yourself shut, which still creates energetic offgassing anyway. So not deadening yourself til your comfortably numb, having a momentary lapse of reason, so disassociated you're on the dark side of the moon. A little Floydian slip there, but basically, it's allowingness without powerlessness. Keeping some slack in the fishing line. Standing still or taking a step back without ceding your authority. It's actually having the self authority, the self authorship, to write your own story, to stand in strong balance or take a step back rather than involuntarily engaging your reactive tendencies every damn time you're poked. Rather than reflexively letting a few energy nibblers, and/or a few thousand microscopic, outdated neural connections, boss you around.

There's something refreshing or empowering about that way of looking at it. I've never thought about how sometimes I'm letting just a few thousand neurons, that together would fit in a pinhead, control my whole mind and body and my decisions and actions when I'm caught in a reaction or in some other old issue.

Yeah, and it's also actually our *own* contracting that clenches around our reactivity and keeps it locked around us, that gives it something to grab on to in us. And that whole thing is a smorgasbord, for our brain patternings and brain chemistry, and for the alleged suckerfish, and even for some people whose structures might get fed sometimes, in some way, by getting a reaction out of us when they poke us.

But if we don't contract and self righteously grab on to that rush of reactivity inside ourselves – like "They *deserve* my self strangling tightness and tension, that'll show them!" – then there's just nothing there for them to grab onto or feed off of. You can't grab onto spaciousness, you can't sink your teeth into nonbracingness. You can't get a good grip on a space of nonresistingness. But contraction and resistance and reactiveness and score keeping, *those* have a hard enough, rigid enough substance that they're easy to grab onto.

You know that cornstarch experiment? Where you mix water and cornstarch until it's maybe the texture of watery oatmeal, and if you hit it pretty hard, it's immediately a solid, and it resists and pushes back, but if you move slow and gentle, it's totally a liquid. Rigidity tends to beget rigidity. Resistance tends to beget resistance. And spacious flow tends to beget spacious flow. So it's the less rigid, less resistant, more flowing, more flexible stance that lets intensifying electric currents pass all the way through and dissipate, like a lightning rod on an airplane. Whereas the static electricity of unprocessed, unreleased, constricted reactivity and resistance can build up and then cause a shock or a bumpy ride. Being flexible like an earthquake-proof building, that can flow or rock back and forth to help it absorb and dissipate and withstand the energy of the ground shaking beneath it.

If a subtle level electric eel keeps sending you little shocks – to try to get a rise out of you so they can feed off the energy your reactivity would generate – but you just relax into it instead of tensing up or fighting it, soon they'll stop wasting their energy and move on. So keeping things as unrigid and flowing and unclenched as you can, when you can. Not powerlessness, not meekness, not martyrishness, not placatingness, just unclenched and un-tensed, and not trapped in a trench. Not as caught in the optional drama. Just practicing your stance of having a solid tree trunk with flexible branches and strong deep solid roots. Developing your sea legs, easefully rocking with the flow, without fight or flight or freezing. That helps there be not as much electrical evaporation for those subphysical electric eels to feed on. Not as much concentrated reactivity juice for the subphysical energy leeches, so they lose interest and go on about their way.

So it gets down to just simply not feeding them, or same principle, not feeding your brain's self perpetuating stress patterns and cycles and chemical dumps. Not driving in those old well worn ruts. Reducing or ceasing the feeding of your reactivity, which in turn helps to cease or greatly reduce the reinforcement of unhelpful and unhealthy neuropathways and chemical releases, and helps to stop attracting the subtle level suckerfish with tasty energetic offgassing sugar water.

CHAPTER 61

And I can tell I'm a little concerned about someone misunderstanding what I'm trying to say here because this is like the third or fourth time to bring this up, but I'm absolutely not saying don't take strong outer action when it's called for, but that's not what we're talking about here. We're talking about those darn pesky energy sucking subphysical fruit flies, swarming around, ruining your picnic, trying to elicit a reaction.

They like to divebomb you and get you swatting at them and get your emotional blood pumping, and then they help themselves to the buffet. If you don't give them any good food they move on in search of the next picnic, just like the seagulls and the mosquitoes, and that coworker who likes to try to get a reaction out of you. And as there's less food around, it's not a big leap that their numbers diminish and/or their individual size withers down, and they get less voracious and less powerful and less able to push your buttons and pull your levers and hit your emotional reactivity knee with a reflex hammer, if they even still bother to hang around. Subtle level electric eels need the friction of your resistance to generate the electricity they feed on. Without that, they go somewhere else to find some tasty electricity sparks for their energy fix. They can't get a free meal if there's no charge.

So it's not about suppressing and clamping down and breathing less and paying them off with your vitality. I like that phrase, not paying them off – in the hopes they'll leave you alone – with your vitality, your aliveness, your life force, your empowered autonomy. Which doesn't ever work anyway. But what *does* work is calming the tasty and irresistible emotional waters you're splashing up, so they're less choppy and less attention-getting and less attractive to the energy nibblers.

And you know, if the goal is settling the ripples in a pond or the waves in a lake, the more you're splashing around trying to stop all those damn ripples or waves, the more there are. The more flies you frustratedly try to get out of your home by opening the door and frantically shooing them out, the more get drawn in, checking out what all the commotion's about.

So just ceasing fighting or ceasing resisting the ripples that are already there, giving them some space without adding to any emotional charge that might already be there. And if you can't seem to help adding to it, giving *that* some space without adding any more charge to it. And then soon it can start to be like a vast lake that has way more room for those ripples, so they become even less of a big deal, even less of anything that matters, even less of anything that you need to react to. A one foot wave is a little less problematic in a lake than in a bathtub.

And with all that space, and no longer being fed fresh agitating energy, the waves calm down a lot sooner, instead of building up and getting even more agitated. Then there's not as much for the energy suckers to nibble on. Or not as much to entice the seagulls to nosedive you, to divebomb you, or not as much for the mind to perseverate on and reinforce and cycle up about and build a whole impatterned neural cluster with.

Ω

So if you feel yourself having a reaction to something or someone, if you're feeling some strong unpleasant emotion, feeling yourself tightening up or seething or fuming or resisting or reacting or shutting down or closing off, the invitation is to not go to war with yourself over it, and not go to war with *them* – not selfishly dumping or transferring your discomfort onto them – but to just, to the degree you're able, in the immortal words of Saint Paul and Saint John, let it be. To just let it breathe, exactly as it is. To let it make the internal ripples it's already going to make whether you want it to or not, and to not get your hands all in the mix. Not reacting to your reactivity when you feel it, and when you do react to it – because we all do sometimes, it's just what happens in human brains sometimes – not reacting to *that*.

Warm, kind, nonresistant allowingness of what *actually* is happening inside you now, without trying to get rid of it or change it or hide it from yourself. You might not *feel* any warmth and kindness, but the intention itself just naturally has that energy whether you can feel it or not. Intending to be like some small hint of Absolute Allowingness in relation to the wave of reactivity and resistance. Letting it pass through inside without colliding with it. Then these ripples come and go more smoothly and quickly, and there's not as much to really deepen the ruts of an old entrenched neural pathway around.

And also, remembering that they aren't your archenemy, those little energy pedicure fish that eat dead skin and maybe once in a while nibble at live skin. They're mostly pretty harmless and don't do a whole lot, we do most of it for them.

What do you mean?

It's our *own* reflexive, reactive movement that draws them. Like maybe if you kick and shake your foot because their nibbling kind of tickles or barely hurts, then maybe they just instinctually get a thousand times more active, and kind of tickle more or nibble more, and cause a little more discomfort, so then you kick more and then maybe there's this whole chain reaction of escalation happening. So just letting them be, without giving them your focus or energy or, you know, reflexively reacting to them. Gradually growing, through practice and intention, a stance of strong, empowered, balanced flexibility.

And also, disengaging – well, first let me just throw in that I know I'm on another monologue roll here, but let me just get a few last things out that are lined up and waiting their turn.

Sure.

Ω Ω

And one is that disengaging, or stopping leaning too far forward, is one tool we could use more than most of us do. There's usually not a real negative side to walking away – for a few minutes or a few hours – from something activating you or hooking you when that's an option. Just moving to a less activating place for a while. Ending that triggering phone call or that in person, increasingly heated argument, with an excuse if needed, or just with a clear, straight, "I'm getting really activated and it's not likely to be a fruitful conversation when I'm this tight, so I'm going to go for now."

And by now it's probably clear, it's the exact same invitation if there's no energy shadow suckers at all, if they don't exist, and it's all just the human brain doing its thing the best it can – sometimes with considerable pressure from someone else or something else outside of us – or if they *do* exist, and it's a combination of the two.

But the main flash packet that opened around these cute little suckers wasn't like here's a step by step strategy you can implement to handle the situation. It was a space, but that space contained all of this information somehow, the core seeds. The sense that was radiating through me was of a stance of grounded, settled, noninterference with inner reactivity, when reactivity happens to arise. Grounded and settled and solid, with feet balanced, when so called negative emotions are blowing around, instead of ping ponging or pinballing all over the place. Letting your roots grow bigger and spread deeper. Letting your trunk become stronger and more solid, your bark thicker.

Not defensively, not knee jerk reactively, not a permanently closed drawbridge that keeps out the world, but in a well boundaried, healthy, solid, mature, autonomous, agented, empowered way. And at the same time, your tree limbs can be flexible, able to flow with the wind instead of straining or snapping when there's some pressure pushing and pulling against them.

So it's standing steady and still and solid-footed in the midst of your emotions having some charge. Not acting those feelings out unless really clearly warranted. Just because someone is hitting a few tennis balls to your side of the court, that doesn't mean you have to hit them back, or that you even have to stay on the court. So yeah, similar vibe as a modicum of Absolute Allowingness. It's an invitation to see what it's like to allow a tangle to be a tangle without tangling it even more by impatiently and impulsively trying to untangle that damn tangle you want untangled.

Or like in a football game, if ten players pile on the ball, and you want that pile de-piled so you can get to it, then you diving onto the top of the pile isn't going to help anything. That just weighs things down and constricts them even more. If you want to unpile things, if you want to untangle the pressure pile, adding your own weight to it and jamming your arms in there for the football isn't going to help. Like I said last night – or I think it was last night – you can't help rose petals open with a crowbar.

So it's taking a step back from the pile, taking a breath, and just not adding your energy to the mix. You can't force the pile to unpile, but you *can* intend to make sure you aren't contributing to its weight and pressure and tangledness. You might feel the pull to, but if you get all in it and compress it more and tighten things up more, that just increases the tangledness.

Or back to the boat, you might feel the waves tilting the boat up, causing a gravitational pull to kind of stumble backwards, but as you develop your sea legs, as you start to roll with the waves more and more, as you develop your stance of solid, grounded, centered, flexible standingness, then that gravitational pull just doesn't have the power to knock you off your feet anymore. You've gradually become stronger and more rooted, while also more flexible and flowing, and instead of futilely trying to steer the boat around every wave that's quickly approaching, you're more and more able to just let go and let be, roll with the waves and make friends with the sea.

Ω Ω Ω

So, finishing this up, it's learning to ignore and relax with those picnic nibbler flies that won't stop pestering you. While you're busy waving your fly swatter around, trying to shoo away the first few, all the other flies in the area think you're waving at them, like "Hey you, come on over, the potato salad's great!" What we have here is a failure to communicate.

So just, inside yourself, even if you can't really step away and take some space for yourself, stopping any contributing to the commotion for a few, outside yourself and also inside, the best you're able in those moments. Ceasing, getting more centered, feeling your grounded strength, even if it feels a little wobbly at first. Practicing your stance.

And not by cramming down the emotions or the reactivity, not by engaging in a battle with yourself. You're in your canoe in a small mountain lake, and the waves are rippling, and you remember you're supposed to not have a lot of waves because they attract mountain lake suckerfish, or maybe the elusive, little known Rocky

Mountain lake shark, so you start beating down the waves with your canoe paddle to try to get rid of them and calm the waters. Good luck with that.

Or you could explore putting down your paddles and just letting the current waves be there, and just sitting back and relaxing for a few, even if a few suckerfish might be around, instead of making more waves as you hopelessly try to stop the already existing waves. Not perseverating on how to stop perseverating. Not piling on the pile to unpile it. All of that creates the static electricity, the friction, to light up the *Buffet is Open* sign. All of that stirs the buffet dishes and rings the dinner bell.

And fifth or sixth time's a charm, and I'll try to stop feeding a full horse here, but of course if you suddenly realize you're heading towards the spillway where you would drop a thousand feet, you paddle like hell, you take action, you use your power to do what you need to do, that's what it's for. When the best way to take good care of yourself is to push back or engage or use your power, then that's the way to move. Part of being on this planet is growing the power to set a good solid boundary when called for. To say a good strong no in a way that's not going to be missed, to take assertive action when needed.

So, the experiential current, under all those flash packet sprouting seeds, was a deeper sense of how it would feel to just be done with chasing after the flies buzzing around, or running from them. Done with bracing against the waves or fighting against them. Having some flexibility in your limbs so they can roll more with life's winds and punches and pokes. Growing and developing the inner stance of deep roots, solid trunk, don't give your power to just spinning when you're in a funk. Not that it's easy, but those muscles can be strengthened, those skills can be developed and honed, that rootedness and groundedness can be deepened over time.

So yeah, that's a theme that's come up several times in the bridging sessions, from different angles, and even if it feels difficult, we *are* able to practice and develop and hone our nonreactivity sea legs. To grow our trunk and our flexible branches. Okay, I think that's everything with that one.

More food for thought. I appreciated you going into it, and trying different arrows or spaghetti to see what sticks.

Spaghetti arrows. Not that popular with archers, but sometimes I noodle around with them.

I'll use that as a chance to practice ignoring and not reacting. Alright, so before we opened that up, you were about to bring in one or two other background threads to Influencing Your Unfolding, beyond the range of things that can influence what happens in our lives.

CHAPTER 62

Yeah, so, let me think where to start. Okay, so we've touched on how everything is *from* Pure Consciousness, is *returning* to Pure Consciousness, and at the Core is never anything *other* than Pure Consciousness. Pure Infinite Beingness is the Most Fundamental Substrate of everything on every level. It's the Source Substance from which all is made. The Absolute Ground is the Source of Pure Beingness, and Pure Beingness is the Source of all that exists on every level of created reality, subtle and dense. But as you go thicker and thicker into form, into heavier and denser levels of reality like this one, the Infinite Everpresentness of Pure Beingness is usually more and more obscured, with less and less conscious connection and less and less perceptual and experiential evidence. Not always, but that's the trend line.

Ice is always water, but when it's ice it can be shaped and chiseled, it can have structures and patterns and solidity and consistency of makeup, and doesn't seem to be anything like water. "What do you mean this is water? Look at it. I can stand on it, I can sculpt it, I can hold it easily in my hand. Obviously it's not water." But even though it so clearly *appears* to be something *other* than water, with no shared properties – nothing in common with flowing, splashing, liquid water – that doesn't mean its true nature is actually extinguished. It's always water, made from water, returning to water and its essence is water, always, even if its current properties are hard and dense. All of that's true at the same time.

And more subtle levels of created reality or formed reality – meaning the higher levels just on this side of the prism or of the two way mirror – they're less dense, so in this imperfect analogy, the ice on those levels is more like thick slush. More easily malleable, shapeable, create-with-able. It's closer to the lower density and higher frequency of Consciousness and thought and intention and creative expression, so it's easier to be *molded* and *shaped* by thought and intention and creative expression.

Consciousness unburdened by heavy density is incredibly powerful in its ability to create and change subtle level form, unhindered. Like being able to easily direct blowing sand to form intricate sandcastles, or like moving snowflakes around to create snow castles, or snow anything. It's like they can 3D print intricate ice designs, formed structured designs on subtle levels of reality, with just slushy water in the 3D print cartridge.

Who can do that? Multidimensional Beings?

Yeah, on those highest levels that are the closest – let's say the closest vibrational resonance to Pure Infinite Consciousness itself, instead of using slushy water to print snow or ice designs – it's all subtle energetics, which is what all form is anyway, fundamentally. Even on our level, particles are made up of waves which are made up of fields of potentialities of energy. On subtler levels, form is much more like flowing energetic patternings, though like I think I've said, they can seem on some levels just as solid on that level as things feel on our level.

So on those more subtle levels, much less dense and much closer to consciousness and thought and the intention to create, there isn't much lag time, if any, between intention and creation. It's all far, far easier. If you can envision it, you can create it. The more subtle the level of reality you're on, or the higher the frequency you're on, or the further into the onion-like reality layers you go – however you want to look at it – the more effortlessly you can create on that subtle level of reality. Or let's say the closer to the warm molten liquid center of a planet you go, the less hard and solid the ice is, or even the rock is, so the easier it is to 3D print intricate slush or molten sculptures, which can then harden into solidness on that level, instead of it having to be painstakingly chiseled from hard ice blocks or granite on the surface.

Ω

So to use twelve confusing analogies in two sentences, another way to think of it is to imagine Old Faithful, or any geyser, shooting hot water way up into the air on a below freezing day, and it comes down and makes beautiful, naturally unfolding ice designs. And then just imagine that process can be deliberately 3D printed, consciously directed, orchestrated, infused with intelligent direction that's consciously controlling how it lands, so that amazingly intricate designs are created.

So the upshot is, Conscious Beings on much more subtle levels of reality can consciously use the medium of the Pure Overflowing Potentiality of Infinite Super-abundant Beingness to create structured designs in subtle level form. To create new form and new formations, new structures. New intricate inter-arrangements and unique expressions. So this boils down to a little mini-formula. The closer to Pure Beingness your consciousness is, plus the less dense the level of reality you're trying to create in, the easier it is to create something you're intending to create.

Would you say that again?

Yeah, so the closer to Pure Beingness your consciousness is, plus the higher the level of reality you're intending to impact, the easier it is to influence or impact or create something you want to create on that level.

As usual, this is a bit hard to get my mind around. Then Oversouls can 3D print on their level of reality? The Omega Being can do that, and does do that? What would they create?

So based on this little theorem, it depends to some degree on what level an Oversoul's wanting to create on, and also where they're residing in the Continuum of Consciousness when intending to create. Multidimensional Light Beings like Oversouls can instantly and effortlessly rise to an even lighter level, a higher vibration, where thoughts and intentions create and alter form on that level instantly, or close to it.

And it's not quite that they lift up higher or actually move, it's not that they rise in altitude to a higher level of the stratosphere like a weather balloon, or take an elevator from their usual 50th floor to the hundredth. They inwardly expand their awareness aperture into a higher frequency that's always available to them along the Consciousness Continuum, that's even closer in frequency to Pure Essence. Closer to the Superabundant Source Substance from which all things arise and are made of and are always surrounded by and immersed in.

Through this through line of Consciousness, Oversouls are always on every subtle level of that seamless, uninterrupted Light Thread simultaneously. So they need only shift their awareness to instantly attune to a more subtle level, where they can even more easily 3D print with slush jets, with slush being like halfway between water and unmalleable ice.

So maybe it's a little like a submarine can be skimming the surface or go down to the depths, as the captain wishes. But actually, scratch that, because it suggests it's either/or, and Oversouls are on every level of the Continuum of Consciousness at once, their zoomed out focus actually lets them be zoomed in everywhere at once, but they can still just shift their awareness to be more fully on one level or another. Like a camera can see every point, but you can choose which point to focus in on the most sharply. Except, for Multidimensional Light Beings, every single point can be in clear sharp focus all at once, all along the Continuum of Consciousness, but they can still kind of lean in more to one level, to more fully tune in to it, even though it's always present in their awareness.

Ω Ω

So bottom line, it's easy for them to create on those higher, most subtle levels, a few notches higher frequency than where they tend to primarily be. But to impact or influence or create through conscious intention on our thick, heavy, strongly bound by inflexible physics level, that's a considerably taller order. We'll come back to that, but for now suffice it to say it's usually much slower, tougher going, even for a Multidimensional Being hanging out on the highest levels of reality, in Conscious Connection with Pure Essence.

It just takes longer to chisel ice than to 3D print with slush. Wet cement is easier to mold than hard concrete. It's like the conditions on more subtle levels keep that wet cement wet and malleable and shapeable way more easily, and even when it hardens, it's not really hard solid cement, it's more like a half solid gel, that retains a gel like flexibility and can be reshaped again and again, or kept as it is.

And this isn't a mixing technology with just the right blend, it's just the nature of more subtle levels of reality. But because of the thicker density or the lower frequency on the cosmic radio dial that our level occupies, it's less responsive to thought and intention. Not absolutely completely unresponsive, but less responsive. More sludgy and sluggish and resistant.

The laws of physics in our little universe are pretty set in stone. Figuratively and sometimes literally. Strong, stubborn forces at play, that don't take kindly to being messed with, and they show it. You split one little atom, you're gonna have a bad time. Things are just more stubborn here to being influenced, which we'll get back to in a few.

But back to what would Oversouls create, there isn't need, and there really isn't strong personal want, there's not like, we won't really be content til this is different or til we have that just right. That isn't happening much when you're already always consciously intimately one with the Pure Infinite Joyful Love-filled Everpresent Consciousness, one with Pure Flowing Isness, your Purest Essence. There's not much to want. But there *can* be participating in the ever-continuing joyful fractaling outward of the expression of Infinite Inexhaustible Potentiality into form. A natural response of delighted creatingness.

And so, I didn't want to try to – or take two, like I've said, we can't really go into everything at once, and I didn't want to throw this into the mix yesterday because we had enough on our plate – especially with all the falling spaghetti and the multidimensional sausage – but Oversouls like Omega not only *experience* different amusement park rides, different snow globe realities – which now that we're using this analogy of water and ice is a nice serendipity – but they can not only *experience* these worlds, by extending conscious autonomous but intimately connected tentadrils, Higher level Multidimensional Beings can *also* actually 3D *print* or *create* structures or even create whole snow globes on some levels of reality.

And then they could potentially tendril into them if they wish, and even invite other Multidimensional Beings to come down and give it a whirl as well. Not so completely different than if someone designs a video game or builds an amusement park, and then explores it, and also opens it up to others.

Or maybe it's a little like creating a model train railroad that you more and more intricately fill out, with more and more buildings and people figures riding the train, plus green grass and trees and so on. And then imagining into life a whole world happening there. So there's not a real need, and there's not even a strong individual self-focused want. There's just sometimes a natural, congruent response, of fractaling outward or tendrilling outward with creative expression, because that's one of the inherent qualities of all Consciousness, and of the Source Substance, the Living Overflowing Superabundant Isness of Pure Existence, the Essence of all that exists, as it expresses and dances into form.

CHAPTER 63

So you're saying Oversouls don't only extend soul tendrils into created worlds, they can actually create those worlds first?

Well this is another one of those both/and paradoxes. Oversouls as I've been speaking of them so far, it's more like kind of a more subtle level Mothership, that sends down astronauts or exploration pods – or sends down tentadrils – that experience living as a physical being on a planet or on some other amusement park ride or unique snow globe world. I mean there's a lot more happening than that for Oversouls, but just to oversimplify it.

And on their usual level, Oversouls aren't really creating worlds or doing a lot of 3D printing. But there's that through line of the seamless, unbroken and unbreakable Continuum of Consciousness. From Pure Conscious Beingness all the way through every level to Oversouls or Higher selves or MLBs, and then tendrilling on down to denser levels including our smaller, more experientially limited consciousness. And again, the delineation between different levels or layers is fluid and flexible and waxes and wanes and ebbs and flows and expands and contracts. Breathes in and out. It's not like pre-delineated, pre-set, precise floors of a skyscraper with pre-existing elevator stops.

So up a few notches, or in a few notches, from the place in the Continuum of Consciousness I've mostly been speaking of when I've talked about Oversouls, at that higher vibrational level of created reality that's closer to Pure Beingness, benevolent Multidimensional Beings of Love and of Joyful Creative Expression can easily and fully be a part of that natural outflowing potentiality. They can participate in creating and co-creating and expressing and fractaling out into created form on various levels.

So up the through line a ways, Multidimensional Light Beings can not only tendril into new worlds, and old worlds, through extending autonomous conscious individual tentadrils that are always plugged into their Greater Consciousness, their Greater Being, whether they're aware of that or not, but up a few notches, Oversouls can also participate in *creating* those worlds if they wish. And something that I've—

—*When you said whether they're aware of it or not, you mean whether individual tentadrils are aware of it, not Oversouls, correct?*

Right, individual soul sparks. Us. And something I touched on yesterday, similar to how Oversouls are in part kind of like a Mothership for individual sparks of consciousness, for individual soul extensions experiencing various formed existences, we could also say, from a more zoomed out perspective, there's a level above that, or a higher vibrational resonance than that, with even *Higher* level Multidimensional Beings or Being Collectives, that are like an Oversoul for Oversouls, like a Higher Self for our Higher Self. Like our supervisor's supervisor, but without all the reminders to keep the breakroom microwave clean.

So from one perspective, it's kind of like pyramiding upwards towards the One Single Pure Infinite Awareness, Pure Beingness, even though the whole pyramid is always made out of the Pure Gold or the Pure Crystalized Honey of Pure Beingness. The higher the level you go – or the higher the vibrational frequency – the closer you are to the One Pure Conscious Beingness, and the fewer individual conscious tendrils of Pure Beingness there are. While the more into form you go, the more offshoots. But from that higher level, these Over Oversouls, these Higher Higher Selves, they can create worlds and snow globes for our Oversouls to go explore and tendril into and experience.

$$\Omega$$

And a quick side note, I'm probably going to keep using the terms higher levels and Higher Selves, but that could easily get associated in our minds with a hierarchical structure where they're like more valuable, above us, superior to us, like "Yes your Highness." I don't really like that image of a pyramid, because it's just too hierarchical to convey the actual situation, and it's just too easy to interpret it as superior and inferior, more valuable and less valuable.

And it's kind of the same with soul and Oversoul. It could imply superiority or aboveness. It just feels more awkward to me to refer to them as like Faster Frequency Beings, that doesn't quite convey it. And Higher Frequency Beings maybe works a little better, so maybe I should throw that in here and there, but to my ear it's a little too radio-ish and technology-ish to really fully resonate, at least for me.

But from the larger perspective, Multidimensional Light Beings are definitely more subtle, higher frequency Consciousnesses, and definitely closer to Pure Beingness, or have less layers obscuring it, but that doesn't mean they're above us in terms of value or worth, or more respect-deserving. Which touches back to yesterday, how the astronaut that has much more limited functioning in a spacesuit on a distant, mostly cut off planet isn't judged, isn't looked down on, isn't demoted, for the limitations and obscurations they so often have to struggle through, that are largely a byproduct of the density of the planet they're on.

So that hierarchical pyramid analogy, that conjures up images of, you know, corporate leadership ranks, it's definitely flawed, and of course it's also flawed because it entrenches the sense of separate beings, when zoomed out or up a little, that's not actually what's going on.

But yeah, back to your question, the creating of worlds and amusement park rides and snow globes, that's just a natural part of the unfolding of the Rich Creative Infinite Potentiality of Superabundant Isness, endlessly expressing and fractaling into structured form. For Beings on those most subtle levels, creating whole snow globes, whole worlds, with their own unique physics and energetics and pre-quantum laws and potentialities of unfoldment and evolution of form and of consciousness, that's a joyful expression of the overflowing creative limitless potentiality of Pure Infinite Living Consciousness.

And are those Over Oversoul Beings really other than the Oversouls I've been talking about? Are these delineations really valid? Is Uber-Omega really a separate, different Being than Omega is? Could that actually just be Omega on a more subtle or higher level of the Continuum of Consciousness? And that's definitely true, that the through line isn't actually different beings on each level. And again, from that larger vantage point, our Higher Self, our Larger Consciousness, isn't *actually* a different Being than *we* are, hard as it is for a finger to fathom, much less directly experience, that it's actually one with the whole body.

Lower level, midlevel, higher level, highest level, they aren't really delineated. But it's hard for us to grok that, and it's one of those both/ands, where we can also see it the more delineated or regimented way, where the we that we're aware of is a tentadril of our Oversoul, which is a tentadril of a more subtle Oversoul, which is a tentadril of Pure Consciousness. But those layers aren't hard stops like elevator floors, they're like gradually changing landscapes as the elevation slowly increases in mountain ranges.

Ω Ω

And back to that not really quite it hierarchical pyramid analogy, as for exactly how many notches up it goes, how many middle managers and executive vice presidents of product development and so on, the answer to that really depends on how we're marking it. The knots in the through line rope of Consciousness aren't stationary. There's always an influxness and outfluxness to it all, an inwaving and outwaving. An outbreathing further into form and an inbreathing closer to Pure Essence, with just as much variation of rhythm as our breathing naturally has.

So it just isn't a fixed locked in system where if you freeze frame it and look at it, you've got it the way it always is. It's more like the Great Lava Lamp of Conscious Beingness, falling down into heavier levels, then rising up again into lighter ones.

And speaking of lava, I'll just add here that maybe a little like when a floating raft of cooled ocean volcano lava or pumice eventually becomes an island brimming with life, this is the place Light and Joy and Conscious Intention come together, with the ability to express Infinite Creative Overflowing Potential.

And once this fractaling outward in ever more complex arrangements and structures and unfoldings in lighter and heavier layers of form, once that's initiated, it can continue to fractal outward in its own unique directions, self perpetuating. It can still be directed, but it doesn't have to be, and it isn't as easy to be. It now has the momentum of self unfolding. Like if you create a new path or channel for a mountain creek to go down, then the gravitational pull will take care of the rest, and that water will find its own natural ways of flowing down and through and past. Or like however the first sparks of single celled life happened on this planet, once it started, it was a runaway snowball that would be hard to shape or control. The inherent nature of outward fractaling is to keep fractaling. That unfolding creative expression has its own momentum once it starts.

So when you said this is the place Joy and Consciousness come together to express and create, I didn't follow what place.

Yeah, probably wasn't clear but I meant that higher subtle level where it's so easy to create, where the Higher Selves of our Higher Selves reside, from one perspective. And from another, it's the place where our Higher Selves or Greater Beings can just shift the focus of their omni-awareness aperture a couple of touches, and instantly open and expand into that higher level even more than usual. And from there, Higher Beings can easily participate in the Creative Expression of Infinite Potential into formed reality. They can participate in the 3D printing or conscious geysering of a 3D slushjet printer, forming ever-evolving structure, that can then keep fractaling outward with ever more complex, creative expressions of structure. The 3D printing of self evolving form, that can continue to create ever more creative, complex form.

Ω Ω Ω

Could you give a specific example?

Okay, so on our planet, simple one celled organisms evolved and evolved, til an amazing variety of complex life and interdependent ecosystems developed, including our species, which learns and experiences and expresses and grows and deepens and integrates and communicates and connects and interrelates, and also creates not only increasingly more intricate physical structures and objects and systems – for benefit and detriment – but for millennia we've also been creating complex customs and cultures and ceremonies and stories and songs and plays, and then tablets and scrolls and books, and then radio plays and movies and TV shows, and video games and virtual online communities and online worlds, and so on. Again for benefit and detriment, but no denying an ever increasing expansion and complexification of creation and expression.

So in created reality, ever-creative fractaling continues to unfold. Infinite Creative Potentiality continues to express more and more, and be more in-formed. Including complex organized structural systems that can self-complexify and exponentially expand the original creative out-fractaling. And when that includes evolving consciousness, that's even better, that's even richer, that's really more of what it's all about.

And like I touched on yesterday, maybe after trillions of years or trillions of inbreaths and outbreaths of entire universes, every created world, every snow globe, in a sense every fractal, slows, stops and reverses direction, and begins to de-structure and de-compose and de-fractal back into the Original Source Substance, back to the other side of the two way mirror, where Infinite, Pre-prismed, Pre-created, Pure Essential Beingness resides or exists or pulses or vibrates or breathes.

Undifferentiated water becomes an individual drop, or an ice bubble, which eventually melts back into the one undifferentiated ocean. Ocean evaporates into sky, which then falls as rain or snow, and then it flows down a stream into a river, and makes its way back into the ocean. And so it goes, the outbreath and inbreath of Pure Endless Love-emanating Essence. All form eventually returns to the Infinite and Eternal Formless Isness, and then returns to the Absolute Still and Silent Ground. And then the upchurning begins again, though it never truly ceased.

I think today might have just officially surpassed yesterday in terms of mindbogglingness.

And if it hasn't yet, we've still got some time. Okay, so now I want to start to transition towards what all this groundwork has been building towards.

Alright.

So it's kind of intuitive that it's easier to blow a smoke ring than to chisel out an ice donut, right? It's easier to impact and shape less solid matter than solid rock. And along the same lines, it's not so easy to alter the fractaling unfolding already in motion on denser levels. It's easier to build with or move around slush or sand or wet cement than already solidified heavy blocks of ice or granite. They could have built the pyramids a whole lot easier if they had just used an industrial sized 3D wet cement spray printer, instead of chiseling out and dragging those pre-solidified granite slabs a hundred miles or whatever it was.

And I've touched on this, but on our level of course not everything is equally dense. Blocks of ice on one end, then snow, then water, then maybe clouds, and even more subtle, thoughts and feelings and ideas and intentions, which largely come from physics in motion, from the electrochemical firing of neural chains influenced by other body systems, and sometimes even by gut bacteria, and maybe by pesky energy nibblers, and some other influences too. And it turns out, thought and awareness can also exist completely independent of the human brain, which like I've said, I used to think that kind of belief was just for people desperately needing to cling to a fantasy to help comfort them over the inevitability of our physical deaths, the poor saps.

And a lot of our neuropathways, both helpful and not so much, are really well worn and habitual, established long ago. But river channels can change and neuropathways can change. Like energy nibblers, if you stop recharging unhelpful pathways through either siding with them or engaging in a tug of war all the time, they can grow weaker and start to have less power. That old unhelpful paved road to nowhere becomes an old grown-over jeep trail, harder to bother traveling down. And if you start to use a new path more and more, the grass gets trodden down over time til it's second nature – or let's say first nature – to go down it.

But just in general, more density means the physics in motion or forces in motion are harder to corral and change course, while more subtle levels have less resistance and more flexible energetic laws of their own, which are more like suggestions, loose guidelines, so they're more easily shaped and reshaped.

And then that little formula I mentioned earlier, the second half of it was the higher or more subtle the level of your consciousness, the easier it is for your thoughts and intentions to impact created reality, particularly on higher, more subtle levels. There's more clarity and focus in your consciousness stream, and there's more connection to Pure Infinite Streaming Awareness itself.

I want to ask, I've been intentionally more taking in what you're saying than jumping in with questions, and you end up answering some of them shortly anyway, but I do want to ask one that's come up four or five times this weekend and just came up again.

Kay, but if we're pausing the main thread here anyway, let's go ahead and take five. Or actually let's take ten. I could use a quick mini-walk outside, and a splash of water on my face, and maybe an apple or a cookie. Or maybe I'll compromise, and have, you know, two cookies. But help me remember magic wand.

Magic wand?

Yeah, for a bookmark to remind me where we were. It was just a quick point I wanted to mention but it's a gateway point into what's next after your question.

You aren't going to say the big secret to impacting what happens in our life is buying a magic wand are you?

No, of course not. It's cheaper to just make your own. I guess I'll just go ahead and say it, that on those higher levels where Higher level Beings, Higher Frequency Beings, can just easily create, it's almost like pointing a magic wand. You point your intention, your desire, and tap into the Superabundant Creative Force that's just part of the makeup of those highest levels of created reality, and alakazam. So who knows, maybe the whole magic wand thing actually came from a deeper intuiting. A physical way to focus your intention and attention and emotion, even though it's a whole lot slower and iffier here. But yeah, let's leave it there for now, and start with your question after the break.

Sounds good.

SESSION 11
CHAPTER 64

Alright. That was a good idea to take a longer break.

Yeah, nice to step outside for a few.

So, like yesterday around this time, during the break I asked if you would be up for going an extra hour, until 11 or so again, if needed, and you said you were, which means we have a little over two hours left for our marathon if needed. Alright, so back to it, the question I wanted to ask you was, sometimes you've talked about the brain and neuropathways, and also brain chemistry. Did that information come from the Omega Being or did you already know about it? Or a bit of both?

Yeah, that's probably a good thing to clarify. So the inflashes seem to be tailored to amalgamize with information that's already in my brain. Some of it I might know I know, and some of it maybe I forgot I knew or never really knew I knew, if that makes sense. And if Omega was wanting to communicate things to someone else with a completely different knowledge set, or from a very different culture or hundreds of years ago, the way things would be explained would look really different, and probably some or most of the topics would be different, or at least expressed from a very different angle, that would take into account what's available to amalgamize with in *their* mind.

So when bridging with me, the information that comes in and the way it comes in is in a way that's a good fit for me and my knowledge base. Like Omega finds contact points where amalgamization can happen, or somehow inflashes are geared towards and incorporate what I already know.

So specific to your question, I'm definitely not like, you know, a brain surgeon. At least not professionally, I mean I dabble here and there as one does, experimented in college. But no, I'm not anything like an expert on the brain or neuroscience, and I haven't meant to imply that I am. But I've mentioned I've always been interested in general science, so over the years I've read or skimmed accumulatively a lot of articles and a fair number of books, watched a lot of talks and documentaries, etcetera, about a lot of different science topics. So all added up I have a very basic, amateurish hodgepodge of science-related information swimming around, or at least, sitting at the shore available to swim around if needed.

And then in terms of brain chemistry and neuroscience in particular, it's always been fascinating to me, that this three pound organ in the head creates and maintains consciousness and self identity, and manages trillions of microprocesses a day – although now I know there's more to the consciousness story than just that – but still, even just of itself, pretty damn remarkable. But it's an area I've always been interested in, and over the years, I've learned at least some of the basics about the brain and how it works, read a few books and quite a few articles, watched some neuroscience-focused talks and documentaries, and even took a couple of free online university courses about the brain and neuroscience. Don't ask me if I completed every single reading assignment, but I did get emailed my virtual blue participation ribbons, pretty much the same thing as a diploma.

But all of that adds up to me having some basic pieces, some rudimentary understanding of some aspects of the workings of the human brain. And then the inflashes use that, they incorporate whatever knowledge I already have that's relevant to conveying what's on deck to be conveyed. Even if I don't remember having some of it in my conscious awareness or I haven't opened that mental folder in a few years, those nuggets can still be used as almost the soil that the inflash seeds grow in. So basically, something new gets introduced to that substrate, and then the amalgam of the new and the old goes deeper and fills out more and opens connections and understandings I never would've or could've come to on my own. Unless of course it actually *is* all just my own unconscious, which again, if it is, pretty damn impressive what the unconscious can do.

Ω

And I've wondered a few times, and tried asking Omega once, what if somewhere along the line I ingested some incorrect facts, or non-facts, how would that play out in a flash packet? Like if I read an article about something and later that turned out to not be accurate but I didn't get the update, would an inflash amalgamize with inaccurate information because in my brain it's inaccurately stored as accurate?

And Omega didn't really clear anything up, just that the deeper points or pointers or map or deeper information that comes through in the bridging sessions aren't dependent on the accuracy of my own knowledge base. My own understandings are used to help connect the dots and kind of illustrate and contextualize, they're helpful connective threads, but they aren't foundational. They're fillers not pillars. So if I had some facts wrong, it wouldn't greatly interfere or invalidate what was coming in to be understood.

And just to finish a thought about amalgamizing, by the time I'm aware of a flash packet, aware of the inflash contents that are unpacking after that first whomp, it's already mixed with what I already knew, in kind of a blended together way, where at that point it's not always easy for me to go back and be absolutely sure what I knew before and what was just now newly introduced. New knowledge builds on old knowledge to create new synergies and at that point it's hard to separate it again.

Like you're making a cake, you have the eggs and milk and butter and flour, and a friend brings over the chocolate and cherries and coconut and vanilla, but when it's done, it's all one seamless cake and you can't cut one piece that came from you and another that came from your neighbor. So yeah, something along those lines. Okay. So where are we? Where to next?

Well, your reminder word before the break was magic wands, but you went ahead and talked about it a bit.

Yeah, I think that's still a good touchpoint to pick things back up. So, intending to impact how things unfold is almost like pointing a magic wand and proclaiming a confident spell, that might or might not have a noticeable impact. It's pointing your intention while connecting with what you're wanting to create, while also feeling your desire or your wanting to create it.

And not just mentally, but including your body, your heart, your feelings. Letting your enjoyment of the idea of it happening really be felt. So allowing that, feeling that, plus connecting with your intention to create it, plus the image or imagination of it, meaning seeing it already existing or already happening, feeling it's already come about. That added together is a little like pointing a magic wand and creating something, just a little slower and iffier and less Harry Potterish.

And based on our little formula, a High level Being on a high level of reality, intending to create on a high level, that's as easy as pointing a magic wand. On those higher levels, thought and creative imagination and emotional focus and intention and desire can easily tap into the Everpresent Overflowing Creative Potentiality inherent in Unformed Reality fractaling into form, to create on those more subtle levels. You think it, you intend it, you feel your wanting of it, you enjoy the thought of it already existing, and on those higher levels, basically it appears.

Ω Ω

So intention plus feeling your wanting of it plus imagining it plus emotional focus plus enjoying it already being so, plus doing all of that lightly, non-tightly, non-contractedly, all that together can help create what is desired, within some parameters and limits and other influences and fine print that I can't really speak about.

You can't speak about those things because you don't know them, or because it's highly classified information and you're sworn to secrecy?

Well, so far Omega hasn't started any data streams with "This flash packet will self destruct in ten seconds." So really I just meant there are a whole lot of different influences on what unfolds, and I don't know much of anything about how all those influences – sometimes pointing in opposite directions – figure into it all and interplay with each other, and just the nitty gritty of how all that works.

And I'm not sure if we've explicitly said this, but what you're starting to introduce now is a way we can experiment with trying to tilt the scale, as you put it, in terms of what shows up in our own lives, and you and I talked about this just enough that I wanted to include it this weekend. So back to it, I'm not clear what you mean when you say emotional focus.

Just really letting yourself *feel* how much you want what you want. That's a big part of kind of the secret sauce that really differentiates this from just thinking about something or just mentally being aware of something or being aware you're wanting something. It's really feeling your *desire* for something to come into form. Feeling your *wanting* of it.

It can be light and ultimately unimportant, what you're wanting, but you can still let yourself feel how much you'd like that to happen, how much you'd enjoy it. And it can be really important to you, but when you do this, you can still intend to keep things lighter for a few minutes. Either way, something that's more light or more serious, consciously connecting to that feeling of wanting it to happen. Dipping into that, letting it be more in your conscious space.

Letting it breathe freely, with the curtains pulled back and the windows open.

And the other big part of the secret sauce is really feeling how it would feel to already have that which you want to have, or how it would feel if or when it shows up. Not just mentally imagining it's already happened, but *enjoying* the sense or the feeling that it's happening or already happened. Enjoying how it will feel when it's arrived. Imagining you're a little in the future and it's happening or already happened and going ahead and getting a real taste of how that would feel in you. Marinating in that. And really bringing in your senses, visual, auditory, tactical, or I mean tactile, and also emotional, heart feeling, the works.

So to the degree that you can, it's full bodied and fully felt imagining you already have what you want, and feeling how that would feel. That and bringing emotional focus are together like the secret ingredients, the bread leaveners maybe, that help what you intend to create be more likely to rise up and fill out into form. And also helpful is to hold it all lightly. Or not even holding it, just allowing it to waft upwards and outwards into the field of creative potentiality, lightly.

Ω Ω Ω

And I started describing these steps as how more subtle beings can create in more subtle levels of reality, but on those levels, there's already so much harmony and in sync-ness that it's not like take Step One, then add Step Two, then be sure to add Step Three. There's no recipe or no series of steps they closely follow, it just flows, all together. It's just part of the effortless fractaling outward into formed expression. A flower doesn't follow steps, it's just being itself and blooming is what happens.

But like I've touched on, with intentions to impact what unfolds, with creating in form, there are gradations of difficulty. A Higher level Multidimensional Being creating in or impacting the most subtle levels of created reality, easy. The same Being creating in or impacting this level of reality, *that's* usually much slower and more difficult and more iffy.

And then our comparatively dense and amnesiac consciousness trying to send some intention to a more subtle level – like intending to help a recently deceased person, that you sense might be lost in a fog, find their way to Clarity and Connection, or sending strong, clear, no trespassing, get off my lawn type energy to sub-physical suckerfish that compels them to leave – let's put all of that in the not quite as easy to have a big impact category since our awareness aperture isn't usually very open, but not as hard as impacting things here. And I don't mean it's hard to just send some warm, heartful, soul-healing energy through the ethers to a loved one who has left their body, that's easy, I'm talking about having more impact than that, though that definitely has an impact, those heart packets or subtle level energetic care packages always reach their intended recipient.

And like I've mentioned, for connecting with and impacting things on more subtle levels, ceremony and tradition can help us find a good runway, can help us focus and get liftoff. For millennia, ceremonies and sometimes sacred plant medicines have been used to help open up awareness apertures, at least temporarily, to help people see more of what's beyond the usual veil, and also to hopefully help them be more able to create through intention. And that's the most difficult, us with our denser and mostly closed awareness aperture and scattered and disconnected consciousness trying to impact our own dense and tightly controlled by physics level of reality. That's usually the slowest and the hardest and the least responsive.

Though again, even on this level, some things are more dense than others, right? I mean if you spend all day thinking about your dream house being built in that empty lot across the street, you might find yourself dreaming about it that night, your thoughts and intentions impacted your dreams. A fully explainable psycho-physio mechanism. But it's not as likely you'll wake up the next morning with that house suddenly actually built in form, right across the street. You almost never hear about that happening on the news. Not so easy. Rome could have theoretically been dreamed up in a day, but it took a little longer to actually build it.

CHAPTER 65

So, Bullet Point One: A lot of different influences and events and situations and just the reality of things here on this level of reality all impact what happens in our lives and how we experience them, and Bullet Point Two: Consciousness can create and influence form, but the denser the consciousness and the denser the level of reality, and the denser the specific form on that level of reality you're wanting to impact, the more difficult it tends to be.

I lost you with the denser the specific form on a level of reality.

Like are you wanting to influence your dreams or are you wanting to turn the Great Pyramids into the Great Cubes? Same level of the Omniverse – ours – but not quite the same level of density or difficulty.

Got it.

So on our level, there are way more detriments, way more competing influences and forces and structures and already in motion momentums, and there are strong and stubborn physical laws and random events and unconscious patterns and other people's dissonant intentions, and maybe planetary influences we don't yet understand, and maybe those annoying but oh so cute energy nibbling suckerfish – and whatever other more subtle influences – plus our own consciousness isn't as clear and connected. So it's more likely to be a way thicker and slower process of intention moving towards creating or shifting things, and it's less likely to complete in form. Less likely to happen. It doesn't *have* to be slow or not happen, but it just usually *is* slow or doesn't happen or doesn't quite make it all the way into form, like a sprouting seed that doesn't quite manage to fully push up out of the rocky soil. The taller the order the thicker the border.

I mean, you could spend 50 years completely focused on imagining jumping out of a plane and flying or floating instead of falling, but unless that opens some eventuality where you maybe have on a wingsuit or a jetpack, odds are those decades of visualizing and wanting it and enjoying the thought of it already happening still aren't going to be a stronger influence than those pesky physical laws of gravity crashing your party. It's just tougher going here, whereas on those highest levels of created reality, open-apertured Light Beings can create with a wave of their nonexistent wand or a snap of their nonexistent fingers.

So obviously, on our level, every single thought we think with some feeling and even intention doesn't automatically and instantly show up in form, which, thinking of the last time someone cut you off in traffic, or the last time you called customer service, you'll probably agree is a good thing, that every thought that happens to bubble up in billions of people all day long doesn't instantly and automatically change external, formed reality on our level. Wouldn't work so well.

On the higher levels where that can happen, consciousness itself isn't so limited and weighed down and split and tangled and sometimes riled up, with so many influences and so many internal mechanisms, and trillions of neural connections firing in all directions. Beings on that level don't have to contend with a physical brain and adrenal glands and the biomicrome – the microbiome, I'll get it one day – pushing us around now and then, and the whole list of influences we're subject to, understood and not yet understood, along with our default, mostly closed awareness aperture. So it's just easier for them.

Ω

Whatever the exact mechanism is on more subtle levels for consciousness to hold memory and consistency and some sense of unique identity while also being deeply connected to Pure Open Flowing Consciousness – however that crystalized Pure Golden Honey or holographic individualizing membrane exactly works – it's all much simpler and more integrated and congruent and unified than our typical consciousness is here, and less fragmented and distorted and cut off and frazzleated. And it's not as dense and self focused and influenced by evolutionary tribalism and tendencies of self preservation at all costs, or by deeply entrenched neuropathway clusters or by very stubborn physics, and everything else that gets in the mix.

And yeah, we can probably agree it's a good thing, that everyone can't win the lottery every single week, or get someone wrongly fired, or make someone like them, just with a two second *Bewitched* nose twitch, or can't instantly – well I'm blanking on another example – but significantly change physical reality in whatever other way with just a whim and a wand. Our consciousness isn't at a high enough level to be able to do that easily, and this level of reality isn't easily kind of herded or nudged or pushed the direction we want it to go. It's unwieldy and hard to get it all to line up the way we want.

It takes a whole nother level of focus and intention and connected desire to – forget moving mountains – just to move one subatomic particle one nanometer on this level. Not generally in our skill set. We just aren't at a level of deep enough congruence with Deeper Consciousness where we're skilled magicians of created existence, and even if we were, this level we're on is harder to wand around, to apply intentional creating to. It's easier to make a snow sculpture than an ice sculpture, and it's easier to make either when you're not so split and spread out and diluted and distracted in your awareness that you hardly remember that's something you're currently trying to prioritize and focus on.

Maybe creating through intention on this level is a little like trying to create sandcastles with molasses instead of sand. You might be able to start to have some impact, but all the other influences are so much stronger, it's not so likely to stick, to stay put, to set and solidify and remain. The force of gravity and the power of the waves win out.

But like heating soft clay bricks to harden them, there are ways to support the potential hardening of our molasses imaginings and intentions into hard sugar structures, it's just a tougher proposition for us here, with our distracted minds and everything else I've named, including the existence of predictable and unpredictable competing factors which have their own influence, their own physics unfolding, their own momentum, their own strength. And they're all to varying degrees impacting some of what happens, with their own predispositions and potentialities and their own thumb on the scale.

Ω Ω

So we definitely can't control every influence or override every influence, that's just not the deal on this level of reality. I mean every moment, every fork point, is an intersection of – I really don't know – a thousand or uncountable influential forces – depending on what's happening and how you break it down – from like how tired you are that day to basic rules of physics to cell biology to a tire that blows out a mile ahead of you due to a faulty tire gauge and hot pavement, causing a massive traffic jam and making you miss a job interview that would've been the rest of your career, or making you miss a date that would've been a serious relationship.

And there's genetic predispositions, microorganisms, government and corporate leaders making decisions, unexpected weather events, unconscious parts of us with other agendas that can bog down our primary conscious goals, and so on, ad infinitum, or near infinitum, all the way out to purportedly real more subtle influences that we can't directly perceive and don't yet understand.

Such as planetary forces and energy suckerfish. And also Beings on other levels wanting to help a bit.

Yeah, potentially all of the above and more. So the basic idea here is that, even though it's way more miss than hit, and even though when it's something approaching a hit it's usually slower and less obvious and less a perfect match than what we had imagined, we can at times have an impact around what unfolds in our life, beyond the usual impact range we're already familiar with.

And if there are a hundred main forces and predispositions and probabilities and potentialities already having a gravitational pull that contribute or could contribute to what happens – each with their own degree of influence – we can make that a hundred and one forces, and sometimes that could just be enough to tip the scale to a greater or lesser degree. Sometimes it could totally just *own* the scale, damn near miraculously, and a lot of times it just isn't enough to bend the current trajectory even a little, that we can tell, with all those other forces, or even just one or two big forces – like pesky physical gravity or an advanced illness – already in motion.

So what would happen if there's a big playoff sports game, where half of the millions watching want one outcome and the other half want the other, and they all tried to influence the game with these steps?

Okay, so let's back it up and say it's a month before the big game, and everyone on one side decides to really try to follow these steps to create the outcome they want, and everyone on the other side does the same. Then when the final whistle blows, whether that outcome was even a little impacted by the millions trying to create their desired outcome is a different question – and it might not have been in the slightest – but at the end of the game, whatever the outcome, half didn't get what they wanted, even if they really tried to create it.

Ω Ω Ω

So it's obviously not as simple as just imagine it and it happens, or if you can dream it then soon you'll see it, because you've got a million fans on each side of the tug of war rope, and only one side wins and the other million fans end up in the fairly sizable mud pit in the middle. And if one of the teams has half their rope tuggers let go of the rope to sit down and focus on these steps to try to influence the unfolding, that's probably not gonna help their cause too much. Physics is gonna phyz.

And again, even if you're about the most focused and clear minded a person has ever been, if you spend a lifetime faithfully following these steps, visualizing jumping out of an airplane without a parachute and landing safely, when it's finally jump day, unless you call a 30 seconds or less trampoline company on the way down, you're probably going to splat right into the next dimension.

And then you'll never have the guts to do that again.

Exactly. Nothing like a good guts joke if you have the stomach for it. Thanks for meeting me on my level there for a second. And to add a non-gravity example, if the odds of winning the lottery are 300 million to one, that's like picking the winning name out of 300 million pieces of paper from a ten gallon hat. That's a powerful pre-existing propensity of unlikelihood, that you're trying to swim upstream against.

Or if someone has a serious and progressively worsening health condition and the clear diagnosis is they're approaching the end of their life, that's a lot to counter and overcome also. There's already a lot of physiological momentum around the direction of their condition worsening til death. That prognosis might not be as rock solid as jumping out of a plane and hitting a solid rock, but in the late stages of terminal illnesses, it's rare – not unheard of, there are cases of incredible spontaneous healings, right? – But it's rare for the momentum of the current trajectory to radically reverse.

So we're not talking about Omega giving me some unfailable step by step prescription or recipe, that if you follow you'll have everything you could ever want in life all the time. You're on the wrong planet for that. Maybe it works out for some people a lot of the time, if all the different influences happen to line up that way, and maybe it works less often for other people. But this is a way to add your own intention, your own wanting what you want, into the mix, and that can sometimes be enough to tilt the scale or open a new potentiality pathway that otherwise wouldn't have shown up.

And even when it *isn't* enough – and this is probably more important than what I've said about this so far – even when it *isn't* enough to tilt the scale, there can still be goodness in doing this when it resonates. It can still support your life in a way that can influence your unfolding in a positive way, which I'll get to, but it looked like you started to jump in with a question a second ago.

I did, but you just said that what you were about to say is important and I don't want to interrupt that.

That's okay, I'll definitely get to because it's at least half the point of Influencing Your Unfolding, probably two thirds, but I'd rather you ask your question while it's fresh and then we'll decide from there.

CHAPTER 66

Alright, I wanted to ask, and I wasn't sure that was the place to do it, but what about the idea that it's selfish to try to bend the world to your will and shape it to your bidding?

Yeah, that's another one I probably wouldn't have thought to include but it's good to bring it in, so let's go ahead and tackle it now. So it's all about where you're coming from, right? Is it selfish for a painter to respond to the creative impulse to paint a particular scene the way they feel pulled to? Is it selfish for a gardener to want to pull out weeds and help the flowers and vegetables flourish? Is it selfish to prune a tree, to clip a bonsai? To plant a fruit tree where there wasn't one before? And also, in a world where scarcity has been a factor for hundreds of thousands of years of human experience, it's hard to really grok how it doesn't have to be my gain is your loss. My good fortune doesn't have to be your bad fortune, and vice versa.

Now if it's like a race, and I shove you down so I can win, that energy and that intention obviously isn't a good thing. If there's one job opening and you're hoping the other candidate gets sick or their car breaks down on the way to their interview, that's clearly not coming from a balanced larger perspective. If a thought like that pops up, you don't wrestle it back into the basement, you let it walk by, brains are gonna brain, but you don't give your energy to it either.

Those thoughts come from parts of us that mean well for us, but they're scarcity based, *me and mine first at any cost* based, like we talked about this afternoon. They're more than willing to shove another person out of the way so we can get on the life raft. Others, outsiders, they're less important and less worthy of consideration than us, for those parts of us. How we treat *them*, how we impact *them*, it doesn't really matter much as long as it helps us get ahead. Like climbing a ladder by shoving someone above you out of the way, not caring if they get hurt when they hit the ground.

Having those places in us doesn't make us terrible people, it makes us human, but just because we have them doesn't mean we have to give them the driver's seat. The energy of Influencing Your Unfolding is much more of an in sync dance, much more in harmony, than that mentality of it's me or them. Much more like a painter or sculptor or potter creating something out of the stuff, the medium, the clay, the paint and canvas, that's available to be used to create something that would bring joy or delight or happiness or peace or a light twinkle to the eye.

Not scarcity based but enjoyment based. Win/win based, without you having to figure out how everyone else wins – that's not on you – you just know it would be off to hope someone else loses. So not putting your energy there at all, even if those understandable me first thoughts show up sometimes, just enjoying the thought of winning that race or getting that job or having that increase in income or nicer home. Enjoying that image, the possibilty of that unfolding. Seeing it, imagining it, feeling how you really do want it, letting that desire breathe inside you.

And enjoying the feeling of, what would it feel like to already be on the other side of that actually happening? How would it feel to already have it? What would that give you? How would that impact your nervous system, your stomach, your heart, your shoulders, your jaw? And your thoughts, your feelings, your morning, your day, your night?

Getting that email or phone call or text with the good news you've been hoping for, feeling your health issue improving, seeing that nice bank account balance, or seeing your credit cards at zero balance. Walking into that new home you've been wanting. Imagining it's in the future some and it suddenly really sinks in that you now have what you wanted, it already happened. What would that feel like?

Enjoying imagining telling someone the great news. How would they respond? Letting yourself pre-feel that delight or enjoyment or satisfaction of finding out it's actually happened. Why wait? Avoid the rush. Why so narrowly limit the time window of when you can enjoy the good news that what you want to happen actually came about?

I mean we certainly pre-worry about possible unwanted future events a fair bit of the time, and a lot of those worries never happen.

So why not give the *other* side of the spectrum a little attention? We're able to feel into and tap into some of that benefit now, of pre-feeling how it would feel if what we want to happen actually does, even if it doesn't actually end up coming about at all.

Ω

And what do you mean by benefit?

So by pre-enjoying having what you want, you're giving yourself, right now, some degree of the same resonance you would have if what you want to happen does happen. If you *do* get that job, if you *do* get those extra funds, if that health challenge *does* improve, if you *do* get that nicer place to live or that vacation or that car or a good relationship or find a happier life or whatever it might be. Even if it doesn't end up happening, you're still giving yourself a little bit of those neural nutrients, a little bit of that feel good, that you would have if it really does actually happen in formed reality.

And nowhere in that is there any shoving a competitor down or wishing them ill or choosing to side with any understandable little thoughts of animosity towards them. Knocking them down so you can get a leg up. It's not actually your business who the organization hires. I don't mean it won't affect you, I mean their selection process isn't your business, to get your energy all entangled with. You don't need to get your head space into that.

It *is* your business to of course do your best to prepare and present yourself as well as you can and the whole list, and also at times, if you wish, to just relax and enjoy the feeling of how much you do want that position, and how good it would feel for that to happen. How that would land in you, sit in you, impact you, change your life.

And of course, there's a lot of different things you could want to unfold, and my examples are just a small snapshot. Could be better health for you or a loved one, financial security or freedom, healed relationships or a new relationship, clarity or healing around an issue, living in a better place, driving a safer, more dependable car, recovering from an addiction, having less anxiety or sadness or heaviness or anger or stress, a heart wish for someone you care about, the resolution of a challenging situation, what else?

Well, a trip to where you've always wanted to go, more happiness and contentment in your life, a deeper purpose or more meaning in your life, psychological healing and balance, spiritual growth or consciousness growth – same thing I guess – but it could be a million things. But whatever it is, not tensing and bracing and clenching to force the issue, just letting yourself enjoy how it would feel to get that which you want, and being humble enough not to presume you can or should tightly force something to happen just because you want it. So enjoying the sense of already having it, without contractively trying to bully the universe or anyone else to your bidding.

And we can feel the difference, right? Between "I am the ruler of the world, ye shall do as I command," and simply being clear that we really *do* want something and just relaxedly enjoying how good it would feel if what we want to happen happens. Then we're feeding our neuropathways some good nutrients, even if it doesn't end up happening. Nothing is lost, something is gained, and we're not sending tightness or conditional demands out into the airwaves, we're not polluting the air. We're not intoxifying other people's space or bulldozing over them to get what we want. Elbowing and shoving them out of the way, even knocking them down, so that we're the first to the dinner table. We're not playing dirty to try to win the race.

Can you say a bit more about neurons getting nutrients?

So whether or not things end up happening the way you want them to, by enjoying the thought of having what you want in your life, by seeing it and feeling it and imagining hearing yourself talk about or seeing yourself typing or texting about how grateful you are that it happened, by seeing it as a fait accompli, as already so, that *does* influence your unfolding in a supportive, life enhancing way, even if what you want to happen doesn't happen.

One thing that inflashed around what happens when we do that was seeing and feeling like a golden light wave or multicolored light waterfall gently pouring down on my head, my brain, my mind, and my whole body, and really feeling how we can get nourished and renewed some, by spending some time feeling ourselves already having what we're wanting.

Ω Ω

We don't have to wait til we know that what we wanted to unfold has unfolded to feel to some degree how it would be for it to have already happened. And the repeated bathing in the feeling of already having what we want to happen actually can impact and change some neuropathways, and thinking and feeling patterns, as though we actually already do have that in our lives.

And as that pre-enjoying grows new neural connections, that can in turn actually open new possibilities in our life, it can lead to our seeing ourselves a little differently, having more of an open flow where there might have been maybe more of a bottleneck in that area before. So it's good for our mind and body even if what we wanted to happen never does.

And also, that opening and shifting and neural pre-imprinting can potentially change the balance of the various forces and influences that are potentially impacting what could unfold in that area, soon or down the road. It can potentially to some degree influence your unfolding, not only in your own inner landscape, but your outer life too. So it just might make it more likely in the future to have something show up in your life that's closer to what you wanted, even if it doesn't happen this time.

It sounds like it can change your programming a bit.

Yeah, that's a good way of putting that aspect of it. You start to inhabit what it would be like to be someone who already has that thing you want, and that can start to change your energy, your thinking, maybe even how you carry yourself a little, your sense of what's possible. Your self identity starts to include and be more in sync with the possibility of having that in your life, and that can help make more space inside you so that actually having what you wanted, actually having that in formed reality, isn't quite as big of a stretch.

There can even start to be to some degree a magnetic or gravitational pull that, like a finely honed metal detector, consciously or unconsciously pulls you more towards the gold of situations that increase the likelihood of what you want to happen actually happening, if that made sense. Down the road a little it could look like you got really lucky or there was an amazing coincidence, but at the same time, somewhere in you it was almost expected. Or because of you spending time really enjoying the sense of it already happening and how that would feel and impact your life, it maybe to some degree actually *was* expected. It already feels familiar, lived in to some degree, because you've already spent time hanging out in and feeding the space of it already happening, so it wasn't a big jump.

I mean, *of course* you're drawn towards that which your inner reality is already resonating with. When your inner tuning fork is tuned to C, then as you walk around in the world, if you unconsciously barely sense the tiniest whiff of a distant C note vibrating in the wind, you naturally steer that way, move that direction, make a beeline and get closer to it, like a dog who's caught a scent that delights them, or like me when I smell cinnamon rolls at a mall.

Then when you bump right into what you caught the distant scent of, the distant sound of, you think it's an amazing coincidence, but just maybe in some cases it was almost inevitable, once you've tuned your inner tuning fork and made space in yourself to have what you want by enjoying the thought and feeling of already having it. And in addition to this just being something that can tune your unconscious mind towards being more receptive, more available for catching a scent that can lead you to what you want to happen in your life, it *also* taps into, to some degree, the magic wand dynamic of consciousness creating in form. It taps into that formula.

CHAPTER 67

And can you say the formula again?

Yeah, so the higher the vibrational level of reality a consciousness is coming from or deeply resonating with, and the higher the level of reality they're wanting to create in, the easier it is for them to create, to impact, to affect, to influence what unfolds on that level of reality.

So it's not usually easy for us to impact our unfolding here through inner wand waving, but that force, the physics, of subtle subquantum intention, still has some magnetic pull, even if it's so subtle it might not be felt or noticed compared to all the stronger forces. For a skydiver, a gentle westerly wind isn't noticed nearly as much as the force of gravity or the wind resistance hitting them from below, but by the time they land, it just might have nudged them over, a fourth mile or more, and influenced how things unfold.

And even if what you wanted to happen never does, you've still spent some time taking in – or integrating, or soaking in the sunlight – of experiencing already having it, to some degree. Enough to have at least some subtle impact. And that can nutrition some new neural pathways some, and help inform who you are and how you are and how you move as a person, and inform what truly feels in the realm of possibility in your future, which could impact how you move and the choices you make, and edge you closer to that which you want, or to something along the same lines. And it just might put in place that subtle westerly wind outside of you, which over time might naturally steer your future closer to something along the lines of what you really wanted to happen.

Like if you find out you're going to be getting an unexpected life changing amount of money in a month or two, you might immediately have a spring in your step, before you see a dollar of it. You're walking around differently. Your neuropathways and your body are already experiencing how it would feel to walk around with money. Then whether you actually get the money or it was all a mistake – in which case you might emotionally feel a lot of difficulty and disappointment – but you still had those moments, and they've stretched your neural connections in new ways, and they created a little smoldering ember with full on flame potential, that if you care for and blow on now and then, it could potentially become a future flame, of having something in the ballpark of – or exactly – what you were really wanting in that area.

Even just psychologically, rehearsal smooths out the road, connects and strengthens the neuropathways. So something along those lines, but deliberately honing those moments of poignant potentiality. Why wait for external circumstances to perfectly line up, which doesn't happen a whole lot with our wish list for most of us, for you to get started?

So yeah, that's the idea, that's the sense of this material that came in. You aren't guaranteed to actually have what you're enjoying the thought of already having in your life, but either way, it can attune you more towards having it, it can increase the chances of that or something along the same lines happening, maybe even something that ultimately turns out to be better for you in that area, that you wouldn't have known to even think of. And even if not – because that's how it plays out a lot of the time – it still can serve to, in a way that's in harmony with all that is, bathe your brain, feed your heart, strengthen your tuning fork towards a new start. At least to some degree. Regardless of whether it unfolds in formed reality or not.

Ω

So maybe you can get at least a little sense, feel a little wisp, of that harmony, that congruence, that non-scarcity and non-me-first-ness. Instead of my win is your loss and your win is my loss. And as I've been talking about this, I've been feeling a subtle little wave of it coming in, that feels fresh and alive and a little exciting and in harmony. Like there's full permission to enjoy the possibility of us contributing to the unfolding, contributing to the creative out-fractaling, because there's goodness in that, goodness in enjoying doing some painting on the canvas of our lives.

We're allowed to do that, we're invited to do that, we're *welcome* to do that. With integrity, and with a sense of balance, and with an understanding it's not an energy or an intention of *I win you lose*. There's real goodness in getting out our paint and canvas, our clay and potter's wheel, our pen and paper, dusting off our old guitar or keyboard from the closet, and enjoying lightly exploring creating with this medium. Absolutely regardless of whether it ever actually does show up in form in a perceivable way.

I'm still just starting to get my head around all of this, but I do see the difference between being willing to bulldoze anyone and everything that might interfere with you having what you want, compared with enjoying the possibility of something you want to happen actually happening.

Yeah exactly. Connecting with what you'd like to unfold, and really feeling your wanting of that and your enjoyment of that possibility, that's an artist painting on a canvas. That's creative expression that's supporting energy moving towards an unfolding that you would enjoy. This is an inherent potential quality within all consciousness, and not to be equated with selfishness just because you're aware there's something you would really like to happen or to have in your life. No one thinks a painter is selfish because they would enjoy adding more blue sky to the top of their painting and less sidewalk and more flowers at the bottom. That's their delight in expression. The expression of their delight. That's one of the delights of being a conscious being. Consciously creating and expressing and building and sharing and connecting, in ways that bring lightness and enjoyment and fulfillment and contentment.

We needn't be shy about that. We needn't be suppressive of it. We needn't feel bad or guilty for knowing we really do resonate with something coming into or leaving our life. I needn't tell you I've never used the word *needn't* before. But there's room for us to enjoy knowing what would uplevel our life in a small or big way, and to lightly and delightedly *yes* into the wide open invitation of playing with it and coaxing it into formed reality, like patiently inviting a wild fox to eat the treat we've placed on the ground a few feet in front of us.

And even if we don't seem to succeed, lightly enjoying the feeling of having what we want can still be a goodness in our life, and help expand our inner world, help nourish and uplevel our neuropathways, help bring us joy and enjoyment and anticipation and belief that we could be more than we've been, or we could have more that we would enjoy – or that would lift our life – than we currently have, or that we could be free of a heavy, tiring weight that has limited us. And all of that can have real value in and of itself. And as a free bonus, it just might also help an inner ready-making and an outer steady sailing breeze, for something along the lines of or as good as or even more fitting or more brilliant than what we originally wanted, to show up in our lives in the future.

Ω Ω

So what about something that legitimately is really serious and important, that isn't light or enjoyable or fun at all? Like getting the money to not be evicted or not lose your house, or to make your car payment so it isn't repossessed so you can get to work and pay for your kid's medication? Or the healing of a health issue you have, or as you said earlier, that someone in your life has? If we really want something to happen in the future, sometimes *it really <u>does</u> matter. It's serious, it's not a game. And then that brings up another big question but I'll save it until after this one.*

Yeah, so the number one thing is not contorting yourself to try to feel what you think you're supposed to be feeling when you aren't. So in those situations, when the stakes are high and the outcome really does greatly matter to you and there's a lot of heaviness and tension, there just *is*. You can't get rid of it because you're "supposed to be" relaxed and light and enjoying yourself according to someone else's instructions. Who the hell are *they* to tell *you* what you're supposed to feel anyway? There's a serious situation you're dealing with here, and they can just back the hell off.

So first is always just being congruent in yourself with what you're genuinely feeling, with where you're authentically at. And then you do this little process as well as you can, absolutely not adding to your situation any extra heaviness or self pressure that you have to stop worrying or stop feeling heavy or you have to do the steps better or lighter.

It can be as simple as just saying to yourself something like, "This really *does* matter to me. It doesn't feel light, it *matters*. So what a relief it would be if I got the good news I'm hoping for around it. That would feel *so* good. That would be *so* amazing, I would *love* for that to be what happens. It would be such a deep, deep relief. I would feel so, so grateful if that money I need came in. If that medical test came back fine. If that relationship that really matters to me started to really heal. If things turn out okay for that person I care about. It would just really, really be so good to get that news or to see that happening."

So just really welcoming any heaviness that so understandably exists in you about something important to you, not fighting with it. Not trying to wrestle worry into enjoyment, letting it really be included just as it's showing up. "Yes, I feel heavy and worried about this, and, what a huge relief it would be if it all turns out the best it possibly can. That would feel so amazing. I would feel so much lighter. I can just imagine telling everyone the good news. They would be really happy for me, and *I* would be too. I would just feel sooooooo relieved." So including that, sincerely welcoming it, I mean it's here anyway, right?

The martial art, Aikido, never fights opposing energy, never battles it. It *moves* with it, lightly *embraces* it, *flows* with it. *Dances* with it. The heavy worry in us holds within it the fuel to really feel how good it would be for that to be relieved. A compressed spring already has within it the potential to be unsprung, if that makes sense. But it's like "Yes, of course I feel tight and anxious, because I *really* want this thing to turn out really well. That would be *so* amazing to have real resolution around this, to be *free* of this heavy worry. I can just *feel* how *good* that would be, for what I want to happen to actually come about. How that would feel in my body. How *relieved* I would feel. *So* much lighter. I would just really, really *love* that so much." So feeling the stakes of what you really want to happen and how much that matters to you, that's not a detriment at all, when it's met and given space and included. So yeah, something like that. And your second question?

CHAPTER 68

The second one was, you mentioned wanting something good for someone you care about. So if you're wanting something to unfold in someone else's life, if you do this for someone else, could that potentially have an influence too? And if so, that could get into some very shaky territory of potentially trying to impose your agenda on someone else, when it might not be theirs, like using this to try to bring about the end of a relationship someone you care about is in because you don't approve of the other person, or possibly trying to get someone to like you romantically, or using it to influence things so that your significant other has to leave a job they love, because it makes them travel too much for your liking, or anything where you're trying to impact someone else's life for your own agenda.

Yeah, that's an important question, and it also brings in that quick, simple practice I mentioned when we started tonight, that I think has some value. So that came up during one of the bridging sessions about all this, and really it gets down to two things. Well, back up, first, yes you can explore using this process to influence the unfolding of something outside of yourself, in a way similar to how people sometimes pray for things for other people, so this same ethical question could apply to both, because in both situations you're sending out something you really want, involving someone else's life, with an intention that it becomes so.

And sometimes people pray for something for someone else that's actually self serving or self-focused, like please make them leave their job so I can be happier, and sometimes they really mean well but they presume to know what's best for someone else and they pray for that to be what happens in another person's life. There's an innocent arrogance. Please help them leave their job because they don't seem happy there. Please end that relationship my friend is in so they can find a better one. Please help them join my religion, since obviously it's the only true one, plus if they don't join this uplifting, joyful religion of peace and forgiveness and unconditional love, they'll be punished in hell for all eternity, which would be such a shame for such a kind, generous, loving, selfless person, but what can ya do?

So, there's two things here with applying Influencing Your Unfolding to trying to affect the unfolding of someone else's life. It's first, are you out of deeper resonance, and second, would it possibly work if you are? So like we talked about, if you're knocking people off the ladder above you so you get ahead of them, treating people like number two so you can be number one, or if you're hoping all your competition for a new position gets sick so you're the only one who interviews, that's outside of deeper resonance. That's scarcity based me first, as opposed to "This is what I would love to happen, I would really enjoy having that job, or at least I would really appreciate the income and security it would provide. I can just imagine having it and how good that would feel." Very different resonance.

Ω

So when we care about someone, we can sometimes feel concerned or frustrated they won't live their life the way it's so obvious to us they should. And sometimes maybe we're actually seeing clearly – like maybe they're in an abusive relationship and their life is controlled by someone else or they're even in physical danger if they don't break free, or maybe there's a lot of evidence they have a destructive addiction that they're not yet fully acknowledging or coming to terms with – and sometimes maybe we're just running it through our own filters and obscurations and brain tangles, and don't recognize there could possibly be another valid perspective about their situation than our own, since, surprise, when we check our own internal answer key it tells us, yep, we're right and they're wrong, case closed. And then sometimes it's more just our own preference and agendas – it's actually, a few layers down, serving ourselves, consciously or unconsciously – and we don't much care to even really check out if there could be another way of seeing it.

So, if someone is like, "Why is my 20 year old kid stupidly dropping out of college? I think I'll try to use these Influencing Your Unfolding steps to set them straight," first, do you *absolutely* know that leaving college isn't ultimately going to lead to a better life path for them? Maybe the odds say yes, but do you *absolutely* know that's how the future will play out in their case? And second, is it really your place to try to strong arm them? You can have your own boundaries around financially supporting them and letting them live with you, but is it your place to try to force – or use The Force – to try to make a young adult do your bidding because you know best and they're obviously clueless?

And for a lot of us the understandable answer to that would be, "Hell yes, I damn well *do* know better than my 20 year old kid about what's going to be better for their life, thank you very much. They just don't have enough perspective and maturity and responsibility yet to make that decision." And you might be right, that 20 years from now their life would be way better if they do what your clarity says. Or maybe not. In almost every case you can't be absolutely one hundred percent sure. Nothing wrong with knowing that the odds are you're right, but that's a little looser of a stance, of a position, than strongly and inflexibly believing their whole future is already set in miserable stone if they leave college. That's quite an assumption to really fully dig into with absolute conviction.

So, one way to think of it, to stay in your own integrity around all that – and this is that little process I mentioned a few minutes ago – is what is it you're *most deeply* wanting for them by wanting this particular thing to happen? What are you *really*, a few notches deeper, wanting them to have by this thing happening that you want to happen in their life? What will that give them? What does it provide for their life that's why you want them to have that first thing? What's more fundamental, more basic, that you believe the first thing will get them?

And then, if you imagine for a moment that they have that deeper thing that you feel clear the first thing would give them, what would *that* give them that's another notch deeper? What would that give them that's more to the root of what you're really *most deeply* wanting them to have? And then what would *that* give them that's *another* notch deeper? That you really, most fundamentally, want for their life? That everything else you wanted for them around this would hopefully steer their life towards having?

Ω Ω

Can you give an example?

Yeah, so like "What do I want for them by wanting them to stay in school? It seems obvious but let me slow down and really check, to make sure I'm really conscious of what it is I'm most fundamentally wanting for them around this. Okay, so yeah, it's just obvious to me that if they don't drop out of college then they can probably get better jobs the rest of their working life. I want that for them." Okay, great, that's the first notch in.

And you might feel absolutely sure that in all of existence there's no scenario where leaving college before graduating could open up a life trajectory that actually turns out pretty solid, or even better than their *stay in school* trajectory, but just in case you aren't, you know, omniscient in your current form, just having the space to ask yourself, what does them having *that*, having better jobs, get them, that's another notch deeper, that you want even more for them, even if it seems obvious. "Well, I feel like it would give them a better shot at financial security." Okay, great, so the deeper thing you're wanting them to have is financial security. If they could get that by winning a hundred million in the lottery, that would pretty much do it, and it wouldn't be about the job anymore.

So financial security is closer to the bottom line of what you really want for them. Just being conscious of what's going on inside you, what's motivating you. Your very strong feelings have focused on they need to stay in school, and now you're just following the thread. It doesn't mean you suddenly are on board with them dropping out of school, but you're just seeing, yeah, so far what's more important to me is that they're financially secure their whole life.

And let's see if that's the end of it or not. Next asking yourself, "What is it I want for them by wanting them to have financial security? Is there something *that* gives them that's a notch deeper to me? One notch more important, more fundamental, that financial security would provide?" And you let that question kind of land in you, land in your chest and stomach – you don't have to find a mental answer right away – and then maybe an answer shows up, bubbles up, maybe in a few seconds or half a minute, like "Well of course, so they can be happy and safe and have their needs met and have more of their wants met and not have financial stress like I've had so often, and to have money to travel and to do the things they love to do, and so they have a comfortable, secure future."

Great, seems like nice things to want for someone. And then just checking, is there anything a notch deeper than *that*? Maybe there is, or maybe that's the final deep layer, you're just taking a look. Just asking and seeing if anything more fundamental comes up. Like, "And if they have financial security and all those things I want for them like money for their future and money to travel, a notch deeper is there anything *that* gives them that's even more fundamentally what I most deeply want for them? Well, I want them to have all that so they can have freedom and safety and happiness and a light, easeful content, happy, carefree, unstressful life. Yeah, that really resonates. *That's* like the bottom line, the most fundamental thing I want for them. Freedom and safety and happiness and lightness. Safe, comfortable Carefreeness. Yeah, that's really what I most deeply want for them. I feel how congruent that feels. That's really the fundamental bottom line of what I want for them."

$$\Omega \; \Omega \; \Omega$$

So when you want something for someone else's life, if you follow it a few notches in, odds are the thing you've been focusing on as wanting for them is a means to an end, so they can have something more fundamental, and *that's* what you *really* most want for them. Not always, maybe you just want them to survive a surgery, pretty straightforward. But with most things, if you follow it a few notches in, you find a deeper, more foundational and universal wanting for them, and everything before that is your assumption of how they have to get there. Could be right, you probably are a lot of the time, and could be wrong, we all are sometimes.

And high odds are still far from a certainty. I mean, if there are a hundred thousand people in a group and each one has only a five percent chance of something happening, that's still 5000 people it will happen to, on average. Not sure that tracked, but just trying to make the point that low odds doesn't mean no odds, and including that in the mix can maybe loosen a little the absolute conviction that you're unquestionably right about what someone else should obviously do. And just to be clear, I'm not talking about naively ignoring odds, but that means not ignoring *either* side of them. The 95 percent or the five percent.

Not long ago, I was talking about investing with someone I know, I'm pretty new to it and he's a successful big time investor, and he started really pushing me to invest most of my available funds into a high return so called sure thing, and I just wasn't comfortable with it. He had no ulterior motive, he genuinely just wanted to be helpful, but he was absolutely sure he was right and that I was just being foolish for not jumping on it before the door closed. But I resisted his considerable pressure, didn't do it, and then two weeks later it unexpectedly really crashed, and if I had listened to him I would've lost about half of my not exactly plentiful investment funds. His high confidence in knowing what I should do turned out to be wrong, even though if you had taken a poll at the time probably 90 or 95 percent of those in the know probably would've completely agreed with him. So just, you know, not equating high odds with a done deal, sometimes literally.

But if you follow what you're wanting for someone a few notches in, a few steps deeper, more fundamentally, then it's pretty much always along the lines of just a small handful of basic, universal, foundational human longings, that we naturally on some level want for ourselves and those we care about, like happiness and contentment, mental and physical balance and health, freedom and lightness and love and connection, including Deeper Connection to Greater Reality when that's part of your experience or intuition or belief system. And basic safety and security, inner wellbeing, and like we touched on this afternoon, deeper meaning – that your life has meaning and matters, and that there's deeper meaning beyond your life as well. And to just be able to freely and easefully *be*, loved and safe and burdenless, without worry or heaviness or unmet needs. I might have forgotten one or two, but these are the pretty universal fundamental or root wantings, for ourselves and for those we care about. They're beautiful things to want for someone else, when they're unwrapped from all the assumptive packaging of how they have to happen, that we usually aren't even aware is optional.

CHAPTER 69

And of course, sometimes if you do this, you might stumble on something a notch or two or three in that's understandably actually more for you than for them. Like, "If they stay in school so they can get a good job, then I could relax and not worry so much about them. Then I wouldn't have the stress and weighed-downness of maybe having to bail them out financially again and again, when I don't have the funds to do that. Then I could just be finally free of the burden of taking care of them. I would really love to feel that freedom. To feel the relief of knowing whatever money I have saved gets to go to my own retirement, not bailing them out for their avoidable mistakes I warned them about and saw coming a mile away."

And if that happens, where you realize what you want for them is actually for yourself, welcome to being human. It's pretty universal, to want others to get in gear and get their lives the way you're sure they should be so you can be happier and less stressed, even though of course that's worth noticing and taking a step back from and separating the wheat from the shaft.

From the chaff.

What?

Separating the wheat from the chaff.

That doesn't sound right.

It's the husk around the wheat. The chaff.

Makes sense, I just, it sounds really strange to my ear. Well I guess now I have to decide whether to give *shaft* the shaft. And actually, what's happening in me right now is a good example of something feeling absolutely right in my answer key because that's what I absorbed long ago. So when I check, the way I've always said it feels completely right, and I feel a palpable resistance to believing you. Even though just logically, mentally, I can admit odds are really, really high you know what you're talking about here and my expectation bias just kept me from noticing anytime someone said it right. But I still feel a stubbornness, a resistance to updating it to what feels so strange and unnatural to my ear.

So it's both, a hesitance to believe you – even though now I would say 99.9 percent chance you're right – and a hesitance to update externally in a way that isn't congruent with my internal long time answer key. So a real time, small stakes example of how we lean more towards our own answer key even at the expense of updated information or evidence or proof.

But anyway, so, yeah, when you do realize, a notch or two deeper in, that you're actually wanting something for yourself, then you can also keep doing this "What do I want from that, another notch in?" process with yourself, which is a nice thing to do anyway. Like, "And if they have enough money so I get to really relax worrying about them struggling or worrying about me having to bail them out, what would that give me that sounds even better? Well, then I could just relax and not worry about that anymore, and I would know that I'll have enough money to take care of my own life, and won't have to use it on them.

"And what does that give me another notch in? Well, feels like it gives me more safety and security and a feeling that I'm more okay and more safe and more secure and more taken care of. And is there anything else that gives me, another notch in? Well, then I can just really relax and feel relieved and be more at ease, and actually *enjoy* my life more, instead of so often being heavy and tight and worried about money for me and for them. That would really feel so, so nice."

Ω

So, once you discover more what you're *really*, most deeply wanting for someone else, then instead of insisting you know the best way the universe should unfold for them to have that more fundamental thing, just going straight to the end point, to what you most *deeply* want for them, three or four or five notches in. Or what you want for *yourself* if that's what got uncovered.

And odds are, once you're at that most fundamental thing you want for them, it's one of those handful of most basic human longings that there's just no doubt they would appreciate the goodness of having, and letting *that* be what you let yourself really feel your wanting around, and what you imagine hearing them tell you they now have in their life, etcetera. A phone call, a text, a conversation, an image of seeing them in front of you while having that quality, whatever. Just imagining and enjoying the thought and feeling of it already happening.

Not getting into what led to it, not insisting it has to be your preferred path to it and only your preferred path to it, not making it your business whether they make a bee line or take the scenic route. Dropping your insistence, and possibly ceasing giving power to unconscious arrogance, that can unnecessarily limit your perception of the number of potential pathways to the end desire, which is what matters more. And just enjoying the feeling you would feel if that end result actually comes about. Giving your mind and body and heart a pre-taste of that now, and savoring it.

What matters really, when you step back, is just the most core thing you want for them. You want them to be happy, great, enjoy the thought of that. You want them to feel safe and secure and to have freedom in their lives. Great. How will you feel when you realize that's really happening more than you ever thought it might? Really enjoying that feeling. Embodying that feeling.

Not zeroing in and attaching to a specific route to it, but enjoying the sense of the end point actually happening. And keeping an eye out for your own assumptions around what having that most fundamental thing you want for them has to look like in someone else. Maybe for you, feeling happy and safe and secure looks like having an extended quiet staycation in a really nice house with a great backyard with a pool or beautiful garden, no drama or excitement, gardening and lounging and reading, the quiet life, with plenty of money in the bank for security. For someone else, it could look really different. Like going on big adventures, taking on really challenging goals, exactly *because* they feel safe and secure and happy, not in lieu of it. We're all wired differently and it's very limited and limiting to try to superimpose onto someone else what we assume having that fundamental quality has to look like.

Ω Ω

So whatever makes sense to really imagine them having the final, final beautiful thing, without risking crossing their own boundaries, without making it your business *how* they come to that deeper level of final result that's what your more surface level wanting for them was *really* wanting to give them all along.

What an indisputably lovely thing you want for them, once you follow it a few notches deeper. So let *that* be what you focus on, and resist the temptation to tell the universe it better follow the route you're so sure is the only route that could *possibly* lead to that beautiful thing you wish for them. You might turn out to be right about that route being really the only viable way for that to show up, or you might not. But you don't have to determine that. That's not your job. It's above your pay grade.

You want them to get focused and start hiking up the steep trail to the top of the mountain of happiness, but they're just casually walking around the base of the mountain, not very focused on that goal. Obviously that's not going to work, and they need to get their butt in gear and start hiking up the direct path, ASAP, damn it. But do you *absolutely know* that's the only path? Maybe there's a gondola just around a couple of bends, that will just carry them to the top once they find it. Maybe not, but you've been so zeroed in on the obvious trail up the mountain, the only one you've ever known about, you can't really say you're one hundred percent positive nothing else could ever work, so like might have been good with my investor friend, it might be good to factor that lack of absolute certainty in, and modulate the passion and absolute conviction of your opinion accordingly.

Or what if your assumption that they need to be at the top of the mountain to be happy – that obviously that's where happiness is found, and maybe for you that means job security and money and stability – what if that whole paradigm is based on a shaky foundation that you can't yet recognize? You can't say with absolute certainty you don't have any blind spots there. So why not leave things more open, more zoomed out, less defined, with more room for a wider variety of potential ways that that particular most fundamental quality could arise in their life, and with care taken that you aren't intruding and infringing on their life with your own narrower, more surface agendas, even if they mean well?

And just to really remind yourself of that, to reinforce your deepest intention that doing this process for someone else is to serve *them*, and maybe doesn't need to look the way you might assume it should, you can add in there, into your intention – and you can do this with intentions for yourself too if you like – a sense of, "May that show up, or whatever most deeply serves their life."

You can say that when you start and finish spending half a minute or a couple of minutes imagining them having that deeper, more fundamental quality you want for them, and/or it can just be baked into the cake, solid in your awareness, like "This isn't about me trying to twist the universe's arm to make it twist *their* arm to make *their* life match *my* agenda for them. I want them to be happy, I want them to feel safe, to feel supported. And since I can acknowledge I'm not currently completely omniscient, I have space for some course correcting here if there's any way I'm off." So in short, "May they have whatever most serves their life."

I really like that. I really like adding that in.

Yeah, it's a nice way to do a little arrogance check, to keep a little humility, and also to keep a space of possibility for Goodness to come into the situation in a completely different way than you were thinking.

CHAPTER 70

And by the way, you can also do this little "And what would that give me a notch or two deeper?" process with things you want for *yourself* whenever it resonates. When you're frustrated, when you're discontent, or just when you're aware you're wanting something in your life. When you feel like it, just taking a couple of minutes and taking it a few notches deeper, all the way to what you're more fundamentally wanting if you really have that first thing. If you have that most outer thing you're wanting, what does that provide for your life that you really want more fundamentally? That you feel like having the outer thing will give you once you have it?

And then repeat that a few times, a few notches in, til you feel like the deepest thing you're most fundamentally wanting through that first thing is really fully unveiled. And then really feel that most fundamental longing, the resonance of it, the rightness of having that. The congruence inside yourself when you just let yourself feel your longing for that fundamental thing.

Like, "if I get the big promotion that I'm so uptight about this week, what does that give me a notch or two deeper that's even more what I really want? Well, then I'll feel more financial security and feel more like a success. And if I have those two things, what do they provide for me a notch or two deeper that's more important to me? Well, then I would feel like I was pretty much enough and my life was pretty much enough. And what would really having *that* give my life, a notch deeper? Well, if I actually, through and through, one hundred percent, felt like I was enough, knew in my bones I was enough, that I really had irrevocable basic value, well, then I would really feel relief and I would feel like I can finally really – maybe for the first time in my life in a way, completely settle and relax.

"Great. And if I can finally really relax and really feel relief, one hundred percent, what does *that* open up for me or is that pretty much the final thing I want around this? Well, as I sit with it a few seconds, yeah, that would help me to be able to just *be*, and not be so tight and so stressed and so focused on having to do more and more all the time, which is exhausting and doesn't ever really seem to be enough.

"And what would finally getting to just *be*, one hundred percent, what would *that* open up for me or provide my life? Yeah, that would really help me to just drop into more of a space of settled beingness and peacefulness, no pressure, no worry, no tightness. That would be really amazing. And is there anything another notch in, that dropping into a space of settled beingness would give me, or is that it? Yeah, it feels like that's really the most deep and fundamental thing that I want for myself by getting a promotion."

Ω

And just by asking those questions and letting the answers bubble up by themselves – not mentally guessing what they're going to be or trying to herd them into the corral, but just letting the question sink down and then letting the authentic answer rise up – there's some degree of pre-feeling that which you're naming that you're longing for, or else you wouldn't even be able to know what that next notch deeper longing is. So some sense, some taste, can start to come in, of the feeling that would accompany having what you're longing for, to some degree, and then you can just enjoy that feeling for a few. You can marinate in it, and that helps bathe the neurons, like we've talked about. Helps nurture ourselves, and give nutrients to ourselves that are really a gift to feel, and that are beneficial to our lives, like in the steps of Influencing Your Unfolding.

And you can do this one notch deeper process with yourself anytime you feel to, with something you're aware you're wanting. And the most important thing is to not try to rush it and intellectually pre-guess the answers. It's just letting the questions land in you, letting them drop in, and seeing what naturally shows up in a few seconds or sometimes a little longer, maybe half a minute or more sometimes, no rush. And just simply doing that can help open a channel to feeling a hint – or sometimes more than a hint – of having what you really most fundamentally long for, just by asking those simple questions and letting the answers rise up in you. That answer is found by resonating with the frequency of what the quenching of that longing would feel like.

Say that again?

When you have a hit, "Oh, that's what I most fundamentally am longing for around this," that happens when your receiver syncs up with the resonance frequency, the wavelength, of that fundamental quality it turns out you're longing for. So just answering the question plugs you in more than you were before.

So, bottom line, when you want something for someone else, really being conscious of where is that coming from and what you most deeply want for them a few notches deeper, that you believe them having that first thing would give them. And keeping solid in the intention of something along the lines of, "This or what most serves their life."

$$\Omega\ \Omega$$

And then to get back to the second part of that two part question from earlier, would it even work if it's me centered? Would it even *work* if you're using this process to try to change the unfolding of someone else's trajectory in a self serving way? Or what if it's just an innocent misperception or glitch or mind tangle, a limited perspective, maybe a touch of innocent arrogance, and you really think you're aligned in trying to change a specific thing about someone else's life that you think would make it better? Is this some powerful technology that can be unleashed for good or for evil? For goodness or for harm? For imposing your will upon other people's lives, like a wizard with a magic wand, but one that just takes some time to really charge up?

You know, when you throw a frisbee the same direction the wind is strongly blowing, it can really go. If you happen to throw it against a strong wind, even if your throwing technique is perfect, it's likely to be a dud and fall to the ground in no time or even blow back towards you and hit you in the stomach. That's just the physics of it. So you could think of it like that. When you extend an intention outward, and it's aligned with the greater subquantum multidimensional physics of – let's say benevolent higher harmonic resonance, it's likely to go quite a ways farther. The wind's at its back. When you extend one that's *against* the physics of higher harmonic resonance, even innocently, it's likely to hit that wind resistance, and just be a dud. So something along those lines.

I don't absolutely know that to be true, but it does resonate. And I really liked what you said a minute ago, about if you do this for someone else, finding what you most deeply want for them a few layers deeper than your initial presenting wish for them, and then making that be your focus for doing the steps. And also adding in a conscious, deliberate intention like, "This or whatever best serves their life." Factoring in your own potential unseen presumptions, or as you said, even unconscious arrogance. I didn't think there was anything you were going to say that would relax my red flag about someone doing this with someone else in mind, but those actually did it. They really resonated with me.

Good. I'm glad we pulled up from that nosedive at the last minute.

So could you methodically lay out the steps, one at a time?

Yeah, so, first just getting in touch with what you're wanting, and then just asking yourself, if that thing I want to happen happens, what does that provide that's even more fundamentally important to me, one notch deeper? What is it that I'm more fundamentally wanting, that would be unlocked if this first thing happened? And then doing that a few more times, a few more notches in, and just let yourself really feel the resonance of those answers bubbling up, and staying with the that deepest answer in particular a while, letting it really resonate in you, and I'm just realizing you meant the steps for Influencing Your Unfolding, right?

Right, but I liked hearing that again, and I think you said it a little differently. Does that one have a name?

Not really. It didn't really have a name that stuck when it came through, but I think in my mind I just think of it as that notching in process. And calling it "What do you want from that, another notch in?" is a little long, so how about just Notching In.

Notching In.

Yeah, works for me. Notching In, or the Notching In Process.

CHAPTER 71

And as for your actual question, take two, the official steps to the exclusive and elusive Influencing Your Unfolding Process, so in a nutshell, Step One is of course getting clear about something you would like to be different in your life or beyond your life. Something you don't yet have that you want. And if it's something already in your life that you want to change, that you want gone, try to frame it as what you'll have once it's no longer in your life. The relief or a fresh start or a lighter step or more relaxed shoulders or more enjoyment in your life or more ability to do more or whatever it might be, that you'll have once it's gone. Having a taste of the relief of that. Having a sense of what its absence will give you. It's a little less vague and a little less salmon swimming upstream to put it in terms of what life supportive thing you *would* have, like the freedom and relief of not having that stressful situation or those monthly bills.

So Step One, getting clear what you want. Step Two, let yourself really feel the truth that you really do want that. You do really desire that outcome. Let yourself feel your wanting of that. Not just a mental idea but also the visceral desiring. It doesn't need to be tight desiring, which I'll say more about shortly, but feeling how the simple already existing truth is, you *do* want that in your life or you *do* want that to happen. You don't have to try to stir up more feeling than you genuinely have, just letting it have some space. Side with it, stand with it, feel congruent with it. Let yourself feel the emotion of it to the degree you authentically can.

So Step One, what do you want? Step Two, really let yourself fully feel that you want it. And Step Three, letting yourself, to the best of your non-tight ability, repeatedly imagine and feel the experience of already having it. Asking yourself, how would it feel to already have right now that which you want? Imagine it's already happened, that you're however far in the future would makes sense, and it's come about. Not just mentally, but like how would things feel different in your day? How would your body feel when you wake up, knowing that it's happened? Imagine excitedly telling or messaging other people that it's happened, if that fits. How do you feel different? How does that happening add to the richness or quality of your life?

Just letting those questions slowly drop in and find their own answers inside you, not trying hard to answer them mentally. How does the sense of already having what you want land in your body? And maybe how does it impact who you see yourself to be? Who would you be if that comes about? *How* would you be? What would your life be like if this was already so? Just lightly asking these questions, letting them drop in you, letting the questions themselves impact you. That can help make space for the answers to land in you, for some degree of already pre-feeling having that which you're wanting to land in you.

And as you feel towards how it would be to already have this thing or non-thing that you want in your life, you can also lightly explore how it would feel to let yourself be pre-grateful. To kind of rehearse the scene or playfully imagine the scene of feeling grateful once you have that thing you want in your life, just to whatever degree that's available. Let yourself feel that relief, that enjoyment. Gratefulness is good for the brain and body, so why limit it until *after* what you want to happen has already happened? Why not pre-feel how that would be? Like I said earlier, we certainly tend to imagine and pre-feel potentially *negative* events when we don't know if they'll happen. No one thinks *that's* unusual or being fake or inauthentic. So why not try the other side a little and see how it goes?

Ω

So Step Three is more than just mentally imagining something as we probably usually think of it, it's bringing in all the senses you can, bringing in your body as you can. A heart feeling of gratefulness, a stomach feeling of excitement and happiness, maybe a feeling in your chest or spine of accomplishment if that fits. Maybe your shoulders are more relaxed and relieved, maybe your face is smiling. Just a little embodied imagination acting exercise.

And if you can't feel any of that, not forcing it, that's fine, but just lightly exploring, how would it feel, and what would it look like, to already have it be so? Imagining yourself in the future, already having that thing you want. Picture a snapshot moment or a short repeating scene of you now that it has happened or is happening. Maybe the moment you find out, or a moment you're toasting or celebrating or telling someone, or a moment the next day as you're really enjoying that it's happened.

And play around with ways to intensify and reinforce all of these things. Like imagining a scene where the camera is looking at you as you get the good news, and maybe also imagine a drone shot from above and a little ahead of you, why not? And a POV shot, a point of view shot where the camera is looking out through your eyes. Hearing what you might hear, seeing what you might see, how the person you're telling the good news to is happy for you, or anything else that enlivens it up.

So just embodying it and energizing it in whatever creative ways you can. Hearing yourself telling someone excitedly that you have it now or it came about. Pre-feeling the relief, the drop of your shoulders, once it's happened. Picturing and feeling posting it on social media or messaging friends or family or however else you might engage in sharing what happened if that's something you would do. Even pre-writing the good news email or journal entry. Pre-videoing a video. Just imagining scenes where you're celebrating it or acknowledging it or feeling how good it is that it's happened.

So it's like preheating the oven to be ready for the real deal. Have imaginary conversations where you're talking about it. Do it out loud even, people will just think you're on a bluetooth call, right? And when you wake up in the morning, half asleep, imagine you're waking up in a near future where this has already happened, and notice how that fills in or informs your whole experience as you're about to start your day.

It's kind of like you're an actor playing a part, and in that part your character is seeing this unfolding happening that they had been wanting, and they're feeling happy and relieved and grateful it happened. They're emotionally and physically impacted by this good news. And how do actors convince others? They feel it themselves, however much they authentically can, even though they always know the situation isn't literally real in their own current life. It's light, enjoyable play acting, and it's powerful, and on some level it can help evoke something real.

$$\Omega\,\Omega$$

And even just physiologically, it's like you're training your brain to make way, to make ready, to make room. I liked the analogy of preheating the oven. You're rehearsing, doing run throughs, doing a dress rehearsal, you're creating the prototype. You're limbering up the pathways, making a road that wasn't there before, starting the process, greasing those wheels, oiling those train tracks. If that's a thing. Is that a thing?

I don't think that's a thing.

Well let's say it's a thing. Oiling those train tracks. And if you ever notice there's tightness in all this, seeing if you can let that relax some, let it go. And if you can't, you can't. No added worries. But just seeing if now and then, two or three times a day or whatever fits for you, for a few minutes – even 30 seconds here and there – just seeing if you can feel how much you really would love for what you want to happen to really happen. And then pre-feeling it, pre-celebrating that it came about. Relating to it. Connecting with how relieved you'll feel if it gets resolved the way you really want or even need it to. Resonating with the relief that would bring, even though of course you don't yet know what will actually happen.

We're not trying to lie to ourselves that we're certain when we're not. It's just some light pretending, and also honestly and congruently resonating with how good it would feel for what we want to happen to actually come about. Like, "I can just imagine how good that would feel. I would feel this lightening of my load and this almost like springtime feeling of a new start. A reset. A new and upleveled life chapter. I would love for that to happen, so much. It would just feel so good to have that in my life."

So just relating to that. Enjoy wading in the warm waters of how nice that would be. Pre-marinating in it. And seeing if you can become so – well take two, seeing if you can lightly and playfully imagine being so convinced that it's already happened, or that it's already absolutely on its way, that you just let it go sometimes. Confident in its unstoppable arising in your life. Play acting that you're confident in its ultimate, definite arrival, and then just letting it go for a few days or a week or so, since it's already on its way.

And yeah, on one level of course you have no idea if it will actually happen, and you don't need to try to change that touchstone of rational awareness, I mean of course you don't know. And there's a thousand other influences and momentums in play around what unfolds in life. But on a simultaneous level, just letting yourself play with trusting and being confident it will happen, and actually enjoying that thought and feeling.

Ω Ω Ω

This isn't hard work, this isn't a task, it's not a chore, it's not a to do list entry to try to cross off ASAP. This is to be enjoyed, even savored, whether what you want actually ends up coming about or not, which you don't know yet. And even though it might or might not actually happen – and there are all those other influences and forces and potentialities weighing in – it's still a worthy endeavor to give your brain and neural network some nutrients and nourishment and new pathways of possibility, and to give your mind and body those feelings and endorphins and good vibes and nutrients of having something new and good and uplevelling, as well as just maybe it actually does influence and tip the scale some, around how things actually *do* unfold.

I like that, new pathways of possibilities.

Yeah, and again, it's actually not even your pre-business whether it happens or not, even though it might really matter to you. Meaning it's not for you to take on being the Ultimate Controller of everything that does and doesn't happen in life, in your life, in the lives of others, and on this planet. That's a touch grandiose and above our pay grade. We can have a lot of control in our lives, but not Ultimate Final Say control. We just don't get to have that.

But we *can* lightly play with imagining and rehearsing acting scenarios where what we want to happen is well on its way, which it might be. Or lightly doing the acting exercise of feeling and believing that it's already done, that it's already so. That on the blueprint level it's already formed, it just might take a little perceived time to get here, to show up here. And letting all of that be light, as though you're enjoying painting a picture or making some pottery or writing a poem or a song or acting in a play or movie where your character is going to have what they want to happen, or as though you're lightly engaging in any other creative endeavor.

And to the degree that you can, actually enjoying the moments of connecting *now* with what you intend to have *soon*. Enjoying feeling into already *having* it. Why wait to enjoy having it in your life til it shows up? Who said that's the best way to work it? All added up, that really robs you of a lot of good potential moments. Some good nutrients. That's such understandable but limited, two dimensional, arrow time thinking.

Maybe what you want doesn't ever happen and unless you pre-feel it, you miss out on ever in your life feeling any hint of having that thing happen, so why wait? Or maybe it *does* happen. And how would that feel? Enjoy the sense of having it *now*, to whatever degree you can. Imagine it's already the future if that helps, but just letting your brain and body bathe in the nutrients and feelings of how it would feel to already have this thing or event or unfolding or change that you want.

Ω Ω Ω Ω

Then, even if it doesn't happen, you still got something out of wanting it. You primed the pump, greased the wheels, got those thirsty train tracks all oiled and ready, which we all know is so important for proper train track maintenance these days. And who knows, maybe some time in the future that thing you wanted, if it doesn't happen this time, maybe it or something like it just comes in a little easier, or damn near miraculously. Serendipitously. Synchronicitously. Super-coincidentally.

And even if not, you enjoyed yourself a little, and gave your brain and body some real nourishment. Real nutrients. They aren't imaginary. They aren't just pretend. They're physiologically and mentally impactful newly organized neural clusters and pathways, and that goes with you into your future, regardless. All of that actually *is* real.

In some ways your body doesn't know if you're running on a treadmill or running down the street. I mean we can get scared watching a movie safe on our couch, right? So some parts of your brain and body don't know if that good thing you're feeling has actually happened yet or not. It's not really your – or put it this way, it's not the thing happening that makes you feel a certain way, it's your brain processing that it's happening or already happened.

And you're far too empowered to let whether or not that which you want to happen *actually* ends up happening determine whether you get to feel some of the good, sweet relief or enjoyment or excitement or accomplishment or enhanced mood, or expanded sense of yourself and your life and what's possible and who you are – and the new, very cool potential trajectory of your future – that you would experience if it does actually happen. Why not go ahead and feel some of that ahead of time, and get some of the physiological and mental benefits, whichever way it actually ends up going in form down the road a little? Why not take the early bird special? Why not avoid the rush, and be pre-grateful, pre-happy, pre-excited, pre-relieved, pre-proud of yourself, pre-infilled? Why not do some ready making?

Then you're already primed and ready and well rehearsed. You're already making space for it, easing into it, living into it, embodying it, creating neuropathways of familiarity, expanding your comfort zone or self concept zone a little, which creates the resonance of availability. And that in turn oils the track, to potentially help that more easily roll into your life.

And even if not, even if it never happens, it offers real nutrients and nourishing in your brain and body, and expands your mental sense of what things might look like fairly soon, what's possible, what the trajectory might be. And that can prime the pump for future good external unfoldings, as well as for enhanced internal mental experiences and attitude and contentment level and optimism and for leaning towards life more and bracing against it less. Regardless of what happens with this particular thing you want.

That really makes sense, even just, as you said, physiologically.

CHAPTER 72

What did you mean a minute ago when you said at the blueprint level?

Okay, so this is another one I'm not sure what to think about, and I didn't get a lot of information about it, but from one perspective, at least per that inflash, there's a more subtle blueprint level that contributes to or partly informs what happens on our physical level, and because it's more subtle it's easier to create changes to those blueprints, which then can impact what happens in form. It creates a – let's say an allowingness of enhanced easefulness, which I don't love but we'll keep it – because while it might seem hard to budge trajectories on this level, if you can alter the subtle level blueprints, that can help tilt the scale of what unfolds on our level.

So what to do with that? Well two things. First, you could just let that concept, the vibe of it, kind of wave in, that maybe it's not always as hard as we might presume to impact things on this level, in that it's easier to change, you know, the construction blueprints than to try to will all the building machinery and construction workers to go against the current ones. Just lightly playing with that, enjoying the possibility that there's something there worth resonating with and just, yeah, playing with it.

And the second thing, basically the second thing you can do with that is – yeah, I lost the second one. The first one was just kind of lightly playing with the possibility that it might not be as hard as it might seem to influence your unfolding, because there's a blueprint level that's more easily impacted by your intentional, emotionally resonant imaginings, and that can possibly more easily shift things in form. And the second one, oh, the second one is that you could just add this to the things you're imagining have already happened. Some kind of imagined representation that the subtle level blueprints are now already rearranged to be in alignment with what you want to happen. Just adding that into the mix as another way to kind of access a sense that what you want is already on the way. That the blueprints are already updated and you'll therefore see the results of that in form soon.

You've addressed this a bit, but what about the perspective that it's disingenuous or lying to yourself to do some of those things? Like trying to muster feeling grateful for something that might or might not happen, and convincing yourself it has already happened, when it hasn't and might not ever.

Well, if you're following these steps, you absolutely *aren't* trying to trick yourself about what's currently factual and what isn't. Not at all. An actor *always* knows the greater situation. You're just playfully faking it til you're making it. You're just letting yourself have a little taste of the arrival of something that you really want in your life, and that can, in a sense, alchemically help transform some of your longing for it into some hint, or more than a hint, of actually having it. It can help generate some momentum, to some degree, towards it actually coming about. And it can kind of – let's say bless your body and brain, with good enlivening nutrients in the meantime, either way. Doesn't guarantee a thing, but you're nutrienting your brain and you're energizing that imagined, desired potentiality more, and simultaneously you're now energizing your lack of having that in your life – that deficit, that deficiency – less and less.

Ω

Say that again? Simultaneously you're...

You're not energizing the feeling of lack, you're not feeding the feeling of *not* having what you want. You're not perseverating on deficit and deficiency. Odds are you've done that enough. You can definitely let yourself feel any feelings that are there, just instead of planting more lack seeds, now you're planting more fulfillment seeds. And even if they don't really seem to get to the stage where they bear fruit, they're just nicer seeds to be planting and watering and nurturing and nutritioning. Because unlike the lack seeds, as the fulfillment seeds start to grow a little, they can actually nurture you back, nourish and nutritionize your mind and body. Support your life. You water them, they water you.

But with lack seeds, you water them, and they need more and more and more water from you without ever giving you anything back. Like feeding the subphysical energy suckerfish just makes them hang around more and poke and prod you more, with a bigger appetite. Give a seagull one little treat and they'll be a *fiend* for life. So it's just kinder all around to take care about which seeds you're planting and watering and shining the sunlight of attention on, and this is one powerful way to do that.

And the whole point of this isn't hoping it actually happens, though of course that can be there and is welcome. But that's maybe half the point or a third of the point. 38.5 percent of the point. More important is the potency of actually bathing your neuropathways and your nervous system, to whatever degree is available, through you pre-feeling what they would bathe in if you got what you want. That can start to shift the frequency, from a brain that maybe sometimes – or probably *more* than sometimes – discontentedly sees what you *don't* have, to a brain that can really catch the vibe of having the good thing or things you really *could* soon have, in a relaxed, spacious, empowered, more authentically optimistic way. A brain that attunes more to the frequency of a more fulfilled life, and less to the lack of it.

And what you're attuned to, you're more likely to encounter in your life, for maybe a few reasons, one of which is it can directly impact what you're putting out to the blueprint level, but also just because, you know, you buy a new car or get a new puppy, and you suddenly see that model or that dog breed ten times more than before, you're just unconsciously more attuned. Kind of like that, but more deeply imbedded. Your vibrational tuning fork just tends to find external matches for internal spaces and beliefs and expectations and biases.

So even if doing this little process doesn't ultimately bear fruit around that specific thing in any way you can see, you were still getting to, at least a little, bathe in the field of having that which you desire, which greases the wheels and oils the tracks for possible resonant future unfoldin s, as well as bathes your brain in new possibility and potentiality and good vibes. Gives it some new, good, healthy more expanded, more potential-rich neural connections.

Ω Ω

It's hard to get from A to Z if you only spend time firmly experientially locked in A, angsting or contracting in a closed loop because you don't have Z, with a giant chasm between the two, which might even just seem to get deeper and wider and more hopeless as time passes, never the twain shall meet. Or maybe I should have gone with A to C, to bring in that it's just possibly not as far away as it might at first feel.

But exploring this process can help build a bridge across that perceived chasm between where you are and where you want to be. A frequency bridge where there's not such a huge dissonance or distance between the two. Or it can help you remove your pessimistic colored glasses, so that you actually *do* see some real routes to potentially get to where you'd like to go, so the predominant inner stance around it isn't impossibility – or damn near impossibility – anymore.

Then you're not likely to be as limited or life limiting in your perspective. You're not a sad, hopeless, hungry stray dog looking in a restaurant window at a steak someone's eating, angsting for something so out of reach and unlikely. You're a filled with *potential*, hungry, currently soloing it dog, a hungry dog filled with positive potentiality, that's pre-tasting how amazingly scrumpdillyicious it's gonna be to have that steak in your mouth, which might happen any minute now, which is so cool! And that gets your tail wagging with a little delight, and that might make you more in sync with a potential unfolding where you get to have that steak, a potential unfolding where you're more available for catching the scent of any arising potential opportunities to actually have it.

Maybe someone leaves the restaurant with a – I didn't plan this, I swear – but with a doggy bag, and they see your tail wagging, and you seem like a genuinely happy dog, and that makes them feel delight and they just naturally give you their leftover steak that they were going to have for lunch tomorrow, cuz aren't you the cutest little furball ever, yes you are.

Or maybe you're a hungry currently soloing it dog that's available for unexpected potentialities, completely focused on actually having and tasting and eating that steak you see through the window, instead of on how impossibly out of reach it seems – I mean there's a dress code and you don't have a *thing* to wear – so then you notice the restaurant door, off to the side 30 feet, and you tailwag yourself right over to it, and as soon as someone opens the door you prance right in, grab that steak from the table, politely say wankwoo, and run back out the door before those oh so loveable but sometimes a little scary humans even know what happened.

Ω Ω Ω

And like I touched on earlier, if you're spending all day telling yourself you'll never get a job, reinforcing that, you're probably less motivated to take intelligent action with some gusto, and less authentically upbeat and confident during a job interview, than if you're feeling how much you want a job and seeing it as already in the process of happening, and feeling how good that will feel to read that offer email and feeling how exciting those first moments of showing up to work will be. How good for your life, to be upleveled in that way.

That pre-occurred experience of success helps feed you now, and also naturally helps give you the confidence and enthusiasm and determination to keep optimistically and good-vibedly working towards your goal. And also, because you've seen it happen in your mind and felt it happen in your body a hundred times or more, when it actually *does* happen, you're not shell shocked or feeling undeserving or like a fish out of water the first time you walk into your new workplace or get that promotion or get your first clients or whatever it is. You're completely on board from day one.

Of course there's still a steep learning curve, learning the ropes and getting more comfortable, but right off the bat it just fits you better than it would've, because you've already worn it a hundred times – this new position – and pre-grown into it. You're more pre-aligned so there's less acclimation time. So it's just not quite as big of a stretch that this is now your new role. You've already pre-lived in it, 50 times or more. If you rehearse it first you start with a burst.

So yeah, it could be interesting to just give this Influencing Your Unfolding process a little fair, reasonable test, and just see if you find anything of value in it. Not "I didn't get ten million dollars this month, I *knew* it was bull!" But a little more subtle or zoomed out than that. "Did this seem to be good for me in any way? Is it worth lightly, experimentally playing with this some more, to feed some seeds?"

So maybe exploring the potential cost benefit analysis of trying out this process for a while – maybe a few minutes a couple of times a day for a few weeks, or whatever seems good – on one or two or three individual things, and then just seeing, not only if anything starts to show up in your life that you were enjoying the thought of showing up, but also, even if not, does it seem good for the ole brain to give it these nutrients and neuropathway upgrades and good stretches and muscle building training more often?

I'm not sure I get muscle building.

I just mean strengthening the neuropathways that are in line with this, making them stronger. And even infusing your sense of self with how it would feel to have this thing that maybe hasn't so far been a part of your identified sense of self and sense of what you do and don't have in your life and what's reasonably possible. Rehearsal makes way for the smoother and easier embodying of that which you're rehearsing. Makes it simpler and more comfortable, because then having that thing you want in your life starts to feel like you more, instead of something foreign and beyond your familiarity zone, that doesn't line up with who you've been or how you see yourself.

CHAPTER 73

And the steps to do that, I'm still wanting to get them pinned down. So far, I think we have first knowing what you want, second feeling how much you want it, and third really feeling how it would feel to already have it.

Okay, so there weren't like big flashing numbers next to each thing that came in, and the last three could be in any order, doesn't really matter, but we'll say Step Four is keeping it light and loose and lovely. I was going to say light and loose and enjoyable, but at the last second I overreached for a little mnemonic alliteration instead. And there's two similar parts to this one. No, there's three, yeah three. First, being light and loose and enjoying it as you go through the first three steps, doing them with light playful creative, anticipatory enjoyment, to whatever degree that's available. And if it ain't there, it ain't there.

And second, being light and loose about whether or not what you're wanting actually happens. Enjoying or at least appreciating, or at the very, very least *participating* in this process, with an intention to be good with either way. There's still the benefit of that other 65 percent or so. Fine to have a preference, fine for it to really matter, but ideally not tightly trying to squeeze it or force it, which is counterproductive.

And third is being light and loose about *how* it might happen. Maybe sometimes there's really only one way, but when there could theoretically be more than one, you don't have to pre-assume how it has to come about or insist the Omniverse be limited to only one route. No need to narrow down the possible potentialities prematurely. Enjoy not knowing for sure how it's going to happen, having space that the route it takes might be a really nice surprise.

Now if you find yourself motivated to be planning something or doing something that could possibly naturally lead to the outcome you want, great, you don't need to stop yourself, that might be how it happens. Sometimes damn hard work is how it happens. That's not an error, sometimes that's the through line to reaching that outcome. But not being narrow visioned about how what you want could possibly come about.

So for instance, if you want two million dollars for retirement, when you imagine having that, not preselecting how that has to happen. There might be five or ten or fifteen general ways it could theoretically happen, with varying degrees of likelihood, or even more ways that have never even occurred to you. And one of those ways could include you starting a business where you're working 50 hours a week for a while to really rev it up, get it off the ground. It's not necessarily all lotteries and unexpected inheritance and finding a Rembrandt at a garage sale. Who knows what route or routes might open up?

So not trying to insist or bully or steamroll how it has to happen, just imagining, hearing, feeling, seeing that you're on the other side of it, that it *has* happened. And being light and relaxed about the *how* and the *if*. A watched pot never boils, and it starts to feel really awkward if you're just staring at it all the time. So keep it light and playful and unconcerned to the best of your authentic ability.

Ω

And like I said, if you *are* uptight and nervous about trying to get something to happen because it's really important to you, then *that's* what's in front of you to be authentic and congruent with. So then leaning into that deep strong serious wishing *exactly* as it is, and doing the process with that staying close at your side, instead of trying to wrangle it into the basement. Instead of wrestling with it. Like, "That's *really* important to me, I would so love that to happen, so much. That would be such a huge, huge relief."

And steps Five and Six are quick and easy, and the order doesn't matter, so we'll say Step Five is just let it all go once in a while, and Step Six is just rinse and repeat. So Step Five is playfully and lightly trying on embodying the confidence that it's so definitely on the way that you can just let it all go for a while, and then just dropping it for a day or a week or whatever, it's up to you. Maybe add it to your calendar for a few days later so you can really let go of even remembering to get back to it for a while.

And this step is as important as all the other steps. Letting it all go, forgetting about it, moving on to other things, with a light, playful confidence that it's already taken care of. Taking your eyes off that uncomfortable pot you're still secretly side eyeing to see if it's finally boiling yet. Just enjoy letting it all go, lightly trusting it's already so. And that should probably be the short version of Number Five, letting it go, lightly trusting it's so.

Just playfully trusting that it's already in motion on the blueprint level, and that it soon will show up fully and completely here, so no need to give it another thought for a while. It's easy to stay contractedly waiting for something, and that can jam up the works. A heart doesn't move blood just by squeezing. It does it by squeezing then letting go, not just one or the other. Squeezing then letting go, that's what creates the flow.

Are these little couplets you've thrown in here and there this weekend pre-planned or just coming out?

Yeah, I don't walk around rhyming in normal daily life, and I didn't spend last week sitting around, thinking up and memorizing potentially relevant, hokey couplets in case the opportunity arises to fit them in somewhere. They just seem to be coming out this weekend, not sure why. I guess chalk it up to both, sometimes trying more arrows or more spaghetti to see what sticks, more passes of the photo printer, and also that languaging change or verbal expression change that happened from the Big Event, where my relationship with words and verbalizing feels different and a little deeper and more creative and maybe more playful than it did before.

And then maybe a third one, unless this is just more of the second one, but it's almost like – well it *is* like – I now have a lot of extra creative energy just looking for something to do, looking for a place to express itself, so apparently sometimes it jumps on some word play. Just kind of happens.

And another question I have cued up, you did a one minute version of the blueprint level. Could you add another minute or two?

Yeah, I mean not much has come in about it, so I don't have a lot more to say, but you know how a 3D printer has a design it follows, first comes the design and then comes the creation of that design in form, right? Like when you send a file blueprint to your regular computer printer, short of a printing glitch, what you send over is what shows up on the page. Same with building a house. The construction workers follow the blueprints, at least ideally. But it's much, much easier to move a pre-created window in the blueprints, preconstruction, than it is to move the physical window after the house is already built.

Ω Ω

So what came in was, that's a little similar to one aspect of what happens, what unfolds, in our lives and on our level of reality in general. We don't have to take it too literally, but you know how a lever uses – well, *leverage,* to lighten how much effort it takes to lift a heavy object. So when we're wanting to create something in our lives, it can maybe make it feel a little lighter and a little more in the realm of possibility if we think of it as just rearranging the blueprint on a subtler level of reality, so that if that blueprint changes, it's more likely to change in form.

That blueprint level is lighter and more subtle, so while our thoughts and imaginations and feelings maybe can't easily do a lot with our dense level of reality directly, maybe sometimes they can influence the blueprint level a little easier, and from there, the rest is more likely to take care of itself. It's just easier to erase a line, and add a line somewhere else, in the construction blueprints than to move an already built window. And it's easier to change where a river ends up by changing the channel it's taking way back up at the start of it. So this is just another way to kind of gain entry into the feeling of possibility that we could have an impact or an influence on what unfolds, another way to work with it. Kind of a consciousness technology, that maybe adds just a little train track oil to loosen things up.

And how does the blueprint level fit in with the level of energy suckers? Which one is more subtle or are they the same?

Yeah, so there's our physical universe, and then a few frequencies over on the radio dial is the higher frequency tesseverse, if it exists, four dimensional physical reality of which our 3D universe is one side or facet or slice, out of hundreds or thousands or millions. And then a little farther over or higher up the frequency dial is energy suckers, if they exist, and then the blueprint level is like farther over from that, if it exists. A higher frequency or higher level that includes blueprints and/or afterglows or after ripples of all that unfolds in all these comparatively more dense levels of reality. I haven't received yet like an intricate, laid out, detailed frequency spectrum map delineating exactly where all these things land, what precise megahertz each exists in on the cosmic radio dial, but that's the general layout as I've understood it.

And by the way, another potential brain boggler I haven't fit in anywhere yet is that we assume, or at least *I* assume, that we're at the densest level, the lowest frequency on the cosmic radio dial, and that's definitely how I've been talking about it all weekend, that's my default way of seeing it. But some higher frequencied levels of reality can feel solid too, like ours does, and they can also have some degree of obscurative veils or partitions in between levels, so those things in themselves aren't evidence we're the lowest frequencied level. Just because we can't perceive any denser levels doesn't mean they don't exist, just like less dense levels.

Ω Ω Ω

You're saying there might be levels more dense than ours? That's – that's hard to imagine.

Yeah, this is definitely another one of those things that's really hard to grok the possibility of. Things feel so dense and solid here, how could there possibly be anything denser? How could there be any world or level of reality that's lower frequencied, and that would see our dense and heavy level of reality as actually more subtle, more wispy, more translucent, as at a higher frequency? And where is it? Is it right here but even denser than ours, like slower, lower radio waves, which can exist in the same space as faster, higher frequency ones? Like local radio stations or mobile phone signals don't interfere with each other even though they're all waving through right here and right now? Not sure. It really is hard to grok, and I can't really get a sense of it. And I'm not saying that *is* the case, just that – partly to keep up our mind stretching exercises and partly to make sure we don't get too, I don't know, complacent or arrogant or trenched in with our assumptions – it's good to hold a little space for that possibility. And my amazing psychic abilities can tell you're about to ask if I've asked Omega about it – impressive I know – and the answer is I have.

Pray tell.

So this sense of radio frequencies and turning the radio dial to different vibratory levels sometimes comes in as an analogy during inflashes, and once in the middle of one of those something popped in, that this isn't necessarily the most dense level that exists, just because it's the lowest that we can perceive. And also the highest we can perceive, for that matter. And first of all, it wasn't definitive that that was the case, and second, with that one it wasn't as crystal clear to me as it usually is that it was an inflash and not something that just bubbled up from or originated from my own mind, and just kind of happened to pass through in the middle of the bridging session.

So I asked Omega, and the answer, once translated, was just "Could be." That was it. "Could be." No real subtext I could discern like wink wink or "You're onto something, kid." And yeah, I've already dinged Omega's Yelp ratings a star or two for being so annoyingly unforthcoming sometimes, especially after seemingly promising during that first bridging session that now all my deep questions would be answered.

What do you mean seemingly promising?

Well, that was the way I took it, but technically Omega didn't *actually* promise to answer all my questions, just to show me more of what I've always longed to know – which the only thing I longed to know at the time was what the hell was it they thought I always longed to know. And also, in fairness, these *new* questions, they just came up in real time, I hadn't *always* longed to know the answers to them. So technically no promises were made and none were broken, but it still has sometimes been between mildly annoying and – like I shared earlier – pretty damn frustrating, when there's no answer, and no explanation about why sometimes that's the case. It's definitely not my preference.

And just one quick straggler from what I just said, you could argue that actually I *had* always longed to know something, and that is, how it all works, how it's all set up, which to me always meant how the universe is set up, how quantum level waves and particles and fields work, those kinds of big questions. I even thought about majoring in physics in college, and maybe having a career where I could get paid for asking the big physics questions, and maybe help chip away at answering a few of them.

So there *has* been that interest or pull or longing in me, to understand how it's all set up, I just never for a minute seriously considered that the big answers to that might include that there was anything beyond our physical reality. Not to mention that there's so much beyond this level that our physical reality is merely one ultra-thin onion layer in an onion the size of Jupiter. So there *was* actually that longing, but whether that had anything at all to do with everything that's opened in me over these months, I truly have no idea.

CHAPTER 74

Have you ever asked Omega why the bridging sessions are happening, or why you?

Yeah. Something close to, "This is just the potentiality that opened when your particular aperture loosened. Everyone has their own unique potentialities as their aperture loosens and/or their hearts and minds begin to release their constricted limitations. Not better or worse, not higher or lower, just unique to them, and these bridging sessions happen to be what has opened with yours."

But one last thought about the blueprint level, is it like a subtle ethereal kind of offgassing afterglow or echo or ripple wave from our physical level, or is it more the precursor to this level, shaping it, instructing it, the pre-existent blueprints of it? Or is it a little of both, where what happens here informs the blueprints of what's next, and the blueprints of what's next inform what happens here?

And when some people seem to perceive something that hasn't happened yet, it could be they're attuned to a much higher level of reality where their Higher Self or Fuller Consciousness has access to the whole film reel, or maybe they're just picking it up from like the ethereal auric blueprint level of what's likely, but not absolutely certain, to arise, just as some animals can pick up the subtle electromagnetic changes just before an earthquake, or your cat somehow knows exactly when you've finally fallen asleep, and then Machiavellianishly pounces on your stomach.

So my sense is they can mutually impact each other, this level and the blueprint one, if it exists. And again, what do you do with that, including the uncertainty of it? One thing is just lightly play with considering that things don't necessarily have to be as hard to shift on our level as they first might seem. It's just a way to kind of gain access to a sense of enhanced possibility. And then what was the second one from earlier? I'm blanking on it again.

Imagining that it's already in motion on that level. To reinforce the sense that it's going to be happening so you can let it go for a while.

Yeah, that was it, nice tracking as usual. So just including that in your imaginings, in any way you want, to lightly imagine that the blueprints have updated so it's done and in motion and already on its way. Just letting it go and believing it's so for a while, which is Step Five.

And Step Six is rinse and repeat?

Yeah, just repeating the first five steps, revisiting them, keep going through them, including letting it go for a while. And you can work with several things in the same week or month, or even the same day, just not in a rushed, cross it off the list kind of way – not that it has to take much time at all – just not, you know, getting fatigued and tight about doing it or having an attitude of it being yet another damn thing to try to squeeze in, or trying to cram in three different things you would like in your life in one mostly mental minute.

And this whole Influencing Your Unfolding process, also known as the IYU Process, as of one second ago, is actually simpler than first impression, because once you have Step One, getting clear what you want, you don't have to do it again for that specific thing, it's done. And steps Four, Five and Six are just keep it light and loose, drop it now and then, and rinse and repeat, keep doing the steps now and then, mostly steps Two and Three, a few times a day or a few times a week, for a minute or two or five.

Ω

So once you've got the first one, the first step, then if those last three are in the back of your mind, it's really just steps Two and Three, letting yourself feel how much you really do want that in your life, you really do want it to happen, and then really connect with and feel and imagine and pre-experience and rehearse how it would be to already have it. So doing those two again and again when you feel like it, that's most of it right there.

When you take walks, when you have a couple of minutes, in the shower, when you sit down to relax a few, before jumping to the next episode of a show you don't know why the hell you're still streaming. And when you're going to sleep or waking up might be good times, the mind can be a little less contracted with daily details and a little more open to imagination, and more in the hypnagogic state between sleeping and awakeness. But trying different times and seeing what seems to work for you to just stop for a few and do steps Two and Three, and checking in on the other steps occasionally as needed.

And I think just one last point with these steps, that I touched on earlier, if we believe a specific future unfolding will give us good feelings – relief, happiness, joy, feeling more secure, feeling safer, more settled, more content, whatever it might be – then how do we even *know* that? How do we *suspect* that? Because on *some* level we can already sense into it, at least just enough to get the inner feedback that it would feel good to have it. How do we even know to want something except that we can already feel, at least a touch, even if it's beneath our awareness, some sense of how it would feel if it happened? We can already glean what it would give us.

It's so hot out today, a nice cold glass of ice tea would just hit the spot. I'm feeling stressed about finances, some extra income would *really* feel like such a relief. Resolving that tension with my friend that's been hanging around for far too long – I mean the *tension's* been hanging around too long, not my friend, unless *that's* what all the tension's about – but resolving that and really resetting things would really lighten my load and feel so settling. Or it would feel so amazing to get that good medical news. We already pre-know that what we want would feel really good to have, because we can already feel a hint of what it would give us. How we would feel once we have it.

So this process is just kind of elongating and elaborating on and con-sciousizing something that we all already naturally do. Stretching that instant unconscious moment and making it more conscious and more infilled. Just slowing down enough to let yourself steep in imagining you already have it, and how good that would feel or how good that would be.

And the vibe that showed up in me as this was all unpacking was a deeply settled contentment that in those moments, you actu-ally get to receive the fruits, to some real degree, of already hav-ing what you wanted, even if you never end up actually getting it. It's like a shortcut to some of the fruits we're so positive we can only access after we get what we want in form. It's so unquestioned and assumed to be obvious to us that we might not take kindly to someone suggesting otherwise. But – and this also touches on that other process that we'll go into in a minute – but we actually *can* take in some of the gifts of having what we want, just by *being* with what we want and feeling that *longing* in a relaxed and settled way.

And it would be I think really common to feel some resistance to letting ourselves just lightly explore whether we can pre-feel a hint of the gifts of having something we don't yet have and might never have. There's some self protection and skepticism that can get activated there. And of course, sometimes we just don't resonate with a particular offering. Maybe a particular invitation or practice or process just doesn't speak to us. But unless it's a clear no, it could be interesting to just not give any resistance too much weight just yet, and to just lightly explore this for maybe a few weeks or so and see what happens. Not much to lose and potentially some good things to gain.

Ω Ω

And could you just take 60 seconds and list the steps one last time, quick and succinct?

Asked the Little Prince, who never once let go of a question once he had asked it.

You <u>did</u> read it.

Yeah, three times actually, and I teared up a little each time. It was the perfect book at the time, heartful and simple and pure. One of the few things that connected me to my heart for a little while, during those first days of being so especially disheartened at what I had lost, so it was a really timely gift. I had never read it before, and honestly I don't think I would've been able to really catch the vibe of it before the Big Event. But okay, the six steps in 60 seconds, start the timer.

So, Step One, knowing what you want. Step Two, connecting with how much you want it. Step Three, feeling how it would feel to already have it and imagining scenes and scenarios around that. Step Four, What's Step Four? Yeah, keep it all light and loose and lovely, including hands off how it happens or *if* it happens. And Step Five, what was that little rhyme for Step Five? Let it be and then you'll see? Not quite.

Let it go and believe it's so, or close to that.

Yeah, let it go and lightly believe it's so. The blueprints are updated, the spillway's already open upstream, the cool refreshing water is on its way even though you can't see physical signs of it yet, it's a done deal, so forget about it for a while. Stop side eyeing that poor awkward cooking pot that's dealing with performance anxiety from trying to boil the water you're impatiently waiting for. Just drop it a while, let it go for a day or three. And then Step Six, blanking again. Getting a little tired.

We'll take an overdue break in a minute, but rinse and repeat.

Yeah, rinse and repeat. Just keep going through the steps, mainly Step Two and Three, til you feel done with it or it feels done with you. And those are the six steps. And, bonus round, if you're doing this for someone else, it's good to start with two – let's call them pre-steps – and you could also add them when you're doing this for yourself if they resonate. So Pre-step One would be doing Notching In, which is just, "If they end up having this thing I want for them, what is it *that* does for their life that's more what I'm *really* going for here, one notch deeper?" Doing that a few times and feeling the answers resonate, letting them come to you, letting them kind of bubble up into your awareness, until you feel like you've reached the most fundamental thing you're really most deeply wanting for them, and letting *that* be your focus.

And then Pre-step Two would be – and instead of a step this could also just be a consistent attitude throughout the whole process – but instead of insisting *my* will be done, having a continuous humble intention of, "This, or whatever most supports their life. Even if it looks different than the way I'm seeing it." An intention along those lines, that you just carry with you, until it just lives in you, and/or you could say it at the beginning and end of each time you're giving this a spin. The same could apply when you're doing the process for yourself.

Ω Ω Ω

So yeah, those are the steps. And there's one last thing about this that I've started to say a couple of times but haven't gotten it out yet, and that is, you know, why did Omega open this whole process up? Influencing Your Unfolding? It's a little different vibe than most of the other things that have come through in the bridging sessions. I mean a lot has come through about a lot of things, in a lot of different areas, but Omega isn't really about, you know, think and grow rich or personal prosperity above all else or anything like that. So why this topic or this instruction? And somewhere towards the end of unpacking all of this, that wondering came up in me, why this? And two things just instantly kind of mini-whomped in and felt instantly clear to me, felt really obvious to me.

And one was, we're invited to participate, we're welcome to participate – you could even say we're *encouraged* to participate – in the unfolding of our lives, not just in the usual, familiar ways, but also through this kind of deeper intentional participation in potentially shaping what unfolds. We're welcome to have things in our lives that make our heart sing, that bring us enjoyment, that lighten our load, that ease our mind. We're welcome to soar while we're here, in little ways and bigger ways. There's no virtue in materialism, but there's also no virtue in stoic lack. So we're welcome to play, to create, to explore intending to see in our lives that which would delight our heart. We're welcome to row and steer the boat, both on the obvious surface but also via the deep subtle rudder, hidden from the surface, that's lesser known in this world.

And the second mini-whomp was, regardless of whether what you're wanting actually shows up, this is a way to beneficially life hack the brain some, to give it some good things, some nourishing and nurturing, some nutrients and newness, when modern human life often isn't so conducive to those things. And that's a really nice gift to offer yourself. And those good vibrations can also ripple into your future, partly through the impact on neuropathways and brain chemistry, and partly through maybe tilting the scale in what unfolds, and that could possibly help you have more of what you really want, a little farther down the road. And even if not, those ripples can still help you have more content richness within, even when things are a little more challenging out there than you would prefer.

Okay. I think that's the whole Influencing Your Unfolding piece. The whole IYU Process. And the invitation is to check it out for yourself if you'd like, give it a fair try if you feel pulled to or if you're a little curious, or if you just want to prove it wrong, prove how ridiculous it all is, and yeah, just seeing how it feels for you. Just noticing how it's impacting you over some time, regardless of your apparent short and medium range success rate of it turning out that what you were wanting actually shows up, since it's also very much about the nutrients and the stretching into a larger sense of what your life could include, within and without.

And that can have long term benefits aside from the specifics of which things on your list do or don't unfold within the next month or the next year. And it can leave you more available and open and more ready to catch the scent of similar things that could potentially open in the future, and just maybe tip the scale a bit. So yeah, I think that's it. Let's call that one done. Whew. That was a *lot*. I'd still like to talk about that other process, if you're up for it, but I definitely need a quick bladder break first.

Yes, I'd really like to hear that last one. I really appreciated you opening up Influencing Your Unfolding, a lot of really rich material. More food for thought as usual. Alright, so it's already a little after 11:30, believe it or not. As you said when we were getting started yesterday, best laid plans.

Yep. So how about if we just take like three minutes or so, and then come back and finish this thing up, while I can still form semi-coherent doorknobs.

Sounds good. See you in three.

SESSION 12
CHAPTER 75

Alright. Back to it. The home stretch. So tell me about this last process.

Yeah, so basically, this came in a couple of weeks after the last Influencing Your Unfolding flash packet. It overlaps with it some, Venns with it, but it's definitely its own thing. And like I've said, so far I haven't been deliberately and disciplinedly trying to do it, I've just kind of found myself doing it sometimes, spontaneously. Probably the handiwork of Omega, or maybe I just took in that flash packet really deeply so something in me got onboard with it in a particularly aligned way. Probably some of both.

And it's had a real impact on my gradual transition from impatiently and jadedly and resistantly waiting to fully return to that amazing sense of Love and Belonging and Acceptance and Relief that I felt during the Big Event – like kids in the back of the car, are we there yet – to more moments of a little more enjoying and appreciating and relaxing into the notably less transcendent ride I'm currently on, of living an often flat life as a person on this planet, who's not very consciously connected to the Beautiful More. There's less chronic resistance to the way things currently are.

And this process starts at the same place, with being aware of something you don't have that you really want, but it has its own approach from there. And the basic theme around it was kind of like almost a gentle, graceful Aikido move, where you actually let your very lack of having something that you want in your life give you, in just a few minutes – at least potentially – an infilling of content aliveness and settledness and even just maybe a hint of Expandedness and Beingness, and that's actually been my experience with it so far, sometimes really subtly, sometimes pretty impactfully.

I know we don't have time for a big tangent, but I just want to ask, both Influencing Your Unfolding and Notching In are about working with when you really want something you don't have, and it sounds like this one is too.

Yeah, that's been a big theme of the last several months in my world, being dissatisfied with my life because it's felt so comparatively lacking and empty without having what I wanted. And to varying degrees, at least at times, discontentment with our life as it is is a pretty universal thing, but I was a poster child for that kind of entrenched defensive space of "Nope, this isn't good enough. You want me to show up and stop resisting what's here, you gotta make it better than this comparatively flat, empty, lifeless, cut off, poor excuse for a life." So it makes sense to me that some support and tools around that stuckness and that massive dissatisfaction with my life were showing up in the bridging sessions, that I could apply if I were so inclined.

Ω

But other invitations have come in too, not focused on that, like I've talked about Simultaneous Awareness Practice, where you gently try to let yourself be aware of two or more things at once. Gently, because it's damn near impossible, but the gentle intention and practice of easefully leaning into doing it can lead to a more settled, grounded, clearer space.

And maybe you remember the simultaneous awareness touchpoint checklist from yesterday, and it really could be anything you can perceive with your senses, but specifically it could include any two, of your hands, your feet, your arms, your legs, your stomach, your chest, your breathing, your shoulders, your neck, your jaw your forehead, any sensations or discomfort in your body, any sounds coming in, anything you're aware of visually, someone you're talking to, a breeze or draft on your skin, any smells wafting in, whatever you might be seeing directly or peripherally, and really anything you can turn your sensory attention to.

But all of it with like a soft gentle, light hearted gaze, not a sharp, tight, effortful trying to keep it all in sharp focus. And the human brain gets bored and forgets and stops doing it, and that's absolutely expected, and so gently bringing yourself back is important, not impatiently or self judgingly, or else *that's* what you're practicing and reinforcing.

And you can do it alone for a few minutes, or 20 or 30 or whatever seems good, as a type of an occasional or regular centering and grounding and connecting and awareness practice or mindfulness practice. Or you can do it throughout the day when you remember and feel like it, or something in between. It's totally up to you how you explore it, if you give it a try, just keeping it stress free and light and gentle – a kind of soft gaze – not tight and strict and zeroed in and hyper focused and self harsh.

And when you're exploring what it's like to bring it along with you on a busy workday or an important project or an intense meeting or a heavy personal conversation or other active times, you can explore applying that 80/20 rule, or 70/30, meaning 20 or 30 percent of your awareness doing this, and the rest focusing on the task at hand.

And it might feel a little wobbly to start, but once you get acclimated to it, instead of distracting you, it can actually enhance and ground you while working or having conversations or being busy. That's been my experience when I find it happening, including sometimes this weekend. I find it supports me being grounded and more present and more capable of the task at hand, rather than hindering or interfering with what I'm wanting to be primarily focused on.

So after an initial orientation phase, it doesn't compete with primary focus, it enhances it. It helps you be more rooted and balanced and centered, instead of leaning too far forward into what your current task is, which usually isn't actually as helpful or productive or healthy as our default settings might think it is. That's been my experience with it anyway.

Ω Ω

So yeah, there's that one, and then another one not based on wanting anything, that I haven't mentioned to you yet, and this one really may have been one hundred percent me, my own unconscious, or not, which like we've talked about, could theoretically be said about everything the whole weekend. But I was waiting for Omega to show up one day, this was about three months ago, and when I was probably five minutes from calling it a no show day, I had a whole cohesive thought stream bubble up all at once, like happens with flash packets, but without any obvious whomp or any signs it was Omega. But I was pretty settled and quiet and it just out of the blue came in, fully formed, for no reason I was aware of. That happens now and then, where something pops in or bubbles up before I'm aware of the bridging session starting, before I'm aware of Omega in the space, and I'm not really sure if it came from Omega or my own mind.

And it was something like, you know, it really could've gone either way there for a few when I not only flirted with death, but gave it a kiss, and if my ticket *had* been one way, there would've been a lot that would've been left really unresolved in my life. A lot of messes, even just in terms of having my affairs really in order, financial records, digital files that stand out as something I would like to make sure people know exist, piles and boxes of papers in no particular order, having all my stuff fairly organized, a current will, having an *In Case I Die* document that spells everything out. And also some unfinished things with people in my life, and maybe a handful of people who used to be in my life that I didn't quite feel totally complete with.

So all this just popped in at once, and along with it or maybe a few seconds later this clarity just came in that I should – well not I should, like a duty or obligation, but like an invitation – that it would be good taking care for me to just lightly – since there's no guarantees for any of us – just lightly ask myself, if I only had a year left to live, what all would I want to be sure to take care of gradually over the next year, and what's stopping me from going ahead and actually doing that?

And odds are high I'll be alive beyond that, likely for years after that, and that would mean I'll get to live with that extra layer of peace that I really did get my, you know, instructions and finances and disorganized piles and haphazard boxes, those kinds of details, in order, and also the extra peace of contacting some people from my past, with maybe an email of appreciation or an apology or speaking my peace or similar, and maybe even have a few calls or video calls or coffees. And also including some people currently in my life and even peripherally in my life. Just cleaning up some residue, to leave things a little cleaner and shinier and more in order. And if it turned out I wasn't around to reap the benefits from all of that, even more important that those things got attended to.

And I don't mean I have to have a big dramatic goodbye with everyone, like "I pretend have some sad news. I pretend only have a year left to live so I just wanted to pretend say goodbye, and get some pretend closure with you, because you've been my pretend friend for a long time." So maybe I share I'm doing a one year deep life cleanse process or maybe I don't, but just, whatever in myself would give me that sense of finishing some unfinished business, bigger and smaller, to the best of my ability.

Ω Ω Ω

So assuming I live quite a while longer, there's just no downside to this. Even just methodically going through everything I own over the course of the year, releasing some of it and organizing the rest, would improve my life some. And since, as Clint Eastwood said – I don't remember in which movie – "Tomorrow is promised to no one," which has not only been more in my own awareness since the Big Event – I mean I didn't just have a *brush* with death, I had a scouring pad – but safe to say it's been more in our collective faces this year than it's been probably in my lifetime, so it's just a caring act, to just set up clear instructions and basic information to make it easier to close up shop. Most of us usually think it won't happen to us, but tomorrow really is promised to no one, it *does* happen to some people, I mean it already happened to me, it just didn't take. The Great Sorter Machine in the sky rejected me for not quite being ripe enough yet. So it's an expression of kindness to loved ones, to have things more in order for them, and it can make your life a little lighter and more enjoyable, knowing you have all that done. And it also helps you keep in your awareness a little more the precious temporariness of being alive.

So that's what – well I was going to say flashed in, but I'm not a hundred percent sure – but that's what suddenly bubbled up or popped in out of nowhere, and it's hard to convey how much it just clicked or resonated as the most obvious thing in the world to do. And I could feel that sense of relief that would come from just having all that resolved and in order in my life. Or at least a whole lot *more* resolved and in order. Why wait til your days are particularly running short to get everything sorted and organized and to say what's left to say? Why not do it soon enough that you get to enjoy the benefits as well?

Reminds me, a few months ago a friend of mine got their house all fixed up nicer than it had ever been so they could sell it, and then they were kicking themselves, like, if I was going to do this anyway, why didn't I do it years ago so I could've actually enjoyed all those improvements myself, while I lived there?

And another reason to do it, that I think would normally apply but not so much with me this particular year, is that it just keeps more in our awareness the truth that no one gets out of this thing alive, it *will* happen one day, so spending some time with that truth, being more present with it, like a poignant kind of dance partner as you go through life, instead of a prisoner locked in the basement of denial because it's a bummer to think about.

So yeah, that was the invitation that popped in, from wherever it did, plus the sense of doing that every five or six years or so. And safe guess this kind of thing has been around a while in different versions, because it's just so obvious – at least it seemed completely obvious to me once it showed up, with several upsides and no downsides, I just hadn't ever thought about it before.

$$\Omega \, \Omega \, \Omega \, \Omega$$

And did you ask Omega if that was a download? Actually, first did Omega end up showing up that day?

No, after that popped in I sat a while longer being with it, and then called it done. But I did ask about it the next session. And the response was along the lines of, "That's a sample of the wisdom that can sprout from you creating the fertile soil of clearing space and sitting in present availability." And yes, if you asked me to say that again I would probably say it a little differently, but that expressed it really closely.

But really, that response wasn't exactly the same as saying it was all from me, and I'm really not at all sure there wasn't a nudge from above, which again isn't really above. Plus would Omega see my wisdom as differentiated from what comes from my Higher Self along the Continuum of Consciousness? That delineation isn't so solid from more subtle perspectives, so maybe Omega was just saying, when you get still, you're more connected to the greater wisdom of higher levels and have more access to that. I don't know.

So I'm not sure the origin, maybe just my own mind had a realization, that's a natural part of life, right? Spontaneous insights. Very possible. But, to me it's kind of like, if every day you sit at a park bench and someone walks by and gives you an orange, and then one day there's an orange sitting on the bench even though you didn't see them come by, odds are probably higher it came from them than not. And that kind of brings us back to, what matters more, where something purportedly came from or how much it resonates in us. And this just really resonated and seemed obvious to do, whether it came from Omega or purely from the creativity of my own unconscious, or if it was something forgotten that I came across sometime in the past that just percolated up again a little refurbished. Or some combination of those.

But the feel of it was, committing to doing like a one year process or practice or experiment – January 1st or your birthday would probably be the most obvious times to start, maybe the first day of spring, but whenever makes sense to you – and just exploring, if you knew this was your last year alive on Earth, what would you want to attend to that would be of goodness? In terms of making things a little easier for other people logistically, and also in terms of your own sense of inner preparedness for the inevitable end of this temporary life. The completion and cleaning up of loose ends that haven't been cared for as fully as would be good, practical things and also more emotional/relational/spiritual things. A one year intentional journey of deep life cleaning.

So that might look like maybe tackling one really big thing a quarter, like bucket list level or something you might really dread dealing with, like getting your will all set, and then one big thing a month, and one medium sized thing a week, and one small thing a day – like 15 or 20 minutes, maybe cleaning out a box of old things or going through some old papers or organizing some old computer folders. And also doing a little reflecting on the limited and continuously falling sand in the hourglass of our lives, spending some time really trying to consciously connect with the impermanence of our life as we know it, which I think in my case is pretty much already checked off, at least for a while. And somewhere in there communicating with people there's some unfinishedness with, and finding some conscious closure or some completion or cleaning up some old messes or whatever that might be.

That really makes sense. On a few different levels. A one year, what did you call it? A deep life cleaning?

Yeah, or a one year Deep Life Cleanse, or Life Spring Cleaning, or Life Completion Prep, or whatever you want to call it. I like Deep Life Cleanse. But it really instantly resonated with me, and I do plan to do it before long. It just felt like a no brainer, to do it while I still have a brain.

That's one way of putting it.

CHAPTER 76

So, a little tangent there, but it does seem relevant to the topic of grounding some of what we've covered this weekend with some potential real life applications and invitations. But let me get back to that last process I wanted to share. So the quick groundwork for this one is just that when we really want something, that wanting is almost always actually comprised of two different things, that we've never really noticed or thought about, or at least I hadn't ever heard of this. And the first is pure unadulterated, unspoiled, unsullied, untainted, simple, singular, clean and clear wanting what you want. No tightness, no tension, no contraction, no discontentment, no frustration, no angst, you simply want what you want.

It's just acknowledging, or maybe it's closer to say it's just being in touch with, the fact that this particular wanting exists in you, and then letting it have a little space inside you, since it already does exist in you anyway. Leaving aside if it's something that would be good for you to go after, or if it's something that's even theoretically possible to have, it's just 101, really basic, purely, simply wanting something without any extras.

And then there's a whole second thing that's usually accompanying that pure, clear simple wanting, that's interwoven with it so tightly we don't even usually notice it consciously and don't realize that wanting is comprised of two separate things. And this second thing is some degree of beneath the surface tightness and tension and dissatisfaction and discontentment. Maybe unconsciously a little tightening and bracing against and being resistant to the current situation because it's missing this thing we really want. A subtle or not so subtle feeling of incompleteness and unsettledness and contractedness, maybe a little frustration or agitation, to some small degree, at least unconsciously.

And one way I saw this dynamic was that wanting – wanting anything – is kind of like a thick climbing rope hanging down from a really tall beam above you, and if you look closer, it's actually two ropes. A straight rope that another rope is tightly wrapped around. And that straight inner rope is somehow actually clear, translucent, like if the clear gel inside an aloe vera plant was really strong and fibrous while still being completely clear, or if there was somehow a completely clear, transparent vine. So the inner straight rope is strong, solid and transparent, and it represents pure, clear, simple, unencumbered wanting. And then I saw the outer rope as red, maybe just to clearly differentiate the two, and it really tightly coils around the clear inner one so that you can't even see it. You wouldn't know it's there from just looking. Are you with me? Usually I can tell, but I'm not sure.

I am, but I just got a bit of a cramp in my leg. I'm going to stand up a minute but I'm listening and following you so far.

Yeah, feel free to do whatever you need to do, stretch it out or whatever, and we can take another break if we need to.

No, I just needed to stand up. It's not a bad one, and it will go away in a minute. Let's keep going.

Ω

Okay, so, yeah, the straight clear rope is just simple, pure, pristine *longing* for something. Simple wanting. Nothing extra. Not unsettledness, not tightness, not squeezing, not contracting, not angsting for what you don't have, it's just a soft, relaxed aching for something, or sometimes it's a powerful and strong but still spacious aching for something. A clear sense of simply wanting something.

And the red rope, it's made of the tightness that we just inherently, naturally, automatically, seemingly unavoidably and involuntarily almost always add to the mix, to some degree, when we want something. We do it so automatically that we don't really notice it as possibly anything separate from wanting. We just think it's part of what defines wanting. Or even *most* of what defines it, if we even notice it at all, which we usually don't.

So the red rope is the inner bracing and grasping and constricting and holding, with maybe some degree of subtle angst or discontentment or discomfort, or maybe some mild frustration or aggravation or agitation or unsettledness. It might show up as any of that, obvious or subtle or completely beneath our awareness. And there also might be things like the stomach muscles or chest tightening some, or breathing becoming a little more shallow, or more tense shoulders, or a clenched jaw, or a tight forehead. The red rope could be any or all of that, more often than not completely unnoticed.

If you think of a desperate and uncontained and pleading three year old at a toy store – that suddenly absolutely *has* to have a toy they didn't know existed 30 seconds ago, followed by a massive meltdown when they're cruelly denied by that big stupid meanie – that's the far end of the spectrum of the potential intensity of the red rope that pretty much always accompanies wanting, at least to some degree, conscious or not.

For most of us most of the time, for most things we want, the squeezing and tightness and discomfort and discontentment is way more subtle and subdued than that. Maybe a one or a two or sometimes a three out of ten. We might not even be conscious of it at all, and it certainly won't feel unusual or unfamiliar or out of place. That's just what wanting something we don't have usually feels like to some degree. A little tight, a little unenjoyable, that just comes with the territory. And the red rope usually is just part of the territory when we want something. But that doesn't mean it *has* to be.

Ω Ω

So, that's the background, and then the invitation or process is to – well first, like Influencing Your Unfolding, just choose something you really do want, so you can either start doing this process because you notice there's something you really want in the moment, or you can sit down, or while you're walking or taking a shower or whatever, and think of something you want in your life that you don't have, that you can do this process around.

Then once you have something, just really letting all your wanting of that show up in you as fully as it already exists. Fully letting that wanting be there, ten out of ten. Really letting yourself turn up the volume if you had been suppressing it or ignoring it at all, which we usually do at least some. Turning up the dial all the way, so that your wanting gets to exist as fully as it already does exist – under some dampening insulation we tend to add to tamp down how much we might want something.

Because the way it usually shows up, with the red rope, wanting something we don't have can at least unconsciously be uncomfortable and unsettling, constricting and contracting, and can bring up lack and deficit and deficiency and not enoughness. So it's letting your wanting really be here in an alive, present, feelable way. Not exaggerating it and also not suppressing it.

Then right after that, letting yourself really be aware of any beneath the surface – or also above the surface – tightness or tension or dissatisfaction or discontentment, anything along those lines that might be accompanying it. That subtle, nagging sense of not enoughness and scarcity and lack, around not having what you want. Or that restless, tight shouldered, tight jawed, resistant, even subtly agitated or aggravated energy, that can be there when something we really want is lacking.

It's different for all of us and different at different times, but all of that red rope contracting is so natural and so evolutionarily automatic and ingrained or embedded in the original operating system that it doesn't feel off or optional, if we even consciously notice it. It just feels like the way things are. It's what mobilizes mammals – and probably most other animals – to not just lie there in the desert when their body is uncomfortable because of thirst, but to get up and start walking towards a possible water source and some shade. Or to go look for food, or to go find a mate, or to keep looking for where you left the damn remote. It's so ingrained and interwoven that we don't even realize these are two different ropes enwrapped as one.

We assume wanting is wanting. We assume without ever even thinking about it once in our lives – at least *I* hadn't – that wanting just by definition includes the usually subtle and mostly beneath our awareness red rope list. The discontentment and discomfort and pushing and pulling and resisting and rejecting. Resisting the way things are right now, usually without being aware of it. Rejecting this moment to some degree because it's missing that thing you want, maybe creating a mostly unconscious sense of your life feeling lacking and deficient and incomplete, and the contrast feels uncomfortable, consciously or beneath our awareness.

And if we really look at it, does wanting something in that tight, dissatisfied way, when we really feel it in the moment, infill us and enliven us a little or drain us and kind of deaden our spark a little, even if we don't usually consciously notice it? Does it help us feel a touch more connected or more cut off? A little more open or more closed? A little more settled or more tense? A little more flowing or more stuck? Does it leave us with a touch more life force and vitality and energy or a touch more numbness and tiredness and closed down-ness? Even just subtly?

And if I didn't say this clearly, that's the next step, the third step. After you connect with something you want and then really feel it, just consciously noticing how that wanting is feeling in you. Does really wanting something we don't have, the usual way we've always done it – a much milder version of that agitated kid in the store – does that actively enrich and inflow our life some, or does it tighten it and stagnate it a little? Does it lighten our load a touch or weigh things down a little more? Is it empowering or disempowering? Soothing or agitating? Plentiful-reinforcing or deficiency-reinforcing? Is it a nice thing for our body to feel, or a little tense and draining, even subtly or unconsciously? And it's one thing to ask these questions based on memory or a hypothetical, but asking them when you're really feeling full on wanting something, just checking it out, and seeing what the answers are.

And if the first time or two the answer is just kind of, "I don't feel much of anything from your strange little red rope list, I just feel like I *really* want my offer to be accepted on that house, that's all I'm feeling, " then maybe it could be interesting to explore how you can tell you really want that, how it feels in your body to really want that, what clues are there that you normally don't tune into, that show up when you really want something. Just noticing.

And what's cool about this little practice to me is, just what if the very thing that tends to be subtly and unnoticedly life draining and burden adding, at least a little, could actually be the opposite? What if being in real connection with how much we want something that we currently lack could actually be, in real time – not after a year of practicing but in real time, in just a few minutes once you have a few practice runs behind you – what if it could become life giving and heart opening and energy expanding and settling and empowering, to some degree? What if there's a deeper possibility here, that just might be pretty quick and simple to bring in? What if we actually can help the red rope to release its tight grip on the pure rope of clear simple wanting, til it just unravels to the ground? How would the pure clear straight rope of simple wanting feel to us then?

So the fourth step, which is the heart of this process, is about, while being aware of really wanting something, while letting that be there as fully as we can without forcing it, also seeing if we can just allow those usually mostly beneath the surface red rope qualities to relax and loosen their grip. Letting go a little more of any obvious or barely perceptible or unnoticed inner bracing and clenching, tightness and tension, grasping and gripping. Just letting any of that begin to relax a little more.

Letting that red rope loosen its very subtle but circulation-inhibiting grip around the clear rope, just a little more. And as you allow that, without fighting with it, the red rope can begin to naturally uncoil. We can let it start to release its grip around the pure straight clear rope of simple wanting, til it begins to unwind, unwrap, and fall to the ground.

And from another perspective, when we stop tightly holding up the red rope with our own grip, it's just naturally free to uncoil and fall away on its own. As we let ourselves still feel the clear simple wanting of that which we want, while releasing any remaining tightness and contraction and discontentment around wanting it and not having it, the red rope begins to relax and de-constrict, and loosen its habitual grip, and then it effortlessly and easefully just unravels and falls to the ground.

That reminds me of the boa constrictor from earlier.

Yeah, definitely the same kind of thing. It lets go of us exactly as much as we let go of it. Your leg's doing better?

Yeah, it's fine now, thanks, I just needed to move it a little. I may get up again and stretch it preemptively at some point, but I'm tuned in.

Sure, do whatever's good to do.

CHAPTER 77

So, the fourth step is while being as connected as you can with the truth that you really *do* want this thing or event or situation that you want, and while really feeling that wanting of it as much as is authentically available, at the same time – in an open, allowing way – just letting any and all subtle or obvious contractions and constrictions and the rest of the red rope list – all of those well meaning unconscious tightenings – all just relax and let go and have a little break for a few.

Just letting that programming in you – the part of you that believes to have that thing you want in your life, or even just to *feel* how much you want it in your life, you have to mostly unconsciously tighten and squeeze and hold tightly and contract, like a more subdued, less apparent version of that three year old in the toy store – letting that part of you just take a breath and take a break. Inviting that subtly gripping or grasping or restless or impatient or stressed part of you to just see if it's really a problem to be off duty for a few minutes. To see if anything falls apart in you if it just takes a little coffee break. Decaf, no sugar, since it really needs to just decompress and unwind a little. Literally unwind, actually.

Just exploring what happens if you let that part – that's in charge of adding the red rope to the clear simple wanting rope – just take a little break for a few, and you know, let it kind of go outside for the first time in a long time, and walk over to some nice trees and relax in a hammock for a few. Shoes off, feet up, head back, eyes closed. So just daring to see what happens if for just a few minutes you let go of the habitual and usually unnoticed automatic squeezing and bracing and rejecting, which habitually and automatically and unconsciously – and seemingly nonnegotiably – usually goes along with wanting something, to varying degrees.

And if you feel like you don't have any of that at all in the mix when you're really wanting something – that red rope list – maybe you're right, or maybe it's there a little more subtly than you're used to noticing or than I'm describing. Maybe it's just so everpresent with wanting that it's hard to even notice it as a distinct thing or even notice it at all. A very subtle, nagging discontentment or energetic constricting, or just a little tension or tightness.

Or maybe in that moment when you checked, you weren't quite able to connect with or generate much of a feeling of wanting in the first place, which is fine, then just try again another time, or go ahead and try again now with something else you really want. Trying to feel it ten out of ten or eight out of ten or however much is authentically available, without forcing it or squeezing it or fer-vorizing it.

Just acknowledging, yeah, I honestly really, really do want that, and then letting yourself feel it and feel the impact of subtly tightly wanting that, and then relaxing and releasing that red rope list, and feeling the clean, pure clear rope of wanting or longing for this thing you really do want, without red roping it. Which you just might find, maybe after a few false starts and seemingly futile attempts, is a really good thing to experience.

$$\Omega$$

So, it's seeing to what degree we can release that continuous sub-tle tensioning beneath the surface that we just automatically carry with us when we really want something we don't have, big or small. Because just maybe, just maybe that deeply ingrained pattern in every human is just a residual automatic reaction – a residual encoding, an outdated evolutionary tendency, a default setting – and not a good fit for most human wanting, and especially for most of the wanting that happens in our daily modern lives. Just maybe, at this point, it's not a feature, it's a bug.

And just maybe there's more potential, more profound possibility, more deep and impactful gifts, lurking right there, right smack dab in the middle of our strongest wantings – and also in our lesser wantings – than we have access to by habitually continuing that old automatic way of wanting. Which doesn't have much room for fresh, vibrant, connected open newness, as the red rope constricts and constrains and limits and drains, and stagnates the vibrancy and rich present grounded aliveness of the pure rope of clear simple wanting.

And that contracted, strangling red rope can only stay up because on some automatic level, *we're* holding *it*, *we're* squeezing *it*. So seeing if the tower guard inside you might be willing to just try, for a minute or two or three, relaxing that grip, and letting the red rope of obvious or subtle contracted, discontent wanting just unwind and fall away.

So it's letting that tightness and tension – that's been embedded within the wanting in a way that keeps us from even realizing it's a separate, optional, unrequired thing – letting that dial down from a ten or an eight or a six to a five or a four or a three. While still connecting with the sense that you really would like to have that thing in your life. And then taking another pass, allowing it to let go of its grip even more, down to a two or a one, and down even more if that's available.

And as that tightness and tension and holding of the red rope begins to fall away, and it begins to relax its grip, maybe it no longer has anything to hold itself together and it just turns to dust and blows away. Maybe it wasn't so strong after all, even though before, it was squeezing and cutting off the flowing circulation of the clear rope of pure simple wanting. It was literally squeezing some of the life out of it. Squeezing any potential gifts out of it. It was draining some of your life force in an innocent but misguided, evolutionarily encoded attempt to support you while you were wanting something you didn't have.

And this is a really risk free process because you can always bring that tightness and tension back anytime you feel it serves you to, instantly, and the odds are high it will come back on its own anyway, especially at first. So why not just check it out, and see what happens if you let that red rope list slowly dissipate for a few. As you let go of the red rope, it will unravel of itself, and let go of you. Gravity will unwind it all by itself, like that boa constrictor. Like the lion cubs that just settle down and go to sleep. Like the subphysical suckerfish that just go on their way. Like the aggressive seagulls that quickly lose interest.

It takes two to play tug of war. The red rope draws its strength from your resistance to what's here now. Your tight resistance and rejection – to varying degrees, conscious and obvious or unconscious and imperceptible – of what's showing up right now, contrasted with what you want. The red rope gets its energy from your bracing against the discomfort and discontentment and dissatisfaction and deficiency of not having something that you really do want to have. Like a subtle level electric eel that feeds off the electrical offgassing from your resistance to it.

So it's about just lightly playing with letting go of your grip of the red rope, and inviting it to let go of its grip of you. And if you lose your sense of clear simple wanting, take a moment and feel it again, how you really would like that thing in your life. And then relaxing any remaining gripping or grasping or constriction or contraction or dissatisfaction or discontentment. Inviting that bracing to just cease for a few.

Ω Ω

So I'm sitting there getting this whole inflash – unpacking it, or really they unpack themselves – and like when Influencing Your Unfolding all opened up, it's just getting downloaded into me the vibe and value of this whole process. The potential impact of it. It's really landing and sinking in, and I can really feel magnified those subtle and not so subtle red rope qualities, that I hadn't really ever consciously thought about or completely tuned in to, and then I feel them really start to let go.

And then I can directly feel what it's like to really fully but spaciously want something, not dampening it down, but without any tightness or tension or resistance or rejection, or the whole red rope list. I can directly feel what it's like to just openly and flowingly and unrestrictedly long for something, cleanly and alively. Really aware of and feeling that pure simple wanting, with a flowing, open – let's call it a wanting aperture. Feeling wanting with a spacious, open wanting aperture, instead of with a subtle, easy to miss, closed, constricted, tight and squeezed and slightly dissatisfied and maybe lightly frustrated wanting aperture, which doesn't *actually* do much of anything for us – at least in adult world – and actually stifles and stagnates and drains some of our aliveness, our life force, our energy, our vitality.

What do you mean at least in adult world? It doesn't seem like it helps kids get what they want either, it usually just frustrates adults when they fully express it, like the toy store example.

Well, think of babies, when they have a need, when there's something they want, it wouldn't work too well if evolution had just skipped the red rope, and they were just spaciously and quietly feeling how strongly they want their diaper changed or want to nurse, or want some pain to be gone, and they just quietly relaxed into that.

The red rope is *vital* for early survival, it creates sometimes huge expressive discontentment and can even build into a rage of irate frustrated expression, and that's absolutely appropriate for a baby. The gradually escalating feedback of the degree of want and need in that moment.

And then young children are in that process of learning that's not really gonna work for the rest of their lives, like having a tantrum from not getting a toy in a toy store. So it's a really important, vital piece, just evolution didn't need to shed that mechanism 100 percent completely for human life to be propagated, so as adults it's still in play, still faithfully carrying out its orders, just more subtly and beneath the surface. And it accumulatively drains some of our life force and limits our vitality and causes us tension and dissatisfaction – and sometimes some beneath the surface contractive unexpressed frustration, with our life as it currently is, not having that thing we want. When just purely and cleanly wanting something, reduced to its most elemental form, can actually be the opposite. It can actually support and enhance our vitality and clarity and contentment in the moment, rather than steal from it.

Ω Ω Ω

Part of it might just be how late it is, and how much we've covered yesterday and today, but I haven't been feeling as much natural appreciation for this topic as I've had for I think everything else this weekend, I wasn't quite feeling as engaged or on board or really getting it, but what you just said made it click. I feel like now I get what you're saying.

Good. Yeah, this one is maybe a little harder to connect with, so I'm trying to kind of approach it from different angles and gradually fill out the overall tapestry of it. So it's really just exploring letting your wanting aperture relax and open and unconstrict, changing the default settings so it's not so tight. A flooding stream can be really turbulent and agitated going through a steel culvert under a road, but as soon as it reaches a big lake, that same amount of water moving can be really open and smooth and flowing and gentle and tranquil and lovely, while still being really strong and powerful, because it has all the room, all the space it needs.

And this is really the deeper point of this whole process. Opening and smoothing out the wanting aperture, and receiving the gifts of that. And during that bridging session, I could really feel this and feel my body relax and my energy expand as I just let wanting be simple and clear and spacious, without the usual beneath our awareness red rope constricting of it. It felt really enlivening and settling and relieving and enjoyable. Wanting something I didn't have actually felt *enjoyable*. There was an unwinding of tension and tightness and discontentment and rejectingness, that I hadn't even been conscious of existing before.

Once I was free of the red rope list, wanting something I didn't have was life giving and rejuvenating and infreshing and soothing and nurturing and nutrienting. It inflowed Aliveness instead of draining it. It inflowed contentment instead of squeezing it. I could just feel pure, clear, simple unencumbered wanting. And it felt like a spacious, flowing, enriching, non-suffering longing. A gentle, non-painful spacious ache. Vibrant and full and connected and congruent and settling. And ironically, wanting for nothing. Lacking nothing at all.

It was so unexpected, what opened when I was being really connected with the wanting of something I didn't have, more connected to that than I had probably ever been before, but without all the usual subtle contractedness and tension that I hadn't ever really been that conscious of before or thought about. I just by default assumed that was what wanting felt like, that it was just part of the whole indivisible package.

But what opened in that relaxed wanting aperture was the opportunity to experience receiving the unexpected gifts that showed up through releasing the red rope list. A sense of feeling some of the same fulfillment and contentment and satisfaction and relief and lift and settled alive alertness, that I mostly unconsciously believed I could only have if I had in my life that thing I really wanted. But the way I was now experiencing the clear rope of wanting, without the red rope, was in kind of a heightened, richer, more connected, more immediate, more congruent, more open and settled and vibrant way, that actually went *deeper*, and landed more *fully*, than even if I suddenly actually had what I was wanting.

CHAPTER 78

So this little process of simply and clearly and spaciously wanting what we want, being fully connected to the pure clear straight rope, while letting the red rope fall away, that can actually allow us to feel some degree of contentment and infilling and richness and vibrant groundedness and deeper connection, just through relaxing into our direct, open, uncontracted wanting of something we lack.

Could you say that last sentence one more time?

So just by feeling our longing for what we don't have and allowing a relaxing of the red rope list, it can, really surprisingly, open up enrichedness and aliveness and spacious okayness and a feeling of fresh rechargedness and contentment, and deep, present enjoyment, *while* we're wanting something we don't have. Not by trying to imagine or pre-feel having what we want, like with Influencing Your Unfolding, which serves in its own way, but with this – just clear simple wanting without the heavy, constraining red rope extras – it can happen from the inside out, just by naturally enjoying the feeling of spaciously longing for what we want, while letting the tight contractions and constrictions of the red rope just relax and fall away.

And you know, how can just simply wanting something you don't have actually give you some of the inner gifts you would have if you actually had it, as well as those peripheral bonus gifts that are deeper and more congruent and more connected than what you would probably feel if you actually had that which you're wanting? It's counterintuitive and sounds almost offensively bass ackwards. And yet, that was my experience during the bridging session, and also all the times I've done this process on my own since. Well, not sure it's on my own, but all the times it's happened since the bridging session when it was introduced.

You're not sure it's on your own because you feel like the Omega Being is helping you do it?

Maybe. I guess I just mean since it just happens sometimes, effortlessly, maybe there's some kind of synergistic help supporting me doing it. Maybe it's Omega, or some kind of resonant Field or Flow that's still doing its work, or maybe like I've said it just really went in deep when the flash packet was opening up. Or maybe something else, but however it happens, I sometimes just find myself doing this process, and it consistently leaves me more deeply satisfied and more landed and more infilled and more content, and more vibrant and alive in the moment. And also more availably present, instead of subtly, unawaredly slightly deflated and resistant and closed off and discontent and deficient and constricted, around the way things currently are. Not having that thing I want.

And I don't mean to oversell it, I don't mean it's anywhere near as amazing as the Big Event, but it *is* really a deeply appreciated kind of visitation, of settled, content, soothing, quiet yet vibrant enjoyment, when that happens. And circling back to that little comparative checklist from earlier, it leaves me feeling at least a little more optimistic instead of a little more negative, a little more enriched and energized instead of a little more drained and depleted, more innerly connected instead of more cut off, and more soothed and settled instead of tight and discontent. Right where I am, and right in the middle of really wanting something I don't have, which in my case has included the usual list people tend to have, but more often than not has been wanting to be reconnected with Pure, Loving, Light-filled Belongingness, melted back into that incomparable Ocean of Living, Flowing Love, while profoundly connecting with Omega.

Ω

And when this process happens, it transmutes tight, dissatisfied rejecting-filled wanting into really rounded, spacious, energized, empowered soft wanting or longing. With a lot of room to flow, like that big lake instead of that tight flooding agitated creek. And then wanting something – instead of it intensifying and accentuating and exacerbating subtle, largely unconscious tension and holding and scarcity and deficiency and not enoughness and nagging lack – this spacious aching for something we lack in our lives can actually be a *doorway* or *gateway* or *opening* to being intimately connected with a *much* richer and more life renewing space than we had access to before we were in touch with lacking that thing that we really want.

So *not* having something we really do want can actually open the door to feeling some real enriched fulfillment, or connected content aliveness, in just a few minutes. Mindboggling in its own specific way. So through this simple process, not having what we want can actually become a gift that infills us, just by letting our wanting aperture finally have a chance to flowingly and uncontractedly open and breathe and feel the sun and the breeze of this unconstricted, connected living moment, through the spacious, relaxed soft open longing for that which we want and don't currently have.

And I resonated with it as it opened in me the first time, as I felt the inflash unpacking in me, working in me, but I didn't ever deliberately set aside a few minutes to give it a try. I didn't muster a little discipline to doing it a few times to see how it went. But now that it's been just spontaneously happening in my life in real time, out in the real world, transmuting moments that had been dissatisfying and heavy and unpleasant and bitter and jaded and tight and tense under the surface, to varying degrees, into pretty deeply satisfying and enriched and energized and grounded and connected and settled moments, it's just been a *really* appreciated gift.

And maybe you can feel the vibe of that, or at least a hint of it, that in those moments of pure simple wanting, instead of not currently having what I really want being – even really subtly – a sore spot containing some or all of the whole red rope list, which is what it was those first months – a lot of tight discontentment and jaded rejection of my life as it was – but instead of that, when I do this process, or when it does me, the red rope starts to uncoil, and to varying degrees – sometimes not that impactful and sometimes more so – it just becomes this really fresh, enjoyable space of open-apertured, clear, spacious, flowing, content, enjoyable wanting what I want. Roundedly longing for it in a smooth, settled, spacious way, instead of mostly unconsciously jaggedly tightening and constricting around it.

It's like I'm being trained – like my mind and body are relearning how to want what I feel is lacking in my life – in a way that almost instantly becomes a pathway to receiving gifts that are sometimes pretty nice and sometimes truly Deeply Good to receive. So as counter intuitive as it sounds, cleanly and spaciously connecting with our desire for what we lack can actually infill us with, in some ways, more than we would have inside ourselves if we actually already had what we want. Who'da thunk?

$$\Omega\,\Omega$$

Say that again?

Who'd a thunk.

Before that.

I had a feeling. So as bass ackwards as it sounds, simply spaciously feeling our wanting of what we lack can actually infill us with having more satisfaction and contentment and other inner gifts than we would've had if we had just immediately gotten what we wanted in the first place. Open apertured wanting can give us more satisfaction and rich alive presence and connected, congruent depth and empowered availability than actually having what we want would likely provide. We might still get what we want, and it might be really nice to have, but this way of relating to unfulfilled wants in an open and flowing and clear simple way, it can actually infill us even more deeply, because it comes from us being in a more congruent way within, and that can sometimes have deeper, more impactful alchemical gifts.

So yeah, who'da thunk? In that big spacious lake, wanting just has no added discomfort, no tightness, no agitation. No suffering or discontentment or not enoughness. No sense of lack or deficiency or frustration. If what you want is for physical pain to go away, that first level pain might not suddenly dissipate, but like when we talked about Absolute Allowingness, there isn't added rejection and resistance and tightening around it, and that can reduce the experience of suffering that surrounds having some unpleasant, not preferred, real and notable pain.

So as we relax the red rope list, and it stops strangling some of our natural spacious aliveness, that can open up gifts, right in the moment, that seemed completely out of reach just moments before and that wouldn't have shown up if we hadn't been wanting something that's missing in our lives in the first place.

I never would've guessed, I could never have thought to investigate, that the very act of wanting something I don't have could bring me fulfillment that's comparable, throughout that experience, to actually having what I wanted, *plus* the added gifts from that open wanting aperturedness. The infilling of revitalized energy and flow and empowerment and capacity, and simply being more vibrantly yet centeredly present in the moment for a while. It just really defies – I mean, it's just so counterintuitive to what we would expect.

And you just find yourself doing this process without effort?

Yes, it just kind of unfolds really naturally, at least recently. But I had the benefit of kind of being blasted – or not blasted but really immersed in the experience of that whole data stream while it was unpacking, and with a Deeper Resonance waving in along with the invitation. So I would expect for most people it wouldn't quite happen that way, so effortlessly and organically, at least at first. So to give it a fair try, it would probably take deliberately doing the process for a few minutes now and then, and seeing how it lands over maybe a few weeks or a month or two or so.

CHAPTER 79

You probably knew I was going to ask this, but can you just lay out the steps for this one again?

Yeah, so first, you do this either when you notice there's something you're really actively wanting in the moment, or you set aside a little time and let yourself tune into something you really do want. So Step One is just zeroing in on something you really want, and then Step Two is could you just let yourself really connect with how much you truly do want that in your life, feeling that wanting as fully as you can. A 10 out of 10 on the dial, or whatever's authentically available without forcing it.

And then Step Three, just noticing how it feels in your body and mind and mood to really want this thing you don't have, the way we habitually or automatically do. Is it a little life giving or a little life draining? Even subtly, barely perceptibly? And is it a little settling or a little tightening? A little relaxing or a little contractive? A little grounding and empowering or a little cut off and lacking? Does it make things a little lighter or a little heavier? A little more enjoyable or less? A little more solid and centered in yourself or less? Just taking a minute and noticing, even if it's mostly pretty subtle and under the surface.

And then Step Four is the main step, and that's gently inviting the relaxing of the red rope list. So while keeping in touch with the feeling of really wanting this thing in your life, or at least checking back in with it regularly for these few minutes, could you now gently – since you can't force it – invite the red rope to relax anything like subtle or obvious contracting or constricting, tightness or tension, aggravation or agitation, not enoughness or lack, dissatisfaction or discontentment, resistance or rejection, just whatever unsettledness or clenching or anything else along those lines that you might be subtly aware of, even if it hardly registers. And we're so acclimated to it, it usually doesn't at all, unless we're really tuning in and checking.

Just inviting the desk guard to take a little coffee break for a few. And from one perspective, that guard is just a part of the brain following some ancient evolutionary encoding, but from another, we could see it as like this lifeless and unsatisfied employee whose only job is to stay in a small, dark, dank basement control room, holding tension and contraction for us when we want something we don't have.

So exploring if you could spaciously invite that guard to kind of go up the stairs from the control room basement, step out into the bright, sunny outdoors, and take a nice relaxing break on a nice lounge chair in the sun or under a shade tree, or maybe sit in a relaxing hot tub for a while, or kick back in a recliner, in a nicely windowed room. Really letting that guard be off duty for a few minutes.

Ω

And one way to think of Step Four is imagining a control panel, like at a radio station or recording studio, that has a volume lever that slides up to ten or down to zero. And if we think of that as our wanting, we've probably always seen it as just one lever, one slider, connected to the intensity level of our wanting. But if you look a little closer, actually that control panel lever is comprised of two half levers, like left and right stereo control, even though they look like just one seamless lever, and they've almost always moved that way. But when you really look at it, they can also be moved individually. So you could move the dual lever up to 10 or so, really feeling your wanting, and then – keeping the pure simple wanting side where it is – you could slowly lower the tightness and tension side, the red rope side, slowly fading it down so that it just settles and quiets and reduces, and then letting it fade out to zero, so it just stops making wave forms all together.

So maybe during the first round of gently inviting all of that to start to relax, we help lower that red rope half of the wanting lever down to a 6 or 7. Then next pass we let more of that tension and tightness let go, and help it lower maybe to a 4 or 5, and then to a 2 or 3. And then on down to as close to faded out as we can lower it without forcing it. So that's maybe another way to get a sense of it, but it's just about helping that red rope, with all its subtle constriction and holding and resisting what's currently here, to get looser and looser to whatever degree it does. A first pass, and then a few more passes of inviting any remaining tightness and tension and bracing to more fully let go.

Asking yourself if you would be willing to just relax a little bit more of the largely beneath the surface tightening and bracing and resistance and rejection that chronically subtly embeds itself with really wanting something we don't have. Relaxing a little more of the muscle tension, of the neuro-physical contracting, of subtly squeezing towards what you want, like a remnant of that tantrumming kid. Just for maybe five minutes or so. Or even two or three. Could you just give it all a rest even for one minute? Do I hear 30 seconds?

So it's allowing the relaxing of the no longer necessary, completely understandable, evolutionarily ingrained, habitual tightening that surrounds pure, pristine, uncompressed, clear, open-apertured wanting. Letting the river gates be wide open, instead of them being mostly closed which causes a lot of turbulence. Opening into spacious longing, instead of some subtle tight bands of agitated squeezing and subtle discontentment. And just noticing what happens as that whole red rope list all begins to unwind and fall away.

Ω Ω

And then Step Five is just, like Step Three, notice how it feels now. Feel again how much you do want what you want, but with that contracted side of the lever all the way down, or at least lower than it was before. Without the red rope list being so active, or maybe not active at all for the moment, just noticing what remains. Noticing how you feel and what you feel for a minute or half minute.

And you just might notice somewhere in your first few tries of doing this little process, that what remains, to varying degrees, is something along the lines of clear, settled, quieting, congruent, flowing, infilling, empowered, deep, connecting, capacity-enhancing, pure simple longing. And you could think of this as just a natural extension of Step Five or as a quick Step Six, but just hang out in that for a minute or two, taking that in. And that's it.

And like I said, this was a – well almost a shock to me – that through this, let's call it mysterious alchemy, you can feel deeply content and enlivened, by just cleanly feeling your longing for what you long for, while letting go of the red rope list and inviting it to let go of you and uncoil and fall to the ground. And that means you can really, really want something, and really fully feel that, and instead of it being a mini-version of the kid in the store, it can actually be really nourishing and settling and opening and enriching and fulfilling and envibranting and life giving.

And can you do the 60 second bullet point version of the steps for this one?

Yeah, nice and neat, Step One, choose something you want, Step Two, fully feel how much you want it, Step Three, notice how that feels in your mind and body, any tightness or tension, is it lighter or heavier, is it more settling or constricting, more life giving or life draining, etcetera. Step Four, do a few rounds of letting any contraction and discontentment and lack and resistance and the whole red rope list just fall away – letting the red rope side of the control panel lever or slider slowly fade down to zero or close to it, while the simple, open, longing for what you want side of the slider stays all the way up. Your wanting aperture nice and open and relaxed and flowing.

And then Step Five, notice how your mind and body feel now, like you did in Step Three, as you still feel the longing for what you want but without the same degree of tightness and holding and subtle discontentment. Notice the space that's here now, any gifts that are here now, without much of the red rope remnants. And then – we'll go ahead and call it Step Six – just marinate in that for a few before you move on to the next thing, before you check your phone or get back to work or whatever.

Ω Ω Ω

And that's it. Just doing that anytime you want to with something you're wanting, and see what you notice, both while you're doing it, and if you do it several times over some time – over some weeks or a couple of months – noticing if it gets easier and/or more impactful, and also if it seems to be positively impacting the rest of your life a little, maybe giving you a little more access to those gifts a little more often, during your regular daily life.

And like I said about Influencing Your Unfolding, why not give it a try a few times, even if just to prove it wrong, and just see if there's anything there for you. And as with everything else this weekend, if not, or if you just have a clear no around it, throw it out, or at least put it in a drawer or in a box on a storage shelf and just forget about it for a while.

And for me, it's of course not anywhere near the same as during the Big Event, being merged with the Contended Belongingness of hanging out with Omega in that Spacious Ocean of Living Loving Light, but it *is* a diluted version of the same ilk, the same vibe, the same energy. And it's while living my life on this planet, with my body alive and ticking – which you know, has its advantages – and it happens exactly *because* there's something I don't have that I want, which I hadn't ever encountered or even thought to wonder if it might be possible, that not having something could be a near instant doorway to some very content, enriched moments.

So when this process is happening in me – around wanting to be back in that incomparable Space of Absolute Acceptance and Belonging and Love, or around some other things I've wanted to be different or wanted to have, that have been more relatively run of the mill things of this world, either way – all the beneath the surface, subtle dissatisfaction and discontentment and contraction and frustration really relaxes and settles and softens for a while. And the peripheral gifts always seem to show up too, at least to some degree, and sometimes a lot. The more fundamental gifts of feeling more settled and enlivened and rejuvenated and empowered and soothed and centered, and satisfied with this exact moment just as it is. Without a hint of suffering or lack or deficit or deficiency, even though there's still something absent that's strongly but spaciously longed for.

And it feels like over time it's becoming easier and quicker and more full and filled out when this process happens, and it's staying with me longer sometimes afterwards. The bridging sessions are great, I'm really fortunate to have them, and they've most definitely lightened and brightened and untightened my life some, no doubt. But they add up to at most a couple of hours a week, so this little addition is really having an impact, and gives me a whole nother level of hope and optimism that I can get more and more re-acclimated to living my life. And not just get through it, not just killing time til time kills me – which has to be the title of a 1950s country song – but that more and more I really might be able to be in this temporary lifetime in a way that's rich and alive and rewarding and enjoyable and actually deeply good. What a concept.

Ω Ω Ω Ω

And how often has this process been happening?

It started with around twice a week or so, but now it's maybe four or five times a week full on, around five to eight minutes each time, counting soaking in it a little afterwards, plus a few times a week of like a quick mini-version, that doesn't go as deep but does offer a quick little reset. Those are maybe two minutes. And I've noticed the red rope list is releasing faster and there's a little more energized settledness for a little longer after it's done than there was at first.

And I was just going to add a second ago, since our instinct is to be restless and dissatisfied when we want something we don't have – as a pre-programmed way of mobilizing enough energy to get to the watering hole, or to get our caretaker's attention to get our needs met as an infant – the idea of relaxing right in the center of lack and deficiency and wanting something we don't have, that's damn near blasphemous to our brains and nervous system, and to a million years of evolution.

Our unconscious holding patterns, AKA the desk guard, faithfully carry out ingrained orders to not let us fully relax and be content til there's nothing more we want. "I'll relax once I've got my wants and needs list all crossed off." That works great for like dogs, their want lists are pretty short and basic, not much concern about retirement or a better job or a newer car, as long as the windows go down, so a lot of times they're simply content. But it doesn't work so well for us modern humans most of the time, because almost no one tends to get all that much of their ever lurking and often nagging want list crossed off for long.

And last point, that chronic or frequent red rope of contracted wanting can really have an accumulative impact on our lives, even though since it's as natural as gravity to us we mostly don't even notice it. Like a constant 50 pound yoke around our shoulders. It can accumulatively deaden and weigh down and cover over and numb out our aliveness and lightness a little at a time. And if we don't ever check this out in some way, and explore it and investigate it a little, you know, the yoke's on us. And at least in my experience, if we do this little process, of really giving space to pure clear simple wanting, and allow the red rope list to relax and release and fall away, again and again, then it can actually – blasphemy alert, reflexive rejection alert – but the very lack of having that thing we want can actually give us the gift of settled, enjoyable, pure, present, content, alive, spacious presentness, simple and life giving and infilling and capital G Good.

So bottom line, our open-apertured wanting can create a proximity to or intimacy with both, that which we want, and a larger enlivened presence, and those two things are enjoyable and fulfilling and life giving and supportive and enriching. So it's a real gift, to feel what we're wanting, with an open wanting aperture, even though that thing we're wanting hasn't happened yet and might not happen.

So yeah, that's that one, and like I said, for me it's been undeniably impactful and feels like it's been a significant support the last few months, up there with the bridging sessions themselves, not in every way, but in terms of helping me to keep acclimating to a mostly pretty ordinary, Earthbound, not so connected human life, after having the heavens open so profoundly and being so completely quenched in inexpressible Belonging and Acceptance and Love and Okayness, and then having to come to terms with living a life without anywhere near full and complete access to that. So your mileage may vary, not everyone responds to the same things, but for me it's been a real gift.

And once more, as you've been sharing, I've been feeling a subtle Presence coming in. It feels like that process has been working in me a bit, or even working <u>on</u> me a bit, as you've been describing all this.

CHAPTER 80

Do you have a name for this one?

The way it seemed to be referred to the most in the flash packet, once it went through my brain's translating, was clear simple wanting, or just simple wanting. And what I saw when this came in, which I think is in the early stages of starting to happen with me, is that over time, there could be a deeply supportive shifting that could start to happen, where the translucent straight rope of wanting gradually wouldn't be as habitually compressed and limited and held back and weighed down and constricted and covered over by the red rope nearly as much. And more and more the life enriching and enlivening gifts of spacious clear simple wanting could arise more and more effortlessly, more of the time in daily life, just by sometimes being with the wanting of something you don't have with an unconstricted, open wanting aperture.

So through the henceforth named Simple Wanting Process, I now have some access to more enjoyable and content and settled moments again in my daily life, outside of the bridging sessions. It doesn't compare to what I experienced when my body got a little depulsified there for a while, but it really is like I'm starting to have the early foundations of a satisfying life again.

And I almost don't want to say this and tempt fate, but maybe not just satisfying, but just maybe I'm on my way to a deeply *good* and *rich* and *satisfying* life, that just might be more content than before the Big Event. More rich and enriching and full and fulfilling. And there's already no doubt that at least for now I'm more *connected* than before. I was pretty much on busy and distracted automatic before the Big Event, relatively not very connected with myself or anything else, pretty much never grounded or present or deeply settled, not a lot really going on under the deeper hood, at least that I was in conscious connection with. More a skipping stone, never going beneath the surface.

And I don't mean now every moment is rich and connected and enjoyable and beautiful and settled, that's not the case at all, but definitely more moments with a little more depth and richness than before the Big Event. And not too many months ago it really felt like I would never have anything like a fairly decent life ever again, not to mention moving towards an actually fairly connected, enjoyable, and increasingly meaningful one.

And it's all always moving and in flux, with some weeks and some days and some hours better or worse than others, and who knows how things will actually go, but first with the bridging sessions, and now with these moments of rich alive contentment via the Simple Wanting Process – which open up not in *spite* of having lack but actually *because* of me spaciously being with really wanting something I don't have and letting it flow openly and simply, like a big tranquil lake instead of a turbulent creek – the graph line has definitely been moving on up.

Ω

And I'm starting to have – and I haven't thought of it this way before, and it touches something in me to say this – but I'm starting to have more and more moments where I'm not withholding from life just because it's withholding Deep Belongingness from me. Where I'm seeing the real possibility of more and more fully living this quick-falling hourglass sand of a lifetime, rather than being a sad, all left alone puppy that's looking out the lonely living room window, with my wagless sad tail, stuck believing my wagless sad tale.

I'm no longer just kind of sitting there, waglessly, desperately waiting for Total Belongingness to come pick me up and give me some love and attention and feed me and take me for a walk. My life is starting to be – I don't want to jinx it – but my life is starting to be good again, and I'm starting to find the balance of one foot a little more fully in my daily life and one foot a little more fully in all that's been opened and continues to open in me, which potentially really opens more richer possibility and deeper possibility for my life than there ever was before the Big Event.

And more and more, outside of the bridging sessions in normal daily life, there's more moments of kind of no big deal goodness, and sometimes I even notice and connect with Deeper Goodness and hints of the Beautiful More, like when we get together to talk about these things, but other more mundane times too now and then. Or sometimes, usually through the Simple Wanting Process, there's just the Goodness of being in rich, content, present Connection with myself in this moment.

And like I said, I don't want to oversell that, still plenty of gray flat hours, and still plenty of times I catch myself comparing and finding things falling woefully short, but it's moving in the right direction, and for that, I'm really grateful. So yeah, I've started to be hopeful again, really just in the last few months or maybe even less than that, that this temporary lifetime in this temporary Earth suit – that actually is really precious and worth such care and kindness – that this lifetime in this denser, less Deeply Connected world, actually *could* have real, deep, growing Goodness.

So, I'm grateful for the gifts that have already come from the bridging sessions, and there's been a lot of things I've appreciated from them, but as I've said, top of the list is being fortunate enough to re-connect, to bridge with Omega, to feel that Presence meet me. And then just below that – well at least for this month's billboard charts, is being shown, and lately having an effortless synergy with, Simple Wanting. And if that ever stops effortlessly arising in me, I would take responsibility for making sure I still do it regularly, for as long as it resonates to, because there's clearly goodness in me doing it.

And if the bridging sessions themselves ever stop, I think by now I'm back on my feet enough to be able to navigate that, though I do feel a little sinking in my stomach, a little dread, as I think of that possibility. But I do just really solidly feel like there's a lot more bridging sessions to come, that the portal isn't winding down any-time soon, which does brighten my day and my week, that they're in my life, probably for quite a while.

$$\Omega \, \Omega$$

And last thought, like I said yesterday, my experience during the Big Event was that I was more fully alive dead than I ever was when I was alive. But as time passes, I do have more genuine moments of actually being grateful to have more time here. And I'm fortu-nate to have the benefit of absolutely knowing, in the marrow of my Being, the Beautiful More that awaits after this life completes. So the invitation while I am alive on this planet – it feels to me these days anyway – is to see if I can be open and willing and available to bring just some small but slowly growing amount of the Greater Beingness, that's always right here, more and more into my human life. More and more into this level of reality, onto this planet, into our species, in a way that's more consciously connected and partic-ipated in and fundamentally recognized, and more and more inte-grated, instead of almost entirely missed.

And that doesn't have to happen with some big huge hero leap, it can happen bit by bit, accumulatively, every time I make – or any of us makes – a few small, solid steps, like when we talked before dinner about digging up and digging out. I mean I'm already here, the time will come I won't be, and it's more and more clear in me not to use up this fast passing blink of a life just tantrummingly and rejectingly wishing I was somewhere else. That's not honoring the rare and precious gift living a human life is, even though of course it often doesn't *feel* like a rare and precious gift at all.

So I'm intending that to be the case, and when I do have resistant dissatisfaction come up, sometimes Simple Wanting just kind of happens, and a few minutes later I'm more plugged in to a living open connection to my life exactly as it is, but without the resisting or rejecting of it or bracing or tightening against it. Without the red rope boa constrictor cutting off my life force. And then it's not so hard to see the remaining life in front of me, however long or not so long it might be, as being rich and good and a real gift to be able to keep experiencing, even though it will have its thorns, it's difficulty and hardship and pain.

So it's not hard for me to really clearly see anymore that it was a real gift that I was brought back to this world, to this body, in spite of my protests and complaints and bitter jaded hurt. It actually genuinely is – and maybe this is beyond obvious to most people, I don't know, but I had to go through some things to get there – but even during tougher, more painful phases, it actually genuinely *is* a gift to be alive.

So yeah, I think that's it. I think that does it for that last piece. So, let's move that over to the done column, and unless you have a burning question, I think maybe we actually call our little weekend marathon finally done.

I liked hearing that last bit, it touched me. And just about every time you've answered a question it's brought up at least one or two related ones, so I think it's a lost cause to try to get them all zeroed out. But it was never my expectation we'd be able to drill down exhaustively into every topic that would come up this weekend. And it's a little after one, so we've been at it for 12 hours today. Which is hard to believe. So we went three hours over tonight, and two hours last night. I feel like we've done what we set out to do, to the best of our ability. So let's finish any last thoughts and call it a wrap.

Ω Ω Ω

Sounds good to me. Hey, we actually finished our little marathon. I've probably never talked in a *week* as much as I've talked yesterday and today. I'm either going to sleep like a rock tonight or be too wired-tired to sleep at all, not sure which, but we actually did it. I don't know how you'll feel about it after some distance, and there were definitely times I just didn't feel like I was expressing things as clearly as I would've liked, and also it was hard to know what to bring in and what to leave out, and how much to talk about what, but like you said, we did our best.

I'm really pleased with what we got down and with how this went. And I do really appreciate you being willing to step out of your comfort zone and into the unfamiliar territory of doing this with me. And sticking with it so late both nights.

Well now that I'm on the other side of it, I'm definitely glad you thought of doing this and that we made it happen. I'm still not sure what to think about this becoming a book, I'm still not that comfortable thinking about it, but may it be of service in some way. And actually, I feel like it already *has* been. It's been good to talk about all this in more depth than we had so far, to have a chance to drill down more, and also to try to talk about some things I hadn't ever shared before. And it's also been nice to feel Essential Presence so much of the time as we tuned in to some of these things, which I didn't expect to happen as much or as strongly as it did, so yeah, nice bonus.

And last thing, I do recognize it's going to be – well, if we're about five hours over total then that's about 21 hours of actual talk time, right? So it's going to be a *whole lot* of work for you to transcribe all of this, plus whatever else is involved with publishing it and trying to get the word out about an anonymous book. It's a lot to add to your already pretty full plate for the next several months or however long it takes. So just acknowledging that.

And, I guess I don't need to say this right now, but it's important to me that you really – well first, I guess I haven't explicitly said this, so spoiler alert, but green light to move forward, I relinquish my 30 day veto rights. Sorry to not leave anyone reading the transcript in suspense about whether it will ever be available to be read. But it was just important to me to be able to ixnay it if it didn't end up resonating, which it did and it does, so yeah, full green light.

And second, it's important to me that you just navigate working on it however you need to, including taking a year or two or more to put it out there, or dropping it altogether, for a while or permanently. You don't owe me putting it out there, this is something *you* resonated with in yourself, I just joined in because of your heart enthusiasm about it radiating my way, trans-rooting in me. So whether you ever finish and how long you take, that's totally up to you. I wouldn't want our marathon to become a stressor or strain or burden on your life. That wouldn't really match the energy of the project, and just wouldn't feel good in me. So please feel free to just navigate it however seems best when considering your whole life and everything else on your plate.

And final final thought, I just want to say that I'm kind of awkwardly humbled, or humbly awkward, that you felt a response to do this and take it on. I'm still getting used to having this whole ongoing connection with Omega, having what I experience to be, you know, friends in high places, and I still can't really quite get my head around how I'm in this exact situation right now, sitting here with you, having spent the weekend talking about these things, which you plan to bookify. Definitely out of my comfort zone and self identity, to be involved at all in anything like this. But it's been a gift to me to do it, and now my part is done, aside from a little title talk, which definitely feels good.

Ω Ω Ω Ω

So yeah, I think that's it from me. Just, I'm glad we made it happen and damn glad we're done. We actually did it. Next time we should probably remember to hit record, but we did it.

Not funny, my heart stopped for half a second. Not quite as long as yours did not too long ago, but still. Alright, I'm really happy you decided you were up for this. It's been a gift to me too, and I'm glad to hear I have your official permission. And yes, I'll take my time and take care, and I'm actually looking forward to listening again, bit by bit, as I gradually transcribe it. Alright. Any elegant and profound last words for all posterity?

Damn, no pressure. I got nothing. Well, how about just short and sweet: Don't be too harsh, we did our best. Just keep what speaks and leave the rest.

I like it. Alright my friend, let's call that a wrap for our–

–Actually, let me try a take two. My last words of the whole marathon. I'm suddenly feeling some performance pressure again here, but what's coming up is just to share again what Omega – well actually first let me just say that I really do get that it might not feel like what I'm about to say could be even remotely possibly true, and I've been there myself, and sometimes I still am. But just, for what it's worth, this is slowly becoming more and more of a steady and growing subtle undercurrent in me – or at least the beginnings of one – where I'm starting to really know it a little, in my bones. In the marrow of my soul.

And it's what I shared yesterday, what Omega conveyed to me at the end of the Big Event, when I was being rudely and joltingly pulled back to my body and crammed back into it. And at the time, I couldn't hear it, I didn't *want* to hear it, it didn't seem like anywhere near enough. I didn't want what felt like empty words, I wanted the continuous irrevocable *experience* of off the charts Love-filled and Light-filled Belonging and Acceptance and Oneness. Call me picky.

But as the months have passed, with the bridging sessions and with Simple Wanting spontaneously happening and supporting things, and even with starting to talk with you about all this in recent weeks, including this weekend as I've shared more in depth, this is resonating more and more in me. Gradually hitting home more and more deeply.

And it's speaking from a deeper view and a longer view, a more zoomed out view, so you know, it's not trying to minimize the very real challenges we can face here. The real difficulties we have to navigate in our lives at times, unevenly distributed between people and between different months and years and decades of our lives. It's just bringing in a larger perspective from a little farther up the Continuum of Consciousness than we can usually see from the density of this world, and from the density of our own heavier awareness here.

So, as I was being ripped away, Omega had what felt like a light Heart smile, with definite care, but no heaviness or concern or sadness or somberness for me. And the sentiment of what came through, and I want to slow down a little and really connect with this as I say it, it was something really close to, "All is well, Dear One. Yes, you have the rare privilege of getting to return to your body for a time, and that really is no time at all. And then you get to come back here. And for us, from where we sit, you never truly leave, and your return to us is absolutely certain. So when you can, enjoy the rest of your fleeting, precious Earth journey. It's not that easy to get a hold of a ticket. And always know that, from where we reside, actually, all is well. All is, and all shall be, so deeply, deeply well." And that's all I got.

I really felt that flow in. Underneath and between and inside the words. A good way to end. Alright. Really grateful we did this. And that's a wrap for our weekend marathon.

Thank you for reading some or all of *The Omega Portal*. If you appreciated this book, please consider leaving a rating or a brief review at Amazon.com, to help more people discover it.

Only communication via TheOmegaPortal.com should be considered legitimately from the publisher of this book.

Made in the USA
Las Vegas, NV
25 August 2021